Best wishes,

Mitchell Smith

By Mitchell Smith

STONE CITY

DAYDREAMS

Mitchell
Smith

STONE CITY

A NOVEL

SIMON AND SCHUSTER

New York
London
Toronto
Tokyo
Sydney
Singapore

Simon and Schuster
Simon & Schuster Building
Rockefeller Center
1230 Avenue of the Americas
New York, New York 10020

This book is a work of fiction. Names, characters, places and incidents are either the product of the author's imagination or are used fictitiously. Any resemblance to actual events or locales or person, living or dead, is entirely coincidental.

Designed by Levavi & Levavi, Inc.
Manufactured in the United States of America

10 9 8 7 6 5 4 3 2 1

Library of Congress Cataloging in Publication data
Smith, Mitchell, date.
Stone city : a novel / Mitchell Smith.
p. cm.
I. Title.
PS3569.M537834S7 1990
813'.54—dc20 90-27921
CIP

ISBN 0-671-66223-6

To the Memory of Zel Lockwood

Some Jews believe, my lord Duke, that hell—spoken as "sheol"—is a manner of levels, in form great circles, each containing the opposite of truth. So being that up is down, and down becomes up; left is right, and right, left; good becomes ill—ill, good; and sunlit noon turns darkest night . . . all and every object found in unseemly misproportion. Therefore, it may be understood, they say, that the truths which are the sense of the City of God, become by this, nonsense—and this city of stone a habitation of devils, whose voices sound in echoes only.

LUIGI LOQUESTO,
Letters to His Grace
Cesare, Duke of Romagna
(Parker Hanley Hewes,
Letters of the Italian Renaissance,
translation by C. M. T. Ruggiero)

Chapter ONE

The river fell down the mountain slope in weighty series, like a carried trunk slipped loose, falling down a flight of stairs. Narrow, cold, dark and deep, the river ran a length along the mountain's shoulder through stunted birch and wind-bent willow to a lip of granite gray as the autumn evening, tripped there and fell again, foaming as it dropped.

The wind carried some of the river's spray over each fall, supported the mist for a moment, then lowered it gently to rejoin the easier water below.

It had been a considerable climb to find a vantage in such high mountains, in such harsh late autumn weather. Bauman's legs were tired, his boots heavy as cement.

Standing this close, his ears were assaulted by the river's tumultuous noise, each sound rhythmic and arrhythmic in its separate way, but all whispering loud as thunder, with a chill, gusting breath. The river turned and twisted, the violent black tongue of a permanent beast of ice, massive, white, still and silent, that lay along the ridge a thousand feet higher.

The wind blew past, around, and over all. It tugged at the opened front of Bauman's parka—shoving the fat down coat fully open, making wings of either side, billowing, blowing it flapping out—and pressed against his chest like a big man's insistent hand, but very cold. The air smelled of nothing but ice and colder stone. It flowed into his lungs like water, and made them ache.

Bauman turned away from the river—the wind now blowing his coat hard against him from behind, cuddling him in it like a lover, wrapping it around him. He looked into distance, and saw a roof of dark trooping clouds filing away ten thousand feet over the peaks of the range—those gray granite steeps, rises and walls, summits snowy as fresh-broken bones marching off to the north until, perhaps in a hundred miles, their heights became only ghosts, shadows, suggestions, the possibilities of more mountains continuing.

Bauman walked back to the farthest edge of rock. Looked down, careful of his balance in the wind, and saw the tiny scarlet dot of Philly's parka a thousand feet below. The boy was climbing very slowly.

This was the highest he'd brought his son. Far below, they'd climbed past a scree where marmots found their refuge amid the rocks—had heard the small animals whistling their alarms, for them or for some raptor's shadow sliding past. There, the boy had asked to try the last long sweeping pitch alone. Bauman had nodded—little danger of a dire fall on that slope—coiled the rope, and climbed away.

Now the wind, perhaps to keep him company, was making a keener sound across the height—wailing a rising then wavering note, but always high—the air's rushing progress snagged nearby at some fault, some spire or buttress.

Something seemed to press against his eyes, and Bauman opened them; he touched one hand with the other to be certain he was awake despite the dark.

Dark . . . and someone screaming.

He sat half up, fumbled over his head for the bottom of Scooter's bunk, felt the wire and springs. "What the *fuck*?" The screaming continued—a high, thin, trilling note, almost beautiful, held the longest time—then stopped abruptly in a gurgle and a sneeze. The red night-lights were out. It was the first time since Bauman had come up that the block had been in absolute darkness.

"Maybe somebody got his butt-cherry busted." Scooter, softly, from above. He sounded even younger in the dark, his voice higher pitched. "—But I guess not."

"Why the hell are the lights off?"

"So somebody could get that shit done up there, man."

Bauman reached under the right edge of his mattress for his watch, and read the circular phosphorescence of the Submariner's dial, big as a silver dollar: 3:47. Murmurs along the tiers . . . murmurs, but no voice calling out. The darkness complete, so unaccustomed, had made cowards of headlong and dangerous men.

Thereafter, it seemed the longest time till hacks' footsteps rang and echoed on the stairs, their flashlight beams swinging curious through the dark.

"You want your Jell-O?"

Bauman was eating breakfast with Scooter and two bikers, Perteet and Stokes. Perteet—bearded, earringed—was a very big man and very big eater. He was in for drugs.

"I can eat this stuff, midday," Bauman said, "but it's hard to swallow for breakfast," and shoved his tray over to Perteet, who, hairy square-backed hand shuttling, spooned the pale green stuff away and onto his own tray, to mingle with his eggs. Their utensils were small and pale orange plastic—the spoons almost miniatures, good for snorting, not much else. It took Perteet several rapid scoops with one of these small spoons to get all the Jell-O.

Breakfast was eggs. Bauman had wondered what was wrong with the eggs when he first came up, had asked a man named Dixon about it, and been told they were powdered. "Bakers' shit," Dixon had said. "—They get too old to sell whole, they grind 'em up an' dry 'em an' sell the powder. They got big cans of that shit comin' in every week. That's how come it tastes like it does. You get lucky, you get a rat turd in yours."

Dixon had gone out on parole a few weeks after that, and stayed out—or gone into other walls, if he'd fucked up.

Breakfast was those eggs, with a piece of white bread. Toast for East mess had been one of the demands the Inmate Committee had made two years previous, when they'd seized a hack and threatened to grease him up and give him a baby. It had been talked out, but the toaster, a huge old machine resembling a mangle, was still usually down.

Breakfast was those eggs, a piece of white bread, and lime Jell-O. Half-pint cartons of milk to drink, and Styrofoam cups of coffee—microwaved and set out on trays, powdered milk and sugar already added. Bauman had a carton of milk.

"This shit's not bad," Perteet said, finishing up, a few little pieces of breakfast in his beard, egg-yellow, Jell-O-green, bread-crumb-white. "—Better'n that banana shit." He meant the banana pudding sometimes served on Sunday. The banana pudding caused diarrhea, therefore "puddin' his pants" as a descriptive.

Bauman ate with the bikers on third shift—morning, noon, and night—but was usually not invited to the back of the mess hall, where most of the club members sat, rowdy, sipping pruno from coffee cups if the shift screws were easy, while discussing business.

Bauman was in on a pass at biker tables, as Scooter's housemate, though Scooter was in on something of a pass himself. A car thief who'd come up on the same fish-chain with Bauman thirteen months before, Scooter had been badly beaten when he'd entered the bikers' clubroom to inquire about membership, had some preliminary discussions, and been attacked then and there—his jaw broken, a kneecap cracked and kicked loose by a Gypsy Joker named Handles—when he'd mentioned riding and appreciating a Kawasaki above a previous Harley. It had taken Scooter months of service and silence around and about the club to expiate, to be accepted as a one-year probationer, pot-mule, and possible candidate for short Sunday-afternoon motorcycle rides around the yard circuit, under the weary gaze of the wall guards.

Another, smaller, very serious group of cons always ate earlier, on second shift, at two tables along the side wall. These eight men were lifers. Mark Nellis was one of them; Brian Wiltz—a much-feared killer—was another. Housed here in B-block, a biker stronghold, these lifers only ate and slept in the building, preferring to spend their days over in C, the Lifer Club's fortress.

Zip had been said about last night's killing across the four-man Formica table bolted, stools and all, to the black and white rubber-tiled floor—this mess-hall floor so dirty, Bauman had found while in Housekeeping, that mopping it made grease soup, smelling like chicken noodle. East mess served all of B, half of A and C; and most of the men eating had at least known the murdered man by sight—"Your buddy Spencer, the little nigger rapo," muttered by Scooter on their way down the stairs from Two-tier—but no one seemed to care to discuss it while eating. An indelicate subject, apparently.

"This hole is bad enough," Bauman said. "Isn't it bad enough without some animals killing people in here? Did that little man bother anybody? I don't think he ever bothered anybody."

This speech, which Bauman immediately felt was foolish and naive, had erupted out of him—out of his fear, he supposed—and was met at their table by a silence not so much chill as smothering. A mattress of silence lowered upon them, and Scooter, sitting opposite, made first a comic face of astonishment, then one of dismay at such bad taste, such bad judgment.

The killing, it appeared, was shop, and not to be introduced at mess. It would be talked about later, more privately, out on the walkways among friends, housemates, family or lovers.

"I went up to look," Scooter, to Bauman after breakfast, climbing the ringing circular steel staircase—painted cream-cheese white, as was all State's steel—to Two-tier for lock-'n'-count. "One of Cooper's guys and that black hack was in there with mops. Looked like it was painted, man. Looked like somebody slung a gallon of red lead all over. That poor little asshole bled out like a pig."

The news had enlivened Scooter, made him hop lightly up the steel stairs, so he was talking to Bauman half over his right shoulder. Scooter—blue-eyed, tall, thin as a pipe rail, pale as paper and very young—was decorated with tattoos innumerable and a wispy, nearly pubic goatee, rust red.

Bauman had been trying to think of eggs over easy, country sausage—ground hot with sage and pepper—and two cinnamon rolls with sweet butter and marmalade. He'd formed the occasional habit of imagining a rich breakfast after State's breakfast, climbing the echoing stairs. A rich breakfast, and Susanne seated across the table wearing only her yellow pajama top. Lank, fox-faced, almost plain without makeup. Long white throat with a small dark mole at its base, on the left, and long hair—thick, very light brown, burnished as poured clover honey, though not yet brushed for the day. Her eyes, pale green, mildly myopic, slightly distracted as she poured the coffee. . . .

"Hard to believe," Bauman said, "anybody would have a reason to kill that man."

"You kiddin'? They don't need reasons, Charles. They make up any reason they want. His roommate—that jig, Burdon?—got sick two days ago. Went to the infirmary with chest pains. You believe that guy had a heart attack, you believe anything, man." Scooter, energized by event, talking fast, stepping up, up, up the stairway.

"I still would like to know just what the hell that little man did, some jackass here had to kill him."

Scooter glanced back over his shoulder at Bauman as they climbed. "Hey, you don't want to be callin' names, Charles. None of our business. Really . . . you know?"

"I didn't say it was our business—my business. But I was doing some work for the man, and he was very shy, very inoffensive."

"Hey, he offended some dude—right?" and, peppy steps ringing off Two-tier's landing, Scooter led the way into the house. "It's a lesson, man; don't borrow fuckin' money. Don't borrow fuckin' anything."

"Right." Scooter borrowed everything he could from Bauman. Usually returned these things, in time. "—Good rule, Scoot. Only I don't think Spencer was into borrowing money."

"So? You did stuff for him. You were helpin' him write those letters. —How was he goin' to pay you?"

"That was only fifteen bucks. He was going to have his wife bring it in. —Not what you'd call really big money." Bauman started making up his bunk. Hospital corners. They'd shown him that in Classification, at Evansville, and he'd kept to it. He'd had the thought that a corrections officer might be pleased, in passing, by such neat making-up, that it might tip some slight scale when a captain asked about Bauman. Might make the most minor difference when the Corrections Report was submitted to the Board. —Superstitious bed-making. A useless charm. The screws occasionally noticed if an inmate didn't make his bed at all. Usually didn't notice that.

"You be surprised," Scooter said, "what some people consider big money. Hey, little nigger must have did somethin'. If he didn't, man, he wouldn' be dead. An' it don't have to be much, what he did."

Bauman smoothed the top of his bottom sheet, exposed a small roach, and snapped it away with thumb and forefinger. The roaches had upset him his first few weeks. No longer.

"He was just a gentle little man." Bauman stepped down to fold over the near bottom corner. "It would be nice, since we're all penned up together in this zoo, it would be nice if a few morons could refrain from killing a con just because he owes somebody a pack of cigarettes, or walks across the wrong corner of the square."

"Hey, Charles, right, that would be nice, but we're in the real world here. An' believe me, you don't want to be callin' names. Guys got their reasons." Scooter, returned from the sink, and having prepared his toothbrush with a neat dab of blue-and-white-striped toothpaste (dollar eighty-six, scrip, at the canteen), held it ready in his hand while pacing the cell up and down alongside the double bunk. Seven feet up to the blanket curtain hanging across the cell's back—sheltering the toilet—then seven feet down.

The wall at his other side—welded steel over original stone—was taped thick with pinups. Flesh and machinery. Highest, a brunette, near middle age and looking tender, held fat-nippled breasts up for regard, vines trellised behind her on some sunny veranda. A glittering bright blood-red hog rested just below, transmogrified from its original Electroglide into a wheeled lance, sparkling, dazzling in coastal sunlight, its gas tank tiny, inconsequential, as if the thing might run and roar on air. Along and up and down the wall—painted white over gray steel—other complementary beauties of women and motorcycles alternately demonstrated aspects of what Bauman supposed must be love and freedom—and all in sunshine.

Scooter brushed past them, pacing back and forth, then leaned in under the upper bunk, while Bauman tightened his top sheet, to smooth some Scotch tape scrolling at the corners of a centerfold. A slender blond girl with short hair and chocolate eyes lay naked on her back, braced in bright beach sand on her elbows, smiling out through the V'd pillars of slim tanned thighs. A sprinkle of sun-sparkling sand lay along the left crease of her groin—sticking in sweat or body oil the photographer had insisted on. This blond girl had a child's face, an experienced woman's genitals—those lips being slightly slack, loosely tucked, one pink frilled edge unfolded to show richer redder color deeper. The patch of decorating hair, blond, sunstruck, was coarse and tangled.

"You see that Cousins pussy out of A, down there talkin' to Pokey an' Pat?" Scooter finished smoothing the tape at all four corners with his left hand, his loaded toothbrush waiting in his right. "I think I'm in love, if I was a faggot. Looked to me like she was givin' you a little eye on the sly."

"Not funny," Bauman said, plumped the thin pillow and set it in place.

Scooter stood out from under the upper bunk and went back behind the blanket curtain. Bauman heard him peeing, the stream hitting the cracked porcelain with one blurred note, slowly falling in pitch. "Hey," Scooter said, over that diminishing sound, "I heard Clarence Henry busted a knuckle in his hand. Is it true?"

"That's bullshit. Clarence hasn't broken anything. —The Beast is ready to roll."

"Good news for my ten bucks," Scooter said, and flushed the toilet. It had taken Bauman two months to persuade Scooter to flush every time, and so at least a little reduce State's cloacal odors—feces, urine, a fairly constant drift of flatulence from the men packed together row on row and row above row in sweaty proximity, where constant tumultuous noise (electronic and human) seemed to meld with the stenches to produce a single seamless, encompassing, and intolerable environment. Bauman had been quite surprised one day to find he no longer much minded the noise, the fecal stinks. Hardly noticed them.

Even so, in that minor way and in others, Scooter had proved a biddable housemate ever since the two of them—three weeks up on the chain from Classification and unafraid of each other—had decided to settle together into Bauman's bought house, the first of the small two-man cells off the stairs on Two-tier. The cell—built for one man, originally—had cost Bauman two hundred and fifty dollars, street money. He'd purchased it from the lifer, Mark Nellis, who'd owned this one and the two-man directly below it on Ground-tier. Nellis still lived in the Ground-tier house with his wife, Betty, a *Latino* inmate with a beautiful mouth.

Scooter at first had wanted to share with three of the bikers in one of the bigger cells along the body of the block—those two-man houses now holding four men each. But though he'd thought himself quite tough on the street, Scooter found the other bikers too fierce to live with, and was afraid they might beat him again, or fuck him if he was convenient after last lock-'n'-count and lights out, when only small red bulbs burned along the block.

A hack named Haley called out, *"Fingerrrs,"* from below, and their cell door, suddenly racing a hundred and nineteen others to close, racked across its short track in dead heat and hammered shut. Eight thirty-one, and twelve . . . thirteen . . . fourteen seconds by the Rolex.

Bauman usually wore the big watch, sliding it far up under his left jacket sleeve almost to his elbow, then locking the band to hold it high and out of sight. That was taking a chance even so, and not feeling particularly lucky today, after listening to Spencer's death—not wishing to have to worry about the watch being seen, some thief or bumper noticing it—he bent down, gripped the wall-side pipe post of the double bunk below his pillow, heaved the whole structure up a few inches, and doubling the stainless watchband close, tucked the Rolex up into that leg's hollow. Then lowered the bunk gently.

"Why the fuck can't they make that stuff with some fuckin' space-age material?" Scooter had said once in the echo of the cell door's slamming sound. "That's a pretty depressin' noise."

"Space-age material," particularly boron fibers, had been ready on his lips since the Italians were written up in *Racing Bike* as considering it for use in the frames of racing motorcycles, to substitute for steel or titanium.

"That'll be the day, man," Scooter had said after he'd gotten his October copy in the mail, climbed up to his bunk to read it. "—That'll be the day, they use that stuff. Too fuckin' much flex. Tank an' fenders,

O.K. Frame, forget it." Had mentioned that Handles and Perteet had already brought the subject up—reference their copies, perused that morning—and dismissed it.

Bauman finished making his bunk, squared the pillow again, then went to his shelf, unwound his razor's cord, plugged it in, and began to shave, hardly glancing into the foot-square mirror over their shelves. Electric razors, ubiquitous at State, being the only sort allowed, were tediously noisy and less and less effective as their blades dulled. . . . Finished, his throat's skin reddened, irritated, Bauman put the razor away, took a fresh pack of Winstons from his carton, opened it, and took out a cigarette—the archaic habit hard to avoid in State, where smokes were cash. He dug in the right pocket of his blue denim trousers for a match, lit the cigarette, then picked up his Sony and went to lie down on his well-made bunk. Tucked the small earplugs in, thumbed the Walkman's start button, and closed his eyes, lying at ease, waiting to be counted.

A Dvorak waltz. Bauman kept his eyes closed, turned the volume slightly higher, and—sealed from the racket of the block—lay slack, smoking, moving his head slightly from side to side as, after its plangent introduction, the waltz rhythm somersaulted in and began to swing back and forth like a bell. Close beside him, unwatched, in unregarded privacy, the young blonde, her left upper corner already curling loose, rested with him, squinting slightly in the sun. Tiny droplets of moisture, infinitesimal, glittered in her pubic hair.

The day's weather was almost his last night's mountain dream's, but not as cold, and with more promise of rain. Bauman—not carrying his knife today—had been able to go straight out through B-block's main gate sally and metal detector, out to North yard, bound for the library. Carrying, he would have had to try the side gate, or duck and dodge out through the kitchen to take the back way out of B, out to the courtyard and then catercorner across to C-block. At the back gate to C, a Lifer Club guard to be consulted for permission to go past their dayroom and office, then out through C into East yard, with only one cop, one fence gate to pass to North.

It had taken Bauman some time, since coming up, to grow accustomed to the detours necessary to get along, to travel the mazy right-angled confusion of the four main-block buildings, the great square court they enclosed, the four wide yards stretching from the building fronts to the wall beyond, yards with their own wire entrance gates and exits. . . .

Almost rain, out on the walkways this morning, its promising odor draped invisible through cool morning air. Sunlight diffused to pearl. Rain would be snow in a few weeks. Bauman's second Christmas at State coming up. Then, one more Christmas to go. Possibly two.

North yard—much longer than a football field and twice as wide—had been planted with new grass months before that had taken well. Cement walkways to the buildings lying against North wall—Administration, the license shop, Evaluation, Testing, and the library—cut the yard in half lengthwise, cut it twice again at even intervals across.

The chill smell of wet stone drifted from the buildings behind him as he walked away, drifted from the granite wall obscuring the lower sky all around. From this great barrier, in summer, echoes of men's shouts as they played baseball in East yard, echoes also of various musics—blue grass, rock, rockabilly, mariachi, salsa, and soul—echoes of footsteps on hot cement walks would sound faintly off the granite, as if ghost prisoners of the hundred and more years past still played baseball, played the strumming music of their times, still strolled the walks.

The big wall had never bothered Bauman as much as his cell door slamming to—the wall appearing geological, a feature of the landscape.

A con, Chris Magliotta, came toward Bauman on the walk, glanced at him, and averted his eyes, as Bauman did, until they'd passed. They'd never spoken; Magliotta was a lifer, a fight fan, a friend of Donny Kenway, who Bauman did know—both of them from C-block.

Magliotta, a small quick-stepping man in State's blue denim trousers and a light blue street sweater a size too large, had a face like a spaniel's—muzzly, damp-eyed, and soft. His eyes had seemed swollen, inflamed as he passed by. Pink-eye or sorrow. Bad news from home, from outside, occasionally made an inmate weep. Bauman had heard a man crying in the block toilet, once, right after picking up mail.

Susanne hadn't wept, but his father had, on the phone—the first time Bauman had ever heard it. (And was sorry not to have seen it.) "Oh, god . . . oh, god . . . oh, god." The father—still taller than the son, though bent, hair remaining somewhat blond beneath the gray, eyes gray-blue as a Hollywood gunman's—had wept over the phone, had also claimed his doctor wouldn't O.K. the trip down to visit. Just not up to it, arthritis much too severe.

"He's got a lot of Frog in him from Yvonne," Bauman's father had said once in the barbershop when the barber, Milton Mathuin, had commented on his son's black hair, brown eyes, his shortness, stockiness, all that Mediterranean aspect. "—A lot of Frog, or Indian. Red nigger country, up there."

"Oh, god, oh, god," had been the song, however, when Bauman called up to Minnesota with the news.

Susanne hadn't wept. Only looked astonished—pale eyes wide, each black-dotted by its pupil, her mouth slightly open, lips hardly pinker than the skin surrounding them (their border always reinforced in daytime with a faint line of makeup pencil to make a mouth more definite). That astonished expression had remained even after following the police car down, waiting at the station house for hours.

"Please change that face you're making," Bauman had said to her over a white plastic phone the next morning, the thick glass between them smeared with spit, he supposed from attempted kisses. "I could use a more interesting expression, if you can manage one." Had gotten tears from her by that, then put his head into his hands and covered his face so as not to have to watch her, wishing the glass was stone—a wish soon to be granted.

Beth had not, he supposed, cried at all, certainly not for him to hear. Certainly not in her two letters since. Hadn't cried at that news—hadn't cried at the news of Susanne, a year and a half before. She seemed to have been waiting patiently for that news for some time.

Beth, in plaid skirt, gray sweater, its sleeves pushed up almost to her elbows, had been grading mid-terms on the living-room couch. She was wearing her glasses. "A graduate student? And young? How novel, how *original*. You want her? Then by all means . . ." She'd turned a page. "I think I'm going to be able to bear your loss, Charlie. I'm sure I will. I think Philly's going to be able to bear it, too." Then she'd turned another page, made a mark.

Later, at the lawyer's, after a calm hour of dividing, she'd suddenly said, "I am a little humiliated about something. I'm very humiliated about it; I'm going to be honest. It really hurts finding out you've spent fourteen years as an asshole—with an asshole."

Bauman had braced himself for a scene—a scene portended by her calm over several weeks—and saw Bob Christiansen bracing himself behind his handsome desk, its tooled-leather blotter holder.

But Beth had said nothing more, except that she wanted her new house (a pleasant old Victorian outside Fort Wayne, only two miles from her mother) to be inspected by a contractor, and any repairs needed then made at Bauman's expense. The inspection fee to be his responsibility as well.

Philly had been settled first thing, before the Victorian house had been found and bought for her. At thirteen, he hadn't seemed to care very much, had been more concerned with the move, his new school. They agreed not to use Phil to fight with, and that he was to remain with Beth. Bauman was to be able to visit him twice a month, five hours a visit, and was required to call before driving up. It had been agreed that Bauman keep the dog, Braudel.

After the divorce, during his visits, Bauman had found Phil resembling Beth physically more than he'd remembered the boy doing. Had also found him remote, busy, casual—smiling away attempted discussions of upset, loneliness, schoolwork, girls—his eyes, Beth's lighter brown than Bauman's, watching his visitor with only slight regard. A somewhat chilly article. True, Bauman supposed, to the sire, and a suitable punishment. When he hugged Philly goodbye after each visit (a rough-enough, manly-enough hug), Bauman would bend his head to smell the boy's hair, his sapling scent.

Beth, more active, more forthcoming than her son, constantly mildly adversarial, had startled Bauman on one visit, just before he and Susanne were married, by leading him upstairs in the Victorian house while he waited for Phil to come home from school on Friday afternoon. Had led him upstairs into her unfamiliar bedroom. Hadn't kissed him, but had—sitting on the side of her bed—unbuttoned, unzipped Bauman's trousers (old chinos, for possible touch football) and served him with her mouth, finally swallowing what he gave her down. Then had stood and walked downstairs, and left him to zip and button up and follow after.

She said nothing at all about it in the kitchen, but seemed satisfied to have had him in her small square strong hands, their firm massaging grip, to have suckled his compliance from him.

"I wish," Bauman had said thereafter, leaving for a movie, Phil already waiting in the car. "—I wish to God I could have you both."

Beth had given him a look of such amused distaste he'd spent much of his five hours with Philly thinking about it, considering she might have been only amused—perhaps warmly amused—and he'd imagined the other. He wished also that he'd caressed her while she did her sucking, had bent to kiss her instead of doing as he had—stayed standing facing her, leaning slightly over, hands resting on her small shoulders for balance as she sat hunched, attending to him, Bauman observing, as from ceiling height, her soft black hair, gray-streaked, caught in a casual ponytail, performing its irregular advances and retreats.

He'd thought about her on the long drive home, recalled her fine details, taken so much for granted when so often granted. Her neatness, smallness, the nightfall darkness of her hair (like his mother's, of course). Her sturdy, strong, round white legs, thatched thickly between—an embarrassment to her in bathing suits, for which the curling edges must be trimmed away—a softest thicket through which her dampness had always to be sought.

During these reconsiderations, Bauman had tried to persuade himself the blowjob had been a salutation and farewell, rather than a gesture of contempt for him, and for Susanne.

Beth had written one letter right after the arrest. Some friend must have called her. And written another after the trial. Both had been perfectly sympathetic, not the slightest satisfaction showing. . . .

The hack at the entrance to Testing and the library, a short fat freckled young man—khaki shirt and trousers freshly pressed—took Bauman by the arm, gripping harder than he had to, swung him to a wall, and patted and stroked him wrists to ankles. Then examined Bauman's book, clipboard, and pencils.

This was a new hack. "Still smellin' of cow shit," Scooter would have said. The man didn't run his fingers around inside Bauman's shirt collar or inside his belt. He hadn't learned his business yet. When he finished, he said, "O.K.," then stood watching carefully as Bauman picked up his book and clipboard, his two pencils, and walked away down the short hall—ancient yellow plaster, paneled waist-high in oak—and on up narrow, worn wooden steps to the library.

"Where's the Moncrieff? Are you returning that, Charles, or what? It's four days overdue, and I expect just a little more responsibility from you, in that area, than from the others."

All delivered by Schoonover after one quick look up from his file drawer. He was sitting against the library's east wall, a small table serving as a desk. "—I expect more from people of the book, where books are concerned, particularly when that book was a special order, specifically requested by you, and paid for out of library funds."

All rehearsed and held waiting the last four days.

"It's an exercise book, Larry, and I need to have it for exercises. I told you that." Bauman walked over to shake hands. Schoonover was formal, liked his hand shaken on greeting.

"What you told me, and what I agreed to, are two very different things." No handshake. Larry Schoonover, alone in his library but for Bauman, was tall, hazel-eyed, and plump, his cheeks dotted with small light brown moles—none disfiguring—and his hair, forming an almost theatrical widow's peak, kept very black with periodic applications of Grecian Formula smuggled in against the no-makeup regulations. Schoonover's denims were a fine faded blue, had been bleached in the upholstery shop, then tailored, starched, and pressed by State's queens at Sweet Stitches.

The librarian, having had his say, sat concentrating on a long wooden file of three-by-five cards and refused to look up, reminding Bauman of old Tomlinson's evasive postures at the university, his doodling during conversations. Dates of return were important to Schoonover.

"The book was out on professional usage, for Christ's sake, Larry. It's not a porno, O.K.?" A low blow, since Larry Schoonover had been writing porno science-fiction for at least three years, trying to get it published by second-rank firms in the West and East. *The Lord of Trades* was the most promising of these works, and almost complete. Adventures of a spacer merchant captain in some perfectly distant time and place—the Pleiades? Laser pistols, very romantic fucking, sacrificial deaths for the sake of love. The women dying for the love of Captain Nate Chabouk. Six and a half feet of black-haired, hazel-eyed, merry-humored murder. No facial moles, but a penis that frightened before it satisfied.

Bauman had read some of it, congratulated Schoonover on the work, and reported it was pleasant to masturbate to. He'd mentioned that Scooter, a nonreader excepting only motorcycle magazines, had made an exception for this novel, and said the same.

Schoonover had not been flattered, believing there was more to *Lord of Trades* than entertainment. He considered it a tragic description of the collapse and ruin of a great intergalactic civilization under the impact of technical developments too freely distributed among barbarian worlds—and for nothing but short-term profit. A lesson and warning, he felt, for our own benighted time.

"I don't consider the captain to be the real hero of the book," Schoonover'd told Bauman. "I consider him a villain. He's really part of the problem." The truly heroic figure, apparently, being a nicely drawn imperial legate—aging, fat, hopeless. Unfortunately, this real hero killed no one with laser or razor whip, and never got laid.

"Then give him a wife, give him kids, a family life," Bauman had said—conscious, as he said it, of possibly uncertain ground.

But the librarian had simply replied that it wouldn't do. "Kwal Katchak is too busy. He sacrificed all those possibilities to his work. . . ."

Now offended personally as well as professionally, Schoonover sat silent, concentrating on his file cards.

Apparently such a promising choice for librarian—an ex–high school social studies teacher—Larry Schoonover had proved not so. The inmates, regarding him as a dangerous ding, tended to avoid the long room, its walls stacked with shelves from corner to corner, the flaking green-painted plaster above the shelves decorated with Magic Markered signs encouraging reading as a path to freedom—external, internal. Decorated as well with photographs of presidents past, a single photograph of the present governor of the state, the state flag, the national flag, and a multicolored very large alphabet cut out of poster paper, its scissored letters in dusty blue, red, yellow, green—then blue, red, yellow, and green again and again, repeated in order left to right from the A almost all the way around the room to a red Z just above a large, framed, faded original map of the prison—this beautifully drawn on thin strong taffy-colored paper neatly crumbling up and down its edges under sheltering glass.

Bauman had studied the map and an accompanying column of typescript, separately framed, apparently a cover letter to a report by some English or Scottish consulting engineer to a British government commission, and dated 1871:

> This colossus of construction—to be administered initially by the Federal military—and intended to confine of all convicts the most treacherous, violent, and intransigent this Territory (soon to be State) affords, over eight hundred armed robbers, murderers, and the like, has been taken after the principles of Vauban to a point of perfection in layering, having at its center four great rectangular buildings of stone—designated 'A,' 'B,' 'C,' and 'D.' These facing the cardinal points—'A' to the North, 'B' to the East, 'C' to the South, and 'D' to the West.
>
> These four buildings—each a full three storeys high, each containing a great block of cells in three long tiers, as well as storage rooms, guard rooms, mess halls and kitchens below—form together the sides of a hollow square enclosing a spacious inner court, to be divided as may please for the creatures' exercise. This central portion, prison enough as prisons are presently constituted, is, however, being augmented by a cyclopean wall—thirty-five feet in height, in thickness, fifteen—that will form its own enormously larger square (one third of a mile on each side) to enclose the whole, leaving within its bounds great fields for the exercise of the gentler sort, as well as plentiful room for

associated buildings, workshops, an infirmary and a chapel, as the commandant might deem prudent and useful. But all remaining within those mighty walls.

In this, as in occasional other evidence of inventive engineering, we may well take instruction from these provincial *Romans*, and so, in time, replace our own archaic penitentiaries with forms at once economical, enduring, and secure.

The map accompanying was State today to the foot—except for the "associated buildings," now crouching, as foreseen, against the foundation blocks of the surrounding wall. The map, with exemplar elevations, had been done in medium blue ink, and perfectly, without corrections. Always pleasant to look at, Bauman had found. A single steady unimportant English (or Scottish) hand, one of the thousands of British competents then ruling much of the world.

This considerable library, packed with almost three thousand donated and purchased books—a few new, most dry, cracked, falling to paper crumbs with age—and including six separate tubs of used paperbacks, had been combed and recombed, censored, winnowed, and sifted by sixteen wardens, their captains and lieutenants, through more than a hundred years.

Only in the last decades had the courts insisted on permitting almost perfect freedom for the shelves, excepting only gay porn, explosives manufacture, and handbooks on methods of personal violence. *The Merc's Menu,* instructions in jungle survival, purification of casual water, wild edibles (birds' eggs at any stage of development, most roots, surprisingly few leaves) and some basics of knife, garrote, and stick fighting, had been lost to the library in State Superior Court, found a proper subject for administrative denial. Schoonover, a strict constructionist on freedom of the press, on freedom of speech, had led the fight along with Buddy Parris (State's convict radical), seen it taken up to that court, and lost.

Ungrateful, many inmates still refused to patronize, except for those unable to get into a club library for law books. Those convicts who didn't mind would come in with their friends' lists, and fill those for them.

"I don't give a fuck," an inmate had said to Scooter when Scooter'd quoted Bauman to him on the virtues of the library. "I don't give a fuck; I ain't goin' to check out shit from a dude went in a McDonald's an' offed some baby. Fuck that!"

He was referring to an evening several years before, when Schoonover, after an ordinary day at school (two parent conferences in the afternoon), had come home at four-thirty, had a glass of iced tea, and proved persuaded of a notion he'd been considering for some time. He was convinced that the fabric of reality, certainly alterable, might —by sufficiently weighty sacrifice—be shoved at least momentarily aside (as the mass of a star dimpled space and on collapse might snap clear through it) to reveal a much completer scheme.

Convinced, and having exercised his hands for the past several weeks—fingering and squeezing a tennis ball with all his might—Schoonover had interrupted his mother, Charlene Kent Schoonover, in the kitchen while she was preparing their dinner, and strangled her. After which—exalted, hopeful—he'd gone into the TV room and performed the same act upon his wife. Then, after a half-hour's wait, watching, listening on the stairs—so evidently the place between, from which any trembling of seeming's curtain might be felt, perhaps be seen—Schoonover had greeted his two young sons when they came in from Little League. He'd asked his oldest and favorite, Walt, to wait in the hall for a surprise while he led Richy away, and so disposed of each in turn. Then—nothing, after all, but a slight seizure of trembling resulting—he'd left the house desperate, determined not to waste their sacrifice by insufficiency. Driving his old Toyota two miles to the strip, he parked at the McDonald's there, and took a Phillips-head screwdriver from the car's glove compartment.

After entering the restaurant, impatient—pacing here and there among chocolate-brown tables and banquettes, their murmuring occupants—he'd passed, then repassed a pretty blond mother of three, and choosing the youngest, a pleasant plump baby at ease in one of the restaurant's high chairs, struck down hard, and with a crisp popping sound drove the screwdriver into the child's skull, so its translucent grip (plastic, corrugated, and merrily yellow) stuck up from the baby's wisp-haired head like a sudden handle, which, properly turned, might lower the volume of its mother's astonished and astounding shrieks.

Convinced then he'd done all that was necessary—and anticipating momentous arrivals, sudden waking views of a landscape in which his family, full of thanks (the baby accompanying), bowed before him in a blue garden, weeping with gratitude as he, with shining ones, assumed at last a true posture—Schoonover strolled through a side door, away from the noise, the shouts and scrambling, and out to the restaurant's small playground. There he climbed to its short slide and slid down it, hands lightly gripping the side rails, large bottom (in tan polyester slacks) barely fitting between, squeaking slightly from friction on descent. Did this several times—climbed the narrow ladder and slid down again—closely observed through plate glass by a few hardy patrons, one absently eating his french fries, but wincing at times in concert with the others at the sounds behind them.

Schoonover, climbing up and sliding down in growing disappointment as the world about him stood unchanged, had continued this exercise until two policemen arrived, came to stand at the foot of the slide, and received him.

The trial judge, though convinced of Schoonover's motive, still found the killings deliberate (performed for gain, though only gain of knowledge metaphysical), so found him sane, and sentenced him to five terms of life, consecutive. . . .

"All right," Bauman said, giving up the Moncrieff, putting it down on the corner of Schoonover's table. "—I apologize. O.K.? It was careless of me. Some of my people needed to work with that book."

Schoonover, head bent, fiddled at his file drawer. No word. No smile. The library was still arranged in Dewey decimal, and needed constant keeping up with.

"I apologize, Larry. I will try to get the books in on time."

"O.K.," Schoonover said, and looked up from his filing. "Just don't take advantage. Friends shouldn't rip friends off, Charles. And as for people, I know what their needs and purposes are better than anyone in this place."

He meant they were keys to a kingdom. Bauman had heard Schoonover out on that just once, and didn't care to hear it again. It was the sort of explanation that kept people out of the library.

"Those workbooks didn't come in? I need the damn things." Bauman wandered over to fiction. A lot of old fiction. Thirty-two shelves. Worn bindings—the cloth covers handled to milky white along their edges—showed where murder or screwing was the subject.

"No, they didn't. And if they didn't come in today, they won't be in till next month. That's their schedule." Schoonover got up to put his narrow file drawer away in the yellow oak reference chest, to slide out another. He carried it back to his table, sat down, pursed his lips, and commenced at the first card, checking order. "I've been thinking about it," he said, "—and I hope you're keeping in mind some notion of guidance for your students. I don't think there's much use teaching a man to read, without advising him what's worth reading."

"Larry, they want to read their appeals, and fuck books."

"I'm not a prude," Schoonover said. "I think they have the right to read anything they want, any trash. If a man can't open the sticky book, he'll open a substitute. . . . You know what I'm talking about. I'm talking about good advice. I think it's part of good teaching."

"Um-hmm. You're probably right." Bauman had learned, over a year, that it was bad policy to argue with Schoonover, and not because Larry controlled library ordering or offered violence in argument. Schoonover had the peculiarity of never admitting defeat in a disagreement unless his error could be proved in a published book. Lacking that proof, Bauman had had to pursue arguments with the librarian that lasted for months—Schoonover, in slow, deliberate terms, reopening the discussions every day they met, with a small synopsis offered first, to recall their subject and positions: the specific effects on the eastern capital of the loss of the themes of Asia Minor; FDR as revolutionary; popular education and the production of an elite—and continuing his thread from there, obsessive as a religious, whatever the matter in dispute.

"Now I'm only a high school teacher, Charles," he would say, "—but logic holds for college professors as well as high school teachers." So continuing, in this odd environment, the petty malice of academic intercourse.

This behavior had struck Bauman at first as funny—later, tedious. Finally, he'd found it disturbing. Schoonover's ambling pace, his careful schoolteacher's enunciation, the measured, tireless repetitions he employed, the simple-minded logic marshaled to small ends began in time to seem sinister, as if Schoonover (if engaged in the wrong debate) might slowly prove to himself a dreadful necessity—as once he had.

"I hear," Schoonover said, looking up from his file drawer, "that you lost a man on B."

"Yes."

"Kenneth Spencer."

"That's right. And I was helping him with some letters, too. Barely literate—wanted to write to a couple of black mayors, some black ministers, trying to finance a better lawyer for appeals. Very shy man. Mainly worried about his family."

"Well, he was here every single Tuesday afternoon—while you were at the gym, playing with that team of muscular morons—here every single Tuesday afternoon using the law library, sitting in that corner puzzling away at the same page for half an hour. I offered to help him research whatever he wanted. 'No, thank you.' That's all Mr. Spencer had to say. I just lost one of my few regulars, is what's happened—and probably to an unpaid debt of two cartons of cigarettes, or some equally earth-shaking obligation."

"He didn't smoke. . . ." Bauman looked along the shelves, slid out a light blue book—its title unreadable, worn away—opened it, and saw it was a Freya Stark work on traveling in Turkey. He read a passage on donkeys (the lessons they patiently taught, of patience) then put the book back and found another—brown, slender, rotting on a lower shelf—a collection of English poetry on crumbling pages, verse evenly divided between garden and orchard sprites, ". . . bobbing in blossoms' cups, through breezy days of May," and reflections on the World War.

Blessed at last with an absence of sun,
And granted that settlement of shade,
The gunners and infantry rest as one,
Dug in beneath their barb-wire glade,
While flare and flashes fill the dark,
Pitch shadows through artillery parks,
From deeper woods, in music bright,
Trumpet tattoos that call to quarters,
All these spangled regiments of night,
To rest from rifles, guns and mortars,
And dream the way to dawn and light.
These sleepers, when required to waken,
Will rouse bereft—furious and forsaken,
To take more lives, and have theirs taken.

"Reconnaissance," *Collected Poems*
Harald Stephenson Ainsworth
Apollonian Press, Coventry

Not, Bauman thought, inappropriate. He supposed that Ainsworth, almost certainly a lieutenant and university man, must have been finally fulfilled by some Mauser, a month before armistice.

"You're losing books, Larry. Some of these things are falling apart."

"That's no news, Charles. If you care to, you might send a letter to the State University people. Possibly the head librarian there will take you more seriously than, apparently, he takes me. They have a complete deacidification setup down there, but they're much too busy to bother with a few shelves of reading material for prisoners. Of course, you could write to your ex-colleagues at Midwest; I'm sure they have the best of everything."

Bauman picked out a copy of a book titled *Follow Me Down*, a shelf higher. He leafed through it—this in better condition. Three pages in the middle of the book were stuck together; he read a passage overleaf of the first of these. A young woman, ignorant, reflective, about to be entered by a goatish farmer. Then the pages stuck together, some inmate having sealed these lovers into privacy with his semen.

"By the way, I've decided to submit," Schoonover said shyly, head bent over his files, "—to Knopf."

Downstairs, the fish hack, fat and freckled, put Bauman to the wall again and patted him down, considering possible contraband from the library, or simply for practice. He left Bauman's ass and crotch strictly alone, and didn't check his socks, didn't have him open his mouth.

The anticipated rain now was drifting down, not much more than steady drizzle spattering along the walkways, falling in mist curtaining across North yard's dun fields of grass. The air was colder. A guard walking along the top of the wall turned his head, looked down at Bauman or near him, then walked on. Too far to see which one it might be. One of the older officers, ready to retire. One of the few veterans.

"Those motherfuckers can see outside," Scooter had said of these once, while he and Bauman were walking to watch some bikers run their machines back and forth beneath the base of the wall—a Sunday privilege for the men in the shop.

"They can't read; they can't talk; they can't even listen to the radio. They just stand around up there," Bauman had said. "I wouldn't trade places with them if that was all there was."

"Shit, Charles," Scooter had said, "you couldn' be more wrong. Those motherfuckers can see *outside*."

They'd walked on across West field, then past the wide front of the laundry building. This building—red brick, three stories high, the West wall's gray granite rearing up behind it—was called the laundry, though only the ground floor contained hot piping, steamy vats, rolling canvas bins, the ranks of mangles along one wall. The building's second floor was Protective Custody. Top floor was Segregation. And, in the building's basement, lay old Cooper's kingdom of Housekeeping, where Bauman had been first assigned.

Past this, State's only building in red brick rather than the prevailing stone, Bauman and Scooter had continued along the base of the wall toward the truck-shop yard. The motorcycle engines were already grumbling, stumbling, barking as the bikers gave them gas. One of the wall guards, leaning on the rail three and a half stories up, was watching them on their way. The metal rims of his dark glasses had flashed an instant in the sunlight as he turned his head.

"You're right, Scoot," Bauman had said, thinking also of the pleasures of his four bus trips with the boxers. "—Because they can see outside. . . ."

Back now across North yard in the rain—he'd tucked his clipboard underneath his jacket. The rain not heavy enough to puddle the walks, soak the grass (soon to be frozen out anyway), not heavy enough to wet Bauman's denims through, just his jacket shoulders, his trouser cuffs.

The walkway yo-yos had backed in under the distant overhangs alongside A and B, and though fewer in this weather, made a continuous dotted line of men there just behind the filmy, beaded curtain of the rain. Most wore bleached denim in various shades of light blue, though a minority afforded street windbreakers and sweaters in browns, reds, and black, and a few dashing dealers sported civilian slacks and jackets. Almost all wore State's gray baseball caps or knit wool watch caps in midnight blue.

They'd be talking football, baseball, boxing, fucking (straight or fag), discussing their families, their kids, their treacherous wives. Boasting of polished remarkable holdups, where courage and luck had combined for rich reward—and talking deals above all. Trading and selling—joints, bags, kids (blowjobs or bungies), leather jackets, magazines, fuck books, uppers, downers, crystal, crank and coke—a pint of this for a pinch of that. Medieval market.

Poor Kenneth Spencer, his throat now cut, must have forgotten where he was, kept careless inappropriate habits from the street. He must have brushed against someone in the halls, or waited for a bill to come in the mail.

Bauman walked down to the northeast corner of B, nodded to two young black men leaning against that corner who'd nodded to him—he'd taught one's housemate to read the alphabet, spell out his name and write it down—then walked past to an open hurricane-fence gate into East yard, and waited to see if the hack in the booth there, a tall ex-farmer named Elroy, wanted to come out for a check.

"Hey, Teach . . . ! You gettin' you ass wet, man!" One of the young black men calling after. Bauman waved an acknowledgment, then saw Elroy look up through the glass and motion him through.

The rain was letting up, pattering in on occasional gusts of even cooler air as he walked the distance down East, turned right to pass through that fence gate to South yard, then walked along the massive granite back of C. This walk was called "boxing" by the inmates—for what reason they were ignorant, some felonious sailor's ancient talk of boxing the compass long lost in grimmer, more entertaining legends.

Bauman felt his damp trousers clinging to him at the knees. Some higher wind was blowing against the clouds, shifting them over. He saw almost a shadow along the grass—the pale momentary sun shining down a wet gray three-story prow, the granite corner past which C-block became D.

D was majority black, and the big block stirred along its tiers in different motions here, sounded along them to different music. The men wandered in thick, slow currents, almost all out of their houses—where many white and Hispanic inmates tended to huddle home if rain or snow made the walkways, the yards unpleasant.

Checked through by two hacks at the steel-barred gate (his building pass examined by a guard named Harrison as if the man had never seen him before, couldn't imagine what a wimp white was doing bringing his act to D), Bauman, carrying his clipboard, walked through these meandering dark streams of silent, murmuring, or laughing men, stepping carefully over the extended legs and feet of those sitting against the block wall, gossiping. He threaded his way, received a few nods, was generally ignored, and climbed the circular stair to Three-tier—careful not to brush the arms or shoulders of men stepping down past him—then walked to cell eleven of the row, a double gone to four-man with crowding.

Wayman Thompson, tall, hunch-shouldered and yellow-eyed, his skin the shade of shadowed lemon, greeted Bauman with real pleasure, homework apparently done—no avoidance, no pouting, no sullenness—shook his hand with a long-fingered grip strong as pliers and seated him on a small crate chair. Then, relaxed, forthcoming (homework certainly done) Wayman offered Bauman a free joint—a rebuilt roach—mentioned with little interest (and no apparent fellow feeling) Spencer's death in Bauman's block, and talked fighting with him for a few minutes.

Was this so-called middleweight motherfucker Muñoz ever goin' wake up he had a right hand—and maybe use it before ever' dude in State lost street money, that Joliet faggot goin' come in an' beat his ass?

Back and forth on Muñoz for a few minutes, Bauman mentioning the jab, the hook—while noticing, as he'd noticed before, on the wall beside Wayman's lower bunk, three photographs (eight-by-tens) taken by some fairly talented pornographer, revealing in close-up series a pretty white girl, her dark hair cut softly short, her pale throat, slight shoulders naked, sucking a black man's penis—her gray eyes (elaborately made-up) blank as a feeding shark's, her jaw opened wide, lips at a painful stretch. In the third of this triptych—all of them torn at their corners by hasty dismounting when hacks had come through on a cleanup pass—in this last picture the man had ejaculated, the girl's eyes now closed (in pleasure, in concentration or relief), chin and cheek slicked, dripping with what had escaped her.

Except for these, Wayman's house was decorous, papered over with torn-out magazine photographs of old-line black celebrities: Diana Ross, Martin Luther King, Bill Cosby, Coretta Scott King, Eddie Murphy, and the Reverend Jesse Jackson. Decorating the cell's corners—to the right and left of the toilet curtain—were action shots of the black stars of professional basketball and boxing, and above those, on the right, one of the Black National Army posters made by the club at State—a large rectangular banner in bright red, divided down the center by a double-edged dagger, black. "B.N.A." printed below as legend.

Agreeing, after some time, to disagree on the usefulness of Muñoz' jab, his double-punching with the hook, Wayman slid two packs of filter straights from under his pillow, and handed them over. Then he bent down, reached beneath his bunk for his book bag, unzipped it, got a green-covered notebook out, and settled to read his story assignment aloud, raising his voice over the cacophony of the block.

Wayman's housemate, Roy—a very big black man, and very fat over the big—lay listening in the opposite lower bunk, dressed in bead-decorated denims. Roy had never spoken directly to Bauman in a dozen visits, never shaken his hand—whether from shyness or dislike. He smiled, but he was always smiling. The other two men from eleven were out walking—always were when Bauman came.

" 'Khalife Goes to School.' . . ."

Wayman Thompson had a pleasant voice, sounding slightly younger than its owner—now serving two consecutive lifes—who had six years before broken into a handsome house (apparently empty) in a handsome suburb, found to his surprise a pretty woman with her pretty daughter, the child kept home from school by flu—and had lost control of himself.

" 'Khalife Goes to School.' . . . Once they was a little boy. He name Khalife. Khalife go to school on the bus but he get off. He goin' say he bus-left. He see a little dog. Dog ax him why you not be in school? I don' want to go, Khalife say. Dog say, You auntie see you she whip you butt. Dog say . . . he say you better go to school. Khalife say, kiss my ass—"

"Right on," Roy said from his opposite bunk, and received a hard yellow look from the interrupted.

"You payin' this man?"

Roy shook his large head, his soft black jowls and chins. Wayman bent his head, studied, and resumed.

"—Khalife go on by. Another dog. He come by. This dog be bigger. This big dog be tellin' him—is tellin' him—go to school."

"Say 'Kiss my ass,' " Roy said, irrepressible—then, at Wayman's fierce glance, wallowed gleeful over onto his right side to hide his face in his pillow, and giggle.

"He a fuckin' retard, man," Wayman said to Bauman, which made great Roy shake harder, so his bunk trembled.

Wayman sat up straighter, examined his notebook to find his place, and continued where he'd left off. "—Khalife say kiss my ass. I ain' goin'—not be goin'. Then a big ol' *monster* dog he come over to Khalife. The dog be hidin' behin' a tree. The monster dog say go to school Khalife or I'm comin' in you house tonight an' eat you legs so they jus' stumps stickin' out. Khalife he go right on . . . to school."

Wayman, finished, looked up at Bauman defenseless as a child.

"Are you bullshitting me, man?" Bauman said, theatrically unpleasant.

Surprise. Shock. "What you mean . . . ?"

"You didn't write that; that's too damn good. You pay some dude to write that story for you? —You did, didn't you?"

"No. . . . No!" Delighted—and his friend Roy delighted for him, rolling back to face them, saying, "He did so. He write that story 'bout them dogs!"

"No shit, now," Bauman said. "Don't waste my time. You wrote that?"

"Every fuckin' word, man. I didn' tell nobody, an' no motherfucker tol' me."

"All your idea?"

"Fuckin' a! It was my idea—them dogs an' everythin'."

"No shit?"

"No sir, no *sir!*" Bad boys momentarily back in school—successful at last, not fools.

"Let me tell you something," Bauman said, happy as Wayman, "—that is very good work. Congratulations, man. You are reading and writing."

Wayman modest on his bunk.

"—Doesn't mean it's perfect. Let me see it. I think you left out your commas. You've got to remember, commas are like taking a breath—you know, hesitating when you say something? You need to put those in. So it sounds like somebody talking."

Wayman's irregular printing was innocent of any marks but several large periods drawn as small egg-shaped O's. Bauman slid his red pencil out of his clipboard clamp, and entered commas. "And you have some words in different tenses—showing different times that things happened?—that need to be changed. Got some work to do. But I'll tell you, it's not bad. That's a good story."

"I got them three dogs," Wayman said, "—gettin' bad."

"That's right. One, two, three—getting worse and worse. One—two—three. Like three strikes in baseball. That's the best thing about your story—that there're three dogs, and they get bigger and meaner as the story goes along. . . ."

Feeling better than he had since Spencer's screaming, Bauman, going down the tier stairs, brushed past a man only a little carelessly.

"Hey! You fuckin' motherfucker! Who you puttin' you han' on?"

"Sorry," Bauman said, quickly as he could. He turned to look back up, and saw a stocky black man in white T-shirt and shorts despite the chill weather, saw the man's furious face.

A taller black man in denims, standing beside the shorter on the steps, and looking down at Bauman, said, "You come back on up here, you ofay faggot, I'm goin' break your fuckin' jaw." And Bauman realized this was the man who'd called down after him, not the other.

"Sorry," Bauman said. "It was an accident." Turned back and went down the stairs, carefully, the back of his neck heavy with being stared at.

" '*Accident.*' . . . You old faggot cocksucker, you better move your pale ass out!" called after him, echoing off steel and concrete, plain through the many voices, the varied musics of the block.

Chapter TWO

Lunch was peanut-butter sandwiches, iced tea, orange Jell-O.

Bauman had been eating alone, then was joined by two fish fresh up from Evansville. One, a thin young Hispanic with a bony nose and slightly bucked teeth, was silent. The other—a sturdy white, and older—occasionally commented on the mess hall, the lunch, trying to seem tough. The white man asked Bauman about a bunk, complained that men were already housed in the cell he'd been assigned.

"If you have some money coming," Bauman said, "—then buy a bed."

"I ain't buyin' shit, man," the white fish said. He had a heavy face, blocked almost square; an upper tooth was missing at the left side of his mouth. "It ain't my first fuckin' time in a joint."

Bauman said nothing more to him, sat silent and finished his orange Jell-O. The white fish also stopped talking. He hadn't finished his sandwich, didn't seem to have the appetite to finish it.

Bauman got up, took his tray to the serving counter's garbage can, scraped it, stacked it, then walked down the basement corridor and up wide stone steps—each gently hollowed, the granite dished almost two inches deep by more than a century of feet, chipped here and there where some earlier convict had dropped the cannonball he carried, its short jingling chain fastened to his leg irons. Up on Ground-tier, a hack, a plump, talkative older man named Carlyle, passed him without patting.

Bauman walked the length of Ground-tier to the circular stair and climbed the white steel, reminded as he went up of how miserably he'd fled down in D—the shouts ringing behind him, the furious face of the shorter man.

Off the staircase landing on Two-tier, he walked into his house, went behind the blanket curtain, pulled down his trousers, and sat on the toilet's bare cold cracked porcelain. An older convict named Metzler—a lifer, and supposedly a very dangerous man—had been knifed to death, disemboweled, while sitting on his cell toilet weeks before.

Bauman imagined he'd behaved differently in D. Imagined he'd had his shank, had turned at the first remark, tugged the weapon out, then hurried up the stairs toward the tall man and his short friend—had seen, as he went up, their twin glances at the knife, their shouts turning to sand in their mouths. . . .

He leaned forward, strained his bowels, and passed nothing—none of the peas, creamed tuna, and cherry Jell-O of last evening's dinner. Nothing of breakfast. He resigned himself to a wait, sat considering the knife.

He'd carried, for a short time, a very fine shank (double-edged and almost six inches in the blade) sheathed in a sheet of folded gray cardboard and strapped with electrician's tape high up on the inside of his right thigh. This because of a disagreement on legal fees with an inmate named Les Kerwin, State's premium jailhouse lawyer, a *pro pers* specializing in appeals. Kerwin—some time ago, before Bauman had come up—had stuck a defaulting client in the eyes with a sharpened length of bedspring wire. That man had been blinded, and Kerwin handed an assault conviction on top of his previous murder-two.

Bauman's problem with the *pro pers* was not so severe—a question of whether a casual conversation on Superior Court findings (having nothing to do with Bauman's own case) constituted a consultation, and was to be paid for.

Kerwin said yes; Bauman, no, Kerwin remaining amiable throughout, uttering no threats. However, Scooter had asked around and found that Kerwin had been equally lightsome with the man he'd finally walked up to and blinded on the West-yard walkway one afternoon. Had stuck the pointed wire into the man's left eye—tugged it free—

and, clinging like a beast, had ridden the screamer down flat, wrestled his head to hold it still enough, then pushed the wire carefully into the right eye, driving it till it went through and stuck in the thin bone before the brain. Then got up and walked away, leaving a kicking ruin in the dark.

Wire removed some time later at the Regional Medical Center in Fort McLaren. Life saved, sight not.

Bauman, over five weeks ago, had started taking his chances of a severe ticket and ten-and-twenty (ten days solitary, twenty segregation) by carrying the knife when he went off block into lonely places or too public places, going elaborately out of his way to avoid the metal detectors at main building–to–yard gates. He'd practiced in their house while Scooter criticized—reaching down into his pants to grip the knife's short flat taped handle, then tug it up and out, ready to use. It took a lot of time, and certainly would seem to take more if a strong man was on him—Kerwin was fit, tall and handsome, with prematurely graying hair, an upper-middle-class professional look—would seem to take much too much time if a strong man was on him and sticking a needle-pointed wire into his eyes.

"You're goin' to have to hold him off with your left," Scooter had said, "while you get that shank out."

"Hold him off, my ass. Run, is what the hell I need to do, if I can get this damn thing out, running."

"You get it out, though, guy's in trouble."

"If I get it out," Bauman said. The blade was one of the best, filed from the machined side-strip off an old stamp press in the license shop. An elderly convict named Boscowen made them and sold them for street money only—no scrip, no powder, no weed, no speed, no ass. The knife had cost Bauman forty-five dollars, street cash, and a spoiled visit with a weeping wife (the small fold of bills—two twenties and a five—knotted into a tiny pink toy balloon, and extracted from Susanne's vagina in a stall of the visitors' toilet). Had cost Bauman more than that, really, since he'd had to give seven reading lessons to a Black Muslim imam (who'd been faking his services from remembered texts) in exchange for the fundamentals of killing with a knife, which, it seemed, involved suddenness rather than style. Fast hard punching, the knife present almost incidentally in the power hand, not the lead.

Bauman had thought he might do that well enough—the punching part, anyway—if he didn't prove so frightened that Kerwin had only to come up and butcher and blind him while he tried to think of something to say.

After less than two weeks carrying, Bauman began to leave the knife at home, slid deep into the works of Scooter's portable TV. The cell's two sizable square vents (warm dry air in, smelling of oil, warm damp air out, smelling of everything else) were set one into the ceiling's center, the other surrounded by the pictures of machines and women on the house's left wall. These large vents, seeming so convenient as hidey-holes, were not. The square vent grills, composed of ten rows of inch-square openings up, ten across, were cut from thick steel plate, and that fastened with twelve face-bolts deep into the stone. —So, the back of Scooter's TV, with barely room enough alongside the picture tube for the slender knife, its tape-and-cardboard harness.

It had begun to seem to Bauman more and more ridiculous, absurd for him to be strutting with a shank, entertaining masturbatory fantasies of combat, and, as well, had worried him constantly about getting a tag for carrying, something that might blot his sheet. He felt that Kerwin was simply not hot enough about the matter for it to be worth the risk. This reinforced when that nemesis, approaching Bauman in the mess-hall line at lunch, had one day casually inquired concerning the progress of Tony Marcantonio.

Marcantonio, a slow, monstrously strong light-heavy—and as one of the few whites on the boxing team, a darling of the Caucasian Union—had been doing very well. He'd bruised even such heavyweight monuments as Clarence Henry and Bubba Betts when, to be reminded of fundamentals, he'd been set to sparring over his class. Les Kerwin had been pleasant discussing this, stood easy and held only ordinary eye contact, not too little, not too much.

"Your ass, Charles," Scooter said one night before lights-out. "Ain't goin' do you any good in my TV. And you're one of the guys can get away with carryin', 'cause you're always runnin' around givin' lessons. Hacks don't never think you got nothin'. —They don't even pat you good."

"It's a chance I'm tired of taking," Bauman had said. "So what I'll do, if he jumps me, is just run. He can't stick me if he can't catch me."

"Then better not let him get you in a one-door place, dude. . . ."

He took vanilla, supposing the chocolate to be more precious to her.

"You wan' two?" Betty Nellis, plump, dark-eyed, dark-skinned and pretty, with penciled eyebrows and no shadow of beard to see—possibly an effect of smuggled hormones—extended her small left hand with another vanilla cookie resting on the palm.

"No thanks," Bauman said, sitting (his clipboard on his lap) on a small furniture-factory rocker—pine, stained cherry, and a reminder of Mark Nellis' eminence. Betty's husband, Bauman's landlord until the purchase outright of the house upstairs, possessed the luxuries commanded by a fearsome reputation—in his case as one of the agents of lifer murder power, and a Caucasian Union officer as well, though Scooter had said Betty'd told him Nellis had retired. This reputation the more surprising since the dreadful Nellis looked perfectly ordinary—medium-sized, sturdy, balding. In his mid-thirties, but seeming, as some men do, to yearn for the comfort of forty, Nellis had mild blue eyes and wore State-issue glasses. However, he'd never been called Four-eyes, not even Specs—not before he'd stabbed a soldier of the Black National Army to death on the South-yard walkway, and certainly not after.

Three years before Bauman came up to State, Nellis had attacked this man, a dangerous jocker and much larger, and knifed him twice in the lower back, then three times more in the man's belly as he turned, trying to defend himself. This soldier of the B.N.A., accompanied only seconds before by friends—two black men as large and powerful, swaggering, on the stroll—had stood suddenly deserted as they fled, had stood all alone in the sunshine with Nellis and Nellis' knife.

Then he ran, staggering along the walkway, stumbling now and then into the building-side, and calling out hoarsely for help, leaving on the granite bright smears and spatters to mark his progress and Nellis' pursuit. Nellis, persistent, stabbed and stuck into the broad back retreating before him until the B.N.A. soldier, exhausted, sat down on the warm cement, then lay down on his right side, drew up his knees, and died in front of a fish guard named Ed Berry.

Berry had later testified, but to a fight—the second knife somehow missing, lost—not a murder. Word was, that before the hearing on the Nellis matter, two of Nellis' home-boys, veteran armed robbers from downstate, had visited the guard's family in Garlin while Berry was on duty. Had visited, enjoyed some conversation with Mrs. Berry in her kitchen, the smaller man holding the Berrys' little girl on his lap, then left without hurting anybody, without threatening. . . .

"You want a lot of milk, Charles?" The "you" pronounced a soft Hispanic "jew." This accent, quite heavy in moments of excitement, added considerably to Betty's charm.

"If you can spare it." His first few visits for afternoon coffee, months before (sometimes accompanied by an ex-banker named Thruston, since paroled), Betty Nellis had called him "Mr. Bauman," apparently out of regard for his former professorship. This had soon relaxed to

"Charles," which she appeared to enjoy pronouncing, the *l* undergoing slight, charming glottal confusions before the relief of *es*.

These coffee hours became frequent and, attracting the envy of other ladies, had encouraged the casual custom of such afternoon salons throughout State, where owners, lovers, husbands permitted. In Betty's case, Nellis, pleased by what pleased his wife, had offered no objection at all. For these gatherings, one or two or three people of previous or present eminence—if presentable and easy-tempered—were invited for circumspect gossip and to drink hot-coil coffee, eat canteen-bought cookies, and, on special occasions such as birthdays or successful hearings for parole, to share small pound cakes baked in the ceiling light fixture of a basement supply closet.

Bauman, when fresh up to State, had been startled, then amused, and finally touched by the efforts of some long-term inmates to create odd and fragile versions of the warm and loving families most of them had never known. These "families," usually built around a necessarily homosexual relationship, often grew rather elaborate, so that a fierce middle-aged murderer might assume a father's role, with an ex-pimp for wife. Their son perhaps a loving thief, daughter-in-law a pretty forger. A nephew, troublesome and charming, a young armed robber.

"I got a lot of milk today." Betty poured a good dollop into a mug, ceramic brown, with an English setter on point baked into its side. "I brought up two cartons from breakfas'. That's one advantage not havin' much up here," gesturing at the front of her white blouse—adapted (fitted, tailored, and illegally frilled) from an original man's dress shirt—where the cartons apparently had ridden up concealed. "I don' serve no coffee without havin' some milk."

Standing at her shelves on the cell's right side beyond the double bunk, Betty lifted her hot-coil from the pan of coffee water, tested the water's temperature delicately with a small brown forefinger, then dropped the coil back in—the instrument's wire draped companionably across her right shoulder on its way up to the multiple plug holding the ceiling bulb as well. "This takes forever," she said. Then, ducking under the wire, stepped lightly back down the cell in white blouse and pale blue denims tailored to slacks, the pants zipper on the side, to perch on the edge of the lower bunk, framed by curtains in a pretty green-flowered print, drawn back and tied for the day. There, Betty settled with a hostess's satisfaction, and watched Bauman eat his vanilla cookie.

"Creme sandwiches," she said, smiling at him across the narrow aisle, raising her voice slightly against the steady uproar of the block.

"What?"

"When they vanilla, they call them creme sandwiches." Her eyes, tender as a child's, were a light sweet canine brown.

Bauman could only nod, his tongue having separated the bite's cookie halves, busy breaking the top against the roof of his mouth. Not as good as chocolate, but good enough.

Betty, certainly eager for some discussion, probably of the killing two tiers up, had made her customary chirping sound from the doorway of Nellis' house as Bauman came down the stairs from one o'clock lock-'n'-count, then gestured him in. Now, her coffee in preparation, she sat on her bunk, hands folded, waiting patiently for Bauman to swallow and settle down. A wedding ring hammered at the truck shop out of steel and tiny jeweled bearings shone on her left hand's plump brown ring finger. She and Nellis had been married by a born-again forger last spring.

"That was the worse thing, man, that thing las' night," she said, and shook her head so that her hair—fine and tarry black, grown long as the administration would tolerate—shifted softly left to right. "That little nigger never bothered nobody. He was a sweet little man. An' now, you los' your frien'."

"Well, not really a friend," Bauman said, and when he saw something like reproach in Betty's gaze for that quick cowardice, added, "I don't mean I didn't like him. He seemed to me to be a very decent guy. I was helping him out, and we ate lunch together a few times. Yesterday too, and he didn't say a word about anything bothering him, other than being in here. It's a goddamned shame. This place is bad enough, without killings."

Kenneth Spencer had, in fact, been shy as a hermit crab, noticeably silent in a city of reticent men. Shy, silent, and ugly, he'd resembled—with his cocoa color, apprehensive eyes, large mouth, large ears—a chimpanzee raised in a human home.

"You like a man, it's rough he get killed." Betty, reflective. "It's scary, le's face it. Figger it could happen to that little dude, could happen to anybody." She seemed upset by Spencer's end, where another killing only five weeks before—of a *Zapatista* named Rosario Coelho, castrated in the showers in A-block, and so roughly he'd bled to death—had been the occasion for her of nothing but interest, interest in the causative transgression, to be sure, not in any particular possible killer.

"And, honey," Bauman said, "—you can bet not a damn thing is going to be done about it. Not one damn thing." The 'honey' had been spoken naturally in conversation with her months before, had been received without comment or complaint (perhaps with pleasure), and since had become customary. "He probably borrowed a little money—I hope to Christ not to pay me with—was a day late paying it back, and that naturally gave some creep an excuse to murder him."

"You don' wan' to call names, Charles. An' Spencer didn' borrow no money," Betty Nellis said in that conclusive tone Bauman had learned signified information received from her husband. "He didn' buy nothin' but candy, anyway." True enough. Bauman had often seen small Spencer standing carefully in line at the canteen, cautious not to bump or jostle, waiting his turn to buy two Snickers, or three of the smaller Hersheys, without almonds.

"Jus' like that guy in D. That dude wasn' botherin' nobody neither."

"Who?"

"Blake. Wimpy little white guy."

"Right." Blake, a burglar, had been stabbed to death five or six months before, while showering alone off the basement corridor of D-block. "I thought he was raped. You know, some people got hold of him in the showers before that ever happened."

"Tha's right. But he didn' do nothin' about that. —Wasn' no reason for anybody to kill that man. Wasn' no reason for anybody to go an' kill Spencer, neither."

"Well, I suppose Spencer could have been a mistake. They could have gotten the wrong house in the dark. . . ."

Another headshake, soft shifting of her hair. "No way. You do somethin' like that, Charles, you count them cell doors goin' down the tier so that don' happen." Professional information from Nellis, Bauman supposed—though Betty, now so gentle, had (as Osvaldo Perez) practiced armed robbery upon fortressed dealers during their deals, and had killed two. "You know what they did, get them night-lights out?" She reached behind her to the open box of cookies resting on the bunk's brown blanket, picked out another creme cookie, and held it out to Bauman, dubious. "You rather have chocolate, wouldn' you?"

"No. That's fine. The vanillas are good."

"You rather have chocolate," Betty said, reached behind her to return the cookie carefully to its place, then stood up and walked back to her shelves. As she passed him, Bauman realized she was wearing perfume—jasmine, or something like it—against regulations.

She stood over at her shelves, rummaging. Her denim slacks were tailored tight, snug up into her buttocks' crease.

"I don't need a chocolate cookie," Bauman said. "—These're fine."

Betty opened one cigar box, closed it, and opened another.

"Honey, would you please sit down," Bauman said. "—These are fine. I do not need a chocolate cookie."

"You goin' have one, anyway," she said, and came over to present him with two Oreos. "Come on, now. Don' make me mad. I got plenty cookies." Standing close, she seemed quite small.

Bauman took the cookies, bit into one, and held the other on his knee, forefinger lightly tracing the carving on its surface as Betty went back to her shelf, apparently found her coffee water hot enough, filled the setter mug (milk and instant coffee already in it) and added three spoonfuls of sugar without needing to ask. Then she prepared a smaller cup for herself, and carrying both, came to present the mug to Bauman and go to her bunk, this time reclining, cup in her right hand. She lay—almost Goya's duchess, in denims—observing Bauman at her ease and his. Sipped as he sipped.

"Good coffee," Bauman said.

"Taster's Choice. Marky won' have nothin' else in the house."

Bauman rocked the small chair in relaxation, noticed two new paintings on the cell's close walls. No centerfolds, no naked pussy on display, only paintings on velvet by Tony Di Marco, State's only class counterfeiter-engraver. All the paintings—there were seven of various sizes—were done in very dark palettes—dark grays, purples, deep carmines, basalt blues. Only touches of white or bright orange where a warning sign was shown bolted to granite. Subjects were: the wall, West mess, the lifers at dinner, a tower that seemed to be the northeast corner tower, Administration (from the inner entrance), an old convict named John Gingold standing in the South yard, and two young bikers Bauman didn't recognize standing arm in arm outside the truck shop, smiling at the artist.

"We don' have no trash in here," Betty said, as she usually did when Bauman looked at her house's decoration. "You like them new ones? Gingold an' them bikers?"

"They're very nice." Not so foolish, banning from such close confines reminders of greater spaces—sunny beaches, swift machines. Women complete in their womanhood. There were no pictures of Betty's family, or Nellis'.

"You know how they got 'em out? —The night-lights?"

"No."

"Carlyle tol' me. Some dude put . . . folded a little piece of Reynolds Wrap. That foil?" Her small hands mimed folding. "Took a little piece of that, stuck it in the fuse box in the gate office down there. How about that? Them cops suppose' to be lookin' out for everybody, a dude goes right in that office an' fixes the fuse box."

"They're out of there all the time."

"That's what I'm sayin'. They not suppose' to be out of there. —That shit suppose' to be their job."

"That's true."

"They don' care. That's what's true."

"So the wrap melted after a while . . ."

"You got it. Three, four hours them night-lights is on—an' that stuff melts an' that's it. Some cowboy can come an' off anybody he wants."

"How'd he get out at night—miss lock-'n'-count?"

Betty transferred her coffee cup to her left hand, reached behind her for a creme cookie. "Now you're askin' the big question, Charles. That's the big one. —An' Marky figures you got to ask some hack. You tell me another way a dude is out in the middle of the night, runnin' aroun'."

She took a bite of her cookie. "Those motherfuckin' cops," Betty Nellis said, her gentle spaniel's eyes belonging for a moment to a different breed, less gentle.

The small chair was a pleasure to sit in. Bauman rocked steadily back and forth. He drank more of his coffee, and started to eat the second Oreo. He'd separated the first Oreo with his tongue to get at the filling. This one, he bit into.

"I heard Clarence hurt his han'," Betty said. "Is that true?"

"No. It isn't true. I don't think Clarence could hurt his hand—unless he sparred that wall out there."

"A lot of money on this Joliet fight, Charles. People don' want to lose to them faggots. —They sure don' want nothin' wrong with Clarence's han'."

"His hand's fine. They're all in good shape; that's the one thing they've all got. Not a lot of style, but plenty of stay."

"You goin' over there today?"

"No, I'm not going over—for a change. The old man gave them today as a down day. I think he'll be working them hard from now on, build a good edge on them for the Joliet people. And he also got Trebona to go over and replace two of the showers today. Wouldn't hurt to put in all new showers; they're rusting away."

"You wasn' so old, you be tryin' out to fight?"

"No," Bauman said, "I wouldn't. I'm not tough enough. I never was that tough."

Betty considered that, made a soft continuous popping sound with her lips, but didn't contradict him.

"I saw your wife—over at visitin'. You mind I say that?"

"No."

"Well—that's touchy, you know, you talk about some dude's family. Your family doin' O.K.?" Betty held her head to one side, interested.

Bauman finished his coffee, the last swallow running through a half-chewed bite of cookie, making the chocolate taste more chocolate. "They're doing pretty well. . . ."

Almost two weeks before, in the crowded visiting room, Susanne had wasted half an hour in earnest conversation—her voice hushed in tone, slightly high in volume to clear the racket in the room—while the two of them sat primly side by side on a torn-cushioned orange couch. Susanne—in gray tweed skirt, blue silk blouse, dark blue sweater—keeping her head turned away from their neighbors sitting directly across the aisle in a straight-back chair. These were an Hispanic dealer in for five, and his wife, a plump young blond girl with milky blue eyes, who, astride her husband's lap, pretended to conversation while posting slowly up and down under the umbrella of her long flowered skirt. A few inches up, a few inches down. Talking softly as she did, he nodding, smiling, listening.

One of the duty hacks, Dubois, was standing half the room away, talking with a con Bauman didn't know. Two little boys ran the aisle beside them; one had something the other wanted.

"Charlie, I need your help." Susanne seeming the most distressed of these many visitors. "I just . . . let me talk with you. Let me just talk with you."

"Of course," Bauman had said. "We'll just visit. —How's Braudel?"

"He's fine. He's eating like a pig."

"He misses me."

"Well, we both miss you."

Bauman saw she'd put on more makeup than usual. There was rouge or something at the fine cheekbones. Bright lipstick, an almost tangerine shade. Eye liner, eye shadow, faint burnt umber. Her eyes, soft in conformation, colored so cool a nacreous green, were complimented by these shades, made almost into semiprecious stones. Spinal, peridot, or opal. And, as opals occasionally were, streaked lightly at their corners—the inner corners, here—with pink.

The blond girl across from them had hummed softly, sat still, and bent her head slowly to rest on her husband's left shoulder.

"You won't be missing me much longer," Bauman said. "Only until late next year. We can consider this just as having been a particularly grubby sabbatical." He'd felt immediately ashamed of speaking so slightingly of State, of pretending to make light of what was in fact so massive, so particular and frightening. Bravado—and probably unconvincing.

"That's not too long." Susanne glanced away as the blond girl across the aisle, dismounting from her husband's lap, shook Kleenex from her plaid purse, straddled, and reached up under her long skirt to mop and clean. A baby, sounding like two babies, was crying through the conversations across the room.

"I'm going to put Braudel on a diet," Susanne said, still looking away at nothing to her left.

"Let Braudel eat." Bauman was imagining the little Brussels griffon—black, spidery, cropped tail stub revealing an innocent asshole, his bright black unfriendly eyes bulging observant above the breed's curious monkey's muzzle. Bauman considered Braudel's freedom to come trotting in and out of their home—coming, going, doing as he pleased through the backyards of the block, then returning, prancing in through the back door, very small, sooty black, nails clicking over linoleum, to bury his flat face in his food.

Their home was the right side of an ugly slate blue duplex on Carteret (the house on Stuart gone to buy Beth's). The left side of the duplex, rented by an Indian woman—plump, middle-aged, a professor of particle physics—produced occasional rich odors of curry and the susurrous thump and jangle of Indian music. Produced as well, once in a while at night, faint hooting cries audible through the bedrooms' connecting wall. These sounds accompanied by soft, hurried creaking, the physicist's bed, acknowledging strenuous activity, responding as Newton had suggested.

"A student," Susanne had said, referring to the lady's partner, and had been more than supported when she and Bauman, up one morning for an early breakfast, had seen two young men (one Susanne knew) walking away through the first of daylight, up the duplex's drive.

"—I took him for his shots, and the vet said he's snapping because he's fat."

"He's snapping because he's a nasty little shit. Let's talk about something else."

Susanne had been sitting nearly at attention, tall, lean, and pale. Of an age with the surrounding wives and girlfriends, but badly out of place, she sat erect and looked at Bauman, waiting for the new subject's introduction.

The blonde who'd just fucked, her skirt now decorously arranged, was reseated in her husband's lap, her round left arm about his neck, her other lying along her right thigh, white forearm glowing, palm up, relaxed.

Bauman had decided well before sentencing, even before McElvey had suggested it, not to tie himself into certain knots, drearily predictable. It seemed reasonable, though, to mention the makeup.

"I assume, from the makeup and so forth, that there's a little bit of sea-changing going on. Somebody being sympathetic? Coming by to visit?"

"To visit?" she said, and glanced at the blond girl sitting safe across the aisle.

"Could be whoever the man is, who's being sympathetic, listening to your troubles—and Christ knows, sweetheart, you have them, and Christ knows I'm bitterly sorry for them. Whoever—"

"Charlie—"

"Whoever this guy is—and he's probably a decent man, a kind man. Paul—right? Whenever Maureen's got a conference?"

"Please—"

"Whoever, the fact of the matter is if he should comfort you by sticking his cock into you, he's performing a hell of a selfish act."

She gave Bauman the look she'd given him at the police station more than a year before.

"I amaze you. I astound you by my crudeness, my unfairness. How could I be so wrong? —How could I be such a commonplace jealous asshole?"

"That's right," she said.

"I didn't say it was happening. I just assume some male, Paul or whoever, has smelled you and is hanging around making comforting noises . . . leaning against the kitchen counter near you while you make coffee. Then, when you come here, you act every goddamn time as if you were coming into the arena. It's all just too, too much for you. These are only human beings, you know, and some of them are smarter even than graduate students."

"There's nobody," she said. "—It may worry you, but it doesn't worry me."

"Nobody's been nice to you? Tried to make things a little less lonely for you. None of your friends have been friends?"

"They've been friends, and that's it."

"O.K. End of discussion. Chalk it up to eyeliner paranoia. Sue, would you like to skip a few of these visits? Are we doing any good with them? I'm afraid we're damaging each other with these goddamn visits. . . ."

"I meant I wanted to talk with you, Charlie—be with you—not come up here just so you can take me into the toilet."

"I see. That's reasonable. You've got a point. You've got *the* point, and I'm getting jailhouse hysteria. Please forgive me. And you're right; we don't have to waltz off to the toilet. —O.K. Let's visit. What did Turley say about the paper? I know what he said. He said, 'Show me amber at those sites.' "

"Yes. He said he needed finds—not beads and perhapses."

"The man's an idiot, but that's all right. Dealing with an idiot's good practice for dealing with the next idiot. —And look, we're talking! See? I don't have to get laid. I don't have to be an aging beast. . . . Sue, I'm happy just to look at you. Really, sweetheart, I am. It makes me feel better." He wanted to kiss her, lick some of the lipstick off her mouth, but decided he'd better not.

Susanne, pleased, smiling, had reached to stroke Bauman's blunt right hand with her long-boned left. Stroked and patted. The visit before—three weeks before—he'd had her sitting on a toilet (an inmate named Webster looking out while Bauman and another convict, whose name he didn't know, dealt with their wives in adjacent stalls). He'd had her there, slacks and panties down and off, her bare feet tender in sandals. There'd been soft damp smacking noises through the partition, the appearance (just visible under the partition's edge) of a middle-aged woman's wrists and hands, hands planted on the floor, fingers spread—the woman taking, it appeared, considerable strain on all fours, supporting shoving weight. Murmuring, "Oh, dear . . . oh, dear, oh, dear . . ." as she was acted upon.

Bauman had turned Susanne's head so she could see those worn freckled bearing hands, the trembling wrists, and Susanne, aroused or obedient, had taken that woman's rhythm up.

"Now," Bauman said—returned from that reverie, he'd raised Susanne's hand and kissed it, "—now, let's see what we can think of for that ass and his amber." And they'd spoken of that till the buzzer. Then kissed goodbye. . . .

"How's your boy doin', Charles?" Betty was chewing a bite of cookie, her soft mouth slightly open.

"Fine. He's all right."

"Well, I wish I had a boy back then. People say boys are more trouble. You should see me tryin' bring up my girls. —I hit 'em. I admit it right out, man. I smack them little mothers ever' time they got out of line. I'm not talkin' about hittin' 'em hard, you know? Jus' on their butts. I didn' do that, them two would take over that house. An' I hit 'em, an' Marita would come after me with her fingernails—you know, goin' for my face? 'Don' you hit my babies!' " Betty sighed on her bunk. "No way raisin' girls is easier than raisin' boys. Dude say that, didn' try it."

"My boy wasn't much trouble," Bauman said. "—He was always very cool. Nothing bothered him much."

"That's good," Betty said. "That's the kind of kid you want, you in here. You don' want a kid gets bothered. You think my girls ever come visit? Never. Know what she says? Marita says they scared, man. You ever hear any shit—you ever hear any stuff like that? Charles, what they got to be scared about? Not even comin' up an' see their papa. . . ."

"My boy hasn't been up."

"That's different. These are girls, man. They suppose' to be full of love. Know how many times I cry at night, jus' because those two little shits wouldn' come up here with their mama? It broke my heart, man—it jus' broke it. Wasn' for my Marky, I don' know what I'd do." Her round soft brown face appeared to fold upon itself preparatory to tears—so completing for Bauman the pleasure of his visit, making her more nearly the ghost of the presence of women—an instrument of tender response, sturdy, pretty, injured and brave. Almost convincing.

"I have to go. I've got a student. . . ."

Betty sat half up, bent her head, and used a corner of her pillowcase to pat tears from her eyes. "I don' know why those dudes can't go to the damn classes. This joint got regular classes for 'em to go to. Why you got to be teachin' 'em?" She sniffled, and lay back.

"Well, it's a job I was able to get. People who won't go to the regular classes—they don't like things that remind them of school, I suppose."

"Charles, ain' nobody likes that shit." Forgetting that Bauman must have.

"It's a job."

"I wouldn' do that shit—that stuff—for a million dollars, tryin' to show them niggers, all them monkeys, how to read." A reminder this was a Union house, Betty's brownness notwithstanding. "—Listen, you know what we was talkin' about, that boy Chris?"

"Right." For weeks, Mark and Betty Nellis had been considering adoption, a serious step and one that had seemed to Bauman to strain their marriage slightly. The object of this—Chris Onofrio—was nineteen years old, looked younger, and perhaps was slightly retarded. A shy, pleasant boy in the old-fashioned hippie style, he'd come up on the chain from Classification at Evansville eight weeks before.

"Marky wants a family. An' I understan' that. I got no objection. It's jus' I already got my kids—you know, Charles? Now, Marky never had no kid in his life. He was married, but nothin' happened. An' now he wants to adopt this boy, this wop kid never did nothin' but steal cars!"

"Um-hmm."

"An' he's sayin', 'Well, this is a boy, an' that's different.' This way, I already got two daughters—now I can have a boy."

"Right."

"But he isn' goin' be raisin' that boy! He isn' goin' be takin' care of him! —I'm goin' be doin' all that shit. An' when Marky's goin' be out playin' basketball with that boy, an' teachin' him poker an' shit, an' takin' him in the business an' shankin' him up an' doin' all that shit—that stuff—what am I suppose' to do stayin' here aroun' this house?"

"It's a problem."

"—That boy's goin' be aroun' here all the time, man. An' I'm talkin' about privacy. What's goin' happen to our relationship, is what I'm sayin'. But Marky don' see that."

"Well, he's a nice boy."

"I know that. I know he's a nice boy. —You know two jockers tried to get him in the weight room? Give that boy some jive they wanted to talk to him. Talk to him in the fuckin' weight room? You believe that shit—that stuff?"

"Not good."

"Marky says we got to take care of that boy. But I don' know. . . . You bet ain' no motherfucker goin' be takin' Marky Nellis' kid into no fuckin' weight room."

"That's right."

"Marky says we got to settle down, be a regular family." She sighed. "I don' know. . . . I never chipped since we got married. Not one time. Man *has* the best goddamn wife in State. —What the fuck does a man want more'n love?"

Betty lay thinking about it. She was wearing white sneakers. Women's sneakers, narrow, with flowered laces. Neat brown ankles above those, no socks, and where the legs of the denim slacks were pulled a little high as she lay, sturdy calves just beginning, shaved smooth, brown as toast.

Bauman then looked up into her face, and saw there, regarding him, acknowledging his regard, the most complete and womanly recognition.

"An' how about you? How you doin'? —You doin' O.K., Charles?"

"I'm doing all right."

"You know, you see that Lee Cousins over here this mornin'?"

"Scooter said he saw her."

"Well, that's not the prettiest lady in here. Prettiest Anglo, maybe, but no way the prettiest lady. Marcia the prettiest lady."

"I'd say you are." A little risky, but surely not much.

Betty was pleased. "Bullshit. I'm too fat, man! Marcia's got those long, long legs."

Marcia was black, and elegant.

"You remind me of Sally Field," Bauman said. "—You look a lot like her."

Very pleased at that, Betty said, "Charles, you full of shit as a Christmas turkey." Very pleased.

"Well, it's true."

"Shit. . . . You know what Marcia says about that Lee?"

"No, I don't."

"She says, 'We boys tryin' act like girls—Lee like a girl tryin' act like a boy.' "

"Could be," Bauman said, restless. It was time to go.

"Tell you one thing, man. That Lee don' know about wearin' nice clothes. Them regular baggy blues, that's all she ever wears. . . ."

Bauman shifted to get up from the rocking chair. "I want to thank—"

Betty didn't rise to say goodbye—lay determined in her flowered sneakers to have her say. "In here, man, this place . . . you got to act natural, you know? What I'm tellin' you is, maybe you got somethin' good goin' you don' know—you understan'? She was askin' Pokey about you this mornin'."

Pokey Duerstadt, a near-dwarf biker with enormous mustachios and one thin gold hoop fastened through the flesh of his right cheek, was one of the popular men in B-block—liked even by lifers for his merry humor. He'd been sentenced for the beating and sodomizing of two young boys who'd wandered to the bike shop where he worked, and stood watching Pokey fiddle with an aged and lovely Sportster with a cough—until, by some grace or attitude, they'd caught his attention. This offense against children, or near-children (an unpopular crime at State), was mitigated by and largely forgiven for his jolly ways.

"—You try an' not try, you see them two chickens. All the time they was cryin' an' carryin' on, them little pink assholes was just winkin', man, beggin' for it. Jesus would have plugged them sugars! An' you gotta remember, man, I used detergent summerweight on the suckers. They got no complaints. Skinny one loved it, man. Croonin' an' creamin'. . . . That punk wanted to marry me!"

This Pokey—called Switchboard, as well—took many messages and relayed them, staying all the time carefully clear of hacks to avoid any snitch-jacket on account of his big mouth.

"Great," Bauman said. "Cousins and Duerstadt—that's all I need."

Betty frowned in thought, philosophical. "Charles," she said, "—you got inside, an' you got outside. You are inside now, man. How you goin' get along without somebody cares about you?"

"Jesus H. Christ. What is this—matchmaking?"

"She didn' say nothin' bad—jus' asked about you. Don' mean people don' have no eyes." Betty plumped her pillow behind her head. "An' you can't tell me you don' look at her, man. Everybody lookin' at that."

"Honey, I'm really not interested. No offense. I'm sure she's very nice."

Betty rested, regarding him with profound dissatisfaction. "You scared," she said. "Ain' that right?"

"Scared of what?" Mark Nellis said, stepping into his home in pressed denim trousers bleached to light sky-blue, a blue denim shirt, and a very nice zippered windbreaker (street), charcoal gray. Nellis had deep lines graven into his face. Bauman had forgotten how deep they were.

"Nothin'," Betty said, and Nellis bent to kiss her. "Hi, sweetheart. You O.K.?"

"Fine," Nellis said.

"He's gettin' a cold," Betty said to Bauman. "—This shitty weather."

Bauman got up out of the rocker, holding his clipboard and the coffee mug. "I'll be getting along."

"Stick around," Nellis said, stared at Bauman for a moment with spectacled mild blue eyes that seemed never to have seen a murder, then went to their sink.

"No, I think I'll take off," Bauman said. "I've got a lesson at two-thirty." He set the empty mug carefully down on the rocker's left arm.

Betty sighed, sat up, and extended a plump hand. "You think about what we was talkin' about, now," she said.

"Not if I can help it." Bauman took her hand. At the sink, Nellis gargled something medicinal—Listerine, by its odor. The sound reminded Bauman of murdered Spencer's last, the night before.

Bauman walked along Ground-tier, then down the wide steps to the basement corridor. He went through East mess into the kitchen and kitchen smells (rancid permanents, and a current fishy odor of slightly spoiled cheese in preparation), and nodded to Rudy Gottschalk, chief cook. Gottschalk, a tall awkward man with richly-waved red hair perfectly tattooed strand by strand onto a bald scalp, had never been seen to eat his own cooking, apparently surviving on canteen candy, potato chips, corn chips, ice cream sandwiches, canned nuts, smoked stick-sausages, canned Vienna sausages, and diet Pepsis and Cokes—this stuff paid for out of kitchen kettles leased to pruno brewers serving B-block and sections of A and C.

The booze resulting from these efforts was always presented in competition with that of the other kitchen, West mess, in D-block—a contest more than a century old, with marvelous brews still recalled by year and brewer.

Bauman, walking past the first in a long row of big Garland ranges—oily, black, radiating permanent heat—was reminded, perhaps by some dank, salty odor, of small Spencer in the dark. Saw the man drowning in his blood, staggering here and there in his steel-walled, steel-barred box, attempting to escape a strangling self, while (vocal cords apparently sliced not quite through) producing that prolonged high-pitched warble.

By way of relief, Bauman considered Lee Cousins' reported and improbable approach. That silent slender person, who seemed in the corridors a dour, tough, tall girl—troubled, attractive—pretending to be a man. Pretending, but betrayed by wary, shadowed gray eyes, pale slender wrists, her dark brown hair short, soft, ruffled as feathers . . . the tender column of her throat.

Bauman had heard many months before, from a maid nicknamed Margaret—with Housekeeping, also a part-time servant at the Lifer Club—how young Cousins, when eighteen years old and fresh up for dealing tabs of this and that, had been taken by force, or on pretext, over to the gym basement by seven B.N.A. soldiers. There, watched by a hack who loved to watch, the boy was beaten severely, thrown to a stack of stained canvas mats alongside the boiler—was beaten again for resisting—then made to drink a Pepsi bottle of pruno. After which, held down, his arms doubled behind his back, was stripped, oiled with vegetable oil from the kitchen in D, and was played with fairly tenderly for some time, the men around him—some already naked, most not—offering mainly awkward, harsh caresses, except for one, who gripping gently with a rhythmic hand, finally produced in the beaten boy, despite himself, an erection. This seen, he was played with more roughly, was beaten again when he struggled (ribs cracked by kicks) and was finally fucked—swiftly, heavily coupled to in hot wrestle by each of the men in turn, until he bled. This completed after almost an hour and a half—one of the men demonstrating for long minutes an exceptional masculine control, before slowly commencing to thrust faster (his friends laughing), then losing himself, hunching in slow convulsions, emptying, groaning all the while with the pleasure of it . . . and recovering, still running sweat, lay weary on the boy.

Cousins, badly injured—bleeding, three ribs broken, a cheekbone cracked in his battered face—exhausted, bruised, naked amid the men, was made to drink a good deal more. Then, on the mats (their covers soaked, stained, slippery in spots), he was hugged, comforted, stroked very affectionately, was petted for the longest time, was deeply kissed by one or two whispering of love as if they held him far from any watchers, private and alone. After a while of which, he was pinned firmly face down to pull the train again through a long, long afternoon, till that day's dinnertime.

Following that, claimed Margaret—sweeping busily, missing the corners while Bauman (still in Housekeeping at the time) emptied wastebaskets—following that, Cousins began to become a girl. Had been the mistress of a B.N.A. captain named Clemens in D-block, had been sold to the Christie brothers of that block, who'd put him in the infirmary—beaten and burned with a cigarette lighter—for refusing to perform for an invited audience. Recovered, and removed from D lest the Christie brothers kill him, Cousins had free-chipped in A-block until on one occasion, naked, walking weeping through the block, drunk and crystal high, he'd been laid down in a Two-tier cell and performed upon (fairly carefully, fairly gently) by all comers, until the block sergeant and six hacks, concerned by the shouting, shoving, the long line, sallied in and broke the pleasure up.

He was transferred to Protective Custody after that, and when released from P.C. to population after some months, was befriended by an older white convict, Barney Metzler. Metzler, a lifer—and, at the time, suspected by corrections of probably killing a possible snitch named Maury Bell—proved unexpectedly gentle with Lee Cousins, and after a while they'd lived in C-block together as man and wife, or rather, it seemed, father and daughter.

"He was her sugar daddy," Betty had supplied later, over a Fourth of July feast of Entenmann's cinnamon buns. (This the fifth or sixth of Bauman's formal visits.) "—He was crazy about that Lee, an' I don' think he ever touched her. Clarice? You know Clarice? She went out maybe a month after you come in. Clarice, she was on C. She say the old guy, he jus' like to watch that Lee move aroun'. You know, jus' walk aroun', do her nails, do her hair . . . shave them long legs. Say he didn' put his hand on her. Jus' looked." Betty, chewing with her pretty mouth open, had then paused to finish a cinnamon bun. (Soft lips, white teeth—churning damp brown confusion between.) "Ain' nobody fuck with her then, Charles, tell you that. That old man was a mean motherfucker."

Cousins, following this protector's death—Metzler mysteriously slashed while sitting on his toilet—now roomed peacefully, it seemed, in A-block, with a shy middle-aged burglar interested only in model airplanes. . . .

Bauman, having passed through the kitchen, went down the pantry hall, met B.B., a kitchen helper, lugging a tray of dubious meat the other way, and walked out through the back door, down six stone steps, and out into the courtyard.

Looking smaller than its ten acres, fenced on four sides by the long granite backs of the block buildings, the courtyard was a worn dirt square, crisscrossed by narrow blacktop paths. It was divided, as the great outer yards were divided, into East, West, North, and South. East court, outside B-block's kitchen entrance—marked only by fading stripes of white paint—was the Biker Club's playground and property, as South was the lifers', West the blacks', and North court an occasional battleground as independents, Latinos, and Indians claimed it.

The afternoon sun shone pale silver-gold through a last spatter of light rain tracking the courtyard as Bauman crossed from East court into South, his denims still slightly damp from the morning.

At the back gate to C-block—hurricane fencing and steel pipe—a fish hack named Billings, very young, interrupted a conversation with a convict Bauman knew, Bud Teppman, to stroke Bauman's armpits and the small of his back, to bend with a grunt to finger his ankles. Teppman—young, short, square, packed into his denims, his long blond hair braided (nonregulation) into one heavy pigtail—stood observing, his jacket collar turned up, his sleeves rolled up halfway to reveal thick white forearms bright with tattooing. A peacock in full color strutted down to his left wrist; a small naked girl, Oriental, pale orange, hugged his other arm to keep from sliding to his hand.

Teppman, a bank robber, had—with a friend—hit a small bank in

Marsdon four years before. They'd taken a young teller with them as they left, and attracted by slimness or softness, by spirit or surrender, had pulled off the road at a rest stop, walked the girl away into woods, and abused her so roughly she'd begged them for mercy, then prayed aloud to God for help—and these pleas failing, had, when the men commenced to practice something agonizing upon her, begun to shriek and would not be quieted.

Teppman, or his friend—their accounts differed before the court—had silenced this racket with a stone.

"Bauman," Teppman said.

"That's right."

"You passin' through?" His manner more a cop's than Billings' had been.

"If it's O.K."

Teppman looked at Bauman eye to eye—they were nearly the same height—the bank robber's eyes a handsome, bright, and empty blue. He glanced down at Bauman's clipboard, and said, "You goin' to make a habit, comin' through here?"

"No, it's the weather. Got rained on enough this morning, figured I'd shortcut it."

"That's O.K.," Teppman said, "you can come through here. You just don't go walkin' through without checkin' in—right?"

"Right. I won't."

"You're out of B?" Billings said. "—Where the guy got killed?"

"Yes."

"I want to thank you guys for knocking each other off in here," Billings said, and smiled. "You keep it up, it'll make our jobs a lot easier."

"That supposed to be funny?" Teppman said to the hack.

"I didn't say it was funny." Billings surprised to have offended.

"It's not funny," Teppman said, sounding oddly out of breath. "We're wards of the fuckin' state. State's supposed to look out for our ass, not let some ding go in a guy's house and cut his apple for him, middle of the night."

"Well, I didn't mean it was really funny a guy got killed. . . ."

"Fuckin' a," Teppman said, very restless. "You didn't mean it, motherfucker, but you said it like it was funny, '—makin' your job easier.' An' you're in *loco* fuckin' *parentis* here! We're not a bunch of dogs in a pound gettin' put down an' not do shit about it. Anybody thinks that, man, he's got another think comin'."

"I didn't mean anything by it," Billings said. "Look, we didn't lighten up in here, we'd all go nuts, right?"

"Christ knows that's true," Bauman said, he and Billings exchanging only the slightest and swiftest of glances—and Teppman, after a few moments spent frowning, staring out across the court, seemed to ease.

"It's a shame," the bank robber said, calm now, apparently resigned. "The guy was a ward of the fuckin' state. . . ." He raised his right forearm level, regarded it closely, and began to make play with its muscles so the tattooed girl embracing it commenced the slight, paced motions of relaxed intercourse, her citrus-tinted buttocks shifting as he clenched his heavy fist. Looking somberly down at this, attending his own performance, Teppman said, "She likes it."

The corridor beyond, dark and narrow, was lined with leaning men the previous drizzle had driven in. They watched Bauman as he went walking by, conversations lowering in volume as he approached, silenced as he passed, resumed in increasing volume as he drew away. The corridor walls were papered with posters—all made at State, and most announcing this or that effort by Growth-Behind-Walls, the Lifer Club's official name, and that by which they applied for their minor federal funds for special counseling, minor state funds for inmate development, minor county funds for small handicraft production and sales.

Through a door on the right as he passed, Bauman saw Jim Shupe, vice president, sitting on a desk edge—lean, neat, snub-nosed, his short auburn hair and beard carefully trimmed. Shupe had papers in his hand, was talking to another convict, seated, a very big man with tattooed cheeks (FUCK on his right cheek, YOU on his left), giving dictation, it appeared, the big man typing as Shupe talked.

Bauman walked down the corridor, across the wide passageway introducing C-block's Ground-tier, then out the block's side entrance to the South yard steps and into light and air, away from immediate gazes. The infirmary building (granite, once whitewashed) stood shining in slight sunlight far across the yard, flanked by the darker stone of the old upholstery shop on its right, the license plant and warehouse on its left—all three buildings lying along the wall. At the foot of the steps, Bauman passed two walkway yo-yos, familiar but not personally known to him, leaning in wan sunshine against the staircase's granite balustrades, their faded denims and pale faces light against a ground of gray.

These men, and others like them, were out on the walks in most weather, lounging, strolling, leaning against the granite building-sides, pretending they had big deals running for hash, or smack, or coke coming into the dairy or shops. Bullshitting about letters they'd gotten from straight women dying to screw a convict, desperate to be with a man who'd known such trouble—who'd once, betrayed by the world, been so dangerous—and now, his lessons learned, was ready for love at last.

They stood exchanging these dreams and lies while watching out for commandos coming by, particularly in bad weather. Lifers, bikers, grim independents bored enough to go down the line looking for some bunny-balls to rip off for a joint or pack. A bunny-balls in a bunch of bunnies. Somebody talking too much.

"Run you mouth—you bendin' over an' spreadin' cheeks, far as them jockers is concerned." McElvey, in an early lecture, courtesy of Adrienne Sonnenstein—who had not come up to visit. . . .

"Run this by me again, Mr. Bauman. It's a little weird for before lunch."

Adrienne Sonnenstein, in appearance a parody of a young Jewish social worker—thin face, large damp brown eyes, frizzed hair as mightily Afroed as if its owner were a Sudanese tribesman—was in fact a tougher article altogether, a parole officer, a veteran at twenty-seven or twenty-eight years old.

Bauman, wearing a blue seersucker summer suit, white short-sleeved shirt, maroon-striped tie and black loafers, was sitting in a yellow-oak armchair directly in front of her desk—a hot seat for her clients, he supposed. This almost in the center of the State Office of Probation and Paroles, a single unpartitioned office-building space (half the fifth floor of the State Office Building), and a maze of white waist-high dividers under blue-white fluorescent light. The noise—tapped terminals, murmurous phone calls—was subdued, sibilant . . . distant ocean.

"—As I said, I'm due to go on trial on a serious charge, Ms. Sonnenstein. In three weeks, if there isn't another delay. In a month or so, anyway." It was a relief, a pleasure to be talking to someone who didn't care. The brown eyes were observing Bauman only as a curiosity. "My attorney believes I'll be convicted. And that being so, it seemed to me it might be a good idea . . . I think it would be a very good idea if I could learn what I'll be up against . . . at the prison." (That had been a delicate pause: " . . . at the prison.")

"Taxes?" said Ms. Sonnenstein.

"No."

"Well, to start with, Mr. . . . Bauman, if you're convicted, you could be assigned to any of several facilities, depending—"

"Well, I've been told I'll probably be going up to State. To the state penitentiary—that is, if I'm found guilty."

"Sex?"

"No."

"But you're out on bail, now?"

"That's right."

"Do you mind if I ask how much bail you're out on, Mr. Bauman?" Now, she was interested. Shades, subtle and delicate, had drawn away from her brown eyes, revealing a denser brown beneath—the Adrienne within the office Adrienne.

Bauman, as he'd found himself doing for the past few weeks with many women—almost all women of a reasonable age he met—fell slightly in love with her, imagined himself lying beside her on an old-fashioned double bed in her studio apartment. Her leotards, pale blue, draped over a chair-back across the room, and faintly smelling, when held to his face, of Chanel and sweat. Adrienne might have danced in college, maybe had dreamed of dancing with Cunningham in New York. . . .

"I'm out on fifty thousand dollars bail. . . . Do you dance?" Bauman said. "If you don't mind a criminal-to-be asking. You look like a dancer."

"No, I'm not a dancer, Mr. Bauman."

"Well, you have delicate hands," Bauman said. "—You look as though you danced in college, is what I meant. Posture, the way you were sitting. I didn't intend a pass, obviously, under the circumstances."

"I'm not a dancer, Mr. Bauman. —Let's get back to what we were talking about, O.K.? I'm very busy, I have a number of appointments, and I don't really see how I can help you."

"Oh, yes, I think you can. —I need to talk to one of your people, a parolee. I think I should talk to someone who's been up there, Ms. Sonnenstein. You know, to give me some sort of head start."

"A head start. . . ."

"That's right. I really don't see any reason for going into this blind, if I can learn some things, get some preparation." He smiled at her. "It's not much use being middle class, if those behavior patterns aren't helpful in a tough spot. You know—intelligence, planning, preparation and so forth." She hadn't smiled back at him, had sat listening without, apparently, much interest. "—And of course, I'd pay."

"What the hell do you do for a living, Mr. Bauman? I'd hate to think you're just some kind of nut who's in here wasting my time."

"I'm not wasting your time. I really do need some help. —I teach. I'm a history teacher. And I'm very well aware that this is all somewhat bizarre."

"High school?"

"No. I'm . . . in higher education."

"Are you a college teacher, Mr. Bauman? An instructor or something?"

"I'm a professor. —History."

"Well, Jesus Christ, don't be so coy about it! Anybody can get themselves into trouble." Ms. Sonnenstein had stopped looking into Bauman's eyes, was looking down at papers on her desk, instead.

"—Until the trial, anyway," Bauman said. "Suspension. I've been suspended. I was at Midwest, and just got tenure, too. Little bit of irony, there—more than a little."

Adrienne Sonnenstein was wearing a thin white summer blouse, short sleeves, white lace at the collar. The slightest dusting of dark down along her forearms. Slender arms and thin wrists, delicate as a ten-year-old's, her hands fragile, long-fingered, every vessel and slight bone revealed. One filigreed silver ring, not an engagement ring. —There was no strength there for fighting, defending herself. Her strength would be in her head, her paperwork, in the marshaled army of police, invisible, ranked behind her. If not for those invisibles, one of the men she saw every day (to question or command) would have long since reached across the desk to take her into his hands.

She was still looking down at her papers, turning one page over, turning it back, perhaps thinking about what he'd asked—perhaps not. Bauman reflected on the petitioner's eternal problem of dignity. Client and patron—along with slavery, a constant marker of social strata in Roman society. Continued so as vassalage up to . . . what? Mercantile societies, northern Europe. And even now—less formally, attenuated—in every office.

A man over the next partition to the right was raising his voice, angry at some thief, forger . . . someone who'd missed an appointment.

"Excuse me, Ms. Sonnenstein," Bauman said, "—would you mind looking at me while we talk? I haven't been convicted yet. I'm still human."

Ms. Sonnenstein sighed, then looked up at him, seeming to take no offense. "What did you do, Mr. Bauman?"

"I killed a young girl, but it was only an accident. An automobile accident. Supposedly, I was legally drunk."

The brown eyes became much less curious. Bored. She would probably have heard someone say something like that only this morning. Excuses . . . accidents. Would certainly have heard it from someone yesterday afternoon. With her long slender arms, her narrow chest,

Bauman thought Adrienne would have armpits deep and tender as a dog's.

"I'm married," Bauman said, "and I have—had, at any rate, a very responsible position and a number of good friends. And it *was* strictly an accident. Two modest vodka martinis at a departmental party are the big legal *cause célèbre*. But I do think it would be sensible for me to talk to a man who's been up there, because my attorney says if I'm convicted, I'll be there for two years and maybe more before parole. So it seems sheer stupidity not to be at least somewhat prepared. Physically as well, exercise and so forth. I used to box in college."

Then she looked back down at her papers—to keep from smiling, probably, because of what he'd said about boxing in college.

"You just take it easy," she said, not looking up from whatever, a report of some sort.

"Well, I'm a little upset," Bauman said. "But it does make sense to me to talk to someone who's been a convict up there. I understand the place is extremely grim."

She didn't look up, didn't say anything.

"I've been asking a number of people to come up and visit me there. People I don't even know, really. Some sort of personal contact insurance, I suppose." He smiled, though she wasn't looking at him.

Then she looked up. Beautiful eyes, but not his lover's eyes anymore. "How old are you, Mr. Bauman?"

"I'm forty-three. Forty-three last month."

"You just take it easy," she said. "—O.K.? I have a client who might be willing to meet with you. Trevor McElvey. He's a physical trainer, part-time, so I suppose you could talk to him about that, too. But it would be his decision, strictly."

"Oh, that's wonderful. I appreciate it." Only one night with her, now. No blue leotards. Panty hose draped over the hand-towel rack beside the bathroom sink.

"His decision, Mr. Bauman, not mine. You understand? He might just say the hell with it."

"O.K. I wouldn't blame him. —I know it's a little odd."

"I'll get in touch with him. And you can call me tomorrow morning, about ten. —You've never been in prison before?"

"No. Of course not."

"Well, you're not being dumb, trying to find out what you can. It'll save you some problems, probably."

Bauman had taken a deep breath and stood up, buttoned his suit jacket. "I appreciate this very much, and I apologize if I was rude. There's a very strange dreamlike quality to all this." He'd smiled at her again. "I don't suppose, if worst comes to worst, you could visit me up there—you know, in a semiprofessional way?"

"Hell, no," she said.

"*Afternoon*." Bauman had to raise his voice over the waxer's noise. Its operator, in pressed and snowy whites, turned and nodded, skated the machine away for one last long run down the second-floor hall to a thudding impact against the wall, then angled it back, leaving a narrow series of rounded brighter green jeweling polished onto a dark green floor. The cleanest floors at State, upstairs and down.

"Hey man, what's your action today?" Turning his waxer off. Tiger, a large butterball black in medical whites, was the infirmary's male nurse and master. Report had it he'd once used a smothering pillow to relieve an elderly convict of further humiliation—the old man having developed a permanent case of sloppy sphincter, not ever being able to hold his shit again. The unkind said that Tiger had tired of changing sheets—but said it not to Tiger.

"Bobby Basket wants to learn to read," Bauman said.

"That what he said?"

"That's what I was told."

"Teach, you was told shit, man," Tiger said, "—but I'm too busy to fuck with you. So you go on in, see what the little motherfucker's tryin'." And turned and lumbered away down the wide corridor toward his dispensary, from which fine grape-jelly pruno flowed at three dollars a quart, transshipped from the kitchens.

Bobby Basket lay on this second floor—the infirmary's first given over to storage—lay here down a verdant left-hand hall, where he rested the last in the short row of chronic cases, able to look out the single wide window—screened, barred, the thick glass (more green than clear) sandwiching chicken-wire in addition. Elderly Bobby made the smallest bump under the frayed white cotton sheet that any man could make.

Bauman passed seven recumbent men as he walked down the aisle of cots—four men on the left, three on the right. He knew only two of these. Lying second on the left, Jomo Burdon, slaughtered Spencer's housemate before chest pains, providential, had removed him from the scene. Burdon appeared to be sleeping. In the third bed, right side of the aisle, lay a lifer named Teddy Rawlins—once a brute, now shrunk by AIDS, sparsely bearded, great-eyed and tender as he died.

Rawlins recognized him, nodded slowly.

"How's it going, Teddy?"

"It's a pisser, man. . . ."

Bobby Basket's face was craggy as a tragic king's, his head startlingly massive, gray-bearded, gray-maned above his cotton-covered little lump of body. He rolled small bright blue eyes and watched Bauman coming.

"About fuckin' time," he said. Basket had seen Bauman once before, months ago, when Bauman was still in Housekeeping, mopping up.

There was a shaky little white-painted chair under the window, and Bauman set it beside Bobby's bed and sat down holding his clipboard, legal pad, and pencils on his lap.

"It's two packs a session, or a pack and half a bag," he said. "Filters on the straights."

"Two packs?"

"That's right. Or one pack and a heavy joint."

Bobby appeared to consider, then his great head nodded on its pillow, something stirred under the covers just beneath his chin.

"O.K. Do you read at all? Can you write just a little? —Write your name?"

"I can read fine, asshole," Bobby Basket said. "An' when I had my fuckin' arms, I could write fine, too! I ain't some dumb nigger, you know."

"Then what the hell did you get me up here for?"

"I could write with my fuckin' toes if I had to, if I had my fuckin' legs."

"Then what did you get me up here for?"

Bobby, armless, legless—all lost to gangrene from diabetes—was nasty, snappy as a spoiled child. Bauman hadn't liked him before, and didn't like him now.

"—To ask you a fuckin' question, if you don't mind."

"It's your packs."

The majestic head nodded across the aisle where an old TV sat blank and silent on a table, turned so the ward could see it. "They had a movie on there—Rome fallin'."

"About the fall of Rome?"

"That's it. We got a bet goin'. Twenty, scrip. That fruiter, Irma? Attendant up here? She says the Romans was O.K. They was just outnumbered, just got their ass whipped, straight military. —I say they wimped out, went queer, an' got too faggoty to last. O.K.? Now, you're the big professor. You tell us why did the fuckin' thing fall, it was such hot shit? An' you keep in mind there's money ridin' on this. So, how come those guys got their asses beat by some boony assholes dumber'n bikers?—one of 'em I hear you're sharin' a house with. You screwin' him, or is he screwin' you?"

"We get along," Bauman said. "—It's not a romance. And that's two questions."

Bobby Basket lay silent, nothing stirring beneath his chin. Bauman assumed there was at least a small stump of the left arm or the right down there, to have made the previous movement under the sheet. Basket's cock had to be lower down. Word was, he paid a tan queen called Nita to come up and suck it for him. —The "Basket" handle dated from before Bauman's time, when the daughter of the then yard captain had provided a laundry basket to transport Bobby—already armless, legless—to the Christmas show in the truck-shop bay.

"Well, get to it," Bobby said.

"This wouldn't be a joke, would it? Somebody like Sarasote suggest this?—thinks it's funny?"

"What's your problem, Professor?" Bobby said. "You think you got the only brains there is in here? Some dude can't wonder somethin', put a bet down? —Or are you a fuckin' fake? That it? You don't know shit about that stuff, am I right?"

"I know about it. Why don't you just be quiet for a minute. . . ." Bauman doodled a daisy on his legal pad. This was the first question in his field from anyone at State. The last question as naive had been asked well before the accident, in some undergraduate survey course. The students not nearly as alert or interested then as after the accident, when for nearly two weeks Bauman had been allowed to continue teaching, had been on display before members of a student body seeming now somewhat despicable in their self-satisfaction, stupid with comfort—a good deal less satisfactory than many of the Calibans he tutored here, who strained to understand the mysteries of the alphabet.

"What the fuck about it?" Bobby, staring at the ceiling, waiting for enlightenment. Two of the men back down the aisle were listening. Not Teddy Rawlins; he seemed to be asleep.

"Well, Irma's more right than you are."

"Shit. . . ."

"There were a lot of factors, a lot we don't know. People assume we know more about ancient Rome than we do. Also, there wasn't just one Rome; there were a series of them as time went by. It changed. A lot of German tribal influence, by the end. Very much so, in the military."

"It fell, didn' it?"

"Oh, yes."

"Well, how the fuck come?" Bobby, though old and a smoker—when he could persuade someone to hold a butt for him—had a clear, strong, young man's voice, the voice of the young man who'd robbed banks thirty-five years before, and was supposed to have killed a policeman in Missouri.

"O.K. The three major factors. First, the empire's fiscal policies were primitive; they badly needed some sort of imperial bank to act as a central clearing house for major transactions, a repository for cash reserves, for issuing credit—"

"A bank?"

"That's right, some sort of monitoring agency for their currency."

"Jesus Christ," Bobby said, "—banks ain't nothin' but fuckin' organized crime. You want to know what organized crime is, forget them wops an' take a good look at a bank."

"And . . . and they hadn't developed their tax system much beyond the sort of simple farm-the-taxes-out policy they'd used as a city. That worked pretty well for a city, but not so well for a territory—and it didn't work at all for an empire. So the bigger they got, the worse their tax problems, and the more social pressure and legal force they had to use to collect their revenue, until, trying to control that, they had to control everything—everyone's work, everyone's income, everyone's position in society. And people got sick of it. A lot of people were glad to see the barbarians come in, glad to have a chance to get out from under the imperial administration, even if it meant living rougher."

"O.K.," Bobby said. "That's a good one. You're makin' some sense about that tax shit. I don't pay any fuckin' taxes to those assholes. Never have and never will. Those motherfuckers can kiss my rosy red."

"Second . . . second, just the way the Romans hadn't developed their financial policies, they didn't adapt their military tactics sufficiently, either. Not soon enough. They were very conservative people. They figured that what had worked so well for so long, was bound to keep on working."

"That's a fuckin' blunder, man. Nothin' stays the same, exceptin' this hole."

"Right on," a man said, down the line.

"—And their army was mainly heavy infantry, which had been perfect for fighting other Mediterranean cities and confederations with.

But heavy infantry was lousy at dealing with hordes of savages, some of them horse people, who drifted here and there, sometimes fighting, sometimes just come to settle. The Romans could win almost every pitched battle they fought—when the tribesmen held still for a pitched battle. But the difference was, the barbarians could afford to lose an occasional battle, then just fade back into the wilderness. For the Romans, it was different. If they lost a battle, it was a disaster."

"No place to run, poor fuckers."

"That's right. When they lost, they lost settled real estate, cities, at least strategic opportunities that would never come again. And that constant military pressure made their army more and more important, politically. Pretty soon, it was more interested in politics and pay raises than trying to fight barbarians, especially when many tribesmen were already serving in the Roman army, and their families mingling, intermarrying with Roman settlers on the frontiers."

"Swamped—right?"

"That's right. They'd needed a lot of really good light cavalry right at the beginning. It was largely Hunnish cavalry that had driven the German tribes west in the first place. But the Romans weren't a cavalry-minded people. They liked their military slow and sure, and they wanted to know what those army commanders were up to every minute. They didn't want them galloping around, doing the gods knew what. Cavalry they did have—Gauls, usually, other tribesmen—was an also-ran until way too late. Caesar was about the only general who used it well. . . . Trajan understood it, too."

"Julius Caesar?"

"That's right."

"Exceptional guy."

"That's right."

Bobby nodded. "The rest of 'em sound like the U.S. Army we got right now. Fat-ass office soldiers and a bunch of bonehead niggers couldn't beat their meat." He lay silent for a few moments, brooding on this decline. "—You in the service?"

"Air Force."

"That bullshit," Bobby said. "You a fly-boy?"

"No. Edited the base paper."

"Jesus *Christ*." The head, disgusted, wagged on its pillow.

Bauman recalled Basket, months before, making much of his infantry service in Korea during an argument with another old convict, hospitalized for heart. "These fuckin' faggots, now," he'd said, referring to Vietnam veterans, "—they got their asses kicked by those slope midgets, an' they been pissin' an' moanin' about it ever since. No wonder we lost that fuckin' war—faggots like that doin' the fightin'. *Heaventh!* They're *thootin'* at uth!"

Bauman, still with Housekeeping at the time, had been machining another layer of gritty wax into the ward's clean snot-green floor, a new fish then, still in shock. . . .

"You got a third one?" Bobby said, back on subject. "I'm not payin' a pack an' a boomer to you, an' twenty fuckin' bucks scrip to that asshole, Irma, for two fuckin' reasons."

"O.K.," Bauman said, "—number three. All the people the Romans took over during those centuries had their own ways of life, all very traditional tribal things. The Romans forced Roman law and imperial administration on these people, and they were very hard-nosed about it. You gave them any trouble, they'd kill you quick."

A grunt and nod from Bobby. "They had that in the movie, there."

"—The result was that a lot of people hated the Romans' guts, hated the empire even when it was to their advantage, even if they'd never been ruled as competently before. So, when big trouble finally came, a lot of people were glad to see it, even if it put their own asses in a sling."

Another grunt and nod. Discontented Jews or Greeks—Christians, must have appeared in the movie, complaining.

"—Similar thing for the Eastern empire later, when the Muslims came along. Aztec empire, too. And in a more diffuse way, the British empire as well. I think it's been a major factor in all imperial dissolutions. A kind of cultural auto-immune reaction." Bauman thought of mentioning that to Schoonover, reference his decaying galactic empire, by way of illustrating the limitations of economic determinism.

Bobby Basket lay silent—thinking about it, apparently.

"They had some of that stuff in the movie," he said, "—but mostly not."

"It's too complicated to put all that into a movie."

"An' that's it . . . ?"

"Those are the major causes we know, the most important causes. There were other factors—problems inherent in a society so completely dependent on slavery. And there're some interesting analyses—short on basis, of course—referring to their agricultural development and transportation network. Probably they did have difficulties, there."

"O.K., Mr. College, then you tell me somethin'. You give me three big reasons, right?"

"Right. Though of course there's bound to be one nobody knows—some factor the Romans didn't see, that we don't see now, either. We can never understand all the important causes for something that complex."

"O.K., I got that. I understand that. You gave me three, though, right?"

"Yes."

"O.K. Now, you tell me which one is the big one. *The* fuckin' reason."

"I would say, taxes. They never could catch up."

"Is this country caught up on taxes, wise guy?" The head held a brain.

"A nice point," Bauman said.

"What a bunch of sad shit," Bobby Basket said, after a few moments' reflection. "An' they didn' just wimp out, go faggot?"

"No."

"Twenty fuckin' bucks to that Irma. . . ." A heavy sigh. "An' they were civilized guys an' everything, an' they still had their heads up their asses."

"Look around you," Bauman said.

"You got a point, too. —I hear you lost a guy in B."

"Spencer."

"A wimp coon, right? Rapo. Called him to the bars and cut his apple for him. Eighth deader this year, man; warden's assholes are goin' to be fuckin' steamin'. This shit's goin' to be on TV!"

"It's a damn shame," Bauman said. "I knew the man; I was working with him. And he didn't bother anybody. I doubt if he ever raped anybody, either. Man only wanted to be left alone. —I'd really like to know who the hell would kill one of the few decent people in here."

"What d'you mean? You askin' me who did it?"

"That's not what I meant—"

"Askin' me who did somethin'?" Bobby said, suddenly frowning from his pillow. "I'm not a newspaper, asshole. I don't peddle no shit off the vine."

"That's not what I meant. I just meant I'd like to know."

"Oh, you just want to know? Listen, man, you come nosin' around here askin' me this an' that—none of my fuckin' business, an' sure as shit none of your fuckin' business!" All stated loudly, as in righteous wrath—the voice that of a young jocker smacker, the moving mouth a feature in a mask of age.

Bauman, after only a moment's confusion, realized this sudden misunderstanding was intended to abort payment. No one had not paid him before.

"You know damn well that's not what I meant, Bobby. Now what about you keeping your voice down, and paying me what you owe me."

"Keep my voice down? I'm not keepin' my voice down, motherfucker—come in here big-nosin'."

"You owe me," Bauman said.

"I don't owe you shit. And I ain't goin' to tell you shit, neither, so get your snitch ass on outta here."

"Don't call me that," Bauman said. "And you owe me one pack and a joint, or two packs."

Veins grew marked as worms at Bobby's temples. "Listen, you sawed-off cocksucker," he said, unconscious of irony, "—you come in here an' ask me who this an' who that an' sayin' I owe you somethin'. You better just get the hell outta here; I'll roll out of this bed an' bite your balls off for you. An' if I can't do it, I can goddamn well get it done! You hear me, you fuckin' kid killer?" Not keeping his voice down at all.

"You owe me two packs," Bauman said, "—or one and a fat joint." He wished he was somewhere else, had never come over. Wished he was in his house, listening to Schubert.

Bobby, his aged noble face now dull red above his beard's gray-white, smiled as if there were still two hundred pounds of young muscle beneath his chin. "I'll give you a fat joint, you bend over," he said. "Get outta here before I look you to death, you fuckin' college faggot!"

"Two packs," Bauman said, "—or one and a joint."

Everyone at State might as well be listening, watching his cowardice. If he got up and walked away, if he did that, then tomorrow or the next day one of his regular students would certainly decide not to pay him—would sit on the edge of his bunk, curious, waiting to see what Bauman would do about it. After that, there'd be no more teaching for him at State.

Bobby Basket glared as if his look could kill, as promised. "You're lucky I'm crippled up," he said louder than ever, carried away with his acting. "If I could get up outta this bed, old as I am, your sorry snitch ass would be runnin' off the ward so fast you'd leave shit behind!"

"You had a question. I answered it. Are you going to pay what you owe me, or not?"

"You suck my cock, motherfucker, maybe I'll give you a rollin' paper for that."

Bauman, short of breath, heart thumping, leaned back to get his right hand down into the pocket of his denims, got a book of matches out, separated three, and pulled them free. Then he struck them alight, leaned down where the frayed edge of Bobby's top sheet hung, and set fire to it.

Chapter THREE

"What are you doin'?" Bobby said. "—What did you do?"

The thin patched cotton lit like paper along its border—charred, flared, then flamed in a swift narrow runner up over the bed's edge and into Bobby's view.

"Oh, hey! *Hey!*" Bobby's lump of body thrashed this way and that under the sheet.

"Jesus! *Jeeesus!*" The shouts had turned to screams, and other men were crying out as well as the sheet began to burn in earnest, short flames jumping up from char all along the bedside. If Bobby'd had a right arm, it would be burning. —A surprising amount of smoke was coming up.

The cripple, writhing fantastically, was trying to roll away, to buck and heave off the bed's left side, when Bauman reached over through the smoke, gripped him on some soft bulging bump, and held the cropped man still. A quick flame rose hissing, and stung Bauman on the wrist.

"I'm gonna pay youuu!" trilled Bobby Basket, his dentures chattering under the notes. As Bobby howled, Bauman reached over with his free hand, hauled the burning sheet to him and off the bed, and revealed a torso, swaddled in a large gray knit stocking, convulsing,

doubling like a great worm in burning grass. The other men were now making as much noise as Bobby.

Tiger, breathless, apparently just arrived from the infirmary's third floor, came down the aisle to this chorus—shouted for silence, almost got it—reached the smoldering bed, and remarkably quick for such a weighty man, snatched howling Bobby up and out of the smoke and set him on his shoulder as a mother might her baby. Then he leaned across the cot, shoved Bauman back one-handed, and tore the last corner of the charring sheet away, dropped it to the floor, and ponderously trod upon it.

"You . . . better . . . have a fuckin' good reason," said Tiger to Bauman while he stomped, panting, "—or I'm goin' to dust your ofay ass, an' you got my *word* on that!"

Two of the sick men farther up the aisle were still exclaiming, still frightened of being roasted in their beds. Dying Rawlins was laughing.

"He owed me," Bauman said, "—and he wouldn't pay."

"What the fuck," Tiger said. "What the fuck—" Bobby being lifted from the fatly muscled shoulder, glared at, being roughly shaken back and forth "—have I told you? This little motherfucker sends out for all kinds of shit; sent out for a fuckin' leather jacket from the craft shop, an' then don't pay up!" Shake, shake, Bobby's kingly head bobbling, wobbling. "I am tired of it!"

"That little motherfucker don't pay for shit." A voice from two beds down—an unstable ding named Cargill, who Bauman now recognized. Cargill, two weeks before, had sliced his left Achilles tendon through with a razor blade, sawing away while his housemate watched, until that sturdy cord had parted with a pop like breaking wire, its severed higher portion snapping up into the knotted calf muscle above, the lower dangling limp, a thick and bloody piece of white tape two inches long.

"He owes me two packs, or a bomber joint and one pack, filters," Bauman said.

"That's it?" Tiger now replaced his patient against his shoulder, absently patted the broad back as if to burp it. Bobby was sobbing softly, undone perhaps by being baby-handled, and so reminded of his helplessness amid the fire. "—That's all he owes?"

"That's it."

"Well, somebody's goin' to pay for this fuckin' sheet, man. An' I'm goin' to have to burn some shit in a wastebasket, cover this smoke. Somebody's goin' to pay for my trouble. —You lucky wasn' no screw standin' round. You had a point to make, am I right? Now, you pay me for my trouble."

"All right," Bauman said. "—I'll pay the pack, and ten dollars, scrip, for the sheet."

Outside, in Tiger's just-waxed hall—the ward settled down, fresh sheets brought for bedded Bobby—Tiger handed Bauman the boss joint, the pack of Camels (plundered from the sniveling patient's bedside drawer) and immediately accepted the Camels back, and a ten bill in scrip.

"O.K.," he said. "—We all square," and shooed two curious fruiter attendants (Paul and Irma) on their way, when they crept down the infirmary's third-floor staircase in tailored medical whites, shuddering at the smell of smoke.

"We thought it was a riot," Irma said—a big man, and (against regulations) lightly lipsticked, subtly rouged.

"Rape time," Paul caroled. The two were married, and Paul the husband, despite being much smaller and only a forger. In that marriage, as in all, strength of character finally told for more than history, and Irma's armed robberies, her killings, stood for nothing when housework and ironing were needed.

"You have a can, here?" Bauman said, after the couple, arm in arm, had climbed back up the stairs to duty on Contusions, a principal ward.

"I got the patients' toilet, but ain' nobody else usin' that. We got AIDS people shittin' blood in that toilet." Tiger pointed out a door at the far end of the hall, on the right. "You can use that one down there. —But don't you mess the motherfucker up. *I* clean that motherfucker."

The bathroom was a narrow bin of chipped gray-green plaster, with a stall shower by the door, a short pinched passage to a cracked-seat toilet at the back, and a small attendant sink.

Bauman kept his denims up, and sat on the toilet with his face in his hands. His fingers felt surprisingly cold; his heart still drummed against his breastbone.

"My choices were limited," he said to himself through his fingers. He felt nauseated, and thought for a few moments—sweating, hands tingling—that he would have to vomit. When he became convinced of it, he stood up and turned to kneel before the small stained toilet bowl, imagining Tiger's rage if he fouled the sink.

In this position, calmer since prepared, Bauman felt better almost at once. "I'm alone," he said, speaking into the toilet bowl. It echoed, sepulchral.

It seemed at the moment almost worth it to have had the argument, to have commenced burning Bobby Basket, to have had the potentially very serious trouble with Tiger. —Worth it to have this time in the bathroom alone. Door closed.

After he'd first come up—had been requested from Assignments by old Cooper, boxing coach and head of Housekeeping—Bauman had at least twice been alone in Housekeeping's huge dark wire-binned cavern beneath the laundry. On both occasions, he'd been set to shifting cartons of soap powder in the shadowed concrete-smelling damp, turning each of the hundred and more light unwieldy boxes upside down to prevent the aging stuff from caking. That done, he'd restacked the cartons in neat square columns ten feet high against the basement wall. At least twice he'd been left alone there for those chores by old Cooper and his cronies—older, sterner convicts than the usual, and often matched in the little man's wire-screened office by one or two corrections officers as grimly veteran as the cons. On those occasions, these men had set down their cocoa mugs—laced with Tiger's best—and in good humor trooped away on one errand or another, leaving Bauman alone with the fading echoes of their footsteps, their voices.

He had also been alone in the showers—a dangerous practice. And been alone in the watch commander's office, once, for three or four minutes.

Bauman knelt at the toilet a while longer, peering down at his dim reflection in the water, feeling better as the minutes passed.

"Could this be worse?" he asked his reflection, was asked by it.

"I suppose so," both replied, looking tired. His reflection's hair was grayer at the sides, he was sure, than it had been only a few months before. Bauman leaned forward, hands on the toilet's chilly rim, to look down into his reflected eyes—deep set, dark brown, dark browed—to find their usual expression of cautious mockery replaced by lingering fright's blank encompassing stare.

"Take it easy," Bauman said to his reflection. "It was just an incident, and it's all over. By the way, I wish you the very best of luck from here on out." He was nodded to in response. Then he stood up to knot the bomber weed into a tiny blue balloon—and unsnap, unzip, and pull his denims and underpants down to commence the uncomfortable business of putting the contraband away. . . .

A corrections officer named Truscott was sitting at the desk in the infirmary entrance, reading a current *Cosmopolitan*. She hadn't been there when he'd come in. Truscott was nearly fifty, great-hipped, dumpy, and dyed blond in starched khaki slacks, khaki blouse. State Bureau of Corrections was abbreviated neatly ("State Bur." above, "Correctns." below) on her blue and yellow sleeve patch.

Truscott roused and stood up when Bauman walked down the stairs, stopped him, checked his pass, and commenced her customary thorough pat-down, while her little two-way whispered on her hip.

"You get aspirin or something?" Pat, pat, pat.

"Nothing."

She took his clipboard and notebook, examined them carefully, then stroked his arms, shoulders, shirtfront, and back, Bauman turning, obedient as her touch traveled, cooperative as a dancing partner. She checked his front waistband, then trailing her fingers down, veered lightly away from his groin—not caring to touch him there, not caring to have him drop his pants and bend over—and so missed a chance to ticket him for the torpedo weed kiestered up his ass.

Truscott stooped, grunting softly, to trace carefully down his legs, then finger first his left sock top, then the other.

It had been Truscott who'd first stepped in to end his only fistfight at State—his only altercation of any kind until now—and that with a young inmate named Wagner who'd elbowed him once, then deliberately twice more, in the movie line. Wagner had wanted to step in ahead to be with friends.

Bauman, since coming up, had avoided trouble very carefully so as to give an impression of tough reserve rather than terror. This had taken great and constant effort through days, weeks, and months—watching out for others, watching himself for proper appearance, proper behavior. It had worn him out and made him more and more frightened, so that when he beat up Wagner, he made a convincing show of frenzy.

After the fight, Bauman had been exhilarated, barely bruised. Chunky young Wagner—short, strong, and slow, a filling-station robber from downstate—had shown no talent for fistfighting. Surprised at being attacked so madly, he'd tried to wrestle, put up clumsy hands to grapple, pawed away—and been hit a nice sequence of punches that split a lip, cracked a tooth, and knocked him finally down.

Truscott, a strong woman under her sheath of fat, was one of the few female hacks ready to deal physically with inmates. She'd hurried across the auditorium's crowded lobby, strode in upon Bauman just as Wagner hit the floor, and alone (an officer named Sawyer still running toward them) had grappled with him intimate as a lover, small strong padded hands searching for his right wrist as they embraced. Bauman had smelled her powdery scent—very pleasant, possibly White Rain—felt the cushioned shove of her large breasts as she found his wrist, gripped it, and twisted with surprising force, attempting to double his arm behind his back for a controlling hold. In this wrestle, he'd at first resisted slightly, still humming with the energy of the fight—and might have resisted still more but for being embarrassed, reminded of his maturity, touched by the fat woman's courage, her earnest endeavor, her breathless panting as she dealt with him. As it was, he'd cooperated, allowed his arm to be hauled behind him, bent, and shoved up hard against his shoulder blade.

Ever since, Bauman had felt that Truscott recalled that minor cooperation—one of the multitude of small and evanescent social debts (to be paid or not, though never acknowledged) incurred every day at State, as they were wherever humans clustered. At the time—perhaps frightened, perhaps sensing his cooperation and angered by that implied insult—Truscott had forced his arm high, and left him an aching shoulder.

"Awesome. Bad fuckin' *ass!*" Scooter, complimenting him that evening at lock-'n'-count. "—Turned that motherfucker every way but loose. What'd he do?"

"He pushed me. Elbowed me on purpose."

"Teach that motherfucker mess with a fuckin' professor, Charles."

That made Bauman laugh, still feeling wonderfully relieved.

"A fuckin' stone jocker," Scooter'd said. . . .

"What's that smell?" Truscott, nearly done, pausing at the back of Bauman's shirt collar. "Something burning?"

"Some paper caught fire in a wastebasket up there. Tiger put it out. —No big deal."

"You didn't get any aspirin? People didn't give you any aspirin?" Truscott's voice was a farm woman's, rich and chortling, as if she had a ready sense of humor, was prepared to smile, but never seemed to find anything quite funny enough for that. She finished with his shirt collar, turned Bauman around to face her, and patted his shirtfront once more.

"No," Bauman said, "—no aspirin."

She took his clipboard and pencils from her desktop, gave them to him, stepped back, and said, "Move out."

Bauman, obedient, walked out the double doors and into a dark-gray late afternoon, its slight sunshine vanished. South yard, stretching vacant, empty of strollers, was being buffeted by a shifting cold breeze that ruffled the shallow sheets of puddle left behind the rain, and persuaded Bauman to pause to button his jacket up.

. . . Once the fight was over, both hacks, Truscott and Sawyer—uninterested in explanations—had signed a ticket on each combatant, ticket dupes delivered to the watch commander's office that night. This was one of only two tickets Bauman had had written on him since he'd come up; he'd gotten the other for dropping a tray of meatloaf while kicking at a fugitive rat in East mess's kitchen. The meatloaf had spattered a hack's right trouser-leg and shoe. —Bauman had had no business working for Gottschalk in any case, Housekeeping having loaned him out to the cook in exchange for some favor.

Chuck Gorney, the watch commander for A and B blocks the evening of the fight—and one of State's relatively few veteran corrections officers—was a small handsome man with a neat iron-gray crew-cut and eyes the color of weak tea. Sporting perfectly tailored khakis, a sewn-on twenty-year service badge, he'd talked to Bauman in his small office off A-block's basement corridor, the office decorated only with a large picture calendar—a field of some growing crop, dull yellow, with a huge green-painted farm machine parked in the left foreground. Another officer had been present, a very thin black man sitting in a straight-back chair tilted against the wall.

"If you're trying to show these people you're a tough guy, Bauman, you're wasting your time. —And that's what you been trying to do, right? Show 'em you're not scared . . . ? You been here what, three months? They know you're an old man. You're forty-three, forty-four years old, right? And you're a college guy. So, whether you beat that inmate's ass or not, don't kid yourself you accomplished anything. He's a nobody around here, and you're a nobody around here. You understand me?"

Bauman had said yes.

"I hope so," Gorney said, "—because if you bother people here trying to act like a tough guy, somebody's just going to kill you.—Far as I'm concerned, this isn't even worth giving you a ticket, but the rules say you get a ticket. You and that guy Wagner are posted for a week—out of your blocks only for your jobs, no privileges, no visitors, no movie, no canteen, no yard time."

"O.K."

"That's O.K. with you, is it?" Gorney had glanced over at the black officer and smiled. "Well, I'm real glad that's O.K. with you. What's that you got up under your sleeve? Hold it over here. What is this, some kind of fancy watch? You don't have any jewelry in here, Bauman. You have religious medals, wedding rings, ordinary wristwatches, and that's it—period. How'd you get this? Look at this," to the thin black officer, "—it's a goddamned Rolex, for Christ's sake! How'd you get this in here?"

"I bet his wife snatched it in," the black officer said, rocking his tilted chair slightly off the office wall. "—Got a twat tells time."

"You want to get your hand cut off, Bauman?" Gorney shaking his neat head, marveling at this new oddity, only the last in a grand series through the years. "You want to get your ass kicked? Well, you just keep wearing this fancy watch, and some con'll cut your hand off for it. Understand me?"

"Yes, sir. . . ."

"He understands me," Gorney said to the black officer. "Listen, Bauman, you turn that fancy watch in to Property, get your receipt, and tell time the way every other inmate does. You get a five-buck digital. If you don't want to do that, there're clocks all over the walls here. Here, everybody knows what time it is. O.K.?"

"Yes, sir. . . ."

But Bauman had kept the watch and sometimes wore it, unfastening the stainless band so it expanded to a larger chain-mail loop, and sliding the Rolex up over his shirt-sleeved forearm to just under his elbow, where his jacket sleeve covered it, hid it from view. It was a beautiful machine. No one else in State had anything as fine. Not the hacks or any of the corrections people, not the richest inmate dealer. Nobody. It was the finest thing at State.

Though chafing at his week's restriction to B-block, and even admitting Gorney's probable good sense, Bauman nevertheless enjoyed for much of that week a great relief from apprehension. He felt himself tried and proved sufficiently to be left alone, to be spared some grotesque bullying that might reveal his terror to everyone. This exhilaration, however, had lasted only those few days. Then, gradually, his fears had begun to pour back into him—slowly, in lonely places out on the walkways—suddenly as if tipped from icy buckets, when he was jostled once or twice in this line or that.

Then he'd thought of conciliating Wagner. Of approaching him in a casual way, making light of the fight, even apologizing for flipping out so far. He imagined that he and Wagner then became friends.

The odors of State, reminders of reality, helped keep him from pursuing this fantasy. The prison's air, though it smelled somewhat different—included tobacco smoke, stale sweat, pot smoke, and spoiled food—still had something of the stink of a hospital about it, strong disinfectant, floor wax, traces of urine. Like a hospital's, these odors—penetrant, weighty, breathed by Bauman as he woke every morning, roused to the commencing uproar of B-block's radios, TVs, tape decks, conversations, shouts and countershouts—were antidotes to wishful thinking. . . .

Jacket buttoned, its collar turned up, Bauman settled his clipboard under his left arm as he walked across South yard, his running shoes almost silent on the walkway cement. He smelled through chill damp air the slightest taint of smoke from his denims, and saw himself, implacable, as he'd set fire to Bobby's bed. Very different from that foolish fistfight. In this case, he'd certainly handled the situation as sensibly as a person could have in circumstances so bizarre, with a creature . . . a cropped oddity like that. Handled it better, he felt sure, than most inmates would have, even the fiercest. Lesson being, of course, get the bread up front.

"Get the bread up front," he said to himself aloud, kicking through a small shallow puddle in his way—but didn't see how it could be done with some. McNeil. Sarasote. In those cases, get the bread up front, if possible. It could certainly be done with the likes of Bobby.

'Why the fall of Rome? You got it. And that'll cost a pack and so forth, and don't give me any bullshit. You ask a major question, you're getting the answer for peanuts.' If Bobby'd then said, 'Fuck you,' Bauman could have said, 'Then try and figure it out for yourself, asshole. And good luck.' —Bobby could not, after all, have come up out of his bed, and was old in any case. Wasn't in a club. Wasn't liked by anyone Bauman had heard of.

Get the bread up front. Wayman, give him credit, always paid up front. Was there any reason, at State, to suffer the casual contempt all street teachers did who hadn't toadied and sweated into tenure, whether grade school, high school, or university? No reason to take here what he didn't have to take, though McNeil and Sarasote might be regarded, like Fanning and one or two others of his students at State, as special cases—like some resentful deans of graduate studies, too dangerous not to be exceptions to the rule.

Bauman prepared with a readying step, then jumped over a fairly large puddle, feeling almost at home at State—as he had momentarily when rewarded by a student's surprising mastery of the alphabet or long division, as he had also, he recalled, when first old Cooper (in his alternative role as boxing coach) had taken him over to the gym.

There, continuing the reintroduction Trevor McElvey had begun outside, Cooper had presented Bauman with boxing's familiar drumbeats—the heavy bag a steady base, speed bag the rattling traps, rope-skippers' footfalls for syncopation—their echoes booming, chattering, shuffling softly from the gym's high ceiling. Had presented the scent of resin as well, of mildewed canvas, rubbing alcohol, the acrid comfort of ancient sweat, so that for a short while Bauman had entertained fantasies of competing there as a boxer on the team. He imagined himself a middleweight whose balance, whose easy moves despite his age were canny as Archie Moore's had been, and so proved able to surprise some young hood with an elegant left hook out of the thirties, forties, the sort of punch Robinson (aging, slender) had used neat as fly-swatting, to knock that tough English kid on his ass.

This notion, fragile enough, dissolved with Bauman's first afternoon's attendance on Cooper's team as trainer, gofer, and water boy. State's boxers had been for several years Midwest champions of all notable prisons—state and federal—for a thousand miles east and west, eight hundred north and south. This excepting only, and likely temporarily, the team of a northern Missouri maximum-security establishment for which at least two outrageous psychopaths had been deliberately recruited—one of whom, at six-foot-seven, three hundred and twenty pounds, was a nasty biter.

State's boxers, by contrast, showed class at every weight, nicely blending the brutalities of seasoned street fighters with a really competent and thorough education in the science, courtesy of Cooper. This old man—sixty-five at least, and probably more, small as a jockey and topped with a beaked bald old rooster's head—had been flyweight champion of the world for two years, before a Panamanian named Petey Nosostro had beaten a blood clot into his brain, and so retired him blind in his left eye. This eye, however, retained the same faded blue as the right, was set in an identical small white wrinkled puff of scar tissue, and moved as the right eye moved—its pupil, however, permanently pinpoint.

Compared to State's boxers, Bauman, even at his best—when young and captain of the Minnesota team, fairly short but strong, and gifted with sustaining anger—would have been far outclassed. Was mainly useful now for instructing beginners in the fundamentals of classic blows, stances, footwork and ring strategy, for routine instruction on the bags (light and heavy), and sparring under the swing weight. With the veterans, he worked on correction of any elementary blunders so consistent that little Cooper—impatient, fierce as the aging fighting cock he so resembled—had, in disgust, left them to the fists of opponent fighters to correct by battering.

Bauman was useful for this, as well as for his corner work, his performance of chores, hurling of the medicine ball, fist and ankle taping, liniment rubdowns and cleanup, and handy—when cuts occurred—at plying disinfectant, butterfly bandages, and razor blade (this item returned to a C.O. after every use). And was responsible, as well, for equipment packing for the team's few trips.

On these rare occasions, State's smaller security bus—its windows sandwiches of Plexiglas and hurricane fencing, its body reinforced by sheet steel painted bird-shit white—was found parked in the Northgate courtyard at first light. The team would be standing waiting, all except old Cooper lightly chained in sets of four.

Cooper, whose baggy gray shorts, snowy T-shirt (size boy's medium) and lanyarded bright steel whistle (never blown) were worn invariably in his role of coach, was free to skip aboard, preceding two corrections officers. The hacks were followed by the first chained set: usually Bauman, the team heavyweights, Clarence Henry and Bubba Betts—both black, both ponderously lightfooted as circus bears, with tempers as undependable—and a scrawny retarded Latino cleanup man named Enrique. Long-suffering, Enrique served as little Cooper's housemate in the last cell on Three-tier in A—a position no one envied him.

After, following set by set, the rest of the team boarded, with two more C.O.'s to follow up and bar the folding door behind them.

Loaded, the small bus was almost full, since each of the team's weight classes was usually doubled for a trip—the second man taken along to look and learn, to enjoy in travel the only recruiting privilege the boxing team enjoyed, to substitute in case some discovered personal or institutional problem made it unwise for a State fighter to engage a particular opponent—and finally, to provide throughout these few contests away, at least a murmur of support against the home crowd's savage thunder.

At last, loaded and locked—its civilian driver(contained with his controls in a little closet of steel and urine-yellow armored glass) setting its engine mumbling, then into gear—the bus would roll out through the great white two-story North gate, which, like their cell doors (but monumental) had racked slowly open into its own left flank to allow them sally.

On these journeys, women could be viewed, though not called to, not gestured at. These women were appreciated, made the subject among the men of noisy, merrily imagined encounters rich with extraordinary postures and indecent revelations, including the woman's complimentary expostulations—her odors as, sweat-soaked, she kicked and struggled in the fucking. Which fantasies—commenced and rapped continuous by the most talented tale tellers, augmented by called-out contributions—quite often came at last to some lazy, tender conclusion, at odds with the initial encounter's unbuckled impact, in which gentleness, affection were discovered. Love admitted to, returned.

These usually good-natured entertainments were, rarely, preempted by a very quiet young fighter—remarkably quiet, even among men so habitually reserved—a tall, wiry welterweight white named Todd Ferguson. After relating, in a loud, determined, hortatory tenor, the desultory rape of the female seen in passing—the act hurried, carelessly envisioned, barely imagined by him at all—Ferguson would then develop and expand upon an extended, wonderfully detailed description of the beating of the particular woman, she shrieking (Ferguson, in sudden falsetto, imitating this with great fidelity). This beating so severe that the bones of her slim arms were broken, protruded through soft skin—shafts damp, slippery, vivid white, their splintered tips a revelatory red.

Ferguson's rapt and energetic descriptions of these events—quite uninterruptable by inmate or hack—always were presented at length, minutely, in rich relief, and were continued until that woman seen walking by was, in narrative, finally still, silent, and dead.

These uncommon presentations were always received—excepting only a few initially responsive remarks by those too stupid to remember Ferguson's last occasion—were always received by the other men in deep and disapproving silence. This silence once, last August, had lasted through the telling of the tale, then through the rest of a summer afternoon, the afternoon's miles, while Ferguson, eased, relieved, slept like a child against a lightweight's shoulder. All had traveled mute, sweating in summer's heat, while their small white bus rode the swells and shallows of numerous hills. Still silent later (farther west, the hills left slowly heaped behind), they rode over prairie—flat, wide horizoned, furred five feet deep with wheat—riding to their evening entrance through whatever walls, whichever gates and towers, what razor wire, what steel bars enclosed their then opponents.

Even unsuited to practice boxing at State's level, Bauman sometimes imagined, when mitting for some swift young beast—its pelt sweat-glossy brown, white, or black, its eyes amber, blue, or ebony, polished with the wet of youth, peering from under a guardian brow thick, obdurate as hickory planking—even so evidently outclassed, he sometimes imagined as he caught their flickering punches, flickering until they smacked and stung the mitts in combinations—that he'd lost the last twenty years, and saw himself twenty-four, standing taped and gloved to show a young hardrock a thing or two.

Just once, very soon after he'd brought Bauman over from Housekeeping, old Cooper had caught him sparring to make a young recruit—a raw black lump-muscled brute named Patrick Coile—look foolish and feel foolish. This new boy held his elbows so wide as he punched that Bauman, having quick-tied on a pair of gloves, was given the opportunity almost at will to step inside those detouring blows and punish Coile smartly, with no great pretense at instruction.

Bauman, on that occasion, pleased in the second ring, went dancing through light and shadow provided by several sunbeams streaming down from the gym's high clerestory, boxing hard, almost fighting the awkward boy, but never quite. Counterpunching to smack him in the short ribs, left and right, right and left. These punches—struck almost full, hardly pulled at all and sounding like dropped duffel bags—were accompanied by young Coile's soft grunts, expressing puzzlement and surprise rather than injury.

Little Cooper, his bald head flushed, good eye and blind eye glaring together, had come upon them, sent slow-learning Coile trotting off to shower—then stepped to the ring and looked up to speak with Bauman, resting his bent-knuckled hands on the bottom rope.

"It's surprisin' to me, Trainer, to see what you was doin' out here with that Coile." Cooper's false teeth—improbably even, white, bared somewhat in anger—seemed to overfill the little gargoyle's mouth, interfere slightly with an articulation always odd, lisping. "—Number one, I thought you was a teacher, and wouldn' be doin' crap like that to a kid, make him feel bad about his fightin'. That's number one. Number two is, I didn' figure you personally had that kinda shit in you, which numerous of them fairy inmates got here now, that you got to fuck up another con so's you can feel better, yourself. I didn' realize you had that problem, Trainer. I figured you was all growed up." He'd turned away then, and strutted his banty's strut off to the lockers, the legs of his baggy gray shorts flapping about narrow paper-skinned blue-veined thighs, each deeply scarred, each not quite big around as the forearm of the least of his light-heavies.

Bauman had taken particular care, thereafter, not to betray one of the men again. And after months of the most determined effort—with the team and his chores for the team devouring his afternoons until he could take only an occasional reading student after lunch—had felt properly rewarded when old Cooper (beaked face on a level with

Bauman's upper chest) stopped him after practice on a Friday afternoon, and standing well back—as was his pattern, as his pattern had been when he'd fought, his head only slightly turned to present his good eye—said, "I notice you been dealin' square, not fuckin' around with nobody, Mr. Trainer. Looks like that shit back there was the exception with you. You know, 'stead of the rule. . . ."

Bauman, almost across South yard—somewhat exhilarated at having set limits to the crap he must take in this castle of crap—approached another puddle, smaller, slightly deeper than the first, kicked through it in spray and felt cold water soak the top of his right sock, then settle deeper into his running shoe.

Holding his clipboard in his left hand—his empty right hand fisted, tucked in almost to the angle of his jaw—Bauman, snorting chill whiffs of rain-washed air, began to shadowbox. He spun to dance backward, backstepping down the walk heedless of puddles, then (ducking, threatening to throw the right) continued to revolve, sparring. His left, hampered by the clipboard, was capable only of slow-motion jabs, no hooks to set the paper flying out from under the clipboard's clamp to scatter on the wet walk, wet grass.

After several in succession of these revolutions, still snorting, having twice thrown the right, Bauman noticed three inmates—Indians, by their darker complexions, their blocky heads (one bound in a beaded band), their thick shocks of coarse black hair—standing in order of size (taller to shorter) far to the left in C's central gateway, staring at him.

Rather than be seen to stop his sparring in confusion, Bauman spun around once more, bobbed, threw the right again, looked across the wet grass to casually wave to those distant three, then ducked, danced through a very shallow puddle, and straightened to stroll on his way with soaked, chilled feet.

He wondered whether it was true that some whites in Indian hands had saved themselves by pretending madness, or if that was simply one of those attractive pieces of nonsense, unsupported by corroborative testimony, that provided fools a cushioned notion of a past. U.S. Army archives at Fort McPherson might be a repository to check for that.

Certainly seemed possible, paralleling as it did shamanism's concern with possession by this spirit or that. Probably had some basis, depending on the year, the particular tribe, the tribe's cultural disarray. The more nearly destroyed the tribe's culture, the more likely that a seated captive—gibbering, lifting his head to yelp, to howl like a coyote, or chuckling, rocking back and forth rolling his eyes and singing snatches of "The Wilton Ram"—would find the charade greeted with vulgar farting noises, great hilarity by the encircling men, drunk, many wearing torn trousers, white men's busted hats. The show appreciated as well by the four Indian women, gap-toothed, bruised, sick from a winter's whoring at the fort. These women, pleased and busy with occasion, retiring with one small slender child (its anthracite hair cropped short) to gather twigs, sticks, odd chunks of punk from a rotted willow stump to feed the lazy afternoon fire up from smolder to purpose. . . .

Most of the few Indians at State stood alone, not clubbed in with lifers or bikers, certainly not with Hispanics or blacks. The only exception to this Bauman knew of, was Eddie Becker, at least half Indian, who was a collector of lifer loans. Becker also ran the sweat huts the Indians used in summer—they being permitted, thanks to some judge's addled notion of their religion, to construct these of canvas, heat them with small fires of scrap from the furniture factory. Becker ran these sweats and collected fees from his fellows—in for drunken felonies, most of them—these Cherokees, Osages, and Pawnees sporting unlikely Indian names such as Bull Elk, Great Grizzly, and Lobo Wolf, all apparently preferred to the more authentic names free tribesmen, a humorous people, had enjoyed the century before: Thunderclap Farter, Eats Anything, or Handsome Only Upside Down.

Reaching C's wall, Bauman turned right—the walkway here emptied by chill and damp—and continued along to the end of the building, not looking back to see if the Indians were still watching. Then, turning the corner and passing through the open gate into East yard—no hack caring to stand there in such weather—he walked left along the front of B to the building's main entrance, handed his clipboard over, and stood framed in the metal detector for some time, held there by a new hack. This one—long-nosed, sad-eyed, awkward, tall, and stooped, too old to be starting new work—was certainly another of the local farmers gone to ruin.

This fish hack stood staring at the telltale dial on the machine's flank—apparently forgetting it had a bell to ring, as well, if something ferric perturbed it—until another C.O., a young black woman named Carson, apparently acting as guide and tutor, tapped the farmer on the shoulder, then gestured to her own ear to remind him of the bell's business.

Carson—an unfriendly woman, quiet, stocky, wearing rimless glasses—gestured Bauman through, handed him his clipboard, and let him go on into B, unpatted.

In the entrance hall, Bauman nodded to a C.O. named Patterson, then went down the right-hand steps to the basement corridor. This tunnel—wide, warm, smelling of steam and hot metal—ran north from B to A, divided at the center (just beyond the mail drop, phones, and canteen counter) by a guarded gate, its pass-through a revolving rack of steel bars admitting only one at a time. The corridor's grimy ceiling was snaked with massive gray ducts, paint-peeled piping, and irregular clusters of long fluorescents—these pale lights reflecting off cracked white-tile walls.

At the foot of the basement steps, smelling the odor of cooking dinner (macaroni and cheese) riding the warm humming blower-driven air from Rudy Gottschalk's kitchen far down to the left, Bauman turned right and walked up to check the length of the line waiting for service at the canteen's window—the length of the other line, for the phones. These long queues of fairly patient men ran parallel almost up to the corridor's dividing gate.

This afternoon, both lines were long—the left too long to wait in to buy his two Bit-O'-Honeys, Scooter's three Almond Joys—the right too long to stand in on the odd chance Norman Silber might be at his office, and even being at his office, would care to talk with him.

Bauman had never called the Silbers' home—had had a great deal of difficulty getting Norman Silber to talk with him at all. The first several phone calls wasted with Silber's enraged abuse, personal threats, and threats to call the police, call the warden's office and complain.

"I'm the last person who saw your daughter healthy, effortful, perfectly alive," Bauman had said on his sixth call to Silber's office. "This has been too disastrous for each of us, not to be spoken about. Isn't that so? Does silence help us, Norman?"

Silber finally proved unable, on persistence, to refuse the chance to hear something additional of his daughter—the opportunity to have described to him Karen's appearance, the smooth circling force with which she'd pedaled, the wind ruffling her short blond hair (bright under the streetlight, blown back from her brow in her speedy passage down the drive and out into the street). Silber—unable to bear not knowing such final details as Karen's frown of concentration while, unfortunately in error, she'd swerved attempting to avoid the Volvo—listened to Bauman for these descriptions at least.

An ex-ironworker and construction foreman, Norman Silber had been out of town when his daughter died, had been surveying sites for manufacturing relocations. He'd received the news calling home from a Ramada Inn in Ohio.

Unable to deny all communication with Bauman, Silber finally (after many months) admitted peripheral matters, volunteering reminiscences of Karen's babyhood, her childhood—discussions which it seemed his wife couldn't bear—and in that limited way recreated her for the duration of his telling. Often, however, after these interludes, Silber would deliver sudden savage promises to Bauman of every sort of injury, of death.

Silber had never asked for vision of the accident's aftermath, never wanted to know what his daughter had suffered, once struck, run over, and dying. Never asked what it was his wife had seen. Bauman was apprehensive during each call that those details might be requested, but Norman Silber had never asked. . . .

Besides the tedious length of this line for just six phones—one or two of which were usually out of service, receivers broken by too emphatic hangings-up—besides the long wait, Cernan, the phone con, now seemed to be having a problem with a man, apparently finished with one call, who wanted to place another out of turn, thus screwing the line out of a move one place up. This disagreement, already noisy on the part of the man demanding, would certainly have become more than that with any phone boss but Cernan, who, very fat and almost fifty—doing ten years on a third conviction for fraud—possessed a con artist's soft voice, his reassuring winning ways. In addition, Cernan had always acted decently in persuading the line when a truly desperate man needed to be moved up front to a phone in a hurry. He persuaded the line, took no scrip to do it, and so had made friends.

In this instance, however, and with no emergency to excuse him, a young Latino in neatly tailored denims, shaven-headed, his stubbled scalp laced dark blue with *pachuco* tattoos, was proving recalcitrant, very reluctant to let his receiver go. And while Cernan quietly worked to persuade, the phone line grew more and more restive.

Bauman—disappointed, after his burning of Bobby, to find this minor disturbance causing his usual mild seasickness of apprehension—took four or five steps back down the corridor away from the phones (grateful each step for its small gift of distance) and saw several other older inmates likewise making room. The whole long line for the canteen quietly shifted over to press against the corridor's left wall, separating itself as far as possible from the phone line, from the chance of trouble in which a bystander, just by jostling at the edges of a fight, and ignorant of any personal offense, might find himself surprised three weeks later by five inches of steel stuck into the small of his back, or a peanut-butter jar's measure of oven cleaner thrown into his eyes while he waited outside the barbershop for a haircut.

Performing his cautious withdrawal, Bauman—who'd fantasized, while coming down the basement stairs, receiving some recognition among the men for his arson, news of which must have been transmitted already by the vine, receiving some indications of respect, at least for a time—stepped backward from the furious shouting, then turned to walk away with several others as if they'd only changed their minds about a tedious wait. He wished now he'd never been so brave in the infirmary with the crippled man, who, shithead though he was, had after all been at State long enough to have made at least one good and dangerous friend.

The shouting at the phones now drowning Cernan's persuasions, Bauman glanced back to see two C.O.'s—one a veteran named Geary, the other a young black man Bauman didn't know—come down the corridor from the basement gate, hurrying, but carefully not running, to the disturbance.

"I am gettin' the merry fuck outta here." A con named Kavafian deserting the canteen line to fall into step beside Bauman. "I had enough fuckin' trouble for today," he said. "I say, get the fuck away from all that racket. Who needs it? You want, Bauman, you come in my house for a Dr Pepper, an' we'll bullshit a little, tell a few lies, pass the time until dinner."

"O.K. Sounds good. But, Mike, no way am I playing cards with you for money."

Kavafian smiled. Shorter, wider than Bauman, a few years older as well, mustached, thick curling hair a grainy gray-black, he was especially well dressed this late afternoon in pressed denim trousers, polished black leather loafers, and a dark gray tweed sports jacket—the last certainly street goods, not cut and tailored by the queens at Sweet Stitches.

"O.K., Teach, you got it. We don't have to play for money. We'll play for toothpicks; I don't give a shit. An' you're welcome to join me and my dipshit roomie at our private table for what I hope to Christ is not macaroni and cheese. Dinner's on the house. An' you want your dipshit roomie to sit with us, that's O.K. We both got crosses to bear far as roommates is concerned."

"You convinced me," Bauman said, raising his voice against the raised voices behind them, and turned again to see the two hacks at the head of the phone line, trying to deal at once with the *pachuco* and the men he'd annoyed. Fat Cernan, out of it, had stepped aside to his lectern, was leafing through his big notebook, this for scheduled long-distance calls due out or in.

The new young black C.O. seemed to know his business, must

have served in other walls. He was standing very close to his object, a thin, restless young white con with the loudest voice present, standing close so as not to be surprised by the production of a knife, so as to be able in that case to grapple with the man.

"You got a pack of animals in here, an' that's all you got." Kavafian, at Bauman's right side, turned with him to walk down the corridor away from the noise of argument, each shout behind them ringing off the passage's tiled walls. "—Not one goddamn minute's peace."

"Too true." Bauman, as he walked, heard the difficulty apparently easing, lower voices, less argument—though even so, several more inmates had left their places in the lines, were walking back toward the mess hall, back to B-block.

"The death penalty," Kavafian said. "You can't tell me that isn't a good idea. Get rid of some of these assholes once and for all." A specialist in robbing jewelry stores—by blowing boxes, not by threat—Kavafian seemed to Bauman to be a reasonable man and fairly comfortable company, unless he was playing poker for money, a circumstance in which he couldn't keep from cheating. Which habit, in their only game some months before, had cost Bauman twenty-three dollars, scrip. Since Kavafian—though supposedly connected or at least acquainted with wised-up people in Illinois—presently roomed with a biker and ate dinner with the bikers at the back of the mess hall, though showing no interest whatsoever in motorcycles, it was assumed he arranged shipments of pot, crystal, or crank for them from time to time, smuggled in.

Bauman thought of managing some conversational opportunity to relate in a humorous way his conversion of Bobby Basket to ready-pay, but could think of no way to tell it Kavafian wouldn't consider boasting, and boasting of bullshit, besides.

"I'm for the electric chair one hundred percent," Bauman said, "if it'll cut down on the noise at all."

"Speakin' of noisy," Kavafian said, "Switchboard—Duerstadt?"

"Yes?"

"—Was talkin' to somebody, sayin' you was pissed off at whoever for offin' the little nigger."

"Well, I thought it was a pretty shitty thing to do. It just occurred to me— Well, it seems to me there really is no damn reason to put up with that kind of killing in here. Seems to me if the hacks can't or won't stop it, then the men should get together and stop it themselves."

"You mean, like they was cops . . . ?" Kavafian, walking alongside, had walked closer, lowered his voice.

"That's right. Why the hell should the majority of inmates have to put up with a few nuts who go around killing people?"

"Hey . . . . hey, hold on now." Lowering his voice again, so Bauman could hardly hear him. "—First, you got to keep in mind some guys are offed for real good business reasons. I mean that; real good reasons. Some people, if you don't kill 'em, the fucks pay no attention to you at all! You don't want to call guys some kind of dings when they're just doin' business. And the other thing is— You like cops? You trust a cop?"

They walked past the mess-hall entrance, started up the stone steps to Ground-tier.

"Not all of them, no."

"So, what do you think con cops would be like?"

"You have a point."

"Be just one more fuckin' club lookin' for some action, an' believe me, we got enough clubs in this joint."

"Then what are we supposed to do?"

"Be glad it wasn't us got killed, Professor. That's what we do." Kavafian barely murmuring as two inmates came down the steps past them. "You know, people are startin' to think you got an interest or somethin' involved with that guy bein' offed, 'cause you been talkin' about it this mornin'—you know, like you was coverin' your ass or somethin'."

"That's ridiculous."

"Sure, but you maybe want to remember there's lots of guys in here believe any kind of shit. Know somethin'? This place is the third joint I been in. I'm not bitchin'; cost of doin' business. So I been in two others, an' neither of 'em was bad as this. You get my drift?"

At the top of the stairs, they walked out into Ground-tier's vaulted space, its smells, its tidal clamor.

"I should keep my mouth shut."

"Hey, is that ever a bad idea? An' I apologize to you for even bringin' it up. Strictly none of my business; you're a grown guy. . . ."

Dinner was macaroni and cheese, lima beans, and rice pudding.

Bauman was eating with Scooter at Kavafian's table, surrounded at the back of the mess hall by the bearded, earringed bulks of all the major bikers—the club's redhaired president, Eric Ganz, being a slender clean-shaven exception, and bearing no tattoos. Ganz, one of those rarities, even at State, for whom extreme violence represented an immediate and natural extension of behavior, had won his office within three weeks of coming up from Evansville.

During his admissions interview in the Biker Club office, having apparently come to some conclusion as to the then-president's qualifications, Ganz had stood, picked up from the president's desktop a heavy white plaster skull with ruby glass eyes, and had swiftly beaten the incumbent to death with it, scattering fragments of white plaster and ruby glass broadcast. Then, the club members present not caring to interfere, slender Ganz had slung the weighty corpse, carried it out to the stairs, and dropped it headfirst down the well, creating the flimsiest passable alibi.

The bikers, led the past three years by this person, a young man ferocious enough to give even the lifers pause, had been enjoying a renaissance of power, influence, and dealer profit. This resurgence was especially timely, since Peter Nash, the legendary president of the Lifer Club, had for the past two years waited penned in Segregation for possible trial in the murders of two inmates—these two garroted by Nash with nylon bootlaces in the print shop, after the club's tribunal had convicted them of disrespect. Their deaths were then presented to the administration, unconvincingly, as the result of a gay suicide pact.

Bauman, trying to fill up on lima beans, was seated across from Kavafian's roommate, Carlo, an absolutely silent young albino who, though he looked dangerous and was a Gypsy Joker, was in fact gentle, passive, detached, his light-pink eyes protected by permanent dark glasses, his tattoos startling cobalt blue against skin white as white bread.

The poker in Kavafian's house before dinner had been ante'd only for toothpicks, though the host (impatient with cards for card-play's sake) had made several suggestions that each toothpick represent a very, very small amount of street money, a penny, at least a penny, or if not that, then a very small amount of scrip.

"The camel's nose does not get into the tent," Bauman had said, seated on an apple crate and dealing to the householder, his roommate, and an inmate named Gordon down from Three-tier—Gordon an amiable gas-station stickup man, who'd almost accidentally killed someone during a robbery netting painfully short money. "—The camel's nose does not get into the tent. Never again will I play cards for money with someone named Kavafian."

"I hope to shit you're not claimin' I cheat, Teach." Kavafian taking no real offense.

"Never. You're just too good, too fantastic a poker player for anyone else to stand a chance."

"Could be. . . ."

"—How many cards?"

By game's end at the dinner bell, Kavafian, though uninterested, had won one hundred and seventy-three toothpicks.

After finishing his lima beans, Bauman offered to trade his macaroni and cheese for more. This was accepted by Scooter, who'd learned how to manage off odors, off tastes—the cheese being off in this case. As usual, it had an odd wet crumbly texture and an odor something like fish, and unpleasant. Scooter had discovered that such food, if it must be eaten, was better chewed and swallowed while gently, steadily blowing a breath of air out his nose. This still left an aftertaste on the tongue, but one less offensive than if the whole bite's odor had been inhaled while chewing.

Scooter made the trade, used his small orange-plastic fork to carefully rake over the barter serving of macaroni and cheese, checking for steamed roaches—then, satisfied, took a bite, softly snorting out through his nose as he chewed.

Bauman offered his rice pudding for more limas, but got no takers. Behind him, at some table against the wall, one of the bikers began to giggle at a pitch higher than conversation. Several others commenced to laugh along, and Bauman, taking only a taste of his rice pudding, felt a large heavy hand settle to rest on his right shoulder. He sat still, somewhat reassured by the gentleness of the grip, wondering if he should turn and look up to see.

When it occurred to him this might be Les Kerwin with his sharp-pointed wire—and occurred likely much too late—Bauman, his heart thumping hard, suddenly lurched half out of his seat, turned with his right arm raised to ward, and saw the biker, Perteet, grinning down at him.

"You are a crazy motherfucker," the huge man said, voice rumbling deep, black beard clotted with macaroni and cheese. And another voice, baritone, sounded from one of the important tables against the wall, seconding that. "—A crazy motherfucker."

Bauman—still half risen, right arm still raised, rice pudding turned to rusty iron on his tongue—looked far right for that voice and with very great relief saw Eric Ganz and an older biker named Bump smiling at him from the officers' table in the corner. —It appeared the vine had finally delivered its tale of Basket's burning, which had not offended the bikers of B, and with good luck would be received so throughout State.

"You are a crazy motherfucker," Perteet said again, his furry hand, large and smelly as a foot, resting across Bauman's shoulder. And

Bauman was struck by the notion—hearing very clearly the slightly different emphasis Perteet had placed on the reiteration—that repetitious phrasing in teenage and underclass speech was only superficially so, with variations in emphasis taking the place of additional vocabulary. —A sort of choral speaking in one voice, nearly a chant, that might explicate the repetitious simplicity represented by choral speech in Greek drama, so often presented as the witness and comment of ordinary people.

"Teach is a fuckin' crazy motherfucker . . . !" This cry from across the room was taken up by one or two others. "Torchy! Torchy!" called out to rhythmic handclaps which caused the two C.O.'s standing by the coffee trays to put their coffees down, concerned.

Bauman, having by this small celebrity made dinner eventful for the block, settled back into his seat and spooned up another bite of rice pudding—so relieved, so absurdly pleased that his throat ached, his vision blurred with almost tears.

"What the fuck did you do?" Kavafian—Scooter and the albino also waiting to hear.

"I just made a goddamn fool of myself," Bauman said by way of preamble, to take the curse from boasting, "—this afternoon, over in the infirmary." Then followed the tale, told as if the scorching had been primarily humorous, a rough joke on a welsher, with no frightened puzzlement for the jokester, no desperation or discomfort in it for him at all. Told once, applauded, Bauman repeated it for two bikers who came to stand by the table to listen, more and more careful as he heard himself, to keep the telling short, casual, offhand—and so, by not trying to entertain, did. It was certainly the best dinner—even though macaroni and cheese—certainly the best dinner Bauman had had at State, if only for the fool's reason that foolish men were giving him regard.

There followed a lightfooted climb for lock-'n'-count, made more agreeable by amused congratulations from Mark Nellis at the foot of the circular steel staircase. His wife, less amused, was concerned for such a dreadfully crippled man, no longer young, and needed to be reassured Bobby hadn't been hurt—Bauman and Nellis exchanging smiles at Betty's excess of tenderness.

After this, fairly satisfied, Bauman climbed the flight and led Scooter off the stairs at Two-tier and into their house to find Herbert Hanks, the watch sergeant, standing with a black hack named Jepson amid the wreckage of their goods.

The house had been very roughly turned—one leg of their stool broken or pulled loose from the rungs, almost all the photographs of motorcycles, of women, torn off the left wall, items from the sink shelf thrown on the deck (Scooter's small blue cap broken) and the blanket curtaining the toilet pulled down. The double bunk had been shifted.

"Hey, dickhead," Hanks said to Bauman, "—now don't tell me you wasn't told. Don't tell me Lieutenant Gorney didn' tell you turn this friggin' jewelry in." Hanks—a big heavy-bellied man, aging, scalp gleaming bald in front, fringed grizzle at the rear, his khaki uniform perfectly pressed—held the Rolex out, dangling from a large liver-spotted fist, its fine stainless chain-mail band catching every light.

Startled at having his minor celebration cut so rudely short, and for such petty, nearly forgotten cause, Bauman saw the Submariner held in another's hand—being stolen was what it amounted to—and not given time to keep his temper, lost it.

"You ridiculous cretin," he said to Sergeant Hanks. "Give it back!" Then put up his fists and stepped across the litter of torn photographs to get his watch.

Hanks, insulted and assaulted in such quick succession and slowed a little digesting the phrase "ridiculous cretin," was surprised enough by Bauman's coming at him to take quick complementary steps back nearly to the toilet. Jepson, the black hack, saying "Hey!" and shouldering forward, was still slower than Scooter, who'd already jumped jittering in front of Bauman, his scrawny arms spread to guard as they must have when he played basketball on his high school team in Tecumseh. Scooter, dancing, guarding, jumping slightly up and down before Bauman, shouted, "Cut this shit, Charles! You just fuckin' cool it, man!" in tones harsh and heavy, intended to placate, substitute for, and render superfluous immediate official responses.

This worked well enough for Bauman to pause and put his hands down—then, very worried, to back up across the cell. At which retreat, Hanks lurched into motion, pushed past Jepson to shove Scooter away against the cell's steel wall, and fetched Bauman a swift awkward left-hand punch, which Bauman accepted, didn't attempt to ward, and during which the Rolex hanging from the striking fist flailed out ahead of the blow to bite a neat small bit out of Bauman's right cheek—perhaps, Bauman was to consider later that night, in furious disappointment with so cowardly a master.

"You motherfucker!" Scooter's contribution, and his last immediate, since Jepson took him by the back of his neck, shook him, shoved him into the wall again so his head struck, and told him to shut his hole.

"What the fuck were you goin' to do? You fuckin' college faggot!" Hanks' inquiry and insult as he punched again with the same fist, but lightly, so the heavy watch swung to only touch Bauman's face.

That night, half asleep on his new, narrower, harder bed, Bauman would imagine this gentle touch an apology for the previous injury.

Now—seized, spun, his hands cuffed behind him—Bauman was impressed by Hanks' strength, certainly not evident in the man's punching. The watch sergeant heaved Bauman out the cell door, hooked a grip through his triced right arm, and hauled him to the stairway, Bauman trotting to keep from falling.

"Makin' a fuckin' fool of yourself, asshole!" Hanks still upset at having backed to the toilet. "You was told about that fuckin' watch!"

Bauman, shock having replaced anger, was tugged it seemed in slow motion through gluey impeding air, surprised at Hanks and at himself for such a fuss over so little, and tried to be careful going down the stairs, which Hanks, wrestling him down the ringing circular way with Jepson following, made difficult.

At the staircase foot, the two hacks took fresh grips, then bucked Bauman along Ground-tier toward B-block's gate. Past the Nellis house first—Betty standing wide-eyed at her bars as he went by. Four bikers in the next house shouted "Cocksucker!" at Hanks in fair unison. A few more men stood at their cell doors, watching, calling this or that as Bauman was hustled past. But most, uninterested, stayed silent in their bunks, watching TV or occupied with crafts—matchstick schooners, toothpick chapels, belts tooled richly as Spanish saddles.

Gorney—spare, collected, his iron-gray hair crewcut closer than usual—was sitting pressed and pin-neat (though apparently into a double shift) looking over paperwork when Hanks shoved Bauman into the lieutenant's A-block basement office. Gorney looked up at once, and seemed satisfied with what he saw.

"Lieutenant, this jerk-off tried an' come at me up there in B, an' all because of this piece of shit!" Hanks slapped the big watch down hard on the metal desktop, and Gorney reached out to pick it up, examine it. Then he put it back down and looked up at Bauman again, apparently finding something funny.

"Well, you got a real tiger by the tail there, Herb, and not just for holding jewelry. What I hear, the champ here tried to burn up old Basket in the infirmary."

"He set a fire . . . ?"

"Sure did. Supposedly damn near burned poor old Bobby right up in his bed, looking for some payout or other. Did you do that?" he said to Bauman. "I sure as hell heard that's what you did."

Bauman said nothing—finding, though not for the first time at State, the rich rewards of silence, containing within itself almost autonomy, the power of so many implied unspoken responses.

Gorney, veteran at monologue, repeated, "Burned poor old Basket right up in his bed. . . ." and sat observing Bauman's handcuffed discomfort, his bleeding right cheek.

"How come you're bleeding there?"

Bauman—who might, simply to annoy, have broken silence to complain about being punched, even requested a grievance interview with the A.W. to inflict paperwork—found himself choosing instead the simpler solidarity of all male subordinate societies, in which appeal to higher authority, even with reason, is not done. The lieutenant and Bauman collaborated in this. Gorney waited for his answer, certain of no complaint forthcoming. Bauman, stayed silent.

Gorney sat looking at Bauman a few moments longer, a regard measuring as a doctor's. "You do understand that this here's not really about this showoff piece." He patted the watch. "What I'm talking about, what this is all about, is you doing just exactly what you're told to do. And I told you to turn this thing in, get a Timex or whatever. Didn't I tell you that? Didn't I tell you that a few months ago?"

Bauman, shoulders hunched slightly to relieve his handcuffed wrists, kept close his treasure of silence, impressed by the random uncertain elements of human relationships—even in their simplest forms, as here between binders and bound—where such a minor disobedience might after months be resurrected to trouble him with an evening's casual humiliation, a cut face and cramped arms, the confiscation—theft—of his watch. Love, he supposed, was an effort to reduce that uncertainty to bearable, often only increasing it.

Gorney picked up the Submariner again, examined it. "Kind of person would spend—how much? How much did this cost? Well, spend a whole lot of money just on a wristwatch, has got to be real rich, or a ding. Wouldn't you say, Bauman?"

Hanks, having kept his grip on Bauman's right arm—awkwardly angled to the cuffs behind his back—yanked once, in vain, to encourage a reply.

"As to that thing over at the infirmary this afternoon, if I had a better handle on that, I would dip you in deep shit; you can believe it. I'd ticket you in for a couple of months. As it is—for keeping this jewelry against a specific order by a shift officer, and because you probably think you got away with that stuff over at the infirmary—I'm going to sheet you over to Seg for a week on Direct Disobedience and Concealing Contraband."

"And Resistance," Hanks said, and yanked Bauman's right arm again.

"O.K. On Resistance, too." He looked up into Bauman's eyes—his own light tea-brown, mildly interested, apparently, in what made this inmate tick. Professional interest and personal interest sufficient, Bauman supposed, to have kept Gorney in corrections as a career. —At promotion's ceiling, though. No advanced degrees, no master's in criminology, administration, corrections, let alone a doctorate.
"—All right, Bauman, you're going in over there for short time, just a week; you don't get out of that cell. Locked down right through. No block time, no time out at all. No visitors. You got somebody coming up—too bad. Your wife comes up, doesn't she? Too bad. . . ." Looking genuinely sympathetic. "Anybody coming up is going to find out they came up here for nothing, because you blew it. And maybe just this little short time locked down is going to alert you to the fact of the matter, Professor, which is that you are really starting to screw up. Do you understand that?"

Bauman kept still, but Gorney seemed satisfied with that particular silence, and nodded as if in confirmation.

"—You're going over right now on administrative. You dumb enough to go for a penalty hearing, you can have it in a couple of days, per regs. You want that hearing?" Gorney waited only a moment or two. "O.K., Herb, you and Bobby take him on over, check him in right now. We're going to see if this inmate can learn a lesson, or if he can't. What do you say, Bauman? You a good learner?"

Taken upstairs, then out through the sally gate from A—out into a chill evening just folded into night, its air frigid and stationary as the deeper waters of a lake—Bauman was no longer cuffed, only flanked by Hanks and Jepson, who, as usual with C.O.'s after trouble, seemed to hold no grudge, were amiable, relaxed, jovially professional. This practice, called "zatching," was believed by the inmates to be hacks' kiss-ass insurance against the possible occasion of being held hostage, when enmity might prove fatal, or if not that, perhaps be the cause of serial acts of anal intercourse, rudely introduced.

The night's new-descended darkness occupied North yard in immense topological sections, oddly shaped by intrusions of tall bright urine-yellow cones of lamplight, by narrow sweeping beams in tints of blue, bright blue-white, smeared blue-green, and by the dull small soft gold of those stationary bulbs burning high at watch station intervals along the crenellations of the wall, burning higher in distant towers.

It was an adventure to be outside at night. Though Bauman had twice ridden into State on the team bus after dark, those entrances had been only through East gate, to stop half blinded under the entryway lights—not at all the same as walking tonight, with a distance to go in passage through such varieties of light, to a different destination.

The men flanking him had fallen into step, their heavy shoes sounding solid unisons on the cement, and Bauman skipped once to remain contrapuntal, though his worn blue running shoes scarcely made sufficient sound for it. They stepped abreast through a bright silver-green sheet of light into vaults of darkness deep across the yards. Here, unlit, unwarmed even by inference, the air presented the edge of winter, smelling like sharpened steel.

In the distance before them, the laundry building lay sited against the wall's western flank, one lamp shining down on its front steps, dim light glowing through several of its first-floor windows, where rows of huge washers, dryers, and mangles now stood silent in air still smelling of steam.

Above, in the second story, where two windows showed light, men particularly despised—stone dings, snitches, the talkative aged—were held in Protective Custody, achieving some safety at the price of stricter confinement. And above them, on the building's third and final floor, unlit, swallowed by the night, lay Segregation. There, men being punished, or awaiting trial for recent murders—or simply those greatly feared by staff and inmates alike—were held separate for a while, or forever, from the four great central blocks.

Hanks, after what seemed to Bauman too short a long walk from North yard into West and across, led past the laundry's wide stone steps—the light from the lamp above, yellow-white, bright enough to reflect in the stone's sparkling mica—led to the flights of a narrower steel staircase beyond them, and began to climb. Bauman followed Hanks up, and Jepson, not crowding, followed after.

Bauman had spent many of his first weeks working in the laundry's cavernous basement, in which Cooper's housekeepers headquartered, kept their supplies. During those weeks, the unsteady rumble of giant kettle washers, the higher buzz of drum dryers had vibrated down from the first floor through the basement ceiling during all days but Sundays—shaking a constant agitated cloud of the finest possible dust down with the noise. Bauman, sitting in the basement one dark morning at old Cooper's desk, had discovered an almost Brownian motion in these particles (thick, roiling, bright enough to have been the light itself) in the beam of the goose-neck lamp.

Rarely sent up on errands from the basement to the laundry, he'd had no occasion to visit P.C. on the second floor, much less Segregation on the third. Now, climbing behind Hanks' ponderous haunches, he found every steel step—whose metal, intended for steps from the start, had been rolled out at the mill with a raised diamond pattern to prevent slipping—found each step, though all were painted battleship gray, to have some individual point of interest—four small grooves in a lower left edge, the diamonds worn to shine on another step, which seemed the same, certainly no older than its fellows. Each step a slightly different step, even only looked at in passing. Absolutely different, Bauman supposed, fundamentally different at some subatomic level where no particle agreed. —A foundation beneath which, however, might lie the buried footing of their perfect agreement after all, the revelation of steel steps too identical in substructure to be separate, revealing all apparent multiples, all differentiations, as too inconsequential to have ever made up anything but one thing—that single structure of which steel steps and their climbers, mistaken for what they seemed and imagined to be separate, were only portions, misunderstood.

The door at the top of the last flight, as P.C.'s on the floor below had been, was a steel fire door, this one painted the stairs' dark gray and set deep into windowless brick. Bauman followed Hanks through it into a large square room, high-ceilinged and brilliantly lit—or seeming so after the darkness—its walls all white-painted steel. There was a faint toilet odor, as if the whispering ventilators were contributing some sewer's air.

The room was divided straight across its half by a wall of dark amber armor-glass, backed by a lattice of white steel bars—this division rising the considerable way to the ceiling and meeting it. There was a narrow single-passage gate, set into the center of the glass wall's complication, that seemed to lead through the wall into a narrow entryway, also glassed and barred—a sort of airlock, an isolation box in which an inmate might be held to be perused at leisure.

"Hey, Hanks. . . ." A microphoned voice.

"What you doin', Frank?" Hanks said, having recognized the voice or the shape of the C.O. rising from one of several desks behind the wall to drift forward, cloudy through amber glass. Bauman couldn't remember seeing this man before. He looked young, slight, and when he came closer to the wall appeared to be dark-complected as a movie gypsy.

The gypsy observed the three of them, his face bisected so a dark eye peered from each side of a narrow upright white steel bar.

"Bauman?"

"Right," Hanks said. "—We're O.K. here." And strolled to the room's right wall, pressed and held a red buzzer's button set at waist height, while the hack behind glass reached left to a complementary. The buzzers sounded together (angry wasps) only briefly, and the narrow central gate slid left and open. At which Jepson, standing behind, put his open hand between Bauman's shoulder blades and pushed him gently to the gateway and in, staying with him the first few steps, still gently pushing, till Bauman entered—then relinquishing, stepping back as the gate slid shut.

Bauman stood inside a narrow closet, a security enclosure only two and a half feet wide, perhaps six feet long, with an exit gate set into its far end. That gate—opening only when the one behind him was safely shut and locked—insured that no convict's passage would be other than solitary and slow, allowing for careful consideration. There were slender gray-plastic posts set in the sides of the enclosure—metal detectors, he assumed. When he turned around to look through the first gate for Jepson and Hanks, as if they were friends of his, he found them already gone.

The small amber space, though translucent, began to make Bauman's breathing slightly difficult. Its air carried a definitely fecal odor. Now another hack swam into view, and Bauman recognized him through the glass. A man named Tanner, tall, round-faced, and tough, his thick dark-brown hair brushed back, blown dry. An unfriendly hack, particularly disliked by the bikers, whose case he seemed perpetually upon—this because, according to the vine, he'd been a biker himself once, before deciding to kiss authority's ass.

The closet's end gate slid open, and Tanner stepped in, took a pinch of Bauman's jacket collar to tug him out into much brighter light, then put his hands on Bauman's shoulders to turn him, march him over to face a green metal desk.

"I hope you ate a big dinner, Bauman," Tanner had a harsh big-city voice, Chicago perhaps, or Gary, "—'cause you sure as shit ain't goin' to get nothin' here for a while. Now, I want you to strip an' show, real quick."

Bauman had nothing to see but the white-painted steel wall, the green metal desktop (two sharpened yellow pencils sited together at its center, a fat white report pad arranged just beside them in neatness very unlike State). Evidence, he supposed, of Segregation's special character.

"Hey—wake up an' get to it!"

When Bauman had taken his jacket off, his running shoes, socks, denim trousers and shirt, had stepped out of his skivvies, he turned to face Tanner—saw the dark young hack (too far across the room for his name tag to be read) standing, watching—then opened his mouth to show Tanner his tongue, curled his tongue up to show its underside, and opened his mouth wider, as if he were yawning, his lips drawn back to reveal as much as possible. Then he closed his mouth and bent his head, ran his fingers through his hair several times (to expose and dislodge razor blades, joints, small paper twists of crystal), then raised his arms high to expose his armpits, brought them down again to hold his hands out to Tanner, fingers spread, palms up, then down, lifted his feet to display their bottoms and, at Tanner's nod, turned around to view the neat desktop again, spread his legs wide, and reached behind him to grasp his buttocks and pull them apart for Tanner's convenience.

Bauman heard, after a moment's pause, a soft snap of rubber. He tensed, felt the officer's strong finger probe at his anus, work painfully deep into it, then abruptly withdraw.

Soft snap as the rubber finger-guard was pulled off.

"Lift them nuts," Tanner said. Annoyed he'd forgotten, had presented the opportunity for such an order, Bauman reached down between spraddled thighs and lifted his scrotum to prove no contraband.

"O.K.," Tanner said, and Bauman turned back to watch the hack stoop to gather up each item of clothing, examine them one by one, then tuck them all into a small white plastic bag, which he set aside. Tanner then attended to the running shoes with particular care.

"O.K.," he said, finished with the second shoe and let it fall. And to the other officer, "Log him in. I'm goin' take him on down to the showers."

"Right." The dark hack—off his microphone—sounded like a teenager, and looked, as Bauman glanced over, almost that young. Several large television monitors stacked in a console on the desk behind him seemed to be showing nothing, or nothing much. Nothing moving. . . . Bauman could hardly think of anything worse for someone young than to be working in a prison, to be educated in so many grotesqueries.

"Move," Tanner said, and put a hand on Bauman's bare right shoulder to steer him to the back of the room, where another narrow gate—armor-glazed, barred in white steel set into a white steel doorway—gave on to a wall of green plaster just beyond.

Through this gateway, Tanner strolling close behind, Bauman found the stench of manure much stronger. He walked on, found no way to turn but right, and passed in a few steps to a very spacious entry where a broad gate of fat white bars, watched beside by a hack in an amber cage, introduced what must be Segregation. This was a wide corridor diminishing into distance behind the bars, with one long row of cells running down its right side—a single-tiered block deeply shadowed, barely lit by the dimmest rosy night-light, its cell doors showing dark as pitch. There was no sound but a faint electric hum.

When Bauman stood still, looking, Tanner gently shoved him into motion straight across Segregation's entry to a short flight of cement stairs running down, up which a breath of ammonia drifted to counter the stink of shit.

The shower room, lit by two small bulbs in a single ceiling fixture, was fairly large, L-shaped, its dirty green-tiled walls stained rust beneath each of the six shower nozzles ranked along either side of the long leg of the L.

It smelled like the showers in B-block's basement—of steam heat, ammonia, laundry soap, and mildew—not unpleasantly, a relief from the stench upstairs. The floor drain, like so many at State, was reluctant to accept, and the room's sunken cracked white-tile floor stood three or four inches deep in dark water. Opposite, across the L's short angle, cement steps led up from the wet to another door, gray steel and streaked with rust.

"Get to it," Tanner said, and Bauman stepped naked down into this tidal pool—relieved to find it quite warm, though littered with floating cigarette butts and a small Styrofoam cup, crushed.

He saw what seemed a piece of yellow soap in a tile niche beneath the second shower-nozzle on his right, stepped splashing over to it, found almost half a bar of laundry soap, gritty, cold in his hand, then turned the shower handle halfway round toward HOT—the word's lettering, on spotted chrome, almost worn away.

The nozzle gasped and vomited hot water at once, so hot and such a flood that Bauman ducked away before reaching in to test the temperature, turn the handle back a degree or two. Then the water was perfect, coming down with considerable force in a single stream, the shower's sprinkler-head long since lost like all the others.

Bauman stepped under, busily scrubbing at his sides, his belly with the stony soap, miming a swift and thorough shower so Tanner wouldn't interrupt it too soon, force him out of such enclosing sound and sensation, such a heavy, pouring richness of touch, of comfort.

Rubbing the grainy soap at his left armpit, then at his right as if some suds might be expected, scouring with every appearance of alacrity, Bauman managed to position his head directly beneath the torrent, so that at the minor cost of mild steady battering, he achieved a bell-shaped wavering curtain of water about him, silver, almost clear—a warm and rushing privacy he attempted to prolong by gestures of continuous soaping, lifting one leg to scrub, then the other, carefully, so as not to tear the fabric of his translucent parasol.

This seemed to last for minutes. He kept his eyes down to avoid meeting Tanner's glance, avoid provoking an end to his shower. It lasted certainly two or three minutes, long enough for pleasure to turn almost to relaxation . . . Bauman imagining he had the opportunity much later of rescuing Tanner from cons about to kill him, saying to them, This motherfucker let me have the longest shower I ever had at State. Man, he let that mother run! So my vote is, give the motherfucker a break. —After which, they might.

The shower was allowed too long, it seemed, so that Bauman finally found worry over interruption interrupting. He turned his head beneath his waterfall only a little to the left, saw that Tanner had grown slighter, standing on the steps—and thrusting his face out in spray through the thin wall of water, saw it wasn't Tanner there, but Gorney, the watch commander.

Gorney's mouth moved, but Bauman couldn't hear clearly enough to understand. Then—as Gorney prepared, mouth open, teeth showing, to repeat—Bauman heard a shout from a different direction, quite loud, through all the immediate noise of water. "Turn that damn . . . *Turn . . . that water . . . off!*"

Obedient, Bauman reached back and turned the shower handle—at first to hotter by mistake, then swiftly to OFF and silence.

The man who'd shouted was standing in steam across the shower room on that side's cement steps. A stranger, dressed in weighty black oxfords, dark-gray slacks, white shirt, wide red-figured tie, a gray-tweed sports jacket, the jacket's material thin, looking cheap. This was a fairly big man, black-haired, tall, wearing horn-rim glasses on a brutal face as broad across the cheekbones as an Indian's—might, probably did have some Indian blood. And, an outsider possessing a convict's face, seemed a cop for certain.

"I'm not interested in looking at your genitals, Bauman." A woman's voice. The woman standing beside this cop, or just stepped down from the doorway to stand beside him—so unlikely, Bauman later supposed, as to have been invisible before she spoke—was staring hard into his face, gaze deliberately high, apparently to avoid seeing those genitals.

"You cover yourself!" the tall policeman said. And Bauman cupped his hands down to cover himself, then looked left to Gorney for support, for confirmation of these apparitions. Support there was not, but Gorney, standing on his steps, did nod slightly, confirming their reality.

Satisfied as to what she might see, the woman took a loaded clipboard from under her left arm, looked over at Bauman, then down at a document of some sort, and said as if she were reading from that, "My name is Grace Hilliard. I'm an assistant state's attorney out of the attorney general's office. The governor's office and our office, and certainly your warden, are good and sick and tired of the killings up here, and we intend to bring that kind of behavior to a screeching halt." She looked up at Bauman, but not so as to encompass his concealing hands, and said, "Is that absolutely clear to you?"

"You bet," Bauman said, casual not from calm but from preoccupation as he looked at her. She had a pleasant voice, the sort of voice his mother had called "ladylike." A fairly tall woman, with short ginger-brown hair done up in a curly permanent. Wearing glasses too, like her policeman buddy, but hers oversized, round-lensed, a fashion statement. Grace Hilliard was a rawboned woman, though seeming slight and softly padded beside her cop. The cop a state trooper, Bauman supposed.

"Are you listening to me?" Some steam still dissipating between them.

"Yes," Bauman said, feeling chilled now that the water was off. His feet were warm, though, in the overflow. "I'm listening to you. . . ."

She was wearing a white blouse, matching jacket and skirt. A suit of raspberry-colored material. Betty Nellis would have given a number of creme cookies just for a look at it. Grace Hilliard's eyes seemed mildly blue; the lingering steam made it difficult to judge. She was not pretty, and probably never had been. He'd seen Susanne recently enough, remembered Beth well enough to be sure of that.

This was a pioneer woman's face—angular, irregular, pinched, belonging to a farm woman who was a bear for work in a century before farm women were fat. This strict face, however, certainly capable of deforming during pleasure.

Bauman, thinking of that, watching the woman's mouth as she talked, was troubled by some stirring where his hands were cupped.

"You better pay attention," Gorney said to him, loud enough to echo slightly off the shower room's walls.

"I am paying attention," Bauman said, and then could hear her voice, as if she'd been speaking too softly before.

"The attorney general's office does not have evidence you're the immediate perpetrator in Kenneth Spencer's death. We do, however, have information that leads us to believe you are knowledgeable, that you had an interest and may be an accomplice."

"Me? What information?" Bauman said. "—What are you talking about? I didn't have anything to do with that!"

"So you say, so you say," the woman said in singsong, apparently pleased by Bauman's denial, "—but we have affidavits from both Spencer's wife and his sister to the effect that Spencer told them he was going to need a sum of money to give to you."

"What amount?" Bauman said. "Oh, listen, you've got this very, very wrong. What amount of money are you talking about?" His legs were cold as they dried—a draft of some sort.

"That amount was to be specified on their visit this week."

"That is all just nonsense, Ms. . . . Hilliard. It's just nonsense! I worked with Spencer on his writing—his grammar and spelling—so he could send letters to the mayor of Gary and some other people, asking for help getting him a new lawyer. And that's it—period!" Bauman wondered why in the world he was even talking to her, when silence would do as well. Might do better in this ironical nightmare. "—Letters to some ministers, too. If you really want to know how much money was involved, it was fifteen dollars, street. O.K.? Now, why don't you just busy yourself trying to find out who did kill him, and leave me alone." He almost added, And by the way, fuck you for pulling this little stunt—having just realized that Gorney must have been told to send him over to Seg on any excuse at all, just for this.

"Spencer was seen talking to you in the mess hall at lunch the day he died," the woman said, staring hard into Bauman's eyes as she spoke to him—apparently a trick of the trade, since the prosecutor at his trial, Bellasario, had done the same. "He was speaking with you alone at a table. Just the two of you. And the man was seen crying right out in public."

"Right, right." Bauman turned to Gorney again. "Can these people do this? Come in here and do this?" Gorney looked at Bauman as if astonished at the question. "—I see. Then what about a towel, Lieutenant?"

"Tanner's getting you your clothes," Gorney said.

"Great. . . . Spencer was crying," Bauman said to the woman. "Whatever snitch you're relying on is absolutely right. The man was crying; he was desperate." Bauman found it surprising how difficult speech became when one couldn't gesture, even in a limited way. He wondered whether he should just stop answering, stop trying to explain, to talk sense to this prosecutorial bureaucrat. He wished he might now retreat under his umbrella of hot water, spend years under there if necessary—he'd need some sort of oil to keep his skin from wrinkling, growing spongy—stay under there warm and safe, watching through constant, falling, wavering water. "—Spencer wanted to complain to somebody. Can you understand that? He was complaining to me about a lack of justice in his case, and so forth and so on. He wanted me to help him write some useless letters he could send to people."

"Now, why don't I believe that . . . ?" the woman said, and went on talking. It struck Bauman, listening to the hurry in her voice, its breathlessness, that being in State was frightening her, companion trooper or no.

"All right," interrupting her—whatever the hell she was saying, "—this has gotten bizarre enough. I would like to speak to my lawyer, if you don't mind. And I'm also really tired of standing here in the water, covering my balls for your convenience."

"You just watch your dirty mouth," her tall cop said. "That's about all we need to hear out of you."

Bauman considered saying, How'd you like to kiss my ass, four-eyes? to the trooper, to see if he'd come down into the water, do something about it, ruin his fine black oxfords. But instead of that, Bauman said, "I want to talk to my lawyer."

The woman leafed and checked through her clipboard. Then, reference found, "O.K. Bauman, you talk to your lawyer, and I'm going to tell you what we'll do then. You complain to Mr. . . . Christiansen. Then we're going to name you a material witness before the sitting grand jury considering this mess up here. A material witness and designated unfriendly—a convicted felon. And that status, believe you me, could last for years. *Years.* This grand jury, the next grand jury . . ." She paused, peered down at him through steamed lenses, then abruptly pushed her glasses up her forehead and settled them gently in her hair. Bauman doubted the steam was doing her permanent any good.

"Let me ask you a question," he said. "Did you get your hair done to come up here?"

"I told you . . ." the trooper said.

"Bauman." Gorney, from the other side. "—Bauman, cut the crap."

"Go on, Ms. Hilliard," Bauman said. "Continue. I'm really interested in observing justice *sub judice.* I will say—presuming this Alice in Wonderland interview is not a dream—that it all sounds like extortion to me. Are you, as an officer of the court, presenting a little sample of threat and extortion?"

She didn't like that at all, seemed genuinely offended. Lips—thin already, though colored plumper in pale coral—now thinned to vanishing, became a straight coral line. "I certainly do not have to defend my office against a cowardly drunk who runs down a child and drives away and leaves her dying, then gets up here and becomes some nasty little *bagman* scooting around the state penitentiary all day pretending to give people lessons so he can collect debts and run dirty errands for some killers!"

"I am not the person you describe so colorfully, Ms. Hilliard." Bauman stood dignified as he could in dirty water, his cock and balls under his hands. He had a dreadful feeling he was about to start laughing, and would find it difficult to stop. "—I don't know who killed Spencer or anybody else up here. And believe me, I'm learning it's strictly none of my business. So you just go right ahead and name me a material witness, an unfriendly witness, anything you want, because I don't like being brought over here simply for this asinine bullshit."

"I told you to watch that mouth," the trooper said. His glasses' lenses were steamed across their upper halves.

"No, no, that's all right; never mind, Bob. —So, you don't mind being named a material witness? Doesn't bother you, Bauman? Well, maybe it should bother you. Because ordinarily you could expect to walk out of here sometime late next year on good behavior—but I assure you that the State Board of Pardons and Paroles would never, *never* grant any early release to a convict named material witness in an ongoing grand jury and homicide investigation. An unfriendly witness at that. Which would mean, Bauman, you would definitely be staying up here for the full five years max remaining in your sentence. And I think our office could probably make a case for an additional year for assault while in custody, considering—in case you think we haven't heard about it—considering present hearsay that just today you attempted to burn an elderly prisoner to death."

"That wasn't serious, for Christ's sake. —The man wasn't going to get hurt!"

"I see," the woman said, "—but you did it. And we understand the subject of that quarrel just happened to be Spencer's murder. . . . Oh, I'm sure we can hold you up here, material witness on at least one homicide, probably more. And no indictment, no charges have to be brought against you at all, Bauman. You'd serve the full five years remaining. Then maybe an additional . . . I wonder how much of you will be left, after that. You're an intelligent man—a lot smarter than I am, right? You better use that intelligence."

"I doubt very much if you could hold me here like that."

"That's a good one," the trooper said.

"Do you doubt it?" the woman said. "—Do you 'doubt it very much'? Well then, you just try us, Professor. You try not giving my office every bit of information there is on who killed inmate Spencer—and why." She pulled her glasses down from her forehead, settled them on her nose, and apparently found the lenses now clear enough.

"What's your problem, Bauman?" the trooper said. "—Do you have a reality problem, or what?"

"If you don't want to give us the information right now, O.K.," the woman said. "Maybe you don't know exactly who committed the homicide. That's all right; we'll give you some time. Take a week or two after you get out of here, ask around—whatever you have to do. Use that fine intelligence of yours. And when you know, when you're ready to let us know, then all you have to do is just start some trouble in the population."

" 'Trouble in the population'?" Bauman turned to Gorney, warm water splashing around his ankles. "—Is she crazy?"

"Just give Hanks a problem if you get something, or Carlyle," Gorney said. "You know, give 'em a hard time, or start a fight with some inmate—you did that before, right?—and they'll be set to bring you right on over. Listen, let me tell you something, Bauman. This is not TV. Lots of inmates you wouldn't believe have got some deal or other going, no matter how tough they talk. And what the rest of those people don't know about, they don't care about."

"Oh, right. Sure. Very reasonable, Lieutenant. —But you know goddamn well I don't have any idea who killed that man, or what the hell they killed him for. It is none of my business. And this state's attorney here has her head up her ass!"

"O.K. You better look out, buddy, I'm tellin' you," the trooper said. "—And I'm not goin' to tell you again."

"Never mind, Bob," the woman said.

"What are you going to do about it, you four-eyed shithead?" Bauman said. He heard his voice shaking—with anger, he supposed. "—Come into this pile of garbage with that so-called officer of the court and threaten people? You wouldn't last a week inside! Just come on down here, cop, get those faggy shoes wet—and I'll give you a surprise." The trooper looked surprised already.

"No? —No? . . . He's not coming down here," Bauman said to Gorney. "And look at this; I forgot to cover my wee-wee. Really shocking for the state's attorney. —This is a fucking comedy, is what this is."

"No, it isn't, Bauman," Gorney said. "It's serious. Don't kid yourself. People are real tired of all these killings in here; it's got way out of hand. Now you listen to these people, or you're going to be in here a long, long time, and I don't believe this is your kind of place, is it?"

"The people committing these homicides in this place are the inmates' problem most of all, Professor," the woman said. "I'd think—"

"I want to get out of this fucking water," Bauman said to Gorney, felt his hands trembling as his voice had trembled, and waded out to the lieutenant.

Climbing naked and alone—Gorney had gestured him up the cement stairs—Bauman found Tanner waiting on the small landing, a bright-orange jumpsuit (apparently Segregation's uniform) folded over his right arm, and Bauman's running shoes, minus their laces, held down at his left side.

Bauman dried himself with the jumpsuit, then put it on damp—a fair fit, but too long in the arms and legs. He slipped his running shoes on, and found with his first steps that he had to crimp his toes to keep the laceless shoes from falling off.

Tanner, with nothing to say, led Bauman up the stairs to Segregation block's wide entry, then—after approval by the caged hack—through a small relief gate in that big gate, and on down the corridor into near dark, lit only to dimmest rose.

The odor of feces was shocking, and apparently prompted by it, Tanner said, "Your buddies up here think it's funny bustin' light bulbs an' throwin' their shit at people." He spoke louder as he walked along. "It's animalistic, is what it is!" and seemed to wait for a possible reply from dark and silent houses. There was none. Bauman had never before known a block perfectly silent.

"Look at this. . . ." Tanner directed the beam of his flashlight along the floor, and Bauman saw a small dark heap formed like fat sausages.

"Is this disgustin', or what?" Tanner said, and led on. Bauman, following close, couldn't prevent his shoe heels slipping off occasionally to flap softly on the floor.

Nearly halfway down the corridor, Tanner stopped, and his flashlight's beam flicked right to illuminate a very narrow place, its barred door open.

"There you go." The flashlight beam moved to a narrow concrete platform, a thin mattress on it—then shifted to show a toilet bowl, its piping vanishing into the cell's wall, with a small faucet set directly above.

"Home sweet home," Tanner said, and anger apparently refreshed by this barnyard stroll, suddenly shoved Bauman hard, so he entered his small house with a rush, nearly stumbling in his loose shoes.

With the cell's door racked slamming shut, with Tanner gone carefully back the way they'd come—his flashlight's beam questing ahead of him like some small bright spaniel—Bauman was left solitary, standing in cramped space, looking out through ghost-white bars into darkness faintly crimson.

Segregation block, which had rung with the noise his cell door made sliding to, now settled back into its silence—a quiet easily translated into peace but for the odor of shit, actively mephitic, working, writhing through the air in several varied and energetic stinks, of which one, particularly, presented a rotted, damp odor of illness.

Bauman stood silent, breathing through his mouth, then felt to his right, and found the rough cold edge of the platform, against which, he supposed, a prisoner without any sort of hope might manage—with some contortion, properly braced—to crack his skull. He half turned, sat, and felt the concrete adamant through the thin foam mattress, its cold plastic cover.

He tried to recall his shower, the spouting head so generously drenching him, the pleasure of his water shield—warm, separating—but poor preparation for remembering to keep his mouth shut. He tried to recall what he'd said, but remembered only a cumulative disaster that assuredly would have been improved by his keeping his mouth shut. Then that cunt could have said what she wanted, and still not known the silent man, or what the silent man would do.

He rested, wrapping shadow and quiet around him to substitute for warm water—and was startled, jerked a little as he sat, to hear from the house beside his, from the left, what seemed at first only sound in shadow (tenor, plangent, and clear) that then resolved itself with no hurry into a voice, and the voice into words.

"That was a *very* long shower."

Chapter FOUR

Bauman spent a few moments thinking what to reply, what to say through his bars into the dark—too many moments. By the time he'd decided on "Right, I got lucky," it was too late to say it casually, too late to say it at all. Silence seemed to have spoken for him.

He sat waiting to hear some further remark, more about the shower. Another remark about anything. The silence, however, appeared willing now to speak for both of them.

He might have said something better. Might have said, "Tanner made me mop up the fucking place." Too late, way too late to say anything like that.

He imagined the man to the left to be only some ding, too weird to run loose in population. Nobody fierce, but happening to possess that strenuous tenor voice, stony, shallow, bright as an Irish balladeer's. The voice had sounded like just such a singer's, the singer speaking over barroom noise to introduce his song, the song already filling his throat, ready to spill.

Bauman shifted on his thin mattress, but carefully, so as not to give away a sound, and slowly lay down on his side, facing the near wall. He thought of himself standing naked in the dirty water under feeble yellow light, hands cupped over himself while the lady state's attorney and her watchdog harried him, Gorney being no help at all—had arranged the damn interview, in fact.

Rolex taken, stuck in Segregation with oddities like the one to the left, and for no reason but an opportunity for a little official extortion, a try at producing one more snitch at State—and who better than a middle-aged joint-virgin (a college professor, for the love of God) and likely the only con at State with nothing and no one—no other crime, no accomplice—to betray to the law for a favor. So, a fresh snitch, and possible results for the newspapers and TV news.

He saw the woman lawyer and her trooper walking back up their cement steps, through the rusty steel door, then down flights of stairs which led to God knew where, perhaps a laundry office two floors below. They'd have smiled, then gone chuckling down the stairs, then laughed till their glasses steamed again, recalling Bauman in dirty water—shouted into concealing his balls, prodded into making a TV-courtroom fool of himself over that Basket thing at the infirmary. Bauman asking the watch commander for a towel, Bauman in dignified withdrawal—trudging away through murky water, revealing his damp, drooping middle-aged ass.

So persuasive was this that Bauman began to giggle, had to cover his mouth with both hands—no pillow to muffle the sound. He laughed for quite a while, very softly, huffing, catching his breath to laugh again. After he recovered, he began to cry, but not much, only to an aching throat, to small comfort.

He thought of his watch for a while, and became enraged at Gorney particularly, who seemed to have betrayed a trust somehow—being a State person himself, at least as far as years and hours lived there proved. Bauman pictured Gorney already beaten (his right eye tearing blood) in bikers' hands, or taken by the lifers into C-block. Gorney begging lively as a girl, "Please, please . . . *please!*" his voice gone soprano, pants fresh-stained with the coffee he'd had for breakfast, while Shupe, Teppman, and murderous Wiltz stood watching, making remarks.

Bauman imagined Grace, whatever her name was—Hilliard. Thought of her kept captive with Gorney, the lifers having taken the laundry preliminary to getting their president, Nash, out of Seg. Had caught the lawyer and her trooper, killed the trooper when he fought for her (not entirely an asshole, after all), killed the trooper and held Hilliard and Gorney.

Bauman fantasized the commencement of a revenge where the lifers turned to him to sentence her—sentence her and Gorney both. But he grew too sleepy for the effort, instead conceived her more simply in his power. Alone, kept with him for some reason—perhaps he'd tried to save her, after all, from what Wiltz and Teppman wished to accomplish. So, weary, disheveled, sweet with that tired-woman smell of fading perfume, of stockings stale from too many stilting hours in high heels, of the richer odors of her skin, her perspiration, she lay down beside him on a steel-deck floor, huddled. Then would rouse hysterical in her fear of death, her expectation of being sacrificed publicly, naked, split wide open by Wiltz's blade for all to see. She'd kiss Bauman's mouth, would deposit with her tongue all her lost future, future's loving—would then accept his hands, take one of them in one of hers to guide it under her opened blouse to her thudding heart, over which a softly spreading breast lay gentle guard (suckled soft by her only child, kneaded softer throughout her life, sometimes roughly, by several men).

Considering this, Bauman rolled onto his back, unbuttoned the jumpsuit's awkward fly, tugged his hard-on out, and stroking as quietly, as slowly as he could, imagined Grace Hilliard's frightened face, her suit's skirt stepped free of, her panty hose pulled down. Then, the conventional position she assumed, stretched on her back, knees doubled and flung wide, her left forearm crossed over her face to conceal what grimaces she might make, her right hand reaching down between her spraddled thighs to demonstrate herself for him with trembling fingers—then murmured something from beneath her guarding forearm, something half heard under the mutter of the lifers conferring outside. Perhaps that she loved him, perhaps something else.

"Gotta do more than that, man!" McElvey, even shouting, had sounded bored. "I don' give a shit what you s'pose know about boxin', man. You problem is you don' know shit about fightin'!"

All this had been heard by Bauman quite clearly, despite his being kept in a corner being hit with very hard punches by a Latino boy whose name he hadn't caught when they were introduced to spar. The boy was a two-hand hitter—bang, bang, bang. Not really a classy fighter, though a pro. Just young, only young. *That's all you have going, you little son of a bitch!* Twice—and more times than twice, but twice was all that came to mind—Bauman'd had chances to set the boy back on his heels. One of those chances he only realized after half a round had gone past it. The other one, he made the try—shifting to lead with his right—but the Latino boy had been too dumb to be confused, might not even have noticed it, just kept banging away. He didn't care what Bauman led with.

Covering up in the corner, just trying to catch his breath, then slide away and get some space, get set—Bauman felt McElvey fiddling with his face, and found himself sitting on the canvas. The Latino boy was bent over him, looking worried.

"I'm still alive," Bauman thought he said. He felt his lips puffing, thought maybe the mouthpiece had slipped while he was being hit. "—No thanks to you, *asesino*. I'm old enough to be your father, for Christ's sake!" This getting a relieved smile from the boy, who'd probably thought he'd killed him.

"Good roun's," the boy said, nodding to Bauman and doing a little shuffle dance, still nodding, to show Bauman how good the rounds had been.

"How many rounds?" Bauman said to McElvey.

"Two an' a half. An' they really shit, man. Minute this Spaniard caught you struttin' all that bullshit college form, man, even this Spaniard smart enough to go in an' kick your ass, you doin' all that posin'."

"Young," Bauman said, starting to feel better. He couldn't remember how many rounds he'd gone with the boy. Three or four, he thought.

"Don't you kid yourself, man. I know three, four men old as you could walk in here and whip your ass. An' one of 'em's white! Didn' you ever learn to come in an' take a punch to throw one? What the fuck did those people show you in college?" McElvey reached into Bauman's mouth and gently took his mouthpiece out. "Look to me like they spent a lot of time teachin' you you wouldn' get hurt you didn' do this wrong an' that wrong. —What they should have been showin' you is you goin' to get hurt, you goin' to get hurt anyway, so make the motherfucker *pay*. You ever hear of a counterpunch, hittin' into a punch?"

"I've heard about it."

"Then that's some shitty college you went to, man. 'Cause you sure as shit don' do it. Man, you fight like you don' want to get *hurt*. Like that's the first thing on you mind. Isn' that right? Isn' that the truth?"

"I understand your point; you don't have to keep repeating it," Bauman said. "—Help me up."

"You are up. You O.K., man?"

"I don't understand it," Bauman said. "I keep in damn good shape. Running, rock climbing . . ."

"That so?" McElvey said. "—Let's see you climb on outta this ring." Several men had stopped training to observe the bout; they still stood a few feet back from the ring, watching Bauman climb out through the ropes.

"You're too old for that shit, man." A contribution by one of the few whites present, suited up in natty black for Korean karate. Met with general agreement.

"Hey," McElvey said, "—you people payin' money watch this fight?" And those observers slowly drifted away to mats and rings, heavy bags and speed bags, strike-and-kick targets of their own.

Bauman now had no trouble walking, and McElvey strolled elegant beside him toward a brown bench along the gym wall, much more friendly now that he'd seen Bauman beaten. Or perhaps that was unfair, perhaps friendlier now he'd seen Bauman fight, or at least attempt to.

That morning, Trevor McElvey'd been distinctly unfriendly. . . .

"Now, I heard the bullshit Adrienne had to say—you goin' pay me for gettin' you in shape to go in the joint. Wise you up, or some shit like that."

"Both," Bauman had said. "I'll pay you for your time."

McElvey—younger than Bauman'd thought he'd be, a tall, slender, dish-faced black man in his middle twenties, with an ugly underslung jaw and a carefully combed and parted old-fashioned "do"—had been dressed very nattily for a gym manager, a "martial arts studio" manager, in a gray sharkskin suit, light-gray shirt, tie woven black and maroon, and black Bass loafers.

"You goin' pay for my time if I say I'll let you pay for my time. This ain't no shit I got to do for nobody."

"I know that."

"Now, what the fuck do you want, man?"

"I want," Bauman had said, "—you to help get me into shape. And I want you to wise me up as to the facts of life at State, because that's where my lawyer says I'm likely to go."

"What you do?"

"I ran a girl over. They said I was drunk. Hit and run."

"They 'said' you was drunk?"

"Right."

"An' did they 'say' you hit an' run?"

"I did leave the scene."

"I jus' bet you did, man. I bet you hauled ass, an' if I was drivin' drunk in this state, I'd sure as shit leave the damn scene, too."

"I wasn't really drunk."

"You tell that shit to your mother, man, don' tell that shit to me. What do you do? You do any athletics? How old are you, man?"

"I'm a college professor. —Was. I'm forty-three. But I stay in very good shape, run two to three miles a day. I do some rock climbing in the summer, ski in the winter. I boxed in college—was team captain—and won six out of eight my senior year. I still spar, occasionally."

"You still spar—occasionally."

"Tell you something, McElvey. I'd be pleased to try and beat your wise ass right now, if you're willing."

At that, McElvey had seemed satisfied. "You calm down, dad. Jus' tryin' to see you got any nuts on you." Then said, "All right. It's goin' cost you forty bucks ever' time you come in. I sure as shit ain' goin' lose money on this shit."

"Done."

"—An' right now, we goin' see what you remember from when you did that boxin'." And led Bauman to the locker room past mildly curious glances by young men furiously active, but possessing during their various exercises the calm reflective expressions of grazing beef cattle. McElvey had stood in the locker room watching with some amusement as Bauman unzipped his gym bag, unpacked his gear, undressed, and put it on.

"That your old college shit you brought down?"

"The shorts and shoes."

"Um-hmm. Well, you not too blubby, but you sure ain' no chicken. Them dudes up there ain' goin' be wantin' to screw your old ass."

"Good news," Bauman said.

"—About all the good news you goin' get."

Back in the gym, McElvey had watched Bauman warm up, skip some rope, hit the bags a bit, then had matched him with the Latino boy, fitted headgear to both of them, and, the fight commenced, had lounged by the ring acting as timekeeper and calling out various remarks while Bauman was being beaten.

"Let me tell you somethin', man," McElvey said as they reached the brown bench at last (Bauman not feeling well), and sat down on it. "—You did the bes' you could, you understan'? Let me tell you somethin'. Ex-champion of the fuckin' world, he hadn't had no fight for four, five years, an' step in that ring with any tough kid gone pro, been fightin' ever' day? What you think's goin' happen?"

"Right. He'd get his butt kicked." Bauman was grateful to be sitting on the bench. If there hadn't been anyone else in the gym, he would have lain down on his side to rest for a while.

"—An' man, that's jus' a fact. No way in this world you goin' up to State show nobody nothin' less he's some real fish. Those people up there—an' they mostly young dudes, man—been fightin' all they lives, an' be fightin' up there with han's, shanks, any kind of shit. An' when they ain' fightin', they plannin' on killin' some dude looked wrong at 'em las' year."

McElvey paused to tighten his tie knot slightly, set it straight without a mirror. (He was to confide the next week, over crullers and coffee at a Dunkin Donuts, a childlike trust in the virtues of natty dressing, particularly in uneasy circumstances. "Cops don' even look at you, man, if you dressed real nice, a nice conservative suit.")

"—An' I'll tell you somethin' else about this fightin' shit up there, man. They's always a piece floatin' aroun' up there some fool's old lady visited in, one part this week, next part next week, carried in in her private place. Between her legs, you understan'? Some shitty little gun—automatic. So nobody knows but they could come up against a pistol. You understan'?"

"Yes, I do."

"An' they got a bunch of shanks an' shit, knucks made with razor blades, an' wire off brooms to choke dudes with. They got all that shit up there. An' the screws find 'em—them dudes jus' make some more."

"I see."

"You want to know what old State is like? —You want a drink of water?"

"Not right now."

"You not lookin' good yet, man. You didn' get beat that bad; you should be up an' jumpin'."

"I'm fine. Just leave me alone for a minute."

"Well, I'm goin' tell you what that fuckin' place is like, man. Ever' joint is the same, an' ever' joint is different. An' State got its particular ways like all of 'em do. It shit sure ain' like them faggy little new joints they got out on the coas', where they take pictures of your eyes 'fore you can move aroun' in there, an' they got a duty hack ever' ten dudes, an' you got TV cameras in the shithouse—an' they all the time havin' conferences, askin' if you suckin' dick, an' givin' you drugs make you sleepy. —Ol' State ain' like that shit, man. An' it ain' like them federal walls neither, where those motherfuckers can lock all the people down for years. Ol' State ain' like neither one. It is a *prison*. You understan' what I'm sayin'? It is the maximum security prison for the whole friggin' state. They have a dude they can't handle any other joint, they send that mother on to State. Now, don' mean ever' dude up there is bad, but does mean jus' about ever' bad dude is up there."

"Wonderful."

"An' ol' State don' have no faggy wire fences all aroun'. That mother got fuckin' *walls*, man. An' I'll tell you somethin' else. State got the most pitiful food you ever goin' eat. You jus' better not get assigned to East mess, 'cause 'mess' is right! An' let me see. . . . That joint's real big, real big, an' it's old. I mean that mother is *old*. Sucker was built back then for eight hundred—check this out—eight hundred old-time badasses. Know how many is in there now—was when I lef'?"

"How many?"

"One thousand an' fuckin' nine hundred an' forty-three, man. An' some of them motherfuckers—they hungry an' got a sharp spoon—they goin' eat your eyes."

"Very encouraging."

"You want to know about ol' State, man, I'm tellin' you. Know how many hacks they got? They had jus' five hundred seventy-two of them fuckin' farmers. What is that, three shif's on them walls, an' Admin, an' down in them blocks? Jus' one duty screw locked in for ever' twenty, twenty-five dudes. You don' think them fuckin' farmers are scared, man? They puddin' pants all *through* the day. . . . Thing is, ever' mother's scared up there, man. Tell you the truth—an' no bullshit con shit—you jus' don' want to be goin' to that joint. But if you do, if you got to go, then you goin' to have to work on your insides, man. Not jus' this gym shit. *Inside* stren'th is what a dude needs goin' up there, man, 'cause that's where he's goin' be spendin' his time."

"I understand."

"You lookin' better. I was scared you was goin' die on me right here."

"I'm fine. I'm not about to die, McElvey."

"Trevor."

"—Trevor."

"Tell you what I'm goin' do for you, man. —You a real professor?"

"I was."

"Well, what I'm doin' is takin' you on at this studio for jus' one thing, man. We goin' get you in some kind of shape—an' about ever two, three times you come down here, I'm goin' get some real strong fucker take you in that ring an' bust your ass. Maybe get one of these karate faggots go in an' try an' kick your nuts off. You probably ain' goin' win no fights, but you sure as shit goin' get used to fightin'; you sure goin' get used to gettin' hit. We goin' build your ass up, inside."

"Sounds very Zen, Trevor. You coming in the ring with me?"

"You got to be kiddin', man. I'm too smart do that kind of shit. —You lookin' fine, now. I thought you was goin' die there, for a while."

. . .

"Good luck, dad," McElvey'd said more than five weeks after that active morning. "Good luck. . . ." shaking hands outside Dunkin Donuts. He was dressed in pongee white suiting, an off-white shirt, brown tie, openwork brown oxfords. "—You in about the bes' shape an ol' amateur white man goin' make." McElvey, in their almost two dozen sessions at the martial arts studio, had had relatively little specific advice to give about getting along at State—other than warning against borrowing anything at all from anybody at all, warning against lending anything at all to anybody at all, suggesting Bauman stay clear of a hack named Simmvitz—which officer, as it happened, left to try farming again just before Bauman came up—and repeating an admonition to "Play like you jus' a piece of window glass, man. You be invisible, an' look out you don't get broke."

Bauman, their last day—two cups of coffee, three chocolate doughnuts to the good—was feeling fairly well, though a white club fighter in his late thirties (an old pro named Bob Michaud) had that morning outpointed him two rounds, then butted him over the left eye and knocked him down in the third and final. Bauman felt he'd done all right, even so.

This handshake, Bauman's first physical contact of any kind with Trevor (ringmaster of such aching exercise, such storms of fighting), revealed the young man to have long-fingered, rather delicate hands, fine-boned, tender-muscled. "You take care, now, Mr. Bauman. You get down from that place, you come see me; we get us some doughnuts."

McElvey'd never said what he'd done to be sent up. Bauman—recalling that beneath Trevor's cool was a strict unblinking attention and abiding interest during hard fights, beatings—supposed his crime, despite his elegant air, his thin stalky body, had likely not been fraud, forgery, or confidence. . . .

Bauman now lay fairly comfortable in rose-umber darkness, despite the concrete slab and his thin mattress, and was trying to become used to the odor of shit, which seemed constantly being cooked to stink anew by old radiators clanking with steam heat along the corridor's opposite wall.

Plumbing—a major mystery. Old Cooper, as head of Housekeeping, had picked Bauman from the other fish at breakfast the second day up—on Trevor McElvey's phoned recommendation, or so the little man said. Then had strutted his banty way, leading Bauman on a tour of Housekeeping from linen to ventilation to piping (water, steam, and drain), then on to garbage disposal, painting, and mop-and-wax, promising to see someday if Bauman could fix a cut, could tape a fist for fighting without a dislocated thumb resulting. Could, perhaps, hold a heavy bag and call punches, so proving himself useful to the boxing team.

On this tour, the gross subterranean tangles of State's plumbing had been partially explicated—the ancient rusting pipes and angles, water lines, steam lines, sewage lines, drains, coils, valves, spigots, pumps and pressure dials, the booming ceiling ducts of anachronistically heavy tin, two and a half feet square, shuddering, blatting air out through thick steel grills to every space—air, warm and oily, driven in or sucked out by monstrous groaning exhaust fans bolted into concrete in cellars below cellars. In each depth, in darkness, these giant fans, their black-cased motors half submerged in trembling blankets of dust decades old, stood in massive rows of two or three, all spraddle-legged over one wide concrete sump. The sumps, of ancient oil mixed more than two feet deep with black bilge-water, were constantly refreshed by drainage from a steady fine drizzle of condensation, filled further when some archaic pipe burst nearby.

The fans and myriad other mechanisms were never cleaned, rarely oiled or greased, hardly maintained for many years. Most were not maintainable, their parts and wiring, springs and switches only to be seen in collections of old machinists' catalogues, the yellowed brittle bulletins of businesses defunct, destroyed during the Great Depression or some recession after.

Bauman was conducted through at least a portion of this buried confusion, its many dark decks, ladders, steps, stairs and tunnels—tunnels sometimes eight feet wide, a quarter mile long, their length lit only by the most occasional bulb, perhaps forty watts, screwed into a chipped ceramic socket to light some particular and long forgotten chore. These larger tunnels, containing major connections of pipes and ducting, containing as well several small spaces used by Housekeeping's seniors as dayrooms, semiprivate apartments, lay crisscross beneath the expanse of State, running often deep below the buildings' basements. And all passages, large and small, presenting a faint, pervasive stench of dead rats.

"What are you thinkin' about, fish?—as if I didn' know." Old Cooper—tiny, twisted tough in an ancient tweed worker's cap, brown sweater, brown pants, brown high-top ironworker's shoes in the smallest of sizes—had paused in near darkness beside a great roaring desperate fan, to shove away a wad of felted dust and pat the thing's massive trembling black casing in encouragement. ". . . As if I didn' know."

Bauman—new-issue denims smeared with grease, back and shoulders aching from nearly two miles of walking stooped behind little Cooper, who strode the passages upright—supposed he knew what the old man meant, and saw no reason to be coy. "Not important to me," he'd said, "—but it does look like a lot of ways out of here, under the wall."

"Ohhh, yeah," the little man had said. "Looks like that, don't it? But they ain't."

"No?"

"No." Like a fairy-tale gnome explicating the mysteries of his underground, old Cooper had paused for effect, patting the ancient fan's shuddering flank again. "No tunnel in State gets any closer to that wall than ten yards—an' it wouldn' matter if they run right alongside, 'cause that wall was started on solid granite fifteen feet down, with granite-block footin's run twenty-five feet across, an' there's no gettin' through that without blastin' an' drillin' around the clock two, three days. An' rock sends sound real good."

Pleased to see Bauman impressed by their fortress, as if its strength were their protection from so chancy and dangerous a world, the little man then led away into the dark to more mystery, still lecturing, lisping slightly, voice ringing back from gloom along the piping. "O.K. That's the tunnels look so promisin'. Now, the pipes an' all that ductin'. English guy worked with 'em buildin' this place, an' he was a real smart guy. Every single friggin' pipeway, ductin', sewer, you name it—everythin', an' I mean everythin', squeezes down to thirteen inches or less goin' through that wall. That's it. Nothin'—an' I mean nothin'—goes through that wall any bigger around than that. Sometimes we got a big pipe broke down an' branched into four pipes, five pipes, each one routed separate through all that rock, an' them four or five each got that thirteen inches diameter, tops. Now what do you think of that?"

"I think that Englishman was a pain in the ass."

The gnome had paused, turned to show Bauman a grimace of appreciation by flashlight. "You're fuckin' a," he said. "Not that the simps they lettin' in this place now even think about it. Inmates is all they are—don't even belong here. Got maybe a couple, three hundred real cons among 'em. . . ."

Later—after many weeks of mopping, waxing, well before his relieving call to gofer on Cooper's boxing team—Bauman was glad he'd been properly reticent with the little man, as such a short-timer should have been, and hadn't much to say of escape, and none of that swaggering. For Margaret the Maid, sweeping before Bauman mopped West mess, had related with relish the history of Cooper's own escape attempt thirty-three years before, legendary at State, legendary in most walls east and west.

Cooper had already served four years of consecutive life terms—for shooting to death two Butterfield men when they'd interrupted the robbery in progress at a Catesburg savings and loan. In those four years, he'd planned with a friend a way past State's rule of sizes, which included bundles, bags, crates, boxes, and packages of all kinds. Only those too small, too flat, or too short to hold any man—even little Cooper—were allowed closed shipment out. This rule, like most rules of durance, then as now was enforced absolutely at State, no matter what other regulations might collapse from crowding or legal latitude.

The little boxer—a champion, once—had met with his friend early one evening in the furniture factory's shipping room, where finished pieces as well as disassembled kits of school seat-desks, folding chairs, blackboard stands, and small worktables were packed for trucking out next morning. The two had pass permission there in furtherance of their small prison enterprise—making fine fiber-glass rods and nattily tied flies for trout fishing. Cooper made the rods—hand-wrapped fiberglass, hand-set brass ferrules, the rods collapsible, strong, and finely whippy—while his friend, Vincent Studely, a large man and a killer, used a rich imagination and delicate touch in feathers, tying original and classic flies.

In the shipping room, pressed for time, Cooper had drunk a quart of prime pruno, the juice having had hash soaking in it as well. Right after which, unable to delay, the little man had stripped to his white boxer shorts and T-shirt, lain down on the loading platform—small legs propped up on a solid coffee table shipping out finished—and waited for his friend Vincent to take the fifteen-pound wrecking bar down from the tool wall.

Studely got this instrument (used to break out lumber bundles), came back with it, and after the preparation of a full backswing, struck down with all his might and broke Cooper's left thigh well above the knee—and after a first blow there had failed, his right thigh slightly lower.

With Cooper still conscious, his friend—weeping, begging pardon—then finished by hand whatever further breakage was needed, folded the legs up from the thighs, and tied their ankles alongside Cooper's neck with twine.

After this, Cooper was unable to speak, though apparently still aware, as his friend used the little man's discarded shirt and trousers for bandaging where, in two places, bone had come through, then carried him to a ready crate (small, rectangular), packed him softly in excelsior, and—leaving openings for air—tacked the crating closed and addressed it properly for express delivery to Cairo, Illinois, where Enid Cooper and her brother Martin, a small-animal vet, waited to receive it.

Late the next evening, at a corporate truck park in Eau Claire, Wisconsin —its driver's scheduled route having been altered by dispatch—the big trailer's right-hand rear door stood open for a minor load. Fueling the truck in the rain, a boy pumping diesel noticed fresh red soaking the corner of a small stacked crate inside. A joke with the trucker about busted bottles of wine caused a casual inspection that ended with the folded man found dreaming, the tip of his tongue bitten off. Taken to Good Samaritan in town, Cooper's life and legs were saved after an eight-week stay. Following which, recovering, his legs in plaster to his hips, he was jailed awaiting return to prison. . . .

Recalling that tale in Segregation's stink and silence, Bauman lay considering six additional years. He supposed he might end after that—if it ever happened, if the attorney general's people really pursued it—supposed he might end too well acclimated to live comfortably outside. Would certainly be savagely resentful. Nearer being an old man, too.

Remembering he'd wiped his palm down across the rough cement of the platform's side, Bauman reached down to feel for it—not caring for the slick to show plainly in the morning. But there was no longer anything there—no semen, no stickiness in any case. And either the smell of Segregation's excrement was lessening, or he might already be becoming used to it. Penned chimpanzees, he'd read somewhere, threw their shit when sufficiently annoyed, or bored.

Two men began an evening conversation far down the corridor to the right, muttered dialogue unmistakably inmates' talk. This was the first noise, excepting his neighbor's single clear phrase of observation, that Bauman had heard from the people on this block, and he lay still, holding his breath to hear it more clearly. Just conversation, certainly not an argument. . . .

"*Caine. Andersen!* You people don't say one more word." Certainly Bauman's neighbor to the left, his remembered stony, high-timbre'd tenor.

There was no more talking down at the right end of the block. Not even a final remark to indicate some fragile independence before obedience.

Lying silent—relieved, as he'd occasionally been before, by a cell's concrete and steel isolating him in so strong a small castle—Bauman wished again he'd thought to answer, 'Tanner made me mop the fucking place,' to the tenor's observation about his shower. If he'd said that, he'd have no problem.

Might also have no problem if he'd let Bobby Basket off without paying, hadn't felt he had to make that demonstration to show what a considerable fellow he was. Or, having done so, hadn't wished himself luck in the infirmary toilet bowl—no location for conjuring good fortune, as any Roman could have told him.

Tomlinson had wished him luck. "Historic luck," he'd said, as head of the department. . . .

From Traynor to Garry Hall—and Tomlinson's office—the walk was lined on either side, irregularly, with eighty-year-old red maples. It was the handsomest walk on a handsome campus; the maples had ranked it evenly in early years, before illness and lightning had gapped their rows.

Few students, out of passing many more, greeted Bauman as he went—the others glancing at him, then gazing away as if the trees in early autumn held wonders higher up.

Cliff Bednar—English major, history minor—one of the few greeting, had then stopped for additional condolence. "Really crappy news, Professor Bauman. Real downer. Could have been me, could have been anybody." Cliff was a wide, strong boy, a wrestler and football player. He was wearing a bulky cable-knit white sweater, oversized, that topped his brown corduroys like sugar icing.

Bauman had observed Cliff Bednar's nascent mustache (nearly blond, aspiring to handlebar) since its inception the previous term. On this occasion, the mustache presented itself almost mature, earnest sympathy being expressed in the small hazel eyes a nose above it. —Considerable curiosity as well, to see how such a great difficulty settled, what differences it made.

Bauman stood awaiting additional remarks while other students and occasional faculty passed, strolling over flagstones decorated in filtered spangles of shadow and gold where sunlight struck down through the tall trees' foliage.

"Really shitty luck. A real tragedy. . . ."

Bauman had considered a rough answer, which seemed to require too much effort, and so replaced it with a conventional "I appreciate it, Cliff. . . ." as if he and this student were old friends, of either of whom a personal loyalty might be expected in any difficulty.

Duty done, Bednar had turned to rejoin his waiting girl, a student Bauman didn't know—short, black-haired, heavy-haunched in a tartan skirt, her round and pretty face still summer tanned. A dark blue bookbag suspended from her left shoulder swung slightly as she flanked Bednar when they walked away. . . .

"Charles, really, this whole thing has been so tragic. Tragic as a death. Well, of course a death was involved. But I was referring to its effect on you, on all of us here. The damnedest thing."

Tomlinson's gray Donegal tweed jacket was off, folded neatly, as was his office habit, along the flat white-painted metal of the radiator cover behind his chair. This custom, on damp winter days, released into his bookcased office a slight smoky odor of warmed and faintly sweaty wool.

"Are they going to back me?—Or am I just out on my ass?"

"You are most certainly not . . . out on your ass. They're going to continue your salary, full salary, until the entire matter's been cleared up. They do think it'll be better for you to take a leave of absence, and I suppose—"

"And if I'm convicted?"

"Oh, well . . ." Tomlinson had shaken his head. "Well, if that should happen, Charles, you'd be out. They wouldn't have any choice about it, they really wouldn't. I'm sure you see that. But I don't for a moment think that'll happen. Nobody does. This attempt at some sort of judicial punishment seems . . . well, it seems only to compound the tragedy."

Bauman, a disappointed suppliant, pretended ease in an oak armchair facing Tomlinson's desk. He had fantasized, though not in convincing detail, an outpouring of support and forgiveness—a refusal, the university's president might have said, to allow one possible lapse of judgment, however sad its consequences, to foreclose an extraordinarily promising career. Now he felt, besides that disappointment, some obscure satisfaction as well, perhaps at being left to stand so central in the drama.

Tomlinson paused, or finished speaking, and remained standing behind his desk and bent slightly forward over it, as if he were waiting for something further to occur to him. He swayed very slightly—less than an inch each way—from side to side as he stood, lean, bald, early elderly, the long sleeves of his pinstriped Oxford-cloth shirt folded neatly up to reveal surprising lengths of slender soft pale arm, furred with gray. He was wearing a maroon and white tie in regimental stripes—British regimental stripes, by their reverse angle. Welsh Guards? Perhaps Welsh Guards.

Bauman supposed Tomlinson had been to some trouble for him, protesting, within reason, to the dean, then the president's office. Admirable, considering he'd never cared for Bauman, hadn't liked his manner of doing history, either. "De Groote and that Princeton crowd. And Schama—trying to trendy the past; anthropologizing without observation."

"Worth a try," Bauman had said. "—We'd all like to live a weekend in past lives."

"A wish is not a try," Tomlinson had said. They'd been standing outside his office talking schedules on a rainy day. "And a try is not a *do*."

Tomlinson had for many years maintained his credibility as department head by careful, narrowly focused scholarship mining the Venetian Republic's diplomatic essays, its attendant trading policies—sifting (when hands-on became the trend) the silt in the city's lagoons for dubious corroded little bits and pieces. He'd maintained it as well by avoiding damaging commitment in any disagreement between administration and faculty, faculty and faculty, students and faculty—avoiding any commitments at all if he could. And finally, maintained his authority by the consideration due pitiful revelation—of his wife's affairs, his position as public cuckold—this displayed in majesty some years before Bauman came to Midwest.

The revelation's occasion was a party of welcome for a formidable British historian named Gresham Parry (a red-brick whiz with an exaggerated Yorkshire accent, specializing in the Glorious Revolution)—a party during which Gwendolyn Tomlinson had been discovered drunk in her laundry room (her upper body bent sharply forward over her Maytag dryer, her dress's skirt thrown up), found in actual congress with an Indian teaching assistant, who, withdrawing startled at the interruption, was observed to leave a slight sticky track behind, to trace down her pale right thigh—both legs being bound at the ankles by her fallen panty hose, and those bonds still taut, stretched wide as she'd straddled to present herself.

This tall slender woman—dressed often in raw silk, her heavy handsome graying hair drawn up in a French knot, her blue eyes faded, mildly interested, polite—had, since Bauman had known them, sided her husband like a sentinel at all their functions, as if to leave him for an instant were to commence to hurry uncontrollable through the house, brushing past guests (jarring their arms so white wine spilled slightly), her hair already slipping loose, falling to her shoulders as she hastened to the laundry room, to whoever waited. . . .

Tomlinson still stood, staring down at Bauman as if something were expected.

"Thanks, John. I appreciate the effort."

"Another thing I wanted to say." Tomlinson stopped swaying in his slight way, sat down, and leaned back in his swivel chair as if the unpleasantness were over, the pleasant part begun. "But first, since I'm sure you'll be resuming your classes in a few weeks, I think we can avoid making a drama out of this situation—for the students, for our whole community here."

"No argument from me."

"Well, I think Frank can handle your European history. The students like him," Tomlinson smiled, "—and he pretty much shares your views. And I thought Hanna Rosenzweig for the American history; she's already got the two afternoons free. Is that— Do you think that poses a problem?"

"No. I'll wake the students up when I get back. If I get back."

"Good. All right. Now, about your ancient history. I thought Richard Chu—"

"Chu's an instructor. And there's the graduate seminar, too."

"I know. I know you've got that seminar as well. I was thinking, and the dean seems to agree, that we might bring Richard into permanent faculty. He's very bright."

"Yes, he's bright. Not what you might call an electric personality."

"Published, many times. Excellent work on all that—what was it? That Channel trade stuff."

"Oh, Richard's bright. That was good work. Truth is, John, he could still get a book out of that, if he dug a little deeper."

"Um-hmm, that was it. Well, what if we do bring him up? He's solid on the material."

"Oh, Chu's very solid on the material."

"Well then, perhaps we'll bring Richard up. As permanent, he could handle the seminar, too, until you get back."

"Chu going to be using my office, John?"

"No, he is not. You're not being replaced, Charles; you're being substituted for. Your office remains your office."

"—Except for those personal items I might want at home?"

"That's right."

"Very reassuring," Bauman said. "And this new regime, when do we start?"

"Why not tomorrow?"

". . . That would be all right. I'd have time to talk to Hanna, and Chu. And I suppose no official announcement is going to be made?"

"To the classes?"

"The students."

"The dean, I think, is going to make an announcement. But not particularly to the students. To the university community."

"Wonderful."

"And there's something else. I've been wanting to say this for quite a while, Charles, and this . . . crisis seems a good time to clear the air. I know that you and I've had, I'd have to say, a continuous disagreement on the whole subject of history, from its definition down." Apparently relieved to enlarge upon these reminiscences of departmental disagreement, Tomlinson did what he usually did at ease, reached out as he spoke to sort idly through the contents of his leather-covered pencil cup, searching, Bauman had always supposed, for a sharp Mongol Number One. Something to etch and clarify his thinking, put an edge on him.

"Not so deep a disagreement as all that, I think," Bauman said. "A matter of method." Considering Tomlinson's casual conversational segue from the subject of his suspension, the destruction of his career—apparently to minimize social discomfort for this occasion—Bauman found it hard to see why the old man should get away with it.

"I didn't want to leave that awkwardness unresolved, Charles. I want you to know I had and have great respect for your work, the greatest possible respect for you personally, as well. If that weren't true," Bauman had heard, in fact, that it was not quite true, that Tomlinson had once described him to other faculty people as "an irritant" "—I wouldn't have recommended tenure for you."

"I appreciated that, John," Bauman said. "—A tenure of a week and a half, but still nice to have had." He settled into the armchair and found, as he usually did, that the factory shaping of that particular seat into an oak buttocks' mold, large twin shallow dishes and a fairly sharp raised central spine, made for uneasy sitting.

"So you see, it wasn't the quality of your work I disagreed with. It was its emphasis—approach, if you prefer. That tendency, I thought, to slight the developmental logic of extraordinary events, decisive battles, and so forth." Tomlinson found at last a pencil that pleased him.

It looked very sharp, the coned wood of its tip light tan, fresh shaven. He leafed through a yellow legal pad on his desktop, found an empty sheet, and still talking, glancing down only twice, drew a large cube, seen corner on. —Rather resembled a Maytag dryer, Bauman thought. Tomlinson seemed to be drawing a door on the front of the cube, a door with a sort of handle on it; it was difficult to be sure, viewing upside down.

"If you're saying, John, that I consider most of your 'decisive' battles, and the other grand determining events you and Rickert are so fond of, simply as noisy commentary on questions already settled," Bauman said, "—you're right. None of them, just for example, has had, or ever will have the impact of the general introduction of preventive medicine. For a truly decisive, and almost certainly catastrophic instrument of historical change, try the World Health Organization."

"But that's prognostication, Charles, not history." He'd certainly drawn a square door in the cube's front, with a handle or knob. Bauman wondered what Tomlinson imagined locked behind it. Underwear, shirts, socks just washed, still warm in the hot whirling drying air? Had Gwen Tomlinson, leaning deeply over the machine, felt that thrumming through her elbows, heard the soft sandy hiss close by her bent head as the teaching assistant—short, plump, and bearded, according to one of the interrupters—shifted behind her, found her damp place, and forced it?

"All right, John, then we'll use an event just past, certainly not prognostication—my little traffic mishap, superfluous as any of your battles, and equally beside the point. A drama with no connection to my past life at all."

"You think not?" Tomlinson said, and glanced down at his drawing.

"O.K. Let's examine it. Last week's little event is sure as hell going to change *my* social and cultural future. Already has. But even so, the event itself remains accidental, theatrical, a disruption of the basic pattern of my life, shared with millions of other fairly ordinary lives. —I certainly never killed a child before. And I'll never kill another one. There was no sexual component, not that she wasn't old enough—the word 'child' here, believe me, is misleading—and no class component either. She was riding one of those mountain bikes. Know what those things cost?"

"But Charles, we weren't speaking specifically, were we?" Tomlinson's bald head was now slightly flushed, unless the maple leaves canopied above the window arch behind him had filtered the afternoon sun rose-copper.

"Oh, come on, John, let's *be* specific. How I came to kill Karen Silber, how disconnected this disaster was from my life's development, and how little resulted from it—except sorrow."

Tomlinson was now sitting at a sort of strained attention, his drafting hand poised in the interrupted center of a strip of shading. The bottom of the cube's door? The top? "Really—really, now," he said, "I think this is all too immediate to be discussed this way, Charles. Isn't it, really? Don't you think so?"

"No, I don't. I think it's perfect. Concerned for my feelings? All the grim details and so forth? Well, don't be. My only emotions in this case, if you want to know, are rage and terror at having gotten my foot caught in the gears. Strictly trapped rabbit. You'll find it interesting, believe you me. —Why not? I find it interesting."

Tomlinson had looked at Bauman as if he liked him less and less, a surprisingly forthright glance, nakedly unpleasant. Then he shifted his attention to his sheet of paper, and made short adjacent jotting strokes along his shading. The cube's door had acquired hinges; he must have drawn them quickly sometime before.

"So," Bauman said, feeling quite relaxed, "—let's examine my little boo-boo, both to note how accurate its official reporting was, that paperwork we're so eager to make into history, and even more interesting, examine to what extent this automobile accident really was connected in any structurally useful way with my life."

"Well, I think this is just very inappropriate. Extremely inappropriate."

"Oh, I don't think so. Seems to me it's germane. Disasters, particularly encompassable disasters, are perfect little labs for history."

Tomlinson had pursed his mouth—a wide mouth, narrow-lipped, that pursed surprisingly small. "I'd be perfectly happy to go into all this another time, Charles. I'd enjoy discussing it. Really."

"Never lie to a man who's just lost tenure, John. You wanted to talk history. You brought it up."

"Really," Tomlinson said, shaking his head swiftly no, as a child might do to prevent its hearing the command to bed. "If you do want to discuss this, I'm afraid I don't have time this afternoon."

"Won't take much time," Bauman said. "And beginning at the beginning, more than a week ago, Thursday evening to be precise, Susanne was at her evening class. The History of Ideas, some crap like that. And as you know, a few of our colleagues, who were supposed to be meeting as the doctoral committee, threw an impromptu celebration of my promotion and tenure at Frank Tobey's house. A quasi-departmental party, an unofficial departmental party and no big deal, as Frank can testify, and Quintana, too, since I had a little conversation on the porch with him about the president and his band of merry men, their handling of the basketball thing."

"This is not helpful. I think this is not helpful, Charles. It's all too recent, too painful—"

"Oh, it's not too painful for me," Bauman said. "At that party I was happy, John, but not drunk—certainly not drunk in the culturally accepted sense of the term. Frank wasn't drunk. Ramsey wasn't drunk. The Philosopher certainly wasn't drunk. Nobody was doing that much drinking; it was just a relaxed celebration. As far as my intake is concerned, we're talking about two admittedly generous vodka martinis in the course of an entire evening. That's all we're talking about. . . . All right, at about nine o'clock—a little after, maybe fifteen, twenty minutes after—I left and drove home. Drove toward home."

"Charles—"

"Wait, let me make my point. —Don't be so impatient, John. You brought up an interesting question, the relationship of catastrophe to the more durable developments of history. You brought it up, let's address it. Don't be so damn impatient."

Tomlinson reached out to his pencil cup for a fresh point. He'd worn the first one down drawing the outlines of his cube, its door and door handle, then shading his work architecturally.

"I drove toward home, and I took that corner into Seventeenth Street very smartly. Not fast, not in any unsafe way. Just routine neat no-nonsense driving. I'm a good driver, John, and I took that corner correctly, at the proper speed. If you ask me why a girl, thirteen years old, chooses to ride her younger brother's bicycle down and out the driveway of their house in the dark, out into the street with only the goddamned streetlight— You tell me, then we'll both know."

"Charles, please. . . ." Tomlinson looked down for only a moment, shaded in an area under the cube's door—it seemed under the door from Bauman's view across the desk. Perhaps he intended to show the dryer door opening, perhaps already half open, so that the shirts, the socks and underwear showed clearly.

"We're talking about a girl who sure as hell had to be already menstruating, that big a girl. 'Child' my ass. In most societies on this planet—past and present—she'd have already been married. Betrothed, anyway. Came rolling down that driveway, just flying. One of those short sturdy muscular girls; you know, tanned muscled legs. White socks and white running shoes, I guess, maybe court shoes.

Strong, that kind of strong leg. Dark shorts, and I think a man's white shirt. Dress shirt, tails out. And pedaling like mad, shirttails out, *flying*. God knows where she thought she was going. . . . All these exercised young girls, all those muscles. It must be difficult to find a soft one."

Tomlinson murmured, nodding slightly, smiling slightly, demonstrating patience.

"Well, all right, back on subject. She rode right out in front of the Volvo. Just pedaled right out in front of the car. Very determined face—young Ingrid Bergman, but not so pretty, a blunt face. Face was the youngest thing about her; you could see some baby fat still in her face. As far as the legs went, strictly mature female. Smooth, very adult. Had her hair cut short—blond. Dark blond. And putting out *effort*. We're talking about a considerable physical effort, standing up off the saddle for more leverage. Just pedaling like mad, right out in front of me! I've had a notion—very bizarre, I didn't feel it was politic to mention it to the police—that the little shit intended to kill herself, saw the Volvo very clearly. Why shouldn't she? I sure as hell saw her! Saw me coming and pedaled right out, muscular little heart maybe broken by some fourteen-year-old moron . . . betrayed her, been untrue."

"Terrible. . . ." Tomlinson had reversed his pencil, held the eraser poised, intending perhaps to erase the Maytag's closed original door, possibly to draw it again, half open, then use new shading for shadow.

Bauman, feeling very well now, realized he must have felt slightly ill before. Nauseated. "—I turned away fast. Hard left. And don't worry about my reaction time. I turned hard left, and I did that very fast."

Tomlinson shook his head, glanced barely down, and commenced gently erasing.

"And the moment I turned left, the idiot pedaled *harder*, trying to get around the front of the Volvo. The more I turned, the faster she pedaled in the same damn direction, kept in front of that car as if she were a suicide, and that's the truth. There's no way I or anybody could have avoided her. You put a race driver in that car, John—I don't care who—he would still have rolled right over her. There wasn't time to do a goddamned other thing!"

"Charles—"

"That's not my point, John. Bear with me. —The point is, when I got out of the car I found myself at a loss. In a place different as subatomic physics. A completely slow-motion world, for one thing. A slow-time world. If I'd had that kind of time before, I could have stopped. I could have steered in the other direction. Hell, I could have backed up and driven around the block. If I'd had that kind of slow-motion time before it happened, it wouldn't have happened."

"Um-hmm."

"John, it was an astounding thing, absolutely the most *actual* thing that's ever happened to me. I'm— Everything else in comparison, let me tell you, let me assure you, is strictly moonbeams. And how we can assume, why we should assume, pretend, that cataclysmic events on greater human scale are even approachable without very considerable submission to simple chance, occasional mischance, odd bad luck, good fortune—"

"No one could have expected you to cope—"

"Events of that sort. . . . You can take it from me, John, something like that doesn't need history. I'm not sure that 'event' has anything to do with history. Trends, slow accretions, developments—O.K. Cope? Of course not. Not a goddamn thing I could do. But they expected me to stay there! Oh, you bet! That pack of thieves in the State Legislature had long ago ruled I was expected to stand in the street and watch that poor foolish young girl—injured by her own damn fault—crawling back across the street screaming her head off, all her intestines just coming out on the pavement."

"Oh, dear."

"She was hauling her insides along, crawling, getting her legs tangled up in them, blue ropes and . . . red paint, all getting dragged on the pavement, and she had her head back, held it up like this." Bauman discovered himself demonstrating—face tipped suddenly up to the ceiling, neck straining—and hoped he didn't look foolish. "And *screaming*. You never heard noise like that in your life, I can assure you. You think you have, but you haven't. Her little brother was running around under the streetlight there, screaming. They were both screaming, making the worst noise you ever heard."

"Terrible." Tomlinson had abandoned his drawing and was staring with real attention just over Bauman's left shoulder, as if there were a third person in the room sitting over there listening, perhaps making faces—clownish disbelief, boredom.

"I don't even know where it came from, all that stuff. I don't know if she tore herself open on the handlebar when the car went over her. I don't know if all that was just squeezed out, right out of her rear end. Tremendous pressures. . . ."

Tomlinson, still staring over Bauman's shoulder, seemed to look to his unseen guest for timely interruption.

"I got out of there. I'll be honest with you, John—just as, by the way, I was all too honest with the police. I just got the hell out of there and drove home to get some help. To call for help. To do something reasonable by way of anchoring myself, I suppose, to keep from drifting away."

Something soft from Tomlinson, a comment of some sort—not, apparently, directed at Bauman.

"Then, when the police came, I told them I'd been in the bathroom for some time, sick, and was just going to call. And I didn't tell them I'd had a drink or two after I got home—which I hadn't, and which my lawyer informs me might have made the drunk-driving thing moot."

"Well," Tomlinson said, dragging his regard away from that other, looking at Bauman most reluctantly, "—you've had a very bad time."

"No, no. Karen Silber had the bad time, John. I had, insofar as this discussion is concerned, a most illuminating time. I've been charged with drunk driving, and barely over the legal limit at that, thanks to those two celebratory martinis—which were not doubles. And I've been charged with leaving the scene, hit and run, even though there was no reason at all for me to stay, and excellent reasons to go. It all amounts to vehicular homicide, so we're told. . . . I left, by the way, because the front door to the house opened and a woman and some other people came running outside into all that screaming. At that point, John—you can believe me—it was no longer possible for me to stay. The circumstance itself, the noise, simply shoved me over to the car, pushed me inside, and saw to it I drove away. An extraordinary sensation, an extraordinary sensation. . . . And, it's struck me since, a fair enough model of any individual, any group, caught up in sudden unlooked-for conclusive change. And often, perfectly accidental. Simply unlucky, and not the product of any definable 'historical' process at all. Somebody, one of those people, saw my license number under the light. Because, you know, there was practically no damage to the car. Very minor. A little paint, and a very small dent in the grill. The bumper was just slightly scraped—the rubber covering, plastic, whatever the hell they make that out of. . . ."

Tomlinson shook his head—and used, Bauman saw, one of those sideways shakes to glance swiftly down at his watch. "Tragedy," he said.

"History, John. Accidental, much more than half of it. Not the history we teach at all."

"Of course some chance is always involved, Charles; that we can certainly agree on," Tomlinson said, dropped his pencil, pushed his chair back and stood, then hurried around his desk to extend a furry gibbon's arm, presenting his hand to shake. "And you know," he said, "—considering your own argument, we do, all of us, wish you the best of luck in this. Historic luck, if you like."

Bauman, starting as if suddenly wakened, had sat looking up at Tomlinson for a moment, then stood to shake his hand, to thank him again for his efforts with the dean, the president's office. Then, trying to remember all he'd said, whether or not he'd made a fool of himself, was ushered to the office door, came to a sudden halt there, as if he'd remembered something important or was simply reluctant to leave, then stepped out again and left while Tomlinson was still saying something.

Trying to remember the conversation—its structure, arguments—Bauman had walked to the staircase and climbed it, grateful for the emptiness, the subdued light, the calming repetition of the risers as he went.

"I would," he said to himself aloud, imagining he might have avoided all this by starting his life over at, possibly, the age of seventeen. He saw himself living through so much again, all that landscape of days—reliving it, aware he was doing so, anticipating every event, all relationships, bearing the crushing tedium of no surprise through those interminable years—and making it a very painful point of honor not to avoid any of the thousand blunders, embarrassments, humiliations he would anticipate all too clearly. —Certainly was willing to do that, and for those many years, and only so that driving home from Frank Tobey's last week he would be able to avoid that single mistake, that one misjudgment only, and would know to take another way. Perhaps even drive the same route, but only slightly slower, slightly more cautious on that turn. Could blow his horn.

"I would. I'd do it," he said again, as if to be certain of communicating the wish, then turned right at the third-floor landing and walked two doors down to his office.

A student named Joan Goss, an undergraduate, was standing by his window, waiting, apparently by an appointment Bauman had forgotten. It was unpleasant. He'd assumed the office would be empty, he'd be alone.

She was a lank stooped plain girl, with an oddly pugged nose displaying almost directly its large round nostrils halfway down a face otherwise narrow, attenuate. She carried her long dark-brown hair braided into one thick rope—occasionally, though not today, wearing it to the front, over a shoulder. Joan Goss sported small breasts, usually, as now, revealed in detail under T-shirts. The soft cones, large-nippled, joggling when she moved, sat, or stood, were presented apparently in lieu of conventional good looks. She carried a windbreaker over her arm, its cloth a darker blue than her jeans.

"You wrote on my paper you wanted to see me. You said my paper was unacceptable." Voice hoarse, perhaps with sorrow, perhaps wrath, the girl presenting as well a possible tear glittering in the inner corner of her right blue eye, struck with sunlight from the window.

"That's right. Sit down." Bauman went behind his desk—gray metal, not Tomlinson's polished brown oak—and as he sat down himself, it occurred to him he might seem just such an ass to this student as Tomlinson had seemed to him.

"I think it's unfair," she said. "I think it's just plain ridiculous."

She sat down in the straight-back chair facing him, the sunlight from the open window behind her creating a nimbus outlining her in gold, revealing a few long hairs seeming to burn in the light, floating, escaped from her heavy braid.

Bauman looked over his desktop for his notes, then remembered enough to stop looking.

"You're wrong, Ms. Goss," he said, thinking it a shame about her nose—appearance so often crucial to a young woman's happiness. Stupid of her family not to have paid attention to it, gotten surgery, a nose augmentation that might have provided her a regal arching bridge, might have made a medieval out of her, Norman-nosed, a long-faced chatelaine. —As it was, Joan Goss would probably live her life reactive to that sad snout.

"—You're wrong, Ms. Goss. That 'unacceptable' isn't unfair, and it isn't ridiculous. I'm sorry to say you earned it showing off your Latin, which is very good Latin, and of course unusual these days. Where'd you go to school?"

"Saint Theresa's."

"In Surtees?"

"Yes."

"Well, the nuns gave you some very good Latin, though not perfect; I think there was a correction on the third page, near the bottom. You brought your paper?"

The girl unzipped the middle pocket of a gray bookbag, slid her paper out. "That was the only correction." She'd presented it, protected by flexible orange covers, with some satisfaction the previous week, apparently certain of its reception. It was her first paper for him, her first term taking ancient history.

"You have very good Latin—bottom page three, I think—but you goofed on that line. Page three, red mark in the margin. As I recall, the phrase should have translated 'would have to have been in the city'; you had it '*was* to have been in the city.' That's probably your source's fault; he liked to use a very elaborate grammar as a sort of rhetorical flourish. —And there were two or three other infelicities, but those were more a matter of your not being faithful to Verinus's style. It's a very florid style, and you needed to elaborate your English a little to indicate that. When you're translating, style is almost as important as sense."

"And just because I made that one mistake—"

"Sometimes, one mistake can be one too many." Bauman saw, as he finished saying this, a slight change of expression, some minor alteration at the corners of her mouth, her eyes. "—As I can testify, if you were thinking about my accident."

"I wasn't. I wasn't thinking about that."

"I'd be thinking about it in your place. It's a situation that's a little difficult to ignore—right? Especially when I asked for it with that cute remark about mistakes."

"I wasn't thinking about it, Professor Bauman."

"Well, let it go. In any case, I didn't mark you down because of problems with your translated passages as such. I gave you an unacceptable rather than fail you; you just need to do it over and hand it in again. I gave you an unacceptable because your paper's nothing but a series of translated passages, with bridges—very short bridges, very sketchy bridges, by the way—of explanation and agreement by you. And that was not the assignment. The assignment was to write discussing the various ramifications of the Catiline Conspiracy."

"That's what I did."

"No. No, you didn't. You went over to the library, found the original text, and loaded your paper with translations of Verinus's version of Cicero and the Optimates saving the republic from Catiline. No discussion, no thought. Just Ms. Goss's solid translation. —You have any idea who Verinus was? After all, you use the guy as your only source."

"He was an essayist."

"Just a disinterested literary type?"

"He knew Cicero. He lived in that period." Tears of anger, if any tears at all, probably only light on the lubricated eyes of youth.

"Oh, Verinus knew Cicero, all right. Your 'essayist' was a freedman. Did you know that?"

"No, I didn't, and I don't see what difference that makes."

"This difference: Verinus had been a slave in Cicero's uncle's house—some sort of steward, apparently—and had made enough money to buy his freedom, then made more money selling sausage wholesale. Before he got his citizenship, his name had been Thraximines—he was a Syriac Greek—and our 'essayist' was, on at least one occasion, represented by Cicero in a court case involving adulteration of those sausages with less costly substances than good pork. In other words, we are describing a *client* of Cicero's, an old family servant grown rich doing that family's less respectable business. We're talking about a man with an ax to grind."

"I didn't know I was supposed to do some kind of biography." Nostrils furiously round, prominent in that pugged nose, a tiny pair of angry black eyes echoing the larger blue glistening ones above.

"In history—in any discipline, Ms. Goss—you need to know everything you can know about a source, particularly when you're using only one. Now, what our literary sausage merchant has to say about Catiline may well be true, but you don't support that notion in any way whatsoever. That paper is ninety percent Piso Verinus, ten percent Joan Goss. And that means it just won't do."

Rough stuffing of the paper back into her bookbag. Harsh zipping-up of zipper.

"What I'd suggest is, that you go back to the library and use that good Latin to read other sources that might indicate where your man was telling the truth, and where he was lying. We're talking about research, here, Ms. Goss. You're no longer at Saint Theresa's with the nuns; you're at a university, one of the best. You've been here two years. You're expected to question, research, and come to supportable judgments. And any time you don't do that, chances are it's going to cost you."

The girl exhaled a heavy, patient sigh. "When am I supposed to turn that in. Am I supposed to turn that in in a couple of days, or what?"

"Turn it in next week. You're going to have— Richard Chu is going to be taking over the class. You hand it in to him next week—Wednesday, when class meets. I'll have talked to him."

"Great. . . ." Pouting, face flushed, the erstwhile Saint Theresa's student, certainly an erstwhile honor student, stood up to go, small breasts trembling slightly with the motion. "Can I go now? I've got a statistics class."

"All right," Bauman said. "You can go."

She walked to the office door, the heavy braid of dark brown hair swinging, tapping at her back.

"Just a minute. Wait a minute."

She paused in the doorway to look back, profiling, as she did, that unfortunate nose.

"If I was unnecessarily snotty about your paper, Ms. Goss, I apologize."

"You were unnecessarily snotty," she said, turned and walked out.

Something about the encounter—perhaps that it had been an encounter—reminded Bauman very forcefully of meeting Susanne the first time two years before, just so, but on a warmer day.

That day's afternoon light had presented Susanne's throat—smooth, columnar, tanned very pale taffy-brown to almost match her hair when sunstruck. She'd held, poised upon this pedestal, a narrow head and face with the long-muzzled lines and angled jaw, the deep-set pale green eyes of a young female wolf. This young wolf, gentlest of the litter, changed to a girl by magic only moments before (her vanished fur having been harsh, thick, streaked in blizzard-white and granite).

A striped singlet had revealed Susanne's bare shoulders, and at her back when she'd turned to go, shown uncovered the slight knuckles of her upper spine. Revealed her armpits also, when she'd gestured—these half-hollows soft, faintly damp, and shaded dark ivory where shaved.

She'd come as Joan Goss was to come, but as a graduate student, to argue about a paper. Austro-Hungarian administration . . . Serbia . . . some unconvincing presentation arguing an enlightened educational policy. Absolute nonsense, since the imperial bureaucracy had taken particular care to prevent implementation of anything of the sort.

That meeting, and the one or two still casual meetings that followed, had left Bauman, to his own surprise, determined to have the young woman under his hand—to have the freedom, any time he chose, to touch her mouth, her slim forearms, the white delicate small folds of flesh appearing before the jointure of those tender armpits when her arms were down, her hands relaxed on her lap.

He began—as in the itchy progress of some disease—to suffer a greater and greater urgency to touch, taste her, stroke the long smooth strait small of her naked back. This need the more relentless for not being solely sexual. The girl appeared to personify a great gift of new beginning, as if, in relativity, her slender body might bend the universe's fabric for him, slow time, even reverse it. On several occasions before he met her, he'd suffered sudden headaches in class and at home in bed at night, and each time imagined the pain increasing, imagined it increasing until a stroke spurted into the meat of his brain to blind and ruin him.

Once, with such an ache, he got out of bed while Beth was still asleep, snoring softly, and went into the bathroom to reassure himself with sight of his reflection in the medicine-cabinet mirror—making a face of frightened inquiry, then responding with a casual grimace, a dismissing shrug implying some contempt for a man so deeply concerned with himself.

Dr. Willabrandt, appealed to casually, had Bauman over to the clinic, examined the pupils of his eyes, fitted a sleeve and monitor to record a series of blood pressures, took two encephalograms some time apart—and diagnosed nothing but a probably causative tension in the muscles at the base of Bauman's neck.

The immediate relief at this opinion was great, but Bauman found the subject of mortality, once seriously open to discussion, never after quite unconsidered except in Susanne Pollock's presence. There, though conscious of the vulgarity of age seeking such anodyne—the common dreariness of thickening curdled flesh at play with moist and tender—he found his attention fixed on the girl. He became increasingly energetic to buckle her to him, and it seemed after a few weeks of this pursuit, that recovery from mopey considerations of dying was only a reasonable and necessary function of new-discovered love. One of its gifts.

This delirium he watched himself accepting—detached as if observing an amusing insect caught in the flood of a draining tub—and more than watched, lent himself to it, felt its tumultuous absurdity and possible damage as a sort of spasm of new birth, certain to change him.

Very soon he behaved toward the young woman as toward property that might be wholly owned. Susanne's nature, her character, the personality driving the intricate body through its days, he found of little interest. It was her physical self that concerned him—her feet, strongly arched, lacily veined, coarse-toed as a farm girl's when finally he saw them bare; her knees, bony as a boy's; her thighs; the whole length of her legs. He admired her modest buttocks, her belly, her sides, where ribs ran up like scales of music. Her shoulders, fragile, sloping, were held braced a little back to support her breasts, which, sized and shaped as moderate pears—though riper, smoother, softer than any fruit—drooped slightly, as if their branch had been stung by frost the night before.

This body, rising from sturdy toes to the small poised intrinsic head—that supported, when her hair was up, a comb-kept heap, light-amber, shining, smooth as syrup—all this seemed quite complete without specific wishes, opinions, memories, information or desire. What banal trait of personality might compete with legs, for example, so definite, complete, and elegantly muscled from calves to knees to the round and solid polish of her thighs? —out of the finer finish of which, their inner softer surfaces spread in display, single great tendons lifted at each side beneath the skin, raised as introductions to the damp, furred complication where perfections came together.

It was her lovely legs that Susanne began to slowly spread one early evening. Lying on her stomach on the white-tufted coverlet of her apartment bed, lying there weary, and wearing only a light-blue bathrobe, Susanne commenced to spread her long legs apart as if in demonstration of their various elegancies—her thighs unlocked perhaps by Bauman's curious hand forced in between, his busy fingers, the slight sound one finger made.

This continued until her legs were spread so wide apart Bauman was enabled to do what he pleased—after a while of which the girl began to hollow her narrow back, raise her buttocks, then raise them higher to make more way for him, the blue robe's material sliding to gather at her shoulders, the nape of her neck, that tender twin-tendoned place already bitten just after dinner, and doing this, she murmured into her soft pillow for some time.

Later—up on hands and knees, mounted, entered from behind, and roughly, repeatedly jolted (each action accompanied by a soft liquid sound), dealt with so her neat breasts, suspended, shook—Susanne had set aside her strangerhood. Face contorted, pale eyes blind with preoccupation, she relinquished herself with a deep tearing grunt, as though accomplishing childbirth. That noise turned to a wavering cry, while her splendid naked legs—spraddled, splayed, toes scrabbling in her coverlet—commenced to thrash the slowest kicking dance about the wet transfixion planted in her beneath, which levered her buttocks higher, lifting them to display between as she shook, to cramp closed as she tried to keep her pleasure in.

Just above her and a little back, sweating, braced on trembling arms, Bauman had rested imperial—his startled heart, forty-one years old, sounding rub-a-dub-dub-dub.

It was this body, its type not after all so unusual among tall young women—certainly not perfect, not, objectively, much superior in sexual articulation to his wife's, which many men might have preferred—

still it was this, her palpable weighty physical fact that Bauman found inescapable, as if there hadn't been and never would be such another. A sort of magisterial totem, unique, perfect all the more for imperfection, and impinging as the weather.

Susanne couldn't have possessed a personality rich enough to have persuaded him to keep any closer to, or farther from her, than the distance best for touching. This desire occasioned an insistence of possession that the girl seemed to acknowledge herself, as if she hadn't the right to deny him, as if she often heard a most persuasive voice insisting that was so.

She'd loved her boyfriend, an instructor in the engineering school—had lived with him for months, even considered marriage, her life alongside his. Bauman had entered that reasonable, predictable social space (containing his wife and his son, Phil, as well as Susanne's boyfriend), had entered that space, been unreasonable, and remained unreasonable until Susanne—by his concentration convinced she was treasure appreciated only now, dearer to herself as her body was dearer to him for every new-discovered detail, flaw or favor—lay under his hand, for a time almost fully possessed. His countryside. . . .

"You are making an extraordinary jackass of yourself, Charlie." Pete Quintana advising Bauman at the Pump, over corned-beef sandwiches. "You don't give a good goddamn about that girl. You don't know anything about her; you don't want to know anything about her. Your only real love object, old buddy, is Charlie Bauman. I'm being honest with you." Quintana'd then relaxed a combative stance to take another bite of his sandwich, which left a small smear of mustard at the left corner of his mouth. "—You're in love with your own craziness, is what it is; you're proud of it! You're on a pandemonium high."

Quintana, tall, bald, mustached, was a very good tennis player, had been almost of professional caliber. He'd also shown some talent for climbing the summer before, staying with Bauman up a difficulty five-nine on the Wedge, near Sumner, Missouri. Now, his footing less secure, Quintana was standing not quite neutral in the Baumans' difficulty, since he'd previously formed the habit of mooning over Beth Bauman at late parties, playing the lonely broken-heart when he'd drunk enough. Alas, it was coming fish-or-cut-bait time, and finding he hadn't the will after all to fish abandoned Beth for a wife or even a lover, once Bauman had left her, Quintana was now proving energetic to save the marriage.

"Doesn't seem to matter who you hurt, Charlie. You care to deny that? Hurting Philly . . . Beth."

"Pete, will you please cut the crap? We both know you'd take care of Beth."

"What?" Cruelly startled. "Are you kidding? She loves you. Beth loves you, Charlie, and God help her, because I think you're about fourteen, fifteen years old right now, as far as responsibility goes. All you're doing—and I mean *all* you're doing—is showing off. The campus romantic hero—an extremely stupid piece, if you'll pardon my French, of self-destructive Byronesque bullshit."

"Hit that nail right on the head, Pete." Bauman had ordered a chocolate milkshake, and discovering a good bit remaining in the metal container, poured it out.

"It isn't funny. It's sad, Charlie."

"Um-hmm. You've got some mustard on the side of your mouth. No, the other side. I've always had the feeling . . . Well, since this appears to be revelation time, I'll tell you a truth. I've always had the feeling somehow, that you and Beth might belong together."

A frightened Quintana staring over his crumpled paper napkin. "Oh . . . oh, come on. You're out of your *mind*."

"No, I mean it. I think Beth really depends on you, really feels she can trust you to take care of her and Philly, if that turns out to be necessary."

"Jesus Christ! You are out of your mind!"

"I . . . I hadn't wanted ever to say this to you, Pete. Maybe now, it's time. I think that feeling, that deep feeling Beth has for you—her reliance, her dependency on you—is a major factor in our breakup. It's not a pleasant thing to realize your wife probably loves another man—a friend. In fact, when I first began to get the picture, I had a very propulsive urge to knock you on your ass. —And I suppose Susanne may be my way of face-saving."

A pale, pale Pete Quintana. "This . . . that just isn't *so*. I'm very, very fond of Beth. You know that, Charlie. I've always been very fond of Beth. But believe me, there's nothing like that—"

"Really? Are you telling me the truth, Pete? —Because if you are, if you really don't love her, I think it would be the decent thing to at least go and tell her so. Not let her go on trusting you, thinking you're going to take care of her when all this is over."

"Trusting *me* . . . ?"

Quintana, distressed—able to finish his root beer but unable to finish his sandwich—had apparently left the Pump concerned that matters must be made clearer to Beth Bauman, that she not be shocked later, to discover his support only that of a friend. Therefore, on

Thursday, after his last afternoon class, he'd walked across the campus, then the three blocks down Stuart to the Baumans' house. He found Beth just come home with groceries, and, in the kitchen as she put the food away, had painfully set matters straight—so very painfully that he'd ended leaning against the refrigerator in tears, wiping his eyes and blowing his nose on the paper towels she handed him, and nearly promised to take care of her forever, after all.

"Unforgivable," Beth had said to Bauman that night, and if she thought it funny—as once she certainly would have—concealed that. . . .

Goss gone, Bauman sat at his desk for a few moments, squinting slightly into the window light, recalling that burlesque with Quintana at the Pump, recalling his initial hunger for Susanne's particular shape of meat and bone—his pleasure later, on finding the young woman quite lovable, gentle, intelligent, someone he might have wanted for a wife even after calm consideration. Sheer good luck. And Bauman realized suddenly, having made no specific connection, that Joan Goss, with her pouting, her injured air, her unusual Latin, was likely to be the last student he would ever teach, and this occasion certainly the last occasion to teach at Midwest—or, probably, anywhere else.

He got up from his desk, went to the door, glanced left and saw no one in the hall, looked to the right and saw Joan Goss at the far end of the long corridor, just vanishing down the south stairs.

Bauman took two or three quick steps out of the office after her, leaned forward to trot for several more, then suddenly sprinted away, conscious of absurdity, grinning at himself and for anyone come back from lunch who might look out into the corridor and see him galloping, his loafers thumping down the ancient wide-board flooring, brown tweed sports jacket flapping open, yellow-brown wool tie streaming back over his left shoulder.

Finding it a pleasure to be running, he set himself to running faster, with great echoing noise down the high-ceilinged hallway—and no sooner was really traveling than had to slow slightly to prepare to grip the stairway newel post, difficult to judge with bright light in his eyes from the window at the corridor's end—to grip the newel post and swing himself half around and on down the stairs.

Joan Goss, startled by the chasing racket, stopped a flight below and stared up the narrow well as Bauman, breathless, came clattering down worn wood.

"Wait. . . ." He stepped down to the landing just above her and stopped to catch his breath, left hand resting on the dark half-round rail, feeling faint dimples of old dents under his fingertips.

"What is it?"

"I came after you to apologize again for that little bit of professorial bullying upstairs; it's an easy habit to get into. And also to suggest another couple of sources that might be useful to you."

She bent to rest her bookbag on the step above her, unzipped the large pocket, and took out a fat red-covered spiral notebook, a slender black-barreled pen. Opened the notebook, resting it on her bent left knee, and looked up at Bauman, elaborately patient, prepared to write. There was really nothing to prevent her being beautiful—pretty, at any rate—but that doleful snouted nose and a sullen nature.

"All right. There's a monograph, *Lex Romanorum*. You'll like it; it's in Latin, written by an Italian priest. Author is Fulmieri. F-u-l-m-i-e-r-i. He's got a passage on Cicero and Catiline as opponents in the law, that you'll find useful."

"O.K."

"And one more: *Class and Social Policy in the Late Republic*. That's by Andrew Marcovic. M-a-r-c-o-v-i-c."

"Professor Bauman . . ." still writing, "I am not going to have time to read all these sources. No way. And just to rewrite a paper I already *did*."

"You didn't do the assigned paper, Ms. Goss, and you don't have to read 'all' of anything. Just locate those passages useful as reference. You'll find that's a good skill to develop, especially for history."

She put her red notebook, her slim black pen away, zipped up the bookbag zipper. "Professor Bauman, I'm in pre-law. I'm not a history major; I'm not going to be *dealing* with history. The basic reason I'm taking this course—which is really, really a very interesting course—is for one of my humanities credits that I have to have to get into law school. And the problem is, if this course is going to take up too much of my time, I'll have to transfer to an advanced English or something, instead. I'm being honest with you. O.K.?"

"I see. And you'll get that credit, too. All you have to do, Ms. Goss, is earn it. In other words, you're going to have to do some work, and not rely on leftover prep school skills like your Latin, as substitutes. And if you don't do some work, I—or Richard Chu—will fail you flat, and you will not get your credit."

"Oh, man." This *sotto voce*. She picked up her bookbag, slung it over her left shoulder, and started down the flight of stairs to the second floor.

"Wait a minute. Just hold on." She paused several steps down, turned to look back. "—What's the problem, Ms. Goss? Do you think you're not going to have to do some work for Jacobean Drama or whatever? Read some plays, at least? Many of them, by the way, full of staircase scenes even more tedious than this one."

No smile from Goss. A little glance at her watch. "Well," she said, "I am going to check some other courses out." And away down the stairs again. Graceful enough, going down.

Bauman couldn't help but discard dignity, followed down three or four steps just to say one thing more. "Listen, Ms. Goss. . . ." Another step closer, trying not to spook her. It was like catching up a pastured horse out at Mr. Murtagh's. "—I can't argue you into history. You had your American history your first year. Now, you probably can get out of college without completing any more history courses at all. What I'm asking you is, Would that be wise? Is it a smart thing to do, or does it just seem to be a smart thing to do?"

"Professor Bauman, I really have to go."

"Ms. Goss, to be ignorant of history is like waking up one morning with amnesia, knowing nothing of your own past, your work, your family, parents, friends—"

"Right, but I do have to go." Unfortunate nose nearly twitching. "Really, or I'm going to be *late*."

"Don't worry about it—I'll write you a note! You understand what I'm saying? People who don't know the history of their country, their culture, their civilization, live like greedy and ignorant children—because a world of which they know only the present, can't ever be fully theirs."

Goss glanced at her watch again, shifted her feet like a child needing to go to the bathroom. "Right. But listen, Professor Youmans doesn't like people coming in after the class starts. She's real tough about it. I'll tell you what I need to know, Professor Bauman. I need to know if I still have to do all this extra work on my paper, because I really don't think I have the time to do that."

". . . Yes, you have to do all that extra work on your paper."

"Well, that's really too bad, because then I just won't be able to keep the class—and it is too bad, because it would obviously be very interesting." A sigh. "Now, I do need to be going." And turned to do just that, trotting away down the stairs, while Bauman started his climb back up, so angry he was short of breath.

On the third floor landing—Ms. Goss's footsteps fading almost away below—Bauman leaned over the rail, could see her white hand, small at the bottom of the well, sliding rapidly down the last length of banister. He leaned over farther and shouted down to her: "*Get that . . . damn nose fixed!*"

After an instant of continued motion, the hand below stopped sliding, almost at the banister's end.

"*I don't care what people have told you. Your parents—whoever. It looks like a pig's snout. You need something* . . . something . . . put in there." Bauman's voice sounding softer despite himself as a silence weighty and cold as the coldest water seemed to rise slowly up the stairwell to him. He bent over the rail to see, imagining the girl transformed to some appalling beast—a tusked sow, snout flowered into a great-nostriled pink platter, gray bookbag dangling down one bristled flank as it swam up through the flood of silence toward him.

—But saw only her hand lying still as carving on the slope of the banister far below. Saw that, then drew back and as silently as he could, holding his breath, commenced a slow-motion flight up the last stairs, stepping carefully on the wall side of each tread to prevent its creaking, so the girl, still and silent below, might not be able to locate him precisely, not be certain he was there at all.

Chapter FIVE

Bauman slept, woke to Segregation's stink, its dimly scarlet light, then slept again and dreamed.

He dreamed a visit to him by Braudel. The small ugly black dog, nails tick-ticking as he trotted through the great South gate, had come visiting on a sunny afternoon—Bauman somehow hovering over. Through the gate, the dog continued across the wide yard—a tiny patch of black casting a spidery black shadow along the walkway's cement to the main entrance of C-block. Passing inside—no iron on him to alarm—the little animal commenced to tour through State, exploring, trotting past inmates, guards, and gates from block to block, Three-tiers to basements. During these passages, turning up his flat-muzzled face to peer at places and men as he passed, Braudel traveled many miles through a palace of error at once State and, from the dog's foot-high vantage, someplace grander than State. Finally at dusk, having crossed West yard (very tired, small black-furred legs trembling), he accomplished the two-story climb from the laundry, past Protective Custody, to Segregation—and slight enough to have slipped the gate, came wearily tick-ticking down the gloomy corridor to sit before Bauman's cell, panting and barely visible, his pink tongue the only portion of him clearly seen in such shadow.

Since he was dreaming, Bauman spoke to the dog, asked him if he'd carried a message in from Beth—or something from Philly to say how much he missed his father, how willingly he'd come to visit him. But the dream's magic was failing, waking was too near, and the little dog sat silent, watching his kenneled master for a while, then stood, walked over to sniff at human excrement, trotted away to the gate.

Bauman woke and turned over onto his left side (not his favorite; someone had told him it strained the heart), felt concrete firm through slight foam against his shoulder and the socket of his hip, and wished for a pillow, some sort of cover . . . then went to sleep again, but too lightly, so his second dream was many dreams, none rich enough, none doored and roofed for dwelling.

He woke the third time into morning light somehow obstructed—pretty light, soft silver, wavering down through rows of glass bricks set high in the corridor's opposite wall.

"Good morning." The figure obstructing the light leaned relaxed against the bars of Bauman's house, and Bauman, blinking sleep away, saw the possessor of last night's clear stony tenor voice. A pleasantly smiling man in his mid-thirties, very tall, shoulders slightly stooped—his hair, neatly trimmed, the thinning, fading blond of many farmers Bauman had known in Minnesota. His eyes also their pale blue, as though worn by weather; face long, heavy-boned, heavy-jawed. His mouth, rube wide, was tucked a little wryly upward at its left corner. The man's complexion was no farmer's, though—rather dull light-gray, the sick child's skin of most of many years spent behind concrete, stone, and steel.

This convict, wearing Segregation's bright orange jumpsuit with clean white sneakers, revealed no wristwatch, no tattoos on pale lean hairless wrists and forearms, where his suit's sleeves had been neatly rolled up nearly to his elbows.

"Good morning," the man said a second time. "Welcome to Seg. Bauman—right?"

"Yes," Bauman said, and sat up. His left shoulder ached, he supposed from the thin mattress on concrete. This visitor was the only man he could see. Might be the only man standing in the corridor. A smeared black lump of excrement lay a few feet behind him, to the left.

"Case you're wondering, we're not usually this messy up here, Professor. Not usually this quiet up here, either." The visitor presented a pleasant smile, revealed large, even, faintly yellow teeth. Horse's teeth. A farm horse, then—lank, spare, powerful enough for medium hauling, a moderate feeder. "—We had a little solidarity demonstration for the powers that be. Finally got a discussion goin' with Admin this morning—which is what I'm doing the only guy walking around block-out—and we came to a real reasonable agreement. Some people'll be cleaning up, this afternoon. . . . You hungry? If you got a hypoglycemia problem, something like that, I'll get food up for you." This was presented in a deliberate easy-paced Midwestern accent, its drawn-out doleful vowels almost musical in their lack of any rhythm, any variation of emphasis.

"No," Bauman said, "—I haven't got that problem." He wished this convict wasn't lounging before his door as if he were a hack instead of an inmate, standing with his left hand on the bars, smiling down at Bauman, who had nothing to do but sit on the side of his platform—a structure, it occurred to him, exactly like those seen in zoos' cages—and be courteously attentive. Precisely as if he were a zoo animal wakened for a tourist's convenience. He hoped the man wouldn't have anything more to say about his shower.

"What happened to your face? Hacks bounce you around?"

Bauman reached up to his right cheek, felt a small fresh scab where his watch had struck him. "No. Yes, but this was an accident."

"You got a complaint, I'll see it's filed."

"Thanks anyway," Bauman said, wondering who this busybody might be—nosy last night, nosy now.

"You don't know who the hell I am, do you?"

"No," Bauman said, "—I don't."

"I'm Pete Nash."

Bauman stood up. This standing, coming almost to attention, seemed to amuse the Lifer Club's president, the Caucasian Union's dreaded chieftain, who had continued to wear those two hats—as pharaohs had their bonnets of upper and lower Egypt—and exercise the powers of both offices, even from this exile.

"Wow," Nash said, leaning so relaxed, so easy on Bauman's bars, "—I didn't know I had a name 'to conjure with,' " accenting the quote a little in dealing with so educated and frightened a man. "Sit down and take it easy." He smiled, encouraging, until Bauman sat, and sitting, reflected on the bent for leadership that so automatically assumed command of a listener's posture, so easily enforced it.

"You don't have to sit down if you don't want to, Professor. It's your house. You want to stand up, stand up."

Bauman had nothing to say to that.

"I just wanted to welcome you to Seg, apologize for the mess we got here. It's a temporary thing, method of keeping the C.O.'s aware of our people's humanity. Messy method, but there you go." Nash's laugh was a rattling tenor, high-pitched as his speech. "—Instrument at hand."

"I see. Smell, at any rate. . . ."

"You're sure you don't need some breakfast—medical reasons?"

"No, thank you," Bauman said. "Not much of an appetite. The odor."

An open-mouthed grin answered this pleasantry, Nash's head bobbing, then held to one side, a countryman's posture in conversation. Nash had long fingers, Bauman saw, where the man's left hand gripped his house's bars. The two cons Nash had strangled in the print shop must have seen those fingers and the bootlace they held as their last clear sight, unless he'd stood behind them, a knee up to their chairs' backs for purchase. That drama, and many others, apparently not without cost. Nash's fingernails were bitten, worried into horny broken buttons.

"Fucked up, aren't they?" Nash said, noticing the observation. "I take out a lot of trouble on my fingernails. And speaking of self-assaultive behavior, besides welcoming you up here to Seg, speaking of that kind of behavior, there's something we're goin' to have to talk about. Couple of things. . . ." Nash paused, looked away to his left, something down the corridor catching his attention. Whatever, it was too far, at too acute an angle for Bauman to see, even if he'd been standing at his door.

"You need a snitch-mirror, Professor." Nash's attention back on Bauman, a very direct look, very interested, nearly a stare, his upper eyelids forming almost epicanthic folds, presenting narrow triangles as settings for his eyes, their pale blue. "I'll get you one."

"Thanks, but that's all right." Bauman anxious not to owe the slightest favor.

"A courtesy, that's all, Professor. Don't worry about it; I'm not trying to lend you up. You weren't locked down the week, I could promote you a radio, too. Administration denies us TV's; allows us radios, but only with earphones." Saying so, Nash continued his direct and constant gaze, as if Bauman were the most interesting thing seen in some time. "Now, if you feel like it, I got a couple things to talk to you about, new boy on the block and all that. But if you just want to be left alone, they can wait."

"No. That's all right," Bauman said. Over the odor of feces, he thought he smelled from Nash some faint perfume, after-shave.

"Hey, wait a minute now. I said 'if you feel like it,' and I meant it. You don't want to be bothered, we can talk later." Very like a Minnesota farmer (or, from his accent, a Kansan), but even more a clever small-town lawyer, a farmer's second son, prepared now to run for the State Legislature. Certain of winning.

"No, it's all right." A vision of this courteous monster suddenly exploding in foaming rage, demanding news of Bauman's long shower, his possible treacherous undertaking.

"So, O.K. for a little discussion? Two subjects?"

"Fine. —Really."

Nash leaned suddenly to his left, head and shoulder out of sight. Bauman heard him say to that neighbor, "Carl, I want you to get in the back of your house there, and hold your hands over your ears. Hold 'em tight."

Privacy apparently arranged—"Carl" certainly not arguing the point—Nash straightened, stared down again through Bauman's bars.

"O.K. Tell me," voice soft, conversational, "—you hear about Barney Metzler, was offed a few weeks ago?"

"Yes."

"You ever meet his squeeze? His punk, is what he was. You know who I'm talking about?"

"Yes, I think so. Lee Cousins." Looking up into the haze of filtered light, Bauman saw that Nash was somewhat older than he'd first appeared. A lace of fine wrinkles etched the corners of his mouth, scored his forehead across, complicated his eyelids. Perhaps the cost of command.

"That's right. Cousins. Well, I understand through a certain party that this Cousins punk thinks the same people that offed Barney back then, also just cowboyed the black guy, Spencer. Understand he thinks Spencer might have mentioned something to you. You ate your lunch with the dude just before he got it, right? Is that so? Cousins seems to think maybe you know something. —What's funny?"

"Nothing. . . ." Bauman amused by his slight disappointment as to the nature of Cousins' interest in him. So much for Betty's notion of romance.

"You found something funny there, when I was talking."

"No, no. Just a personal thing."

"Well, let me make something clear to you, Professor." Nash was speaking very softly, apparently mistrusting the deafness ordered to his left. "Ordinarily, in a killing, crime of passion and so forth, I would have no interest. No interest at all. None of my business."

Bauman nodded, wondering whether he should stand to talk to Nash rather than stay sitting on his mattress like an idiot, looking up over his shoulder. Instead of standing, though, he turned a little as he sat, to face the man.

"You see, we got big ears in here," Nash said. "In here, let me tell you, you grow real big ears. Anybody comes in here, he don't even know he's giving you information, but we get the news. We listen real hard." He stared at Bauman, examined him more closely. "—You sure this discussion is all right with you? We could talk tomorrow."

"No, no. Really. It's all right."

"Well, the reason I bring up the Spencer thing—and this is business, you understand, not just curiosity, or I wouldn't be troubling you with it first thing your first morning. Don't have to tell you this conversation is strictly between us." A confiding smile. "Very strictly." Nash's long fingers tapped and played at Bauman's bars. "—Reason is, Metzler's punk thinks some hack had a hand in killing her old man. Now, what do you think of that? Cousins was outside, escorted over to Garlin to have a couple of wisdom teeth out at the dentist. And Barney was locked down alone in his house, because he didn't want to go see the game. Basketball, right? For ol' Barney that was a boring game, except for betting. Betting on that and football and the fights was all the sports that interested Barney. So there he was, alone on Ground-tier in C, and locked down. People on Three-tier heard him yelling—and he was dead. Caught him on his crapper, and cut him wide open across the front. Now, what do you think of that?"

"I didn't realize . . . I didn't know what the circumstances were."

"That's what they were. You sure you're up to this—a discussion like this?"

"Sure. It's fine."

"Now, you see, when that first happened, we figured Barney was stepping out on that Cousins. He's out of the joint for the afternoon, so Barney gets some inmate in there and tries to bang him, and gets offed. Then when the game's over, block's opened up, whoever it was just strolls out and mingles. That's what we figured at the time."

"I see." Bauman wondered if he should say anything more, try to contribute, then decided not.

"Right. But Cousins says, not so. Said not so at the time, too. Said Barney wasn't that interested in sex, anymore. Cousins' opinion, nobody was in there with him at all until one of the hacks opened up his house and let some dude jump in there on him. Or maybe the hack went in and did the job himself. Caught him on the crapper."

Nash paused, looked at Bauman in an expectant way, as though certain of hearing something interesting from him.

Bauman kept his mouth shut.

"—And Cousins thinks that black guy, Spencer, the same way," Nash said. "That one, there had to be a hack, had to have some cop let the dude out middle of the night to do it—or maybe the cop did it on his own." Bent the same expectant look on Bauman.

Bauman wished he'd kept as quiet in the shower, as now.

Nash watched him for a few moments, grinned his wry countryman's grin, and said, "You trying to stay out of trouble?"

"Damn right," Bauman said, and Nash appeared amused, his left hand's long fingers playing piccolo at the bars.

"Well, you have to understand the problem I got here, Professor. See, the trouble with being an inmate rep—being the lifer president, the Union thing—the problem is sometimes you have to deal with things. It's expected."

Bauman nodded.

"And if—just possible, you understand?—just possible the punk is right, and some screw is interfering in inmate business, or on his own is offing people, helping off people, well, that is way out of line."

Bauman nodded again. Could certainly agree that was out of line.

Nash abruptly sounded his rattling laugh. "We're the dudes supposed to do the killing; those dudes are supposed to do the guarding. They're in *loco parentis* here. Right? Isn't this what you call a social contract? Isn't it?"

"I suppose it is," Bauman said, and regretted speaking.

"Well, there you go. I don't think my position on this is off the wall, is it?"

Bauman shook his head no.

"These corrections people—or one of them, anyway—are violating that social contract. They're usurping our prerogatives. That the right phrase?"

"Yes," Bauman said. "That's the right phrase."

"Well, I can't let it go by," Nash said. A mournful shake of the head. "I wish I could let it go by, but I can't."

Bauman nodded. The smell of shit was stronger than it had been, he was sure. Warmth of the morning.

"Can't let it go by. . . ." Nash took his deliberate concentrating stare from Bauman, gazed instead down the corridor to his left. "I don't think I'm being dingy on this," he said, and turned his head to look at Bauman again. "You been segged for a couple years, you can lose your perspective. You know, get paranoid? Well, that's something I really try and avoid. In my position you have to be very conservative, very responsible, use real good judgment. People depend on you; they rely on your judgment. Does that sound funny to you, Professor?"

Bauman shook his head.

"Oh, I bet it does. I mean you're so short-time. Another year, you'll be out, and this'll just be something to write a book about. *Psychopaths I Have Known*, right? A *Year or Two in a Zoo*, right? But you know, we have to operate on the basis of the reality we got."

"I know."

"Now—and this is strictly confidential—there are some other organizations that might have wanted Barney Metzler. We're talking about an executive, an important guy. And there were also a few people who didn't like Barney just because of his natural functions as a club officer. Felt he had disciplined somebody in too permanent a manner, had some other bone against him. —However, as to that black inmate you were friendly with—Spencer? I can tell you in confidence we had nothing against the man. Period."

Bauman nodded.

"Well, what's all this to you—right? Especially so early in the morning."

"No, I can see it's important."

"It is important, and it's real tiring, a real pain, because no way, no *way* I can allow any hack to be helping off an inmate, or maybe killing the guy himself. I allow that, those administration people—over a lot of years, maybe—sure as hell goin' to start dealing with inmates that way as a matter of routine. As a matter of routine." Still gripping Bauman's bars, Nash slowly straightened his arms and leaned back away from the door at a considerable angle, swinging slowly from side to side like a bored child playing at a schoolyard fence. "It's just human nature to take advantage of the easy way. I learned that, if I learned anything. Go the easy way all the time. Inmate gives 'em trouble, they'll just off him. Oh, not always, not yet, but after a while, in a few more years, when they get used to it. Doesn't that sound likely to you, the way an administrative structure would behave if offing people became a sort of accustomed thing?"

"It's possible," Bauman said, "—given time. Solution to overcrowding, troublemakers. Still, it would always have to be *sub rosa*—done secretly." He stopped talking. Apparently only an appeal to his vanity, his lapsed venue as teacher, was required for him to forget to keep his mouth shut. Bauman was surprised at his own childishness, revealed so painfully by these confrontations. Last night, and now. And of course with Bobby Basket, too. It seemed impossible he'd been such an ass out on the street. Improbable, at least. —Of course, he hadn't been so frightened there. Not this frightened, at any rate.

" '*Sub rosa.*' " Nash apparently liked the sound of the phrase. As if on that cue, he pulled himself upright again to stand against the bars. "O.K., you agree with me it's possible," he said as conclusively as that Kansas country attorney might have, having led his reluctant witness to an inescapable conclusion. "And in my opinion, more likely probable. No way can we let this go by.

"Now, there's something I'm goin' to bring up," Nash said, his voice, pitched at that penetrating tenor, still very low in volume, "—and pretty embarrassing for both of us. So I'm only goin' to mention it just this once, strictly between you and me. I never, never, never talk about a man's personal problems behind his back. For me, that's a real no-no. What I have to say, I say to his face." Nash paused, seemed expectant, and Bauman nodded to show he understood and believed in Nash's observation of that nicety. "Anyway, get it over with, it's pretty sad to hear the way I heard last night, you were beating your meat. Because not only is that a real waste of spinal energy—if you believe in that stuff—it's also a major bummer for anybody up here hearing you to realize you don't have any more pride than that—letting a little time, letting the administration turn you into a creepo."

Schoolmasterish, Nash waggled a long pale right forefinger between the bars. "Things like that—losing your pride, letting 'em turn a distinguished guy like you into a dirty-minded little kid—something like that hurts everybody on the block, makes everybody feel bad about themselves, this situation we have here. So do yourself a favor, and cut that behavior out."

Bauman imagined himself standing a distance away, somewhere down the corridor watching Nash against a house's bars, talking to a prisoner. From where Bauman was standing, he couldn't see the prisoner at all.

"That kind of behavior may be acceptable out in population," Nash said very seriously, "—but it don't go in here at all, unless you want to room down in P.C. with the trash. You're an educated guy, and I know you understand my explanation on this, why it's important. —Now, I won't ever bring that up again, and we can forget I had to mention it at all. O.K.?" And on that, apparently relieved to have the subject over, he smiled, leaned over to his left to call, "O.K., Carl," then gestured a graceful goodbye and strolled away out of sight to

Bauman's right, apparently toward what had interested him before.

Sitting on his thin mattress, facing a white steel wall, Bauman wished profoundly to be anywhere else. Wished he hadn't masturbated for that murderer's ear, revealing himself entirely. He imagined Nash lying still and silent in near dark, listening with amused contempt to the professor's busy fist. On the other hand, Nash hadn't mentioned the long shower again, hadn't made it necessary to consider that absurd drama with Grace Hilliard, her cop, and treacherous Gorney. It didn't bear thinking of. Five years more? Six years more? But the role of informer—the cowardly teacher eavesdropping, reporting, betraying his students, even (especially) these sad troglodytes—also did not bear thinking of.

He stood up, left shoulder still sore, took the two steps to his toilet, unbuttoned, and enjoying the distraction of pissing, decided not to think of it at all, decided to wait for whatever circumstance would permit no more waiting.

He was buttoning the jumpsuit's fly when some shift in the quality of light through his door's bars caused him to turn his head to look.

Pete Nash, returned, stood facing the corridor wall opposite, the pale, tendoned back of his long neck revealed by his short haircut. He bent, picked something up from the floor, and began to print in large block letters, smeared brown on white plaster, WELCOME PROF. Then seemed to run out of color. Nash stepped to the left and bent to pick up another small lump of excrement, then went back to the wall and resumed to completion. BAUMAN.

Finished, Nash wiped his hands on the trouser legs of his orange jumpsuit, turned, smiled at Bauman, then strolled away again to the right and out of sight, to no acknowledgment, no remark, no laughter from any house, to no sound at all but his footsteps.

After a short uneasy nap—as if last evening's weariness had been too profound for one night's sleep's recovery—Bauman woke and passed what seemed to be several hours, must have been several hours (impossible to be certain, his Rolex keeping its fabulous time in some desk drawer's dark). He saw no one, heard nothing through his narrow door of bars, only observed the sunlight's slow slight variations through the warp of the glass bricks inset high along the corridor's opposite wall. This became an enjoyable occupation, paced slow as evolution, and after a while he was able, as Newton had, to find soft rainbows refracting through the glass, though these were disordered, not neatly prismed out. He imagined himself in this small house, alone except for Nash, for several months. For years, for a decade or two. What strange Bauman would be sent for by the new warden? What strange Bauman would appear in the new warden's office? A bestial saint of some sort, possibly, educated very nicely as to the nature of time and time's changes. And so a wonderful historian at last, if not judged too old, too odd, too dangerous even for two-year colleges.

In those decades together—Nash wandering up and down the corridor on endless visits with no one, Bauman always stabled in his house, always certain of his own company—they would watch each other growing old. This equilibrium only broken if Bauman came too near the bars in conversation one afternoon in their seventh year, or seventeenth, so that Nash was able to loop a length of twine fashioned from frayed cloth around his neck, or drive a hoarded pencil, beautifully sharpened on cement, into Bauman's throat while discussing dinosaurs—whether they were warm-blooded or not, whether they lumbered or flew at a gallop, whether they cared for their young—so assuring for himself a perfect solitude.

For these morning hours Bauman felt he had little to complain of, except the lack of breakfast, the scent of shit sharp as cheese gone rotten-ripe.

He had, after all, considerable peace, almost privacy. And silence too, for which he would have paid street money any time in the last year—relief from those TV's and tape decks, the tumultuous, grating, slamming noises the other inmates had grown up with as music, the shouts as conversation with which they felt at ease. Whereas here—if not for the smell and no breakfast, if not for Nash, if not for that incident in the showers—there seemed almost nothing to complain of.

He did notice the extreme smallness of his cell. Remarkably narrow. He could touch either wall, standing, spreading his arms out to the side—could almost rest his palms flat against those opposites. White-painted steel. What was worse, he could touch the cell's ceiling, too, though only with his fingertips. The lighting fixture was a single small bulb, the whole assembly recessed into a sort of shallow steel dish above a thick disk of Plexiglas or something like it, preventing his reaching in, touching it.

A man, Bauman supposed, who'd spent ten or fifteen years in this close house would probably one morning ask the hacks, for the very first time, to please unlock the door, please rack it back, please allow him only the shortest walk outside the building, or if not that, then only a few minutes block-out in the corridor, so he might see something he hadn't seen so many times before, might reassure himself other things were there. A man who asked that sort of favor and was refused it, might after all decide to travel by bracing himself between his small house's wall and concrete platform—then, contorting in terrific effort, slamming his head down into the platform's edge several times, listening amid the dull internal sounds of impact for the cracking noise of something breaking for his journey.

A man so obsessed with travel might also roll his thin mattress for a step and, gripping one of the bars, reach up to shove a wet finger into the socket of any fixture not guarded by Plexiglas, or whatever, in reasonable precaution.

Bauman, depressed, no longer as pleased by peace, by privacy and quiet, was still relieved in contemplation of his single week. One week locked down. No question he could do that standing on his head, as half-mad old convicts talked of taking ten, fifteen years, doing those times standing on their heads.

Bauman, as an experiment, tried a change in relative perspective to enlarge his house. Seated on his platform, he imagined this narrow space expanded miles in size, grown to a light-shattering canyon, its walls become cliffs—sheer, smooth, storm-washed white as paint and immensely high—its close ceiling exploded away into a vault of sun-bleached sky. The toilet distanced to an odd feature miles away—gigantic, wind-carved and water-sculpted into that comedic figure writ large. And he a tired climber perched on this infinitesimal ledge, weary, worried about the long climb down and uncertain of its route, staring out across a whistling vacancy through which high winds blew constant crosscurrents ruffling, strumming, buffeting. A climber who, wishing at once to wait for dark to make this day's descent impossible, and dreading even more the night to be spent blind, so meagerly supported, thrust out into black and empty air, would have been happy to have traded all his sense superior for a bluejay's wings. Would trade the majesty of this humming gulf at once, for imprisonment.

This lasted pretty well—and after all, seen by a fly on the wall, the space would have looked just so—but Bauman's legs, their size, their easy reach down to the floor, the awkward looseness of his laceless shoes, kept shrinking his canyon to a cell. And when he sat for a while with his legs tucked up on the platform, he found himself then distracted by the toilet, which looked like nothing else after all, far or near, wind-worn or not.

He lay down on his right side and closed his eyes. Eyes closed, he might have been anywhere. The cell, not seen, not tried against, was good as gone. He might be anywhere. . . .

After a while, Bauman opened his eyes thinking of a spun cocoon, a winding twirl of silver silk he might spin about himself by reciting some spell, spitting out magical saliva, or giving up sperm into pearl-silver threads that wound around and around him while he stood in the cell naked, turning, spinning like a skater until he was enclosed completely. Then he would see and hear but wouldn't need to move—encased by material so unbreachable, though soft as warm water, that the cell became as entirely beside the point as the larger prison, and the prison as pointless as the containing state, the containing nation, and those successive envelopes pointless as all the universe, while he lay safe and free within them.

This notion lasted, he was sure, till noon, then, outworn, left him contemplating the brute fact of bars that so effectively prevented even a walk down the corridor. Perhaps instead, a walk up the corridor to see what had interested Nash. It seemed nonsensical that so coarse a structure could prevent him; surely there must be—though so many so desperately had sought it—must be some astoundingly simple means of passing through or by so primitive a barrier. A simple means not simple enough for man, as a closed door remained impenetrable to even the cleverest dog, for whom the concept of latch was deep metaphysics, unfathomable.

It was possible, of course, to simply change one's point of view, so that the space enclosed by his cell was "out," and the corridor and larger prison and all the world were labeled "in." Whichever, he was being denied entrance, transition to the more spacious territory. It was passage being denied him. He wished to pass through, and State was preventing it.

The relationship of this being-held-static to Karen Silber's death and his two or three martinis, seemed very odd. He didn't consider it lying to have omitted one of his three martinis in recounting that evening. The fact of sobriety was there, his knowledge of it so casually certain it would have presented a very false picture if he'd said, 'I had three drinks that evening, but none of them were doubles.' That would not only have sounded bad, it would have given an absolutely incorrect impression. It would have been a lie-in-effect, as if three moderate martinis must make for drunkenness, criminal responsibility—and that assumed, lead to imprisonment's brutal logic, forcing the killer to emulate (by stillness, solitude, and slow rot) the instances of death.

"You cocksucker. You murdering cocksucker!" had been her father's first response, teary with rage at Bauman's telephoned common sense. A response which had impressed Bauman at the time with its directly sexual nature, possibly the mourning shambles of an attraction Silber had felt for his sturdy daughter, her strong smooth-muscled legs, her tousled dark blond hair, cut short. Bauman could have said something to that point, but hadn't. Even now, perhaps as the result of such reticences through several months of occasional conversation, nothing was settled; Bauman knew Silber still blamed him. Had to blame someone—anything less horrific than casual mischance to have crushed his daughter like a bug, a screaming bug, its insides out. An exit that mimicked in its wet, its bulging mess, the girl's entrance thirteen years before, as her cries must have imitated with reasonable fidelity her mother's shriek as Karen, fat baby cauled in red, tore free.

Bauman was getting hungry, and deeply regretted he hadn't at least a Bit-O'-Honey candy bar. Or if not a candy bar, then some salted peanuts. Even Jell-O would be acceptable, anything but lime. There was nothing in the state's regulations which permitted State to stop serving food. Especially to someone railroaded in, railroaded up here, who hadn't tossed manure at anyone.

Wishing he had his watch, Bauman lay back on his stern mattress and performed several sit-ups, careful to keep his knees bent, feet planted as firmly as the laceless running shoes allowed. When he finished twenty-four sit-ups, finding his abdomen already slightly sore, he stopped and lay still, trying to relax. It seemed to him the block was being kept too hot, smothering, even besides the smell of sewage. The air was warm enough to be difficult to breathe. Not helped by the smallness of the cell. . . . Bauman saw himself collapsing into panic, commencing to screech and whinny, struggling with his door's bars, trying to beat his way past them or, if that hurt too much, trying to wriggle through. Even if he got stuck, jammed in between, at least his arms would be out, one of his legs might be out into the corridor, kicking, stepping a repeated step in air while he made his sounds.

There was all the difference in the world between B-block and this. The constant noise, mingling music, and general uproar made a great deal of difference, and, of course, knowing you were getting out after lock-'n'-count. Out for sure. Scooter also made a great deal of difference, as if the mysteries of another human presence provided physical space as well. People and their noise made all the difference in the world.

"Can't live with 'em, can't live without 'em," Bauman said, lay back and closed his eyes, imagining himself away, recalling (from a summer four summers before) those long rolling hills covered in grass the shade of shade that swelled and sank alongside the Columbia as it flowed toward its own great constraining wall at Grand Coulee. Such marvelous space. A man out alone in that wide country—even in winter—trudging through snow that numbed his legs to the knee, through gusts of hissing sleet blinding him as they blew by, reversed, and came again, still was a lucky son of a bitch. Bauman imagined himself walking in such weather, severe enough to concern him despite his boots, his warm wool pants, shirt, sweater, a canvas jacket to shed the dashes of sleet. They bounced off like tiny tennis balls, away into the feathered tips and clusters of black grass just showing above the sheer white sheets of snow drifted deeper between the hills.

Bauman imagined he walked over that surface, felt it crackle and give to dents beneath his boots, smelled the sharp light odor of cold, then was staggered by a fiercer wind come booming over the hills, come spanking between the hills to shift more snow and gather sleet to crack him backhand across the face. This wind was blowing the night in, bright grays unfolding to deeper grays, to deeper than that, and dark. Stupid to freeze to death wandering blind past the cabin and his waiting wife—how sad for Beth to have a husband revealed a fatal ass, a show-off ending in a chill black-frosted lump nearly concealed within a drift of white—tufts of its dark hair still stirring in concert with the prairie grass when the wind blew back—its jacket, torn at the only surfaced shoulder, revealing where a coyote had nibbled an icy bite or two away. This frozen fool to be nudged in two months by a dimly curious steer, and discovered at last weeks later when a fence fixer jeeped that way, saw small birds seeking spring suet there.

Bauman wondered if he would choose any warmth and safety over this—a too-late start in furious weather over wide country he didn't know. Freezing's searing pain at his face, his hands, his feet—turning later to no-feeling, to touching wood with wood. Bauman wondered if a jail cell might be preferred—a small snug temporary cell to which dangerous and interesting creatures were free to come, and in which, in warmth and surrounding company, even questions of courage, of honor might be considered. He wondered if this might not be preferable to freezing.

This fantasy worked fairly well as long as Bauman's eyes were closed, and continued to give some comfort even when he opened them to his narrow house, admitted the stink and smothering air. But it didn't seem possible to maintain imaginings that elaborate, exhausting, for only half an hour's relief. A horse's acceptance was what was required, to whom the stall was a mystery not worth unraveling.

Even so, the first voices he heard—after another hour? two hours?—were resented. Footsteps with them, and a familiar squealing sound coming from his left, the block gate, into his solitude. Some crowd coming to annoy him. He would certainly have welcomed the interruption in a while—but not yet, while he was learning to be alone.

After some moments of listening he stood up, went to his bars, and was able to watch at an acute left angle as three men came into view—first a young black hack he didn't know, then, following, two inmates in population blue denims. The first convict towed a big rolling mop bucket, the squealing of its small wheels familiar from Housekeeping days. The other lugged two mops, a plastic gallon container—likely ammonia, a stack of newspapers, a yellow plastic dustpan, and a large white-plastic garbage bag. —It was Margaret the Maid hauling the big bucket along, Bauman as pleased to see him as if that mournful fat gap-toothed gossip (straight despite his nickname) were the dearest friend come calling. The other con was Enrique, the boxing team's gofer (scrawny, bustling, busy and forgetful).

Both men looked slightly larger than Bauman remembered them, had almost a bright halation at their edges, like Irish heroes come to fight. As if he'd seen no one, been deprived of any human company for years, Bauman noticed at once many small specifics in their faces, many shades of difference in the background colors of each man's skin, in the cerulean variations making up their denims' united blue. Their walking seemed to him almost dancing.

"Listen up! —Listen up!" The young black hack had stopped, was calling into the silence and watery glass-filtered sunlight as if the air's stench was an uproar needing to be shouted over. The hack was a large man, looked fairly strong.

All three had stopped while the young hack called, a dollop of soapy water sloshing out of Margaret's big bucket at the halt.

"You assholes better listen! We got some people here to clean this shit up. An' if you people do this again—make this kind of mess—the A.W. says O.K. to bring in the fire hoses an' clean it up for you. A.W. says O.K. to hose your asses right down the fuckin' drains, cause of dangerously unhealthy conditions. Michaelson says O.K., too!"

Silence.

Bauman had met Ron Michaelson—one of four local doctors on call at the infirmary—had met him the first time old Cooper sent him over there to mop and wax. Michaelson, a bulky orthopedist with severe acne scars, apparently taking Bauman for one of the civilized and knowledgeable elite, though sadly fallen, had complained to him at length about primitive conditions at the infirmary, about what he was required to put up with. Bauman, work interrupted, had leaned on his silent waxer and commiserated—momentarily one of superior two.

"*No problem.*" This reply in his neighbor's clear tenor, after that pause for effect, came from the immediate left, Nash apparently locked down again after his morning hour block-out. And while Bauman watched, a short stumpy-legged convict with a shaved head came ambling down the corridor from the right, and into view. "No problem." Nash's voice projected like an actor's. "—Mr. Parris and I have come to a rare agreement." The shaven-headed man, his pug face and scalp pale enough to show stubble dark as sprinkled pepper, strolled on by Bauman's house, silent.

Bauman had heard of Buddy Parris from Schoonover; this prison radical and revolutionary a special favorite of the librarian's for his support, for clever briefs submitted in argument for convicts' freedom to read anything they chose. Ironic, Bauman thought, now having seen the men, that Peter Nash—a dark lord—looked and spoke so well, while Parris, self-taught socialist, Wobbly born too late, was the image of a shambling convict brute.

Parris, when he'd gone walking by, had barely glanced at Bauman—a time snob apparently, requiring a man to be serving life or near it to be worth talking to. Give Nash credit for more political instincts, probably contacting all and everyone for whatever use they might be to him in whatever future.

His announcement made, the black hack had turned to walk back down the corridor, was out of Bauman's angle of vision in a moment, and Margaret and Enrique, towing and burdened, came on, Margaret neatly wheeling the big bucket clear of a turd that lay in its path.

They came up the corridor to Bauman's house and paused there, at the bars. Enrique handed Margaret the mop, dropped his stack of newspapers and his plastic bag, then took the top off the ammonia and stepped to one of the two nearest offenses to splash it lightly. Margaret dunked his mop deep in the bucket's suds, thrashed it while he muttered, just loud enough, "Man, is old Cooper pissed off at you. Got three weeks before the big fight of the season—the Joliet fight—an' you get your ass stuck in here. . . ."

"Tell him I'm sorry for the inconvenience," Bauman said, quietly as he could. "Tell him I've worked Tony on the speed bag " ('Tony' being Anthony Marcantonio, cruiser-weight and white hope). "I've worked him and he's actually got some hand rhythm going. Still can't move his legs much, still crummy with the rope. Man simply can't pick up those feet."

"You hit like that wop, you don' need an' move your fuckin' feet." Enrique, brandishing his dustpan, squatted before his chosen mess, splashed it again with the ammonia, scooped up what he could with his dustpan, transferred it to a wad of newspaper, then swiveled, still squatting, to stuff that into his big white-plastic bag. "Cooper like' that puttin' ol' Bobby on fire," Enrique murmured as he stuffed. "—Say you actin' like a convict, anyway. Say keep that shit up, you goin' belong here! He like that shit, man."

"What the hell do you know?" Margaret said softly to his partner, and bent to wring out his mop. "No way is the old man happy, never mind what he said. Team comes first. Old man's really pissed off; he's not goin' to send us over here to clean up any more of these people's crap, either. 'This is the last time,' is what he said. 'Do that again, they can damn well live in it.' "

"Hey! —*Hey!* You people talkin' up there?" The black hack's voice. He hadn't left the corridor.

"No, man, we ain' sayin' shit!" Enrique, standing to go to a second chore.

"Well, stop that talkin' and do your goddamn work!"

"O.K., O.K.!" Margaret, having called obedience, stooped to reach into his bucket, brought a small flat package up out of the suds, dropped it to the floor, smacked his sopping mophead over it—and in a casual mopping motion sent the package sliding neatly under Bauman's bars. Then shoved his big bucket squealing farther along. Enrique, finished with the second pile, stuffed his plastic bag with soiled newspaper, winked goodbye, and trotted after.

Bauman, heart thumping, anticipatory as a child at Christmas, kicked the small package (black plastic wrapping, glistening wet) behind him, stepped back away from the bars, picked the package up and tucked it underneath his thin foam mattress. It made a very visible bump.

Bauman tried to imagine what might be in it—food, probably food. He went to his bars, put his face against them, and looked left down the corridor. He saw no one there, the hack apparently too far down, at too acute an angle to be seen. Up the corridor to the right, only Margaret's back as he mopped, Enrique's as he stooped, scraping.

Bauman stepped back, took the package from under his mattress and picked at the wrapping, sealed with electrician's tape, until a corner came loose enough for him to bite at, then tear and tug away. He put the package down on his mattress and opened it.

Two Bit-O'-Honey candy bars; three sticks of pot; seven Blue Tip wooden matches; five Oreo cookies separately wrapped in a page torn from an issue of *Elle* (those certainly from Betty Nellis); and something folded in a sheet of yellow legal-pad paper.

Bauman sat on his mattress, unfolded the paper, and found writing on the inside of the sheet—and a watch.

> Dear Charles,
>
> Herewith a beforehand Christmas present, of course not as elegant as the one taken from you, and not, perhaps, the most wholesome gift for a prisoner. Still, if you must keep track of every moment lost in this wilderness, I suppose you must.
>
> See you in a week.
>
> Very truly yours,
>
> Byblos
>
> P.S. Has it occurred to you, Charles, that you may be acclimating all too well to this durance vile?

Byblos was Schoonover's *nom de plume*. The watch was one Bauman had seen on sale at the canteen—the most expensive they stocked, he supposed. Twenty-five, thirty dollars, scrip. A princely gift, expressive of Schoonover's loneliness, outcast by outcasts. A Timex Triathlon digital, odd-looking, displaying the correct date above, We 11 19, and (meticulous Schoonover) the certainly correct time below, 1:51.06 . . . 07 . . . 08, its semicircular face resting on a squared base presenting two small gray rectangular buttons. The watch was encrusted with buttons—the two gray at its base, one orange on its left side, and two black on the other. Folded with it, a small sheet of instructions promised many ways to mark and arrange the passing of time. More manipulations than the beautiful Rolex could accomplish, and in a form unanalog, so odd, light, and flat, so different from the Swiss watch there seemed no point in comparing them, no reason to be disappointed, no need to feel disloyal to the Rolex, put away in a drawer somewhere. That heavy watch, after all, had scarred Bauman's cheek. And there seemed to be many things this watch could do—sound an alarm or an hourly chime as reminder; time laps, an obscure procedure by the instructions for it; display the twenty-four-hour system; count down a measure of minutes; and probably keep by printed circuit a time as precise as the Rolex's fine machinery was able to. Perhaps more precise.

Bauman put Schoonover's note and the instructions down, strapped the watch to his left wrist—it was much, much lighter than the Rolex—

and ate one of the Oreos. Then he ate another one. He wrapped the last three Oreos in their page from *Elle*, on one side of which a sketched woman, achingly slim in charcoal, hair up, her stance spread-legged, hands on hips, displayed a slender suit, its material drawn as fine cross-hatching representing tweed. The other side of the page contained the listing of the magazine's editorial staff. A long list. Bauman imagined them—women in the magazine's New York headquarters, their subdued chatter of business conversation, their passing back and forth from office to office, pacing down hallways on production errands, editorial errands, all dressed for business, appearing sufficiently elegant in the morning, less so as the day wore on. Their offices redolent by afternoon of a dozen scents, powders, a trace of perspiration (from tension, not exercise)—and on certain days, in near concert for three or four, the faintest odors of spoiled blood.

And what if a middle-aged convict were magically transported to them? If this creature, rather short, stocky, his hair beginning to gray, were found lying on the hall carpeting, gaudy in his bright orange jumpsuit, the suit might start some minor fashion flash. Convict blaze-orange—modeled for *Elle* by a distinguished felon, erstwhile almost expert on tribal politics extant in Periclean Athens; on Sassanian herd and livestock taxes; on Trajan's campaigns and the tradition of Roman arms.

Bauman imagined himself appearing in those offices and becoming, over several complex weeks, these women's protected toy and mascot, concealed from all outsiders, concealed from all the magazine's males excepting only two fashion photographers, and expected to lie in the mailroom closet with each woman in her turn (descending in office hierarchy). He would become at last an aging Pan, an office Lar, a ready object upon which any of the editorial staff—suit jacket and skirt off and neatly folded on a carton of computer paper, half-slip hiked, panty hose rolled down and tossed aside—might sweat away her resentment of age or plainness or fat, or a love affair or marriage too miserable or too tediously comfortable to be borne.

After a year or so, Bauman supposed, he'd be too worn to be useful—would be fed several slices of take-out pizza with diet Coke at a celebration office lunch, then be danced by the women out into the hall and down it, to be tossed out that window blaze-orange into daylight, with the bright busy street so far below.

Bauman folded up his package and slid it under the mattress again. He decided to wait until tomorrow to eat the first Bit-O'-Honey, have another Oreo then. Have the fourth Oreo and half the last Bit-O'-

Honey the day after that. Save the other half of the Bit-O'-Honey and the fifth Oreo for the day after that.

Examining his new watch—very fond of Schoonover for it, sad for the madman's loneliness—Bauman thought of instructing the Timex to sound its alarm for each occasion for eating cookies and candy, and perused the instructions, dense in small type and diagrams, to arrange it.

However, he grew too hungry before he'd worked out the programming, so stopped pushing the watch's small buttons, rolled over to reach beneath his mattress for the package, unwrapped it again, and ate one of the three Oreos. Then, rather than have another Oreo at once, and so spoil the singularity of the cookie's taste, he unwrapped and ate a whole Bit-O'-Honey bar.

When he'd lain still on his back for quite a while, left wrist held up, watching the Timex's seconds parade, one more cookie seemed appropriate. And a few minutes after that, the second Bit-O'-Honey appeared too remnant to struggle to keep.

The last Oreo was eaten in celebration of all the rest.

Alert by sugar, Bauman got up and went to stand at his bars to watch Margaret and Enrique finishing their task—scooping, scraping, sprinkling, mopping it all away. They scrubbed his name off the opposite wall. He watched them up the corridor until they left his angle of vision—had observed them, according to his new watch, for thirty-seven minutes and either nine or eleven seconds, he wasn't sure which.

Later, they came trundling their bucket back down into his line of sight, waved cheerily as they went by, and resumed their cleanup near the block gate, slowly scrubbing out of his view. Twenty-nine minutes and thirteen seconds later, finished, they left. Bauman heard the big gate's small relief door swing open, hinges faintly moaning, pause, then moan again and hammer shut.

In the silence following that iron close, Bauman thought he heard, then was certain he heard a sound new to him. It was the lightest constantly modulating whisper, thin, twisting, continuous as a length of picture wire laced up and down the block, pervasive, sounding on the verge of conversation or music. Standing at his bars, Bauman held his head cocked like a listening dog's to present his best ear, apparently his left.

The whispering, with which whispering music was sometimes woven, resolved itself, and he realized the men—their protest and its perfect silence over, their waste washed off the block—were listening to earphoned radios, only traces of sound escaping into the air.

He stood at his bars attending to this softest noise for a while longer, then went to his mattress platform and lay down, examined his new watch, observing the seconds trooping on its face, then turned on his side and slid into a sleep too shallow for dreaming.

He was wakened at five twenty-three by the thud and rattle of what, after a short wait by the bars, he saw was a heavy burnished stainless-steel cart, its racks loaded with small tinsel-colored trays.

The hack, Tanner, his khaki uniform slightly wrinkled, pale round face petulant as an owl's, was shoving the cart along. He stopped and stooped to slide one of the narrow trays under the bars of a house two houses down, stood to push the cart another length, stooped to slide Nash his dinner, then came on to Bauman's and did the same, before shoving on along to Carl Whoever's and beyond.

Aluminum-colored paper, not really foil, was stretched over three small sticky heaps on the cardboard tray. The yellowish-white was certainly chicken, creamed chicken or something like it. The green heap, string beans. The last, a dull-orange portion, was either cooked carrot rounds or sweet potatoes sliced the same way.

On the tray's right side rested a half-pint carton of milk. With it a frail white-plastic short-handled spoon, the front of its small bowl carved into four blunt teeth—a spork. A folded white paper napkin lay under it.

Bauman sat on his platform, this meager dinner on his lap, and tasting the colors in turn, found the creamed chicken edible, though smelling of lighter fluid or something like lighter fluid. The string beans tasted too odd to eat. The sweet potato rounds—they were sweet potato—were not bad at all. They had a toasted caramel taste, really good.

Once the sweet potatoes were gone, he pictured some kind cook in the midst of a food factory's steam and stench, producing for jails, for State, for the grimmer hospitals, asylums, a school for the untrainable mentally retarded, all places with dark green or dark yellow corridors, bars, heavy mesh, glass resistant to any effort—imagined this kind cook able to prepare only the sweet potatoes as he wished in these five thousand institutional feedings, a forlorn token of his talent, a gift for those lost ones, their unkissed mouths.

Affected by this conceit, Bauman, to his amusement, wept a few tears of self-pity, salting several inedible string beans. Finished with what he could eat, the milk drunk, he didn't know whether to keep the tray until it was called for, or slide it out under his door bars for pickup, so he compromised, stooped, and placed it just under the door's bottom member (a narrow, flat steel strip) but not so far under as to intrude it into the corridor.

Some of the block's lights had come on, these—sulfur yellow beams from oval armored sockets in the corridor's high ceiling—apparently uninjured in yesterday's action. As he watched the paler daylight mingle then fade into this fiercer, more directed glare, it occurred to Bauman that Segregation, especially when silent, was the heart of State—the penitentiary's main blocks and noisy workshops only anterooms, purgatories, having in their tumult, trade, their myriad relationships, more to do with the outside than the in.

Forty-one minutes by Timex after he'd finished eating, placed his tray down, he heard the crash and clack, the rumbling as some cell doors slid open. Heard conversations commencing just after that, as the prisoners scheduled for evening block-out—this group, for various good reasons, separated for their exercise from those freed in the morning—began to call out to friends, to speak among themselves, in one or two cases sounding cheerful.

Bauman, who'd been so lonely that Maid Margaret and Enrique had appeared haloed demigods strolling down the block, now grew shy. Mindful of the ways by which his neighbors had earned their exiles, mindful of Nash in particular, though that convict seemed to be loosed in mornings only, he lay down on his mattress and pretended to doze—then thought that transparent, unconvincing, and instead began to study his new watch's instructions, trying to discover what sequence of buttons must be pushed to time a lap.

"How're you makin' it?"

Bauman looked up from his instructions and saw a slight fat-faced young man in Seg's bright jumpsuit standing at his bars—a boy no older than Scooter, with muddy brown eyes, long oily black hair, and a ragged beard. The boy wore earrings made from pop-top tabs, and had at some time lost a serious fight, part of his upper lip having been torn away so his left incisor and some gum stayed visible even when his mouth was closed.

"Carl Sorenson," the boy said, and held his hand in through the bars.

It took Bauman a moment to realize this must be his next-door neighbor to the right, the selectively deafened Carl. He put down the Timex instructions, stood up and stepped to the bars to shake the boy's hand. Carl Sorenson's hand was dirty, thin as a girl's, but wire strong. The boy stood almost an inch shorter than Bauman.

"Going O.K.," Bauman said. "Just in for a week."

"Shit, I know that." Carl Sorenson had a harsh back-of-the-throat accent, was probably from Chicago or Kansas City. "I know who you are. Call you 'Teach,' right?"

"That's right."

"Was wonderin' what was goin' on with Henry's hand. Big nigger goin' to fight?"

"Damn right he is," Bauman said. "There's nothing wrong with Clarence Henry's hand."

Young Sorenson considered that for a few moments, then nodded. He had a rank odor about him, sharp as used Kitty Litter. Bauman would have been happier knowing why this boy was in Seg. In the population such information was rarely vital, except in the case of killers; on this block, matters stood otherwise.

"Well, how you doin'?" the boy said, as if he hadn't asked before.

"Fine."

"O.K." The boy held his thin hand through the bars again, and Bauman shook it. Then Sorenson nodded and strolled away to join two other men, both white, both older, leaning against the corridor wall farther down, toward the gate. One of these men was huge—had a bloodhound's mournfully drawn-down face, and sported an NCO's haircut, cropped close on top, shaved clean at sides and back. This man was even bigger, it seemed to Bauman, than Perteet the biker, and Perteet stood six feet six inches tall, weighed two hundred and ninety pounds.

This big man glanced up as Bauman looked at him, and stared back directly, black eyes small in a pale massive face (bits of coal stuck in a snowman's head). The giant smiled at Bauman, then his heavy lips pursed in a slow exaggerated kiss.

Bauman gave this man the finger, wished at once he hadn't been so hasty, then was greatly relieved as the creature, apparently not offended, smiled again and turned back to his friends' conversation. The reflex of aggressive reaction, State's primary code of conduct, proved again.

Heart thumping, Bauman went back to his platform, lay down, took his pulse and found it rapid, then resumed studying how to time a lap.

He supposed Susanne would come up on Saturday as planned and would be disappointed—though perhaps not greatly disappointed to be missing the posturing of a man attempting to maintain his balance on a wire too slender and strung too high for him. He doubted, for example—if he decided to tell her—doubted Susanne would take that shower-room threat very seriously. "Why in the world don't you call Bob Christiansen? I'll call him. Those people can't get away with that!" And saying so, or its equivalent, might even be right—and he the booby, misunderstanding this world, taking its grotesqueries seriously.

He imagined—as he told her of Spencer's death, his trouble with the attorney general's people, how accidental his own relationship to that—imagined Susanne's face slowly draped with another and final veil of fatigue, contempt, and disappointment, seeing her harsh insistent lover, her notable scholar, resolving more and more clearly into a whining fool, primed for any catastrophe, any mischance, insecure from these even under lock and key.

After which, out of pity, Susanne—dressed in a red long-sleeved blouse, dark pleated skirt, boots—might go into the visitors' toilet with him, some convict standing guard in return for the pleasure of listening.

Bauman thought he'd already demonstrated too much to her on her visits—pretending to be tough, and looking older, shorter, unluckier, more cowardly with every pose he struck. This last ill luck—commencing at a lunch with the sniveling Spencer protesting his innocence, a lunch concerning the most minor business relationship with an idiot about to get himself killed (probably for some profoundly uninteresting reason)—this last ill luck he might manage to keep to himself. If Bob Christiansen needed to be called, he would call him. Presuming Christiansen could be of use. The man he should talk to was Les Kerwin; the *pro pers* was exactly the man he should talk to, certainly knew more prison law, release law and so forth than a fucking divorce attorney who'd needed a trial lawyer's help even to lose a case, send his client up here for years. . . .

Kerwin, of course, now an enemy, and perhaps dangerous, pointed wire in the eyes and so forth. At the saving of what? *Amour propre?* A fee of twenty-five dollars, scrip? That had been very well done, very intelligent.

Of course, Ms. Hilliard might also have played her game with one or two other inmates—probably had. Probably had arranged with Gorney for a private audience in one of the supply rooms, or the furniture factory, or Administration, or over at the gym, wherever. Handed these inmates—chosen from the out-of-place, the cowardly, the fresh fish, the talkative—the same hard line she'd handed him, then sent them on their way and waited to see which one came sweating, squealing. It might be perfectly possible for him to tell them nothing—or anything—play along on gossip and maybes and I'm-not-sures until they got tired of it. If he did that—and it might not be the best thing to do, probably wasn't the best thing to do—he'd have to be very careful not to involve some inmate by accident, just running off at the mouth. The traditional response, of course, was no response at all. Centuries of convict wisdom recommended that.

An inmate laughed in the corridor, and Bauman, lying on his side staring at the cell wall's changeless slight imperfections rather than his new watch's restless face, was annoyed with himself for considering that shower-room farce after all, for worrying about it, when he'd already decided not to. The convict laughed again, and Bauman found that now there was noise and company on the block, he longed for the loneliness he'd possessed before, with only his own company to bear.

A buzzer woke the block next morning, its harsh raspberry lasting longer than necessary. Bauman lay for a few moments trying to recall his dream—something about a forest, an animal of some kind. Then he stretched on his slight mattress and sat up feeling fairly well, interested in what the day might bring. It already presented the background sibilance of earphoned radios, and a quiet conversation down to the left, nearer the block gate.

He stood, unzipped his jumpsuit, worked his arms free, pushed the material down his legs, and stepped out of it. Naked, he took two steps to his toilet and sat down on the chilly porcelain. He'd noticed, as he grew older, a tendency to sit for both his functions, wanting the rest, he supposed, a standing piss no longer provided.

His seating successful, after a wait, he wiped himself with State's harsh toilet paper, then stood, flushed, and washed his hands at the single faucet on the wall above the toilet—cold water running through his hands down into the toilet bowl.

He splashed handfuls of water—one under his left arm, one under his right—then bent to a double handful, rinsed his face, combed wet fingers through his hair.

He saw the mirror, a small bright rectangle fit for a woman's purse, while he was drying himself with his jumpsuit. The mirror, placed certainly by Nash or a friend of Nash's just inside his bars, lay flat on the gray steel decking, reflecting a tiny image of white bars ascending into morning light.

Bauman wriggled into the damp coverall, zipped it closed, then stooped to pick the snitch-mirror up. He held it out through his bars—through the center course, above the flat tie-band running across at chest height. What he saw was so small as to need interpretation—certainly, to the left, the big gate at the end of the block . . . and something moving, wagging up and down as he tried to tilt the mirror for better viewing.

One of the things wrong was he was holding it too far out from the bars, almost at arm's length. Made the reflection too small. Bauman bent his elbow, brought the mirror near, and bumped his forehead on the bars trying to see better. "Take your time," he said aloud, and recognized the temptation to be constantly talking to himself, keeping himself company. A tendency bound sooner or later to lead to self-comment, then self-criticism, then argument with himself—and finally to an injured silence even lonelier than the quiet before.

Waggling the small mirror slightly from side to side, Bauman suddenly saw his own reflection, startlingly close. A middle-aged man's transitory face—wrinkled forehead, sallow skin, hair going salt gray above the visible ear, a flash of bright orange as the mirror dipped for an instant to include the side of the jumpsuit's collar, and some sort of attempted communication, inquiry perhaps, in dark eyes set too deep for ease.

Bauman steadied his glass for the corridor's reflection, and at the same time noticed with relief that the smell of shit had been almost supplanted by an astringency of ammonia. Margaret and company had done a thorough job. Another day or two, there'd be no toilet odor at all.

The mirror thing was a knack—mainly of relaxation, as most knacks were. He now had a really good reflection of the gate, the whole corridor leading down to it, and was able to watch in bright miniature the food cart come shoving through the sally door in the gate's left wing. There were several inmates out already, even before breakfast, standing talking in those orange suits. It seemed a little sloppy, letting inmates just wander around down there. The food cart was in; as he watched it, he could hear the trays rattling. He didn't recognize the hack pushing it. An older white man. The mirror was wonderful, made the place much more interesting.

Bauman transferred the mirror to his left hand, pressed his face to the bars, and looked up the corridor in the other direction. Longer than he'd thought it was—a diminishing geometry of barred cell doors. Two convicts were out up there, walking up and down, talking . . . arguing. He heard their voices, disassociated from the tiny orange-suited dolls striding in his hand. As he shifted the mirror slightly, then moved his face to the right, between another pair of bars, Bauman was startled by the quickest flash of silver. He stared into his glass, and saw in reflection a distant orange arm extend into a caterpillar with one bright eye the color of daylight, a small mirror that flashed again as he watched it.

Embarrassed to be observed observing, he drew his mirror in between the bars and set it carefully down on his mattress. He wondered if it was contraband in Seg and should be hidden—glass, after all, could be broken for an edge—but hiding it hardly made sense when men's arms were stuck through their bars holding the things out for any hack to see. He supposed the mirrors were one of those several minor unofficial reliefs State's system afforded, allowing the otherwise unbearable to be borne.

Bauman had never seen the cart hack before—Carey, on his name tag. A plump sparse-haired man in his late fifties, early sixties (age blotches on the backs of his hands), he looked like one of those veterans usually posted on the wall to await retirement. Carey stooped with a soft grunt, slid the tray under, glanced at Bauman, and went on his way, shoving the cart ahead of him.

Breakfast was three small pancakes, a small sausage patty, a plastic cup of syrup, a plastic square of margarine, and a Styrofoam cup of coffee, black. The meal, still hot from the microwave, smelled quite good when its lid was first torn off, smelled less appetizing after that. The pancakes, peculiarly gluey, left patches of light brown skin on the spork's small white bowl each time Bauman took a bite. They were better in aftertaste than when first chewed, though the syrup was very good on them. He put the syrup's emptied little plastic cup in his mouth, sucked on it for the last drops.

The sausage was disappointing. It smelled like meat, but tasted like a wet gritty biscuit. The bites—there were two—came apart on Bauman's tongue, dissolved into little bits of some kind of cereal. When that happened, the smell was spoiled too.

The coffee, however, wasn't bad. He wished he'd saved some of the syrup; with syrup, the coffee might have been quite good. And it would be wonderful, of course, to have one of the Bit-O'-Honeys or an Oreo for dessert, but yesterday's Bauman, careless and greedy, had stolen that pleasure from today's.

Finished with what he could finish, leaving a piece of one of the pancakes, he slid the tray half under the door bars. And supposed he'd positioned it well enough the evening before; it must have been picked up while he slept. Then he sat on his mattress reviewing the breakfast, considering the bites he'd taken, how satisfactory or disappointing each had been. Bauman decided it wasn't the worst breakfast he'd had at State, decided he wouldn't mind having another one just like it. Thing to do was skip the sausage, have two of the pancakes with a lot of syrup, and save some syrup for the coffee.

After he reviewed the breakfast—not caring for some reason to fantasize a wonderful one—Bauman re-examined his new watch, finding it a little too insistent on marking every single second by number, making the progression seem endless, as of course it was. Otherwise, the watch was fine. Being without one in this situation would be unbearable; someone without a watch would very soon be begging people for the time whenever they passed the cell, for fear time had begun to slow, or had stopped.

He lay on his mattress and read the Timex instructions again. Really impenetrable, as far as timing laps went. He supposed the translation from the Japanese or Korean or whatever had lost all logic in the transfer. Everything else was fairly clear, but not timing laps. The diagrams were no help at all. Bauman thought of starting a company—Instructions Limited—organized to provide instructional clarity from language to language, culture to culture, country to country, company to company, company to customer, literate to illiterate, and leisure class to professional class to clerical class to working class to a (welfared) leisure class again.

He thought about that for a while, during which three convicts passed his door without looking to the side to see him. Two passed together; the third followed several minutes later—four minutes and twenty-three seconds later. The first two had looked Hispanic. Bauman considered it and decided an instructions company was a sensible business notion, particularly for a teacher ineligible at most institutions. Certainly the future would require more and more of such customized manuals, directions, and advisories. Also, the project might be an opportunity to discover a few fundamentals, strip some of the bullshit from teaching. "How to succeed at welcome and unwelcome instruction. How to break into brains."

Bauman picked his mirror up again, stood, and went to his bars. First he scanned up-corridor, saw several inmates strolling, sitting against the corridor wall. He wished he had a magnifying mirror; that would be a major improvement. He watched those convicts for a while, the group miniature in reflection, watched also for that arm holding out its own glass, extended by some inmate scheduled block-out in evenings only. Or not scheduled out at all.

When Bauman changed position, transferred his mirror to his right hand to view the corridor's other end, he saw very clearly—as if the man had been waiting some time for this cue—Peter Nash, leaving several lounging convicts behind him, come strolling up the block.

Watching this reflected approach, for some reason certain to come straight to him, Bauman was suddenly reminded of his father's walk—his father's walk that was, before the weight of years—just such a tall man's hunch-shouldered ambling stride.

Stopping sure enough at Bauman's bars, and looking larger, unreflected, Nash gripped them, leaned way over to his left, and said, "Carl . . ." no longer needing, apparently, to say more for young Sorenson to cover his ears, move obediently to the back of his house. Nash swayed upright, his attention now on Bauman, who'd retreated to stand by his toilet—had done so without realizing it was retreat. Nash stared very intently, as if he weren't certain this Bauman was the same man he'd spoken with the day before.

"Thanks for the mirror." Saying so, Bauman noticed Nash had changed out of his shit-smeared jumpsuit. This one was clean, starched, ironed.

"Forget it, Professor," Nash said. "Up here, the more information a guy's got, the better off the guy is. Mirror's a little part of that—you know, watch out what's goin' on around you. And . . . and, speaking about information, I had a real busy morning, all about information."

Bauman had forgotten how rural Nash's accent was, supposed he was some modern transmogrification of the old Midwest bank robbers—Dillinger, Floyd and the rest.

"First thing I guess I better say," Nash said, "strictly my fault for overestimating you a little, Professor. A classic boo-boo—I made an assumption. I assumed you already learned—you been up here about a year, after all—assumed you already learned to be thinking inside-out . . . not like people on the street, thinking outside-in about a joint." Nash nodded, agreeing with himself. "And I really do consider that my mistake, to make that assumption. My mistake, and I admit it. Leadership can't admit mistakes is bound to be heading for a fall." Nash had been speaking softly, and, apparently wishing to be certain of being heard, tucked his right hand in through Bauman's bars and beckoned him closer with a curling forefinger.

Bauman was perfectly willing to do that—go closer—but didn't see the need for it. He could hear Nash very well. "That's O.K.," he said. But Nash's forefinger continued that slight curling motion, as if Bauman were some sort of sea creature needing first to be lured and beckoned in—then by the same instrument, hooked.

Rather than make this invitation more important than it was, rather than require Nash to order him near, Bauman took three steps closer, until he stood alongside his mattress platform only a couple of feet from the bars. Close enough for anybody.

"Result of my mistake has been a real bad misunderstanding between you and me," Nash said, his long forefinger no longer insisting, now curled quietly around a center bar. "I already told you my mistake. Now, your mistake was to still be thinking outside-in, where you figure the inmates and convicts in here don't know what the hell's goin' on out in the world." Nash ducked his head slightly to the right, his countryman's mouth tucked momentarily up into almost a grin, a confiding expression, quite friendly, while his blue eyes—so narrowly set, intent, examining—regarded Bauman as visual mechanisms might, or as the eyes of an alert and witless monster, an octopus perhaps, at sight of a crab. "I notice," Nash said, "—I notice you're not asking me what I'm talking about."

Bauman wished this time was all gone by, that he was remembering it a week from now, was telling Scooter about it. . . .

"We are not fools in this joint, man," Nash said.

"I know it."

"Now, you know it. Now you're goin' to start thinking in a realistic manner. Up to now, you been playing tourist in here. Isn't that right? Isn't that what you been doin'?" He stood leaning slightly against the bars, waiting for an answer.

Bauman thought of saying, 'I wish you'd just leave me the fuck alone,' but didn't say it.

"Answer me," Nash said.

"I suppose I have."

"I know you have." Nash stood at the bars looking in at his object as if there was now little left to learn from it, so that Bauman felt he'd disappointed by collapsing so readily, felt he was now regarded as inconsequential.

" 'Bauman,' " Nash said. "Is that a Jewish name?"

"No. I don't think so." And though innocent of what sounded like a charge, still felt uneasy as a Jew might have at the question.

"You don't think so?"

"It's a German name," Bauman said. "My father's. My great-grandfather emigrated from Germany. My mother was French Canadian."

"O.K. O.K. . . . You thought I was goin' to say something anti-Semitic, right? Well, I wasn't. So if you lied to me about it, more shame on you, man, because I have all the respect in the world for

Jewish people. My opinion, they're just as brainy as people say they are. The reason I thought you were maybe Jewish, is that sometimes those people are so intelligent they forget to be smart." Nash paused, as he apparently often did, for some response of approval. It was, Bauman saw, gamesmanship—the respondent's confirmations serving, nod-by-nod, to build Nash's case for whatever end he had in mind.

"I understand," Bauman said. Certainly no agreement in that.

"No, I bet you don't," Nash said, not satisfied with 'I understand.' "You think I'm a racist, right? Don't like Jews, don't like black guys, Hispanic guys. Right?" Nash smiling slightly at such denseness, such lack of discrimination. "Well, you're wrong. I admire the Israeli army, especially. Those people learned to kick ass at last. And I also think blacks and Hispanics are fine people. They may be short on brains, but as far as I'm concerned they make it up in heart. —You don't believe that? You want an example? I'll give you an example. You take Little Richard. Now there's a guy who not only is a great musical talent—one of the greatest as far as I'm concerned—the guy's also a very fine, decent human being. Tell you this. I'd a *hell* of a lot rather have Little Richard in there instead of that so-called white man we got as president right now. —What's the matter?"

"Nothing."

"You think that's funny?"

"Damn right I think it's funny," Bauman said, "—but I agree with you."

"See? Those people aren't the problem. They're not the real problem at all. I'll tell you the problem. —Know what I'd do if I was president of the country?"

"No," Bauman said. "—What?"

"Man, first thing I'd do, I'd have them build a camp in Arizona, one in North Dakota, one in Connecticut, and one in Alabama—and I'd start sending wimp whites there as fast as trucks could take 'em. Wimp whites, and dumb whites, and fag whites, and chicken whites and all the retarded white people—any whites let down the race. Biggest mistake Hitler made was trying to kill off the Jews. If that guy wanted to do something really great for Germany, it was the whites he should have whittled down, got rid of the deadwood."

"I see."

"Right. That's why it's interesting to talk to a well-educated person. They get your point a lot faster. Anyway, if Hitler had gassed five or six million of the trashiest Germans—and I don't mean anything personal against your people—they'd be in really great shape today.

You know they tried to do that? Some German doctors? Those guys were killing retards and old people, getting rid of a lot of bad white blood—hospitals, asylums, places like that. Hitler'd stuck to that program, he'd have been all right."

"That's a lot of crap," Bauman said, surprising himself with such foolishness, after all his care.

But Nash seemed pleased with engagement, appeared to consider it part of the learning process. "No," he said, "—it isn't. But I understand your thinking. You think it's a crude approach, right?"

"I think it's horseshit." Bauman, emboldened.

"Well, I don't believe that. I don't believe you aren't concerned about your own bloodlines. Those, you have to be concerned about. What you're saying is it's too violent, but believe me, you're wrong. It's the most merciful way there is; it would save a hell of a lot of blood in the long run—no pun intended. Same as it would save a lot of trouble in the future if we just let those clowns in Africa starve, instead of feeding 'em to have more kids to starve worse, later. You see, right now we're standing in historical quicksand, and the way you get out of that, you build a bridge of blood over to your new age. That bridge, believe you me, is goin' to have to be built out of the purified muscle and bone of the white man—and the white woman, too. And that's exactly what I'm goin' to do, when I get the chance. You see, your expertise is all about the past. That's your area of expertise, right? O.K. Well, the future is where I'm goin' to be comfortable. I got the future already in every atom of my being. You look at me—a guy ready to make the real decisions—you're looking straight at the future."

"I hope to hell not," Bauman said, and was rewarded, and pleased, by Nash's rattling laugh. Approval from any source . . .

"Well, Professor, you got a long way to go."

Bauman nodded. Could certainly agree that was so.

"My big mistake," Nash said, confiding, "—and man, it was a real major blunder, was in pursuing my ends with the gun. Stupid. I was a young man very concerned with honor—that was the instrument I felt I could use on life, you know? Then, one day, a guy deliberately broke his word of honor to me, *deliberately* broke it, and instead of doing what he said he was going to do, he went and called the cops. Called the cops—and he'd sworn up and down he was going to get the cash and bring it right back. Guy lied to us faster than a dog could trot. I was very naive, then; I thought, if a guy told you he was goin' to do something, he was goin' to do it. Then the cops all pull up in front of the guy's house—and I mean an army of cops—and they want us to come out and so forth, and I couldn't believe that banker had gone back on his word! Shows you how naive I was. A *banker*. Absolutely naive. So my guys walked on out of the house—you know, a gotcha is a gotcha—and I found myself still in there, still in the kitchen trying to digest that kind of betrayal. That a man would give his word, and then go on and break it in that type of situation!"

"Umm." No harm in a nod, reference the honor of bankers.

"Well, then I was stuck," Nash said. "I was stuck with whether I do what most guys would do in that situation—just accept I trusted a man and he broke his word, and I'm the goat. And right then I made a very important decision, a vital decision, even if it caused me a lot of trouble since. I decided, right then and there, I would *never* treat any human being—particularly a white man—would never treat a man with the contempt that I expected him to be untrustworthy, that I expected him to break his sworn word of honor. I decided, right then and there, I wasn't goin' to let that behavior influence me even a little bit. I decided no matter what, even in that situation, to keep my word of honor—even if the other party doesn't keep his." Nash's narrow blue eyes were now half closed in reminiscence. "I told him what would happen if he strayed off the straight and narrow, and believe me, that's exactly what happened, just what I said. I put one right through his wife's head—poor lady was sitting right there at the kitchen table. She had a tough morning, poor thing. Put one through her head. Put one through the boy's head, too. Did her first, so she wouldn't see the boy get his. Kid was fourteen years old, and his life was over, all because his father was a liar, the kind of guy thought he could always play an angle, absolutely the worst representative of white people. It was a tragedy, is what it was, and it was entirely unnecessary. Stupid. And I'm paying for my gullibility back then. That right—gullibility?"

"Yes, that's right."

"Well, I paid for that decision back then; those cops beat the hell out of me right in the front yard. So much for their vaunted professionalism—all that vaunted professionalism. That's when I lost any respect I had for cops."

"Understandable."

"—And that was a situation, by the way, where a really good attorney would have got me out with short time, pleaded me right out, because of their use of that sort of brutality. —You notice they didn't beat the hell out of the liar who *caused* the whole damn mess. As it is, the guy I had defending me I'm still paying for with this kind of delay in here.

But just like Hitler, I'm putting my incarceration to good use; I don't waste a day. I figure if a man with my present disadvantages can damn near run State—from a base position, a convict—I figure I can sure as hell run things from the top out on the street. For that, though—believe me, I'm very realistic—for that I'm goin' to have to get some felony convictions overturned, just to run for office. Maybe go to law school. Then, I can get the message out."

"Big job," Bauman said.

"The biggest, and that's why I have my people dealing harshly with the bikers, with the black guys—that B.N.A. asshole, Perkins; old fart's about the only black guy in here can read a book, and he thinks that makes him some sort of leader. And with those Zapata people, same thing. I got nothing against them personally; their problem is I'm using them like tackling dummies, you know, team practice. That's exactly what I'm using those people for. I wish there was a Jewish club in here, or the warden and the administration were Jewish, or maybe Japs, because then I could work out dealing with real sharp minds instead of just a bunch of dodos, which, face it, is what these corrections people are. —If these hacks didn't have steel bars and that wall to hide behind out there, how long do you think they'd last? I'll tell you—about one afternoon, before we found the last cop and sliced his apple for him."

"Wouldn't be surprised," Bauman said.

"But you figure no way, right?"

"I didn't say that."

"You thought it, though. How's this con ever goin' to do diddly on the outside? Man's a joke, right?"

"I didn't say that."

"You thought it, though. Now, wise ass," the first time Nash had been rude, "—I'm goin' to tell you just one way it could happen. You ever think there's goin' to be a war? A big one? Put it to you differently. You think there's any way there *isn't* goin' to be another war? Hydrogen?"

"I think it's possible."

"Certain."

"Perhaps, in time."

"Right. Now, if it happens the next few years, and if—this is the big if—if we don't happen to be locked down when those warheads come boomin' in, then who the hell do you think are goin' to go charging out of these walls into that mess? My people, that's who. We got a firsthand knowledge already what hell's like, Professor. That stuff out there isn't goin' to bother my people a bit. We're goin' to be nice and secure behind stone walls, under concrete when the bombs go off—then we're goin' out there and make a whole new world."

Finished with what seemed a veteran speech, Nash waited, as was his habit, for a positive response. The fingers of both hands piccoloed at the bars; the twisted small button of nail on Nash's right forefinger, picked or bitten at recently, displayed a tiny bright red droplet of blood.

"I suppose that might be possible," Bauman said, ashamed of replying at all.

"More than possible," Nash said. "It could absolutely be a done thing if—and that's the big if—we don't get caught wrong time of day, locked down. If that happens, if the war starts with us all locked down, you can bet the administration will bug out, go look after their families and just leave the population to die in their houses in here. People'll die of hunger, is what I suspect is goin' to happen if that happens. Water'll probably keep coming in, gravity-fed from the tank, but no food. That'll mean some real rough scenes where you got two, four men in a cell. Very rough scenes, as time goes by."

"I'd say rough scenes," Bauman said.

"—And of course, we could take a hit ourselves. The Third World as smart as I think they are, they'll figure the possibility of the population getting out of here and setting up as a real formidable force—you know, being the core group of a very formidable force under real good leadership. And they don't want that to happen, right? They don't want a bunch of very violence-familiar white guys out there mobilizing, getting an admin set up. So, they *could* send a warhead our way. And if they're smart enough to do that, then we all go, get fried hot enough so you just melt and stick to the bars, is what I believe will happen under those circumstances."

Bauman, caught up imagining tiers of molten convicts, once they'd cooled, stuck like burned syrup to their bars, nodded to that possibility.

"However . . . however, if they don't send one our way, and we aren't locked down when the stuff starts coming in, then I don't see a reason in the world we couldn't organize a completely independent state right in this area. Wouldn't be the first convict-founded state now, would we?"

"No, not the first." Bauman seeing himself—of all career advancements the most bizarre—acting as adviser, *eminence gris* (careful to avoid Wolsey's fate), acting as grand vizier to Nash as the new-crowned king of that scorched and savage middle kingdom, risen out of ruin.

"O.K.," Nash said, and blinked, rousing from his vision. "That's enough about the future. We have right now to consider. And first, I'm goin' to show you just how dumb convicts are not. Then, I'm goin' to tell you what we're goin' to do."

"O.K.," Bauman said, pleased that Nash intended a future for him. He was sorry he was standing up—afraid Nash might notice his legs trembling—and wished he had the nerve Marshal Ney had had, to make a joke of it. Nash would probably like that, find it amusing. Might like him for it.

"First," Nash said, his right hand's fingers stroking, pinching at Bauman's bars almost affectionately. "First, you're segged for stowing a wristwatch? —Come *on*. And the Basket thing? Not even a ticket written up on that? No filed charges? You come up here, and Tanner—a hack never left a man alone in those showers ever—comes up for your jumpsuit, and leaves you down there more'n half an hour? Come on, Professor, that's really insulting to our intelligence. —I mean it. It's just like a direct personal insult. You think inmates don't talk to hacks, and hacks don't converse with inmates? You think that, man, you don't realize we're all in this joint together. You don't know that, means you're missing the most important thing there is to know about this community—which is it's a place built out of rules, full of guys can't obey 'em." Nash paused, said nothing for a few moments, apparently allowing that observation to be absorbed. Bauman thought Nash might have made an excellent high school teacher. Good remedial teacher for a college, for the athletes.

"My information this morning," Nash said, "—my information is the A.W. had two guests for dinner in the Admin dining room night before last. Bobby Tulachek served the whole thing. The guy guest had seconds on pork chops, by the way. They get pork chops; we get shit. And this same guy already checked a firearm over the counter goin' through Station One. My information, a big fat Ruger wheelgun with a six-inch barrel, GP-one hundred, to be exact. Now, Professor, you tell me what kind of cop is dumb enough to wear a big duty pistol like that, plainclothes?" Nash paused, but Bauman wasn't sure he wanted an answer.

"I'm waiting for you to answer me," Nash said.

"A state trooper?"

"That is absolutely right," Nash said. "—Are you goin' to be sick?"

"No."

"That is absolutely right. A state trooper. And when do individual state troopers come up here? I'll tell you. Only on escort. If they're coming up on cases, on investigations, they come up in pairs." Nash was speaking as if to a slow learner. "—O.K. We got a state trooper up on escort. And who's he escorting? Probably he's escorting some lawyer from the state's attorney general's office, because it's usually the state people come up here." Nash paused, appeared to wait for some comment, some contribution.

Bauman said nothing.

"Professor, the only thing I'll buy excusing this kind of insult," Nash said, "—that you didn't speak up to me immediately, right a-fucking-way, if you pardon my French, that you acted out a lie all the time we were having our conversation yesterday morning—the only thing excuses that insult is you're a one-year fish and a real slow learner. You think because these people keep us in here like a bunch of animals, we are animals? You think that?" Nash hadn't raised his voice, still spoke rather softly, confidentially.

"No, I don't."

"Well, we're not. Some of us maybe did animalistic things in the past, but that's the past. And some of the stuff that was done—and I'm not talking about dingy stuff—some of that, those actions were just what straight johns would like to do themselves, if they had the nuts for it. Did it ever occur to you it's jealousy as much as any other reason people are taken by force and put in correctional institutions? We're the kind of people made this civilization from the ground up. You read any Ayn Rand at all? Even though she doesn't treat prisoners as a class."

"Yes, I've read her." Bauman found himself interested in this jumbled intelligence, which offered, like a handful of razor blades—some bright and new, others rusted from various uses—such troublesome notions, nonsensical and nearly so. He found himself eager to engage, inform, rationalize and refine this mind, see what sort of person might be made by patience, by Socratisms requiring Nash to reflect, to define his terms, to come to realizations of the symphonies sounding beneath simplicity's rock an' roll.

"And now—" Nash, still speaking softly, was speaking more quickly, as if he were in a greater and greater hurry, his tenor perfect for a priest (a priest, by his accent, raised in Kansas or Oklahoma), eager to impress his certainties. "—Now civilization's wimping out, the faggy majority conspires to keep us locked up. That make sense to you? If they'd let us out, let us start tearing down the shit they built up, we'd build you people some wonderful world. I don't guarantee it would be a comfortable world, no way—but, man, you'd be hopping. People wouldn't be bored, I guarantee that. Shit, we'd jump off this planet like fucking kangaroos. It'd be *'Look out! Look out, everybody!'* . . . For now, though, we're just human beings under pressure, and we cope with that pressure as well as we can, and in my case and the case of my people, that is real good coping. Such as I can have about any fool in this joint killed, and I do include that faggot Ganz running those bikers. —Do you understand me?"

Bauman nodded.

"I really do hope you understand me," Nash said. "—You misunderstand me once more it'll be your last, you cocksucker snitch." No change of expression at that, no great emphasis.

Bauman, embarrassed for both of them, lowered his eyes so that no glance, no expression might offend at even so unfair a charge. He hadn't agreed to anything of the sort. Had resisted very bravely, offering to fight the cop if he'd come down into the water.

"There are two lady lawyers—two senior lady lawyers—in the attorney general's office," Nash said, "and we got a lot of experience among us with people in that office." He was speaking more slowly now. Bauman supposed he'd nearly lost his temper, before. "One's named Louisa Marbela; she's an old lady; she's about sixty. And the other one is divorced—Hilliard. She wears glasses; the woman visiting night before last wore glasses. It was Hilliard—am I right? Or am I wrong? Brown hair, got red in it. Short auburn hair? You tell me."

Bauman said nothing.

"You eat lunch with some nerdy black dude, and he's crying. That night, he gets offed. Next day, you got a lot of remarks to say about that, which was none of your goddamned business *anyway*. Then you get a ticket for bullshit, get sent over here after dinner, and that state's attorney and a cop come and visit—and don't see any inmate for the record. Not one. They just come up here and visit, come up here for the pork chops—and you get more'n a half-hour down there in the shower, all by your lonesome." Nash's fingers gripped at the bars, no longer playing. "Checking snitches is my first duty. Don't you know that?"

That seemed a rhetorical question, and Bauman kept quiet.

"—First duty that punk Ganz has got. First duty Perkins and Vargas got." Perkins, colonel of the B.N.A. Vargas, the current Zapatista *Patron*. Bauman wished more than ever for his special cocoon, imagined it twirling softly about him like smoke, slowly occluding him from Nash's vision.

"Only question I have is, What is my duty to my people, far as you're concerned?"

"I wasn't going to do what they wanted."

"Any pigeon is goin' to say that," Nash said very softly, confidentially.

"—And in any case, they didn't leave me a lot of choice."

"Right. What you're saying is it comes down to your ass, or another convict in here you can snitch over. Isn't that the truth?"

"In a way, I suppose."

"You better give me a better answer than that," Nash said, looking concerned, "—or I'm just goin' to have you put down."

"All right. That's true." Bauman was surprised to hear such an important conversation sounding so ordinary, occurring in clear, unremarkable morning light, and supposed that most of Tomlinson's great moments in history had been ornamented by no special prose after all, most of those fine phrases being tossed back over history's shoulder by historians needing good quotes.

"O.K. That's better. You got no more excuse than any snitch ever had, isn't that right?"

Bauman hoped to have a nod accepted.

"Say it."

"That's right." And, Bauman supposed, looked at from another point of view, it might be. He was comforted by the rigor of such judgment, and supposed he might have leaned on those considerations, told Ms. Hilliard a simple no, and accepted his possible years additional as consequence.

"You getting the picture?"

A nod yes was now acceptable.

"Far as I'm concerned, you do have three mitigating. First, you didn't snitch yet, or I would have heard about it, maybe somebody charged on your say-so. Second, you're ignorant. Ordinarily that's no excuse at all, but you're so ignorant of the right way to behave, I'm goin' to take that into account. And third, sticking you wouldn't find me that hack that maybe was involved in doin' Metzler an' your nigger—and him I got to have. We all got to get hold of that son of a bitch, liquidate that individual, and instruct these fuckin' corrections people as to their proper role."

Bauman, remarking in Nash's face what seemed fatigue, noticing anew the fine indications of worry printed there, felt surprising sympathy—and ventured another nod, supportive, much less provocative than speech.

"I been thinking about this," Nash said, "—and I believe I see a way to go."

Bauman nodded when he didn't need to, as a way of staying in tandem with Nash, following his thoughts, wishes, close as a reflection.

"I don't see a single reason we shouldn't try it," Nash said, "—because if it don't work, we always got you." He ducked his head slightly to the right, grinned his country-lawyer's grin.

Bauman, once he was certain of the pleasantry, cooperated with a smile of his own, acting best as he was able as a frictionless bearing, in perfect accord.

"So," Nash said, "I think we're goin' to give it a try." His long right forefinger lifted from the bar its hand was gripping, and curled to beckon Bauman closer than he'd come before. Bauman did what the finger indicated, stepped close enough to smell the faint sweet astringency of Nash's after-shave.

"What I'm goin' to do," said so softly Bauman barely heard it, "—what I'm goin' to do, is hoist corrections on their own petard." This near quote, intended to impress with Nash's reading, his sense of style, expressed a nice complexity—the cat still anxious for the mouse's good opinion. It seemed to Bauman that much of human intercourse, even in desperate circumstances, perhaps particularly in desperate circumstances, involved such exchanged exercises in vanity. He nodded to Nash again, smiled as he nodded to show his appreciation.

"We're goin' to make you a double agent, Professor. Administration's goin' to think you're their guy, but you're really goin' to be ours. We're goin' to deputize you, so you can run a little investigation for us. —I know the bikers are goin' along, because they already been talked to this morning, and I'm pretty sure the other club guys will, too. No skin off their asses; they got exactly the same interest I got, far as a hack coming in offing inmates is concerned." Nash was speaking more rapidly, warming to his presentation. "So, you make like you're doin' exactly what corrections wants, exactly what the attorney general's people want. That'll make 'em real happy; they'll figure, Well, we got the jacket on him." Nash paused a moment, watching Bauman's face, and seemed to be amused. "What do you think of that? Is that cute, or what? See, you do exactly what they tell you. You nose around, find out who offed Metzler, who did the black guy—maybe same guy did both. If you find out it was a convict, that comes to me, to the other club presidents, and that's as far as it's goin' to go. Period. You are not bein' deputized to snitch some convict over had good reasons to put those people down, even if Metzler was one of our own. You will *not* give that convict's name to corrections. You understand how seriously I mean that?"

"Yes, I do." The situation so bizarre, Bauman found, it was difficult not to laugh.

"—What's funny? Believe me, it's not funny."

"With all due respect, it's fantastic nonsense, is what it is. If I even thought of doing anything that stupid, the first thing that would happen is the hack or whoever would come and kill *me!*"

Having said that, Bauman received from Nash a look contemplative, mournful, profoundly adult.

"Could be," Nash said.

"Oh, that's wonderful. Fabulous."

"Come on, won't be that bad. You're goin' to have somebody with you on it. We're goin' to put somebody with you. Besides, it's your job to get that motherfucker, or anyway mark him, before he does you or any other con. Right? That's what you're goin' out there to do."

"Fine. You get somebody else to do it."

Nash paid no attention to that. "But remember, anything you find out comes to us. We'll tell you what shit to pass on to the corrections people. And if it turns out a hack was in on those, that also comes to us. And by the way—and this is strictly a need-to-know matter, goes no further—we do have a couple, maybe more than that, tame C.O.'s. These are hacks we got who work with us on certain supply and transportation problems, help us deal with those difficulties."

"I see."

"One of who, by the way—you talk about how sharp Barney Metzler was; it was his idea—one of who was contacted by us outside, and hired by us to come up here and apply for his job. Dude's collectin' a salary from us, and a salary from the state. Nice? Is that nice or what?"

"Great. That's very nice."

"Now, we already checked with our cops, and they say they don't know from nothin' about a hack wastin' inmates."

"That's very helpful. Look, what if I choose not to do any of this bullshit—for the administration or for you people? Supposing I just tell you to take a running jump? Let's suppose I do that."

"*Good*, there you go. I'm glad you asked that. You hadn't asked that question, I'd be worried about you. First, if you're thinking you can go back to the administration with this, and get off our hook and their hook, forget it. All they'll do is try and turn you again, send you right back in population. And second, even if they do let you off, what do you figure? You figure they'll put you downstairs with the geeks and the other snitches, maybe transfer you downstate to some other joint, and I can't reach you?—You think that, it just shows your ignorance, Professor, because I wouldn't even try to reach you. Believe me, I learned a long time ago you want to punish a guy, you don't kill him. You only kill a guy for a lesson for other people. —What I'd do if you tried crossing back over the tracks? What I'd do? You got a boy, thirteen, fourteen years old, out of state, goin' to junior high in Fort Wayne. That kid can be reached, I absolutely assure you of that. You go ahead and try and hide him, move him around—take him to Canada, take him to Mexico, take him to Brazil—won't make a bit of difference. Hide-an'-seek is a specialty, the people we know. In a week or a month, maybe even a few years, that kid would be reached. He'd *have* to be reached—be a matter of leadership credibility, every club in State. Matter of honor. And we got all the time in the world to get it done. And money." Still speaking softly, Nash released Bauman's bars and took a step back from them. "Man, don't you know a lot of business gets done out of this prison? Scag and bets and shit, all kinds of cash goes back and forth. Believe me, you'd be surprised how much money. I can think of a guy—well, two people I know of out there—be glad to find your kid, deal with him. One of those people would enjoy that better than anything; he'd pick your boy up in that van and take him out in the country with his scissors and shit, and God help him."

All Bauman's conversational nods and smiles, all his grimaces of agreement were frozen on his face. It was odd, because he intended to do something, thought of reaching through the bars, of somehow strangling Nash before Nash had time to discuss Philly with anyone else, before he mentioned the notion to any of his people. But Nash had already stepped back, attentive, and Bauman imagined himself grunting against the bars, reaching through, trying to clutch at Nash, looking ridiculous. He wished Nash had threatened Susanne, instead. Had threatened Beth. Both of the women were at least old enough to have done things deserving of punishment—though not perhaps, such punishment.

"Now," Nash said, pleased by something, perhaps Bauman's inaction, his silence, "—now you're starting to think inside-out. Right? Aren't you? Now you see what I was talking about, when I said we weren't just animals in here?"

"You better not," Bauman said, and had to stop to clear his throat. "If anything happens to my boy at all, any kind of accident or anything. Even if he just gets sick, I'm going to kill you." He said it softly, pitched like the rest of their conversation, in which it seemed no subject was worthy of increased volume. It wasn't what he'd intended to say, but seemed all right. It reminded him of Silber's threats on the phone in defense of his daughter, though those of course had been despairing, too late. "I'll kill you," he said to Nash, "—and I'll kill your family, outside."

"You got to be kidding . . . !" Nash surprised, eyes wide, incredulous. "You taking this personally? Because if you are, you are way, way out of line! This is business. I thought you understood that.—I got three hundred and forty-one people in here I'm responsible for. And that's just my immediate people, not other white cons take it for granted we're goin' to stand up for 'em. You think I can let you run around snitching on people? Let some hack maybe take a walk on wasting inmates? You think that, you got another think coming. Really now—Hey, really, Professor. It's time for you to start thinking about somebody besides yourself. We're all in this shit together, man. Even the blacks—everybody. You don't know that, what the hell do you know? I'll tell you, and I don't mean to insult you, Professor, but really you're goin' to have to start thinking about other people's needs, not just old number one."

"You threatened my son."

"Threatened him?" Apparently startled at the notion. "That was no threat; I don't even know your kid. That was a *commitment*. You have my personal word of honor I'll have that young sucker's head cut clean off and thrown in here over East wall—and you out there trying to catch it before it hits the dirt. —And I like you personally, Professor. But that's exactly what's goin' to happen if you continue this kind of obstructionism. Because that's all it is, is ego-centered obstructionism, and if you ever read Mrs. Rand the way you say you did, you know just what I mean."

Nash had spoken without breathing, and now, staring down from at least a three-inch advantage in height, he took a deep breath in silence. Bauman supposed that some of his own behavior—the boxing, rock-climbing—must always have been reactive to a usually slightly taller masculine world. He smelled Nash's after-shave very clearly, saw between the bars—low on the left side of Nash's throat—a spot of faint blond stubble the electric razor had missed. There was no odor of tobacco on Nash's breath. It was warm, clean as a child's, its owner probably avoiding smoking as undermining. Nash looked into Bauman's eyes as if in search of something specific—then grinned and leaned in, lounging against the bars, apparently no longer concerned about being strangled.

"So," he said, "as of right now, you can consider yourself deputized. You know, a private investigator, sort of an inmate cop. No reason all the cops should be on the other side, right?"

"You kiss my ass."

"Come on, that's just your temper talking." Nash tapped his forehead with an index finger, the one with the bleeding nail. "You need to be using gray matter, Professor. When it's a serious situation like this, you don't want to be thinking with your nuts.—I believe this is goin' to work out just fine. Those attorney general's people are goin' to figure they got the jacket on you, figure you're nosing for them, so they'll stay off your ass for a while, give you back those block passes you go around teaching with. Keep the hacks off you. And all the time, you're really goin' to be working for us. And you're goin' to do it because—one, if a hack's offing people, hey, you could be next. And two, because you love your boy. Two good reasons. And three—last but not least—gives you a chance to show off what an intelligent guy you are, how you really don't belong in here at all. Three good reasons, right?"

Bauman said nothing, imagined that as Nash had relaxed he'd caught him flat-footed and yanked him hard into the bars, then—with great effort, Nash proving very strong—had got his thumbs over the man's adam's apple and managed to break the cartilage in there. If he'd done that, now he'd be standing watching the hacks cluster outside his house, bending to see the last of Nash's life explode with slight popping sounds out of his ruined throat, out of a mouth opened wide enough to breathe for all the world. —Bauman thought of that, and thought he would certainly have tried it if Philly had been up to see him only once—against Bauman's wishes, against Beth's—had only insisted and come up once. Then he would have remembered the boy too well not to have killed Nash, at least tried to kill him. It seemed it was difficult, after a year, to kill for two photographs—one of Philly suited up for baseball, and one of him kneeling on the back lawn of the Stuart Street house, holding Braudel. (The dog a puppy then, still wailing from his cardboard box some nights until Bauman, cursing, got up to go into the kitchen to cuddle him, talk to him, present a finger dipped in milk to nuzzle.) —If he'd seen Phil this year, just given him a hug, this thing with Nash would have been very different. And of course in another year, or two or three, it might be possible to kill even for photographs. Nash had caught him between presences of his son.

"So? Three good reasons, right?" Nash ducked his head a little, smiled pleasantly, the small-town attorney completing a conversation with a friend after church. "We'll swear you in tomorrow . . . next day. Tell you what; I'm goin' to figure out some kind of a badge. Then, you go back in population, you report to Jim Shupe. He'll fix it up so you can ask our people anything you want. And we're goin' to fix it so you can talk to the other clubs' people, too. That punk claims to run the bikers already says O.K., long as no legitimate business gets blown. And that's a good point; you remember who you're looking for." Nash paused, seeming to consider the difficulties of so strictly channeled an inquiry. "Say, for example, you find out about a matter isn't any of your business, doesn't have anything to do with Metzler or the nigger? Well, you just forget that, whatever it is, right there. But I'll tell you something; I think this investigation is goin' to turn out to be a real progressive step, kind of a total inmate leadership effort."

"Just ridiculous," Bauman said. "Ridiculous. . . ."

"And," Nash said, paying no attention, "—in case you're still thinking outside-in, and decide to go with the attorney general's people after all, and try and fuck over your fellow inmates? Well, if you do that, Professor, and after a little while you get that package over the wall? Then, if you want to make it a personal thing, you get out on release you can go look up my sister. Lives in Moline, married an insurance guy, Don Craigie. Three fat kids. —You do every one of that bunch any way you want, I'd be obliged." Nash winked, stepped away from the bars, and strolled off up the corridor and out of Bauman's angle of vision.

Chapter SIX

"Go on! Blow all them suckers out!"

Betty, beaming, round brown face refulgent in candlelight, bent offering the small cake to Bauman, setting its seven candle flames dancing close enough for him to smell the burning wax.

An occasion, and prepared for with considerable effort, the cake having been baked—from a recipe and with ingredients supplied by Rudy Gottschalk—in the basement supply-closet light fixture. This attended, according to Mark Nellis, by such an anxious Betty that she'd popped in and out of that closet close to a dozen times in the course of the morning, had missed her counseling hour and missed gas-furnace repair, a valued course.

Nellis now lay easy as a noonday lion, medium-sized, balding, and spectacled, along the top of their double bunk, its edge bordered by the hand-sewn valance and ruffles of their lower bunk's green-flowered curtains.

Bauman drew in a deep breath and blew the candles out—each representing one of his days in Seg—a touching notion, and apparently Betty's own. Candlelight gone, only the simpler shadows of the house's single yellow bulb radiated from the ceiling's center.

"All right." His hostess set the cake—a small round classic pound, iced with melted Hershey bars—down on a four-legged stool, then hustled over to her sink, produced from somewhere a slim shank, and bustled back to slice the treat very neatly, very quickly crisscross and then again, into eight equal pieces.

Bauman, sitting in the rocker—nervous in the crowd of eight, pressed in upon by Scooter standing on his left, Kavafian sitting on a stool to his right—accepted the first piece of cake, apparently to be eaten hand-held.

"Go on, go *on.*" Betty stood suspended, waiting for a verdict. She was wearing tailored jeans, one of her ruffled shirts, pale peach, and pink plastic-mesh shoes—women's shoes, and strictly against State's rules.

Bauman ducked his head to take a bite, careful to include some icing, and hardly had time to chew, so ready was the portion, rich in eggs and butter, to collapse softly in his mouth, the icing, sturdier, to linger a little longer, its chocolate textured with sugar.

"So?" She watched him chew, nodded as he swallowed. This party planned, in part, to recompense Bauman for having missed Thanksgiving and Rudy Gottschalk's heroic efforts at roast turkey and cornbread stuffing.

"Fabulous. *Wonderful. . . .*" Still tender from the morning's change from Segregation to this noisier, busier, more spacious life, thick with racket, movement, and casual encounters, Bauman felt tears come to his eyes at the cake's softness, sweetness, at this cozy gathering of friends. The week's exile into Seg—its nightmare within a nightmare—had made B-block into that much more a home. He supposed there must be jails on earth so grim as to do the same for Seg, so that prisoners would weep with relief on returning to it, on donning their orange suits.

Schoonover had been invited to this afternoon celebration of the coming out, but had declined. Only a fairly narrow social passage saw the librarian (a baby killer, after all) safely through his days—from A-block, where he roomed with a retarded credit-card thief named McAvoy, to West mess, then to work, and at day's end, return by the same route. Nellis had invited him for Betty's sake, since he was Bauman's friend, but had expected a polite refusal, and received it.

"Unfortunate to miss your anabasis, but I appreciated the gesture," Schoonover had said that morning, when Bauman walked over to the library to thank him for the watch. "—A courtesy, even from a thug, is something to be treasured these days, in prison or out. You don't look as well as I've seen you look, Charles. I thought it might be something of a pleasure to have the solitude."

"No pleasure," Bauman had said. "But I appreciated the watch. Cost too much money though, Larry."

"Well, I don't have a great deal in the way of expenses, Charles." Schoonover was dusting shelves, the books stacked neatly on a work-table beside. "And while I think your obsession with the correct time is probably unhealthy, it didn't seem the proper occasion to deny it to you."

"Face it, Larry, we're friends. The watch meant a lot to me."

"I suppose we are friends," Schoonover said, and began returning books to the new-dusted shelf, then paused, frowning, to examine a volume with a badly frayed black cover. "Casual friends. I don't think we're close friends, though, are we?"

"Perhaps not very close."

"No, I don't think so. I don't think it was given to me to have a really close friend."

The morning walk to the library had almost equaled in pleasure Bauman's first stroll at dawn down the steel stairs of the laundry building, and away from Segregation.

A yard captain named Vermillier—a younger man than Gorney, livelier as well, something of a humorist in aviator's dark glasses—having charge of all changes of work shifts, all movements of prisoners to the furniture factory, the old license plant, all assemblies at the gym for basketball or boxing or a movie, had been the captain signing Bauman's release back to population. This paperwork, and the exchange of the jumpsuit for his old denims (cleaned and pressed) as well as his shoelaces, had been accomplished at a desk in Seg's glass-walled entrance.

Bauman, dressing there—putting his shirt on quickly, so no notice would be taken of his arm—was relieved there'd been no reference by the hacks to the attorney general's people, that whole can of worms. He'd been unpleasantly surprised when Vermillier, walking out of Seg with him, had paused at the bottom of the long steel staircase and said, "I hope you don't fuck up now, Professor. I sure as shit don't want to be seeing your smiling face up here the next five, six years," then strode away, a busy man.

Bauman, walking across West yard to the blocks—enjoying the sunrise just striking over the top of the wall, enjoying with it a mingled breath of cold night and cool morning air—had tried to believe those remarks referred only to his having been segged, had had nothing to do with the other matter. He was able, aided by his exhilaration at the expanse he crossed, by the wonderfully available choices of which way he would take to travel those great spaces—whether he'd amble or march, which entrance he might choose, the main of B, or the side—was able to persuade himself Vermillier had only referred to behavior in general (no more fancy jewelry or burnings of Bobby) and not to necessary cooperation, not to Spencer's killing. Would Vermillier have even been told about the attorney general's people, when it wasn't any of his business at all? Doubtful, very doubtful.

Bauman checked in with Carlyle in B-block's office, and, after a long delay while the hack spoke on the gatehouse phone, received his block and building passes from that pleasant older man as if their return were only the routine necessity of his teaching rounds. Carlyle, though they were alone in the office for almost half an hour, said nothing to Bauman about any scheme to report, didn't wink, nod confidentially, or treat him in any way as a possible informant.

Bauman didn't think Carlyle had been told a thing, the long phone call probably concerning duty schedules. Didn't think Vermillier had been told a thing, either. It seemed very possible that Segregation's schemes tended to remain in Segregation—and probably largely in the imagination of both convicts and corrections there, spoiled alike by days lived through fantasies of ferocious freedoms, of suppressions even more complete. Neither Ms. Hilliard nor Nash seemed quite solid now, compared to State's acreage, its monumental buildings and wall, its customary people's beehive routines, and all in such clear, cold, well-defined weather.

Bauman, absorbing the odors and noises of home—stale sweat, steam heat, some oily breakfast scent rising from the basement kitchen . . . shouts, laughter following, a constant low rumble of conversation over the rhythms and melodies of seven or eight musics—absorbing these, he'd climbed the circular staircase to Two-tier pleased by casual greetings, pleasantries from convicts hurrying down past him, done with morning lock-'n'-count.

Scooter was already out when Bauman reached their house—likely at the truck shop being some casual help, lounging, listening to the bikers' tales of thousand-mile runs, epic combats, extraordinary dope (uppers, downers, coke and bombers), of gang-bangs after which the victim, introduced to the world of the senses at last, came staggering out into the street naked but for her sweat-soaked blouse, her socks, begging to ride, to be carried away at speed, sitting postilion and hugging the rank muscle-packed leathers of the most forward and savage of her assaulters. Wheeling away, whirling away from being only Cheryl to becoming a mama—soon to be decorated in many ways, perhaps as Bauman had been decorated, soon to become less pretty (two or three teeth vanished, small nose, in time, to be broken), but becoming, in those months and years, beautiful in another way, whittled by windstream and beatings, beers, lost loves and throttle noises, into an elemental.

Bauman, roaming his narrow quarters as if to reacquaint himself with every simplicity, had found the house almost completely recovered from the hacks' destructive turning. Pictures of women and motorcycles had been repaired with Scotch tape and returned to their places, the sunstruck dark-eyed young blonde lay once again at rest on her beach above his bunk, transparent tape shining across her ripped belly. The house was nearly neat, all of Bauman's possessions where they should be, except that his electric razor was turned the wrong way on his shelf, had apparently been used more than once, and not cleaned.

Bauman stepped behind the blanket curtain, flushed the toilet—which Scooter had forgotten to do—peed, then flushed it again and came out to take a Mozart tape, a sonata in G, from his shelf box, snap it into the Walkman, and lie down on his bunk. The bunk seemed to have been sat on and messed up all week, then recently remade, not very well. For some time, lying still, feeling his muscles slowly ease, once taking his pulse by measure of his new watch, he'd listened to the piece in G, its lively measures sufficiently ornamental, at volume, to overlay and enamel the companionable noises of the block.

He'd been roused from this by Mark Nellis, his unremarkable face lined remarkably deep, come up with the party invitations—one for Scooter, too. Nellis had confided as he was leaving, one man to another, that Lee Cousins had been asked as well. Betty's idea, for Bauman's own good. Nellis then had left Bauman to turn off his Mozart, whisper to himself awhile into his pillow (humor, encouragement), then get up to go thank Schoonover for his watch.

From the library—leaving Schoonover muttering over duct tape, trying to repair the black book's binding—Bauman had walked over to East yard, to the gym. The sun was up, and a slight breeze blowing from the surrounding wall (as it did many mornings—convection currents, Bauman supposed) was almost warm. He thought about getting a new pair of running shoes. The ones he wore were only a few months old, but seemed to him to have been spoiled somehow by being worn without laces, to have contributed to his humiliation by flapping and falling off like runover slippers.

The boxers were working past the far end of the basketball court, the team's weights, bags, and practice rings set up in the considerable space between the high backboard and the building's wall. The busy shuffling, thumping sounds, old Cooper's noisy lisping correction—he was trying to persuade Ferguson to hook off his jab, instead of the other way round—the odors of sweat and Curry's Liniment, all provided for Bauman a flush of warmth and familiar comfort.

"Well, here he is. Here he *is*." (Both 'is's sounded slightly like 'ith's.) Little Cooper, leaving Ferguson's blunder to his sparring partner's correction, had trotted over to Bauman, his quick-footed bobbing gait increasing the bald old man's resemblance to some featherless but energetic rooster, not quite past it. "Well, here he is," and stopped before Bauman, peering up into his face as if that might have undergone some change in the week past—a different eye color perhaps, more or less of cheekbone, or a different mouth. "—Tryin' an' act like a convict, did you?" Cooper said. "Fat chance." The old man's false teeth, chalk white, seemed to shift in his mouth as he spoke. "You don't belong in here, yet. An' if you wasted enough time with them faggots in Seg, how about you doin' some work for a change—like with that dumb wop you like so much, can't even hit the friggin' speed bag, so all the boys is laughin' at him." Referring to the cruiser-weight, Marcantonio. Old Cooper, having as a flyweight been so handy, was hard on his bigger boxers, necessarily slower with their fists.

"O.K.," Bauman said, considered himself welcomed, and went in search of the cruiser-weight—found him at the heavy bag hanging behind the far left practice ring. The practice ring and the gym floor around it were vibrating from transmitted energy as Muñoz and Washington, both soft-helmeted, sparred a fight.

Enrique was holding the heavy bag, steadying it for Marcantonio's punches—these coming right and left in turn, rather slowly, very visible, each impacting with a loud lingering thud, each jarring Enrique back, forcing him to half-step in again for balance. Marcantonio—his curly hair a black ram's, skin mushroom white (swollen with muscle), dark eyes dull as pond water—noticed Bauman watching, then refocused on the big bag and continued his slow tattoo. Hard to hurt, Marcantonio was in consequence a difficult boxer to teach, learning few lessons from fights.

"Tony. . . ."

"Hey, dude—" *Bang*. "Where you been?" *Bang, bang*.

"Took a vacation."

"No shit." *Bang*.

"I hear you're fucking up on the speed bag."

Marcantonio had nothing to say to that, appeared not to have heard.

"Tony?"

"I do the speed bag." *Bang.*

"Old man says you've been doing zip. And let me tell you, you need the rhythm you pick up off that."

"Tha's right." Enrique, hugging the heavy bag.

"I don't need shit." *Bang, bang.*

"You tell him, man." Bubba Betts, heavyweight, black as licorice, padding by from one press bench (unsatisfactory for some reason) to another, carrying a bar hung with four fifty-pound platters.

"Tony," Bauman said, "—you hit plenty hard. But you need to keep in mind you're going to be fighting lots of men hit plenty hard. You don't want to catch everything they throw, do you? —Do you? That happens, you're going to get out of here with your face all messed up. No girl's going to look at you."

"Shit." *Bang, bang.*

"Tony, light bag's good for your hand speed, good for your rhythm. It's easier to pick off a punch than duck one."

"Tha's right, man." Enrique.

"—What's the matter? You think you look dumb on the speed bag, just because you missed it a couple of times? Lots of people miss that bag a few times."

"Only guy I ever saw miss hittin' that bag," Enrique said. "An' it was jus' hangin' there, man."

"Enrique," Bauman said, "—we're not talking to you; why don't you just stay out of the conversation, O.K.?"

"O.K., O.K."

"Tony, will you please stop worrying about how you look on the speed bag? The other guys were just kidding around; they miss too, believe me. You've got a good natural hand rhythm. —You don't look dumb on the speed bag; you look dumb with the jump rope. That's where you really look dumb. You look like a real asshole with the jump rope."

"Ha-ha." Marcantonio, polished with sweat, put his hands down, stepped away from the heavy bag and stood still, an engine idling. "Ha-ha. That's real funny."

"O.K. Can we get serious? You need to work on the speed bag, and we're going to go do it right now. We're going to work on that bag until you can dance with the damn thing, and that's all there is to it."

Marcantonio sighed as he must always have sighed, persuaded to this or that by a good talker. And rocking into motion, he walked beside Bauman across the gym floor to the speed bag, going along (only two or three inches taller than Bauman, but nearly twice as wide) as reluctantly as a child to the dentist.

"And the center of the ring?" Bauman said. "—You keeping that in mind?"

Marcantonio nodded.

"Remember, fights end on the ropes, but they're won ring center."

"I know that shit."

"Right. So with this Joliet guy, you always go to the center of the ring and work out of there. Don't just keep marching around the ropes, because if you do, the guy's going to back to the center every time, and he gets away from you."

"I got it."

"I know you know it. You're not dumb. You're smart as any guy here. But I want to see you *do* it in this Joliet fight. Don't forget. You own the center of that ring. Period."

"O.K. Right." Marcantonio now stood uneasy, facing the speed bag, a fat leather teardrop hanging high.

"O.K.," Bauman said. "Now I want you to take it easy, and just start slapping this sucker around. Just use your left. Don't worry about getting it going, just start smacking it a little. Don't try to hit it hard. —Tony, will you relax? Nobody's looking at you. Believe me, they all have better things to do."

After lunch—Scooter having bounded in from the truck shop effusive, hugging the prodigal hard enough to hurt his sore arm before they went down to the mess hall for watery chili and cherry Jell-O—after lunch, Patterson, one of the pleasant hacks, walked past their house for lock-'n'-count and welcomed Bauman back to the block. Scooter then had changed to his best denims, and they'd both checked themselves in the sink mirror, Scooter spending several minutes combing his ginger hair.

Ready, they stood and waited for the block's bars to roll racking back. Then, with that clangorous echo, left their house and went down the circular staircase to Betty's.

The party was silent during the eating of the cake.

Betty, sitting cross-legged on the lower bunk, framed by her verdant bed curtains, sliced her piece in half and handed a portion over to Bauman as extra, frowning hard at his initial refusal, maintaining the frown until he accepted.

Across the narrow house, three guests leaned against the wall beside one of the paintings on velvet, the one of a con's back as he observed a distant guard tower. Chris Onofrio, the Nellises' putative adoptee—a tall uncertain teenager with stringy hippie hair—finished his slice of cake, then licked his fingers and the palm of his hand as naturally as a dog might for any taste left over. To his right, the albino, Carlo, stood silent, snow-white fingers toying with his belt buckle—an inmate handicraft with a large light-blue S for State sewn in beadwork on the buckle's red-lacquered leather face. On Onofrio's left, in the cell's corner, Lee Cousins stood eating cake, taking bites neat as a cat's, and appearing slightly less beautiful now, Bauman thought, than he seemed when passing in a hall. Cousins' dark brown hair was cut fairly short. This haircut, however, revealing the shape of his skull, accenting the fine bones of his face, did not make him seem more masculine.

Cake gone, and Betty congratulated thoroughly on it—Kavafian offering to sell as many as she'd make—she propped her blaster at the back of her bunk, slid a tape into it, and turned the volume up on a Porfirio Escalante version of "La Bamba." Then, a busy hostess, and dressed for it in peach and pink, her music thumping hard through the cell's cement and steel, she knelt to open a small cardboard box stored under her wall shelf, and produced individual servings of pecan-sandy cookies and speedball, and a half-gallon carton of rapidly softening vanilla ice cream procured from the dairy's delivery people at a considerable markup. Products from the dairy, a minimum-security establishment quite separate from State, and four miles east outside the wall, were strictly forbidden by State's rules to be sold or received privately outside mess-hall service, the hacks devoting as much time and attention to discovering fresh ice cream, cheese, and yogurt, as to confiscating casual pot or the usual multicolored pills and capsules imported for resale.

While his wife dug into the carton with an orange plastic spoon, shoveling the ice cream into paper cups, Nellis went behind their blanket-curtain and returned with a plastic gallon jug of pruno, dark amber, foaming as he opened it. This from a special West mess production featuring California raisins, canned Del Monte apricots, and fresh brewer's yeast—and called Lifer's Choice. It was an expensive beverage, vying with Tiger's Sickbay Special—created from crushed seedless grapes, grape jelly, yeast, and pinches of ground pot—for place as State's classiest.

The party, though so lavishly supplied—cake, pecan-sandy cookies, vanilla ice cream, and a speedball cap each, washed down with paper cups of Lifer's Choice—had commenced quite subdued, reflecting perhaps the Nellises' tension over Chris Onofrio's adoption, reflecting Lee Cousins' unaccustomed presence as well. But the pruno, offering a syrupy taste that shifted to pepper, and likely the speed, slowly cooked the party into life, enlivened further by Betty's dancing, commencing with tentative hesitation steps of combination salsa, cha-chas and barrio shakes, for which she had more talent than the center of the cell had room.

Bauman had never cared to try prison dope—pot excepted—and would have preferred to skip his capsule (light blue, banded white), but for the expense Betty must have gone to, concern for her feelings. The speedball went down, therefore, with his first cup, along with a pecan sandy, and seemed to him to have no effect at all.

Betty, warmed to the loud, strumming music, finished a series of small intricate steps with Kavafian clapping quick time, then paused in front of Bauman making little gestures of invitation, these seconded by her hips. Nellis—glanced to for permission where he lounged on the top bunk—nodded, and Bauman stood up and began to dance with her, hoping the speed might come to help him, loosen him for this little pleasure at least, aware that Cousins was watching, the young man eating his portion of ice cream as nicely as he'd eaten cake.

Bauman liked old-fashioned dances best, had preferred those dances even in high school, for the opportunities they provided for holding girls, feeling the sleek muscles of their backs as they stepped along. Separate dancing, all its posturing, had seemed to him an empty sort of display—late fifties and sixties stuff hung on too long. The pleasure he found now in dancing with Betty, despite his sore arm—he'd intended a couple of turns, then sitting down—came as a surprise. He made no attempt to match her steps, couldn't if he'd tried, so simply moved along enjoying her joy in the music, and by doing that, danced with her quite well.

"Look out, Marky," Kavafian as he clapped, "—Teach's fallin' in love!"

Bauman, not aroused by Betty at all as they danced, grew more and more fond of her instead—the speed and clipping grace she showed using every inch of her house to dance in. He danced along with her, a lesser satellite, felt his muscles move, felt the same easeful effort and sweat that only boxing had given him at State. He warmed himself before her as they turned and turned in their small space—as if, brown eyes bright, eloquent in makeup despite regulations, she were a small fire of merriment.

Dancing, Bauman considered Nellis a lucky man, and not only for the sexual favors Betty could at times be heard to surrender, when occasionally, at night, she might give distant notice to neighboring houses by softly protesting the pleasure of what her husband did, then accepting it with the sweetest cry.

Dancing fast as he could, Bauman forgot his arm, forgot the music's beat in favor of Kavafian's contrapuntal clapping, then forgot that, even Betty's shining face—as if he might forget himself by dancing, and like a dervish dance away any troubles due him.

He only noticed after she'd done it, that Betty had reached out on one of her turns, taken Cousins' hand in hers, and danced him away from the cell's wall to join them before she fell back on her bunk to some applause—a number of cons and a fish hack having drifted down the block to Nellis' house to check this private party out.

Cousins was a cautious dancer, awkward, angular, uneasy enough to almost spoil the dancing, but Bauman, finding himself the more at ease, supposing also the speed and pruno had some effect, was able to dance almost as well as he had with Betty. Was really not embarrassed, since it seemed Cousins was embarrassed enough for both of them.

"What the fuck," he said to Cousins, and the young man relaxed a little, almost smiled, and gradually, Bauman playing nearly the fool—so actively he stepped and twisted and shook his butt—gradually Cousins commenced to move less and less self-consciously, to dance more and more slowly, and finally only in half-time to the music—its smacking energy, its cheery noise and falsetto choruses outlined, emphasized by Cousins' refusal of speed, his slow dancing from curve into curve. After a while, as if by magic, a young man in blue denim trousers, a fresh-pressed blue denim shirt, had danced himself into a girl—truer in gentleness, in seriousness, in innocent self-absorption than Betty had accomplished for all her generous ways. And not only dancing as a girl, but doing so with just the slight awkwardness an Anglo woman must have demonstrated, a shade too diffident for Latin music.

This was done gradually, apparently unconsciously, until Cousins, face turned a little to the side, gray eyes heavy lidded, danced as dreamily as any girl in love with dancing. Bauman, growing uncomfortable, moved farther and farther away as they turned together. Feeling crowded now by the cell's small space, he finally took advantage of a pause in the music to pretend to be more breathless than he was—to break off dancing, laugh, wipe sweat off his forehead, and find his seat in the rocking chair.

Cousins danced alone for only a few moments after that, turned, turned, danced slower and slower, then stopped and stood apparently confused. His applause was silence in the cell, silence as well among the watchers outside it.

The party recommenced as gossip, Betty's blaster, fed new tape, pouring out a three-trumpet accompaniment with male voice-over as they talked. Cousins standing again with Chris Onofrio and Carlo against the cell's wall, all three silent, listening, sipping their cups of pruno as Betty, with Scooter's interruptions, Kavafian's running commentary, filled Bauman in on block and population events occurring during his segged week.

Excepting Gottschalk's catastrophic Thanksgiving dinner, during which some bikers threw platefuls of blood-rare turkey and dirt-crunchy dressing (B.B. had dropped the tray) back into the kitchen—an uproar almost requiring the entrance of State's Response Squad of pick-handled hacks—there'd been two events of note, one amusing, one sad.

Big Bruce, the smallest of the bikers, almost a mascot—no taller than the dwarfish Pokey Duerstadt, without Duerstadt's squat strength, his spade-wide hands—had attempted to collect protection money for walkway dealing from an independent. A relative fish, up less than a year, Big Bruce hadn't known, and as a rough joke hadn't been told by his friends, that the independent, a bulky young brooder named Errol Vernon, was a deep ding, given to terrific violence on little account. Result, the treacherous bikers had gathered in North yard to watch while Big Bruce was sprung upon by this ding at the very first words out of his mouth, and offered a fearsome beating, in the course of which, drowning in kicks and punches, bitten a time or two as well, the little man had screamed to his brothers for aid, and found them too weak with laughter to assist him. Big Bruce thereafter formally resigned from his club for failing in brotherhood—this word delivered by Paul and Irma from Contusions, in the infirmary. And he was quite right, Betty said, to do it. "They don' treat him like a real member, fuck the little guy over like that."

The other affair had occurred out on the street, and been reported in. An old con named Gunther, who Bauman had seen many times with the remnant Maintenance people, using a long pole-and-gripper to change ceiling light bulbs, had just the week before hit the street from a ten-to-twenty, paroled to live with his daughter and son-in-law, to work in the young man's business, a body shop.

Their very first evening at home together, there'd been a family quarrel. The young husband, uneasy perhaps at his father-in-law's presence, and anxious to demonstrate his rule of the house, had brusquely ordered his wife to bring him a beer while she was still occupied with ironing. After some words back and forth, the girl's father, not caring for her husband's manners, had picked the iron up off the ironing board and killed the boy with it.

This was seen as traditional tragedy in State, where murders *en famille*, and so often swiftly following release, were painfully common. Gunther, according to Betty, was widely pitied, as was the girl. It was felt the young husband had been out of line, had asked for trouble and gotten it.

This street event was discussed for a while, cooling the party until Betty, bored, jumped up, turned the volume of her music higher, and began to pluck at Onofrio to dance. But the boy, very shy, resisted, shook his head, almost clung to the door bars, and finally had to be dragged out into the cell's small floor space by his indomitable hostess, who then set into a sweating salsa that might as well have been fucking, the boy trying to keep up, getting neatly bumped at and ground upon out of a storm of music, while Nellis lay quiet along the upper bunk, smiling, watching, his glasses' lenses reflecting tiny twin birdcages of curved white bars—and at their centers, spinning activity too tiny to be made out.

Bauman glanced across the house at Lee Cousins during this dance, just at the moment Cousins glanced across the house at him—a look that married couples exchange visiting the home of friends in relationship precarious. Bauman looked away at once, glanced back again, and was annoyed to find Cousins had done the same.

Salsa over, Betty—beaming, soaked with sweat, her perfume scenting the cell's air—left the boy standing, tripped over to the bunks, and leaned up to kiss her husband, who'd bent down to her. "*Mi amor,*" she said to him, so softly Bauman supposed he was the only one who heard it.

The party, after that, settled into a relaxed affair, general conversation, gossip, and a long discussion of dogs—animals owned, admired, loved, loving in return. Carlo offered his only conversational contribution here, in praise of a pointer named Barkis, named, Bauman supposed, by someone better read than Carlo. Bauman—once Barkis had died on the vet's table of age, a heartworm condition, and injected barbiturate—described Braudel to them, his small size and ugliness, his catlike coldness and independence, his avoidance of even the most casual caresses, to find that Kavafian had known dogs like that, kennel-bred and a pain in the ass. This subject ended with birds, and Stroud at Alcatraz, all present agreeing that parrots, at least, would make good prison pets. Songbirds, not so hot.

All this, through the last of the afternoon, was discussed at very high volume, since the music still chattered and thudded, with more cookies served, more pruno poured, Betty neatly tucking the jug under her bunk every time a lounger beyond the bars whistled bulls-coming-along, until, nearly time for the dinner bell, Nellis slid down to the floor, poured most of the remainder out for his guests, then tilted up the jug to finish the last to their applause, just short of the sludge of yeast residue.

"Charles," Betty said, amid departures and thanks, "—you walk Lee home, O.K.?"

This request, not seeming as bizarre at the moment—in the party's last glow, the flush of pruno and speed—as it would a few minutes later walking Cousins home to A, Bauman acceded to, more amused than annoyed.

Cousins, slighter than he'd seemed dancing, walked alongside through the basement corridor, silent as if there were tension between them—concern over an end-of-date kiss, perhaps some awkward moment at A's tall gate.

"They got a real problem," Cousins said.

Puzzled for a moment, Bauman then realized Cousins was referring to Betty's dance with her soon-to-be-adopted son, under Nellis' eyes.

"Tryin' to make him jealous," Cousins said, "—so he'll back off takin' the kid on." Cousins had a smoker's dark voice, very like (as Betty and her friends had observed) a girl's pretending to be a man.

Cousins' observation—delivered as one of a settled couple commenting on the party past, the difficulties of their friends—seemed to Bauman very much out of line, part of the boy's (and Betty's) bag of tricks. Part of the fakery all State's ladies indulged in, echoing the voices of women lost, separated from, only remembered.

"Tell you what," Bauman said, just after they'd been O.K.'d through the basement corridor's narrow turnstile by two black hacks. "—I'll tell you something. I would really rather you didn't play your game with me, O.K.? I know you've had a very bad time in here, but your way of getting along just doesn't interest me."

Cousins, silent, went up the A-block stairs beside him as if Bauman had said nothing.

At the entrance to A's gate, Bauman thought he saw Schoonover's bulky height—his dyed black hair arranged in its near ducktail at the back—amid the crowd of inmates filing in before dinner. Thought he'd seen him, then thought not. He took Cousins by the arm and steered him clear—the boy not resisting the grip—into a corridor alcove on the right. Cousins' arm felt exercised, slender under his sleeve—a tall girl's who played very good tennis.

"What I *would* like you to do," Bauman said, "—is please try to keep your mouth shut from here on out, concerning Metzler's being killed, concerning Kenneth Spencer too." Cousins looked at Bauman with only the slightest interest, seemed impatient at the lecture. "I understand your concern about your friend Metzler's death, but there's not a damn thing you can do about it now. And believe me, your going around talking about it, about some hack possibly being involved, has already caused me a lot of trouble—a lot of very serious trouble."

Cousins, who'd seemed to be watching Bauman's mouth as he said this, now looked into his eyes. "I loved Mr. Metzler," he said, and turned to walk away with the crowd through their great gate.

Dinner was hamburgers and fruit cocktail. Opinion on the hamburgers was divided—some of the bikers liking East mess's hamburgers very much, and holding gobble contests at the back of the mess hall, eating the extras more delicate palates had rejected. Bauman found the hamburgers to have a disturbing odor of liver, and to leak a sticky carrot-colored juice. When he'd asked Rudy Gottschalk about ingredients during a domino game with the cook one Saturday evening, Bauman had been told he didn't want to know what was in them. On Bauman's persisting, Gottschalk (who ate none of his own cooking, ate no mess-hall food at all) had said only pigs sucked slops, then won the game with a neatly finished T-row.

Bauman was weary after dinner. All B-block's activity and noise—and the party—had tired him. Pruno and speed. And that last absolute nonsense, with Lee Cousins behaving as if, hammered sufficiently by the B.N.A. soldiers, he'd been forged from an unreliable boy into a considerable woman. The whole day had been a lesson, coming out of only a week in Seg, a lesson in how fatiguing it was to deal with people *en masse*, to rapidly pick out their faces, to observe their size, their age, to judge humor, attitude, intention. These appreciations no busier than those he'd made out on the street, but here crucial.

It was a relief to have only Scooter and the last of the evening to deal with. Bauman, lying easy on his bunk after lock-'n'-count, and wanting familiar conversation, asked Scooter if he'd come closer to deciding on his machine. The machine being Scooter's dream motorcycle, to be purchased (with cash magically bound to appear) within one or at most two days after his release—that due in one more year. Two years, tops.

"Hey, I'm glad you asked me, Charles. You know those Jap bikes I was speakin' with you privately? I was thinkin' brand-new, man, right out of the fuckin' showroom—an' fuck that dude, Handles." The last said softly. "I don't give a shit what he says; you talkin' machine, them Jap bikes got the refinement."

"Scoot, you're going to be riding the thing. You get what you want to ride. Get what's going to make you happy."

"Right. Get what makes me happy, right?"

"That's it."

"Well, Charles, that's what I mean. I got a surprise for you. I was talkin' to Bump," referring to the bikers' gray-bearded guru and chief mechanic, "—an' he laid down the fuckin' law, man, as far as enjoyin' a bike goes. Bump tol' me, 'Dude, you fork a bike, you're forkin' fuckin' history.' He tol' me that, an' I figure who should know better than you about history, right? Is he right?"

"No doubt about it."

"Now don't make fun of me, man. Listen—"

"I'm not making fun. I'm listening."

"Bump says to me, 'Every motherfucker in the bikers knows you still got your head up your ass about Jap bikes.' He's tellin' me, right, like I wasn't the guy got his fuckin' jaw busted."

"Right," Bauman said, relaxed, feeling pleasantly sleepy.

"O.K. Bump says to me, 'I'm goin' to give you the word, man. An' the word is history, an' you better listen up.' I said, 'O.K., I'm listenin'.' An' he says, 'You fork a Jap bike, an' you're ridin' a smooth machine; nobody says the Japs don't build good. But I'm talkin' about forkin' a fuckin' Harley, man, 'cause when you ride *that* machine you are ridin' the history of our country. You are ridin' with fuckin' Custer, man. You are ridin' with Brando an' Smacky Jack an' Tiny an' all those old dudes.' "

"He's right. Absolutely right."

"I know it," Scooter said, standing by the far end of the double bunk. He was hanging on to the outside round steel upright with his left hand, swaying out slightly into the cell's open floor space, gesturing for emphasis with his right.

Noticing this, Bauman realized that State was full of these semi-brachiating poses, aborted swings and climbs and dangles from bunk uprights, from gates, from the ubiquitous steel bars—the monkey house revealing the monkey in the men.

"—I tol' him, 'O.K., I see your point. You're sayin' it's more'n just ridin', right?' "

"Right," Bauman said.

"An' he says, 'Right. A shitload more'n ridin'. It's a fuckin' commitment to your country, dude.' Said, 'You don't think a Jap bike's goin' to make just that little move goin' to save your ass in a slide, runnin' up some square's pickup?' "

"Good point."

"Bump says if you ride American, your Harley's goin' to give you that little extra effort, 'cause the American spirit is expressin' itself through the machine. An' that's called spiritual balance. Spiritual balance. —An' that's the edge the American machine got over some Jap bike don't give a shit if you live or die. What about that, Charles? What do you think about that?"

"I think Bump's right," Bauman said. "I think there might be an advantage there."

"Well, O.K. I'm goin' to do it." And, speaking very softly, added, "That fuckin' Handles could'a kept his fuckin' hands to himself. 'Cause all I ever needed was a decent fuckin' explanation, man." Scooter swung slowly forward, slowly back. "You know, an explanation it wasn't just the friggin' machinery we was talkin' about. Because nobody can say the Japs don't build a great bike. Nobody," Scooter said. And continued *sotto voce*, though with great emphasis, "—I don't give a fuck how tough he's supposed to be! I mean, now I can see that asshole Handles thought I was comin' out against America, when all it was, was I didn' have the full picture of everythin' at the time."

"Well, you certainly have it now," Bauman said. "Bump is no fool."

"So . . . So I'm goin' Harley, day I get out of this fuckin' hole."

"Right on."

"Bump knows a guy goin' to piece me up a total took hog."

"Every part stolen?"

"You know it, man. Bump says outlaw is the way to go real American—you know, stay off the economy an' all that shit. An' I'll tell you somethin', Charles; I can't see where he's wrong."

"Neither can I," said Bauman—and was startled by the sudden noisy racking-back of their bars.

"You got a family emergency call." Harrison, usually a D-block hack and not friendly, stepped into the house and beckoned Bauman up and after him. Harrison was a tall man, balding.

"What's the matter?" Bauman's hands and feet were tingling as he sat up, as if suddenly cramped asleep. He saw Beth dead of something. "What is it?"

"You get up off your ass and come find out," Harrison said. "I couldn't care less." He waited, then slammed the bars shut behind them as Bauman walked out. "I can tell you this—your people better not pull this shit again. You aren't supposed to get any calls on the block. She hadn't called the A.W. and had a shit-fit, you wouldn't be gettin' this one."

Bauman hurried beside Harrison down the circular stair, then, on Ground-tier, moved a little ahead. Harrison reached out, took him by his collar, and pulled him up short. "How would you like to get your inmate ass right back up those stairs? You just keep fuckin' around . . ." the hack said, and deliberately slowed his pace.

A faggot officer named Edwards (and nicknamed Peaches), plump, pale, in his fifties, his hair dyed an unlikely mahogany, was sitting in the gate office reading an old *Silver Screen*. He looked up when Harrison buzzed, looked at Bauman, then pushed the unlock to let them in, pointed to a phone over on the second desk.

Bauman picked it up, said, "Hello," and heard nothing.

"Push nine," Edwards said. He was the hack reported as having watched through a window in the furnace-room door two years before, when the B.N.A. soldiers brought young Cousins to the gym.

Having pushed nine, Bauman still heard nothing, then a harsh click, then Beth's voice. "Charles? —Charles?"

"Not Philly," Bauman said. "Not Philly."

"Charles. . . ."

"Yes."

"He's all right, you bastard," Beth said, her voice wobbling so in tone Bauman thought she might be sick.

"Are you O.K.?"

"Phil's all right; I'm all right—and, as far as I know, so's your child bride."

"Then—then what the fuck are you calling for?" as if he'd seen her last just yesterday, rather than more than a year ago, as if she'd called him from class, from an exam, for nonsense.

"I'll tell you," she said, "—and then I'm probably going to report it to the police. I'm going to tell the people up there all about it. A man came up to Phil this morning at school, out on the field where they were practicing, and said he had a message from you to give to me."

"I do not know what the hell you're talking about," Bauman said, and realized, halfway through the phrase, that he was lying.

"I'm talking about your sending some disgusting friend of yours—Philly said the man told him he looked really strong, and started squeezing his arm. Charles, I could kill you for this! I'll never, *never* forgive myself for marrying you. Let me tell you something. Knowing I did that makes me physically sick. How could you? How *could* you send a creature like that with that stupid note? —And he put his hand on my son!"

"I didn't—"

"Philly brought that note home and it just said, 'Regards.' Regards! What in God's name did you mean by that?"

"Beth, sweetheart—" Bauman's heart was hammering as if, rather than only standing and holding the phone, he'd been running, running faster and faster as she talked. "—It was just a stupid misunderstanding! The man's perfectly harmless; he's absolutely harmless. I had no idea he'd do anything like that. He's just a pickpocket and he was on his way out to the Coast and he asked if I wanted him to do me any favors outside, and I stupidly said, 'Yes, give my regards to my wife.' "

"I'm not your wife."

"—And that's how this happened. He's perfectly harmless, and by this time he's all the way out in California. He lives out there with his mother; he's a perfectly gentle guy, and he'll never be back. Whole thing was just a careless blunder on my part, not really the poor guy's fault at all." Bauman was surprised as he finished his lie, by the embellishments he'd added: California, a gentle pickpocket living with his mother. . . .

"Charles, if ever again anybody—"

"There won't be any 'agains.' There won't be anything like that."

"I was just petrified. It just froze me. Phil said the man parked in a green van and watched them for a while. Then he came over. —It just froze me."

"I know, I know. Sweetheart, it won't ever happen again. Nothing will ever happen. He was just a sad, gentle guy. Never harmed anybody. And he's gone. Gone to California."

"Well, it terrified me. I just couldn't believe you'd do that."

"Of course not. Just a stupid remark the poor booby took seriously. Don't be frightened. Don't be frightened. Nothing will ever happen again."

"Charlie . . . Christ, it's all such a disaster! I have no idea what it's doing to Phil, you being in that place. He will not, he absolutely refuses to talk about it. Just goes up to his room and closes the door. Whenever I try to talk to him about it, he goes right up to that room and closes the door, and I don't know if it's destroying him, or really if the subject just *bores* him. He's exactly like you. He's like a book with a lock on it—you know, one of those really beautiful books out of collections? A beautiful book with a lock on it. Well . . . it's a disaster."

"Losing you was my disaster," Bauman said. "—Throwing you away, that was the disaster. After that, all this seemed to follow naturally."

"Charles, I don't want anybody from up there ever even coming close to us."

"Nothing like that. Never. You can just forget it; it'll never happen again. . . . Have you been all right—except for this nonsense? Have you been all right?"

Harrison walked over to Bauman. "Get off that phone," he said. "You got no emergency there."

"Well, except for that," Beth said, "we're all right. I just called about this thing with Phil. I told the assistant warden—is he the assistant warden?—I told him it was an emergency thing about our son, very, very important, and he said all right, just this one time. He seemed to be a decent man."

"He's not so bad," Bauman said.

"You hear me tell you to get off that phone?" Harrison said.

"And don't worry," Bauman said. "Nobody will ever bother you in any way. You won't be bothered by anything."

"Well, you can't guarantee that, Charles. You can't guarantee 'by anything.' "

"Yes, I can. I love you, Beth."

"I didn't call to listen to that."

"I love you, Beth," Harrison said, apparently to Edwards.

"I know," Bauman said to her, softly, turning to try to shield the phone from them. "—But I love you just the same. I'm not trying . . . I'm not betraying Susanne. I do love her. I love her, too."

"I love Susanne, too," Harrison said, and Edwards started to laugh.

"I'm being honest; I'm being honest with you. She was even more beautiful than you are," Bauman said, "—and she was intelligent, but ignorant of so many things. A terrible temptation for a teacher."

"I'm hanging up, Charles."

"Even more beautiful than you," Harrison said. He and Edwards were both laughing.

"Is there somebody else there?"

"No," Bauman said, "—it's a radio. I've missed you. I have no right to, but I've missed you just the same. I know I have no right to. Believe me, no one knows that better than I do."

"Charlie, I don't want to hear this."

"If it's possible for you to love a—even a little—to love such a jackass, my sweet girl, darling, my darling girl—"

"Charlie, I know what you want. You want everything. And I have news for you, Charlie. You can't have it."

"If you could love a jackass, sweet girl, darlin', darlin', *darlin'* girl," Harrison said, and he and Edwards laughed so loud Bauman didn't hear Beth hang up. Bauman said, "Beth? —Beth?" into the phone several times.

"If you could fuck a jackass," Harrison said, "—oooh, oooh, my darlin' girl!"

Back on Two-tier, longing for lights out, Bauman lay in his bunk listening to Schubert, his string quartet in A minor, the Walkman's earphones providing privacy, providing relief from Scooter's questions and continued conversation. Bauman had said it was a false alarm, his ex-wife worried their boy might have appendicitis.

He wondered as the music sang along, whether it would have been better to tell Beth the truth, to beg her to call the police, to call Christiansen and tell him. He imagined he'd done that, and Beth had taken it all very calmly, had been fatigued but not disgusted by this new mess, this dangerous mess he'd gotten her into, had gotten Philly into. Had taken it all very calmly, perhaps seen in its senselessness some evidence of Susanne's bad management, even at a remove.

And tomorrow morning, two courteous FBI agents (one Bauman's age, the other much younger) would see Bauman after breakfast, or maybe have him brought over to Admin for breakfast in the dining room there (eggs over light, link sausage), or take him into town for breakfast (the eggs and link sausage, and hash browns and whole-wheat toast with orange marmalade) and let him know Phil was under guard, had been moved to someplace quite safe. Beth and Susanne being guarded as well, and they'd mention a continuing investigation of conditions at State. Talk about the whole thing over a pot of good coffee, a cinnamon roll and some butter. The whole investigation by a federal judge. And an investigation of the attorney general's office right along with it.

And he'd be placed in the Witness Relocation Program, be sent out to the West Coast, or perhaps New England. And with perfectly forged, deliberately ordinary credentials, perhaps be accepted to teach in some small lovely provincial college—the history department of which would shortly find, to their surprise, that in their new instructor they had a tiger. His first book, a classic study of the American penal system, *Durance.* His second, *Rome in Dacia, Policy and Politics.*

And, of course, Beth and Phil would be with him, Susanne perhaps teaching nearby. . . .

It became difficult to sustain this vulgar little fantasy while listening to Schubert, so Bauman turned his Walkman off to picture a small white two-story house set in a grove of birches. A bright house outside, a darker house indoors, a sea of secrets where Beth, a possible mermaid, sturdy and beautiful, her black hair streaked with gray, walked or swam through shade among fine furniture, as yet undecided what form—finned or forked—to take forever.

And Susanne visiting, so he was held safe, suspended between them. Sustained by the judgments of women—their importance derived from what, that he should regulate his actions even to life and death, by their approval, by what disgusted them? Importance that might lie in men's suspicion that women held the secret of death as well as life—but refused to reveal it, and died themselves out of spite, and to maintain their treasure rather than share it.

He recalled the look Cousins had given him at A's gate. Hammered into a woman by the B.N.A. Learned the uses of vulnerability, that variable weather of response which no man could be sure of following, being ready to meet, as outclassed in that as a permanent beginner.

"Saw what?" his mother had said, just for example. Had been lying, a withered stick, with a scarf on her head where her hair was gone from chemotherapy. "Saw what?"

Bauman closed his eyes the better to recall his shame on the side porch of their house on Millard Street, a recollection as twinging, as painfully pleasant as biting gently down on a sore tooth. He'd found over many years it was better deliberately to re-create it than have it surface several times a week, sometimes several times a day, to be swiftly buried by concentration on something else.

Something else, such as Beth's resemblance to his mother, in everything but that slight apprehension of manner a woman had who'd been beaten. A resemblance noticed for the first time—so obvious he must have avoided seeing it before—when he and Beth had taken Philly to Kendall Park to play in the autumn's fallen oak and maple leaves, kick his way through their rustling color. Four years old then, and a strong rollicking little boy, not silent and self-contained at all. A little pitcher pouring out affection and interested observations even upon strangers who encountered him.

That afternoon, Beth, radiant in chill, blowy air, stood beneath the trees wrapped in her red Hudson's Bay blanket-coat, wearing her white wool-knit ski cap. Her face burnished by the wind, beaming, as she watched Philly play. She'd called something to him. Calling not a command or warning or encouragement—only a call as a sort of cord of gold, to maintain her connection with her son over that small distance.

Then Bauman had noticed—as he'd noticed himself ignored, nonexistent for her for the moment—how strongly she resembled his mother. Her dark eyes, but lighter than his own, her rich black hair—only a wave of which was visible under the thick-knit cuff of her ski cap (around the margin of which, small green reindeer trotted)—all her complexion seemed suddenly to echo his mother's, only being less definite, less marked, less particular. Not authentic as his mother's cedar-brown Chippewa skin had been, her heavy soot-black horse-mane hair, her large nose, which nearly spoiled her beauty, her eyes—almost almond-shaped and a liquid brown much deeper than Beth's revealing amber.

Still, Bauman had seen the clear resemblance while Beth was calling to her son, as if he'd found and married his mother's much younger sister or perhaps her cousin, the Indian blood diluted by one more measure of white.

In this circuitous way, as he almost always did, often by way of Beth—Bauman arranged as he lay on his bunk, eyes closed, to recall his preparation for a date with Elaine Heffernan. Elaine had let him feel her up in the car two dates before, her sweater and her blouse under it both unbuttoned, her bra pushed up so that small small-nippled breasts had been visible in moonlight, the nipples looking darker for the breasts' soft silver. She'd let him do that, then on the next date had unreasonably withheld the favor. And wouldn't touch him either, even through his pants.

The notion of Elaine looking at his cock, maybe bending over the driver's seat to suck it, had caused Charlie Bauman to jerk off in the bathroom, which afforded such relief he was worried he wouldn't be able to do anything if Elaine changed her mind, suddenly wanted to fool around, maybe go all the way. . . . Bauman remembered that concern very clearly.

He'd called, "I'm goin'; back by twelve," down the front stairs, then went down the back and out through the kitchen. Dressed for a Saturday late date, not just driving around on a school night. Dressed for Elaine's father, really—brown trousers, brown loafers, shirt and tie and a Sears tweed sports jacket. The sixth time he'd taken Elaine out, and if he hadn't had the Chevy, forget it. The Chevy sort of a gift from his dad for very low payments—twenty-five dollars a month earned sweeping the showroom, vacuuming the offices every Sunday afternoon—the four-door an old demonstrator they kept around the agency for years to drive back from delivering new cars. Same car he'd learned on when he was thirteen, and now he was sixteen, and it was his. Same car.

Early-summer evening, Minnesota still cool in May, the evening dark enough already so the light from the house windows fell across the side-porch floor in five pale yellow rectangles containing four outlined squares in each. He'd walked past two—the kitchen windows—before he heard something through his parents' bedroom window, open a few inches at the bottom, that sounded like the TV, until a *smack-smack* sounded weird, and he looked in.

He thought at first his mother was sick, got sick in the living room and his dad had carried her back to their bedroom. She was kneeling down on the floor by the bathroom door, and his dad was holding her by the back of her neck. Then his dad swung his right arm around and hit her in the face. Slapped her, really. He didn't make a fist.

What surprised Charlie more than anything, more than his mother getting hit, was how big a fool he'd been not to know of course his dad beat her up—and not only that one time at Easter. Then, his father had just pushed her, so it was more of an accident than anything.—And his father never had hit him, no matter what he did. His dad made fun of him—and had beat up two men in town Charlie knew about. One guy at a party a long time ago, and one guy out at the agency. A customer, a real asshole, called his dad a thief, which was one thing he wasn't, and got punched out. But his dad had never hit him.

Ralph Bauman—much taller than his son, and always would be—held Charlie's mother by the back of her neck. "I told you, Yvonne," he said, and Charlie could barely hear him, could tell he was speaking softly so nobody would hear what was going on. But when he hit her again, that made the same loud *whack* the other time had, and when Charlie's mother put her arm up to try and protect her face, he pulled her arm down out of the way. "Didn't I tell you?" he said, and drew back and hit her with his open hand so hard her head banged sideways into the door frame, and her long black hair—and not all black but gray in it too—came loose from the way she pinned it up and fell down around her shoulders.

Charlie put his right hand up to his own head, as if he'd been hit there too, wished it was a dream, and saw himself shoving the window all the way open, climbing in across the sill, and saying 'You dirty son of a bitch,' and just charging him, drive right into him like in football and knock him on his ass, see how he liked getting knocked on his ass.

When his dad hit her again—this one more like a punch, really—it made such a loud sound that Charlie was stopped from even thinking about opening the window so he could climb in over the sill. He was scared his dad would hear him just start to open it. His mother's head had hit the door frame again, and she screamed a quick little scream, but not very loud, as if she didn't want anybody to hear her. Her mouth was bloody and her nose was bleeding too.

His mother tried to get away, crawl away from him, but Charlie's father said, "You're really asking for it," followed her, leaned down and hit her on the head two or three quick times with the side of his fist, like he was hammering. These were comic kind of punches, not as serious as the other one had been. They were sort of teasing punches and seemed worse to Charlie, because they were making fun of her. His mother put her hands up over her head to keep him from hitting her there—and when she did that, she glanced sideways and saw Charlie standing out there on the porch looking in, watching.

No doubt about it. Saw him really close. Watching, but not coming in to help her. There was blood on her chin. No doubt at all that she saw him. Then, and really fast, she looked away, looked away as if she never saw him after all, and Charlie knew why she did it. She did it so he could think maybe she hadn't seen him, so he could think at least she never knew he was there—and he wouldn't have to be so ashamed he didn't go in and try to help her. Didn't even yell at his dad to leave her alone.

When she looked away like that, pretended she never saw him, Charlie wished she would die from getting beaten up, so she wouldn't be alive to know all this about him. His dad hit the top of her head again—little bonk bonk hits, not real punches. "Can't I get anything into that thick red-nigger head of yours?" *Bonk. Bonk. Bonk.*

Charlie stepped back out of the light, thinking if she looked again and didn't see him, she might think she imagined it and he really hadn't been there at all. He went quietly back the way he'd come, went all the way back to the end of the porch, then climbed over the porch rail and walked across the yard in the dark, over to the garage to start the car and go on his date.

While he was driving over to Elaine's house, he thought of driving on out of town instead, and starting a new life. He thought of getting a job on a paper out in California. Just driving around the coast. Drive along Big Sur. Just drive out there right now, and the hell with them. If that didn't teach them to act civilized to each other, it wasn't his fault. And they had a real privacy problem, pushing things in his face that were no way his business. Like this crap tonight, which was exactly both their faults. His dad's fault for hitting her at all, and her fault for not doing shit about it, expecting Charlie or somebody to go in there and get into trouble because she didn't have guts enough to just call the cops, just leave him, if she didn't like getting beat up.

And she might like it, anyway. Like that woman Carl's friend told Carl about, who wanted guys to spank her like a kid before she'd screw somebody. If he'd waited at that window a little while longer, they would probably have started screwing like bunnies. Some parents. . . . And that was something he knew from personal experience, not made up. He knew that from almost a year ago, when he got up in the middle of the night to pee, probably because he had some beer with Larry, and Carl and his brother. Got up to pee, and heard that noise, somebody making noise outside—a little noise. Went to the bathroom window to listen and heard his mother saying something in their bedroom downstairs, then heard her make that noise, a pretty weird sound, as if she was sick. That's what he was dumb enough to think at the time.

He listened to that for a little while and suddenly got the idea they were fucking, that his mother was getting fucked. He got that idea right out of nowhere, and when he thought of that, then that's what it sounded like. And he got a hard-on listening, which is about the most natural thing that could happen to you.

He turned off the bathroom light, went back into his room, and opened the door out on the landing and went out there in his underwear with this big boner sticking out. Stood out there in the dark listening so hard he heard a humming sound. Then he heard his mother say something pretty loud, and went down the stairs in the dark all the way, really scared he was going to make the steps squeak or something, and his dad would hear.

At the bottom of the stairs—he remembered it really clearly, could smell the floor wax and everything—he could see the bedroom door was closed after all. But he listened anyway, and in a minute he heard his mother say right out loud, "Oh, you're fucking me. Oh, you're fucking me." And it felt like an electric shock to hear her say that, and he could actually hear the bedsprings too, a little, and thought he could hear a kind of soft clapping sound. He supposed his dad had his mother on her hands and knees, like the picture, and was fucking her that way. After a little while he heard his mother say something, then she said louder, "That hurts . . . that hurts me." Then she said, "Oh . . . oh . . . oh . . . Jesus, I don't care." And Charlie had pulled his underpants down there in the dark and started rubbing his cock, listening. He was really overstimulated as an adolescent in that kind of situation, which it would have been nice if they'd kept in mind. If they'd kept in mind that they weren't alone in the house. He remembered thinking, I can't help it, and wishing he could open the door and watch what his dad was doing to her. That's how overstimulated he was.

When they were quiet—except he could hear his father saying something—he went back up the stairs really carefully, to not make any noise, and had to wipe his hand on his underpants.

In the morning he rinsed his underpants in the shower, then put them under his bed to dry.

And at breakfast his mother looked just the same as she always did. He looked at her feet; she always went around barefooted in the morning, and he imagined her getting screwed, her feet kind of kicking while it was happening. . . .

"I saw what Dad did to you," he'd said when he went up to see her in Montreal in the hospital, years, years later. "—I saw it through the window. And I was too frightened to come and help you."

"Saw what?" she'd said, lying thin as a stick, a scarf over her head where all her hair was gone. "—Saw what?"

Breakfast was cornflakes and bruised bananas, but Bauman didn't go down with Scooter for it. He made his bunk, and when the last men had filed past off the tier, went behind the blanket curtain to pee. He came out, shaved, and brushed his teeth. Then, still in his underwear, went to the open cell door and looked both ways down the tier before he stepped up onto their stool—shakier since Hanks and the black hack had broken it—turned Scooter's small portable TV (kept at the foot of his bunk even though it curtailed his leg room for sleeping), pulled the plug, then popped the fiberboard off the back of it. Bauman carefully fingered in past a tangle of concealing wires to fish his knife in its cardboard sheath from beside the picture tube.

Then he replaced the fiberboard, plugged the set's cord back in, and stepped down from the stool. He took a change of clothes from his second shelf, and went behind their curtain to tape the sheathed knife high on the inside of his right thigh. A strip of the duct tape stuck to some hairs on his leg till he pulled it free. Bauman put on his denims and shirt, still favoring his left arm, tucked his shirt in, put on fresh socks and his blue running shoes. Then he walked out from behind the curtain and paced the cell—twice up and down—to check the weapon's fit, make certain it couldn't be seen, wouldn't be felt either, except by the most determined and curious hack.

He was lying on his bunk listening to Mozart on the Walkman when men began to troop by from breakfast, Scooter, a few minutes later, coming in complaining about the breakfast bananas.

After lock-'n'-count, Bauman got up, put his jacket on, and went downstairs.

He walked out through the mess hall, then the kitchen, passing the ranks of black ranges, the shivering air above their hot iron already smelling of lunch (chipped beef). As he passed, Bauman saw Rudy Gottschalk standing in the narrow aisle between stoves and ovens, talking very seriously with a scrubber named Fields, an older man, a forger. Fields had his left hand up to his mouth, as if he was afraid of being hit—or being hit again. Bauman, walking past, heard Rudy say, "I said sugar; I didn't say salt."

Billings, the young fish hack, stood at B's courtyard gate—usually standing wide, unguarded—below the kitchen steps. He checked Bauman's block pass, and let him through without a word—not talkative as he'd been the week before, at C's gate with Teppman. Billings, a quick learner, seemed to have already discovered the risks in extended and friendly conversations with inmates—familiarities often breeding their contempt.

Bauman stepped out into the inner court—and a cold pretty morning, its high riffle of cloud colored the same as a live trout's side, soft ribs of gray marked with faint crimson where the rising sun first touched them.

He walked diagonally across the bikers' yard, then the lifers' yard to C's back gate, where two young cons were standing, watching him. One of them—tall, wearing an untidy mustache—was Kyle Smith. Bauman didn't know the other.

"Where you goin'?" the other man said. He was plump, shorter than Smith, his light-brown hair neatly combed, parted low on the left in the old style.

"Tell Shupe I'm here," Bauman said.

"Vice president didn't say he was expecting you or anybody else, Teach," Smith said. "Don't you have a weather run through our area?"

"That's right."

"Well, this is a real nice morning. No rain or anything. —I think you should just go back in B, and walk around."

"Go tell Shupe I'm here," Bauman said.

"What do you think?" the plump man said to Smith.

"Oh, go on an' tell him," Smith said, and to Bauman, "I don't guess you're goin' to waste Mr. Shupe's time."

Bauman didn't answer, and Smith, his partner gone, seemed content to stand in silence by the open gate, looking down at Bauman, mildly curious.

After what seemed quite a while, the plump man came back and said, "He'll see him."

Smith led Bauman into the building hall, past lounging men, past posters advertising Growth-Behind-Walls. He stopped at the club's office door, knocked, opened it and gestured Bauman in, then stepped back and closed the door behind him.

There were three men in the office. Shupe—snub-nosed, handsome in a slightly popeyed way, auburn hair and beard cropped short—was sitting at his desk staring down at an open loose-leaf notebook. He was wearing a khaki street safari jacket over his denims. Tips of several different-colored pens showed at the top of the safari jacket's upper right pocket.

"I don't agree with that," he said. "They're not trying to screw us."

"I didn't say they were tryin' to screw us." Brian Wiltz, whom Bauman had never met personally, stood leaning against the far office wall, his ankles crossed. "—What I do think is, they're gettin' screwed on the price, so we're gettin' screwed on the price."

"Bauman," Shupe said, looking up at him, "I'll be right with you." And to Wiltz, "—You say they aren't taking advantage?"

"Right. They're just bein' stupid, that's all."

"So?"

"So, I say let's tell 'em to look for a source isn't goin' to screw the both of us."

"I'll buy that," Shupe said. "I'm tired of us practically losing money with this shit." He looked at Bauman again, spoke to him. "Silk-screen supplies. Cost of paper's a pisser."

The third lifer in the office was the huge man Bauman had seen typing there before. He wore drooping mustachios, had FUCK tattooed across his right cheek, YOU across his left. He was sitting at a second desk, facing Shupe's, and hadn't stopped typing at Bauman's entrance, was still typing.

The office's atmosphere—the bare bulbs in its ceiling fixture, the slight drifts of fog-gray cigarette smoke, the dead white walls plastered with posters, slogans, graphs—all reminded Bauman, as often at State, of scenes from forties films, in which all was shades of gray, and everyone smoked and talked tough.

"Something we can do for you?" Wiltz said. A man in his thirties, not exceptionally large or powerful, Brian Wiltz—lifer vice president for accounts receivable—had an almost comic adenoidal air, his large nose shadowing a small mouth always held ajar so its lower teeth showed. His black hair was crewcut close. His eyes were a very dark gray.

"You can do something for me," Bauman said.

"Now what would that be?" Wiltz said. "—What could we be doin' for you?" Wiltz, the most feared instrument of lifer murder power, was a man who'd found his talent late. Sentenced for multiple rapes—or so Bauman had heard—Wiltz, once in State, had discovered in himself a knack for killing. Though reputed a wonder with a knife, his preferred style was to step up behind his target in a poorly patrolled line or crowd, then fracture the man's skull with a fourteen-inch length of one-inch PVC pipe poured full of cement and set—this weapon, carried taped to his right lower leg, alerting no metal detectors.

Wiltz, arrested twice in State and released both times for lack of evidence, had killed at least four men in his seven years incarcerated, and might have killed six—two of them stabbed (one found in the A-block showers, hung with his own intestine). An amiable man to deal with, never nasty, never bullying, he was feared all the more for this good nature, which broadcast no warning.

"Step up here and speak your piece, Bauman," Shupe said. "We're busy."

Bauman walked to the desk. "You can leave my boy alone."

"You bet," Shupe said, closed his loose-leaf notebook and gave Bauman his attention. Shupe had mild hazel eyes. "—Our organization would regret having to off a kid plays the good shortstop your boy does."

"Leave him alone. Don't ever bother him again."

"Nothing easier than that," Shupe said. "And you can believe this or not, but I'm glad we won't *have* to bother him again. That sort of thing is the worst part of my job."

"How's your arm, Teach?" Wiltz said. "Something like that—you get an infection, you're in trouble."

"Don't ever send anybody to go near him again," Bauman said, speaking a little louder, as if Shupe were hard of hearing.

"You bet," Shupe said, shoved his chair back a little, and stood up. Then he bent to stub out his cigarette in a small white ashtray, a cracked old souvenir piece, with STATE printed around the edge, and a guard tower painted in blue outline in its shallow bowl. "Now, as regards the job you're going to be doing for us—"

"You didn't listen to me."

"Sure I did," Shupe said. "Now, you listen to me."

Bauman felt a great impatience, an impatience that rose as he felt it, so he seemed lifted as the commencement of an ocean wave would have lifted him. It hurried him so he didn't have time for the knife.

"I already did a little ground work on this," Shupe said. And Bauman, worried about having to hit with his left, was able to lean over the desk, swing a roundabout right, reaching a little, and hit Shupe hard on the left side of the head.

"Uh, oh," somebody said, and Shupe, knocked off balance, stepped back into his chair, knocked it over, and fell awkwardly down onto one knee.

"Uh, oh." Wiltz.

"You'll listen to that, motherfucker!" Bauman said, and was suddenly covered from behind by what felt like a fall of weighty canvas, a tremendously heavy cloth that wrapped itself around him so he couldn't move for the burden. He smelled sweat, looked down, and saw immense forearms hugging him, great spatulate hands. The tattooed man had him from the back.

"What the fuck," Shupe said, getting up. "—What in the *fuck* do you think you're doing?" He was holding his hand over his left ear. "You cocksucker, you could have damaged my hearing!"

"What do we do?" The tattooed man spoke high over Bauman's head, his enveloping hug hurting Bauman's sore arm, his weight bearing hard.

The office door opened so swiftly it banged against the wall; Kyle Smith and the plump man stood in the doorway.

"Who asked for you guys?" Wiltz said. "We didn't ask for you guys. This is an officers' meeting." He seemed more annoyed at them than at Bauman, and the intruders stepped back and out of the doorway like a dance team, Smith reaching out to catch the doorknob, pull the door closed behind them.

"You college weirdo," Shupe said to Bauman. He was rubbing his sore ear gently. "Is everybody in this fucking place nuts, or what?"

"How's that ear, Jim boy?" Wiltz said.

"You people send anybody else—bother my son—*anything!* Next time I'll have the knife in that hand." Bauman felt oddly safe in the tattooed man's arms. "—I'll cut your brains out for you."

"I hate it," Wiltz said from his wall. "—I hate it when a cultured guy gets down an' dirty. What the fuck is civilization for, if a guy can drop it that fast?"

"What do we do?" the tattooed man said.

"Nothing," Shupe said, stepped around the side of his desk, set himself, and kicked Bauman's left shin. He was wearing lace-up leather shoes.

Bauman had jerked his leg aside as the kick came, but it caught him on the shin anyway, with a sharp whacking sound. The pain was surprising. Shupe stepped back, then stepped forward and kicked him again, not seeming angry as he did it, handsome rust-bearded face only impatient. Even though Bauman had moved his leg as much as he could—worried about being kicked in the same place—that was what happened, probably by accident. The pain was greater with this second kick, and had a sickening quality to it, as if the bone, bruised the first time, was now damaged. When Shupe stepped back to step in and kick again, Bauman didn't know whether to try to move the leg away or not. He decided not, but couldn't stick to that and moved it anyway. The kick struck his left ankle, and Bauman was relieved enough at it missing his sore shin, that he didn't mind. The fourth kick, delivered by Shupe in a more athletic high-swinging style, and with a soft grunt of effort, caught Bauman solidly in the crotch.

"Ouch," Wiltz said from the wall, and Bauman, despite the tattooed man's great strength, slowly doubled forward, contracting, until he'd bowed to Shupe in the most elaborate fashion. Bauman felt—he was certain—that his testicles hadn't been smashed. The pain had a certain familiarity about it—the anguish of a low blow, seeming to draw his insides down, tug them out of him in intimate agony. But suffered before. Bauman had been hit there—and, if anything, even harder—by a young black middleweight the fourth or fifth time he'd gone down to McElvey's to train. That blow—accidental, the boy in a hurry to put this old white sucker down—had indeed put Bauman down for half an hour, and set him to walking carefully the rest of the day.

Bauman bowed to Shupe for ten or fifteen seconds—then, though it felt he might be hurting himself, slowly straightened up.

Shupe, standing in observation, nodded, said, "O.K.," and went back behind his desk to pick up his chair and sit in it. "Let him go," he said to the tattooed man.

"How's that ear, Jim? Gettin' hit that way could damage your hearing," Wiltz said.

"Very funny, Brian," Shupe said. And to the tattooed man, "Jerry, let him go."

Bauman was released slowly, the thick arms around him loosening, then withdrawing as if reluctantly, parting, sliding away at either side.

"Just remember," Bauman said, still working at standing up straight.

"Oh, you bet," Shupe said. "Isn't every day we deal with a ding like you. Now, you finished playing games, why don't you just sit down and let us get done with this bullshit. O.K.?" Shupe tapped a fresh cigarette out of his pack and lit up. "Sit down."

Bauman heard typing recommence behind him, looked back and saw the tattooed man—Jerry—at his desk and back to work. There was a second wooden chair by that desk, and Bauman pulled it over and sat carefully down. His shin felt as if one of the kicks might have chipped the bone. He could feel his heartbeat pulsing in that injury, but not in his aching groin.

"O.K." Shupe very businesslike. "First thing is, we're a paramilitary organization—not like those assholes in the other clubs got no real stake in the joint. We're doing the heavy time, so we're real serious about chain of command and all that. O.K.?"

Bauman nodded. Shupe, erstwhile Cadillac salesman, was serving two consecutives for kidnapping and killing his boss and his boss's wife. Her father had refused to pay.

"Now, President Nash is of the opinion—and he could be right—that some hack might be offing people, cutting himself a piece of action where he's got no business, for reasons of bread or dope or an Admin power trip or whatever." Shupe reached up to tug gently at his sore ear. "I personally have my doubts the administration had the same kind of hard-on with that nigger, Spencer, they had with Barney Metzler. On the other hand, looks to me like the nigger couldn't have been offed without a hack at least looking the other way—which, far as we're concerned, is just as out of line as if the hack cut the coon's apple himself. O.K.? Follow me?"

"Yes," Bauman said.

"O.K. You're set up to snitch—to Gorney, Vermillier—we don't give a shit. You got your passes back, and they're going to cut you some slack. Fine. Go and do it. Find out why and find out who. Then tell us, and we'll tell you what to pass on to the pigs. You heard of a double agent? Well, that's what you are. You are an inmate representative—don't ever forget it."

"I'll do it," Bauman said, "—just as long as nobody bothers my family again."

"Deal," Shupe said. "Now, we already contacted that jig Perkins, runs the B.N.A. We contacted the greaser, Vargas. And Brian here had a little talk with Ganz, and the bikers O.K. it, too. Nobody wants some hack using his position to off inmates. Period."

"What about the Indians?"

"Fuck 'em. —There's what, twenty, twenty-five of those guys? Becker's their big chief, and he does what we tell him to do. And by the way, Perkins and the Zapata guy and Ganz. Each one of those mothers wants to talk to you, have you pay your respects, probably checking to see if we're trying to pull some swifty on 'em. You will do that. Tomorrow'll be O.K."

"Great guys," Wiltz said. "You're goin' to like 'em."

"And if," Bauman said, "—after all this, there's no corrections man involved?"

"You got the star, big mouth," Shupe said. "Go find out who *is* involved. And by the way, this is strictly officers-only info, all clubs. Far as rank and file is concerned, clubs gave you a warrant—you not being connected-up to any of 'em—to look for some deep snitch been giving us all a hard time. Far as rank and file is concerned, we're paying you good bread to stick your nose in. Is that cute, or what?"

"It's too cute. It's Wizard of Oz, is what it is.—That's what all this nonsense is."

"In Oz, asshole, nothing's too cute," Shupe said. "—You don't know that? You haven't learned that yet? The weirder it is, faster inmates are going to believe it."

"Got that right." Wiltz, from the wall.

"Now," Shupe said, "—I think we spent enough time on this. How about you get out of here and get your ass in gear."

"Backup," Wiltz said.

"Oh, right. You run into something, somebody starts giving you a hard time—"

"You mean kills me."

"—Any kind of hard time, you let that biker, Duerstadt, know about it. Guy's right there for you—same block, eats in the same mess hall, same shift. Handy guy. In fact, any information you get, you give to him. Now what does that tell you, smartass?"

"It tells me Switchboard is making too many calls."

"It should tell you we aren't fooling, here. Pokey Duerstadt's ass, as of right now, is hung on your line. Your responsibility. Ganz finds out he's a source of ours and cuts his balls off, means you fucked up."

Bauman thought Shupe might have more to say, so sat waiting.

Shupe stared at him for a few moments, then said, "What are you doing sitting there, Bauman? You got work to do."

"I was waiting for you to wish me luck," Bauman said, stood slowly, straightened up, and tested his left leg for weight bearing.

"I'd wish you luck, Teach," Wiltz said, "—but I don't give no luck away."

Bauman had tried not to limp leaving the lifer office, but his ankle, which hadn't felt too bad while he was sitting, had pained him sharply when he stood, and forced him to limp just a little. His testicles ached, but felt better if he bent slightly forward as he walked.

At C's back gate—Smith and the plump man still standing guard, a hack named Werbner talking with them—Bauman heard someone calling behind him, stopped and turned to see an inmate trotting after. This tall awkward man was a ding lifer Bauman knew by sight. He'd seen the man out on the walkways, striding, gesticulating, talking to himself, the conversations difficult to follow since the man spoke only his responses to his imaginary interlocutor.

"Hey, Teach. Hey!"

"What do you want?"

"Hey, you know I was wonderin' could you spend some time teachin' me writin'?"

"I'm a little busy right now," Bauman said.

"Hey, your own good time. Your own good time. Name's Hull." He held out a dirty hand to shake. Hull stank of urine. He seemed to suffer from a sort of rhythmic tremor that, commencing in his legs, swiftly worked up through his body in a wave, to end in sudden horselike shakes of his head. Hull's head looked rather small for his size and considerable height. His face, faded as an old photograph, was streaked with dirt under long, matted hair. His eyes were a watery brown.

"I'm a little too busy to take on another student just now, Hull." Werbner and the two lifers were listening, amused.

"Well, I'd sure appreciate it—boy, I'd sure appreciate it. I go to the regular classes an' I sit there all mornin' long, but Mr. Bannerjee says I'm too scattered. That's bullshit. I'm no way too scattered to write my fuckin' name. And that's somethin' I know for sure!"

"How do you know that?" Bauman said. "Bannerjee's a good teacher; maybe you're just not ready to learn writing yet."

"The reason I know it," Hull said, "—is I used to be able to write my name an' anybody else's name, too. So I don't need somebody to teach me to do it; I need somebody to teach me to do it again."

"I understand," Bauman said.

"When I get started writin' again, I can write everything down. I got too fuckin' much to remember, unless I can write it down."

"Hey, geek, leave the man alone," Smith said, Bauman having risen in status by virtue of his stay in Shupe's office.

"You leave *me* alone," Hull said. "I can talk to somebody if I want." But his body denied this, his legs making abortive shambling movements of turning around and walking away against his wishes, so that, his balance upset, Hull had to twist back around at the waist, thrash his arms in small unsteady circles to keep standing in place.

"You come to my house," Bauman said. "Two-tier, B. And we'll see if we can remind you how to write, Mr. Hull."

"O.K." Hull's arms were rowing slower, his hands describing very stylized large gestures in the air, almost but not quite like the sign languages of the deaf. Bauman supposed these signs were meant for Hull's invisible companion, and suspected this companion could write. Hull appeared to hear some query from the air above his head, heard it out, then said to Bauman, "He wants—I want to know how much is it goin' to cost?"

"Your friend'll pay me," Bauman said, turned away and went on through the narrow gate past the lifers' grins, the hack's.

He felt—once he was walking, limping, out across the courtyard—that he'd done fairly well, and found himself even enjoying his predicament, his injuries, as if they affirmed a certain importance. "Vanity," Bauman said to himself, but more softly than Hull spoke in his solo conversations. He was glad he hadn't had time, hadn't had the opportunity to get the knife out. He wished he'd hit Nash, though, up in Seg—instead of Shupe, who was only Nash's shadow. It took some of the honor from the punch. Most of the honor from the punch.

• • •

Bauman went back into B-block where he'd come out. Billings, still standing there, incurious about the limp, patted him very lightly down—avoiding his groin, and so the blade—then nodded him through into the kitchen, to pass steamy deep steel trays of bubbling chipped beef and tubs of strawberry Jell-O in preparation, then through the empty mess hall and down the wide basement corridor to the phone line, which was very short this early in the day.

Bauman had forgotten whether Susanne had a class Tuesday morning—but she didn't.

"Where were you? Where *were* you, Charlie? All they told me was you were in 'administrative disciplinary confinement,' and no visitors!"

"I was segged for wearing that Rolex."

"And now you're out?"

"Now I'm out."

"God damn it. God *damn* it! I told you not to take that—that stupid thing up there."

"And you were right. Believe me, I've learned my lesson."

"Is this going to keep you there longer? Is it a bad mark on your record?"

"No. An administrative confinement. It shouldn't make any difference as far as getting out of here goes."

"Well, you don't sound too depressed."

"I'm depressed about missing you, and about your driving all the way to hell up here for nothing, honey. My fault."

"I'm happy to drive up to see you. I have to do that, even if sometimes it makes us miserable to be together in that awful room. Charlie, I'm happier—even being miserable—when I'm with you."

"An elegant compliment."

"And I know, I know you see yourself as the selfish old seducer of the almost practically virginal young grad student."

"No, I don't."

"Yes you do, Charlie. Sure you do. You've always thought that. —And I want to tell you a little secret, Professor. That wasn't precisely the way it was."

"Another elegant compliment. How's Braudel?"

"Oh, he's been an unbelievable pain in the ass. You know all he'll eat, now? Cat food. I didn't give him any for two days, and he lay on the kitchen floor and moaned, and when I made the big mistake of bending down to pet him, the little bastard bit me!"

"You hurt?"

"No, no, just a little dent on my wrist. And the funny thing is, the shittier he acts, the more I like him. Like master, like dog, I suppose. . . . Poor women."

"What about the amber-trade thesis?"

"I don't know yet. I didn't get the paper back, but I think it puzzled him, anyway. He didn't sneer at me yesterday, and he went on and on about nontextual analysis, so maybe you've got him worried."

"No. We have him worried."

"Well . . . please, please behave yourself up there until Saturday."

"I will," Bauman said.

"I'll be up there in that dreadful room, and you can take me into the bathroom and completely have your way with me—if we can find a free stall. I love you, Charlie."

"And how could I not love you?" Bauman said.

Hanging up, he thought of asking Cernan if he could sneak a second call—against State's rule of one call a day except on weekends—but, undecided what to say to Mr. Silber, decided not, and limped across the corridor to wait in a fairly short line for the canteen.

He spent three and a half in scrip for two Bit-O'-Honeys, a SKOR, and a small tube of Crest—then unwrapped and ate one of the Bit-O'-Honeys, slowly, section by section, on his way back down the corridor to B, up the basement steps to Ground-tier, then up the circular stair to Two, to tuck the shank and sheath back into Scooter's TV.

His shin and ankle both hurt him as he climbed down from the stool, and Bauman put his foot up on the side of his bunk, tugged his pants leg up, and examined his injuries. His ankle showed nothing; you couldn't tell by looking he'd been kicked there. The shin was a cloudy light rose-purple, several inches up and down. Swelling slightly. The skin hadn't been broken, though. Standing, letting his pants leg fall, Bauman unzipped his fly, reached in through his underpants, and gently felt his testicles. They were sore—one was, particularly—but didn't seem swollen, or not swollen much.

He zipped up, unwrapped the SKOR, threw the wrapper into their little cardboard trash box, and went out of his house and down the stairs, chewing the chocolate-covered toffee as he went.

Clean now to pass through the North-yard gate, still limping, but the ache in his groin faded so he walked easily upright, Bauman considered going to D-block to review verb tenses with Wayman, thought of going after that to drill McNeil, in A, on survival English—then decided that both men, having waited a week, could wait another day or two.

He started down the right-hand walkway over to East yard and the gym, but after a few feet—still feeling his pulse beat in his injured shin—he turned back, smiled at a friendly black convict who smiled at him in passing, then walked the long stretch along the front of A-block over to West yard, then down the walkway to South.

Bauman showed his pass to Elroy at the yard-gate booth. Elroy, amiable enough, a failed farmer, was getting a lot of outdoor duty. He examined the pass with some care, then waved Bauman through into South yard.

The infirmary, even with its ancient whitewash fading, seemed almost sugary in autumn light, the more so with the South wall's granite, storm-cloud gray, rearing behind it. . . .

"Don't bother me, man. An' I mean don't bother me. I got a man dyin' in here all las' night an' all this mornin', an' I don't need no shit from nobody." Tiger, sorrowful in blood-dappled whites.

"Who is it?"

"Teddy Rawlins, AIDS dude. Poor asshole's bleedin' out. Now why don't you get your firebug butt gone from my infirmary."

Past Tiger's shoulder, Bauman saw Ron Michaelson and another town doctor, Tracy, halfway down the chronic ward, with Irma standing by holding a small steel tray. The doctors were bending over Rawlins' bed, doing something—one of those medical procedures glossed over in popular drama, intubations, forcing of airways, deep interventions with long large-gauge needles for which considerable force was required, and during which the patient, an object stunned by event, grimaced, strained, made soft humming sounds as if to add his strength to the accomplishment.

"I'm sorry," Bauman said. "I wanted to talk with Spencer's buddy, Burdon. Jomo Burdon."

"Teach, you ain' talkin' to shit on that ward. —Man, don't you know I got no other place to put those people in there? Those sad motherfuckers got nothin' to do but lay on their beds in there watchin' that poor sucker's blood come out ever' openin' he's got." Tiger stood upset, his round black head and broad black hands completing a body otherwise snowy in medical whites, bulky, blood-spattered as a polar bear's just fed off a careless seal.

"Bad timing," Bauman said. "Sorry."

"You want to talk to that fool, that's O.K., but you come visit another time," Tiger said, and reaching out as Bauman turned, to usher him on his way, lightly gripped his left forearm—and was startled when Bauman grunted and jerked the arm away.

"What the fuck's the matter with you, man? —Is that a sore arm or somethin'?"

"It's a little sore," Bauman said, and started off toward the stairs.

"Wait a minute. What the fuck you talkin' about? Let me look at that arm."

"No, it's fine," Bauman said, but Tiger, tenderer perhaps for losing one patient, was determined on another.

"Show me that arm."

"It's fine. There's no infection or anything."

"What the fuck you know?" Tiger said. "You don't know shit about medicine, man. Don't waste my time, now. Show me that fuckin' arm."

Bauman pulled up his jacket sleeve, unbuttoned his shirt cuff, and pulled that sleeve up as well.

"Mother-*fucker*. What the hell you do that for? You do that?"

"No," Bauman said. "And it's not infected."

Tiger sighed the deepest sigh. "You come on with me," he said. "You fuckers in this place are drivin' me out of my mind." He started back down the hall, saw Bauman hadn't followed him, and said, "I tol' you to come on!"

Bauman walked behind Tiger to the end of the hall—noticing the green tile floor needed waxing again—and through a door on the right into the infirmary office and examining room. The room was large, its walls egg-shell white, and—with three tall, barred windows—was almost airy despite the clutter of white-painted chairs, stools, the examining table, a row of medicine and file cabinets along the wall.

"Sit down an' take them top things off," Tiger said, went to a glass-fronted cabinet, opened it, and began searching its white shelves—his hand a great black spider among the folded linens, small white boxes of bandages, frosted white plastic bottles and brown glass jars of this and that.

Bauman took off his jacket and hung it on a hook on the wall behind him, unbuttoned his denim shirt, took that off and hung it up, then sat on an old metal stool—white paint chipped to show a gleam of stainless steel beneath—and waited while Tiger closed the cabinet, a brown plastic bottle and a small blue box in his hand.

". . . I count twenty-five," Tiger said, bending over, examining, dabbing gently with a cotton ball he'd wet with hydrogen peroxide.

"Twenty-seven," Bauman said. "—It was a few days ago. They're a lot better."

"You know you got bad second-degree burns here, man? Shit, maybe they third degree. —They blew on them butts, I bet, 'fore they burned you."

"They blew on them," Bauman said, watching Tiger work, grateful for the attention, for someone to share the burns with. Each burn was small almost as the end of a pencil eraser, and, under its fat little red-black blister, almost an eighth inch deep. The burns formed together a large fairly neat five-pointed star dotted across the underside of his forearm, the pattern centered there and extending halfway around the arm on both sides. The star lay against a background of inflamed skin, a duller red, less angry than it had been. . . .

Bauman had been taken as a fool. Carl Sorenson, young neighbor to the right, block-out to stroll and stopping by to visit, had said good morning, held his thin dirty hand out to shake. Then, doing that, suddenly gripped much harder, yanked Bauman's hand and arm through the bars—and was just able to hold on until two other men (one, the giant who'd blown a kiss two days before) had joined him, gripped the arm more firmly.

Three more men came quickly after—talking, laughing, enjoying their morning block-out—to stand alongside Bauman's bars between the arm holders and the block gate, so it would seem only a social gathering.

Bauman had punched out through the bars with his left and hit one of the holders hard before that arm also was grabbed—was the arm they'd really wanted—and after a quick wrestle it was held harder than his right, extended, its elbow fulcrumed against the horizontal bracing of the bars; then the shirt sleeve was unbuttoned, pushed up. Bauman tried kicking, but a flat steel member across the bars below blocked his feet.

"You can always yell for the cops," Nash said to Bauman. He'd strolled up last, then stayed to watch while the giant, intent on his work, turned—by leverage of his own terrific grip on Bauman's wrist, by the aid two other men gave him in holding—turned the left arm advantageous for careful burning, so as not to spoil the pattern.

"You can always start yelling," Nash said again, observing, after two or three holes had been burned.

But by the time Bauman saw clearly how sensible it would have been to yell, to call the hacks, it seemed too late. Rather, new rules appeared in order, as an accommodation to the five, six men who clustered—talking, laughing for the gate hacks—while giving him such concentrated attention, delivering to him pain so severe he could no longer distinguish any particular burning, as if his arm was being sawed through, rather than burned. Bauman felt he almost owed them his silence against the risk they ran that he might have shouted, have gotten them into trouble, that he might have embarrassed this close-knit society formed with him against his bars, destroyed it by calling on strangers, and revealed himself a coward.

In lieu of yelling, there were sounds he made, attitudes permissable after a while. A sort of humming sound with his mouth tight closed, that ended in a gasp when he needed breath. No one seemed to think those noises were wrong, or that he was wrong to strain his head back, as if to get his most essential self as far from the arm as possible. No one thought that was odd, or made fun of it. His body also wrestled and twisted from time to time against the bars, as if to move for its arms, that couldn't.

Bauman became dreamy after a while, just after his pain became more important than he was, felt himself floating and was able to study the giant's pale sweating bloodhound's face as, concentrating on his pattern, the man absently accepted another cigarette, puffed its tip bright ruby.

"You're sworn," Nash had said to him later, before they all went away, left him to lie down. "Now, you got an official capacity. . . ."

"How bad does this shit hurt you now?" Tiger, dabbing.

"Not bad. Sometimes when I pick something up. —Hurt a lot, day or two after it happened."

"Tell you somethin', man—" dab, dab. "Dude gets this fucked up, he's been dealin' with the wrong people. Jus' a word to the wise. Any motherfucker burned me like this, I'd have that motherfucker's ass no matter took me ten goddamn years." Tiger finished and straightened up. "Truth is, ain' shit anybody can do for this shit, now. Jus' keep it clean. I mean *clean*. I'm goin' give you a bandage—an' you jus' put it over loose. Loose, like I'm doin'. Keep dirt off it." He finished his bandaging, taped the gauze neatly on, then stepped back and screwed the top on the hydrogen peroxide bottle. "You goin' have that star on you day you die."

"Bad company," Bauman said.

"You show me some good fuckin' company in this joint," Tiger went back to the cabinet, put the hydrogen peroxide away, and returned with a larger bottle, white plastic, and three white tablets in the palm of his hand. "Aspirin," he said. "Take 'em." He watched while Bauman put the aspirin in his mouth. Then he unscrewed the top of the white plastic bottle and took a long drink before handing it to Bauman. "Teach, you gettin' bottle in bond. That shit's too good ever to leave the infirmary."

Bauman took one swallow to wash the aspirin down; the pruno was very good. It was clear colored, like vodka, had vodka's alcohol sting to it, but with a rough fruity edge. Bauman took a second swallow, for pleasure, then handed it back.

"I give me some of that to men goin' to die up here," Tiger said, screwed the top on, and went to put the bottle away. "You believe in Jesus?" he said, and closed the cabinet door.

"Possibly there was a man," Bauman said. "One man, maybe two brothers who were simplified into one man." He stood up to put on his shirt and jacket.

"Jus' a man?"

"—If he existed at all. There's no contemporary record of him. Only some elaborated cult tales written about three generations after his supposed death."

"Jus' a man. . . ."

"An interesting man, if he did exist. Probably illegitimate, a mama's boy. Became a country rabbi and a first-class preacher. Maybe took himself a little too seriously, got mixed up in politics."

"Jus' a preacher," Tiger said. "Well, I say that's right, from what I see. My mama an' my auntie believe all that shit." He shook his head, doleful. "—But it sure is bad news for Teddy Rawlins."

"What's in those files, Tiger? Medical records?"

"Oh, yeah. They's a load of stuff in there. —You come on, I need to be gettin' back."

"Would you have Spencer's report in there—the autopsy?"

"Who Spencer?"

"Man was killed last week."

"Oh, yeah. —We got him."

"Let me ask you something," Bauman said. "—Wouldn't take much time. Could I see that report?"

"Your ass! I ain' goin' show you shit, man. You got no right in there, an' I got no right lookin' in there, neither."

"I'd pay you."

"How much? —Fuck you, man. I'm not gettin' my ass fucked up."

"Twenty-five, scrip."

"What for? What's that got to do with you?"

"Just something I need to know."

"Man, I hope you know you could get into some deep shit."

"Just a quick look—and Metzler, too. Just a quick look at those."

"Metzler? A 'quick look' for you, an' my black ass is out of a job, back in population like a dummy!"

"Don't do it, if you don't want to do it," Bauman said.

"You fuckin' a I'm not goin' do it if I don't want to do it. —An' I'm damn sure not goin' do it for no twenty-five scrip!"

"Twenty-five, street."

"Shit." Tiger went to the second white file cabinet, bent to look at the cards taped to the front of the drawers. He unsnapped his heavy key ring from his belt, selected a key, and unlocked the cabinet. Reaching down, he pulled the second drawer from the top partly open. "You better get your ass over here, you want to see somethin'!"

Bauman found Kenneth Spencer's thin file, tugged it out and opened it, leafed through psychological tests and test scores, weight, blood type, and medical history—and saw four pages stapled at their upper left corner, of which two pages were eight-by-twelve photographs in color. Spencer was a lighter brown than he'd remembered, had an odd expression on his face, as if he were about to wake up—and had been opened and then roughly stitched closed all the way up from a shriveled penis to his neck, where that wound (postmortem) met his cut throat.

"Hurry up," Tiger said beside him. "That's that poor little motherfucker all right. —Look at that." Bauman followed the thick black pointer of Tiger's finger to many little lines across dead Spencer's slender forearms, the palms of his hands. "Look. . . ."

"What's that?"

"Man, where you been? That's defense cuts. You know—" he stood, miming, "—where he was tryin' an' keep the blade off him."

"That looks strange. . . ."

"Shit. I seen that shit plenty." Tiger held up a white-sleeved arm, tugged the sleeve back, and demonstrated three, four very thin white lines marching around black-skinned muscle from wrist to elbow. "Think I don't know about that shit? Dude comes at you with a fuckin' blade, man, you don't give a shit he cuts your arms. You happy he be cuttin' them an' not cuttin' you."

Bauman looked back down at the photograph. "But so many?"

"Little guy didn' want to go."

Bauman looked down at Spencer's dreaming face, full of the knowledge of emptiness. "Could a man have held him to his bars with one hand and used the shank with the other, even with him being so slight?"

"He ain' shanked."

"What do you mean?"

"That ain' no shankin'. That's a— Could be a razor, or one of them carpet knives, you know? Somethin' real sharp edge."

"I don't understand."

"Put that fuckin' thing up an' come on here an' look at the other one. One of them people goin' be comin' after me in a minute. That

Irma faggot can't wipe her ass without I'm tellin' her how to do it!" And he jerked the file from Bauman's hand, closed it, bent to fit it back into place, and slid the file door shut.

"But why not a shank?"

"Come on over here!" Tiger stepped past one file cabinet to the next one down, unlocked it, and tugged the top drawer open. Searched through the files. "Ain' no shankin', 'cause with a shank, maybe you got a real sharp edge, but it's pointed. An' that's what you use, that point." He pulled a folder, handed it to Bauman. "You got it sharp jus' so you can get it down inside a man, an' he hardly know it. But you want to kill the mother—you understan' me?—you stickin' that point in there deep, two, three times; you goin' into his heart to kill the motherfucker! Offin' a dude jus' by cuttin' is a lot of trouble. My gran'daddy do that kind of shit, him an' his frien's. This dude here maybe had him a point on that blade, but could be he couldn' get a good position on that nigger, or could be he was jus' playin', wasn' in no hurry get it done."

Metzler had been an older man than Bauman imagined, surely past his killing days. His face—wide, rather froglike, deeply lined (Bauman thought of Mark Nellis), and not composed into mystery—was a slack shambles of gaping mouth, cut left cheek. His eyes were almost open, a crescent moon of white revealed of each. Metzler's barrel chest, furred thick with gray—the same gray as his crewcut—showed, Bauman thought, very similar wounds to Spencer's. Several—many fine lines striping him at either side of the autopsy's vertical stitched seam, until that met a terrible wound—gross, so deep that black vacancy appeared within its gape, and running all the way across a considerable belly, just below its navel. Some fine lines traced across the dead man's hands as well, deeper across one palm; that hand, Metzler's right, turned up as he lay on his steel table, as if to beg a favor.

Bauman imagined the man—alive, squat, truculent—lying in his lower bunk watching Lee Cousins sitting holding a mirror, brushing his hair.

"Same shit," Tiger said, looking over Bauman's shoulder. He pointed to the deep cross-cut. "That's the one done it. Let his insides out. Now come on, put that shit away."

"No stabbing?"

"No way. That one's same as the other one. Jus' all cut up. Hadn got that one across him, across his guts?—them others wouldn' kill him. Dude did it couldn' get a position on the man, or figured he had the time to play, that's all."

"But both the same?"

"Look like it. They both greased up, too."

"Greased up?"

"That's right. I remember both those motherfuckers come in, they was greased. Vaseline, or KY. Had grease on their han's in all that blood."

"But why? What the hell was it for?"

"Maybe they was faggots. Them sissies got to grease up, they goin' fuck."

"What did the doctors say about that?"

"Shit, them motherfuckers don't care! They don't know nothin' about bein' in a joint, anyhow. Now, give me that shit. You got your twenty-five bucks' worth, man, an' I expect that bread delivered this afternoon." He took the file away just as a lady's voice spoke from the door.

"Oooh, you bad, bad boys!"

Irma, in medical whites subtly ruffled at the throat, stained red lower down, stood in the doorway, accusing, as Tiger replaced the file, slammed the drawer shut.

"I saw what youuu did."

"What the hell you doin' in here? Why ain't you with the patient?"

"Oh, Tiger," Irma said, "—Teddy's dead." And apparently struck by the telling, tugged from her white jacket's side pocket a small yellow-flowered handkerchief, touched her eyes very lightly, then blew her nose.

Chapter SEVEN

That night, Bauman slept fairly well. His testicles ached, but not enough to prevent his sleeping. His left ankle was still sore.

He dreamed of Beth. She lay on their old living-room sofa, talking with him. She was wearing white shorts, a white T-shirt, their plain chalk accented by the complex living paleness (white woven with the faintest shades of pearl, tan, and pink) of her throat, her arms, her sturdy legs crossed at the ankles. Her brown eyes were darkened further by their accustomed shadow, as if she watched through shade.

In his dream, Bauman sat just opposite. While he watched, she uncrossed her legs, straightened them, and they slowly became longer. "You like that?" she said. "—You like them better?" Her face had become longer-jawed; it melted, stretched as Bauman watched. Became nearly Susanne's face. "How's that?" Beth's voice spoke from Susanne's wider mouth. "—Look at this," she said, and reached down to lift her T-shirt hem to reveal her breasts. One, the right, still Beth's soft drooping moderate teat, aureoled in brown; the other, the left breast, presented itself firmer, pear-shaped, its long nipple pale pink.

"I can do anything," Beth said through Susanne's mouth. "—Want me to take my pants off? I can smell like her, too. I can change everything." She turned over on the sofa, lay on her stomach, and pushed her white shorts down. Her narrow back was Susanne's, her small buttocks. Beth in Susanne turned her head to look over her shoulder. "—Do you think this makes me a different girl?"

"It's certainly a different ass," Bauman thought he answered—but woke doubting he'd said that to her in the dream. It sounded like a clever afterthought as he'd surfaced, drawn up out of sleep by the morning bell. It was too bad no notice was taken of the funny things said, the decent things, the brave and kind things done in dreams. It seemed a shame to waste them.

Susanne would be visiting, tomorrow. He'd be able to be certain of her face for a few days after that. Certain as he no longer was of Beth's or Philly's. Beth growing older. His son growing up. . . .

Breakfast—the mess hall noisier in the morning, echoing with more shouted conversation than Bauman had recalled. Breakfast was hot chocolate—sandy, sour, nearly undrinkable, but religiously provided at least once a week in place of coffee. With that, several slices of white bread, damp and fragile, and two slices of what was called Pennsylvania scrapple.

Once, while he was scraping his tray at the mess-hall entrance, he'd asked Rudy Gottschalk what the scrapple was made from. Gottschalk, tall, cadaverous, had stood surprised by Bauman's question, its naivete, its rudeness. Gottschalk's tattooed hair—its fine dark-red strands inked in curving ranks across his bald sweat-shiny scalp—was not at all convincing on close inspection.

"Teach," he'd said, "Teach—you fuckin' amaze me. You just fuckin' amaze me." And never answered the question.

Perteet, apparently grown used to finding the grazing good at their table, and sitting massive at breakfast again to take advantage of the prodigal's finicky appetite, was happy to receive first one, then both of Bauman's slices of scrapple, warding Scooter's tentative little orange plastic fork away with a "What the fuck you think you're doin', man?"

"I don't want all this bread," Bauman said to Scooter in recompense. "Want some?"

Scooter, prideful. "Shit no; I don't want that shit, man."

"I'll take it," Perteet said and reached, but Bauman surprised himself by saying, "Will you cut that crap *out?* What am I here, a fucking supermarket?" And was further surprised when Perteet took this correction with a sigh, silently withdrew his large left hand, his own tiny orange fork, and sat, feelings apparently injured, staring glumly at his plate.

"Pete," Perteet's first name, "—you want one of these slices of bread?" Bauman said. "Then eat that scrapple. You finish four pieces of that, you're still alive, then you can have the bread," Bauman heady at instructing so formidable a figure.

Perteet, however—reminded perhaps of some harsh, even violent corrections at table as a child, in whatever mobile home, whatever den—only nodded sadly and set himself to steadily forking away at the scrapple. The fourth man sitting with them, a small silent convict named Hathaway, glanced at Bauman and shook his head slightly at this sort of chance-taking.

Bauman, agreeing, supposed his week in Seg, the visit to the Lifer Club's offices had affected his judgment. He sipped the hot chocolate, managed to swallow a little of it, then ate one of his three slices of bread. Considered, as he chewed, a vision of State as an immense creche, where nearly two thousand injured children—grown magically, bestially bigger, older and dangerous—were penned to yearn enraged for kindness and constancy never known, only dimly believed in. Now they sat in their cells, wrapped in weight-room muscle, staring at their hands—so oddly large, proven capable as children's should never be.

Perteet finished his four pieces of scrapple, but never claimed the slice of bread. Rather, after a brooding pause, picked up his tray, stood, and left the table without his usual "Take it easy. . . ."

"Livin' dangerously, man," Hathaway said to Bauman, then got up, took his tray, and went on his way.

"Chicken shit," Scooter said to Hathaway's diminishing back. "We don't have to take that, assholes takin' our food at the goddamned table!" He nodded at Bauman across their brown plastic trays. "Hey," he said more softly, his narrow face assuming adulthood, wispy red goatee extending his nod. "Last night I noticed that bandage, on your arm? O.K. if I say somethin'?"

"Scoot, give me a break," Bauman said, stood and picked up his tray, the last slices of bread going to waste—or out to unlucky pigs penned at three neighboring farms. He threaded his way through tables, many inmates lingering over their hot chocolate and scrapple, went to the big garbage can by the mess-hall door, scraped his tray into it, and tossed (against regulations) his Styrofoam cup of hot chocolate in after, delivering to the pigs an amusing variation. Then, not limping this morning, his shin and sore ankle feeling better, went up the basement's scarred stone steps to the block.

White-painted pleats of radiator clanged softly as Bauman walked past along the wall opposite the cells of Ground-tier, a musical indication that the weather outside, fall so far, was turning to winter.

Scooter, jittering, caught up with him on the circular stairs.

"I wasn't bein' nosy, Charles." This, very quietly, confidentially, as inmates stepped carefully past them, climbing up to Two and Three for lock-'n'-count. "Your business is your business, man. Word is, Knute was sayin' . . . he was sayin' the clubs give you a badge to go after some snitch." Knute was one of two inseparable and retarded young bikers—the other known as Toot—brothers by association, caught and sentenced together after a parade of violent holdups of convenience stores downstate. "Knute was sayin' you got a license you can do anything you want, goin' after this snitch!" Scooter all agog.

"Will you for Christ's sake give me a break!" This on the staircase with others passing by. "—You want to believe that shit?" Bauman said. "Then go ahead, believe it, but don't bother me with it anymore," and went on up to the landing, and off it into their house.

Scooter followed him in, posture apologetic, hands up, palms out. "Hey, if I was out of line, I'm sorry, man. Not my business. I know that shit's none of my business. I don't mess with any club business, man, and that's with me bein' a biker, practically a made member. I get my membership three, four more months. But I understand club business is not my business at this point in time. . . ."

"Will you just drop it?" Bauman, bent over his bunk, arranging nice hospital corners in the lower end of his bottom sheet. "Just drop it, Scoot, O.K.? You don't know what's going on. And believe me, you don't *want* to know what's going on."

"Got that right, Charles. I don't want to know. That's the only way to go in this fuckin' joint. I don't know, an' I don't want to know."

"Now you've got it." Finished with his bottom sheet, very tight, nicely tucked in, Bauman began to spread and smooth his top sheet.

"*Fingerrrs. . . .*"

Their barred door stirred, then racked swiftly shut.

"Dude must have snitched off big, though, they get a real-life professor after him," Scooter said in the last of the steel's echo. "—Fuckin' Wyatt Earp Bauman, man."

Bauman stood up from smoothing his sheet. "Are you looking for trouble with me?"

"What?" A surprised Scooter.

"I asked you to drop this shit, and I goddamn well want you to do it! I want you to shut your mouth about all this 'snitch' bullshit. About all of it." Bauman, growing less angry, became embarrassed by Scooter's startlement and confusion. "—Just do me a favor, O.K.? I'd appreciate it. Just don't talk about this at all."

"Hey, man, O.K. I got it. None of my fuckin' business. An' I don't *want* to know, man. You keep this shit strictly to yourself, 'cause I don't want to hear about it."

"O.K. Good." Bauman bent over his bunk again and adjusted his top sheet, listening to Scooter's activity at the sink—splashing, wetting his long stringy hair, its red almost pink, in preparation for strenuous brushing. Another redhead. Shupe, Scooter, Ganz—Gottschalk's tattooed maroon pompadour. Bauman wondered if prison populations in general displayed more redheads. A genetic marker, and traditionally so for bad temper.

Below, a hack—sounded like old Carlyle—was calling names and numbers down the Ground-tier. Carlyle always counted aloud.

"I just want to say one more thing," Scooter said.

"O.K. What?"

"One more thing, that's all I want to say. An' then, man, don't mention that shit to me, 'cause I don't want to hear nothin' about it whatsoever."

"Right, right. What is it?"

"Just this, man. Look out. That's all I got to say on that subject. You look out, 'cause I'm tellin' you, those motherfuckers could be just usin' you, you know. For strictly their own selfish reasons. An' I'm not bein' disrespectful callin' those club guys motherfuckers, 'cause I'm practically a biker myself, which is the best club in here, an' great guys. I mean just the way the leadership operates, you know. They got no choice; that's what leadership means, bein' some kind of motherfucker, accordin' to Bump."

"Scoot, you have a point there. You and Bump both have a point, and I appreciate it. I'll be damn careful, starting with not talking about it at all, right?"

"Bet your ass. From here on out, strictly silence, man." Scooter, relieved of disagreement, commenced to brush his hair with exceptional vigor, staring at himself in the sink's mirror as if anticipating a wonderful transformation.

"Go to the movies, tonight."

Handles—Gypsy Joker and enforcer, reputed one of the notables of biker murder power—had come up to Bauman and Scooter as they reached Ground-tier after lock-'n'-count, ignored Scooter, and delivered his phrase of instruction. He stood in front of Bauman for a moment afterward, staring slightly down at him. Handles perhaps five-ten, shaggy-haired, his features poor matches—mild milky blue eyes, a small impudent Irish nose, a weighty shovel jaw—his long pale arms, lumpy with muscle, densely decorated with multicolor tattoos of patriotic trumpets, unfurling flags, stands of arms, slogans mainly Marine.

Handles had stared that additional moment, then strolled on by, brushing Bauman carelessly with a hard left shoulder as he went.

"Asshole," Scooter said, so softly Bauman could barely hear it. Then, "—Remember what we was talkin' about, Charles." And went off to B-block's gate on his way to the truck shop, and a class in camber.

Bauman, worried—supposing this movie meeting a fresh indication of the reality of Nash's nonsense—sought refuge in considering what he might say to Fanning this morning, to encourage that fat man in his writing. Fatty Fanning, obese as his nick suggested, and looking a natural victim, was no such thing. He was a lifer, and a violent one. Had bitten a man's ear off the year before, after a remark had been made about Fanning's table manners. He ate his food with his fingers, believing forks unnatural.

Fanning was dyslexic, and tended to mirror-write, reversing his letters—his script primitive, in any case, a labored square-block printing.

At his first lesson with Fanning, on Two-tier, C-block—his new student sitting mountainous on the bottom bunk opposite, great bellied, great breasted in Fruit of the Loom underwear—Bauman had tried to introduce the notion of written letters only as pictures of sounds, almost a musical notation, with no particular meaning being placed on those groups until the song of communication was ended. He'd persuaded Fanning to first sing a sentence, sing it again, then, humming, try to write it down. Bauman had hoped, ignorant of any proper method of dealing with dyslexia, that this primitive system might make the fat man's communications less labored.

This had helped Fanning—at least with simple sentences. Bauman's student was willing at first, not even embarrassed to be singing, "Dear Carrie, I am being real good on my diet. I am going to be real thin when I come out. I know I was a hundred percent wrong. From now on, I will be a hundred percent right. Yours truly, Matthew."

But as the sentences had grown more complex, so, necessarily, the songs, until Fanning—standing to sing, huge, billowing, teetering on tiny feet in yellow running shoes—had found the involved song too difficult to recall, too complex to write down without its collapsing across the page in scrambled letters, with a word or two perfectly correct, though reversed, perfectly readable in a mirror.

As difficulty increased, so good humor and cooperation decreased, until the fat man was surly at every lesson, breaking pencils—once tossing a broken pencil at Bauman's head—and tearing his notebook pages into long even strips while he complained of unfairness, of being taught all wrong, of being treated with disrespect.

Schoonover had ordered a workbook for dyslexics ("More of them here than you realize."), but this hadn't yet arrived.

Bauman thought of skipping Fanning for this morning. Lessons held in abeyance more than a week might safely be delayed a little longer, perhaps until the workbook came. But the alternative being to worry about the meeting at the movie tonight, to worry about Nash's plans, about the attorney general's, to worry about the fine cuts on Spencer's hands, the fine cuts on Metzler's hands, Bauman walked down the basement stairs concentrating on Fatty Fanning's reversal of P's, S's, and L's. He wondered if Fanning might not discover something about his own difficulty if required to write while looking at his page in a mirror.

Walking through the empty mess hall, then into Gottschalk's kitchen—the kitchen quieter than usual, its shouts, the clang and rattle of trays, pans, and pots subdued—Bauman started down the aisle of stoves and steam tables already smoking and bubbling with lunch. A hot lunch. Stew? (Yesterday's scrapple, mashed potatoes, other vegetables, hot water.) —Or Rudy's Special Soup? It smelled more like stew.

At the kitchen's back door, a slight black man—balding, bush-bearded, starched denims decorated with touches of gold braid on the shoulders, at his jacket's cuffs—stood leaning against the doorjamb at ease, observing B.B. and the other kitchen handies shuffling back and forth with steel trays of food, brown plastic trays to be scrubbed. This black man smiled at Bauman, beckoned him on, seemed to be expecting him.

Two other black men, unfamiliars here in B-block's kitchen—both very tall, so similarly lank and heavy-boned they might be brothers—stood to this decorated man's left, leaning against the kitchen's stained wall and staring at Bauman, expressionless.

Bauman stopped walking, glanced around, and saw Rudy Gottschalk across the kitchen. Rudy looked very busy—was supervising a cook named Carl Nemeier working over one of the soup kettles. Rudy was very busy with Carl at the soup kettle.

Bauman, wishing for his shank—so treacherously at ease up in Scooter's TV—turned around and started walking out of the kitchen.

He was careful not to hurry, not to look back. The smells of cooking lunch grew stronger as he went, as if bidding him goodbye—certainly Rudy's Special Soup, not stew after all. The kitchen sounds faded, were subdued, muffled, until they were barely noises at all, were more indications of kitchen noise, like background sound in a television show—a restaurant comedy, perhaps. Bauman, walking faster despite himself (his body not caring what reputation he maintained), gripped his clipboard down at his right side as if it might turn with its attached pen into a weapon terrible enough to protect him.

Not mightier than the sword after all—certainly not at the moment.

Just before he reached the kitchen's swinging doors, a black man stepped from behind a battery of double ovens to face him, this man not so much black as dark yellow, almost golden.

"Wayman," Bauman said, "—what's up?" thinking surely his own pupil wouldn't cooperate in killing him.

"No problem. No problem, Mr. Bauman," Wayman said, concerned to comfort this aging white man, recognizing his teacher's fear as clearly as if Bauman had started screaming and running for the mess hall, hoping that some bikers, bearded and burly, returned after count for another cup of coffee, might charge to his rescue.

"Ain' no problem. . . ." Wayman reached out, took Bauman by the right arm in a grip remarkable for the strength only suggested in it, used this to steer his teacher into a slow full turn back the way he'd come, then lightly lifted the grip from his arm.

The decorated man stayed leaning at the kitchen door, waiting while Bauman walked back toward him. Slender, almost completely bald, much shorter than his companions and likely in his late thirties, early forties—the bushy beard just dusted with gray—he didn't smile, didn't make fun of the attempted flight.

"Professor," this man said, his ropes of braid enhanced to egg-yolk by the kitchen's fluorescent lights, "—pleasure to be meetin' you." The voice a surprising basso, issuing from so slight a frame. Bauman thought this might be Perkins, the Black National Army's colonel, except that Perkins had the reputation of never leaving his house, or rarely. This possible Perkins was holding out his hand, and Bauman took that, felt a light momentary grip as they shook. Then, with the most casual and confiding air, the man—his eyes a milk-chocolate brown, large, glossy with intelligence—took Bauman's right arm in the crook of his own left and commenced to stroll behind a rank of refrigerators, the two of them preceded by the two black men who'd been leaning against the wall, and followed by Wayman, well back.

In this narrow sheltered corridor behind humming machinery, in the drafts of warm flatulence the tall refrigerators emitted, Bauman felt his breath come easier through his throat. He supposed if they'd had a reason to kill him they would already have done it—and was humiliated at thought of the Chaplinesque figure he must have presented, walking briskly away, rigid with fear, pretending to dignity.

"It's a genuine pleasure to find a white person possessin' prudence," the man beside him said. "An' alert to his whereabouts, too. Most people don't pay no attention what's goin' on around 'em."

Certainly was Perkins—the colonel showing exactly Nash's swift apprehension of his subject's weakness, his subject's great concern—in this case, as probably in most, a fragile self-regard.

Bauman kept quiet, walked along until gently brought to a halt at the massive burnished steel door to Gottschalk's meat locker. Its large round steel padlock, known to surrender only to Rudy's complicated key, now hung open on the hasp.

One of the two B.N.A. men walking before them stepped aside to take hold of the locker's long handle—revealing Lee Cousins standing beyond him at the aisle's end—then opened the big door and swung it out, so that Cousins, having been revealed, was as quickly concealed. There'd been no expression on the boy's face.

"Come on," Perkins said to Bauman, and, as if they were very old friends, arms still linked, he stepped up into the locker bearing Bauman with him. The big door swung heavily inward behind them, wheezed against its sealing gasket, and clacked shut. Bauman was left with the colonel under a small ceiling bulb's feeble yellow light, and was grateful for it—the light spilling like syrup across the black man's balding scalp.

The cold of the place closed about them, and Perkins released Bauman's arm and drew a little away, almost against the nearest of the crowding carcasses, looming, dangling from their hooks in two tight rows to left and right. The beef in this light appeared black, its casing fat dull-yellow. Bumblebee colors.

Looking at this enclosing meat, though certainly of only commercial grade—difficult to chew, fibrous, knotty with gristle—Bauman was impressed with the treasure at Gottschalk's command, though, to be sure, a hack was always present in or near the kitchen before meals, probably to monitor how much of this was un-lockered and portioned to serve.

But there'd been no hack in the kitchen just now—as if a messenger breeze had blown to the captain's office, suggesting East mess's kitchen be overlooked for this little time.

"Privacy," Perkins said, his breath faintly frosting the air, "—that's the mother hard to find in a joint." His voice was almost startling, theatrically deep.

"I'd say we have it here," Bauman said, saw his breath clouding.

"You know who I am?"

"Perkins."

"That's right. My men call me Colonel, but you don't have to. That's a honorary title." A touch of the South in his voice—Southern born, for certain.

"I'll call you Colonel."

"O.K." Perkins paused, apparently to reflect either on the provenance of his title or what he intended to say. He gazed off into the carcasses for some time, perhaps half a minute, seeming to feel no social spur to quickly continue the conversation on Bauman's account. The colonel was not a particularly striking figure. Except for the bright observant eyes, he wouldn't have looked dangerous or remarkable in any crowd of inmates.

"I make a habit," Perkins said, at first addressing the sides of beef, then in mid-phrase facing Bauman. "—I make a habit of keepin' isolated even from my own people. Stay in my house all the time, 'cept I come out a couple times every year," he smiled through his breath's small fog of frost, "—like that groun' hog."

Bauman congratulated himself on only nodding, smiling in return, keeping his mouth shut. Learning the courtier's art in a harder school than Castiglione's. The locker's cold was becoming impressive, sinking slowly down through flesh into bone. Bauman supposed if he annoyed or disappointed Colonel Perkins, he might be shut in here for the rest of the day and all through the night, his disappearance a mystery, cause for official alarm, the inmates served a vegetarian supper by a reserved Rudy Gottschalk. And discovered at breakfast—a teachsicle.

"I hear you got a star burned on you. —On the arm."

"That's right." Bauman supposed Perkins would ask to see it, require him to take his jacket off, roll his shirtsleeve up. But Perkins seemed satisfied with the question and reply.

"I stay alone as much as I can," the colonel said. "It's a leadership thing. Man beats you playin' checkers, jus' one game, he's goin' lose a little respect." Puff of frost at the *p* in respect.

Bauman nodded, serious, not smiling.

"But all that shit sure gets tiresome." Colonel Perkins, only slightly taller than Bauman, and looking weary, smiled pleasantly. A confiding look. "I'm sayin' that to you, Professor, 'cause you're such a short-timer you're really not a con. You are really standin' aside from the shit we deal with in here on a decade-type basis. You bein' aside from the politics, is what I mean."

Nod.

"Such as—jus' an example—such as that in a few years in here, your black inmates will outnumber your white inmates. Long-term politics is what I'm talkin' about. An' gettin' in a proper political position to take advantage of that situation in an organized way. That's real tiresome shit, but it needs to be gettin' done."

Nod. A careful nod.

"Hadn' escaped your attention our situation is a microcosm?"

"How so?" Bauman said, and regretted asking.

"We are like a egg, laid by that world out there. A poison egg. An' that egg can't hatch out no diff'rent than the chicken laid it. Politics, an' the power in politics therefore got to be the same inside as out. Isn' that so?"

"I believe it is," Bauman said, thinking that the lifers and bikers both, for all their ferocity, were going to find themselves in increasing difficulty dealing with Colonel Perkins.

"Tell me," Perkins said, bright brown eyes examining Bauman. "You had you some long talks with Nash over there in Seg. Tell me, is that man a nut-case or what? Tell me your impression of that man."

"He's crazy like a fox," Bauman said. "A rabid fox."

Perkins seemed startled, then delighted by that description. His mouth a childish O of pleasure, he threw his head back and laughed an odd clucking chortle. He'd moved against one of the carcasses, and it shifted and swung slightly behind him. "Crazy like a crazy fox! An' damn if that's not jus' right. That fool's too much trouble not to be crazy!"

Bauman noted that he was pleased to have pleased this intelligent hoodlum in blue denims and braid. Something to do with having tried for his father's approval, he supposed. He noticed that the meat hanging close about them, however cold, nonetheless sweated a slight steady carnal scent, a sweet suggestion of spoilage.

"An' true you got you a snitch-jacket? You was goin' to snitch, an' Nash turned you. That right?"

"I never said I'd snitch. They tried, that's all, then Nash sent somebody to say hello to my son."

"You blame him for that?" The colonel seemed surprised. "I'd do the very same thing. I'd do that, myself! I don't give a shit about your boy. Position of the black people in this establishment, is what I give a shit about. Don't think for a minute I give a shit about some old white dude an' his boy. That's not my duty whatsoever, any way, shape, or form." None of this said in anger, rather as instruction. Breath frost had settled on the colonel's beard. "—So, you wasn' goin' to snitch?"

"I don't think so."

"You don't *think* so?" Colonel Perkins shook his head, amused. He seemed essentially a good-humored man. "Well, I'm goin' to go along with this shit, Professor, 'cause you're too fuckin' weird do us a double, an' because that Spencer was a black man an' my responsibility in that sense. An' because maybe a hack *is* workin' out of line. —But most of all, 'cause I'm curious as to what in the world that Nash is tryin' on, bringin' a fish like you into business, gettin' all the clubs to go along with this shit." The smooth light-brown of the colonel's face was grayed with cold.

"I don't know," Bauman said.

"Oh, I *know* you don't know." Perkins paused another long while, gazing away into the carcasses. After a while, he looked back at Bauman and said, "My guess, the motherfucker is tryin' an' get lined up with them bikers, for later on. All them bikers want is gettin' a pop of somethin', an' make some money. Don't do much thinkin'. Know Lenin? Them bikers is goin' to sell me the rope to hang 'em with."

The colonel stared at Bauman as if anticipating a comment. Seemed annoyed when none was forthcoming. "—An' what the shit you're wastin' time teachin' a white crawler like that fat-ass Fannin'? That piece of shit is exactly the picture for me of all kinds of white people. Fat an' nasty. Nasty white, like somethin's insides. That's what all that white on you people is like, jus' like you was turned your insides out." He shook his head, distressed at this unpleasant vision, then suddenly stepped toward the door, brushing past Bauman, and reached out for a thick white-painted steel handle there, which Bauman hadn't noticed before, and was relieved to see.

Perkins paused, gripping the handle. "You go on ahead an' find out who put Spencer away—an' that ol' white dude, too. I'll talk to my people, an' if they want, they can talk to you. But you jus' better keep in mind the political aspects of this shit. You better not mess with any political aspects."

"I won't."

Perkins pulled the handle down, put his shoulder to the locker door and shoved it a little open. Cold air hissed out past him. "An'," he said, apparently remembering, "—you got this pogie chick out here wants to go lookin' with you. Lifers O.K. that, an' I know her. So while I'm gettin' to know you, you jus' take her right along."

"O.K."

"All I know about you, is you maybe got a jacket snitchin' for Vermillier or one them hacks."

"It was Gorney."

"I don't give a shit! You were seen kissin' Vermillier's ass comin' down them Seg steps. I don't know nothin' about you, fish, except you come over an' teach bloods readin'. I suppose you do that 'cause you like to be teachin'; makes you feel like you're better'n other people. An' doin' 'em some good, same time."

"Could be." Bauman tried not to continue, but couldn't stop himself. "—Like being a colonel."

Perkins, however, was not offended, found it funny. "Could be," he said, and chuckled frost as he swung the door wide, leading Bauman out into warmth, where Wayman, the two tall black men—and behind them, Lee Cousins—stood waiting.

Having operated so at ease in enemy country—a majority-white block, a biker block—Perkins and his people were leisurely also in retreat. The colonel strolled over to a kettle, holding out a hand for the ladle one of his tall guards quickly found for him. Perkins dipped to bring up a portion of Gottschalk's Special Soup, sipped at it, and said, "Sweet Jesus." Then he and his men sauntered away to the mess hall's back door, and out of that to the courtyard. And across the courtyard, Bauman supposed, to D-block and safety.

"I ain't seen that little black motherfucker for three years." Gottschalk had come to stand beside Bauman and Lee Cousins to watch the colonel and his men depart. "He don't hardly ever leave his fuckin' house, for Christ's sake. You see the face that little fuck made tastin' my soup?" The tall man's scalp rosy beneath the complications of his tattooed hair.

"They're used to West-mess cooking," Bauman said. He no longer blamed Gottschalk and his people for treason—standing aside so passively for whatever the colonel and his men might have had in mind.

"That's exactly what I mean," Gottschalk said. "—You ever smell the nigger shit comin' out of that kitchen? They cook fuckin' bugs over there, man. That Clifford can't *cook*."

Lee Cousins—who'd brought, or at least accompanied the colonel and his men—stood by with nothing to say. He'd gotten his hair cut or, if not, now combed it differently.

"Tell you somethin', man," Gottschalk said. "Ganz or some of his people come in here for coffee or somethin' else,"—meaning pruno, "them bikers would have killed some niggers sure, an' the other way round. Wouldn' have been no fuckin' lunch today."

"A loss," Bauman said. "No Rudy's Special." He noticed he was still gripping his clipboard harder than necessary, and decided to carry his expensive knife from now on whenever he could, wherever he could avoid detectored gates.

Gottschalk walked away muttering something to himself, went over to the soup kettle where Perkins had tasted, hovered over that immense battered steel bucket, then snapped his fingers for a ladle of his own, which B.B., deferential, swiftly brought.

"You've gone to a lot of trouble setting all this up," Bauman said to Cousins, so angry he was short of breath. Angered further by Cousins' stillness, his contained silence. "And you caused me a hell of a lot of trouble doing it, going to Nash's people, the B.N.A. people, and, I suppose, other clubs too. But if you're stupid enough to make a mess like this, then come and step in it yourself, then you're welcome. And I hope to God it's you who gets killed, and not me, because man—or lady or whatever you want to be called—you sure as hell are asking for it."

Cousins looked at Bauman for all the world like a woman wronged, misunderstood, being treated unfairly—gray eyes no longer a boy's eyes, soft dark-brown hair, pale wrists, slender hands no longer a boy's. "I'm sorry, Mr. Bauman." The slightly hoarse smoky voice, Cousins' delicately-boned face, its tender brow and temples, all seemed to Bauman a mask of womanhood the more distressing for its verisimilitude, deeply false in a way Betty Nellis' frank masquerade could never be.

"—I'm sorry. I know you got involved, here. But you don't have no way of knowin' how much—how good Mr. Metzler was to me." The grave girl's face—long, solemn, almost plain, its presentation ladylike—at odds with the working class accent and grammar, still those of the boy she'd been.

"Are we talking—" Bauman lowered his voice under the noise Rudy Gottschalk was making at the kettle, shouting for chili powder, black pepper, and powdered milk—shouting, Bauman supposed, to reestablish his primacy over his kitchen, after fading so during the colonel's visit. "—Are we talking about an old convict who was a well-known extortionist, a Caucasian Union officer? A fucking murderer is what we're talking about, right? Isn't that who we're talking about? I understand he didn't screw you, right? Was that kindness on his part?

I mean you brought this crap up, so I'd really like to know, since apparently it was worth getting these club maniacs involved—Perkins, Nash, the whole fucking bunch. Getting *me* involved. I'd really be interested in knowing about what a great guy Mr. Metzler was, what a terrible loss for everybody when some other asshole killed him."

Got some eye-blinks out of Cousins with that, some distress—and a reply Bauman couldn't hear over Gottschalk's racket, so he took the boy's arm, drew him a little away down an aisle of deep steel double sinks facing two black stoves.

"O.K. What did you say? I didn't hear you back there."

"I said Mr. Metzler adopted me. He made me—"

"Made you his what? Not his son, surely?"

More distress, but bravely borne. A solemn girl injured by a coarse, hurtful remark. "No. I'm Mr. Metzler's daughter."

Bauman—who'd hoped, as his temper cooled, to somehow persuade this oddity at least to attempt to contact Nash, speak to Perkins, take back his notions of plots, of possible murderous hacks, and change their minds about so stupid an undertaking—now gave up any chance of that by starting to laugh. The "daughter" thing had started it, but having started, he found himself unable to stop. After trying to stifle preliminary giggles, he began to make honking sounds that sounded all the funnier to him, and laughing at his laughter, he staggered back, bumped his rear end against the hot edge of one of the Garland stoves, and started away, singed and laughing even harder at the slapstick. All the while, he was making apologetic gestures to Gottschalk and his assistants standing staring across the kitchen, and shaking his head at Cousins to indicate that most of this was not on his account at all.

"I'm sorry," he managed to say "—it's just nerves," and immediately started to laugh at that. Not helped by Lee Cousins starting to smile, seduced as people were by others' laughter, as they yawned to accompany another's yawn.

Bauman laughed, and Cousins laughed along with him, a companionship enabling Bauman to begin to control himself, to take deep breaths, and after only one more, shorter eruption, to stop laughing entirely and say, "Jesus. . . ." His eyes had teared so, he had to wipe them on his sleeve.

"That's what happens," he said, "—when you get scared shitless, and some guy says he's somebody's daughter."

Cousins smiled, looking beautiful. "I know it sounds weird," he said.

Bauman, recovering, took a deep breath, then said, "As apparently you and your friends knew, I'm scheduled for a tutoring session over in C this morning. If that interests you—and I suppose we can talk about this other nonsense afterward—then you can come along."

"O.K." A pleasant nod. Seemed perfectly happy to come along for that. "You O.K. there? You get burned?"

"Nothing serious," Bauman said.

Fatty Fanning's housemate was a child molester and murderer named Phillip Herberts, whose crime—as was not always the case—had been revealed to the population, or discovered by it. A slender man, very quiet, with dark, avoiding eyes and narrow hands furred along their backs, Herberts spent most of every day lying in his upper bunk, silent. Sentenced for having used a pocket knife to facilitate his connection with a five-year-old girl named Jennifer Musmanno, and afterward killing her, Herberts had been assaulted in State several times, his bones broken—left arm and jaw—and his left eye damaged. He'd been promised murder as well, by two men with reputations for reliability.

Because of the beatings, the promises, Herberts clung to his bunk throughout the day, every day, going out to only one meal at West mess, and there often having his food spat into by passersby. Once, he'd been urinated on while he sat eating.

True to form, this man now lay silent in his upper bunk, didn't turn his head to watch Fanning's tutorial, didn't appear to listen.

Fanning had been surly on greeting, not particularly interested in Lee Cousins, either. Had nodded them both into his house, he wearing only his tent-waisted blue denim trousers, allowing his upper torso exposure—a cascade of white-marbled trembling meat, blubbered armpits, huge hairless breasts.

"You have a snitch-mirror, Matthew?"

"I got a mirror."

"Well, get it out. We've been wasting time, last couple of classes. I don't want to waste any more." Bauman noticed Cousins seemed amused at this taking charge, the boy seated on an apple crate at the cell's back, watching, listening.

While Fanning fumbled at his loaded shelves, he opened a subject certainly more important to him than reading and writing. "I hear that Betty—that Nellis broad? Faggot lives over in B?"

"What about her?"

"She bakes a good cake, that right?" He found his small mirror, held it up, then waddled over to hand it to Bauman. Fanning's eyes—almost buried in flesh, a sleepy bear's if bears' eyes were very dark blue—were now direct, concentrating to a degree that would have pleased any teacher. "She do from scratch, or a mix?"

"Damned if I know," Bauman said, and had the notion of using food as subjects for all of Fanning's lessons.

"Scratch," Lee Cousins said from his apple crate. "But Gottschalk mixed 'em for her."

"Shit," Fanning said, "—that's not no way to bake a cake. Cook does everythin' A to Z. That's the way to go an' bake a cake."

"O.K. Matt, sit on your bunk. Put your notebook on your lap. Where's your notebook?"

"On the shelf."

"Well, go and get the damned thing. Am I wasting my time here, or what? It's your cigarettes, Matt. . . ."

Fanning muttered, then lumbered back to his shelves and commenced fumbling there again. His back was presented as a sheeted wall of fat, behind which came sounds of searching, sorting through small bundles, heaps.

"And a pencil," Bauman said.

More muttering, noises of leafing through, discarding.

"Used a half-cup chopped pecans," Cousins said. "An' brown sugar."

Fanning, very interested, looked back, turning his round crop-haired head so it stuck submerged to its chins in the pale flesh of his right shoulder. "Brown sugar? Where the fuck Gottschalk get brown sugar?"

"Traded Clifford five chops."

"Pecans and brown sugar?" Fanning, still looking sharply over his shoulder, maintained that awkward posture—less work, apparently, than turning entirely around.

"Pound of butter," Cousins said.

"Bullshit. —Margarine."

"You two mind if we stop the cooking class? This one's reading and writing."

"Butter," Cousins said to Fanning. And to Bauman, "Sorry."

"Bullshit. That's a fuckin' lie from Gottschalk, that's all." Fanning turned his head back to his pencil hunt.

"Pound-of-butter-from-the-dairy," Cousins said swiftly, to minimize the continued interruption. "Carlyle hacked it in for ten, street." And made a little *moue* of apology to Bauman.

"Whenever you're ready, Matthew," Bauman said.

"A pound of butter," Fanning turned massively from his shelves and padded back to his bunk with a large blue-covered notebook, a short pencil. "An' pecans an' brown sugar. . . ."

"Marky loves her," Cousins said. "Betty wants a party, he sees she gets the best."

"*Must* fuckin' love her," Fanning said, and sat ponderously down on his lower bunk, which wailed softly as it took his weight. "Brown sugar an' a pound of butter."

"Is the Betty Crocker hour over?" Bauman said. "We finished with that? Because we have a little work to do. You two want to talk recipes, wait till we're finished."

"Sorry," Cousins said from the apple crate. Fanning sighed and began leafing through his notebook with snowy sausage fingers.

"O.K. Now, Matthew, I'm going to sit here opposite you." Bauman reached behind him for a sturdy stool, built apparently to take Fanning's weight, and sat down. "Now, I'm going to hold the mirror up right in front of your notebook. See? Tilting down? O.K. Now, you look into the mirror, just the mirror; don't look down at your paper. Just look into the mirror. See your page in there? All right. Look into the mirror, and I want you to write, pecans—that's p-e-c-a-n-s. Just start writing it while you watch what you're doing in the mirror. All right. Do it. . . ."

"*Peeee,*" Fanning sang in a pleasant baritone.

"No. No singing on this one, Matt. This one we just do in the mirror, silently." Bauman glanced at Cousins, whose face—pleased, interested, eyes wide in amusement—now looked more like a boy's, less like a girl's.

Fanning sighed again, bent his round head down to study his notebook page, glanced up into the small mirror, then down again, and carefully, cautious letter by letter, printed out a word Bauman had never seen—took a moment to realize was pecans, with each letter reversed.

"You just looking into the mirror, Matthew? Don't look down at your page at all. Let's try that one again."

Fanning groaned softly, rolled his head on his shoulders to ease what must have been a perpetual stiff neck, then settled himself into his fat and hunched over his notebook.

"Try sugar, s-u-g-a-r."

Sugar, reversed, looked very interesting, a mad Esperanto adverb.

"We still haven't quite got it. Matt, you're really doing very well. I know this is hard, hard work. Really hard mental work. Try to look only in the mirror while you write. Pretend you can't see your notebook at all."

"But I *can* see the motherfucker!"

"I know; that's why this is so hard. Can you hold your other hand over your page? You know, so you can't see the paper. —Then you *have* to look into the mirror."

Fanning lifted his puffy right hand from his notebook, causing it to slide off his mighty thigh onto the floor, pages splayed. He presented Bauman with a fat boy's severe pout.

"Let me help." Cousins stood and came over to the bunk.

Fanning, with a terrific grunt, picked up his notebook and fussily arranged it on his thigh again. Cousins, standing beside, reached down and angled his left hand to cover the page from Fanning's sight, leaving for him only its reflection.

"O.K.?" Bauman held the small rectangular mirror still.

"O.K.," Cousins said.

"I can't see to write," Fanning said, complaining, the whole point lost to him in those few moments' delay.

"Will you cut the shit, Matt?" Bauman said. "Just look in the fucking mirror. Look in the fucking mirror, and write. Butter, b-u—"

"I know how to spell butter."

"Then do it."

Fanning sighed a very deep sigh, rich in self-pity, bent a little lower, peered into the small mirror, and slowly began to write, his short pencil's gnawed eraser describing odd motions, angles, hesitations. After quite a while, the fat man sat suddenly up and back with a sort of heaving motion, breathed out gustily.

"Look at that." Cousins. "Fanning, that's beautiful!"

Bauman got up, still holding the mirror, and stood beside the fat man to look. The three of them examined a perfectly spelled 'butter,' in kindergarten print.

"Is that right?" Fanning said.

"It's perfect," Bauman said. "*Perfect*. Matthew, you've done it. And I knew you could. I knew it, because you're such a hard worker, and you're nobody's fool." Said that, and received from this monster his reward—a look so open, helpless, astonished by praise, that the huge, doughy, brutal head became for a moment that of the jolly fat baby he'd been, surprised by a loving treat.

"—And we're going to work with that mirror from here on out, until we just don't need it anymore."

"All *right*. . . ." Fanning sat massively pleased, staring down at his perfect word—while above him, in the upper bunk, his housemate kept his silence and stillness both.

"I know why you do this," Cousins said, as they stepped down the circular stair from C's Two-tier.

If Bauman hadn't known different, couldn't confirm it by glancing over, that might have been a young woman's voice, hoarse from a cold, perhaps. "I do it for cigarettes. And to keep my hand in."

"Not true. You do it because you like makin' people feel good, feel like they're better'n shit. An' that makes you feel like you're better'n shit, too. Am I right?"

"Some days, maybe. I also do it for cigarettes—and to keep my hand in."

A lifer named Burnside, one of the oldest men in State—in his seventies, Bauman supposed, nearly eighty—greeted Cousins as they reached Ground-tier.

He hugged the boy, kissed his cheek. A hack far down the tier called, "*Cut that shit out*. . . ." and the old man gave him a casual finger.

"How you keepin', honey?" Burnside said. "You ready for my big one?"

"Too much for me," Cousins said. "But I sure love the owner." He put his hand up to the old man's weary face (sad, soft, wrinkled as a Chinese dog's). "You O.K.? Nobody hasslin' my lover?"

"Shit, no. None of these fuckin' inmates fuck with me. I used to know cons make all these faggots pud their pants."

Cousins smoothed the old man's sparse hair back from his forehead, arranged and patted it into place. "You tell me if somebody takes your scrip? Some people are botherin' you?"

"I'd tell you. Ain't nobody fuckin' with Billy Burnside, honey. I knew guys could bust these faggots' backs. Better not try an' fuck with me. . . ." Burnside gripped Cousins' slight shoulders with trembling spotted paws. "—What about you? You O.K.? Ain't nobody puttin' the rush onto you, not treatin' you like a lady?" He gave Bauman a rheumy glance of inquiry.

"No, no," Cousins said. "—I'm fine. Really. You know this man? Teach?"

"Yeah," Burnside said. "I think I seen him around. Teach, right?"

"That's me," Bauman said.

"Well, you treat her good. This is an angel, here."

"You goin' down to eat every meal, Billy?"

"Honey, I can't eat that shit," the old man said. "They used to have real good food in here. Food got bad in the sixties. Those fuckin' hippies. . . ."

"You go down an' eat, anyway. You need to be keepin' up your strength so people can't walk all over you."

"Ain't nobody walkin' on me! I knew guys— You remember Waldron?"

"Before my time, Billy," Cousins said.

"Well, you should have knowed him. Big, big handsome guy. Premium bank robber, an' real gentle unless somebody fucked with him. Then, look out. Some motherfucker stuck him in the back, years, years ago. Shit scared to come at him from in front. There was a guy would've took real good care of you, sweetheart. Handsome guy. Real gentle guy. An' a friend, a solid con. You could do a lot worse; I mean it. You'd be crazy about the guy, an' I know he'd fall for you, take great care of you. . . ." The old man's eyes teary, spilling over. "I hate an' admit it, sweetie, but truth is I can't take care of you. You know? I act tough an' all that, but it's all show—it's all show, is all it is. These fuckin' kids don't respect nothin'. Sweetheart, they take my candy. I get two Nestles, and them young fuckers take 'em. Come up to me right at the fuckin' gate an' take my candy. . . ." He wiped his nose on his right jacket sleeve.

"You tell Shupe?"

"It's his friends do it! They take my candy just for fun. Don't even eat it. I seen 'em put it down on the passageway an' step on it. 'Come on, Pops, eat that shit!' That's what they say, an' then they walk off. I'll tell you somethin'. If I could be young just for a minute, they'd be real sorry. I'd kill me one or two of them fuckers. I'd beat their brains out on a radiator. An' I know I can do it, 'cause I did it before— an' Sturgis was twice the con any of 'em is!"

"You don't think maybe you should check into P.C.?" Cousins said. "—Just till you're feelin' more like yourself?"

"I couldn' do that. I never been in Protective Custody in my life! All they got over there is faggots an' snitches. Shit, my friends'd roll over in their graves they hear Billy Burnside was doin' P.C. time. I couldn't do that."

"I'll talk to Wiltz," Cousins said, and leaned forward to kiss the old man's cheek. "He'll tell 'em to cool it."

"Don't you do nothin' dirty for me, honey. You don't have to go chip on that Wiltz. I don't want you givin' out no blowjobs in that office on account of me. I mean it. I'd rather die than have you doin' that."

"No, I won't have to. I won't have to do anything."

"O.K. I jus' don't want you doin' nothin' like that. Fuck the candy. I can lose the fuckin' candy. I'm due out of this hole anyway, got maybe two, three more months."

"Oh, that's great. Billy, can I ask you a question?"

"You can ask me anythin' you want."

"I was wonderin'. What do you hear about Mr. Metzler? You know, the Union guy I used to go with, that got offed?"

"Sweetie, that's the only thing I blame you for," Burnside said. "Goin' with that guy. That Nash bunch gives all lifers a bad name. If a guy was a hour late payin' up on somethin'—a game or somethin'—then god help him. That guy Metzler didn' have no regard, an' the man was old enough to know better. Give a con just a little break on a bet or somethin'—but not him. Only mistake you ever made, even if he did treat you gentle. What are you askin' for? I sure hope you ain't stickin' your nose in."

"No," Cousins said. "I was just wonderin'."

"It was some bet; that's what it was. Dollars to doughnuts it was some gamblin' bet. Pro football pool, or basketball, boxin'. Money is what guys get offed for—fuckin' love or fuckin' money. Or a grudge. Got us all in trouble in here."

"I guess you're right, Billy," Cousins said. "It's sad, isn' it? But listen, we got to go now. You goin' to be all right? You goin' to go down to meals?"

"Oh, sure. I'm goin' to do that. —You're a great gal," the old man said. "You're sure as shit the gem of this fuckin' collection."

"Sure I am. You goin' to take care?"

"Oh, yeah. You bet," Burnside said, wiped his nose again, and started slowly stepping away from them, drifting off with an odd sliding, sidling motion to the left, waving goodbye as he went, as though he were being carried away by a very slow and silent train.

"He needs to be out of here," Bauman said, as he and Cousins walked to C-block's gate. "Good thing he's only got a few months."

"Mr. Bauman, he's got the rest of his life," Cousins said. "He killed a hack in nineteen forty-seven. Stuck him in the heart in South field. They're never goin' to let Billy go."

"I see. . . ."

Two cons walking past nodded to Bauman, and he nodded back—then placed them as McNeil's housemates, men who'd together raped and murdered several young prostitutes. They were always considerate about turning down the TV when Bauman came for a lesson. Considerate, or afraid of McNeil. A State celebrity for having shot two

FBI agents to death in the office of a motel in Davenport, McNeil had led a furious chase across the state line, and killed another officer, a local deputy-sheriff, before being wounded and captured. The last killing had earned McNeil fifty years to life at State, after which, if there was an after, he'd owe an additional life in federal walls.

Tall, powerful, harshly handsome—Hollywood's notion of what a bank robber and gunman should be—McNeil, illiterate, had struck Bauman as dangerous mainly because so stupid, not really capable of thinking of the consequences of any action beyond immediate reward. McNeil had wanted to learn to write in order to send letters to various cheap supermarket tabloids, appealing for women correspondents.

At C-block's main—and metal-detectored—gate, they stopped to wait in the short line passing through. A hack was giving some inmate a hard time, ahead.

"I bet you didn' know you was talkin' to a celebrity back there," Cousins said.

"Who?"

"Billy Burnside."

"Celebrated for what?"

"First president of the Lifer Club. He's the one organized the club. Ran the joint, too, so they say."

"Christ."

"Hard fall, right?" Cousins said. "No fun gettin' old, in or out."

They'd reached the gate, and the hack motioned them to him. He was a short blond man with wide shoulders and a thick neck; he looked as though he worked out, tried hard to stay in shape. Bauman didn't know him.

"You heard me when I yelled at you down there. Didn't you hear me?" the hack said to Cousins. "You heard me, all right. I saw that obscene action down there with that old man. Kissing him. That's strictly a no-no—not on any block I'm working. Any of that obscene stuff, you can just keep to yourself." He leaned forward to read Cousins' name tag—a new hack, for sure—then took out his report pad and wrote out a ticket. "Shift captain is going to be speaking to you about this behavior. This queer behavior. Don't try it again any block I work."

Cousins said nothing in reply. Took the ticket stub, and put it in his jacket pocket.

Past the block gate, out into the entranceway, Bauman said, "You going to see Wiltz about having those people lay off the old man? I've met Wiltz; he's got a rich sense of humor. I doubt it'll do you any good."

"Brian's not so bad," Cousins said. "He'll tell 'em to ease up."

"Just as a favor? Must be a friend."

"A friend?" Cousins said. He stopped and turned with an expression Bauman instantly recalled from Gottschalk's face, when he'd asked the cook what the scrapple was made from. "No friend of mine," Cousins said. "An' not about to do no favors, neither." He started walking again, Bauman catching up as they passed out through the entranceway to the building's steps and into clear cold morning, flashing with sunshine. Bauman imagined what the boy might be required to do to persuade Wiltz to intervene for old Billy Burnside. Lee Cousins dancing naked to slow music in the Lifers' office, lipsticked, his gray eyes shadowed with darker gray. . . .

"Getting cold." Bauman offering this change of subject as they started down the block's front steps out into South yard. A number of men were out on the walkways, wearing sweaters or jackets with collars turned up, most wearing wool watch caps.

"What do you think?" Cousins said, buttoning his jacket. "What do you think about Mr. Metzler's gettin' killed over a bet?"

"I think it's extremely likely. And when you've said that, what have you said? I imagine a great many people dealt with your kindly Mr. Metzler."

Cousins appeared to consider that for a moment. Then, "Where we goin'?"

"Over to the library. I should have some workbooks come in, and I forgot to pick them up, yesterday. —You don't have to come along. I'm not going to do any detecting over there."

"I'll come along, if it's O.K."

"All right."

They walked left along C's front, then out into East field, and were passed by a silent female hack named Heineman through the fence gate into North. In North field, though no wind was blowing, Bauman buttoned his denim jacket, turned the collar up.

They passed two walkway yo-yos at the crosswalk, neither known to Bauman. These two—Latinos—made soft kissing sounds to Cousins as they passed. Cousins seemed not to notice.

"If not for a bet," Bauman said, "—then what?" They walked down the sunny cement side by side, the boy nearly as tall as Bauman.

"If Mr. Metzler had trouble with some dude about money, he would have told me. Mr. Metzler didn' want no trouble with anybody."

"Are we talking about a retired executive, here? Nellis? Like Marky Nellis?"

"Barney couldn' retire," Cousins said, strolling along, hands in his jacket pockets. "He was secretary treasurer."

"Of the Union?"

"That's right. No way he could retire."

"I thought he was just an officer, some nonsense like that."

"Secon' vice president of the Lifer Club, secretary treasurer for the Caucasian Union."

These grandiloquent titles, aping those of the greater world outside, Bauman first found amusing—then appalling in their possible complications.

"Are you telling me this man Metzler controlled all the Union's money, and was also on the Lifers' board?"

"Right. Mr. Metzler was an important guy. I told you."

"But then, why the hell didn't they go after who killed him? Weren't they worried about their money? That doesn't make any sense at all!"

"Wasn't no money missin'," Cousins said. Bauman noticed the boy's breath smoked slightly as he spoke, a minor reproduction of Colonel Perkins' puffings in the meat locker. "Wasn't no money missin', so they figured it had to be a personal thing, an' fuck him."

Bauman's kicked leg was beginning to ache from walking. "All right, then we have this saintly old treasurer. If not for money, then why?"

"I think it was outside people. I always thought it was outside people."

"Outside? What outside?"

"*Outside.* Outside people hired a guy or some hack in here to do it, scared Barney was goin' to talk about 'em!"

"Talk about them. . . ."

"Barney didn' do that killin' he got sent up for. Another dude did that one, killed that guy."

"Oh, man, come *on*. Please, please don't give me this Metzler-the-innocent routine. Half the cons in this hole are innocent! The man was a fucking known murderer, O.K.?"

"He didn' do that one," Cousins said, a little sullen, breath wisping.

"Then who the hell did?"

"A friend of his. Guy named Lonnie Green. Mr. Metzler an' this Green was partners, workin' a loan operation out of LaSalle."

"And this Green killed somebody, and Mr. Metzler took the blame?"

"That's right, but he didn' have no choice, 'cause this Green had fixed it he had an alibi, an' Mr. Metzler didn'. An' it was Mr. Metzler's borrower got killed."

" 'Borrower.' Like in library?"

"You think it's funny, Mr. Bauman? Come up here for somethin' you didn' do?"

"All right, it isn't funny. Your Mr. Metzler and his friend were loan sharks, right? In business. And Metzler's friend murdered one of their customers, got Metzler sent up for it, and now he has the business all to himself. Right?"

"That's exactly right."

"And of course, Mr. Metzler had never—just in the course of business—never had hurt anybody, never had anybody's arms broken, never had anybody killed. . . ."

"If he did, it was just business. People borrowed, they knew what they was doin'."

"But what Green did to Mr. Metzler wasn't just business?"

"No, because he was a partner, he was a friend, an' he was married to Mr. Metzler's sister. Still is. Her name is Janice. Janice Gilman Green."

"All right, presuming that's all true, why would those people suddenly decide to have him killed in here?"

"Scared. He told me a couple times they was scared he'd talk about some other stuff they all did before this happened. His sister was the smart one. Mr. Metzler said his buddy, Lonnie, was too dumb to set up a frame, anyway."

"Well, it's something to think about. I suppose it's possible."

"You better believe it. Darn right, it's possible. People been killed in here from outside before. An' the other way around, too."

"So I gather. And of course, this Janice had been Mr. Metzler's favorite sister."

"Hey—" Cousins startled. "That's right. How'd you know that?"

"I went on the supposition that what hurts worse, is likely to be true."

Silence as they walked the rest of the way to the library, and up the library steps.

In the entrance hall another hack sat at the desk, replacing Mrs. Truscott. It was Officer Elroy, the farmer assigned indoors at last.

"Congratulations," Bauman said. "—Looked as if they were going to keep you out there till you froze."

"Yeah," Elroy said, getting up from behind the desk. Tall, middle-aged, weighty with farmer's fat and muscle. "Keep your mouth shut, things work out all right." He gestured Bauman to hold out his arms, then turn slowly to be casually patted, stroked sketchily down a leg, then up it. Bauman supposed Elroy represented a family tragedy—

land lost after three generations, or four, the family reduced to working for wages. "O.K.," Elroy said.

The hack glanced at Cousins—had only glanced at him when they'd come in—nodded and said, "O.K." Didn't care, it seemed, to touch him, run his hands over him. That was a useful bit of information—the sort, Bauman supposed, most convicts filed continuously. Elroy the hack didn't care to touch Lee Cousins, was unlikely to search him.

They walked down the high-ceilinged hall—wood-paneled perhaps a hundred years before, the yellowed plaster above the wood spalling in small sandy craters—then up the narrow stairs. On the landing before the door, Cousins paused. Balked.

"You go on," he said. "I'll wait here."

"What's the matter? It's just a library."

"You go on."

"What is it, Schoonover?"

"You go on."

"Listen, you can cut this crap out right now. You want to come with me? Fine. Then you come with me. There's nothing the matter with Schoonover except he's a homicidal maniac, and believe me, that puts him ahead of a number of really disgusting people in here, as you should damn well know. Now, come on." Bauman opened the door and went in, Cousins, after a few moments, trailing.

Schoonover, alone as usual, was sitting high on an old wooden ladder, teetering slightly as he bent forward to thumbtack a new enormous letter A just over the doorway, to the left. This new letter A, scissored out of a great sheet of bright-red poster paper, appeared the beginning of a new alphabet for the library, the old one faded and worn by lack of attention.

Bauman wondered if Schoonover, so close above the doorway, might not have heard the exchange outside.

"Larry. . . . A new alphabet. Good idea. Let me introduce Lee Cousins, if you haven't met."

Cousins nodded.

Schoonover, perched high above them, looked like a large lumpy bird in blue denim—glossy dyed-black pompadour, sleek black wings of hair swept back, tucked neatly around his ears, his large pale oval face spotted with moles, prominent nose serving for a beak.

"People," he said to them, "—who overhear conversations about themselves, rarely hear anything good." He reached up to thumbtack home the last loose leg of the A. It was a big A, bigger, redder than the old one had been, even new. "I forgive you, Charles, assuming you meant well," he glanced down and over at Cousins, "—and were addressing invincible ignorance." Schoonover hovered on his creaking ladder, staring down at Cousins. "Boy," he said, "you are striking, physically, the more so since most inmates look exactly like what they are. Is there a brain behind those eyes?"

"You're goddamn right there is," Cousins said.

"Good." Schoonover settled on his perch as if he might spend all the lifetimes of his sentence up there. "—Then let me teach you what this more exalted teacher has failed to. What you don't know is likely to be more valuable than what you do know, so always be interested to learn, even about a 'homicidal maniac,' who, by the way, must always have had his reasons. Maybe better reasons than yours."

"I'm sorry, Larry," Bauman said. "It was a stupid thing to say."

"Forgiven and forgotten," Schoonover said, rearranged himself, and slowly climbed down the shaking ladder, reluctant, it seemed, to descend. Bauman thought perhaps Schoonover's ladder acted for him in much the same way as the shower's warm parasol had served over in Seg, to separate and hold him in an existential safety, removed from the prison's harsh intercourse.

"When I came over to thank you for my watch, I forgot to check for any workbooks. . . ."

"Good news," Schoonover said, descended. "—Why don't you look through the shelves here, Cousins. I'd be surprised if there was nothing to interest you." He ambled over to his work table, crowded with narrow card-file drawers. "Two of them came in early." He lifted a card drawer, slid two large soft-covered books free, handed them over to Bauman.

One was a series of exercises in speed reading; the other a primer for adult reading, its alphabet illustrated by Ample, Barter, Cumulus, and Delight.

"Nothing for dyslexics?"

"I wouldn't be impatient, Charles. Pennsylvania publisher. I'd look for those end of December," Schoonover said.

"Pain in the ass. . . ."

"They're not in any great hurry to serve us. Really, it's a very active prejudice. Don't you realize that?" Schoonover sat at his worktable, fortressed behind file drawers. "Well, you will realize it once you're released. We're the bad dreams of those people outside, no matter that many of them are far worse than many of us. Perhaps all the more, because of that." He waggled a forefinger at a straight-back chair in front of the table, and Bauman sat, leafing through the workbooks.

"I think this speed reader'll be good. . . ."

"I would have thought a slow reader challenge enough."

"Larry, I'll just teach speed reading, slowly. Similar technique, I thought it might be applicable to learners."

"Give it a try. Didn't occur to you to check with Medwin for materials?" Gerald Medwin, young, apprehensive, was State's superintendent of education and did, by general consensus, a fair job at it, with major emphasis on vocational courses just barely out of date.

"No," Bauman said.

"And not Bannerjee?"

"No."

"Prefer not to be told what to do with your materials?"

"—With my students," Bauman said. "They're not much, but they're my own. Medwin's people couldn't handle them, so they passed them over to me. And that's all he has to do with it."

Cousins called over to them. "What's this one about?" He was standing by fiction. "*Beach Red.*"

"I don't know it," Schoonover said to him. "And of course I should. Look inside at the jacket copy."

"No jacket," Cousins said. He leafed through it. "It's a war book, I think."

"It's a novel about the Pacific war," Bauman said. "The Second World War. They're invading an island held by the Japanese."

"When was this?" Cousins said, reading.

"Nineteen forty-four. That was very savage fighting."

"Lots of sunshine," Cousins said. "—Hot out there."

"Very hot, very humid," Bauman said.

"I don't think this country ever fielded better troops than our Marines in the Pacific, then," Schoonover said.

"Civil War."

"I bow. Civil War. Confederates."

"And the Westerners."

"I bow again," Schoonover said, being uncommonly agreeable. Then, voice much lower, conspiratorial, "A beautiful young man—well, hardly a man at all. And what in the world are you doing with him? If you don't mind a casual friend asking."

"We're partners in an enterprise," Bauman said, keeping his own voice down.

"Um-hmm, all that snitch-hunting baloney. Even I've heard about that, and frankly don't believe a word. I just don't—I simply don't understand what the hell you're doing mixing in this sort of nonsense.

Those club people with their fantasies of running the prison. The poor devils can't even run their own lives! All they can do is sell to each other, rob each other, kill each other. And by the way, kill you while they're at it. It's the kind of Renaissance plotting this place is swampy with."

"No question."

"—No thought for any sort of spiritual reality, higher reality. These people don't even *know* the life of the mind. A reason I'd miss you very much if some cretin stuck a knife into you, left me with no one to talk to."

"Try Sarasote."

"Sarasote doesn't come to the library, can't even read. I'm not interested in talking with a brilliant animal. And let's stick with the subject, if you don't mind. It's simply stupid of you to become so involved."

"The less said."

"And this boy?" Asked very quietly, a slight flush showing in Schoonover's pale cheeks. "—Unless it's none of my business, a personal situation that's certainly none of my business."

"There's no 'situation,' Larry. It's a temporary partnership. I'm not on vacation in Venice."

"Has this— This has something to do with Kenneth Spencer's being killed, doesn't it? And I warned you about it, didn't I? Didn't I say in my note you were becoming all too well acclimated, adjusting too damned well to this place? It is not necessary to participate, Charles, in order to prove to yourself you can!"

"The choice wasn't mine."

Schoonover stopped talking, sat behind his file drawers examining Bauman.

"They threatened you . . . ?" Said very softly.

"More serious than that."

"Your wife. —Your first wife, of course. Your boy?"

Bauman said nothing.

Schoonover sat silent for some time, then said, "If I hadn't been so cowardly, if only I'd continued to force the door, this would be a more sensible plane. And so much more beautiful." As if struck by a sudden wind, the librarian rocked slightly in his chair and seemed about to cry, his small hazel eyes filled with tears. "So much more beautiful. . . ."

"I didn't mean to upset you, Larry," Bauman said, and reached out to grip Schoonover's denimed arm. "It's all really more tedious than important. A demonstration or two, and it'll fade away. There aren't many long attention spans at State." He patted Schoonover's arm, let it go.

"Good book," Cousins called to them, still standing over by the fiction shelves, reading. "Poor guy's scared to death all the time."

Bauman looked over at the boy. "What does that remind you of?" he said to him.

Cousins looked up. "Right here," he said. "Right here, too damn much." He looked down at the book again, then closed it and reached up to put it back on the shelf. "I never like these good books for long," he said. "—They're too fuckin' good."

Bauman and Schoonover exchanged the pleased glance of parents at some proof of their child's capability.

"We need to get going, anyway," Bauman said, and stood, his kicked ankle hardly troubling him at all. "Thanks for ordering these workbooks, Larry."

"Have you given any thought to my acid problem?" Schoonover said, standing up, tall and bulky.

For an antic moment, Bauman thought Schoonover was referring to some indigestion, then recalled the deterioration of the library's books.

"I'll call Midwest, see if the librarian there can give us any help."

"I'd appreciate it," Schoonover said, walking beside Bauman to the door, Cousins following. "—And you," to Cousins, "—come up here and visit. I have plenty of books that aren't so good. Plenty that are simple pleasures."

"O.K. I will." Cousins looking at Schoonover with what Bauman recognized as the curiosity he'd felt—others must have felt—examining this large awkward man with his dyed black hair, small myopic eyes, pale, mole-spotted face. Curiosity as to what dream might drive a man to what measures. Curiosity about limits, Bauman supposed. Behavioral borders, *the* problem for the inmates of State. Problem for all human societies, all social organizations, human—and animal? It seemed possible that the equations for behaviors, social and individual, might be found in fractile mathematics, with its elegant iterations and redundancies. . . .

Cousins, stepping down the library stairs at Bauman's left side, said, "What are some other books about that war?"

"*The Gallery*," Bauman said. "—*From Here to Eternity*. *The Weight of the Cross* . . . and for a funny book, *Catch-22*. But all those are good books."

"Was that before the Korean war?"

"Just before."

Elroy, comfortable behind his desk, listening to a palm-sized radio just interrupt its broadcast of country-western music for a crop report, looked up at them, then waved them past and out of the building.

"Where we goin' now?" Cousins, on the steps, buttoned his jacket against the cold. The morning had produced a wind that, recoiling from the wall, blew steady but for slight flutterings, like a wind off the sea.

Far across North field, yo-yos lined the walks, well into their day of gossip, plots and plans, reminiscences. Blue denimed, most of them, with here or there a sweater or street windbreaker in yellow, red, or green—and in one place, against the front of A-block's building, a spot of the rarest deep brown, where someone had conned, saved-for, or extorted a leather jacket.

"Let's go over to the gym. If I can get my work done this morning, then maybe this afternoon we can really start working on the big murder mystery. See if we can make any sense out of it, save some time."

"Save time for what?"

"Ah, right. Good question. Well, in any case, I've got some work to do, so let's go over to the gym." He supposed he might be anxious to show Cousins off, to demonstrate he could attach such an exotic object, then not even need to use it. It occurred to him, just after, that Cousins might not care to go to the gym, be reminded . . .

"Would you rather not go over there? I can go this afternoon."

"Let's go *somewhere*, Mr. Bauman," Cousins said. "I'm freezin' my butt."

"Let's forget the 'Mr. Bauman' stuff. Why don't you just call me Charlie?"

Cousins smiled. "You're not much of a Charlie. I'll call you Charles."

"Done. O.K., let's go over to the gym." Bauman buttoned his jacket and led off to the right, down the wall walk.

Cousins trotted two steps to catch up, changed his stride to match Bauman's, side by side. "Why? You think I didn' want to go 'cause I got turned out over there?"

"It occurred to me."

"I go over there all the time—you know, play handball? It don't bother me." The wind brought Bauman a trace of Cousins' odor. Soap, scented soap, perhaps lily of the valley.

"Listen," Cousins said, "I'm callin' you Charles, you call me Lee."

"Lee it is," Bauman said, stopped walking, and held out his hand. Cousins' narrow grip was firm, strong as a strong boy's. That small ceremony complete, they walked away together. Bauman wondered if he was pleased to have this eccentric company, then supposed he was. Reflected that the human need for companionship—accompanied by irritation with any particular companion—made for an uneasiness expressed in all relationships, personal, social. An inherent instability, occasionally collapsing (personally, sometimes socially) into chaos. And if consideration of chaotic states (chaotic states, fractal borders; it even sounded like an historical analysis), if consideration of these proved useful for analyzing the tumultuous behavior of human relationships, individual and societal, necessarily in constant flux, then why not for societies past? For History? Why not the future . . . ?

Old Cooper was making a speech at the far end of the gym, the first of a series of traditional addresses commencing a couple of weeks before each match, whether home or away. The little man, up in a practice ring in his shorts and T-shirt, lanyarded whistle jouncing on his narrow chest, was strutting back and forth along one side of ropes, below which his boxers had gathered to be exhorted.

Bauman, Cousins walking a little behind, went down the east-side wall, past stacked practice mats, horses, parallel bars, past this week's two gym hacks, a fat veteran named Wostenholm and a crewcut younger man.

Cooper, apparently having paused for breath or inspiration, saw them coming, his bald rooster's head half turned, cocked to observe them, the beaky nose pointing almost their way. Several of the men then turned to look, stared for a moment at Bauman's companion.

"You don't mind," Cooper said to them, that inattention apparently providing him a theme. "—You don't friggin' *mind*, we got a little business here. Hey, you! Ferguson!"

Ferguson, the tall white welterweight—expositor of beatings and maimings on the team's bus trips—had not turned back to attention, instead stood staring at Cousins in an odd head-bobbing sort of way, as a house cat did, focusing intently on a length of playful string.

"What the fuck are you looking at, Ferguson?" Bauman said to him. "Turn your ass around and pay attention." And like a sleepwalker, somewhat dreamily, Ferguson did. Bauman supposed a really good animal trainer, a circus man experienced with bears and big cats, would do very well at State.

"Payin' fuckin' attention!" Cooper was launched, his small body jerking in recoil from the volume of his shouting. "Some stupid shits!" (His slight lisp almost transforming this to Thome thtupid thits.) "Some stupid shits don't think they need to pay attention! They're too fuckin' smart to pay attention! —Well, I got some news for assholes like that. Them Joliet faggots ain't too smart to pay attention! They're listenin' to every fuckin' thing Burt Cafone is tellin' 'em. An' Burt Cafone knows his fuckin' business! Man is a frien' of mine of long standin'. A convict, not a bunch of fruity inmates like we got here."

Bauman wondered if old Cooper heard his own lisp anymore, whether it reminded him each time he did, of the endless hours bleeding broken-legged in his little box so many years before. And biting off the tip of his tongue, instead of screaming.

"What Burt's tellin' that bunch of niggers he's got for boxers—an' I call 'em niggers 'cause they ain't self-respectin' black men like we got here at State. That bunch of niggers Burt's got, they think they can whip any ass in any ring—home or fuckin' away. An' now they're comin' down here an' try an' whip the ass of self-respectin' black men an' Hispanic men an' white men. Well, well I got *news* for them motherfuckers. Big news! This is *State*, motherfuckers! An' we are the best of the fuckin' worst! We are gonna pay attention. An' because we pay attention to our coach, an' Marcantonio stays in the middle of the friggin' ring, an' Betts keeps his left up 'stead of scratchin' his nuts with it, an' Muñoz remembers body punches win long fights, an' Ferguson remembers to pay *attention*, we are goin' to kill us some nigger motherfuckers!"

The response of the men to this appeal—and Bauman had heard Cooper's variations of it many times, and other coaches' many more times in his own high school and college days—the response of these men to this sort of appeal was instant, united, and savage to a remarkable degree. A coarse slamming bark, very deep and almost in unison. It had made Bauman start the first time he'd heard it, now made Cousins start a little at his side.

"Sooo . . ." Cooper was crooning. "Sooo . . . Sounds like them sissies is due a little surprise. Think you can bust a man's jaw with a punch?" (This the beginning of a ritual of question and response, familiar to the men.)

"*Bet you fuckin' ass!*" In rich unison.

"Think you can bust in his cheek?"

"*Bet you fuckin' ass!*"

"Think you can bust out his eye?"

"*Bet you fuckin' ass!*"

Bauman had never joined this chant. Had no right to in any case, since he didn't fight.

Cooper wound himself up for his climax. "—Think you can kill him, if you have to?"

"*Fuckin' a, fuckin' a,* fuckin' a!"

"Hello, girlie, how're you doin'?" Cooper, half a foot shorter, turned his wrinkled left cheek up to be kissed, and Cousins bent gracefully to do it.

"Hello, Mr. Cooper. I'm doin' all right."

"You with my so-called trainer, here? —You didn' come in here chippin', did you? 'Cause that I can't have."

"No, sir," Cousins said. "I'm not chippin' anymore, Mr. Cooper."

"Well, I'm glad to hear it. Nothin' worse for your health than all that sexy stuff; drains you down. That's why I can't have you doin' that with my people. You understand?"

"I understand."

"You goin' with this trainer here?" A swift hard glance over at Bauman, Cooper's first direct look since he'd seen them walking in. "—So-called trainer, doin' his schoolteachin' an' goin' up to Seg like he's a hard rock, when he's supposed to be at the gym, workin' my people."

"Couldn't be helped, Coach," Bauman said.

"Don't give me that shit. You got a responsibility here, Mr. Joe College. —You duck it, you gonna have to tell me why."

"I'll do the work."

"So you say," Cooper said. "An' so I better see, or you're gonna find your ass back behind a broom! You goin' up to Seg—an' what's this other shit you're lookin' for some snitch? What the hell is that your business, anyway?"

"Couldn't agree with you more."

"You're not even a real con, for Christ's sake. I don't know you even belong in here.—What was that? Fuckin' careless drivin'? I don't know you even belong in here, comin' in the gym with your girlfrien' while my boys are trainin'."

"She's not my girlfriend."

"I don't want no chippin' in this gymnasium!"

"I'm not chippin', Mr. Cooper," Cousins said.

"I know, I know, honey," Cooper said, and reached up to pat Cousins' cheek. "You're a nice kid, an' I don't mean to be rough on you. But you see, you get a good boy ready to go, an' some piece does a blowjob on him, or screws him or somethin', an' all the juice goes right out of that boy. Happened to me in nineteen an' fifty-one. Screwed those nasty sisters in Omaha, Elaine and Whats-her-name, same time, in the same room an' everything. Next night I got my ass whipped by some little greaser didn't know beans when the bag was open. Caught me a lucky on the forehead. . . ."

"Third eye," Bauman said, and the old man seemed surprised.

"That's right. How'd you know about that?"

"I'm a professor, Coach."

"You *was* a professor. Now, you're just a fuckin' inmate. I don't know what the hell people like you are even doin' in State."

"I'll just stay out of the way," Cousins said. "I won't cause any trouble."

"Then it's O.K. In that case, you got my permission. I'm not against women in a gymnasium; I don't want you to get the wrong idea about that. Can even be a good thing, have some split—no offense—some lady hangin' around. Boys work harder. Showin' off, I suppose. Never made no difference with me, no matter who the hell was watchin'. Them punches. I didn' think about nothin' but them punches. You want to be a champ like I was? You better not have shit on your mind exceptin' that."

"I'll stay out of the way," Cousins said.

"I know you will, honey," the little man said. "You're a sweetie, an' you got you some real class, comin' back after how bad you was treated. O.K. O.K., enough of this shit. Trainer, I want you should go over there an' take Mr. Wise-ass Muñoz, so proud about his left hook—like Robinson couldn' have hooked his fuckin' head off for him, not even thought about it. You think you can get that asshole think about throwin' a body punch? I'm tellin' you, that nigger Cafone's got—that Willy? Dennis Willy?"

"I've heard about him."

"Well, a few days here," Cooper glanced around to be certain of privacy. "An' you," to Cousins, "—honey, this is a confidential conversation."

"I'm not listenin', Mr. Cooper."

"O.K. Good. Trainer, what I'm sayin' is a few days from now that nigger's gonna start shootin' for Muñoz' head. Straight shots, too. No bullshit hookin'."

"Not good."

"Not good? We're talkin' a lost fight, here! An' all the time that nigger comin' in standin' up. Standin' *up*. Cafone goofed with that boy. An' let me tell you, Burt Cafone don't goof much. Friend of mine; man was a premier bank robber. Light heavy. Nothin' much in the ring; couldn' move to his right. So, what I want to know is, Can you wise Muñoz up? That spic don't listen to me 'cause I called him a son of a bitch. 'Talkin' about his mother,' is what he said. Is that spic a dummy, or what?"

"Let me see what I can do."

"Asshole is a fuckin' headhunter. He don't think a body punch does shit. Won't throw a body punch save his life. You know, he looks like he's throwin' 'em, sometimes, but he ain't for real. Puttin' nothin' on those body punches whatsoever. An' all the time that Dennis Willy—who's a real good boy, give him credit—all the time that nigger's gonna be comin' in standin' up. Beggin' for body shots."

"I'll give it a try."

"O.K., O.K.," Cooper said. "I don't have no more time to fuck with him. You get to it. We got short of two weeks before that fight, an' we got to rest 'em last day an' a half."

"Leave Muñoz to me."

"O.K., O.K." Cooper reached out to grip Bauman's right arm with a small, big-knuckled hand, and said to Cousins, "Sweetie, you're welcome in this gymnasium any time, long as you behave." Then turned—quick as a Border terrier—and trotted off on bare white paper-skinned little legs, the scars encircling his narrow thighs revealed deep and pale blue.

Chapter EIGHT

When Bauman motioned a young black man named Jerry Johnson (who'd been sparring with Muñoz) out of the left practice ring, Muñoz turned to see why. Saw Bauman, then Cousins standing some distance away, and took his mouthpiece out. "Don' tell me nothin' that little fuck-face say—call' my mother a name. An' you take you fuckin' girlfrien', man, an' leave me alone. Day I can't kick that Joliet dude's ass, day I quit."

"Oh, I think you can beat him," Bauman said, took off his blue denim jacket, folded it over the lowest rope, then unbuttoned his shirt, took it off, and made sure his T-shirt was well tucked in. His bandaged left forearm was unlikely to be hit, held behind his back. "—You can beat him, Paco, but it's going to be very hard work, and you'll catch plenty of punches. It's going to take you a lot of rounds to pile up those points." Bauman took his belt off, leaned against the side of the ring to bend down, roll his trouser cuffs up a couple of turns. He stayed bent over to untie, tighten, and retie his running shoes.

"What you doin', man?" Muñoz hovering above, smoothly muscled brown arms relaxed on the top rope, gloved hands hanging down. He was a handsome young man, his looks spoiled only somewhat by a slightly receding chin. He and Johnson, as per Cooper's requirement for prefight practice, had been sparring without headguards.

"On the other hand . . ." Bauman finished tying his shoes, stood up and looked for Enrique, saw him by the heavy bag and waved him over. "On the other hand, if you catch Dennis Willy walking in on you standing up straight—and that turkey must think you're a real boob, come in on you that way—then you have a chance to give the guy a boxing lesson. And that's a chance you should never miss. . . . Enrique, get me an eight-ounce right glove and a mouthpiece."

"What for?" Enrique said, eyeing Bauman's bandage. "—Ain' that arm still sore for you?"

"Just do it," Bauman said, and Enrique shrugged and set off at his nervous trot.

"What you goin' to do?" Muñoz said.

"I'm going to try to show you that a body punch is a hard punch to take—and an easy punch to throw. Most important thing is, it's a hard punch to miss with. You can miss rights and lefts to a man's head all day, but when was the last time you saw a good fighter miss when he was punching to a man's body?"

Bauman reached to grip the middle rope, put his right foot on the ring edge, and hauled himself up. A longer haul every year.

"What the hell you think you doin', man? You ain' comin' in this fuckin' ring with *me*."

"Scared you're going to kill me, Paco?"

Enrique had come trotting with the mouthpiece and glove. Bauman leaned out, took the mouthpiece, then held his right arm down so Enrique could fit the glove and lace it.

"Fuckin' a you could get killed, man. You sure as shit don' belong in no fuckin' ring with me."

"Two-handed, you're right. You could have whipped my butt best day I ever saw. But what interests me, is how well you're going to do without that left hook you like so much. Enrique, take off his left glove."

"Fuck that, man," Muñoz said.

"Will you just give him your hand, Paco, and cut the bullshit? You know everything about fighting? Nothing you don't know? Day a man stops learning, he's heading for the tank."

"I jus' don' want to fool aroun' with you, man." Muñoz held his left hand down between the ropes so Enrique could reach it to unlace the glove. "Screw aroun' like this, I could get a injury before the fight."

"Ha, ha, ha." Marcantonio, the speed bag deserted, had come over to see what was up. "—That's a good one. 'Injury before the fight.'

That's a good one. You're scared Pops is gonna make you look bad."

This was the first time Bauman had heard the 'Pops.' He supposed some of the boxers had been calling him that for some time.

"What's goin' on?" Bubba Betts, deaf in one ear, his head cocked slightly to the right, had lumbered over, the sheath of rubbery blubber on his huge body slick with sweat, black as a pilot whale's.

"Pops is gonna show Muñoz somethin'," Marcantonio said.

"Fuck that," Muñoz said, but hopelessly, now that this cheering section had developed. And to Bauman, "—You want to box with me, man? Show me shit that way? Fuckin' fine with me, man. You get hurt, ain' my fuckin' fault."

"Paco, we're not going to box. That takes two hands. We're going to have a fight. Just a two-round fight. And if you *don't* hurt me, then there's something wrong with your punching, because I'm sure as hell going to try to hurt you."

"Hey, O.K. for Pops!" Marcantonio at ringside. Bauman wished he'd drop the 'Pops' stuff.

Up in the ring, Bauman exercised a few times, holding the corner ropes—deep knee bends, stretches—trying not to look absurd, only casual, workmanlike. The ankle slightly tender. . . . A shaft of sunlight from the clerestory windows high above stood at an angle almost beside him, its bright column hazed with swirling motes. Done with his stretches, Bauman saw other boxers nearby pausing in their work to watch, saw Cousins standing over by the gymnasium wall, watching. It occurred to Bauman, unpleasantly, that he might be showing off.

"Enrique, time us. Regular rounds. We're going two." He put in his mouthpiece, made sure it was settled.

"You *think* you goin' two, man," Muñoz said, fitted his mouthpiece, then watched Bauman put his left hand behind him, tuck it down into his trouser waistband at the back—and did the same, tucked his left hand into the back of his shorts.

"*Time!*" Enrique, below them at ringside, consulting Cooper's fat steel-cased stopwatch.

"Go on, Mr. Bauman, kick his ass!" Bubba Betts.

Muñoz, at Enrique's call, had already stepped his neat Indian-footed way half-circle to Bauman, had already changed his one-handed phantom lead to right. He jabbed twice, hit Bauman very snappily with the second, and hooked off that to graze the top of Bauman's head as he ducked, sidestepped away into the center of the ring. Muñoz came with him like a dancing partner, set himself so quickly it was hardly noticeable, hooked again, missed, jabbed and hit Bauman surprisingly hard with that punch, so that his eyes started to ache as if the light were hurting them.

Bauman, grateful for his shortness, waited for the next hook, which still surprised him it came whipping in so fast. He ducked just in time, the punch whuffling past overhead—and holding his right cocked far back, stepped down and into Muñoz' fast-moving brown body (an impression of ladders of muscle, swinging, passing) and hit the man as hard as he could, as deep as he could dig, down into the short ribs. Even so, even as it landed, Bauman felt the punch whisked away as Muñoz spun to avoid it, as if the blow had been struck against a spinning upright cylinder, solid and smoothly ridged, that was whirling too fast to damage.

Now, Bauman yearned for his absent left hand, with which he was certain he could have caught Muñoz going away—and instantly paid the tax on regret, on inattention, by being hit with a sliding overhand right that shoved him stepping back, and then a right hook to follow, Muñoz happy to demonstrate that quick hooking talent, ambidextrous.

Bauman got on his horse, backed to take a breath, noticed how eagerly the middleweight came after him, and thought he might catch him (as Muñoz should catch Dennis Willy) coming in too carelessly, standing too straight. Had hardly time to think that when Muñoz hit him another jab that really hurt, made the bone in his nose crackle, then threw a hook off that jab that jolted Bauman so his left foot lifted a fraction off the canvas. He supposed that punch had hit him on the side of the head, guessed it had missed his jaw or he'd be down.

Muñoz, pleased, danced a little away, the unsteadiness of character that had landed him in State betraying itself in that moment of self-congratulation, detrimental to the work.

Bauman caught his breath, reminded himself to stop thinking, and made a short rush, swung his right at Muñoz' head, then again—the first punch missing, the second caught in midair by Muñoz' own right glove on a cross and slapped aside so hard Bauman's elbow ached.

Moving away, Bauman stopped, stepped in and faked his left shoulder as if that hand and arm weren't tucked away behind him, but were free, coming in to punch. And Muñoz, betrayed by his own splendid reflexes, tucked his chin, raised his right to guard against the ghost, and allowed Bauman to stretch and swing an awkward right into the middleweight's face. A pretty good smacking punch.

"*Oooh-ow-wow!*" This gallery, so slow at civilized skills, so uncomprehending there, were bright as foxes in observing violence, had seen the shoulder feint and appreciated the result.

Muñoz, his pride injured, came at Bauman jabbing and hooking off his jab, and enabled Bauman to duck, step inside, and dig his right in where the young man's ribs diminished. This punch was the only one worthwhile Bauman had thrown in what he hoped was a full round—what he profoundly wished to be a full round—and it hurt Muñoz. Bauman sensed that injury, as undoubtedly Muñoz had sensed Bauman's injured nose, his confusion after he'd been hit so hard in the head—as if their swift gloves, so deceptively padded, were instruments of music playing in duet. Bauman saw, even as the middleweight hooked with his right again, Muñoz' tethered left arm try to lower, its elbow yearning to be free to guard his ribs.

Glancing at that cost Bauman the reception of another jab, which struck and hurt as if his nose had been a ripe boil. Bauman tried to right-hook back, a variation, a new punch which might do something for him. He was startled at how slowly his right arm moved. It appeared to have aged in only moments, become sore, grown heavy.

Muñoz slipped that slow, slow punch, hit Bauman a straight right hand, jabbed into his nose again—then turned, as if in contempt at such defensive incompetence, and walked away. Bauman almost said through his mouthpiece, 'You come back here, motherfucker!' Then realized Enrique had called the round.

Turning casually to the ropes as if he'd heard the call, Bauman tugged his left hand out from behind his back, and put that cramped arm up alongside his aching right to rest on the top strand of rope.

Bubba Betts looked up at him. "All riiight," he said. "You hang on in there, Teach."

Bauman was relieved not to be called Pop. He thought of turning to look at Muñoz, thought of thinking about the fight, but both seemed much too tiring. He had to concentrate for a moment even to remember what the fight was all about, then recalled Muñoz' foolish arrogance about body punching. "I'm going to break one of that asshole's ribs," he said—to himself, he thought—but Bubba answered from below, "All *riiight!*"

The fool Enrique called a *Time!* that must have been much too soon, and Bauman left his rest on the ropes, doubled his left arm behind him to tuck its hand away, turned and got his right up barely in time to catch Muñoz' overhand. Just that counter hurt unfairly, made his elbow ache, and he was shocked by how little the first round had meant to the middleweight, who now jabbed, hooked off his jab, and hit Bauman a crisp cracking punch on the left temple.

"*Ooooh!*" Bauman heard the spectators very clearly. He couldn't recall hearing them as clearly before, not while he and Muñoz were fighting. There was a very strong smell of sweat and mildewed canvas. He looked down at the canvas, its fine weave very detailed at only an arm's length away, and realized he was sitting, propped on that right arm. He was surprised how dirty the canvas was, and supposed he'd have to see the bout canvas was scrubbed. He looked around, realized Muñoz had knocked him down, and immediately got up onto his knees, steadied himself with his one gloved hand, and was able, with what he supposed was a sort of rising-camel motion (buck an' sway) to get up onto his feet.

"Coun' *eight*." Enrique, from ringside.

Bauman looked for Muñoz—was startled to see him standing near, directly under a shaft of sunlight, so he seemed a fighter of gold, topaz eyes staring over his right-hand glove. Bauman checked to see if his own left was still tucked away behind him, found it was, got hit a snapping jab on the nose, ducked, and was missed by the same right hook that had put him down. The identical punch.

Move, Bauman said to himself, and obeying his coach, sidestepped to Muñoz' right, turning the man, taking a just-touching jab as he went, kept sidestepping, was hit a light straight right hand, kept sidestepping, was missed by another damn hook—and was finally able to backpedal away out into the center of the ring.

Nothing was wrong with his legs. His sore ankle was holding up very well. Bauman felt grateful, as for a special gift; his legs felt fine. It was the right arm that was tired.

Muñoz' hook—right-handed but nifty as his left—arrived before he did, a sort of swift introduction that smacked hard across the top of Bauman's head. Bauman feinted with his left shoulder, bringing Muñoz' right hand automatically up to guard against that mirage left, then faked a high right to the left side of Muñoz' head, ducked, stepped in, and remembering to keep the punch short, tried with all his might to break Muñoz' smallest, lowest left rib.

He was rewarded by the softest grunt. Was then hit in rapid succession by several punches, what sorts he didn't know, and—surprised to find himself once more low and inside to Muñoz' left—delivered with enormous swift effort that same punch he had before. Received for his endurance a similar grunt, barely audible.

Bauman's right elbow felt as if it were breaking at the joint, that it might—if he hit Muñoz hard just one more time—break entirely with a splintering sound, and fold all the way in the wrong direction.

Now under a storm of punches which thumped and thudded into him—striking his head, his shoulder as he ducked and drove in—Bauman was very grateful for being short, for being able to bob and weave, stooping low, legs churning (he thought of the Little Engine That Could). So grateful not to be tall, not standing high enough for Muñoz to get balanced punches into his face, the bones of his face. And finding himself again where he wanted to be, he threw his punch, which certainly seemed to break his elbow but must not have. Missed that solid hit, *missed*, and butted into Muñoz, head down, driving in as if the man himself were the best shelter from his blows. Bauman saw the sweat-slick brown, the muscled rack of ribs, and set out to break his right arm against them—tried to break it, hitting so hard it should have broken right there at the elbow. Felt as if he'd done it, too. Muñoz jolted away, taking a long breath as he went, which Bauman heard quite clearly.

"*Oooooh!*" The spectators.

Muñoz came swimming out of a bright beam of sunlight, landed with a clubbing right, then a straight right, and then, Bauman thought, one of the hooks.

Cursing his cowardly left hand—so far out of it, so far from any trouble—Bauman tried a jab of his own, Muñoz running onto it for fair contact. Tried another, and the middleweight slapped it away, stooped suddenly, and hooked up into Bauman's belly, almost an old-fashioned uppercut. Nothing much. It certainly didn't make Bauman dizzy. He couldn't, however, catch his next breath of air, so instead put his head down and drove into Muñoz again, feeling against his aging body an almost rejuvenating contact with the middleweight's packed and whipping torso.

Thankful for the strength in his legs, Bauman, staring down at Muñoz' swift-shifting dancing black high-lace shoes, did his best to partner, his best to stay in close as to the sweetest date, to duck down under, where Muñoz' punches only whacked and banged into the top of his head and where, when he was lucky, he was able to throw the right into the same lowest rib two or three times. This before Muñoz unfairly spun and stepped far away, reached in to hit Bauman on the mouth, straightened him up—and, it seemed, having gotten his attention—stepped in to avoid a feeble jab, hit him somewhere in the head, and knocked him back into the ropes and down.

Bauman, on his knees, leaning against the ropes, tried to count to eight for himself, after which he was pretty sure he'd be able to stand up. He tried taking a breath, knew he'd better be able to do that, and was very pleased to find he could. Was able to take a short shaky little breath. He thought he was at six, with two long wonderful numbers yet to count, when Muñoz came two-handed—one bare, one gloved—and helped him up.

"Saved by the bell, man," Muñoz said, his mouthpiece already out.

Bauman found he could stand up fairly well against the ropes. He took the mouthpiece out with his gloved hand and was able to get a deeper breath. "Like hell. I'm ready to go, asshole."

"Sure, sure," Muñoz said. "You didn' do too bad."

There were calls of congratulation from ringside—Marcantonio particularly animated—as Bauman, now very relieved it was over, tugged his captive left arm free from behind his back and stretched it to relieve the cramp. These noisy congratulations were then terminated by Cooper's harsh, lisping cock-a-doodle-do. "Thow's over, get back on them fuckin' bagth!"

Enrique held Bauman's denim shirt in through the ropes for him, and Bauman took the shirt and shrugged it on over his shoulders. "Come here—" he said to Muñoz, touched the middleweight's left arm, solid as metal, and persuaded him to the far right corner of the ring for some privacy. On the way, in those few steps, Bauman felt as if he was going to be sick, took a deep, deep breath, and felt better.

"You nose is bleedin', man. Gettin' on you shirt."

Bauman wiped his nose with his right forearm, painting a bright red smear along his wrist. The nose felt numb. "It'll stop, or I'll get Enrique to pack it." He leaned against the ropes beside Muñoz. "So, Paco, what do you think?"

"I think you got you ass whipped, man. You too ol' for this shit." The boxer was barely sweating.

"No doubt about that, but let's forget me. You couldn't whip me, you couldn't whip anybody. Let's talk about you in those two rounds. You have something to say?"

Bauman watched, interested, as Muñoz pondered, trying to avoid anything uncomfortable. It struck Bauman that the men in State, a large majority of them, were entombed in perpetual routined discomfort precisely because they'd already found those same conditions, civilization's repetitive tediums, obediences, and mild fatigues, unbearable.

"You got maybe one good shot in there. Nothin' much, man." Said very grudgingly.

Bauman didn't answer, employing State's most useful weapon, that silence into which anything might fall as endlessly as into the astrophysicists' proposed black holes. And out of which might, as from Hawking's white fountains, rise anything at all.

"—Maybe a couple shots. Didn' bother me."

"And what about a real in-shape boxer coming at you, getting in low, banging on those ribs the whole fight? Think that would bother you?"

"Jus' move away, man."

"—And he keeps coming after you. When do you get to throw the hook?"

"I make time, man." A good fighterly answer.

"And supposing you didn't throw hooks? Supposing straight punches were your style. Standing up tall, and coming in with straight punches."

"Maybe dude give me some trouble."

"Well then, maybe you should give Dennis Willy some trouble, Paco. Far as Willy knows, you can't body-punch for shit. You think he doesn't know how you fight? Staying middle distance and throwing those fast hooks? You mix in straights, crosses and jabs; but hooks are your thing, Paco. And too many people are getting to know it. It's your M.O., and everybody knows it. Why do you think Burt Cafone picked Willy to come down here? Willy's expecting to stand up straight and throw bombs at you, while you're trying to figure out how to get that little bit closer to throw a hook."

"I can beat that dude's ass."

"I think you can, even fighting dumb. You'll take a lot of punches; you'll get hurt. You won't be as smart after the fight as you were before. But I suppose you can beat him, even fighting dumb. Question I have—and no offense—but the question I have is, Why do you want to? Why don't you want to fight smart, give that asshole a nasty surprise, something Burt Cafone didn't tell him about? Surprise the mother. And when he comes stepping in trying to throw those long punches, just come down out of that stance you like so much, put your head down, and go *into* that turkey!"

Bauman backed away to demonstrate, ducking low, shoulders hunched, legs well under, and huffed out six short punches, lefts and rights, hurting his sore right elbow considerably.

"—Into his guts, man! He's begging for it! And you don't have to be doing that the whole fight. I'm not talking about that at all. You fight—then, the second or third time he comes in standing up straight like that, looking to land a big one—well, Paco just isn't *there*, man.

Paco is suddenly down an' dirty and way inside, driving in," demonstrating again, "—boom, boom, boom. Make Mr. Dennis Willy a very confused fighter, and with a sore gut getting sorer all the time, wearing him down."

Bauman straightened up, came to lean on the ropes beside Muñoz. "What do you think, Paco? If it doesn't make sense to you, all right. You're the man going to be fighting. Got to be your decision."

"You know what that old motherfucker said? Cooper said somethin' 'bout my mother, man."

"Paco, Paco. . . . Don't you understand that Anglos don't know any better than that? That's just ignorance, talking about people's mothers. That old man thought he was calling *you* a name; he didn't mean anything about your mother. —Wouldn't that little man be nice to your mother if she came up visiting? Wouldn't he? He'd be very polite to her, isn't that so? Cooper'd love to meet your mother. Believe me, he'd behave correctly. *Respetuosamente.*"

Muñoz brooded on the ropes, considering.

"Paco, listen, a place like this you have to make allowances for ignorance. Many of these men haven't had the advantage of a loving mother. They're to be pitied. My own mother was a little dark angel. She had *Indio* blood, from up in Canada, and was sometimes cruelly treated." Bauman, to his consternation, having begun a condescending piece of nonsense, found himself caught up in it, this ridiculous conversation offering him an opportunity he seemed to have long required. "What I'm saying is between us. You understand me?"

The middleweight nodded.

"My father, who was a strong man, didn't treat her with the respect he should have. He beat her."

A dark, dark look on Paco Muñoz' face, recalling something unpleasant.

"I blame myself for not protecting her," Bauman said, exhilarated at such exposure to what was, after all, a barely comprehending idol. "—I saw him once, when I was a boy. I looked in a window and saw him beating her. I wanted to stop him, but I was afraid. I was afraid of him, so I didn't do anything. Nothing. I watched, and then I ran away. That cowardice has been a shame to me my whole life. And too late now, to do anything. My father is an old man . . . my mother's dead." Bauman found, with some astonishment, that his eyes filled with tears—an emotional aftermath, he supposed, of the beating he'd taken.

Muñoz turned to him, and Bauman was almost, but not quite amused to see tears in those grim amber-colored eyes as well.

"O.K. I fight the fuckin' fight your way. At leas' you a man, not a little *alacrán* like that one," an indication with his head out to where Cooper was active, instructing a cruiser-weight sparring with Marcantonio in the other practice ring.

"Good," Bauman said, interested to find he now—undoubtedly temporarily—regarded Muñoz as a friend. "Doesn't mean a big change, Paco. Your style's still your style. Only just a few times—he comes in standing up like that, thinks he's about to throw the big one—then you go downstairs, see what he had for breakfast. O.K.?"

"O.K."

"So next week, we spend time on the heavy bag. I'll work with you tomorrow afternoon. We're late getting this done, but you're a natural, Paco. You'll pick it up very fast. Fast enough to do you some good in there, when you want to use it. Give that guy a little surprise."

"O.K."

"O.K." A handshake, their right hands still fatly gloved.

"Nose is bleedin', man."

Bauman had seized the opportunity to shower. Cooper disallowed that for trainers, gofers, unless they'd sweated more than enough to earn it. But, pleased enough with Muñoz' tutorial, the little man had quite readily nodded Bauman away to shower.

Congratulated once or twice on his way, Bauman saw Lee Cousins, standing beside Enrique near the heavy bag, raise a hand in casual salute.

The gym showers—plumbing recently repaired, concrete floor patched as a courtesy to the expected Joliet people—were cleaner than most at State. Paint, however, had not been wasted on the walls or ceiling.

Seeing—quite correctly—the showers as a behaviorally delicate location, Wostenholm, the fat gym hack, ambled into the locker room after Bauman and said, "You sure took a beatin' out there." He waited, humming the same scale two or three times while Bauman stripped. Then, strolling into the showers with him, saw only Clarence Henry—mountainously brown, decorated like a massive chocolate cake with festoons of suds for icing—and turned and ambled out.

Bauman knew enough not to try for leisure in this shower. Boxers bathed fast in Cooper's gym, or the little man made sudden magical appearances, accusing them of wasting hot water, the health of the gym's elderly boiler always on his mind. —And reappeared, if they remained unmoved, to loudly accuse them of being faggots and cock-peepers, then order them out.

One of State's worn, stained, scratchy locker-room towels around his waist, his blue denim shirt, blood-splattered, in his hand, Bauman tested the controls of the second shower in from the door, found them working, adjusted the water to fairly hot, dropped the shirt to the concrete floor under the spray, then hung his towel on a hook and stepped in, a scrap of sandy yellow soap in his right hand. His left, its bandaged forearm, he tried to keep somewhat clear of the water.

"How's it going, Clarence?" Clarence Henry was three showers down.

Henry turned, cascading soapy water. Immense, very oddly shaped—his torso a slab so broad and thick through that even columnar legs seemed inadequate to support it—Henry had a soft undistinguished face, his broad nose flattened, his small dark-brown eyes sleepy raisins. The heavyweight presented a patient, quiet, thoughtful manner, that rather than lessening the impact of his size and animal strength, only reinforced it, making his interlocutors the more careful not to disturb that calm. Bauman, as he supposed most men were, was slightly afraid of Clarence Henry—wary perhaps a more comfortable word—as any man must be, faced with a creature that can maim him.

"Goin' all right." Henry had thought before replying. The big man had the high-pitched reedy voice many boxers acquired through being hit in the throat. "—I s'pose." And, on that, turned off his shower, took his towel down from a near hook, and began to dry himself, a considerable undertaking with a towel so shrunk by comparison with its object.

"Henry, there something wrong with your hand?"

Bauman had barely finished the casual question when Henry, still toweling, answered, "An' what the fuck difference that make to you?"

"A lot of difference."

"I don' have shit wrong with my han'."

Bauman, supposing this monument to be having a bad day, these common enough at State even for resigned prisoners, decided to keep his mouth shut. And soaping speedily, he stepped on his shirt in a stationary circle under the shower water, trying to tread the nosebleed out of it. It was an issue shirt; he had one more, and two bought. This one shot, he'd have to buy another.

"Hear you lookin' fo' a snitch."

This was unexpected, Henry usually not taking much interest in State's gossip, usually not volunteering conversational gambits, either.

"Supposed to be," Bauman said, making as little of that frail alibi as he could.

"They's plen'y of 'em." Still busy drying away at a broad brown belly, Clarence Henry raised his huge head, looked at Bauman in a startlingly unfriendly way, a frown dark and lowering as a bad-weather front.

"Probably true," Bauman said, wondering where this circumspect conversation might be leading. Worried about where it might be leading. . . . He grew tired of trampling on his shirt, stooped to pick it up, wring it out, and reached to hang it over the faucet of the next shower nearer the door.

"An' worse'n snitches," Clarence Henry said. "Killin' folks. . . ." Dried sufficiently, he set himself into motion massive as a vault door's, went past Bauman, and left the room and a mystery behind him.

'Killin' folks?' Bauman, starting to rinse, supposed the lifers' flimsy cover story for him was already coming unraveled, the publicized search for a snitch already understood to be actually a hunt for a particular killer, hack or otherwise. That, or Henry'd had some unlikely personal concern. —And surely not over the simple fact of murder. Clarence Henry (muscle for a hijacking ring) had killed three men himself, beaten two truckers to death with a tire iron taken from the trunk of his Impala, and later killed a third with his fists, so earning life plus fifty.

Bauman shut off his shower as Ferguson and Jerry Johnson walked in, towels around their waists, arguing about baseball. —Whether Johnson had earned third base last season, and might expect to take Terry Gower's position away from him in the spring. Johnson, a pleasant young black man, saying, "Goddamn right!" Ferguson saying, "Bullshit. You hit good, but you wasn't playin' that base. Wasn't playin' the base—got no fuckin' right to the position."

"Wasn' playin' the fuckin' *base?* What the fuck is that, man? How many steals I pass?"

They both appealed to Bauman as he was toweling, Ferguson not appearing to bear a grudge for Bauman's correction when he'd been staring at Cousins in that odd way.

"Damned if I know," Bauman said. "—I don't know baseball. Jerry seemed to me to be doing O.K."

"There you go," Johnson said.

"Man said he didn' know baseball." Ferguson, when not in one of his odd moods—recounting, for example, his murderous fairy tales on the team bus—was a popular member of the squad, a natural athlete, able to meet the black inmates as an equal. Convicted and sentenced for an extraordinarily brutal crime, the prolonged murder of a pregnant woman—her husband beaten, then tied to observe—he boxed, nevertheless, in a controlled and elegant fashion, and was one of State's finest welterweights of memory. Ferguson would have diagnosed Dennis Willy's weakness for himself, would have met that Joliet notable (had they been in the same weight class) with a precise attack to the body, without having to be persuaded to it.

Slender, pale-skinned, pale-haired, pale-eyed, Ferguson was solitary except for sports, belonging to no clubs, not even the Lifers', for which he was richly qualified. He was one of the very few inmates Bauman knew, apart from such physical monuments as Henry, Betts, and the huge biker, Perteet—such fixtures as old Cooper, or Bump, the biker's guru—who seemed genuinely at ease in State. Quite unafraid. This quality in Ferguson presented itself oddly, as if he appeared and acted only as a sort of projection, brightly defined and effective, of a being essentially untouchable, standing serene in the lens's depths.

"And Gower was sick a lot," Bauman said. "Doesn't he have a kidney problem?" Dry, he wrapped his towel around his waist, picked his shirt off its faucet, and wrung it out again.

"Even sick," Ferguson said, "he can outplay this asshole." Slipped off his towel, and threatened to snap it at Johnson.

"Look out, now, man—don' be fuckin' with me!"

Bauman left them to that familiar jock humor, and walked into the locker room. The team's two lightweights were there, speaking Spanish as they unlaced their shoes. At his locker, Bauman shook the shirt out, saw the stain down the front untouched by all the soap and hot water, and put it on damp. He stepped into his trousers, buttoned up, and stuffed his sweaty underpants in the left trouser pocket, his sweaty socks in the right, then slipped bare feet into his blue running shoes.

Cousins was waiting for him outside, holding Bauman's denim jacket folded over his arm, and looking, Bauman noticed, improbably fine featured—large gray eyes contemplative, dark-brown hair unlikely in its short-cut elegance. All so apparent a contrast to the fighters' worn, nobly-battered faces. Of these, even the best defended, by the fastest hands, showed—at the eyebrows, the corners of the mouth, the bridge of the nose—at least a slight thickening, a modest coarseness where the weather of other men's fists had eroded some edges away. The storms that had struck Cousins were revealed only in his eyes.

"How come you're wearin' that wet shirt?"

"Because it's the only shirt I have to wear. Let's go get some lunch." Bauman felt pretty well—had the faintest steady ringing in his ears from Muñoz' punches. His nose, feeling much larger than it had looked when he passed the locker-room mirror, seemed to throb in concert with his pulse.

"What did you do? Didn' you try an' get that stain out?"

"I tried to get the stain out, O.K.? What is this, a laundry quiz?"

Cousins fell into step beside him along the west wall of the gym, glanced over at the shirt in disapproval. At the double doors—the crewcut young gym hack nodding them out—Cousins said, "Didn' you use cold water on that? That's what you got to use."

"I used hot water." Bauman's ankle was aching slightly.

"Well, you jus' ruined that shirt," Cousins said, and displayed to Bauman a commentary glance strikingly reminiscent of those Beth had used, that look in which a woman mingled satisfaction, affectionate contempt, and wonderment at the grotesque gaps in men's knowledge, their lack of common sense in matters of immediate importance.

"—That's what you got to use, Charles. You got to use cold water for bloodstains."

As he would have with Beth, Bauman dropped the subject, suspecting that protest—a reference to the unimportance of shirts and stains—would be met with the previous glance's duplicate.

They stepped out into brass-bright daylight, warming past noon.

Lunch was Rudy's Special Soup, and—prompted, Bauman thought, by Colonel Perkins' grimace on tasting East mess's cooking—grilled cheese sandwiches almost as good as real snack-bar sandwiches. The cheese in these was certainly from the dairy, not government surplus. Everyone was served a sandwich, placed in the center space of his brown plastic tray. Rudy's Special Soup, in brown plastic bowls, rested precariously in the tray's upper right hollow, meant for vegetables.

Dessert was banana pudding. Bauman, Cousins, and Scooter skipped theirs. The fourth at their table, a young white fish nameplated Thayer, was persuaded to accept all these treats.

Scooter had been upset at Cousins coming into lunch with Bauman—upset or shy—and hadn't had much to say until Cousins asked a question about light bikes, displacements of 250 cc and less, that might be appropriate for a slighter rider. At that, after careful consideration, being assured Cousins was serious, Scooter had opened like an umbrella, glanced around to locate the nearest biker, then, voice very much lowered, recommended one of the Italians. "—If you can afford the mother. But you really got to be able to ride." And more specifically, almost inaudible, suggested a Ducati. "—A Ducati?" smiling Cousins had said out loud, and been told to "*Keep your voice down, for Chrissake . . . !*"

Their lunches over, the grilled cheese sandwiches eaten fast, Bauman, Cousins, and Scooter sat watching the white fish, Thayer, finish their servings of banana pudding. "Where you roomin'?" Cousins said to the boy. "You got a house?"

Thayer, blond, flat-faced and stocky, a politely tough country boy by his manner, and probably a dedicated car thief, was pleasant enough. "I'm bunkin' in with Suchard an' Robbins."

Cause for covert amusement at the table, Peary Robbins and Earl Suchard being very fastidious old cons, though straight, who'd driven many housemates out by constantly cleaning, painting, and touching up their four-man, making decorated shades for their ceiling light, occasionally burning sandalwood sticks in their one green-glass ashtray. These men had likely picked Thayer as a clean, clean-cut respectable and respectful housemate.

"You want some more of that puddin'?" Scooter said.

"It's real good. . . ."

"Hell, I'm goin' get you some more." Scooter got up and trotted away toward the serving counter.

"You know," Cousins said to the boy, "—that puddin' can sometimes make you sick." Ignoring Bauman's indignant look at such joke-spoiling.

" 'At's O.K. I got a cast-iron stomach, Mom says."

Cousins looked dubious, and might have said something more but for Bauman making a second, even more strenuous face.

"Here you go." Scooter arrived with two more servings of pudding spooned into Styrofoam coffee cups. A small roach, disoriented by its ride, scooted halfway around one cup's rim, and Scooter flipped it away with an absent forefinger as he set the puddings down beside Thayer's tray. "Eat up!"

"And welcome to State," Bauman said. "You have a good sense of humor?"

"Sure do. . . ." Already spooning up one cup of pudding.

"Glad to hear it."

"I have to go for count," Cousins said, stood, and picked up his tray.

Bauman stood up as well. "Walk you to the gate." And, perhaps having gotten up too quickly, suddenly felt slight nausea, like cloud shadow, swing over, then past him. A momentary sickness from exertion, from taking punishment. He'd felt it occasionally playing high school football, and later, boxing.

At the mess hall's double door, Rudy Gottschalk stepped over and touched Bauman's left shoulder. "Could I talk to you?"

"Sure."

"I'll go on," Cousins said.

"Want to get together this afternoon?" Bauman's sensible question sounding to him, because of Cousins' affect, like a casual request for a date.

"O.K."

"Come up to my place after count. Two-tier, right above the Nellises."

"O.K."

Bauman watched Cousins wend away through the crowded basement corridor, saw two men turn to look after him. Cousins' walk had none of Betty's or State's other ladies' hip-swinging. It was a tomboy's walk, deliberately straightforward.

"Rudy—what was it you wanted?" Interrupting the cook's own observation of Cousins' departure. Bauman supposed Gottschalk had something to say concerning Colonel Perkins' early morning visit to the kitchen.

"It's about the lady."

"What lady? —Oh."

"Listen, I wouldn' say nothin', but some screw's goin' to get on my ass about it. The lady can't be comin' over here for meals. She's Three-tier, A. All them got to use West mess."

"Right. Right. . . ."

"You got to get a pass for her, you know? Block sergeant or somebody's got to give her a pass. She ain't even supposed to be comin' on this block without a pass."

"All right. —Listen, Rudy," Bauman said, and glanced around to be certain of privacy in a shifting crowd, the clatter and noise as convicts filed out of the mess hall past them. "Tell me, what about that hack, Carlyle? I hear the old man does favors. That's just what I hear. You think he could arrange it? Get her a pass?"

Gottschalk made a considering face, which slightly wrinkled his tattooed pompadour, then said, "Could be," the equivalent, at State, of an absolute yes.

"All right, I'll give it a try." Seeing, as he said it, the faint settlement of conviction on Gottschalk's face regarding Bauman's relationship with Cousins. An annoyance, but for the duration of the Great Investigation, probably a convenience as well.

Gottschalk satisfied, Bauman went through the doorway, up the worn stone steps to the block, then walked along Ground-tier to the circular stair. Passing the Nellis house, he smiled at Betty, who smiled back, sitting cross-legged on her curtained bunk, crocheting an orange and black afghan. (This a long-term work, something like Penelope's weaving, its patterns and progress shifting with Betty's whims, occasionally being unraveled in anger.)

Bauman climbed the spiral stair to Two-tier and home, went in, and said, "Good lunch," to Scooter. His housemate, resting at Bauman's eye level in the upper bunk, had settled to read *Racer*, a specialized journal of professional motorcycle racing, fairly technical, and containing no chapter on tattooing, no pages of motorcycle mamas straddling their pillions behind bearded big-bellied brutes. In less pretentious journals, these girls and women were often posed with the hems of their yellow Harley-Davidson T-shirts tugged up to reveal tender teats—a delicate nipple occasionally impaled, like Pokey Duerstadt's right cheek, by a small gold ring.

"Great lunch, man." Scooter absently absorbed in what looked like a graph of gear ratios to engine power output. "That fish goin' pud his pants awesome, eatin' all that banana puddin'."

Bauman took off his stained shirt, accepted it was ruined, and stuffed it into their small trash carton. Shaking out a fresh shirt from his second shelf, he put it on, stood buttoning it while perusing the row of cassettes along his top shelf, and was deciding between Schubert and a late Stravinsky piece when their house door clacked, rumbled along its track with a rush, and slammed weightily shut.

"That fuckin' noise," Scooter said.

Bauman—drifting up from a dream of slicing into a piece of fruit outdoors in the summer, seeing its sunny yellow rind, its white pith that smelled so mildly bitter—was embarrassed at being discovered asleep, napping his exertions away like an old man. He sat up angry, swung his feet down to the floor. Cousins was sitting on their stool—its damaged leg a bit crooked; apparently had been there for some time, lock-'n'-count over.

"Don't you knock?" Bauman said. "—Make a little noise when you come into someone's house?"

He made this complaint, but couldn't hear it, since the Stravinsky was clattering aimlessly in his ears. Bauman took the Walkman's earphones off.

"I'm sorry, Charles," Cousins said. "I figured you could use some rest."

Bauman found himself annoyed at the now casual conversational use of 'Charles,' and supposed he'd have to commence with 'Lee,' in some upcoming sentence. He'd been dreaming of grapefruit—not the sweet pinks, but one of those more traditional, with pale yellow-green meat. He'd cut the thing, been eating neat little spoonfuls, savoring—off the spoon's small cool silver bowl—the sour-sweet taste, the quick fountains of juice filling his mouth at every bite. A dream, as he recalled it, more concerned with nuance than appetite—that dulled, probably, by Rudy's grilled cheese sandwiches. It did seem, in an area fairly central for produce shipping, that the state penitentiary could afford a few thousand grapefruit or some sort of citrus for breakfast more than two or three times a month. Not too much to ask. Certainly the capital's zoo animals were served citrus. Apes, chimps supposed to be very fond of grapefruit.

"You was exhausted, man." Scooter's contribution from behind the toilet curtain, followed by the toilet's flush. Scooter shoved the curtain aside, came out, and stood regarding his housemate critically. "I got to tell you, Charles, doin' boxin' with a guy like that spic is takin' a big chance you're goin' to get hurt."

"Scoot, you could be right," Bauman said. "Don't you have to be getting over to the truck shop?" The nap, even if a minor humiliation, a reminder of age, had had its effect. Bauman felt achy but brisk, really quite well. He didn't have any pain in his right elbow until he moved it.

"Goin', goin'," Scooter said, reached his blue denim jacket down from his personal hook, put the jacket on, then went to putter at his shelf, looking for something. "See my Chapstick?"

"No."

"An' I got a lighter I'm goin' to need. . . ." More fiddling at the shelves, things picked up and put down. "Can't find that friggin' Chapstick."

"Scoot, I think they're waiting for you over at the shop. You don't want to be late for the brake seminar."

"Cylinders an' blocks."

"Right. Well, you don't want to be late for those, either."

Someone down the tier, certainly on this tier, began to yell. Hoarse high-pitched shouting. It was difficult to make out the words, even though the block quieted somewhat as people reached to turn down the volume on radios, tape decks, and TV's, the better to listen.

"Need that friggin' Chapstick, Charles. Can't be givin' out blowjobs without my Chapstick. . . ."

"Right. Scoot, I'll lend you scrip for a Chapstick."

"Nope. Nope, I got it." He held the small tube up to demonstrate.

The shouting down the tier had become even louder. Some words quite clear, now. "You eat shit, motherfucker! I trust . . . a dirty fuckin' motherfucker!" At which, judging by ancient experience of these matters—when, after a certain amount of noise, assault or murder became much less likely—the block, almost in unison, raised the volume on their TV's and tape decks.

"Now," Scooter said, "where's my fuckin' lighter? That's what I want to know," and transferred his search to his bunk, stretching up to search through messy blankets.

"Scooter."

"Can't go without my lighter, Charles." Scooter searched his bunk for some time, then bent to the foot of Bauman's mattress to lift its outer corner. "You didn' use my lighter, did you?"

"Scooter. . . ."

"O.K., O.K., I'm goin'," Scooter said, and Bauman noticed his bony housemate and Cousins exchanging one of those swift glances of complicit youth at the teasing of grouchy age, just woken from its nap. It first annoyed then pleased Bauman, seeing Scooter at ease, enjoying Cousins' company, not offput by the boy's girlish looks. Their youth, of course, a quality in common above all.

"Scooter, go or stay. I really don't care."

"Shit," Scooter said, and pretended to discover his red plastic lighter in his left pants pocket. "There all the time."

"*Knock, knock!*" A stocky Latino stood at their house's racked-back door. Smiling. This handsome man, with straight black carefully tended hair, a neat mustache, rather small brown eyes, was wearing a yellow street windbreaker with his blue denim trousers, brown running shoes. A handsome man, and might have been more handsome with a face a little leaner, less plump. "—This a bad time?"

"It's a good time," Bauman said, "—whoever you are. I was about to commit a major felony on a roommate in here."

"Come on in," Scooter said. "I'm goin'." Then was interrupted at the door by the man's outstretched hand, and shook it.

"Jaime Vargas," the visitor said, and at this name—neither Scooter nor Bauman having recognized the man's face—Scooter said, "Oh, shit. Nice to meet you," ducked out, and went on his way down the tier.

"There she is," the Zapatista *patron* smiling as he stepped past Bauman to the stool, bent, took Cousins' hand, and kissed it. "We see you too seldom," Vargas said. *Muy elegante,* Bauman thought, but surely inaccurate, since most of the Latinos housed on A-block, as Cousins did.

Bauman saw three men lounging outside his house. All Hispanic. Two young men in denim trousers, tan sweatshirts. The third—much older, fat, with a face like a turtle's—was wearing an oversized brown suit jacket over his denim shirt. Bauman had seen the older man out on the walkways. He didn't recognize the other two.

Vargas, gracefully energetic (might have made a good boxer), turned from Cousins, swept the toilet curtain aside to be certain no one was behind it, and finished his turn by holding out his hand for Bauman to shake.

The grip was a practiced politician's, warm, dry, firm.

"Now—go on, sit down." Bauman had stood up to shake Vargas' hand. "Sit down an' tell me, Professor," voice lower than it had been, "—what the hell are those nuts gettin' you involved in?" He indicated the bunk beside Bauman, and on Bauman's nod sat down. "Unbelievable, right? Bad enough to be up here on a bullshit thing like you got." Vargas had only a slight accent, spoke his English in a swift easy Midwestern gallop. "Bad enough bein' up here on that, and then get mixed up in this Metzler shit." Vargas shook his handsome head.

"No great pleasure," Bauman said. Vargas, who looked so clean, seemed to be wearing unwashed socks. Their sly nasty odor coiled between them.

"I bet it isn't. I bet it's 'no great pleasure.' " Vargas demonstrated a pleasant laugh, revealing even teeth stained only slightly from smoking. "—Well, I didn't come up here to pull a power trip on you, Professor. For example, you notice we are not havin' this conversation in a meat locker." A merry glance. "And, for another example, I have no intention of foolin' around with your family, outside, which I sure as hell could do if I wanted."

Followed a thoughtful pause, rather theatrically demonstrated. Vargas, in profile, with wrinkled brow, gaze somber . . . removed. Then, "One thing you need to understand is—white, brown, black people, I don't care who they are—people in here long enough are never, never real right in their heads. You understand?"

"I understand." The odor of Vargas' socks was wafting so that sometimes Bauman smelled it, sometimes not.

"Well," voice very low, "—this stuff now about some screw snuffin' people? I suppose it might be so, but, hey, is that the most important question we got to answer about this place? Who's killin' who? Shouldn' the question be *why?* That's the real question, am I right?"

"Both good questions, I think."

"Oh, yeah. But the 'why' is better." Having made the point, Vargas appeared to consider it, then nodded in agreement with himself. "You know what I said about that, about people bein' crazy if they spend enough time in here?"

"Right."

"Well, I been in here eleven years. What does that tell you?"

"That you're an exception."

Vargas smiled. "Nice to meet a smart guy," he said. "And I don't mean a wise-ass. I mean an intelligent man. Short supply, in here." And to Cousins, "Your buddy's an intelligent guy."

"Professor," Cousins said.

Vargas nodded, looked at Bauman. "But then on the other hand, middle-aged man like yourself goin' rounds with Paco Muñoz. Maybe this joint's gettin' to you, after all."

"That wasn't serious," Bauman said, and recalled using the same phrase in the shower over at Seg, excusing his burning of Bobby to Grace Hilliard and her attendant.

"In this joint," Vargas said, still looking very agreeable, "almost anything can get serious." He stood up abruptly, looked down at Bauman. "They put a badge on you, right?"

"Right." Bauman rolled up his left shirtsleeve, then carefully peeled back two strips of adhesive tape, and folded his bandage aside to reveal the large star gripping the inside of his upper forearm, its small still-angry component dots.

"Will you look at that?" Vargas said, shaking his head over such nonsense, half turning to Cousins. "Will you look at that? A bunch of overgrown kids, secret signs and all that crap."

Bauman taped the bandage back into place, then rolled his shirtsleeve down and buttoned it. He couldn't forbear glancing at Vargas' right hand, where, at the angle of his thumb and forefinger, a faded *pachuco* tattoo was nestled.

"That's what I mean," Vargas said, having noticed the glance. "Kids' bullshit. But in this case," raising his hand to better display the small tattoo, "—in this case, a sign of minority pride. *Latino* pride. We're a minority in here too, an' therefore we got to be cautious every way but one, an' that one is, anybody fucks with us is dead." He smiled. "Of course, sometimes we can't get that done. But we always give it a good try."

"I see." Bauman was relieved not to be smelling Vargas' socks.

"Professor, I like you. You got a sense of humor. I already heard you was a decent guy. For example—" Vargas, his yellow windbreaker glowing gold beneath the cell's single light bulb, took three steps to the toilet curtain, turned and strode the three steps back, then turned again, his own madness (certainly present after eleven years despite the good humor, the smiles) perhaps expressed in constant motion. "For example, was I you, I'd be really pissed off at pretty Lee here for her bringin' all this shit up, especially to the lifers, when that Nash is a total *loco*. Nothin' personal against Nash."

"I'm not angry with her—him."

Cousins sat still on the cell's stool, watching Vargas pacing.

"What this little lady needs to remember," Vargas said, approaching the toilet curtain again, then turning, "—is good looks is a responsibility all by themselves. Good looks is a power, right? Well, a responsibility goes along with that."

Bauman nodded, was surprised to see Cousins, at ease across the cell, wink at him while Vargas was turned away.

"So . . ." Vargas returned, stopped and stood still, looking down at Bauman. "So, here's the situation. You got my sympathy with this bullshit. An' by the way, don't know if you thought about it, but this cover that you're lookin' for some snitch? 'Cause you aren't a clubbed-up guy, and you're so smart and so forth?"

"Right."

"Don't know if you thought about it, but there's a lot of snitchin' goin' on in this joint. An' every guy snitchin' is goin' to be scared you're looking to find *him*—an' turn him in to Nash or whoever, an' have him offed. Guy thinks that way, is maybe goin' try an' put you away before you can find him. You think of that? You realize that cover they gave you about snitches could get you in trouble just by itself? Even forgettin' the people offed Metzler and the black dude."

"No, I hadn't thought of that."

"Well, maybe you better think about it. For now, we wish you well, and that's official. My people will talk to you, you come around with a question. Except, *except* you start to finger some *Latino*. Then, you better come check with me. O.K.? An' that's not a request."

"I didn't think it was."

"—But I have to tell you, your ass starts goin' down the pipes, Professor, I have to tell you there isn't goin' to be any brown hands reachin' out to catch you. We're washin' our hands." He made a brisk washing motion, square hands cupping, stroking each other, wringing each other out. "O.K.? You understan'?"

"O.K."

Vargas leaned down to grip Bauman's left shoulder in a companionable way, squeezed fairly hard. "It's a pleasure talkin' with a man don't have to hear everything twice," the *patron* said, and indicated, by a sort of energetic leaning toward the house's door, intention to depart. "—Oh, one thing. I'd be interested your impression of the *Negro*, that Perkins."

"He's very intelligent. A planner."

"Um-hmm. That's what I heard, guy's got a long head. But let me tell you somethin' about plannin'." As if the word were a cue, Vargas turned and strode away to the toilet curtain, turned again and came back. "—Two things. First place, Perkins is a smart head on a black body—body gettin' bigger, stronger every year. But cut that smart head off, an' all you got left is hamburger. Which Perkins knows, an' which is why he sits up there in his house for months, only goes out once or twice." Vargas' pacing accelerated slightly. "An' the second thing is, Perkins don't know what real long-range plannin' is. That poor little dude is plottin' about maybe someday runnin' this stinkin' joint." Vargas halted, stood still before Bauman's bunk as if waiting for his speech to catch up with him. Broad-shouldered, fairly short—perhaps a little shorter than Bauman, he looked quite strong. Looked older, though, than he'd seemed coming into the house.

"Want to know what real long-term politics is?" he said. "Well, Professor, it isn't plannin' at all; it's what I call a natural process. . . ." Giving Bauman that sort of steady, staring attention he'd received from Nash and Perkins. An acute regard, Bauman now realized, quite bogus, the glassy steady stare of some stuffed animal lost in dreams of life. "—You don't know what I'm talkin' about, do you?"

"No," Bauman said, wishing Vargas would resume pacing. "No, I don't." Wishing also these hoodlum princes would find some other academic to hear their orals, those expansive plans for futures that could never be theirs.

"—I'm talkin' about our people comin' over the border, an' I'm also talkin' about them squeakin' bedsprings in every friggin' *barrio*. Them wets, them bedsprings—all that *Latino* fuckin'—are takin' back every mile you people stole. Those brown babies are goin' to shove your Anglo asses all the way to Canada, man! With the fuckin' polar bears! No offense. . . ." The *patron* (face flushed to saddle-leather brown, dark eyes polished darker) seemed more relaxed, relieved of the burden of good humor. Less restless to stride here and there. "—That Perkins got a lost cause, Professor. Forty years from now, this is goin' to be a bilingual country, Spanish an' English, an' where do you think the *Negros* are goin' to be?"

"Damned if I know," Bauman said.

"Well, Professor, I'll tell you. They're goin' to be right where they are now—bottom of the barrel. They just don't have enough Perkinses to go around." He paused. "Well, what do you think? Bullshit or what?"

"It's not so much that your notions are bullshit," Bauman said, "—it's that they're not very interesting, as presented."

Vargas laughed, a humming laugh, almost under his breath. "That's exactly what I mean," he said when he'd laughed enough. "You Anglos are so far gone, so friggin' decadent, you can't even defend yourselves. You can't defend your own country's borders, for Christ's sake! You think *Los Mejicanos* let any assholes from Guatemala come sneakin' over their borders to work, or for any reason? Well, they don't. They blow those motherfuckers away! Men, women, children, they don't give a shit! Now, I point out to you—a *history* professor—I point out to you exactly what's goin' to go down in the United States, an' all you got to say is criticize the way I said it!"

"O.K.," Bauman said. "—Let me ask you one. What the hell slightest difference is future continental politics going to make to you?"

"Oh, it makes a big difference to me right now, man. It soothes my *Latino* soul. Do you understand that? It lets me go to sleep at night, just like all them little brown babies was my own. . . ."

Bauman found no answer to that, and supposed the dreams of prisoners might be useful indicators—barometric readings for the simplest, saddest, most dreary of futures.

"No wise-ass answer?"

"I wouldn't argue with a man's dreams," Bauman said.

Vargas nodded, apparently satisfied, then abruptly turned and stepped across the cell to make his slight bow and kiss Cousins' hand, then turned again to shake Bauman's.

"You take care now, Professor," Vargas said. "Step light, you know?" And he left, his myrmidons forming in his wake—the two young men side by side behind him, the older, turtle-face, ambling after.

"Seems like a fairly decent guy," Bauman said into the vacuum of Vargas' departure, and received exactly the look his ruined shirt had earned him.

" '*Knock, knock,*' " Cousins said.

Bauman sighed, got up to go to the bars to check the tier, then stood on his bunk's side-rail to reach Scooter's TV, unplugged it, pried open the back, and tugged his scabbarded knife free.

Cousins said nothing. Said nothing as Bauman went behind the toilet curtain to pull his trousers down and tape the knife high on his right inner-thigh, imagining himself a warrior arming in an eccentric religion's chapel, while outside waited . . . what? A polymorph.

"Oh, man, it's got to be love. Love in *bloom* . . ."

Young Sarasote—in old-fashioned blue-and-white-striped pajamas sent him by an aunt convinced of his innocence—lay looking down at Bauman and Cousins from the cell's upper bunk. The upper his choice in a two-man house shared with a shy burglar named Pat Lafourche, who lived with Martin Sarasote in the style of a small reef fish privileged with safety amid a sea anemone's poison tentacles.

Sarasote had a tested IQ, on the Stanford-Binet scale, of one hundred and seventy-four—a score he'd managed to introduce into the conversation when Bauman first met him while mopping the laundry's floor. There, young Sarasote, slim, brown-eyed, big-nosed, long dark-brown hair slicked back—and looking, in unpleasant suppleness, very like a weasel—had been working at one of the huge mangles, pressing mattress covers while quoting Whitman at the top of a boyish light baritone, singing the virtues of an uncomplicated life of labor.

His IQ score was no small triumph, since Martin Sarasote couldn't read. The Stanford-Binet test had been taken in oral question-and-answer, except for the math, with which he had only a little trouble. Sarasote's considerable, if uneven, cultivation was the result of a constant influx of educational tapes and recorded books of all sorts on all subjects. These texts, dealing with every discipline (though on mathematics, only through set theory)—novels, technical manuals, histories, biographies, geographies—were all ordered from the Lighthouse or other organs for the blind.

This was an elastic and markedly superior intelligence. Sarasote, half Bauman's age, had beaten him embarrassingly easily in four of the five games of chess Bauman had tried against him. Then, introduced to the game of Go—in Bauman's self-acknowledged hope of vengeance—had learned the fundamentals in one afternoon, and a week later and from then on had beaten Bauman more and more decisively the nine games they'd played.

Sarasote had used this intelligence—overused it, perhaps—in plotting his parents' deaths while home for the summer from a private school where progress past such learning disorders as his had been guaranteed. His parents had been a wealthy couple, a little too old to have had such an energetic teenager, and too reluctant to offer their Marty the freedom and financial security he required at seventeen.

The murders had been elegantly conceived—his dad to perish of electric shock in his shop, where the banker produced lovely handmade knives, and his mother, Dorothy, to die a heroine, electrocuted attempting her husband's rescue despite a shop floor puddled with the poor man's urine as he lay jittering. This last was both the stroke of genius and young Sarasote's downfall, since the local sheriff, a dullard, knew no way of investigation but the painstaking methods taught him years before in the FBI school at Quantico.

The sheriff tested everything. Had both corpses closely examined, discovered the banker's incipient diabetes—then discovered in the fatal urine no such indication. There, only Martin's particular proteins and wholesome hormones were revealed.

Tripped by his healthy piss into a double homicide conviction, the boy had for nearly two years behaved quite well in one of the state's remote rural compounds reserved for underage criminals. In the late autumn of the second year, by young Sarasote's own account—related, humorously, to Bauman after their second lesson—in that autumn, during a disagreement over a broadcast of professional wrestling in the TV room, Martin had lost his temper, picked up a ballpoint pen, and struck a boy in the throat with it. Wrenching this free, he'd stuck it in again, this second time directly and deep under the boy's ear, so his carotid artery ruptured and squirted blood halfway across the room.

On being interfered with by a guard, young Martin—in so many ways an accelerated learner—had used the ballpoint pen in exactly the same way on him as well. Both victims, in that bucolic setting, had been too far from first-class medical help to reach it alive, and Martin Sarasote was sent up to State, a menace proved. There, despite his youth and slightness, he was left carefully alone even by the most ferocious jockers, desperate for feather-free ass. These brutes, on approaching him, discovered in his chatter, his jokes, his rudeness and nastily accurate insults, a want of caution, a disturbing fearlessness.

It had not escaped Bauman that Sarasote, a brilliant boy who couldn't read or write, had picked a pen to murder with.

"*Looove birds.*"

"You can cut that out," Bauman said. "It's a working relationship."

"Oh, sure. Holmes and Watson, 'Case of the Secret Snitch.' Dude, you believe that shit, you'll believe anything. And by the way, man, how was Seg? Old Teach was in with the big boys!"

Sarasote wriggled his head and shoulders farther over the edge of his bunk to confront Bauman, to better examine Cousins, his sleek head thrust out and down like some tree creature's, curious.

"Old Barney's daughter. It's a real honor. This visit is a real honor."

"Get off it, Martin," Bauman said.

"Excuse me if I offend," Sarasote said to Bauman. And to Cousins, "Pretty pussy, you shave your armpits?"

"Yes," Cousins said.

"Angel food, if it wasn't for a lingering concern about AIDS," Sarasote said, "—I'd be tempted to slice a piece off you. Because if you aren't juicy ass, I never saw juicy ass. And I suspect—really hope I'm not offending—I suspect you love it when somebody makes you take it. Is that why you look so sad? You ashamed of digging it? All those stiff needy dicks, those, oh, all-so-different dicks greased right up that sweet white ass?" Sarasote said this in a swift intimate fashion, as if continuing a familiar and friendly conversation.

"You squeal?" Sarasote said. "Or do you like let them hear you moan, just a soft *mmmm*, soft moan when you take it all?"

"You interested in a lesson this afternoon, Martin?" Bauman said. "—Or displaying some sexual problems?"

"I try an' not make any noise," Cousins said, went to the cell's wall and examined several of Sarasote's paintings fastened there with duct tape. "More noise you make, longer it lasts."

Sarasote's paintings all consisted of variations on the theme of delicately drawn proliferating angles, bends, curves, twists, intersecting turns of all sorts, done in black ink on cream poster paper. Each point where any figure touched another, overlapped, even approached a second, was scored with a dab of blaze-orange paint—roadwork signs on secret highways.

"Frigid," Sarasote said, "—what a shame. But very authentic." He swam lithely around on his bunk, followed Cousins with great attention. "The real thing, no doubt about it, Teach. Like pretty soon she'll be talking to you about responsibility, commitment, getting some insurance. . . ." He turned to look down at Bauman, and grinned. Otherwise very neat, well-groomed, young Sarasote never used a toothbrush, and in conversation exposed large even teeth, caked yellow-green.

Bauman pulled the cell's one chair—a furniture-shop rocker, twin to Betty Nellis'—over near Sarasote's perch, and sat down. "Where's your pad?"

"Where it always is, Teacher."

Bauman reached under the cell's lower bunk, found Sarasote's large pad of drawing paper and, clipped to it, a Magic Marker.

Bauman printed F-R-I-G-I-D in large black block letters across the pad's top sheet. When he'd finished, he held it up for Sarasote to see.

"What's that?" Sarasote's attention, so weaving before, now fixed on the printed word as if on a possibly valuable artifact, just uncovered, its use a mystery.

"Think about it, Marty. Repeat the letters to yourself from left to right. Sound each one out, then try to picture all of them together, a unit." Bauman had noticed before, was certain it was significant, that Sarasote's attention—everywhere else wandering, erratic—was, in matters of spelling and sense of words, bizarrely fixed, as if his disability locked him to a focus too narrow, too acute for sense.

"F," Sarasote said, dubious, sounding certain his attempt would fail. He was peering at the pad, bright-eyed as a bird.

"F . . . R." Bauman prompting.

"Don't help me," Sarasote said. "I know the alphabet!" But not the word the alphabet had made, not how to identify it again, not how to use it in a sentence. Another clue, Bauman was sure, to his difficulty—which Schoonover, secondhand, had diagnosed as a selective aphasia masked as a decoding problem.

Their last lesson, Bauman had spelled several words out loud for Sarasote. He'd hoped that alternately printing a word on the pad—particularly a word just used in conversation—printing it, then spelling it aloud, perhaps then printing it again on a fresh sheet, might rock some blockage loose in Sarasote's understanding, as a car run forward, then back, forward, then back, might be rocked out of mud. But that had accomplished nothing.

"R," Sarasote said. "I . . ." He paused, hopeless, lost as any woodsman ever was in darkening forest, his neat narrow head beginning to cant slightly to the side in his effort. A vein grew marked down his forehead as he stared.

"It's all right here on the pad," Bauman said. "You just used it conversationally."

Finally, after almost a minute more of silence, and an effort of concentration that in that time turned his breathing stertorous and slowly rubbered his face into a tragic mask, Sarasote shouted out, "T!" Cracking that out very crisply, spitting as he said it, so that Bauman, three or four feet from him, felt the cool prickle of saliva.

Into the exhausted silence following this, Sarasote took a deep breath, said, "Fritter," then asked if that was right—knowing as he must from Bauman's face, from Cousins', his answer before he asked.

"Well, you have the first three letters of the word," Bauman said. "But you don't have the word. Marty, wouldn't it be easier not to try to spell it back? Wouldn't it be easier just to put the letter sounds together?"

"That's what I did, man."

"Fri—" Cousins prompting from beside the wall of paintings.

"Bullshit," Sarasote said. "You just keep your pretty mouth shut over there."

Bauman, as if the pad were a sacramental object, lifted it into Sarasote's line of vision.

And at this cue, Sarasote again stiffened on his bunk, instantly reassuming that sorrowful expression, that bright-eyed attachment to the printed letters—as if certain this time magic would come to aid him. Another long pause, almost a minute, during which Bauman found himself, as usual, first bored, then inescapably interested in what odd currents, what billions of misfires were occurring in the young man's brain. And whether it had been entirely chance or cleverness that had led Sarasote to murder his parents by electrocution, or if some deep unsteady notion had supposed their obliterating currents might regularize his own.

Sarasote, eyes fixed on the printing, slowly began to turn onto his right side on the bunk, rotating along his own line of sight. It was an odd behavior, one that Bauman had seen two or three times before, and as apparently unconscious as the humming some musicians indulged in, trapped in their music.

The turning continued, Sarasote rolling slowly over, tucking a little as he turned so as not to roll off the high bunk, head thrown back during this rotation, to offer his eyes the truest line to that printed-on pad where he wished his answer—a sensible unity of letters, the word understood—to appear.

Sarasote's face convulsed in slow motion as he completed the full worming turn to lie on his belly again. His expression had altered from its customary malice, alert and present, to a flushed, dreamy mask of sorrows, doleful and disturbing. Bauman, glancing aside to see what his partner might be making of this, saw Cousins standing with his left hand up to his face, covering his eyes as a child might at a horror movie, anticipating some monstrous change by moonlight. Behind him, Sarasote's paintings presented a wall of haphazard intersections.

Bauman supposed Lee Cousins had seen about all he wished to see in life, except the very calm, quiet, and regular. —In which case, of course, he shouldn't have started the Great Investigation.

"Friiic-*tion*," Sarasote said, the syllables pulled out of him at first like the inching presentation an infant made, the crown of its head starting from its mother's vagina—then, like the infant's, a wet rush at the last.

"No," Bauman said.

"Same number of letters!"

"Not the right word; not the same number of letters."

Sarasote looked to Cousins from his tangled bed.

"It wasn' right," Cousins said, using his raised left hand to brush his hair back, as if that were why he'd raised it. "Word he gave you was 'frigid.' "

"Man, if I decide," Sarasote said, looking fatigued, exasperated, older than twenty-two. "—If I decide you two dickheads are just having some fun putting me on, I'll kill you."

This threat, the first Bauman had heard from the boy, all the more impressive for its casual utterance. Easing slightly in the small rocker, Bauman slid his thumb and forefinger along under the front of his waistband as if adjusting his trouser fit, and was able to touch the tip of his knife's handle. "I wouldn't waste my time playing tricks on you, Marty. So why don't we deal with the problem, and not your bullshit."

Sarasote lay silent, digesting that.

"And Marty, as far as your problem is concerned, we're not doing very well. I've been up here a dozen times. It's cost you a lot of cigarettes."

"—*And* scrip." A sore point. His carton of Camels empty one Wednesday afternoon, Sarasote had had to pay Bauman with scrip, a deprivation he still occasionally recalled, money seeming particularly important to him. Must be very important, Bauman thought, for him to have murdered his parents in impatience for it.

"Right, and scrip. We've tried this exercise several times. We've tried it more than several times, and it makes no sense to you at all, even the simplest words. And I do mean 'dog' and 'cat'."

"They make sense to me, man."

"No they don't, not written out. Only if you hear the word spoken—and I have a feeling that even then, you understand it better if it's supported by context."

"And if that's true, so what?"

"Damned if I know. . . ."

Sarasote sat up on his bunk, legs crossed so the vertical stripes of his pajama trousers made a series of X's. "And I'm supposed to pay you for admitting your ignorance, right? Classic example of what's wrong with education in this fucking country."

"Damn right you should pay me."

"Listen, Teach, I have news for you. Your ignorance is no fucking use to me!" The young man—slender, absurdly dressed in gift pajamas, perched cross-legged up on his bunk like some curiosity from *Through the Looking Glass*—had taken on a weightier aspect, as if 'use' and 'me' were keys with which he might unlock anything.

"An admission of ignorance is very useful to any teacher," Bauman said. "And what's of use to me as a teacher, will very likely prove of use to you as a student. —Tell you what. Why don't you reduce my ignorance. When I printed 'frigid' for you, what did you see?"

"I saw the letters."

"One at a time? Or all in a row, together?"

"Well, that's a good question."

"Answer it."

"I don't think you're on the right track at all, man." Sarasote looked across his house at Cousins, and said, "You think he's on the right track?"

"I don't know."

"You don't know, and you're too cute and too rich to care, right? I get in trouble trying to arrange some bread from my so-called parents, get warehoused in here by a bunch of retards, *with* a bunch of retards, have to beg bucks from my fucking aunt for Christ's sake. And you just throw your ass around in here, and get rich in the joint! How much did you get?"

"How much what?"

"Let's stick to the subject," Bauman said, and turned in the rocker. "Lee," noticed he'd used Cousins' first name, "—no conversation, O.K.?"

Cousins shrugged.

"A few thousand, street. Right?" Sarasote said.

"Marty, let's stick to the subject."

"Didn't you know that? You had to know that. Not only is this the most awesome pussy in State, but she's got bread."

"Marty, stop wasting my time. Answer the question."

Cousins stood away from the wall of paintings. "Maybe I better go, wait for you downstairs."

"That's all right," Bauman said.

"No," Sarasote said from his upper bunk. "—It isn't all right. Miss Rich-bitch can just get her sweet ass out of here."

"I'll wait downstairs," Cousins said.

"—Hey, hold it," Sarasote said, as Cousins went to the door. "Just stay loose a minute, just be cool, O.K.? Don't be so fucking touchy.

So I don't happen to have like a great smooth line with chicks. I admit that. I'm lonely. Aren't you lonely? You're lonely, right? I'd just like to ask you a question. —And here's the question. Do you think you can really rely on this act old Teach is putting on? You know, that he's this terrific brain and has a lot of balls and he's going to take care of you? I mean this dude can't even take care of himself. I'm really serious. . . . If you're looking for security—and I'm not trying to run a number on you—I'm just saying like maybe you ought to consider a younger person who just happens to be considerably more intelligent than the professor here, and who also is afraid of no one in this joint. Doesn't that make sense to you?"

"I'll wait for you downstairs," Cousins said to Bauman, walked out the cell door, and away down the tier.

"*Shit,*" Sarasote said. "—Not too cool, right?"

"I would say, not too cool."

"Oh, come on, man, you're not going to take a few minor insults personally. I was just trying to persuade the chick! Nothing personal."

"O.K., Marty. Can we get back to business?"

"O.K."

"Then answer the question. Do you see the letters only individually, or all together?"

"I see the letters, man, one at a time."

"You see each letter separately? Don't even notice the ones on each side of it?"

"I already saw the letter on the left, man, and I'm going to see the letter on the right."

"And when you do look at the next letter, do you still remember the one that went before?"

"I— Could be I have some trouble there, Teach. Because I really haven't got the habit, you know, of remembering the one that went before. To that extent, you could have a point. A very minor point."

"And when you see still another letter, you have to forget about the second one to think about the third? Forget the first two to concentrate on the new one?"

"I wouldn't say that. I could be too busy thinking about each new letter, and just forget the other ones. A remote possibility. I'd call that like a very remote possibility, which, I suppose, you want to charge me a couple of packs for?—that fabulous insight?"

"Marty, the really interesting question is why this difficulty in organizing symbols should confine itself to words, and then only to written words. You don't have any trouble recognizing tunes, do you?

Hearing a series of notes in succession, then recognizing the theme, the song?"

"I can do that, man. No problem."

"And I know damn well you have no difficulty understanding logical series, information defined in process."

"No problem, except once, urinalysis." Sarasote winked and smiled such an engaging smile that Bauman smiled back.

"Then—then, why should the letters of a word, just another symbolic series, why should they give you so much trouble? Why should you be in such a hurry to forget each letter? Are you afraid of what their word might turn out to be . . . ?"

Sarasote seemed to be jolted erect on his upper bunk. "*Shit*, man! And I thought you had something going! No such luck. Professor, you just hauled ass on a little professional problem. Hauled ass all the way to psychiatry—last refuge of the terminally puzzled."

Bauman, happy with such a classically confirmatory reaction, said nothing and sat at ease, pleased to let the matter stand, let Sarasote's one hundred and seventy-four points of IQ worry it, chew on it, try to bite it into pieces small enough to swallow and forget. —He did wish Beth might somehow be a witness to these little triumphs, have watched him playing Daniel in this small white steel den under a single bulb's bitter yellow light. Still teaching, after all. She—perhaps safe in a floating bubble of armored glass—could have observed young Sarasote's fixed glare of concentration, his grimaces, exposing plaque-encrusted teeth, his sad, slow contortions. Behavior too odd—in a young man so preternaturally breezy, malicious, and direct—too odd not to indicate a difficulty associated with his murders. She could be watching the boy now, as he sat up cross-legged in his striped pajamas, eyes almost closed, apparently reviewing the lesson.

Bauman thought it unlikely that Beth, in her new life, had discovered anything as interesting as State was. Unless, of course, someone—taking advantage of Phil's being still in school until three-thirty—was fucking her, had lifted her sturdy familiar legs, spread them, was making her broad bed sigh, forcing from Beth small grunts of acceptance. Who? Almost certainly an old colleague driven up to visit while giving a class at Kilburn. He'd be trying to erase Bauman, fuck him away, drive years of Bauman out of her. . . .

"And that's it?" Sarasote, eyes open, review finished, seemed disappointed. "Like that's your contribution for the day?"

Bauman stood up, leaving the rocker to rock two or three times without him. "Just something for you to think about, Marty."

"Nothing for me to think about, man." Really annoyed.

"Then try *not* to think about it," Bauman said. "—And that's two packs plain, or one, filters."

"I should pay you shit, old man," Sarasote said. "Zero, zip! What do you do? Wait for the end of the month, sell these cheap to the niggers?" But nevertheless turned on his bunk and reached down over the head bar to pick a carton of Camels off his shelf, open it, and take out two packs.

Sarasote, no smoker himself, not even in Bauman's occasional fashion, rarely bothered to buy filters, usually didn't buy out his ration at all. "Here." He handed them down. "—And definitely unearned."

Bauman took the packs and stuffed them into his jacket pockets, noting that Sarasote, gently raised, had said 'niggers' in a peculiarly separated way, setting the word off. Bauman thought it might be interesting to start with the word 'nigger' next lesson—use emotionally loaded words throughout, see if Sarasote found it more difficult not to recognize those collections of letters.

"What in the hell," Sarasote said, relaxing now his lesson was over, and perhaps because Cousins had left, "What in the hell are you up to, *Herr* Professor? I've been hearing really remarkable bullshit about you trying to detect some snitch."

"That's roughly the truth."

"How roughly?"

"Roughly."

"You silly old shit," said almost affectionately, "—would this all be part of your continuing macho bit, aging but heroic? Don't hesitate to confide in me, dad." Sarasote, pleased, showed verdant teeth, used them to nip the end of his sentence off.

"No."

"Annoyed?"

"No."

"You're annoyed, man. Any senile fantasies about your buddy? She's supposed to be awesome in action. Like she took on a whole tier—you hear about that? Drunk, crying, screaming a couple of times when it got really good for her. Cum flying in wads, man. An epiphany, State in delirium. I was still in Classification, down at Evansville."

"And if you hadn't been?"

"Dynamite question, dude. That 'aging macho' bit definitely pissed you off. If I'd been here, and was on A . . . ? Oh, I would have listened for a while, then I would have gone to sleep. I like missing things. Don't you like that, Teach? It's like biting on a tooth that hurts when you bite on it. Doesn't everybody like to do that?"

"In moderation."

"Far as I'm concerned, man, missing something lasts longer than just enjoying it."

"Then you'll do very well in here, Marty."

"Ooooh, pissed off. It was the 'aging' part that really fucked you up, right?"

"Calm yourself. I'm only forty-four. Younger than your father was."

"*Really* pissed off." Sarasote rolled over onto his back, stared at his cell's ceiling. After a few moments, he said, "What do you think about the Romans using that sacred cut just about every time they designed a public building, like an apartment building, whatever? What do you think was the reasoning behind that?"

"There was no reasoning behind it, Marty. The Romans were superstitious as savages. They thought that nearly squaring the circle was mathematical magic. —Now, let me ask you one. What have you heard about Spencer's killing?"

"I heard he owed money. Not that that makes him different. Made him different."

"And that's it?"

"You expected some awesome revelation? I never met the dude. But he wasn't a major star at State now, was he? Just a nerd coon, right?"

"And Barney Metzler?"

"Ah, that's better. Now you're into asshole royalty. Let me tell you something, Teach. You want to know who killed Metzler? I have the answer for you: Like anybody who had the chance. That's who killed that old fuck."

"Any particular reason?"

"Metzler was a slow-pay, quick-collect guy. He was a bookie. You knew that, right?"

"I knew he handled lifer money."

" 'Handled' is very good," Sarasote said. "Like he *was* lifer money. But why the hell are you asking me? That pussy you're showing off knows all about it. Who do you think ran for Metzler sometimes, made a few deliveries and pickups? Miss Rich-bitch, that's who."

"You ever deal with her—deal with either of them?"

"Did I bet? What have you been, Professor, asleep your whole year up here? Everybody bets in this hole."

"With Metzler?"

"Big bets with Metzler. Little bets with other dudes. Where the hell have you been, man, not to know that? I can see that absent-minded-professor thing isn't just a cliché."

"Thanks. I'd heard of Metzler and betting. But who's collecting for the lifers, now Metzler's dead?"

"Teppman. Bud Teppman."

"Teppman? I wouldn't have thought Teppman was smart enough, just keeping track of the arithmetic. . . ."

"Man, you'd be surprised how well dumb guys keep track of cash people owe them."

"And with that much betting, there'd be big losers."

"Hey, depends what you think is big money. What do professors consider big money?"

"Any amount I don't have is big money, Marty."

Sarasote smiled. "I can't fault that answer, dad; I really can't. Let's see. Humongous losers . . . I think you could say Ed Lesnovitch, like just for example, was a big loser. As big losers go. I heard Iron Eddie was into Metzler and company for about three thousand."

"Are you kidding?"

"Nope."

"Street? Street money?"

"He's shocked," Sarasote said to the air. "He's shocked and amazed."

"Three thousand dollars? People kill people in here for thirty dollars."

"Oh? Is it a killer you're looking for, not a snitch? A killer? Well," Sarasote said to the air, "in that case, I think a great light has just dawned at 221-B Baker Street. I think the Great Detective just realized he's looking for a needle—in a needlestack."

"And Lesnovitch paid that—he was able to pay it?" Lesnovitch, a plump, placid, crewcut lifer in his fifties—in poor health now, and on crutches—had been a master electrician on the street, and was now State's senior electrician. This an important post, with perks to share or sell. Lesnovitch was one of the last survivors of the lost empire of Maintenance, sadly subsumed on its last chieftain's death, years before, into Cooper's Housekeeping.

"Oh, Professor, I'm sure he was able to pay it. There is some moderately high-rolling money in this joint. Hey, people just don't have that much else to do with their time."

"But not that much money."

"No, not *that* much. Like I hear the football pool for all the major joints across the country really doesn't get much above half a million, but that's not counting the championship game. And that's joint sports, of course; a lot of people put something on professional games, too."

"Half a million. . . ."

"Across the country every weekend—depend on it, dude. And in this state, about, oh, thirty, forty thousand. And in our own little home away from home, I'd guess about fifteen thousand on a big weekend."

"That much?"

"That much, man." Enjoying instructing his instructor. "Now, not every game is a big-bet game. Like there're weekends they don't handle half that, and, of course, the action goes down for baseball. And also, some hacks are in there, too."

"Hacks."

"That's riiight. You think only cons space out in this place?"

"And you bet like that?"

"I'm not quite as stupid as your average meatball in here, Professor. I don't throw my bread away. Sometimes I bet reasonable amounts, whatever extra my loyal Aunt Patricia is good for. —You know, I'm trying to get the old fart to jerk me off in the visiting room. She's only fifty-four, doesn't look that bad. Looks a hell of a lot better than my mother did. I think she's going to do it, too, you wait and see."

"If you don't mind, Marty, I will wait and see."

"Man, I was begging her and begging her—got some tears up and everything, and you know I put that skinny hand on my dick, you know, still in my pants? And don't think she didn't leave it on there for a little while, just a few seconds. I don't think she's felt a hard one in twenty years."

"Marty—"

"What would you say, like what would you say the odds are I can't get old Aunty Pat to jerk me off? I don't think—man, I don't think even a blowjob is out of the question, if she really loves me. I mean, she knows I didn't do it."

"Marty. . . ."

"What was your question?"

"All this betting, was my question. For example, what has the average inmate in here even got to bet?"

"Are you kidding? Like his ass, for a start. Scrip, street money, dope, his cigarettes, tapes, VCR stuff, a porn tape, his radio, his deck, his TV—anything they O.K. to back the bet. And if he has to, he can bet outside stuff—his parents' car or his brother's car or his wife's car, or some cash. And she better raise it to pay that bet off, or somebody is going to come looking for her ass out there—because man, the money goes in, and the money goes out."

"I see."

"Let me ask you something, Professor Almost-as-Intelligent-as-I-

Am. What did you think? You think all these dudes are throwing their muscles around here just for fun and games? Well, it's partly that, I guess. But, Teach, a lot of it has to do with mmmmoney."

"I understand that. I just hadn't realized it was that big a deal."

"What other deal is there in here?"

"A point."

"Now, some people in here don't bet. But I'd say most do, small bets now and then."

"Like you."

"Like me. A bet every now and then. Now let me guess, just let me guess what your next question was going to be. Did I bet with Barney Metzler? Right? And like how much and what happened?"

"You're right."

"Teacher, you're so *good* at this. You're really quick, you know that? I bet with the deceased three times. Football."

"Pro football?"

"Not that shit. Joint ball."

"But we don't have a team." State's football team—the terror of the Midwest—had been disbanded by corrections two years before Bauman had come up, four of State's players having murdered a fifth, quarreling over a dope deal in the locker room at the Ohio State Penitentiary during an away game.

"Right. But we still have basketball and boxing, and other joints do have football. I bet Colorado–Utah and Colorado–Kansas. I bet those Cannon City people twice, I lost twice, and I paid up. Then I won on Alabama, and Barney didn't want to pay. That was his style, give the winner a hard time, a little delay, see if he has the balls to collect."

"And what happened?"

Sarasote smiled, showed mossy teeth. "What happened was I had a talk with old Barney in the showers. I had this double-edge Gillette stuck in a bar of soap, and I showed it to him. Told him I was surprised he valued his life so little as to look for trouble with me, try to keep my money. Old dude was startled. Like, hey, he was used to having people shit-scared of him. —I don't know what happens to these old cons. They lose all sense of proportion, start dreaming they're something special, don't have to pay a dude the money they owe."

"And?"

"And the real bad Brian Wiltz was in there with him, but Wiltz just thought it was funny, man. He said, Wiltz said, 'Pay or die, Barney.' "

"What happened?"

"Old Metzler paid. He wanted to live, just like I thought. He didn't want to die."

"You didn't think you might be getting into a little trouble with those two?"

Sarasote considered the question. "You think I should have, right? You think I should have been concerned?"

"Most people would have been worried, Marty."

"I can't understand that," Sarasote said, and abruptly sat up on his upper bunk facing Bauman, chin propped in his hands like a child. This change in position—representing, Bauman saw, a change in his temperament's weather—was accompanied by the same strained expression he displayed when faced with a written word.

"Man, like what in the world," Sarasote said, "—is this creepy obsession people have with living, crawling around on this downer planet eating pizza and shitting it out? What's the big deal? Will you tell me that? Am I the only reasonable human being around?"

When Bauman came down C's circular stair, he saw Cousins waiting against the wall of Ground-tier, talking with a young lifer Bauman recognized, but whose name he didn't know—handsome, swarthy, with a weightlifter's neck. His State denim jacket was carried negligently over his right shoulder, hanging from a hooked forefinger. Bauman supposed that Cousins, in the weeks since Metzler's death, had found some consolation, some protection. It would be the natural thing to do, and this dark convict seemed a strong enough man. A little young. . . .

When Bauman reached Ground-tier, the man had drifted away, left Cousins leaning against the wall alone.

"You were up there a long time."

"I was doing what we're supposed to be doing for this bullshit investigation. —Asking questions. And, by the way, finding out a few things you should have told me already, such as that you were a runner for good old Barney Metzler, your adopted dad. And, that he just happened to take bets and whatever in the amount not of hundreds, but of many thousands of dollars a week. It would have been nice to have known all that, before I made an ass of myself with a student." Bauman started walking toward the Lifer Club corridor and C's back gate; Cousins had to trot a few steps to catch up.

"I would have told you that; I don't know what you're so pissed off about. I thought you knew how much bread Mr. Metzler handled. I would have told you I ran for him. —So what? I didn' think it was a big deal. I ran for Mr. Metzler. I wanted to; that's how I earned some money. I didn' want to be takin' money from him."

"Do me a favor. I'm not pissed off, but do me a favor. *You* tell me about Metzler in the future, O.K.?"

"O.K., O.K. I don't know what you're doing goin' up there anyway, tryin' to teach that weirdo. Nobody can tell that shithead anything."

"One of the things the weirdo told me, was just how big-time the betting is in here. I knew it was around; I knew it was going on. I just didn't know it was big business. I didn't realize how important your 'daddy' was."

"It was just his job. He didn' care about that, nomore."

"Right, right. And by the way, is it true Bud Teppman took over for him?"

"Are you kiddin'? That ding say that?"

"Yes, he did."

"Well, that's just bullshit. Becker's got to be collectin' for Nash now Mr. Metzler's gone. Becker always worked with dad."

"Also, Lee," Bauman said, "—Marty called you 'Miss Rich-bitch.' What did he mean by that?"

"Nothin'. Well, two, three hundred bucks is what Mr. Metzler left me. That's all the money I got. Sarasote's a ding, is all, just like that Fanning an' Schoonover. Don't you know anybody in here isn't off the wall?"

"You didn't like Schoonover?"

"Oh, he's O.K. Schoonover's O.K. He's just real sad, that's all. Dude lost it for a little while, an' now he's stuck with it. He's not like them other two."

Bauman had a swift vision of Lee Cousins up in the library next week or the week thereafter, talking of this and that with Schoonover—not being cautious at all. Then, some disastrous subject having been introduced, saw Cousins, so slight, in Schoonover's large white dusty hands, that squeezed and squeezed the slender throat until slowly, reluctantly, Cousins showed the large man the tip of his tongue, then more and more of it, his pale face gone scarlet with strangling.

"Listen to me," Bauman said. "—Don't kid yourself about Larry Schoonover. He's a nice man, he's a friend, but he's also insane. Be very careful what you talk to him about. If he starts acting upset, agitated, just get the hell out of that library."

The men lounging in the Lifer Club corridor stopped talking as Bauman and Cousins walked by. The club's office door was shut, but Bauman could hear someone saying something inside as they passed it. Hard to tell whose voice it was—Shupe's perhaps. Or Wiltz, telling a joke.

The afternoon air had warmed to comfortable, the courtyard full of the sun's blazy yellow light. They walked across the lifers' yard, and catercorner into biker territory. A tall balding man named Jack Mogle—a lifer in for stabbing two bound gas-station attendants to death with an icepick—walked toward them, looked hard at Cousins, then made a long wet kissing sound. "Suck mine," he said to Cousins as he passed.

"Suck your own," Bauman said to the man before he thought, then was struck with fear.

"What?" Mogle said, stopped walking and turned around. "What did you say to me?" Bulky, and despite near baldness, handsome in a sandy sort of way, he put his hands on his hips, waiting for an answer.

Bauman thought this shouldn't be happening—not right now, not in such bright sunlight. Wouldn't have happened if Mogle hadn't walked by, or Bauman had spent only a few seconds more in Sarasote's house. If Cousins hadn't been along, it certainly wouldn't be happening.

"Forget it," Bauman said, although his body had turned to face the man as if, feeling fierce, it was in sudden rebellion, determined to betray its intelligence. Mogle's forearms, revealed beneath his jacket's rolled-up sleeves, looked round and dense as table legs.

"Forget it?" Mogle said. "You shit-eatin' faggot. . . ." And began to walk back to Bauman, had taken several steps when someone called from B's kitchen doorway.

"Hey, buddy! You—the bald guy! You're standin' on biker turf, you know that? Maybe you might want an' take that into consideration."

This voice—welcome to Bauman as Charlemagne's more timely trumpets would have been to Roland—he turned to see belonged to Monte Fitch. Fitch, only medium-sized, quite young, his dyed burnt-orange hair punked high into a rooster's comb held in place with sticky gel, was Eric Ganz's friend—his only friend. Fitch was rumored responsible for serious actions against welshers, deadbeats, any inmates who delayed payment for biker crack, crank, or crystal.

Now, this executive stood lounging in the kitchen doorway's shadow, a cup of coffee in one hand, his cigarette in the other, his medieval costume of denim jacket (studded with hammered pennies), greasy jeans, and black and brutal boots at perfect ease upon him.

Fitch said nothing more—not needing to—and Mogle, accepting

an untenable situation, shrugged, turned away, and walked the few yards out of the bikers' territory and back into his own club's.

Bauman turned to stroll casually beside Cousins again, taking the quietest deep breaths he could to still his heart, which had begun to pound as if just realizing how close difficulty had come.

"I don't want you ever to go an' do that again," Cousins said to him. "—You aren't my husban'. You aren't even goin' with me! Comes to that kind of a thing, I want you to mind your own business. You understand that? You understand me?"

"You bet," Bauman said, as if he weren't furious at such ingratitude, lack of appreciation. "I was out of line." He took another deep breath. "I think Schoonover was right," he said, as if Cousins would understand the reference. "I'm acclimating to this place too damn well. It's going to get me killed. . . ."

"That mean gettin' used to State?" Cousins said as they went up the steps and through the kitchen doorway—Monte Fitch, leaning relaxed against the jamb, moving slightly aside to let them pass. He glanced at Bauman, didn't seem to notice Cousins. Bauman thought of saying something to Fitch about the incident—not "Thank you," but something. Then decided not.

"Is that what you meant?" Cousins, as they walked down the kitchen's long aisle of black steel stoves, bright steel kettles. "You're gettin' too used to this place, an' that's why you did that back there?"

"Right." Shepherd's pie for dinner. The potatoes smelling all right; the beef smelling like warm dog-food, that tobacco odor. "—Too used to it."

"No way, man. You think that, you better think somethin' *else*," as if it was urgent for Bauman to correct the notion. "All that shit back there showed, is you're not used to this place at all."

They walked out of the kitchen and into the mess hall, where two bikers lounged at a back table drinking coffee, talking business or motorcycles. The tall young fish hack, Billings, was standing by the serving counter looking bored and diffident at once. A new boy at school. He seemed pleased to see Bauman and nodded, encouraging conversation. But Bauman, in no mood for it, and not eager for the bikers to see him chummy with a hack whose ways nobody yet knew, only nodded back and walked with Cousins on out of the mess hall to the corridor.

"You heard about Ed Lesnovitch owing Metzler a lot of money?"

"I knew he bet. I ran bets to him a couple times."

"You knew he owed three thousand dollars? Street?"

"I knew he owed some white money. It wasn' three thousand. Maybe fifteen hundred, two thousand. Ed bet with Mr. Metzler a lot. Sarasote tell you that?"

"Lesnovitch ever pay that money?" Side by side they began to climb the scarred basement steps rising to B's Ground-tier.

"He will. He's good for it."

"Um-hmm. We're talking about a man who put seven sticks of dynamite in a cabin cruiser up on Lake Hope, and blew his wife, her sister, and his brother-in-law into small pieces, just to collect some insurance. Isn't that right? Isn't that what he came up here for?"

"Suppose' to be," Cousins said. "People don't know what half these guys are up here for."

"Lee, that one was in the papers years ago. O.K.? Can we assume it happened?"

"O.K."

"What I want to know is, why the hell wouldn't a man like Lesnovitch just kill someone he owed that kind of money—which is a fortune in here? Or at least try to kill him? Why would he pay up?"

"I'll tell you why. —Because he wants to play, Charles. He wants the action. He wants that more than he wants the money. He starts offin' people to welsh a debt, man, nobody's goin' to play with him. Then what the hell's he goin' to do in here?"

"O.K. I'll try to believe that. . . ."

"That's why I never thought any guy bet with Mr. Metzler, killed him. You got a debt, you got a debt. Somebody's goin' to come an' collect it, whether my dad's dead or what."

"That's fine, but your average inmate in here isn't all that good at thinking things through, right? I would say a lot of people get killed in here for very dumb reasons."

Cousins had nothing to say to that as they reached the top of the basement steps, and walked out onto Ground-tier. This long, ample three-storied space, almost deserted by inmates for the bright day outside, and echoing to the footsteps of the few strollers, was bright with light streaming down from very high windows along the top of its left-side wall. The wall's surface, yellow-tiled up to ten feet, plastered in yellow above that to the height of the roof, formed a field down which sunlight flooded enhanced by the opposing three tiers' complications—infinite small Mondrians of white-painted bars—so the great vault glowed rich as butter, a brutal cathedral's sunstruck nave.

Here, as they walked along, Bauman enjoyed an abbreviated fantasy of his destruction by Mogle. In this drama, Fitch never having appeared, Bauman imagined himself overwhelmed, still tired, aching from the two rounds with Muñoz. He saw himself being beaten to the ground, kicked as he tried to rise to fight, never even (out of some scruple, honor) drawing the knife. Kicked several times, his ribs broken—until, finally hauled off by hacks, Mogle left him bleeding at the mouth, dying. A lesson for Cousins. Bauman's last lesson. . . .

Discouraged by this painfully adolescent playlet, Bauman enlarged on it, nonetheless—with Beth, Susanne, and his son at the funeral. They, everyone, then realizing what sort of spirit had been held captive in State. . . .

"Hey, Teach." A convict named Staples, passing by.

"How's it going?" Bauman said, and to Cousins, "Speaking of debts, I owe some money to Tiger. Want to go over?"

"O.K. I'll go over with you." Cousins apparently taking the notion of partnership seriously.

"About Lesnovitch," Bauman said. "Tiger says the same person definitely killed both men, at least used the same method. I saw those autopsy pictures—Tiger showed them to me for a considerable sum of money—and I think he's absolutely right. Both men were murdered the same way. Could be Spencer was eliminated because he knew who'd killed Metzler. Maybe it was Lesnovitch, and maybe not, but I'd like to talk to that pay-up, stand-up guy just the same."

"Definitely both done the same?"

"I'd say there's no question about it." Bauman wondered if Cousins would ask for more details, or not. Would want to know as much as possible about the instances of Metzler's death, or as little.

"All right, Charles . . ." the tone a perfect pattern of womanly resignation to the foolishness of men, "—if you want to go over there to Electric, we'll go."

As little, apparently. "—Let's go over tomorrow morning; I've got a visitor in the afternoon. Maybe it's true Ed Lesnovitch wouldn't dream of spoiling his sporting life just to save a few thousand dollars, street. But I'd be interested to hear him say it. And if you're right, and some people outside hired Metzler's killing done, who better to hire to kill Barney Metzler, than a man who also owed him money?"

"O.K., Charles. O.K., we're goin'. But Ed Lesnovitch isn't goin' to be spillin' his guts to us. Some inmates O.K., but not him." Cousins sighed, demonstrating patience.

"Lee," Bauman said, "—have you got something to contribute to this? You know State a hell of a lot better than I do. If you've got something to say—you're the one who helped create the fucking mess we're in—if you've got something to contribute, believe me, I'd love to hear it."

"O.K., Charles. Great. I can actually have an opinion, here? All right. My opinion, we ought to check the records down at the canteen. That's what I think we ought to be doin'—give Ramos some bread for a quick look at them chits an' sales. 'Cause I'll tell you, inmate gets a lot of cash from outside all of a sudden, that's where he's goin' to spend some. He's goin' to go down there an' buy them sugar-powdered doughnuts, an' some cartons, an' pickles, an' a six-pack of Dr Peppers. He's goin' to buy a new toothbrush an' electric razor. An' not just buyin' at the canteen. He's goin' to buy some dope—pot for sure—an' maybe crank an' shit from some biker."

"O.K. That makes sense."

"He's goin' to buy fuck tapes from Harvey Brown; he's goin' to buy some fancy shank from Boscowen. An' maybe he's goin' to get Michaelson or one of them other street doctors give him a note he's liable to get colds in his chest, so he can buy a leather jacket. You understand what I'm sayin', Charles? I'm sayin' in here is just like out there. A guy gets bread—he spends it." Cousins skipped once to stay in step beside Bauman. "—An' that's what I think we ought to be doin' instead of tryin' an' pump some smart old con knows his way around a lot better'n you or me. An' he's sick, anyway; I don't think he's even goin' to talk to us."

"Lee, you're right. It's a very good idea to check the canteen and so forth. I didn't think of it. But let's also check Lesnovitch out, just while we're at it. Face it, the man had three thousand good reasons to waste your beloved dad."

"An' I want you to cut that shit out, too," Cousins said. "You didn't know him, so Mr. Metzler wasn't anythin' to you. But he was a lot to me, so you don't have to insult him."

"O.K.," Bauman said, "—you're right. Out of line again. I didn't know the man, and I shouldn't insult him."

"All right. . . ."

They turned from the tier, walked down the corridor past the Biker Club and out through B's side gate, where the lack of a metal detector—dismounted to be sent for repair months before, after repeated false alarms—was replaced in theory by thorough pat-downs, occasional strip searches.

Bauman was stroked very lightly by a small black hack named Cunningham, who then waved Cousins past, untouched, to join him.

They walked down B's side steps into an afternoon light already seeming softer, a paler gold than had filled the buildings' court only minutes before.

"They don't check you very good," Cousins said.

"They think I'm the peaceable teacher type. And they see me go back and forth several times a day. They don't check you at all."

"It embarrasses 'em to be rubbin' me," Cousins said. "Scared they're goin' to enjoy it."

"All right, all *right*." Tiger very pleased to receive his twenty-five dollars, street—which sum left Bauman with seven real dollars concealed in the back cover lining of a heavy book on Baltic late-medieval trade. Bauman kept this book in plain view at the end of his shelf. Several others, innocent, lay stacked in a small dusty carton under his bunk, to absorb hacks' attention during inspections. It would be necessary now, to get more street money. Necessary, and unpleasant, to have to ask Susanne to bring it in again.

"Tiger. . . ."

" 'At's my name." Tiger, looking large as an iceberg in medical whites, stood at ease in his infirmary hall—floor freshly waxed and polished, Bauman noticed—stood relaxed, a creditor just paid.

"—How about letting us have a little talk with Jomo."

"I could do that."

"Could, or would?"

" 'Could' for a favor, 'would' for cash."

"Just a minute." Bauman motioned Cousins aside for conference.

"—This nonsense is going to wind up costing us money."

"I got money," Cousins said.

"Street money?"

"That's right."

"O.K." Bauman went back to Tiger. "—Two dollars, street, to see Burdon for a few minutes."

"Five bucks, an' see him ten minutes. Dude could have a shitty heart, man."

"Could have, or does have?"

"Teach, you don't ax me no questions, an' I'm not goin' tell you no lies."

"I'm good for the five," Cousins said.

"What I hear, honey, you better'n good, an' for a lot more'n five. . . ." Said good-naturedly, Tiger patient, holding out his hand.

"I have to get it," Cousins said. "Can I use the bathroom?"

"Hell, sweet thing," Tiger said, "—I'll be happy take that bread out for you."

"Bathroom . . . ?"

Tiger sighed and pointed off down the hall. "Go on down there at the end, on the right. You don't want to be usin' the patients' can. An' don't mess that motherfucker up. *I* clean that motherfucker." And to Bauman as Cousins walked away, "—Damn if I know why I can't make no time at all with no sissies. I can't be doin' no good with 'em at all. Why you think that is?"

"You make fun of them. They don't like it."

"Shit, man, on the outside I was makin' fun of pussy all the time. An' I didn' have no trouble gettin' me some."

"Tiger, women know they're women, no matter what you say. These people in here aren't so sure."

"I'm hurtin' their feelin's. . . ."

"You're hurting their feelings."

"You sayin' I treat one like a woman, she goin' act more like a woman."

"You got it."

"That's absolutely right! We are human beings, with feelings!" Irma the Aide had tiptoed down the stairs to eavesdrop.

"Will you get the fuck up out of there!" Tiger said. "Don't you have no fuckin' work to do standin' aroun' listenin' to private conversations?"

"You wouldn't talk to me that way if Paul was here today," Irma said, and was probably right, since her husband, though only a forger, was feisty fierce and loved her dearly.

"But the little fuck ain't!" Tiger said, and in pretended fury, lunged for the stairs to punish her—moving, Bauman saw, remarkably fast for so big and bulky-fat a man—and Irma, shrieking in delicious terror, scurried up the stairs and away.

"Well, you damn sure mus' be doin' somethin' right," Tiger said, returning. "Mus' be, get up close to that," indicating with an inclination of his large round head the end of the hall, where Cousins had gone to retrieve the five dollars.

"We're working together, not sleeping together."

"Um-hmm."

And, as if having heard a cue, Cousins appeared, walked to them down the hall, and handed a five-dollar bill, street, to Tiger.

"I'm sick, an' I *was* sick. An' I don' know shit about nothin'." Murdered Spencer's erstwhile housemate—blockily built, roughly bearded, his skin a slatey uneven black—didn't look sick. Jomo Burdon's eyes, an odd off-amber color, were very clear. His bare forearms, lying above his neatly arranged top sheet, were round, dimpled with muscle, looked hard and resilient as raw rubber. "So, why don' you an' this punk fuck off, leave me alone."

"You look tough, Burdon," Bauman said, standing to the cot's left. Cousins, on Burdon's other side, was sitting in the chair Bauman had used before the burning of Bobby. Bauman had kept his voice low, even though no other patient lay close to them. Three men lay nearer the door on this side of the ward; there were only two others across the aisle. Cargill, of the self-severed Achilles tendon, was sleeping, and—in his accustomed place at the ward's end, near the TV—lay Bobby Basket. That snow-bearded con, his regal head propped on two pillows, had stared at Bauman and Cousins as they came into the ward, his face stiff with rage.

"You look tough, and you sound tough, Burdon," Bauman said, "but if you aren't sick—and you certainly don't look sick—then somebody must have scared your ass half white for you to fake a heart attack and come running in here. Leave your buddy to get his throat cut."

"Wasn' no buddy of mine, man. Spencer wasn' nothin' to me. I got a real bad heart."

"No doubt about that," Bauman said. "But are you sick?"

"Kiss my ass."

"Jomo," Cousins said, "you remember me?"

". . . I remember."

"Charles," Cousins said, "—why don't you just let me and Jomo talk for a while."

"Well?" Out of the infirmary, they were walking across South field. The sunlight was fading from gold, and chill breezes blew across the field as if the lesser light had freed their motion. The tower at the southwest corner of the wall showed dull red at its windows, predicting sunset.

"Ghostses."

"*Ghostses?*"

"That's what he said. Said ghosts told him to haul ass out of that house."

"And what the hell does that mean, Lee? Are there Klan people in here? Some people running around in sheets?"

"I never thought of that—Klan guys. I didn' ever hear there was Klan people in State. You know, the Union is for guys like that."

They walked past a touch football game. Ten men on a side, and the 'touches' very forceful. The grassed earth trembled slightly beneath Bauman's feet as a runner, a young white man with a shaved scalp, the football tucked firmly under his right arm, galloped past them pursued by black inmates and white—Latinos, too. Very noisy, the men shouting more loudly, with more passion than even so fast and active a game seemed to require. Bauman found it interesting that convicts who were wary of jostling in a crowded corridor—particularly wary of offending across racial or cultural boundaries—ran here so free and easy, happily clubbing each other, this violence labeled 'play.'

"Well, probably wasn't Klan people at all. Just something that occurred to me. —And that was all the idiot had to say?"

"Jomo's not dumb."

"Right. He's a whiz. And he had nothing else to say? That was it?"

"Nothin' else about Spencer's gettin' killed. And he didn' know nothin' about Barney, neither. He heard about it, but that was all."

"You know. . . . You do understand, Lee, if we only get bullshit answers like that, it's highly unlikely we'll ever find out who murdered Spencer—hack or whoever—or who killed your Mr. Metzler, either."

Having said that, and waiting for Cousins' response as they walked along, Bauman was suddenly aware of a strange noise—which, he realized an instant later, was no noise, the diminishment to silence of all sound around them. He turned in this peculiar vacancy to see Cousins staring at something across the field.

Bauman looked, and saw there an odd cloud shadow drifting. The shadow was a great dark gray round, elongated by the sun's inclination. A much smaller shadow kept company just below it.

"Look," Cousins said. A distant wall-hack was shouting through a loud-hailer.

Bauman looked up, and saw floating just overhead—perhaps fifty feet above them—a huge bright blue balloon. Gigantic . . . its slowly turning azure striped with brilliant red, crimson stripes that spiraled slowly down with every turn. And the whole thing sailing. Sailing past.

Three people in the gondola were looking over, peering down as they drifted, silent.

Bauman heard the loud-hailer, incomprehensible, imagined hacks were running out along the crest of the wall with rifles, in case of some mad scheme of escape. He didn't care to turn his head to look for them, didn't care to miss any moment of this wonderful blue, this flying wonder already passing over and away.

"Oooh," Cousins murmuring beside him.

Bauman wondered if the three riders would make any sign, any gesture from so perfect a freedom to its opposite. These three, darkened to outline by the sinking sun beyond them, might have been men or women, might have been angels passing on other business.

The balloon wafted over in silence—its huge shadow running ahead of it —and as one of its passengers waved at last, waved goodbye, was over the wall and gone.

Bauman, looking down as if the sun had been in his eyes all the while, so they needed a more restful sight, saw the field scattered with several hundred silent men still staring up, their mouths all slightly open at the wonder. In the sky—borne on a high and steady wind—other balloons of the regatta, gaudy as Christmas ornaments, sailed the free air.

Chapter NINE

Dinner was shepherd's pie. Dessert, orange Jell-O. Cousins had gone back to West mess, and Bauman ate his shepherd's pie and Jell-O listening to Scooter complaining through the whole meal about missing the balloons, about lying on his back under a truck in the truck shop the whole time. Finished—having comforted Scooter by saying the balloons would probably be passing over again, some day—Bauman left the mess hall, went up the stone steps to B's Ground-tier, and along to the block gate. Change of shift was due, and he expected Carlyle—senior enough to have his choice—to be standing third shift, to midnight.

"What do you want?" Manning, one of the minority of veteran screws, grizzled, bulky, and reliably unpleasant.

"I need to talk to Carlyle." Bauman stood at the guard box well inside the gate, away from the metal detector.

"You do, huh?" A weary glance at Bauman—to Manning, only another of the tens of thousands of inmates seen over more than thirty years at State. "Well, get your ass back there," gesturing to the stretch of wall just behind the armor-glazed gatehouse, "—an' you got no note to be missin' count, either."

"Right," Bauman said, and went to lean against the wall's cool dirty-yellow tiles. His sore ankle was aching a little.

Six inmates (two walking together, then a casual group of four) had passed, noticed that short conversation, had seen Bauman sent to wait for additional attention. —Which meant he'd have to publicize, and none too subtly, that he'd gone to the gate and talked to Manning-the-hack about talking to Carlyle-the-hack about getting a note so Cousins could eat in East mess. Contacts by any single inmate with any of the hacks at distances less than six feet (and at volume less than calling-out-loud) being regarded with suspicion, whereas two or three cons together could freely enjoy a conversation with a cop.

After a short wait against the tiled wall, Bauman saw the gatehouse light flash from dim to bright, saw Carlyle inside, still wearing his winter uniform coat—khaki wool, three-quarter length, with a large flap pocket at each side.

Manning gestured Bauman over, watched as he went to the gatehouse's steel-framed door, knocked on the armor-glass.

Carlyle looked up, stared at Bauman for a moment, then buzzed the door open. "You got something for me, Bauman?" He was behind the narrow counter, hanging his coat on a hook.

For a moment misunderstanding, Bauman said, "I only have scrip."

"I'm not talkin' about that, you stupid shit." Carlyle's face—aging handsomely with a light raspberry flush under neatly-brushed white hair—flushed darker, to port wine. "You *got* anything for me?"

Bauman suddenly realized this old hack meant 'something' for Hilliard, the assistant state's attorney, something for Gorney . . . the whole mess. It came as a shock, as if in granting the club bosses their wishes, in boxing Muñoz, in at least answering Jack Mogle back in the courtyard when he'd insulted Cousins, as if by these means he'd somehow earned forgiveness for any other demand. This asking for 'something' seemed a grave unfairness—like the taking of his Rolex—and he felt, and knew he'd assumed for Carlyle, that stubborn put-upon resentful air all inmates presented to corrections officers.

"Well . . . ?"

Outside the brightly-lit guardhouse, passing inmates and Carlyle's companion-hacks of the third shift appeared as through an aquarium's thick green glass, viewed in mimed presentations of evening pat-downs.

Bauman had imagined this contact—when he'd still imagined it, thought it probable—had supposed it would be somehow indirect, indicate more respect for him, less routine impatience.

"I was supposed to talk to Gorney, go over to see Hilliard."

"Come off it," Carlyle said. "—What you got to see anybody?"

"Metzler and Spencer were killed by the same person."

Carlyle didn't seem interested in that at all, drummed short fingers on the gatehouse's green metal counter, his fingers the same plump, crinkled, flushed rose as his face.

"I don't know why," Bauman said.

Carlyle snorted in disgust, impatient at such incompetence in snitching. "You're doin' real great," he said. "What the hell's the matter with you? You got your head up your ass, or what?"

"Then you try to find the fucking killer!" Bauman embarrassed at having failed, having that pointed out so directly and at such a low level.

"Hey, you're the jerk in jail, pal," Carlyle said, surprisingly unfriendly for a friendly hack. It occurred to Bauman that Carlyle, forced to deal with informers, found it distasteful.

"It's all I have, so far," Bauman said, ashamed of adding the 'so far.' He could have just said, 'That's all I have,' and let it go at that.

"Isn't good enough," Carlyle said. "I can tell you that. Not near good enough."

"I'm doing all I can. If it isn't good enough, they can just go fuck themselves."

Carlyle might as well not have heard him.

"Isn't good enough, pal," he said, and reached down beneath the counter for a small steel-covered clipboard. He opened it, took a black pen from his khaki shirt's starched breast pocket, and made an entry as if noting then and there, for any corrections people to read, that Bauman had proven incompetent, even as a stoolie.

"And I need something," Bauman said, watching Carlyle make the entry, probably only change of shift. . . .

"You an' everybody else," Carlyle said, looked at his watch (a digital, not as nice as Bauman's Triathlon), and wrote something more.

"I need a building pass for Cousins, and I need a note so he can eat in East mess."

"Cousins? That faggot ain't goin' in East mess."

"I need him there. He's a source for me, knows a lot about Metzler."

"Sure, sure." Turned to a new sheet, wrote some more.

"He has to be able to come over here, and stay for the meals. And he has to be able to get in and out of blocks with me, and not have to worry a hack's going to call him on it and write him a ticket."

"I'll bet," Carlyle said, tore out his second sheet, closed the clipboard's steel cover, and put it away under the counter. He capped his pen and tucked it carefully into his breast pocket.

"I *need* him over here," Bauman said. "—We're working together. Metzler meant something to him." At which the hack offered Bauman a satirical glance, as if his shift, otherwise tedious, had just been enlivened.

"No way," Carlyle said, and folded the torn-out sheet. "Now, you move on out of here." He gestured 'out' with his right thumb.

"I need it. I need a note."

"Hear what I said? I said move."

"Listen, if it's necessary, I believe I can get twenty, maybe fifty dollars, street—"

"Don't say that shit to me," Carlyle said.

"I need a note."

"Get out of here," Carlyle said. "—An' I'm not goin' to tell you that again."

"All right, then. Then fuck you!" Bauman said, and turned to go.

"Hey," Carlyle said. "Hey! Where you goin'? Take your shit with you." And slid the folded sheet of paper over the counter.

It was a note for Cousins—block and building pass, and permission to take meals in either mess hall through the last week of November, first two weeks of December. Carlyle had signed it, scribbled Vermillier's initials after that.

"O.K.," Bauman said. "I guess I owe you."

Carlyle just stood silent behind the gatehouse counter, looking at him. Then, when Bauman opened the steel and glass door to go, said, "Why don't you wake up?"

Walking back down Ground-tier, Bauman folded the note, put it in his right jacket pocket, and thought about how to ask Susanne to bring in more cash for him. It needed to be a routine thing, a very casual request, not an excuse for the tragicomedy she'd made of it the last time.

He saw Sammy Miles—one of the A-block people assigned to East mess—heading toward the gate, and walked across the corridor to intercept him. Sammy, very tall, a clean-cut ex–Little League coach and accountant, was just finishing two of five for fraud and misappropriation. State's assistant baseball coach, Sammy was one of the prison's many very careful inmates, those doing cautious time, quiet, avoiding trouble, avoiding attention—avoiding club people if they could, if they needed no loans, no dope, no ass. Needed no protection . . . had no bad luck.

"There he is. Education with a capital E. How're you doin', guy?"

"How's it going, Sammy?"

"I'm going, man. The board loves me. Yours truly is damn near out on the street."

"How long?"

"Two unbearable months. I'll be out three weeks after New Years. Six months' parole, two years' probation."

"I'm happy for you."

"And none too soon. It was getting to be weird-time for Samuel Miles, I'll tell you."

Bauman recalled hearing from Betty Nellis that Miles' wife had divorced him the year before. The wife had taken their children away to Florida, a permanent thing.

"You know who your officer's going to be?"

"No."

"You get the chance, try requesting Sonnenstein. Adrienne Sonnenstein. She's O.K."

"You hear she's O.K.?"

"I met her. She's all right."

"O.K. How you doing?"

"Keeping busy," Bauman said.

"Yeah, that's what I hear," Miles said, "—that snitch stuff. I wouldn't touch that with a pole, man. I really wouldn't."

"Well, you're not always left with a choice."

"None of my business," Miles said, not wanting to hear any more about it, getting restless to walk on, get off B-block and back home to A for count.

Bauman took out Carlyle's note. "I've got a hack note here, Sammy. I'd be obliged if you'd take it over to Cousins."

"I don't know, man," Miles said. "I think I'd rather not, if it's O.K."

"For Christ's sake, Sammy, it's a hack note! An assignment note. I didn't write the fucking thing!"

"Hey, you know, I really have to be extra careful. . . ."

"Here, read the goddamned note. Go on, read it!" An inmate passing them—another A-blocker going home—glanced their way.

Miles took the note, said, "You have to understand my position," and read it.

"O.K.?"

"I guess it'll be all right. I really would prefer not to do it, though, if it's all the same—"

"It isn't all the fucking same," Bauman said. "Will you stop this shit, Sammy, and just give Cousins the note? Carlyle wrote the goddamned thing. It's not a fucking love letter; it's business! O.K.?"

"All right," Miles said. "All right." This last said very softly, to encourage Bauman to lower his voice.

"I gave you Sonnenstein's name—a decent officer you can at least try to get assigned to—and you give me this crap in return. I wouldn't ask you to do anything that would get you into trouble."

"I know," Miles said very softly. "—I know that. Well, I've got to go."

"And tell Cousins I'll be at the movies, per the bikers' request, in case he wants to come over."

"Right."

"And tonight, Sammy. Not next week."

"I said I would, didn't I?" Miles said, and put the note in his jacket pocket. "Well, I've got to go. If I don't see you . . ."

Bauman supposed Miles would go out of his way to avoid seeing him, avoid being asked any more favors, large or small.

"You take care, Sammy. Have a ball out there. And look up Sonnenstein; she'll remember me."

"Right, right. Take it easy," Miles said, turned and walked away toward the block gate. He looked glad to be going.

Bauman walked back down Ground-tier thinking Sonnenstein probably wouldn't remember him at all, not personally, only as the nutcase who'd paid McElvey for training in joint-ology. Useful training, by and large. He tried to remember the color of Sonnenstein's eyes—brown, certainly some shade of brown. And whether he'd smelled her, smelled at least her perfume. He thought about her, to avoid thinking what a fool old Carlyle had made of him, until that became inescapable. It was painfully obvious the old hack had handled dozens of snitches, deal makers, stoolies—reluctant or eager. Could likely do it in his sleep. And finding Bauman nothing special in the line, had confirmed him as an informer by treating his information with contempt. Whereupon, anxious to prove himself satisfactory, the tenured professor had whined and defended his goods, hinted at more. . . .

It was a revelation nearly unbearable—a self so vain, so foolish and nasty. Bauman walked along wishing he had some opportunity to kill Carlyle, so no one else would ever know. He was certain he could deal with that notion of himself, as long as no one else knew of it.

He imagined the other gate hacks distracted by something—a fight, some disturbance—imagined he'd drawn his knife, suddenly leaned over the counter and driven that acute, fine-ground point snappily into the old man's left eye and through the bone behind that. The steel sliding so easily its full length into the brain that Bauman's surprised and sickened glance met Carlyle's—the old man's right eye then comically crossing to observe for an instant the handle of the knife that had killed him.

The movie, a recently released comedy, had drawn a crowd.

A considerable number of inmates still loitered to smoke and socialize cautiously in the auditorium's small lobby before joining the lines of men being passed or casually patted by hacks at the theater's doors as they filed in. The auditorium—cramped, low-ceilinged enough to have been an architectural afterthought—had been placed just beneath the gym's generous professional space for basketball and boxing. Below that great court and its high, flanking bleachers—and just above the basement boiler rooms where Cousins, and others through the years, had suffered their Gethsemanes—the administration showed weekly films, each carefully chosen to avoid excessive violence, inflammatory sexual situations, racially adversarial scenarios.

These strictures left not much of current production available to the inmates at State, except for sugary 'family' entertainments (which often disappointed to rage and demonstration), some comedies, and those few restrained romances, thoughtful treatments of espionage, or tediously accurate portrayals of police work sure to calm by boredom the most adolescent observer.

State's audience, though fairly free to stay in its small houses observing any sort of film on VCR's—including (against regulations, but plentiful) tapes of real fucking or realistic murder—nevertheless enjoyed theater-going as an occasion, especially those interested in the semi-public cock-sucking they might witness or encounter under dim blue light. And of the films chosen by corrections, an occasional one from the forties or fifties, even from the thirties, did please many.

The prisoners, fairly quiet except for the softest liquid sounds, an occasional moan, would sit staring at these old films, absorbing their quaint criminal and street slang, the romantic back-and-forth then current, all their archaic attitudes. This audience was wonderfully relieved by even a single screen kiss, in which very obviously no tongues were employed. And was pleased by a screen shooting of the most archaic and antiseptic sort, where some gangster—just finishing dinner at a little restaurant with checkered tablecloths, bottles of wine in straw baskets, and a painfully Italian owner (short, fat, and funny)—simply, at the shot, clutched the lapels of his dark, tight-fitting double-breasted suit, grimaced as if at the clam sauce, and collapsed, perhaps knocking over a table. The camera, a shy voyeur, then shifting its attention to a fallen wine glass, observing it rolling in crisp black and white to the painfully arched shoe of a woman diner.

Bauman, coming down the gym stairs with the last of the gathering crowd (odd-numbered houses, blocks A and B, tonight) had been talking with Henry Grassle, a bulky young embezzler (fallen from bank branch officer), and lobbyist for the construction of a racquetball court out of administrative funds. Grassle had been arguing that space existed below the auditorium for that, the warden's office replying formally, in letters, that no further funds could be allotted for athletics this year. Perhaps, however, next year, or the year after.

"—Or the year after that," Bauman said.

"If there was a reason for it, for not using that area, I wouldn't mind so much," Grassle said. "There's no damned reason for them to say no; that's what bothers the hell out of me."

"Hey, guy—still waiting for that fee!" Les Kerwin, tall, gray-haired, handsome as a soap-opera lawyer, stood lounging against the stair-landing wall, smoking, as they came down. He'd been talking to a big blond man with tattooed hands.

Bauman found he'd grown tired of Kerwin's insistence, and conscious of his knife taped high on his right thigh, where only a moment of fumbling beneath his waistband would produce it, stopped on the landing and said, "Les, will you cut the crap? The conversation we had was about the application of statutes. It didn't have a goddamned thing to do with my legal problems. You want twenty-five bucks? —Fine. I'll give you twenty-five bucks. Then, right there, I'll *charge* you that twenty-five bucks for having given you my opinion of the historical development of statute law."

Kerwin laughed, though not for long, and shook his head.

"Teach," he said, "—you're wearing me down. Fiscal year's ending, and I'm about to give up." He sighed, and said to the big blond man, "Never debate fee with a professor. Those people are used to winning all their arguments. . . ."

Bauman went on down the stairs, Grassle trailing.

"They are never going to build that racquetball court, Henry," Bauman said, "because only you and Frank Forlini want to play the damned game."

"Hey, that's just not true. Murphy wants to learn, and Ed, uh, what's his name. He's a player."

"Ed Scott's a squash player, Henry. He's a preppie. He doesn't want to play racquetball." Scott, a bulky cheerful middle-aged man—good-humored even in State—had followed his wife to her motel meeting with his business partner, then entered their room with his skeet gun and killed them.

As they walked into the theater lobby, Bauman saw Cousins waiting by the back wall just as Cousins saw him, and started over through the crowd.

"I really have to get out of this place," Grassle said, watching Cousins walk toward them. "I'm not kidding. It's really getting to be imperative."

"Lee," Bauman said, "—Henry Grassle."

"Hi," Cousins said. He'd wet his dark-brown hair to comb it. It lay contrasting—darker, damp—against the white skin at his temples, framed more specifically the fragile bones of his face, his shady gray eyes.

"I'm really pleased to meet you," Grassle said, attentive, intense. His wife—very loyal, Bauman had heard from Margaret the Maid—his three nice kids, his possibility of return to a liberal-hearted bank as junior teller (under supervision), were all for the moment forgotten. "It's a real pleasure. . . ."

"Thanks. Nice meetin' you." Shy eyes, hiding . . . what, from Henry Grassle?

"A real pleasure," Grassle said. "—I've heard, I've heard you're a very interesting person."

At this gaffe, this too-eager fumble at introduction, Bauman watched Cousins' lovely eyes become less lovely, become only a convict's eyes, a young man's who'd sold coke to a cop.

"Be seeing you, Henry," Bauman said, to spare Grassle Cousins' probable unpleasant response.

"Oh, right. O.K."

"Goodbye," Cousins said, and Bauman was amused to see the ex-banker take that as some sign of favor, as if 'goodbye' must someday be complemented by 'hello.'

"Bye-bye," Grassle said, and stepped away, then looked back and waved casually before he was gone into the crowd.

"What a dork," Cousins said.

"You get the hack note?"

"I got it. Thanks." Cousins observed Bauman closely, as if he might have changed since the afternoon. "How're you feelin'? Feelin' O.K.?"

"I feel fine. —Why? The nose swollen?"

"A little—An' some bruises. You took a beatin' in there."

"I've taken them before. It's no big deal." Bauman found this exchange particularly annoying, since he was certain there were damn few inmates at State, of any age, who'd be pleased to go two rounds with Muñoz, or any other boxer on the team.

"O.K. . . ." This said in a woman's annoying way, a question postponed, not disposed of.

"Let's go in," Bauman said. "I don't see any bikers here for the big conference. . . ."

But, as they joined the diminishing line at the theater's right-side double door, two bikers Bauman knew by sight, Gooch and Bad Bob—both rumored important in sales-and-distribution in the bikers' retail drug trade—walked out of the auditorium and toward them, certainly by appointment, cleaving the crowd to either side as they came.

"Pussy sits separate," Bad Bob said as they arrived. He looked lank and deceptively mild with blond handlebar mustache, a pigtail, and gold-rimmed granny glasses. The only biker who'd attended college, Bad Bob was a reader of Regency romances. "—Horses an' carriages and that shit," according to Scooter.

Cousins glanced at Bauman—for what cue Bauman couldn't imagine. Protest? Argument? . . . Refusal?

"You heard him; get the fuck outta here." Gooch to Cousins. Gooch, rubbery fat, bearded—always bringing with him an exhaled breath roughly acid as a belch—was the mouth, the insulter, the threatener of the two. Bad Bob fulfilled.

"Go on, Lee," Bauman said, obscurely pleased after all that Cousins had waited to be advised by him. And the boy nodded, then drifted away into the last knot of inmates passing the doorway hacks.

When the two bikers took Bauman through, last to leave the lobby, neither hack delayed or patted them down.

The auditorium lights were already dimmed to a mild milky blue, hazed further by forbidden smoking in the crowd of almost four hundred men packed into the ranks of seats shoulder to shoulder.

"Right there," Gooch said, and Bauman saw that bikers, apparently early arrived, paved the auditorium's last three rows from side to side. Three long files of dismounted knights—slightly ponderous off their steel stallions—beefy, bearded or mustached, tattooed, grease-fingernailed, and armored in dirt-stiff denims and heavyweight jean jackets or vests studded with metal (copper pennies or brass, so as not to disturb detectors) and painted in the colors of their street clubs—the Gypsy Jokers, Hell's Angels, Ringtails, Bandidos, and Boogaloos. All also wore on their jackets' right sleeves, or vests' right shoulders, obscure under oil-smudge and grime, the small white skull on wheels of the Biker Club at State.

"—Right there," Gooch said again, and gave Bauman a quick jarring shove in the direction indicated, toward the one empty seat in the center of the second row from the back. Bauman (who assumed afterward his two rounds with Muñoz had gone to his head) turned back toward Gooch immediately, intending he knew not what—but found himself facing Bad Bob instead, as if that silent spectacled hoodlum, responding to whatever swift animal instinct, had simply materialized on only this rumor of trouble, where once Gooch stood. Bauman, confronted with that height, that drooping pale mustache and mournful face, sad with violence done, digested Gooch's shove and obediently turned and edged down an aisle of iron knees toward the empty seat.

He saw grizzle-bearded Bump, the bikers' guru and executive officer, seated just behind that place. And beside Bump, sitting to his right—young, clean-shaven, lean and redhaired—Eric Ganz, Bump's master, the master of all these men.

Bauman reached his seat in bluish gloom, and, easing into it, found Perteet sitting bulky to his right, Handles to his left. This arrangement apparently another sample of club theater—those dramatic tableaus of disciplined hierarchy, of presented peril. Here, the ranks of armored brutes in place of the lifers' murderous office staff, or Colonel Perkins' more economical rows of butchers' hooks, the meat locker's arctic cold.

It made Bauman appreciate the Zapatista leader's relative informality, whatever that might conceal. *Knock, knock*. . . .

Sitting as directed, inescapably in contact with Perteet's weighty left arm and shoulder, Bauman was impressed by that sheer mass, the ancient potency of bulk and muscle so recently devalued by firearms' mean advantage. There was a fallen nobility to that heft and power—still celebrated, of course, in watching heavyweight fights, wrestling, professional football, in which size and strength still told.

On Bauman's left, very modern, Handles sat much slighter, his pale right arm's knotty muscle paved with patriotic tattooing, visible but veiled by the auditorium's cigarette smoke and dim blue light.

"First things first." Bump, leaning forward to murmur into Bauman's left ear, breathed a faint odor of peppermint—York Peppermint Pattie, it seemed to Bauman.

"—First things first. We have an information you insulted a made member. What do you have to say about that?"

Bauman, too surprised to be worried, turned his head to the left to look behind him. "Insulted who? I didn't insult anybody!"

Said this apparently too loudly, because Bump tickled the back of his neck with a rough fingernail, and muttered, "Turn around, and keep it down."

As if in response, the auditorium's lights dimmed from milky to near midnight blue—a shade so shadowy, it seemed the administration had some purpose in allowing near privacy for encounters here, or as if the yearnings of generations of inmates for the chance at even such semi-private blowjobs (or less loving attentions with knives or whatever), had slowly, over the decades, by some metaphysical weight, pressed the dimmer down.

"I didn't insult anybody."

Another tickle at the back of Bauman's neck. "Not our information," Bump said softly.

"Well, your information is wrong."

The next tickle had a scratch to it, traced down the back of Bauman's neck. "You insulted brother Perteet at breakfast."

Bauman paused to remember the incident of the grabbed-for bread. "Are you kidding me?"

"Keep it down."

"Are you kidding me? You ask Perteet if he had that coming. Just ask him! The man, who I consider a friend," referring to that massive subject as if he weren't sitting beside him, "—you just ask him if he wasn't out of line, taking bread from my tray without even checking with me. Man was out of line. And no insult involved."

Silence in the back row. Then whispers, perhaps consultation.

"Petey." This out loud. Bauman felt Perteet start beside him, apparently at having his neck tickled.

"What?" Perteet said.

"You hear that?"

"Uh-huh."

"Well, is that right or is that wrong—you reached for the man's bread like that?"

Perteet sat silent, attempting to recall.

"I asked you a question, brother. Is that right or wrong?"

"I guess so."

"You guess which?"

"I guess I did."

Silence behind them, whispers.

The fingernail scratched the back of Bauman's neck.

"Teach, we are goin' to let a possible insult to a brother pass, because the brother could be was out of line. We're goin' to let that pass."

"Great," Bauman said. Below them, in the rows nearer the auditorium's small screen, several inmates began to clap, impatient for the film to begin.

"Now, you two shake hands, an' we can get on to other business."

The clapping was slowly becoming more general.

Bauman turned a little in his seat, against Perteet's obtruding mass, to get his right arm free enough to offer his hand into azure dark. It hurt his sore elbow a little to do it.

The hand was found and seized in a huge hot enveloping grip, that squeezed it very gently.

"Sorry," Perteet said, and squeezed again, gently, to show how much he meant it.

"Petey," Bauman said, "—you can have some bread anytime you want."

"O.K."

"O.K. Now, let's talk some business." Bump's breath, certainly refreshed by another bite of York Peppermint Pattie, drifted over Bauman's left shoulder. "First, we hear you had a problem over at the lifers. An' what we want to know, was it personal or political?"

"Personal."

Some convicts, black men by their voices, were beginning to call out for the movie.

"That's all right, then. That you got kicked in the nuts and so forth. That's not our business."

"Right."

A very large black man in a gray sweatshirt stood up several rows down, visible through hazy blue, and turned to call up to the projection booth. "You goin' start this fuckin' movie or what?!"

At which—as if his seat had been electric, and shocked him—Handles stood suddenly up from Bauman's left. "Hey, you! Jigaboo! You sit your black ass down an' shut the fuck up!"

Bauman imagined at once a desperate battle in near dark, the few hacks swiftly swamped, and he—not so young, not so large or strong after all—quickly trampled down, his bones stomped splintered-white out of his chest into deep blue light. And slight Cousins, of course, who'd wanted to stay with him, destroyed even sooner.

"You ofay cocksucker!" the large black man called back. "—You come down here, I'm goin' bus' your fuckin' back!"

"All right, now. You people cool it. . . ." A hack's rather distant instruction.

Bauman then was jostled left in his seat as Perteet, a hill in motion, surged up and onto his feet, so tall that a sudden preparatory lance of projected light from the booth above nearly touched his shaggy hair, did touch it slightly, lit it to dim silver.

"Bailey, you say one more word down there," Perteet said, voice full of his thick chest's resonance, his pronunciation careful as a child's.

"—Just one more word, an' I'm goin' to come down. I know you, Bailey. You ain't nothin' but a nigger, an' that's that. Don't you make me come down there. . . ."

"Sit down, you black-ass ape!" Handles' lighter voice the rattling traps to Perteet's kettle drum.

It would take, Bauman thought, quite a man of any color to push conclusions with such bookends as his. (He was amused to find himself taking comfort in the ferocity of his companions, as if they challenged for him.) And Bailey, it seemed, was not quite such a man. Bauman, and the auditorium, heard a subdued "*Shit*. . . ." Saw the big man sit down in front in blue silhouette. Heard muttering. Then nothing.

Handles and Perteet, satisfied, sat back down at Bauman's sides, wedging him comfortably, warmly in.

"—Second thing. . . ." Bump's murmur recommenced with a breeze of peppermint just as the movie began—producing, with a blare of lively sound-track music, a bright flashing daylight view of the Los Angeles freeways, buzzing with cars.

"—Second thing. Is Shupe still doin' what Nash says from over in Seg? Or is he doin' what Wiltz tells him, right there?"

Bauman thought of protesting his election as war correspondent, purveying club gossip that had nothing at all to do with the killings. He thought of protesting that to Bump, then decided not.

"Shupe is doing what Nash said to do."

"An' Wiltz goes along . . . ?"

"Wiltz thinks it's funny."

Silence behind him. Perhaps whispers. The movie's title was taking a long time to appear, finally did appear as painting—in bright reds and yellows—across a huge billboard high on a tall building's side.

Medium shot of a sign painter on that dizzy scaffold, just finishing the last giant letter of the last immense word. Then, a close-up of the painter—revealed to be the film's star, a young television performer famous for portraying a wealthy weakling, a lightweight, self-reflective WASP (to the amusement and comfort of those whose class, culture, or color set them under WASP heels much more weighty, much less amusing).

Bump's breath again at Bauman's left shoulder. "Who'd they say to talk to? Who'd Shupe say to report to over in B-block?"

A delicate question. Bauman, captive as he was among four dangerous running packs—five if he included the attorney general's people—thought it improbable that direct lies would last for long. Would more likely get him killed. Let other agents sweat their own safety out. . . . "Pokey," Bauman said over the movie's noise. "—Pokey Duerstadt."

"That so, Poke?" Bump out loud to Duerstadt, who apparently was sitting farther down that row.

"What?"

"—That so, that you're barfin' to the lifers?"

"Bet your ass. An' gettin' scrip for it, too. You ain't tellin' me old Teach has stooled me over?"

Some laughter down the row. Bauman thought Nash had been too long in Segregation, had left delicate matters in incompetent hands—unless the lifers had known that the bikers knew, and held someone besides too-public Pokey as their real informant. An accurately tedious miniature of the intelligence work of nations.

There was a whispered conference behind Bauman that came to silence—and a moment later, over his right shoulder, he heard a different voice altogether, young Eric Ganz's uninflected light baritone speaking to him softly, confidentially.

"Gettin' back to Shupe, an' Wiltz. So Wiltz thinks it's funny. What do you think?" There was no peppermint with that question. Ganz's breath had the faint sharp slightly spoiled smell of a cat's.

"I think some people got killed—Metzler and Spencer, by the way, were both killed by the same people, or person—and I suppose a hack may have had a hand in Spencer's murder, anyway. Besides that, what I think is, Nash's whole investigation is a foolish waste of time."

" 'Nash's investigation,' you moron," Ganz said in the same even baritone, not raising his voice, "—is basically a try at some cooperative effort by the clubs in dealin' with pig administration. It is also a try at tryin' to locate any corrections person dealin' into inmate affairs. It is also a try at treaty-makin' between the white clubs for the day when they're goin' to have to stand up against a swarm of niggers. —You hear what that black dude said down there? You think even ten years ago he would have stood up like that in here?"

Bauman had listened to little of this, had been chewing over being called a moron. He certainly acted stupidly from time to time, but just as certainly was not a moron. It was particularly galling to be called that by this young psychopath, a thug who probably couldn't complete the crossword puzzle in *TV Guide*.

"—Get the picture?"

Bauman said nothing. Then heard, over the movie's dialogue—shouted dialogue, the star (as billboard painter) calling to a friend on a neighboring scaffold—heard Ganz, behind him and to the right, lean back into his seat and say to Bump, quite clearly, "Teach is poutin'. I hurt his feelin's."

"Is that right?" Bump leaned forward to Bauman's left shoulder to query, his breath now hardly smelling of peppermint at all. "—Is that right? The president hurt your feelin's?"

Bauman, hearing that malicious echo, was reminded how adept at bullying most of these convicts were. And why not?—they likely having been the terror of their schoolyards for many years.

As a boy, Bauman had been bullied seriously only one term in junior high, bullied so that his bike ride to and from school became for those months a sort of darkness in daylight, though his enemy was only a grinning boy, slightly taller, a few pounds heavier, but possessing the weapon of unreasoning aggression, and the pleasure of it.

Ralph Bauman had sniffed that flinching out in his son, perhaps smelled the odor of cowardice, familiar to one who was a prime bully himself, fearless in insult and fistfights since his own schooldays. One Tuesday morning he'd asked his son why he wasn't going out to the lake in the afternoons, to swim. Had asked, received evasive answers, and tracked Charlie down to his avoidance while spreading marmalade on a piece of toast.

"Charlie, you're having 'some trouble' with Murray Saenz? Having trouble with Murray *Saenz?*" He'd seemed to find it hard to believe. "Scared you'll get beat up? Why, son, what's that? Just a busted nose." He'd paused to eat his toast. Finished the whole slice while Charlie and his mother sat silent at the sunny kitchen table. "A man," Ralph Bauman had said, after swallowing, "—a man who lets his nose make a coward of him, well, he just isn't a man at all. And never will be."

Charlie—too nervous after that to await an occasion—had ridden out to the lake after school the next two days, to meet Murray Saenz. Had finally seen him Thursday afternoon, had hung around near him until Murray said something casually insulting. Then Charlie, with the greatest relief, had attacked him—and been beaten very easily, as if all his forethought had turned his arms to water.

"More like it," his father had said that day at dinner, satisfied with Charlie's face. "That wasn't a big deal. —Was that a big deal? Getting punched in the face?"

Charlie Bauman had said no.

"Otherwise," his father said, "—who knows? I guess I could have taken you out in the back yard and showed you what a real punch feels like." Then he'd smiled to show he was joking. "I guess you wouldn't have been so worried about that Saenz trash after that. Whole family's garbage, anyway. I'd love to see them try and skip out on payments to the agency the way they do with Carl at the market. Not that that bunch could afford a new car. . . ."

Bauman heard Bump talking behind him, not bothering to keep his voice down, raising it over the movie's dialogue. "Guess you did," he said, apparently to Ganz. "—Guess you hurt his feelin's. Teach don't have nothin' to say at all."

"Sure I do," Bauman said, just as loud, and turned half around to his left to see Bump sitting behind him, smiling at him through the speckled colors of the movie's reflected light. "First thing is, you're just an old asshole with a big mouth, who barely finished grade school. Second, I know—and everyone knows—you always hide behind tougher people when you have something to say. And those are the facts about you." Bauman's heart was cantering in his chest so it seemed to strike his ribs. "As for your boss, the 'President' there," Bauman saw young Ganz (draped in moving mottled light) watching him with only slight curiosity, "—who at least is genuinely dangerous, if he's so fucking intelligent, what's he doing stuck in this toilet with the rest of us?"

Silence, as Bauman turned back around in his seat—to see Perteet's great bull's eyes roll to goggle at him.

"Got some points, Bumpo," Ganz said from behind, and all the bikers near them laughed.

Ganz leaned forward to Bauman's right shoulder. "One for you," he said. "—Don't ever try for two."

Bauman, in Fruit-of-the-Loom underpants and T-shirt, stood at the sink brushing his teeth to the tumult of a night moto-cross race from Scooter's TV. Scooter, lying still on the upper bunk, silent, concentrating, was drinking in those dusty revolutions as if their snarling noise, their leaping energy under egg-yolk night-lights soothed and relaxed him by contrast, so he lay boneless, staring, drowsy, as the riders raced, skidded, and raced again.

"No ordinary day," Bauman (aural privacy assured by that noise) said to his reflection. "—No ordinary day," his enunciation interfered with as he finished brushing, then rinsed. He stood his toothbrush up in his mug—heavy white ironware decorated with Midwest's crest, a unicorn and bison rampant on a field corn-gold, and mottoed below, For Love of Learning. He set the mug carefully on his shelf above the sink, then stepped behind the curtain, and sat down on the toilet's cold porcelain, though only to pee.

His elbow was feeling better, recovering from that frantic punching at Muñoz' armored ribs. But his left ankle still ached a little—the spite in Shupe's kick producing an effect greater than all Muñoz' skill, strength, and speed.

Bauman wiped himself from habit—State's toilet paper gray as its walls, almost as adamant—stood, flushed, and came out through the curtain to wash his hands at the sink, and dry them on his T-shirt. He hung the damp T-shirt up on his hook, then went to his bunk to turn down his blanket and sheet, and climb into bed, the bunk's primitive springs protesting softly as he settled.

He checked his Timex. It was less than two minutes to Lights. Less than one and a half minutes, actually. And, except for his sore ankle, he felt quite content, felt he was handling a bizarre situation fairly sensibly (the unpleasant scene with Carlyle excepted). Wasn't concerned about the bikers, the meeting at the movie. The antics of these prison baronies as tediously provincial (however dangerous) as the power-grubbing of petty medieval landlords must have been.

As for the film, it had proved comic only when someone was falling down, and then only if the fall were serious enough (if real) to have crippled or killed. The movie's only point of interest had been the blonde (her name escaped him)—small, small-breasted, snowy-skinned, with bright blue eyes and a triangular face drawn to a pointed chin—and that interest had diminished through the evening. This girl's appearance, greeted at first by State's audience with satisfied grunts and sighs, met with no increasing applause at each reappearance. There'd been no loud, smacking kisses, and only a few obscene remarks which, at other films, had provoked threats from the auditorium hacks to shut the movie down.

Proved so disappointing, this evening's pretty blonde was one of those girls whose careers had been made in television—which, as if by black magic, had sucked the sex from between her legs and replaced it with a sort of ectoplasmic panty-hose, impermeable. Perhaps she'd been the subject of too many eyes—each viewer stealing, through her image, an infinitesimal sip of her essence. Tonight's reaction quite contrary to that only a month or so before, to Priscilla Lane (starring in *Four Daughters*), whose bright two-dimensional ghost of half a century past—so perfectly the good girl, and only moderately beautiful—had called forth from this convict audience a strained silent attention, broken only by the soft sounds of a few inmates publicly masturbating to her, lost in love.

This evening's film, like its heroine, had been unimpressive. Its 'meet-cute,' the hero's plunge from his collapsing scaffold, forty stories down onto the closed canvas top of the blonde's new convertible—wrecking the car while sustaining, himself, not a scratch—had proved a sadly accurate prophecy of the rest of the thing.

And considering the improbable, what of Jomo Burdon's directing ghost or ghosts, with their orders to him to flee to the infirmary? It seemed possible that Perkins (or Vargas) might have found superstition useful—*Vodoun, Santeria*—to keep their followers in line. To curse the opposition as well, *a la* Papa Doc Duvalier. State certainly a grim and shadowy-enough castle for those or any other horrors, a zombie walking through D-block, the black men sitting along the walls casually moving their feet out of the way of the thing, as it stalked by. . . .

The Lights bell rang shrill as a fire alarm. "Shit," said Scooter, and his mattress bulged down above Bauman's head as he knelt to turn his TV off, interrupting the fury of the race.

That noise, and the output of all the block's electronics—TV's, radios, tape decks and ghetto blasters—ended abruptly, leaving only human sounds, called-out comments, a low, steady murmur of conversation . . . one man laughing far down the tier as the day-lights went out, the red night-lights flickered softly on.

Lying at ease in dim maroon, Bauman was almost able to recall the scene with Carlyle at the gatehouse, his own confirmed snitchhood, only as an incident in a busy day, part of a structure more and more complex and interesting. As if his introduction to the prison more than a year ago, and even the accident (or tragedy or whatever) occasioning that, had proven worthwhile, introducing him to a wilderness of possibilities—perilous, various, and interesting.

The history he'd read for its rich recollections of human monstrosity, courage, comedy, and determination—this as a possible key to further understanding of all humans, and necessarily himself—appeared to him wonderfully present at State, but a history here distilled, compressed, concentrated, accelerated, molded by the penitentiary's pressures into an intricate jewelry of human endeavor, its stones beautiful, hard enough to cut glass, and in refraction wonderfully revealing.

Bauman imagined he stood exposed by this magnifying mechanism as no one (so far) very unusual, and supposed the more he was involved in it, the more he would learn about himself, and more swiftly, if only how little of importance there was to learn.

State's was a history in which—defined, like time, by action—an individual's contribution, however evanescent, might be seen to operate.

His boyhood, his college years, his work at Midwest, most of his life, except for the turbulence of his parents, and women, seemed simple, plain, uninteresting as a mown meadow compared to State's dark forest—so dense, strange, deep and dangerous, inhabited by creatures each a minor jungle in itself.

Bauman raised his right arm from his covers, and exercised his elbow in the dark, bending the arm, straightening it. It was much better, and his left arm's bandaged forearm, burns healing, didn't trouble him at all. There'd be a scarred pattern to show Phil's children in fifteen or twenty years, if they asked.

"You know, Scoot," he said, into almost dark, "—this place may turn out to be good for me."

"Jesus Christ," Scooter said, almost whispering, above him. "I'm gettin' concerned about you, Charles. . . ."

Bauman, almost happy at what must be considered an adventure, at least the chance for adventure through a realm secret, dark, more sinister than any fairy tale's, fell into sleep as if his bunk had rocked very slowly up and over to the right, rolling him over into a pool of sleep, warmed to receive him.

Later, he dreamed one of the balloons had returned. Returned for him. But not the blue and crimson. This balloon, the color of earth, was hung about with fine silver chains of small silver harness bells that shook and chimed in soft crashing chords as the balloon turned, turning slowly down the morning wind across a yard greener, wider than even State's yards in spring. His father had come to take him fishing. . . .

Bauman woke to the sound of someone shouting, and sat straight up, afraid Scooter was getting his throat cut at the bars. Then heard the shouting farther away.

"*Get in . . . fuckin' toilet!*" was what it sounded like.

Scooter turned over in a squeak of springs above him. "You hear that?"

"What is it?"

More shouting from down on Ground-tier, indecipherable, then clearer. "*In toilet. Get in, you* something . . . something *fucker.*"

"You know who that is?" Scooter, gleeful. "It's fuckin' Peary Robbins, man! That fish Thayer must be shittin' banana puddin' all over their fuckin' house!"

It seemed to Bauman too good to be true, but listening to the bellows of rage—furious injunctions to stay in the toilet—he grew certain it was Robbins shouting.

"That fuckin' banana puddin'!" Scooter, ecstatic.

Bauman found himself laughing as he couldn't recall doing since he was a boy, laughing without complication, he and Scooter laughing in the rosy dark, together as a team of horses at the trot. And laughing harder—along with many ignorant laughers and whistlers along the tiers, hungry for amusement by any cause or none—at the shouted conference between silencing hacks and Robbins and his finicky housemate, their neat lodging apparently spattered with banana pudding.

"Are we enjoying ourselves, or not?" Bauman to Scooter, after the block had quieted to near silence.

"Hey, Charles," Scooter, settling above on twanging springs. "—a joke's a joke. Don't mean we're fuckin' *happy*."

Bauman woke to the morning bell, its sound so harsh, shrill, and continuous it seemed to set the days on edge at their beginnings.

The double bunk heaved as Scooter performed his usual convulsive sit-up on arousal—stuck long bare bony legs straight out over the upper's side, then launched himself in grimy jockey shorts, flailing, to land hard on the concrete floor.

Up and down the tiers, through the whole of B-block, an enormous slow swell of sound began, rose, then broke in a surf of racket as TV's, radios and tape decks welcomed the morning, their owners beginning the day's tide of talk, catcalls and shouting.

Bauman shoved his covers down, then, as he started to sit up, was shocked by a sudden severe pain across the small of his back. He could barely move, seemed bound, buried in sand.

He thought for an instant he'd had his stroke at last, his lower parts paralyzed, hanging on him like dead meat. Then, even lying still, he felt a charley-horse ache deep in the small of his back, dull at first, then sharper, then so sharp he had trouble catching his breath.

Bauman tried again to sit up—and wheezed out a grunt as the pain caught him in mid-movement and held him still. All of Muñoz' punches, all Bauman's desperate efforts in the fight seemed to have been deposited yesterday and held overnight to gather this morning's dividend.

He managed to push his covers down, then sat up very slowly, grunting his way up the degrees of inclination, until he could swing his legs out, get his feet down on the floor's cold concrete.

Scooter flushed the toilet, came out from behind the blanket curtain, and caught Bauman—just out of bed, still in his boxer shorts—standing bent at the waist, trying to straighten up.

"What's the matter?"

"Nothing. . . ." Trying to demonstrate that, Bauman caught himself in mid-straighten with an exclamation he transformed into throat clearing.

"You got a chest pain? Feelin' of tightness?"

Bauman, rather than answering, bent forward a little to catch a deeper breath.

"—Like a clampin' feelin', pain goin' down your arm . . . ?" Scooter's china-blue eyes were slightly popped in apprehension, his meager, rusty goatee quivering.

"Will you please shut up. . . ."

"Man, man, we got to move fast! Every minute—"

"Will you shut up? I'm not having a damn heart attack!" On his second try, straightening more cautiously, more slowly, Bauman managed to stand almost erect. "—Just a little stiff," he said, and walked carefully past Scooter and behind the curtain to the toilet.

"I'm tellin' you, man, I'm jus' tellin' you." Scooter's voice lower pitched in relief, as he called through the curtain while he dressed. "That fuckin' fight. You ain't no kid now, Charles. I mean it. You should'a known better."

"Scoot, why don't you go on down to breakfast, O.K.?"

"All I'm sayin' is there's an element in there about showin' off. That's all I got to say."

"Good."

"Sure you don't need no help in there?"

"I don't need any help in here." A lie. Bauman would have loved to have some help—a masseur with heated gloves, who might have laid him down on the cold concrete floor, then bent over him to dig and turn up and smooth again all his back's aching muscles, as if preparing a garden for spring planting.

"You sure . . . ?"

"God damn it!"

"O.K. All right. If you don't need no help, you don't need no help. Excuse me for askin'."

Bauman, leaning against the cell's back wall beside the toilet, raised his arms above his head to slowly stretch.

He rested a moment, arms still in the air, and stood listening to Scooter roam their house, getting ready for breakfast.

"You want any breakfast, Charles? You want some, you better get movin'."

"I don't want any breakfast, Scooter."

"Nothin' feels tight in your chest?"

"No."

"O.K. . . ."

"My muscles are just a little sore."

"O.K. Look like more'n a little sore to me."

Arms still raised, Bauman stretched, reaching higher. That worked pretty well; he was able to get a good stretch, up onto his toes. It felt as though something caught in the small of his back, then slowly released so he could stand straight, bend slightly to the left, then the right. . . .

He dropped his arms to his sides and relaxed, took a few breaths deep enough to make his lungs ache. Each time he breathed, he was able to breathe a little deeper, felt less discomfort in the small of his back. —He couldn't recall such severe soreness after boxing at McElvey's. Not quite this bad. . . .

"That do you any good?" Scooter's head in through the curtain, observing.

"Nothing's falling off," Bauman said. "That's about all I'll say."

Their house door clacked and clacked again, as all the cell doors were doing along the tier and through the tiers above and below. Then, their door and all the others—sounding like the running-gear of trains—rumbled slowly wide and crashed open to their stops. The barred doors made essentially the same clangorous sounds opening as closing, but Bauman, leaning against the wall resting, recalled no inmate complaining about the noise that opening made.

"You don't want to go to breakfast?" Scooter still peering in through the blanket curtain.

"This morning, I'll skip it."

"Want me to bring you somethin' up?"

"No, thanks. You go on."

"O.K." Scooter pulled his head back out through the curtain. "You know," he said from the other side, "—you know, you could've got hurt bad foolin' around with that spic. Just somethin' keep in mind. . . ."

"Thank you." Bauman stood up straight, then attempted a very slow bend forward from the waist, back rounded, arms dangling loose, his upper body relaxed as he could make it. He felt a series of small tugs and loosenings in the lumbar area, some aching pain, but was able to do it, able to get down far enough to almost touch his toes, then touch them, then touch his fingers to the floor.

Once there, he decided to stay down, let his back stretch out slowly.

That seemed to work; he was fairly comfortable. But when, after a while, he did try to straighten up, he met with such sudden sharp agony across the small of his back it took his breath away, and he stayed half bent over, afraid to straighten further and afraid to bend all the way down again. He thought he might have a ruptured disk, something wrong there he'd made a lot worse trying to exercise, work it out. Bauman saw himself walking in constant discomfort through State's corridors, up and down her crowded stairways, frightened that some young jocker would carelessly, or deliberately, shoulder him so that his back, so precariously balanced, would be twisted into spasm, and he collapse to call for help from a prison of pain smaller, lonelier, more confining than any cell at State.

Allowing himself to bend slowly down, he went cautiously to all fours, turned carefully onto his back on the floor's rough chill. He drew his knees up high to hug, and lay there taking deep breaths, trying to allow the muscles of his lower spine—so apprehensive—to relax at rest along the floor. Bauman felt very sorry for himself for missing breakfast, probably on that once-a-month morning when Rudy Gottschalk extended himself to fried eggs, frozen dinner rolls heated so only the small knots of their doughy insides were still icy, and small Valencia oranges, sweet and packed with seeds.

After a long while it seemed his back felt better, and he tested that by letting go of his knees, allowing his legs to straighten out, to lie along the floor. That didn't hurt. He rolled slowly over onto his belly—the floor's concrete colder to his belly than it had been to his back—and felt no objection. He lay there imagining the layers of hot blood-soaked muscle resting in darkness side by side along his spine (shot through here and there with fat, slightly tendonous with age) gradually uncoiling, unknotting their striated regiments, un-kinking, easing, easing to sleepy relaxation so the blood dammed in these muscles leaked, spurted, then ran free, waltzing through them to the rhythm of his heart.

"Charles?"

Bauman lay silent behind the blanket curtain.

"Charles . . . ?"

It was Betty Nellis. Bauman imagined the idiot Scooter busy confiding over that rich breakfast to Betty and whoever else, "Poor old dude, I thought he was havin' a heart attack," and so on and so forth. Bauman wished he had a tougher housemate, some old convict who took pride in keeping his mouth shut.

"Charles, I'm comin' in there."

"Just a minute," Bauman said. "—Just a minute," and got up onto all fours. "Can't a man take a goddamn crap in peace?" He tried to stand up from that position, but his back didn't like the attempt at all, and made him grunt under punishment. Instead, he went on all fours the three feet to the toilet, and using that as an aid, pushed himself up onto his feet.

Once he was up, his back felt better. He flushed the toilet as if he'd used it, then stepped out from behind the blanket curtain to find Betty Nellis and Lee Cousins standing waiting for him—Bauman regretting in the instant appearing in his foolish undershorts, revealing his bare chest and belly, slightly tallowy with age.

Cousins wore the accustomed plain pressed blue denims. Dark brown hair fresh-combed for breakfast, worn a little too long, Bauman thought, seeing it now the third day in a row.

Betty Nellis sported her pink-laced tennis shoes, tight-tailored black denim pants, and a man's oversized white dress shirt, its sleeves folded up, revealing round brown arms, its collar raised a little at the back the better to frame her face. She stood beside Cousins, darker, stockier, her black hair denser, gleaming—as if between them, and better than either might alone, they represented what creation's winds might blow from North and South, what forces coincide to approximate a woman.

Betty carried a big brown paper bag at her left side. "Are you O.K.? I see you still got that bandage where them fuckers burn you." She peered at him, slightly nearsighted, as Bauman took a folded pair of denims from his second shelf, shook them out, and put them on, balancing carefully on each leg in turn, favoring his back, then zipped the pants fly up, sucking in his belly slightly as he did.

"I'm fine. Just a little stiff from boxing, yesterday." He took his last clean blue-denim shirt from the shelf, put it on—then realized he usually put his shirt on first, before his pants. He had to unbutton the trousers and pull the zipper down a little to tuck his shirttails in. Supposed they were watching him, amused.

"You shouldn' *be* fightin'." Betty, looking angry about it. And to Cousins, "You shouldn' be lettin' him do shit—stuff like that."

Cousins didn't answer, stepped over to the house's wall to look at Scooter's collection of photographs, and seemed to examine the motorcycles and the naked women impartially, one by one, not lingering.

"An'," Betty said, "an' what's this other shit—this other stuff you goin' lookin' for somebody?"

"Don't worry about that." Bauman saw his blue running shoes under the edge of his bunk. He didn't look forward to sitting there and bending over for them, staying bent over to put them on and tie the laces. He delayed by getting a clean pair of socks, State's thick dull-gray cotton, from a shoebox on his shelf. His second-to-last clean pair.

" 'Don' worry about it?' —'Don' worry about it?' What you think, Charles? You think you goin' show up some snitch? You think they ain' more'n one snitch in this place?"

"I'm sure you're right." Bauman sat down on the edge of his bunk. The sitting didn't hurt him, though his lower back felt tender, like a sprained ankle just healed, but prepared (if stepped on wrong) to double over in reinjury more severe.

"I jus' thought about somethin' I bet you didn' think about," Betty said. "You didn' think maybe ever' one of them people snitchin' is goin' believe you after his ass, personally? Find him so the clubs can kill him? Man thinks like that, what you think he's goin' do?"

Bauman raised his right leg, casually as he could, to set his heel on the bunk's side rail and get his sock on. "Honey, you're not the first to make that observation. Unfortunately, it's a point that's beside the point." He lowered his right foot to the floor. Putting the sock on hadn't been all that bad; he supposed he was loosening up a little, back becoming less stiff.

"You gotta do it, man, is what you sayin'."

"That's right. And it's not that big a deal, so let's not make a big deal out of it." Bauman raised his left foot, and got that sock on quite easily.

Betty looked at Cousins. "You in it with him, isn' that right?"

"That's right," Cousins said, still looking at the rows of photographs.

"I'm talkin' to you," Betty said, but Cousins didn't turn around to look at her. "You get him into this shit he suppose' to do?"

"No," Bauman said, and bent carefully down to reach just under the bunk to pick up his left shoe.

"I had somethin' to do with it," Cousins, apparently finished looking at Scooter's collection, turned to Betty as if interested in any further comment she might make.

" 'Somethin' to do with it,' " Betty said. "An' you let him fight like that, too."

"Betty," Bauman said, "—forget it, O.K.?" He raised his left leg and managed to get the running shoe on that foot.

"Forget it, my ass."

Cousins said nothing.

"I mean it," Bauman said. "It's more complicated than you think. So just drop it, O.K.?" He started to lace the left shoe, but his back began to ache, and the ache got so rapidly worse he sat up straight and put his foot down on the floor. Could always tie the shoe later.

Cousins stood watching Betty a moment longer, apparently ready to listen to anything more she might have to say, then looked at Bauman. "You all right?"

"Fine," Bauman said. "Just a little stiff." He bent carefully down again and picked up his right shoe.

"Give it to me," Cousins said, came over and held out a hand—then, when Bauman hesitated, took the shoe and knelt before the bunk.

"Not necessary," Bauman said, drawing his foot a little under the bunk. "Thanks anyway."

But Cousins reached for his foot, lifted it rather roughly, and worked the running shoe on. Laced up that shoe, then laced up the left.

"Thanks."

Cousins didn't acknowledge that, stood briskly up. "Betty's got somethin' to show you."

"No, I don'."

"Yes, you do," Cousins said. "Go on, go on behind the curtain and put it on."

"What is it?" Bauman wiggled his toes in the running shoes. Cousins had laced them both a little tight.

"I don' wan' to put it on."

"Bullshit, Betty," Cousins said. "—Go put it on."

Betty sighed, and went in behind the toilet curtain carrying the big brown paper bag.

"What is it?"

"You wait an' see," Cousins said.

"I don' wan'—" Betty, from behind the curtain.

"Will you put that *on?*" Cousins said, and after a short pause, Bauman heard the faint pop of a snap unfastening, then rustling and soft footfalls as Betty stepped out of her trousers. More sounds of cloth. Additional rustling, sharper-sounding steps. Then, quiet.

"Betty?" Cousins glanced toward the house's bars as three men passed by, come up from breakfast. "—You ready?"

Silence behind the toilet curtain.

"Betty, I got to get out of here, go over to A for lock-'n'-count!"

"O.K. . . . I'm ready."

Cousins impatiently gestured Bauman up, watched him stand without much difficulty, then held the toilet curtain aside for him. —Stepping into those cramped quarters, Cousins close behind, Bauman was confronted by a plump brown flustered lady, her round throat oiled with nervous sweat above the neckline of a tight, blazing-red ruffle-skirted dress. It was the sort of dress—resembling a great hibiscus blossom—Bauman had read of or seen on television being worn by Latino women on celebratory occasions, weddings, christenings. There was also a pair of bright red high-heeled shoes, in a fairly generous size.

"It's red," Betty said, apparently to encourage and warm a chilly perception, Anglo and educated.

"My favorite color," Bauman said, though his favorite color was blue.

"You don' like it. . . ." Soft brown eyes uneasy.

"I *do* like it," Bauman said. "It's lovely, Betty. It's like a fire, a fire burning on a dark cold night. And you're perfect in it. *Perfect.*"

"Isn't she beautiful?" Cousins said behind him, and stepping close to see past, to admire Betty's dress, put a hand on Bauman's shoulder. "Sue an' Jolene made it in Sweet Stitches. An' that hack, Edwards—you know, Peaches, the faggot? He brought in the shoes."

"Cos' me more'n a hundred fifty," Betty said, "—the shoes an' the material an' for the girls makin' it. It's for the adoption. We're goin' have it in the chapel in two weeks."

"Beautiful," Bauman said. And so Betty almost was, but for arms, though round, too roundly muscled, but for shoulders, though smooth, too wide. She'd stuffed cloth or Kleenex into the dress's bosom. "—You're the most beautiful girl in State."

"Marky's goin' to fall in love all over again," Cousins said, "but Jesus, it's a double ticket, you get caught."

"Listen," Betty said, "I don' give a rat's ass. Goin' be a private occasion; ain' no hack goin' see it. An' what right they got, anyway, tellin' me what I can wear please my husban'?" She suddenly raised her arms and spun, so the dress's full skirt fanned out in a bright circle, filled the narrow, curtained space around her. She spun and stamped as if to a guitar's most plangent chords.

The phone line was fairly short so soon after lock-'n'-count. Bauman nodded to Cernan, received the phone con's genial nod in return, and after a ten-minute wait stepped into the second booth. The booths had no doors—corrections feeling even so cramped a private space might be abused.

Susanne still held sleep's hoarseness in her throat as she said hello, questioned who her caller might be. Bauman was struck by a shocking sense of loss—that he hadn't shared, hadn't been permitted to share her sleep, to rest in their bed beside her. The pain as acute as if the night just past had been their only possible night, and he'd lost it.

"Sweetheart. . . ."

"Charlie, is anything wrong? Can't I come up?"

"You can come up, and I'll be grateful to see you."

"All right. Is anything wrong?"

"Nothing. Nothing's wrong. I just think I ought to tell you that I'm not such a fool I don't realize what a gift you are."

"That's very nice."

"And let me follow that tender—and true—submission, by asking you to bring me up a hundred bucks, concealed in the most humiliating way."

". . . All right, Charlie; I know you must need it. Why in the world don't they let you have money up there? Of course I'll do it. And there won't be another scene, Charlie, with me acting like an offended nun, adding to your problems."

"Listen, you make all the scenes you like. It is humiliating for you, and it damn near kills me to ask you to do it."

"I know. . . ."

"But, I need the money up here. It's important."

"You aren't in trouble?"

"I'm not in trouble. But I need that money."

"You don't have to tell me anything else, Charlie. I love you, and I'll see you this afternoon—with a pussy full of twenties."

"You're a wonderful creature, aren't you? But listen, roll the bills tight, and use a rubber or a little balloon. You don't want to get an infection."

"Charlie, I won't get an infection."

"Well, be careful."

"I stopped being careful almost three years ago, Charlie. And I don't regret it."

"See you this afternoon."

"Bye-bye. . . ."

There was a black inmate in line for the second booth, a young man, looking sleepy.

"Excuse me," Bauman said, "—I need to make one more quick call."

"I don' give a shit, man; jus' hurry the hell up."

"Men, let's keep it movin' down there." Cernan, from his lectern, holding open his fat notebook of scheduled calls.

"O.K.?" Bauman said to the young black man.

"Jus' make the fuckin' call, man!"

Bauman stepped back into the booth and dialed Norman Silber's office.

"Locations. . . ."

"Is Mr. Silber in?"

"May I ask who's calling?" A secretary or receptionist. Bauman recognized her voice.

"Charles Bauman."

". . . Mr. Bauman, Mr. Silber is not in. Mr. Silber will not speak to you again, ever."

"I understand. But I do have a message for him. I'd like you to give him a message for me. O.K.?"

"I don't think so."

"You tell Norman that I admit I haven't been completely candid with him. I wasn't completely honest. Tell him I had three martinis that evening. But they weren't doubles, and I was not incapacitated. Will you just give him that message, please?"

"No, I certainly will not."

"Yes, you will—because he's going to ask you what I said. And please tell him something else for me. Tell him, tell him I understand that even if it was only a little bit my fault, that little bit is unforgivable. Will you tell him that?"

"I'll tell *you* something. You stop calling here. You leave Mr. Silber alone! He's a wonderful man—and you're just an animal."

"No, I'm not," Bauman said, but she'd hung up.

The air out on the walkways was colder than yesterday's had been. Morning's light lay bright as polished metal over West field's grass, bitten brown, laced with the last of last night's frost.

The wall presented its high horizon—gray as a sea gull's back—across the field as Bauman walked, his denim jacket buttoned to the collar. At his right side—much taller, constantly having to shorten longer dancing strides—Hull, the madman, kept him company. He'd attached himself as Bauman left B-block's side gate.

Cadaverous and grimy, stilting alongside, Hull was engaged in a three-way conversation with Bauman, himself, and his invisible companion—always located slightly above his head and to the right.

Bauman's suggestion—that Hull's companion, who apparently could read and write, might help him do so—had borne its first fruit. Hull, demonstrating how his doppelganger had taught him to write his name, was inscribing as he walked, with a darkly dirty right hand, a huge slow unmistakable H in the air. This was followed by a giant U and two immense L's.

"How about that?" Hull said, lalloping along beside Bauman like a wolfhound pup in need of a bath. He had a strong sour smoky odor, not really unpleasant in the open air.

"That's good. Damn good, Mr. Hull." Faint puffs of breath visible at that, less definite than they'd been in the meat locker with Colonel Perkins. Despite the morning's chill, Bauman was finding his lower back less and less tender as he strolled along, the pain slowly easing away, the muscles warmed with walking. His ankle felt fine.

"I write my name!" Hull said. "And I'm thankin' my friend, and you too. *I write my name . . . !*" He skipped ahead of Bauman, then turned to face him, dancing backward, and drew his name again, very large, letter by letter in the air.

"That's it," Bauman said. "—You've got it," noticing the pupils of the madman's eyes were dissimilar, one enlarged, the other nearly pinpoint as he stared up, watching his sooty hand pace through H-U-L-L. The man might have been beaten once too often, too severely, and received some damage to his brain.

"Mr. Hull, that's wonderful. You getting ready to write something else?"

"My buddy didn't show me how to write nothin' else." Hull, calming, turned again and fell into step beside Bauman.

"I bet he will, though," Bauman said. "He seems like a good friend."

"Are you bullshittin' me, or what?" Hull said. "I just make that shit up."

"Then who's teaching you to write, Mr. Hull?"

Hull softly hummed a minor descending scale. "Good question," he said, once the last note had died away.

The morning was cold enough for Bauman to notice the slight breeze stirred by his forward motion. He'd planned to continue wearing only issue blue denims at State—the notion being to blend into background—but now, back still stiff, sore-muscled, saw the uses of a padded street windbreaker. Perhaps one of the leather jackets, their linings softly quilted, that a few rich convicts wore—at least those too tough to be casually robbed of them.

As far as blending in was concerned, that likely ended with the burning of Bobby Basket. Had certainly ended in whining and bluster in Seg's showers. . . .

"I really don't know who's teachin' me, man," Hull said. "Damn if I know the motherfucker's real name."

"Ask him," Bauman said. "And ask him how to spell it."

"Oh, what's your name, what's your name? What's your name, what's your name, what's your name?" Hull sang, to a melody Bauman didn't know. The tall man then turned aside and trotted suddenly off to the right across the grass, his large, clumsy feet—in torn high-top black basketball shoes—crunching faintly in the frost as he went, leaving dark damp footprints behind him.

When he was some distance away, he began to sing again, "My name is Richard, my name is Richard, my name is Richard," to the same melody as before. He faced Bauman, transcribed in the air a probable large R, then turned and jogged away.

The electrician's office was a separate and much smaller bay behind the truck shop, the building lying hard against the West wall's base. The truck shop—long, wide, tumultuous with radios and tool racket—functioned as job assignment for many younger mechanically minded inmates, especially the bikers. There the club members kept and continually worked on the three battered motorcycles corrections allowed them—and allowed them, on Sundays, to ride roaring back and forth under the shadow of the wall.

The electrician's office was a very different space, one Bauman had visited only twice, both times on errands for Housekeeping when he'd first come up. In that narrow bay, peaceful as a library, several old cons held quiet court. These men, in their fifties and older, remnants, Bauman understood, of the ruined empire of Maintenance—which little Cooper had over decades gradually undermined, broken, and absorbed into Housekeeping—still held the electrician's office as their own. There, they relived ancient bureaucratic battles (occasionally violent) and held, with Lesnovitch their chieftain, the electrician's office as last redoubt.

Bauman, in from chill and bright morning, his entrance announced by a buzzer connected to the door, was cozied in warmth, momentarily half blind in dim light. His eyes adjusting, he saw an old hack named Wrightman sitting drinking coffee and reading the Garlin paper at one of the bay's two long counters, which ran down the sides of the narrow room to the back, where a shorter counter was set across to connect them. Wrightman turned on his stool to look at Bauman, then turned back to his reading—the local town's paper the only daily newspaper at State. The penitentiary's own had been discontinued some years before, following an exposé—not submitted to Admin for prior review—of the sexual habits of the then warden's sister, a lesbian lady.

Cousins, standing at the back counter talking with an elderly con named Waggoner, waved him in, and Bauman walked down the bay's narrow length, its long walls to left and right decorated only by a complex dado of spotless pegboard, on which all electricians' tools and items—cutters, cappers, fuses, pincers, testers, pliers, plugs and junction boxes, coils of electrical wire in several colors and rolls of tape, all black—were fastened precisely over a red-painted outline of itself.

"Charles," Cousins said, "—Mr. Waggoner."

Waggoner, a fragile, crumbling seventy-something, had lost almost all his white hair. His glasses' frame had bitten deep into the bridge of his nose, the thin metal strip almost buried in irritated skin, puffed, red, and flaking.

"Mr. Waggoner. . . ." Bauman held his hand out over the counter.

The old man, his worn denims faded glossy blue-white, looked down at Bauman's offered hand, apparently out of primeval caution, glanced over at Bauman's left, as well, which held no knife, no razor blade or piece of pipe, then reached out a cool frail hand to shake.

"Who are you?" Waggoner said.

"I told you, Uncle Jake," Cousins said, raising his voice a little. "—This is Charlie Bauman. The professor."

"Oh, yeah." Waggoner's blue eyes, oily wet, their whites dull yellow, studied Bauman through the punishing spectacles. "I make you, now," he said, and Bauman wondered in what old cons' house or den he'd been referred to, then dismissed.

Waggoner, who'd left his gentle hand in Bauman's as if to rest there from the labor of shaking, now withdrew it.

"Uncle Jake says Mr. Lesnovitch is downstairs." Cousins lifted a short hinged section of the counter, went through, waited for Bauman to follow, then lowered it behind them. "Says it's O.K. to go on down."

Bauman brushed past the old man—Waggoner smelled faintly of urine—and followed Cousins down a very narrow hall, its walls dull gray heavy-duty corrugated metal, its low ceiling perforated fiber tile. Cousins, certainly knowing his way, walked past three closed sliding doors along the hall's right side, then stopped by another at the corridor's end.

He waited for Bauman to catch up, and said, "Know what he did?" Smoke-gray eyes lit with a tale to tell, an inclination of the elegant head to indicate old Waggoner back at the bay's counter.

"No," Bauman said, and heard a muffled electric buzz, a soft clack-click in the closed door's lock.

Cousins pulled the door sliding open, and led Bauman through. The door slid closed behind them, left them standing in the dark.

"What he did," Cousins (a voice only) said, "he shot a snitchy con back in nineteen fifty-four. He was one of them club robbers—you know, go in some bar or a gamblin' club after hours, line everybody up an' rob 'em?"

"Right." Bauman was acutely conscious of Cousins beside him in the dark, oddly, since his beauty was unseen, only his low-pitched tough-girl's voice presented.

"Well, when they put him in here, he got hold of a piece someway, an' they took a hack an' that snitch, an' held 'em."

Cousins was standing close; Bauman caught a slight scent of breakfast coffee from him as he spoke.

"—State cops came in and said no deal, an' Waggoner took that piece an' blew the snitch's brains right out on the floor in the big linen closet. You know where Sweet Stitches is, over in D-basement?"

"Right."

"That's it. That's where that linen closet was. Warden—guy was warden then—was watchin' the whole thing. You talk about pissed off. That old man's goin' to be in here forever. Even after he's dead, they're goin' to keep him in here if they have to stuff him. You know, taxidermy."

"Poor old bastard. —What now? Do we get some lights on in here, or what?"

"Turn 'em on in a second. How's your back, Charles?"

"My back's better. It's working out; walking helped it. What I'd really like is to get some lights on in here."

As if someone had been listening—and he supposed someone might have been—a red bulb blinked on just over their heads, and Bauman saw he and Cousins had been standing on a short landing at the head of a steep, very narrow flight of wooden stairs. The small bulb gave only the dimmest sort of light. Below, at the bottom of the flight, the steps sank into dark.

Cousins, who must have made this trip many times, running bets for his adoptive father—or perhaps to meet some lover whose attentions were less fatherly—went swiftly, smoothly down the stairs. Bauman, following carefully, his lower back not pleased with descending stairs, imagined Cousins naked in that deeper basement dark, palely naked except for his shirt, which powerful hands had not left him time to unbutton.

"Careful."

Bauman slowed, became tentative out of the glow of the small bulb above, felt for the next step with his left foot, found it, was careful stepping off the one following—then stood on level flooring, cement gritty under his running shoes. He heard, or thought he heard, a phone ringing some distance away.

It was cool in this lower darkness, the air heavy with the basement odors of cement and damp wood.

Waiting beside Cousins, Bauman could hear him breathing, could, after a little longer, hear that mostly-felt tympanic rhythm of his own blood pulsing through his inner ears. The darkness and silence made a wonderful privacy—at least for a time. To be placed in a dungeon, in just this darkness, this silence—broken perhaps by a rat's scuttling, by dripping water. How many men and women, who'd never dreamed such a thing could happen to them, had found themselves in just such shadow and silence. Probably imagined hot sunlight, flower-beds, the spacious sea in every color of green. Probably imagined friends, restive horses they'd raised from colts. Panting girls, strenuous young men. Then, later, only dreams of release—jolted awake to a sharply imagined clatter at the trap door's bolt, almost blinking in fantasy's sudden, blazing lantern light. A dream to swiftly die away to silence, its lantern light to dark. . . .

After a while, another light bulb—small, red as the first—was switched on just beyond them, and revealed a long, shadowed basement room, its low ceiling the concrete structural members of the floor above. The basement was stacked from either wall with crates and smaller cardboard cartons, leaving only narrow passageway between them.

Cousins led that way, and Bauman followed, having to edge through sideways here and there, causing twinges in his back. He noticed no stenciled legend on any crate or carton—deliberate, he supposed, to enhance the mystery of the electricians' trade, strengthen their cult and make them less dispensable.

"Here we go," Cousins said, and they left the second light bulb's province and walked into more dark. Cousins took Bauman's arm, tugged him to the left, and said, "Steps."

This flight down was short, and ended where a third red bulb glowed over a small square space crowded by an old black iron furnace and riveted boiler. Bauman heard someone laughing.

There were two wooden doors—both painted white, the ancient paint flaking like dandruff—the nearest just to their right, the other across the room, beyond the furnace.

Cousins walked to the nearest, and knocked.

"*O.K. Come in. Come in.*"

Bauman followed Cousins out of dimness into light radiant, shimmering gold, and saw, as his eyes adjusted, a small bright-faceted entry light, and beyond it two table lamps and a floor lamp burning in a good-sized low-ceilinged room furnished as a real living room might be—and convincing but for the run of massive ductwork hung from its ceiling. At the room's center—occupied, and leaned against by a pair of aluminum crutches—a fat-cushioned sofa upholstered in brown corduroy faced two generous armchairs covered in the same material, their common coffee table of some wood oiled smoothly dark as chocolate syrup. Magazines were scattered across the coffee table, with an ashtray of heavy sharp-angled crystal. An occasional table displaying what appeared to be several pieces of antique china, faded, cracked, and elegant, was placed against a wall opposite. A long low bookcase—in which, Bauman supposed, Schoonover might find one or two hundred of the library's long-missing books—stood along the wall further down, with two small bull's-eye mirrors hung over it, reflecting the room in little. The floor was carpeted a deep maroon, small vases woven into the pattern, each vase with a bouquet of curling flowers. The room's wallpaper also a floral pattern, of dandelions or buttercups, blossoms small and gold in sprigs of green. At the room's far end, beyond the sofa, a card table had been set up with folding chairs around it, ashtrays, pads and pencils set at four places, and two unopened packs of cards.

During the subterranean tour conducted by little Cooper, Bauman had seen two or three gussied-up basement niches, storage closets or lumber rooms appropriated for daytime relaxation, boozing, and card games by old cons with sufficient juice. None had been near the equal of this. Lesnovitch, through many years, had taken full advantage of his princedom of electrons—and its profitable opportunities for barter, black market, substitution, and repair—to create this private living room of light.

"Hi, sweetheart, you heard this shit?" This was spoken with a liquid sizzling sound in the speech—as if the speaker had half a mouthful of water—that made it difficult to understand the end of each word, the beginning of the next.

The man sitting propped with cushions on the plump sofa, his crutches leaning beside him, was middle-aged, balding, lamp-tanned and sturdy in a tweed street sports jacket, tan street slacks, and oxblood loafers. He hung up the phone and smiled at them as well as he could, his right arm moving slowly to deposit its hand back in his lap. The right side of his face hung slack, right eyelid drooping to show its red, the right corner of his mouth sagging, lower lip hanging open to expose teeth and produce a fine glistening strand of spittle spilling to his chin. From this wreckage, bright brown eyes looked out curious as a lively dog's.

"Hear that shit?" he said to them in his difficult, slurring way. "—Infirmary coon lost a patient last night. Jig strung himself up in the toilet."

"Jomo Burdon," Bauman said, without even thinking about it.

Chapter TEN

"You heard that already?" Lesnovitch examining Bauman, interested, ready to be amused by the answer. His civilian clothes, complete from shoes to sports jacket, gave this damaged convict an air of worth, of social weight most inmates had to conjure out of size or reputation.

"—What do they call you? 'Teach,' right?"

Bauman nodded, deciding to commence with reticence. The master electrician's face—only half a face, really—reminded him of his own night fears of years before, the anxious attention to every headache, any possible disturbance of vision that might prove prelude to a stroke. This half-a-face was what he'd feared to see when, risen from Beth's side in the dark, skull cracking, he'd stood before his bathroom mirror.

"Reason we came over, Mr. Lesnovitch," Cousins, courteous at Bauman's side, "—is we just needed to check up on Mr. Metzler's bets, you know, before he died."

"Now, why'n hell you want to do that, sweetie? Is that your business, or what?" Lesnovitch sat up, careful of the creases in his trouser legs, and patted the cushion to his left. "Come on over here, sit beside old Ed. Keep me some company."

As Cousins went to comply, Bauman chose the nearest twin armchair, walked over and sat down, the cushions exhaling softly, accepting him. The chair was almost painfully comfortable, made all other chairs in his year and more at State meaner, harsher by contrast.

"Why don't you sit down?" Lesnovitch said to him, annoyed. "—Make yourself at home in my place?"

"Thanks," Bauman said.

"We were just checkin' on some of dad's bets, Mr. Lesnovitch."

"Now, that's surprisin'." Lesnovitch patted Cousins' hand. "What I heard, your buddy here got a badge go after some snitch. Was that bullshit the way I figured it was bullshit, or what? An' this about my bet; is that any of your business, sweetie?" He patted Cousins' hand again. Held it. "Is that your buddy's business, here?"

"This is a beautiful room," Bauman said. And it was, even on more leisurely inspection—except for the big duct along its ceiling, and a damp odor of basement. "It's the only civilized place I've seen at State. I'm surprised, though. I'm surprised you don't have any pictures up."

"Yeah?" Bauman watched Lesnovitch struggle swiftly between pique and pleasure, make his choice. "Yeah? —Tell me about it. You don't think I thought about that? But it just so happens I don't want some fuckin' paintin's on velvet in my apartment."

"I understand. But what about some drawings? Two or three good drawings, nice frames. Nothing more pleasant in a fine room, except really first-class watercolors or oils."

"O.K., O.K., now you're talkin' somethin' besides shit. Good oil paintin's, right? An' where the hell am I goin' to get 'em? That wop don't do nothin' but paint on velvet like he was doin' 'em for asshole tourists in Hono-fuckin'-lulu. A forger, what do you expect? You think he could even do a good oil paintin'? That'll be the day that wop does a quality oil paintin' on canvas. An' I could get him the canvas; I could get quality oil paints. I could get him anythin' he needs, an' I wouldn' charge. You think a painter, a artist, is grateful you give him a chance?" Lesnovitch paused, apparently brooding on the patron's lot. "Like hell he's grateful. 'I work on velvet, Mr. Lesnovitch.' Period. Like money don't mean nothin' to him. . . ."

"Then go outside," Bauman said. "—Have something sent in."

"Some piece of catalogue shit? You think that, you don't know what I'm after at all."

"I know exactly what you're after. You're after the look, the feeling of a casual living room in some handsome old country house, here or in England. You're after whatever takes you farthest from State—a room reflecting beauty, balance, comfort, and calm."

"Well, well. If you ain't a crazy motherfucker," Lesnovitch said. He patted Cousins' hand again, then let it go to lean forward to the coffee table, pick up a small silver bell, and shake out several bright notes. He put the bell down, sat back, and took a white handkerchief from his jacket's breast pocket, dabbed away a slender run of saliva spilled from the lax right corner of his mouth. "An' you look in a catalogue," he said to Bauman, putting his handkerchief away, "—you got a fat chance seein' what a paintin's really goin' to look like in this room."

"Some paintings, that's true. Good hunting prints, though, I think they'd be perfect."

"Huntin' prints. . . ."

"Fox hunters. Red jackets, green jackets, dogs and horses."

"Oh, I got you. Right. I know what you're talkin' about. But tell me, an' I want your honest opinion, here. Good prints. We're talkin' quality prints, right? But most of 'em, they're what—shit for some square john's den, right? Cheapos?"

"A lot of them. You'd need the best, two really first-class reproductions."

"Man, wish I could afford originals."

"For originals, you have to win bets, Lesnovitch. You have to win big bets. Losing bets gets you zip, gets you reproductions."

"Very cute, very cute. I lost thirty-one hundred on that Ohio guy eight weeks ago—fought Wajid Coleman? Joliet? Man, Coleman nearly killed my guy. Never bet a white guy against a nigger."

"And you paid up?"

"Damn right."

"To Becker?" Cousins said.

"No. Teppman was collectin' when I paid. Becker came around, but what the fuck—both collectin' for Nash, right? Why? Are you people sayin' we got a problem here, or what?"

"No problem," Bauman said. "Something we have to check with Teppman and Becker."

"Well, go check it. —Teppman says I didn't pay up, he's lyin'. Go ask Becker; he had his ass in a uproar. No business of mine. Those people need to get their act together."

"Stubbs," Bauman said.

"Who?"

"Stubbs. British. He's the artist you want. Classic paintings of fine horses."

"Stubbs?"

"Stubbs. I'd say you could order really good reproductions from New York or London."

"London. . . ." Lesnovitch seemed pleased with the notion.

"Or New York. Each reproduction, framed, would probably cost you four to five hundred dollars."

"That's all right . . . that's all right. How do you spell this guy?"

"S-t-u-b-b-s."

"What do I need, a catalogue? Pick 'em out of that? Providin' the stuff looks good as you say."

"Go over to the library and see Schoonover; he'll order a couple of catalogues for you. Then you make your choices and send for them. You'll want to be careful about the frames you order; good ones might be narrow old-gold leaf—"

"Listen, don't you tell me what fuckin' frames to have with nice prints. What do you think, I'm goin' to get some neon, lights up like a beer sign or somethin'?" The juicy hissing pronounced in Lesnovitch's speech as he grew angry.

"No," Bauman said, "—I don't think you'll do that." He hadn't noticed a doorway set into the room's far wall, the doorway unframed, door covered with the walls' paper. Now he saw it swing open, at first a little, then all the way, and a serving cart—made of the same fine dark wood as the coffee table—was shoved rattling through into the room by a very tall beautiful black woman in a maroon dress with dark-ivory lace at wrists and neckline.

Bauman had never seen Marcia Simms in full drag, so tall, spare, lean as a licorice whip. This changeling's face—long, elegantly Nilotic, the still, unreflective black of ancient ebony—was also the face of High Sonny Simms, pimp and throat cutter, and contained its womanly and manly secrets both behind silence.

"We got coffee here," Lesnovitch said. "—Real coffee. An' we got cheese danishes fresh out of the hacks' mess. You two got to help me polish off them danishes. Marcy, why don't you pour coffee for these people, O.K.?"

Marcia, stalky, bent like a heron over her serving table, sorting through snowy china with midnight hands, fingers improbably attenuated. She turned her head—turbaned in mustard silk—to Cousins and said, "Miss Lee. . . . Cream? Sugar?"

"That's a rich guy," Cousins said into a brisk buffeting wind. "Know what Marcia charges be with a guy like that, maybe all day?"

"A lot," Bauman said. This late autumn wind blowing confused temperatures across West yard—some gusts chill, some warmer. Just behind them, loose metal sheeting on the truck shop's walls boomed softly.

"A lot is right. —Well, what do you think?"

"I think we need to go over to the infirmary."

"No *way*." Cousins buttoned his jacket, turned its collar up. "You got to be kiddin', Charles. There's goin' to be cops over there an' everything! We sure as shit don't want to go over there today. These buildin' passes ain't goin' to mean a damn thing over there today."

"All right. Then let's go to the furniture factory, see Becker. —Doesn't he work over there? Or go to C, talk to Teppman. I don't think delay is going to help us with this improbable manhunt. In fact, I think the sooner it's over, the better."

"Charles, tell you somethin'. Long as we get out of this wind, I don't care where we go."

"O.K. Furniture factory."

"O.K."

There was only one con out on the West-yard walkway, a small black man Bauman didn't know. This man, in State denims, a gray, padded street parka, approached and passed them, saying nothing.

"Franklin," Cousins said, skipping once to get into step alongside.

Despite the weather, a baseball game was going on when they reached North yard, inmates—bundled in State sweatshirts, denim jackets, street windbreakers—arranged out on frost-burned grass in the game's pattern of play, calling insults, shouting advice to a large white man poised at the plate, bat cocked over his right shoulder. A hack was umpiring—there by regs in any case, whenever a bat or other possibly lethal instrument had been checked out for a game.

Another hack—unpleasant Harrison from D, less pleasant now that he was out in the weather—was sitting in the small unheated guard box mid-fence between North yard and East.

"You two got passes?"

"We don't need yard passes."

"What you got? You got buildin' passes?—walk around like you own the place. Show me them passes. I saw you come out of Electric over there. You lookin' to find somewhere play patty-cake? That it?" Harrison stood in the narrow doorway of the guard box, stepped back as another gust of wind came blowing. "Goddamn hurricane out here," he said, and read each pass in turn, their small paper fluttering in his hands. "Bullshit," he said, and handed the passes back. "Get outta here." He retreated into the guard box, shut the door, and buzzed the fence gate open.

"Why in hell," Bauman said, raising his voice a little, talking into the wind as they walked along. "—Why in hell would a hood like Jomo Burdon hang himself?"

"Maybe he really was sick. A lot of guys can't stand bein' sick."

"He didn't look sick to me, or to you. And he didn't look sick to Tiger."

"Still could'a been."

"I don't believe it." Bauman didn't remember the weather being quite as blustery last autumn. Even the winter hadn't been very severe—snow, but not much wind. And not terribly cold. This winter coming up was looking fiercer. He thought of asking Michaelson, or maybe the other doctor, Tracy, who didn't seem quite such an asshole, for a coat prescription. Susanne could buy him a leather jacket lined with that fake beaver fur—fur collar, anyway. Or, perhaps a sheepskin jacket. . . .

"—Some guys just get fed up."

"What did Burdon have to serve? Know his sentence?"

"Oh . . . he was in for some armed-robbery shit. Already been in here two, three years."

"No killing?"

"No killin'. —Not sent up for that, anyway."

"So, we're talking about a man had maybe— What? Only two more years? And he didn't seem like the sensitive type to me."

"Well," Cousins said, "couldn' be too much of a hard rock, gettin' run out of his house day before Spencer got offed in there. I knew him before."

"That's what I'm saying. He could be scared, and he was scared." Bauman, his back hardly troubling him now, twisted slightly left and right as he walked, testing, and felt little discomfort. Exercised out. . . .

"Not scared by me, an' not by you neither, Charles."

"But by somebody, right?—or something."

"Somethin'?"

"A ghost, maybe. What he thought was a ghost come up to those bars."

"That'd have to be somethin' special. A real special ghost, make that dude off himself."

"It already ran him out of his house."

"That's what he said. Charles, you can't believe nothin' anybody tells you in here. Don't you know that? Ghosts. . . ."

As they walked across East field, the capricious wind brought news of the baseball game now distant behind them, confused shouts of mingled celebration and disappointment. . . .

The furniture factory, three long stories of gray State granite lying along the East wall, exhaled a sweet sticky scent of glue and sawdust—these odors accompanying a faint soprano of saws.

The factory office was on the ground floor, a long room to the right, just past the entrance. Warm, lit by rows of blue-white fluorescents, its air redolent of glue, sawn wood, oil and turpentine, the office was busy with the factory's clerical work—voluminous enough, since this was the only one of State's enterprises that made any money, supplying, for the last century, the state's public schools with blackboards, tables, and desks and chairs in various sizes. The counter edge, where Bauman leaned his forearms, vibrated with a high humming buzz, the subsound of saws on the factory's second floor whining, slicing through lumber.

A con Bauman knew fairly well, an extortionist named Pat Pacelli, was at the service counter making entries from a stack of waybills. There were no computers in the office, none used in any inmate endeavor at State. No need here to conserve labor, hours.

"Hey, Teach, what can I do you for?"

"Pat, how's it going?"

"I got no complaints." Pacelli glanced over at Cousins.

"Pat, we need to talk to Becker."

"Do, huh?" Pacelli had a face from a Renaissance crucifixion—one of those lupine, unshaven, gap-toothed condottieri in shabby half-armor, standing in for Pilatus' legionaries.

"That's right."

Pacelli picked up the counter phone, punched three numbers, and winked at Cousins as he waited for connection.

"Hey, Toby? Got a guy—Teach, out of B? Down here lookin' for Becker. That's it. Lady with him—Cousins. That's right. That's right, me an' you both. I'll send 'em up the back." Pacelli hung up. "Third floor, storage. You guys go in the back, take that freight elevator up there. Save you climbin'."

"Thanks, Pat."

Pacelli gestured out and down the corridor with his thumb. "All the way back."

"O.K."

The corridor, quite narrow, ran straight along the building's length, its high ceiling lined with a double row of fluorescents filling the hall with light at once blue-white and feeble, so it seemed quite bright but left detail faintly fuzzed. Bauman and Cousins walked past dusty office and storeroom doors on either side, some closed, locked on silent rooms, others half open, one or two inmates lounging at desks or resting against ancient file cabinets, turning their heads to watch Bauman and Cousins pass.

A hack was sitting at a desk alone in one of these rooms, the fat freckled fish hack who'd patted Bauman down more than a week before at the library. The hack was sitting at a desk drinking coffee, a magazine in his lap, his feet up on a half-open drawer. He watched Bauman and Cousins walk by—didn't offer to get up, check them or their passes.

"There's a nothing-much cop," Bauman said. Thirty feet and several closed doors beyond, when they came to the freight elevator's wide battered black metal doors, he pushed the worn UP button twice. After a pause, as if the weary machinery were considering the matter, they heard the distant thud and moan as the drive wheel turned into motion. The elevator began its slow descent to them, and, a while later, thumped home and rebounded slightly behind its wide doors.

When the doors slid open (the big elevator's interior unlit, dark), Bauman stepped in—and was taken hold of and yanked forward so sharply his head jerked back at the acceleration. As this happened, a terrific blow struck his belly, then he was hit hard twice on the side of the head, and his feet kicked out from under him. He fell onto a chill steel floor with some textured pattern stamped into it, and was kicked two or three times in the side as he lay there—kicks so forceful they lifted him a little, made him grunt, and rolled him hard against the freight elevator's back wall. Padded—musty padding. He opened his mouth to shout, scream—then didn't, afraid he'd be kicked again, kicked to death.

He hadn't heard the elevator doors close, but supposed they must have, since the elevator was rising, making faint groaning noises.

Bauman was kicked once more, a very unfair, hard kick. An unnecessary kick. It caught him in the back, and for a moment he thought his back was broken, then decided not. He wished this was happening in the light, where he could see something.

Lying in darkness, facing the wall, he reached down along torn padding with both hands to find his knees—found them, gripped them, and pulled them up tight to his belly. Anybody could break his back now, but they couldn't kick him anywhere else, except the back of his head. He supposed they could do that. He waited to see if the person would kick him again, but instead felt the elevator slowing for a floor, second floor or third. He let go of his right knee, and still doubled like a fetus, dug his right hand under his waistband for something—recalled it was a knife just as his fingertips touched the tip of the handle. This object his fingers crawled down and curled around as if they'd found something to hold to through any flood. Then, the elevator's lights came snapping on.

Bauman closed his eyes and wished for the darkness he'd had. He remembered Cousins, was certain Cousins had stepped back, had run away down the corridor and left him alone.

"Hey. —Hey. What are you doin' down there, cocksucker?" This a weighty solid voice above him, a little hoarse.

"Lookin' for his nuts." A different voice, lighter.

Bauman kept his eyes closed, hoped he'd be thought unconscious, out of consideration. Maybe dying.

"You hold fuckin' still." Another voice. A third.

"—Hey, what are you doin' down there? I asked you a question." The man nudged him with his foot, with what felt like the toe of a running shoe, not hard leather. Heavy shoes apparently weren't necessary for hard kicks; must be the power, the velocity that did the damage. Running shoes, regular shoes, boots . . . it seemed to make no difference.

"I have a star," he said, not very loud—and it sounded ridiculous as he said it. He wished he hadn't said it at all.

The three men started laughing, laughter sounding very noisy in such an enclosed space. Laughing at him for saying something that stupid, for just lying there with his eyes shut. They could laugh at him all day; he didn't care. Then he opened his eyes anyway, saw dirty khaki padding on the wall beside him. It was torn, a small flap hanging open just above his face, revealing yellow cotton batting.

Bauman lifted his head, looked over his right shoulder, and saw a man he knew standing against the elevator's opposite wall with Cousins. He was an Indian named Manny Elk Antler, a Pawnee, supposedly. He was a short man, rather lean, almost dark as a black, with a large nose and attached upper lip that together seemed a beak. His lower front teeth were missing, and he held Cousins from behind with an arm crooked around his neck. His other hand, the left, was slid under the front waistband of Cousins' trousers, moving in there. "Oooh, that's nice," he said.

Cousins stood relaxed in the Indian's arms, his eyes closed as if he were dreaming.

The man standing above Bauman nudged him again with the toe of his shoe. "You want to keep lyin' down there, it's O.K., buddy. I don't give a shit. —Any of you guys give a shit if this asshole just lies there, he's got him a star an' is a deputy an' all?"

Bauman looked up and saw Eddie Becker standing over him in denims and a brown nylon windbreaker. Becker, a bank robber, was very tall—a powerful man, smoky-eyed, his high-bridged nose broken at least once, Indian-dark hair clipped into a stiff crewcut.

"Don't bother me, he stay down." This third man was also an

Indian—short, plump, dark, his thick round shoulders straining a red windbreaker, tarry eyes popped enough to look perpetually surprised.

"This is the faggot we want to talk to," Becker said, smiling down at Bauman, indicating Cousins with a turn of his head. "What you got there, Manny?" he said to Elk Antler.

"Nice stuff." The Pawnee's hand active in Cousins' denims. "He ain't gettin' no stand, though."

"Don't have to," the third man said. "—Ain't his party."

"Faggot," Becker said to Cousins, who, eyes closed, might have been asleep in the Pawnee's arms. "Faggot, you're goin' to tell me just what the fuck is goin' down on bettin'. An' just why, when we go to collect last couple weeks—from which collections, by the way, we make our fuckin' living—I get told that asshole Teppman is already picked up!"

"I don't know," Cousins said, eyes still closed.

Bauman saw the Pawnee was holding something small and bright between the thumb and forefinger of his right hand, where his arm was crooked around Cousins' neck, as if he intended to try some bauble—a silver earring, perhaps—against the boy's pale cheek. Looking more carefully, Bauman saw it was a single-edge razor blade. Seeing that, he felt grateful to be subsidiary, almost only a bystander, so nearly out of it.

"So, Metzler never said nothin' to you about plans before he got offed—about plannin' to take our collections, give 'em to Teppman, any asshole Shupe says? He said nothin' to you lived in the same fuckin' house, was the guy's fuckin' *squeeze* for Christ's sake?"

Cousins shook his head no.

"An' comin' over here for what? Find out how we're takin' this shit? Hell, you want to know that, that's no problem. Here's how we're takin' it." Becker stepped in and hit Cousins in the face with his left so hard both the boy and Elk Antler were jarred back against the elevator wall.

"What do you think about that, faggot?" Becker said, and stepped back beside Bauman as if to better judge effect. "—That give you a little intro what happens you lie to me about this?"

Bauman rolled over onto his belly, wondered if he should have stayed still, but found himself getting up on his knees in any case, tired of lying down. He got up that far despite his better judgment, but stayed hunched over as if he were badly injured, his right hand absurdly wedged down into his pants, refusing to let go of the knife.

"Dad," Becker said, "—you be real smart an' just stay down." He reached out with his left hand and patted Bauman on the head, three casual pats. *Pat, pat, pat. . . .*

Bauman took no umbrage at that, really didn't. The knife, however, seemed enraged—moved in Bauman's hand, struggled, then torn and born up out of his waistband, flourished in the air as Bauman jumped to his feet, hanging on to it.

Except for Cousins, whose eyes were closed, all in the elevator watched the knife as if it were the only source of light.

Bauman followed his knife to Becker as fast as he could—flicked the blade left and right as the big man attempted to slap the weapon aside—then lowered his head as he had with Muñoz, and drove in. He felt the smacking impact of Becker's great heft and muscle in resistance, smelled the warm odor of tobacco and strange male as their footsteps slid stamping, ringing through the elevator's steel—received two smashing blows (on the back of his neck, the top of his left shoulder) and with all his might lifted the man's weight a little and drove him back into the elevator doors with a heavy slamming sound. Then, from beneath, straining close against Becker as the big man shouted and struck down trying to knock the knife away, Bauman brought the blade tip up to Becker's throat just above his blue shirt collar, and stuck the point in half an inch.

Becker put his hand on Bauman's wrist, and Bauman said, "Look out!" as if the big man were a friend in danger. Becker slowly took his hand away. He was standing with his chin slightly raised, the back of his head against the elevator doors.

"What the fuck," Becker said. "What the fuck do you think this shit is goin' to get you? Other than dead, I mean." If he hadn't been standing so straight, his head back, a little blood staining his shirt collar, Becker would have seemed hardly concerned.

"Hey, motherfucker," the Pawnee had set the razor blade against Cousins' throat, "—lookie here!" The razor blade tugged slightly to the right, and sudden bright red beads rose from white skin behind it to coalesce into a short bright red line.

Bauman wanted to rest for a moment, but the knife prevailed. Its blade left Becker's throat with a sudden licking motion, spanked against his mouth as he tried to turn his head away, then slid its narrow point up into his left nostril until something there resisted and began to bleed a run of droplets down the steel and onto Bauman's hand.

"What the fuck's your name . . . ? Bauman," Becker said, calm voice only slightly nasal. "Let's use a little judgment here, Bauman,

O.K.? You're gettin' way in over your head—an' on a matter of business got not one fuckin' thing to do with you. *Business*. . . ."

Bauman found that though he'd moved very quickly, it had somehow slowed his thinking. He felt he needed time to think.

"I'll cut her fuckin' throat," the Pawnee said.

"Just a minute," Bauman said. "—Let me think," and took a deep breath, then another. His heart was beating very fast. Then he said, "All right," twisted the blade in Becker's nose, and shoved it a little higher.

Becker hummed and stood on his toes, his big hands raised to either side, describing slow small circles in proximity to the knife, his nose.

"Now," Bauman said to Manny Elk Antler, "now, you red nigger, you listen to me. You go ahead and cut her throat, and watch what happens. I'll stick this knife right up this asshole's brains and then I'll come over there and kill you. You have my word of honor. —It'll be a pleasure." He hadn't meant to say the last; it just slipped out.

The third Indian, the fat one in the red windbreaker, was standing against the elevator's side wall as Bauman supposed he'd lain against the wall in back, hoping to be out of it.

"You're really goin' overboard on this," Becker said, sounding as if he had a very bad cold, sinus trouble. His head was tilted so far back he was speaking to the ceiling light. "Way overboard. . . ." The blood from his nostril had run down the knife blade and over Bauman's hand. He could feel some trickling down his wrist under his shirt cuff.

"The star I have on my arm, motherfucker?" Bauman said, "—I earned it. And as far as you and your buddies are concerned, I am an officer of the fucking law. All the law there is in this shit pile."

"Whadever you say, ace," Becker said.

"—And you make up your mind," Bauman said to the Pawnee, past Cousins' dreaming face. "Do it, or don't do it, but make up your mind."

"Hey, come od . . . come od," Becker said, and tried with little tentative spittings to rid himself of the blood apparently tickling his upper lip. "I'm dot spittin' on you," he said to Bauman, "—so don't get id a uproar."

"What do you want me to do, Eddie?" Elk Antler said. "Want me to go for it, or what?"

"Maddy," Becker said, "maybe you didn' dotice I got a disadvantageous position here."

"Throw that blade away, cocksucker," Bauman said to the Pawnee, "—or use it. Go on, cut her throat. Do it, see what happens." When he said that, Bauman noticed Cousins' eyes were open, watching him.

"What a pain in the ass," Elk Antler said, and flicked the razor blade away so it spun, bright and small, across the elevator to fall with a 'tick' on the stamped steel floor. Then he shoved Cousins hard away from him to stumble into the padded back wall. "You got a date with me, buddy," the Pawnee said to Bauman.

"Sure I do," Bauman said, and pulled the knife blade down out of Becker's nose. The point had stuck into something up there, and had to be tugged a little to free. Then, the knife still in his right hand, he turned Becker, unresisting, and pushed him gently away, back toward his friends. "Right now, if you want. Want to have our date right now?" He felt confident as a demigod might, contemplating some contest with a mortal, as if a steady strong wind was blowing at his back, certain to multiply his strength to any requirement.

"Come on, Eddie," the fat Indian said. "We held the elevator a long time, now. Some hack's gonna stick his nose in."

Becker was holding his head back, pinching his nostrils shut with thumb and forefinger. There was blood on his chin, drops of blood on his brown windbreaker. "Do be a favor, Freddy," he said. "Don't use the word 'dose,' O.K.?" and grinned at his joke.

"Push the fuckin' button," the Pawnee said to the fat Indian. "Let's get the hell away from these fuckin' fruitcakes."

The door rattled open onto another corridor—shadowy, barely lit, stacked with cartons and crates as far as could be seen. Becker gestured his two friends out ahead of him, turned in the doorway, still pinching his nose to stop its bleeding, and said to Bauman, "You deed to be sure you don't let this go to your head, man. One lucky break don't make a policy, udderstan'?"

"I understand."

When the door slid shut, Bauman went to the panel and pushed the button marked 2.

He said nothing, and Cousins said nothing until the elevator had sunk one floor and stopped—until its door had opened again.

"Let's get out of here," Bauman said. And when Cousins moved very slowly, took him by the arm and hurried him out of the elevator, down a dark corridor past four closed doors, and through a fire door sheathed in red-painted steel out onto a stair landing. There was a dusty window at the landing that allowed daylight down the steps. Bauman heard the sounds of saws vibrating through the building afresh, as if there'd been a hiatus, as if the trouble in the elevator had stopped all other activity.

Cousins was standing where Bauman had left him, his hands clasped together at his chest. His hands were shaking so it seemed it was the sound of the saws—their vibrations—causing the tremor.

"All over now," Bauman said. "Take it easy. Over and done with, and frankly I feel just fine." Which was true; his lower back didn't hurt at all. He felt very well, exhilarated. "I think I've discovered a treatment for lower-back pain," he said, and reached out to take Cousins' arm, lead him slowly down the stairs. "—You just get some really big mean motherfucker of a convict to kick the shit out of you. And I'll tell you something, the technique I used up there? I'll tell you something, very classic Tenth Legion stuff, and it still works. You have a big man, a barbarian, a Belgic Gaul or whatever, and you go right into him, low, get in close so he has shit for leverage and you have plenty."

At the landing, the turn of the stairs, Bauman had to tug Cousins' arm a little to keep him moving, start him down the next flight. "You have a short handy thrusting blade that's just perfect. Close. Close is the secret for effective infantry. Israelis, North Vietnamese, same thing. Get in close—negates a lot of the opposition's firepower. Boxing, exactly the same."

Cousins stopped on the stairs, and when Bauman gripped the boy's wrist with his left hand, he found it icy cold. "For Christ's sake, it's *over*. And it was no big deal. It might even occur to you to say a word or two of thanks, unless I offended you by interfering up there. If I offended you again, I really, really apologize." Bauman turned to lead down the stairs, took two or three steps, feeling as if he had to burp—then was surprised at how sick he felt, how suddenly his mouth was full of vomit. It was so full, some came out his nose.

He leaned out over the rail and vomited down the stairwell, spattering the front of his jacket, the banister, and the steps below. He heaved as he vomited, straining so that he rose on his toes to do it. He was able to draw a whooping breath, then vomited again and took some steps down the stairs right into it. It looked as though there was stuff in his vomit he'd never eaten.

His stomach was empty very quickly, and he leaned over the stair rail and gagged, his body trying to vomit some more, trying so that he rose on his toes again, his stomach aching unbearably. Someone was hugging him; Cousins was hugging him, holding on to Bauman's waist as if leaning so far out, gagging, he might fall over the rail.

"Holy cow," Bauman said, and rested his forehead on the stair rail even though there was vomit there. He didn't care. "Oh . . . oh, boy," he said. "Oh, boy. . . ."

"You were really brave up there, Charles." Cousins let go of Bauman's waist and gently patted his back, stroked Bauman's back in gentle circles, as if some pain were there.

"Oh, yeah. Oh, yeah. No doubt about that." The vomit smelled awful, but Bauman didn't feel like raising his head off the rail. He felt much better just where he was. "—My belly knows all about it."

"I don't care. You were brave," Cousins said, and took his hand away.

"Sure. You bet. I was just too scared to be scared, that's all. That's all that was." After a little while, Bauman lifted his head off the rail. He put his hand up and felt a smear of vomit on his forehead. "Do me a favor," he said, starting to feel better. "Let's just get out of here. I hope to Christ there's a bathroom on that fucking ground floor. Let's just get out of here—and look out where you step." He leaned over to spit. The vomit smelled terrible; he was stinking with it. He looked down and was surprised to see he was still holding the knife in his right hand. He'd forgotten he was holding it. It was stuck to his hand in blood. He rolled the knife's handle in his palm to unstick it, held his waistband out with his left hand, and slid the knife down into its sheath with his right. Then, starting slowly down the stairs, he took his bandanna out of his jacket pocket and dabbed at some vomit on his pants.

At the fire door to the ground-floor corridor, Bauman stopped to blow his nose on the last possible corner of his ruined bandanna. "We make some team. As a team, you and I are really out of sight." He hadn't intended it as funny when he'd said it, but started to giggle when Cousins did, so they went out into the corridor laughing, trying to keep quiet.

The long hall, dark here with its ceiling lights off, was narrowed by stored planks stacked on either side.

"Where's the bathroom?"

"If you go aroun' to the right," Cousins said, "—then you take a right again an' you're at the office. They got a can down there on that corridor somewhere."

"Let's get to it," Bauman said. "I need to clean up." Now that he felt better, everything seemed quite comfortable, the air containing—besides the distant song of saws, the rich odors of glue and sawdust—an easy pervasive warmth, a barely visible glow.

Cousins walked a few steps ahead to a right turning in the corridor, leaned slightly forward to look down that way, then straightened up, said, "Hack's comin'. —Gleason." He took Bauman by his cleanest arm, steered him back through the fire door at the foot of the stairs, and closed it behind them. They stood there against the closed door, listening as footsteps came slowly nearer, passed, grew distant, and were gone. "You O.K.?"

"I'm fine," Bauman said. "I'm fine." A little annoyed at the question, but not very annoyed. He smelled god-awful.

"Try again?"

"By all means."

Cousins shoved the fire door open—then led out as if Bauman's disarray and slight reluctance to move constituted a sort of abdication.

They reached the right turning again; Cousins leaned out to look down it, then walked that way, Bauman following. They passed more small stacks of rough lumber piled first on one side of the hall, then the other, and Cousins stopped twice to try doors along the left side of the corridor. Both locked.

"I know they got one down here," he said, stepped over to try a third door, found it open, and looked in. "—Got it. Come on."

There were three grimy sinks in a line against the narrow room's tiled back wall. One of the sinks—the far right—had been used to clean brushes, was striped and stained with caked colors. The only toilet was severely cracked, seatless, filled almost to its rim with a brown-black mixture—feces, soaked and sinking folds of paper, and a cluster of cigarette butts, barely submerged and oriented by some slight current as a school of tiny ornamental fish might have been. The room smelled less of shit than tobacco and paint.

"What if somebody comes in here?"

"Somebody comes in here, we're mindin' our own business an' they can do the same," Cousins said. "You O.K.?"

"I'm fine."

"Let me have your jacket; I'll clean it up for you."

Bauman, obedient, took his jacket off and handed it over, watched Cousins run water into the second sink, use his hand to rub traces of vomit off the jacket's right sleeve under the faucet.

"Why don't you wash up a little, Charles? You want to be gettin' that blood off your hand, first. O.K.?"

"You got it," Bauman said, stood watching Cousins scrub the jacket sleeve a few moments more, then sighed and went to the near sink, turned the hot-water faucet on, and after a wait discovered only cold water forthcoming. He decided to use the cold water anyway, unbuttoned his shirt cuffs, unbuttoned the shirt, tugged the tails out of his trousers and took it off. There was some vomit down the front. He put that part of the shirt under the tap, and rubbed at the stains.

"You got some thanks comin', Charles," Cousins said, picked the denim jacket up and shook excess water off it. "Not bad now," he said. "It's wet, but it's O.K. You're still goin' to have to put it in the laundry."

"Oh, I know that," Bauman said, drew a deep breath and sighed again as if he were sad about something. He was feeling less dreamy, now; the cold water flowing over his hands was waking him. The blood on his right hand was slowly flaking away with the water, peeling away.

"Charles, I owe you some thanks about up there," Cousins said, folding the denim jacket over his arm. "An' after I mouthed off about you buttin' out of my business—you know, not bein' my boyfriend or whatever."

"Forget it," Bauman said. "—I'm trying to."

Cousins put his hand up to his throat, fingertips tracing the thin line of stippled red where the Pawnee had lightly cut him. He looked along the line of sinks as if for a mirror.

"That's not bad," Bauman said.

"Don't look bad?"

"It doesn't look bad at all, just looks like a scratch. There shouldn't be any scar from that. Get some pruno when you go home; rub a little on there, lightly. Get it clean, then just leave it alone." Bauman lifted his shirt out of the sink, wrung it out, then put it under the faucet again. He found some vomit on it near the breast pocket, rinsed that off. "—I'm going to get pneumonia, running around in wet shirts."

"Wasn' I right?" Cousins said, cupped his hands beneath the next sink's faucet, and lifted the water to his bruised face. Then he ran his wet hands through his hair and took a comb from his back pocket to arrange it better. "—Wasn' that other shirt ruined, you used hot water on that bloodstain?"

"You were right. It was ruined. —How's your eye?"

"O.K. It isn' hurtin'. It's sort of numb." Cousins put his comb away, and examined Bauman's jacket for more mess. "—You know somethin' funny, when we was up there? An' you looked at me, you know, told Manny Elk he could jus' go ahead an' cut my throat?"

"I seem to recall that." Bauman took his shirt out of the sink, wadded it up and used it, wet, to wipe down the front of his trousers. "—That sounds familiar."

"I got the idea up there you wanted Manny to go ahead an' do it. Is that weird, or what? You had him an' me both goin'."

Bauman used the shirt to wipe vomit off his blue running shoes, then put it back in the sink, ran water on it. ". . . Lee, as I believe you know, or you wouldn't be bringing it up, I did want him to go ahead and do it.—Now, what do you think about that? If I were you, I wouldn't be too quick to thank me for anything." He picked the shirt up, then wrung it out, shook it out, and put it on.

Cousins had nothing more to say, stood watching Bauman as if he'd been revealed, as on a zoo-cage label, a slightly rarer animal, more interesting than he appeared.

Bauman reached down under his waistband, found the knife's handle, and tugged it out. It was painted with drying blood. He held the narrow blade under the tap, turning it slowly in the stream, rinsing the red away. When the blade was clean, Bauman reversed the weapon, and holding the blade lightly, careful of the honed double edges, let the tap water run over the taped handle. Below the knife, the sink's dirty porcelain was drifted over by a mist of rust red, then ran clear again. Bauman turned the water off. "I need to dry this blade."

Cousins came to him, held out his jacketed left arm, and Bauman, careful not to cut the denim, stroked the flat of the slim blade down across the cloth, turned it, and dried the blade's other side. Then he held his waistband away from his belly, to put the shank away. He was sliding it carefully down into its sheath, which would have to be untaped and cleaned at home, when the bathroom door swung open. A tall middle-aged convict Bauman didn't know walked in, glanced once at them, then turned his head away and went to stand at the toilet, unbuttoning his fly. The man wore State-issue glasses, and had short blond hair fading to gray. He wore blue denim coveralls, dirty, smeared with paint.

Bauman sheathed the blade, adjusted his shirttails and tucked them in, then took his jacket from Cousins and put it on.

The tall con—his face turned slightly away from them—began to pee, the narrow stream stirring the school of cigarette butts into motion.

Bauman gestured Cousins through the bathroom door ahead of him, stopped in the doorway, and said to the tall man's back, "We weren't here when you came in. There wasn't anybody here."

"That's right," the tall man said.

The wind, blowing over East yard, chilled Bauman's wet shirt against him under his jacket's weight. His back felt fine, didn't trouble him. There were sore places from the beating, from being kicked, but that was all. "—Who was that came into the can?"

"He wasn' nobody." Cousins walked at Bauman's right side, thoughtful, or still recovering from Elk Antler's attentions in the elevator, from Becker's punch. "—No lifer anyway. I think his name's Chambers, Chamberlain. Nobody, not even a armed robber or anything."

"That eye hurting, now?"

"Yeah, a little. That side of my face."

"Bad?"

"It's all right, Charles."

"Just tell me. How bad is it? That was a hard punch."

"Charles, it's all right. It feels sort of numb."

"Want to go over and see Tiger?"

"No, I sure don't. I been hit before, Charles."

"Well, if you get a bad headache, trouble with your vision—"

"*Charles*. . . ."

"All right, all right. So, where are we now? We have a pissed-off Eddie Becker and his noble savages. And since, I gather, a lot of money is involved in those collections— What's the collectors' share, by the way?"

"Five percent to pick up, twenty-five percent if they got to do somethin' to collect. That's regular bets. Personal debts, they get fifty, collectin'."

"Adds up to a lot of money, right?"

"Good money, Charles. Not great, though, if people pay off up front."

"Even so, with the crowd we have in here, there'd be a lot of people paying late, or not wanting to pay at all."

"Right," Cousins said. "It's a good job."

"And Becker lost it—thanks to Barney Metzler?"

"I see where you're goin', Charles, but that's no good. Becker was Mr. Metzler's guy."

"And Metzler didn't fire him?"

"No. I would have known if he did that, 'cause Becker was always comin' around."

"O.K. So Becker lost his job after your Mr. Metzler's death. Well, who profits from that death? If not Becker, then who else but the con who got his job."

"Teppman."

"He's making the money. Becker's lost it."

"I don't know. . . . Teppman's a bad guy, but I don't know if he'd figure somethin' like that on his own."

"Why don't we ask him? —And speaking of asking him, why in hell haven't Becker and his people already done that? Why don't they go over to C, go into the lifer office, and ask why they're out of a job?"

"Not goin' to do that."

"Why not? If I was Becker, and it was worth that much money to me, I'd damn sure go over there. I wouldn't waste time asking you in some elevator in the furniture factory!"

A swifter, colder gust of wind came bowling across the yard, buffeted them, then blew away.

"He can't go over there to those guys."

"Why not?"

"Well, it's a pride thing. 'Cause Eddie and his guys were in on a pass, anyway. Mr. Metzler let him in."

"And why in on a pass?"

" 'Cause he isn't a white guy. He's half Indian—an' his guys are hundred-percent Indians. Union didn' want Mr. Metzler to use him at all, any more than usin' black guys or Spanish guys."

"But I thought Metzler was in the Caucasian Union."

"Officer."

"Right. An officer."

"Mr. Metzler let Eddie in 'cause he wanted people who felt an obligation—you know, show some loyalty an' be his guys, personally. But now, Eddie can't go over there an' start askin' Teppman an' those Union people why he's out. Him an' his guys aren't white guys, an' now they're out—period."

"But you're saying Metzler was big enough to get away with using them."

"That's right, with Nash sayin' O.K."

"Well, maybe what happened to Metzler is it suddenly stopped being O.K. Stopped being O.K. with somebody."

"I don't know. You got to understand how big Mr. Metzler was."

"Maybe too big. Maybe somebody said to Teppman, 'I think Metzler's getting a little too big, got his own army of Indians,' and so forth."

"I suppose that could be, but it don't seem right."

"O.K., Lee, then what happened? Because something happened to upset somebody's apple cart—Becker's for sure. And we're discussing people who tend to action in those circumstances. Isn't that so?"

"Yeah. . . ."

"Well, this is what I think; I think we have our best chance of getting this foolish and very dangerous investigation over with as fast as possible, by simply following the money. Make sense?"

"I guess it does, except for Mr. Metzler's partner, outside, framed him for that killin'."

"All right, Lee, we follow the money, but keep the treacherous partner—and his possible hired hack, hired killer—in mind as alternatives."

"O.K."

Two inmates came toward them on the walkway—new fish, Bauman thought, very young—and bikers, by their scraggly beards, tattooed hands, the heavy boots showing beneath the cuffs of just-issued denim trousers. These boys, one dirty blond, the other ginger-haired, ginger-bearded, walked with sauntering swaggers, the gusting wind blowing from behind tangling their long hair, tossing strands of it forward past their faces.

They stared at Cousins as they approached, then glanced at Bauman and looked away as they walked past.

"—I've got gym this afternoon, and then a visitor. But if you're free this evening, we'll follow your suggestion, go down to the canteen and check with Ramos about anyone suddenly getting rich, spending a lot of cash. O.K.?"

"O.K."

"And then tomorrow morning, we can go see Tiger at the infirmary, find out if he has any idea at all why Jomo Burdon killed himself just after we started to ask him some questions. —Maybe ghosts, if you think anything could frighten that animal to death."

"Lot of hard guys scared of somethin'."

"That scared? So, we'll check with Tiger. There shouldn't be any cops still over there by then."

"An' after that, we go over to C—just ask Teppman right out, how come he got Becker's job?"

"That's exactly right, Lee. Why not? Teppman got the job; he's collecting the bread. Damn right we're goin' to ask him how come."

"Well, all that askin', I guess we'll find out somethin'. . . ."

Change of shift just past, a different hack, a man named Pruhasko—sturdy, middle-aged, and silent—was manning the guard box between East and North yards. More than a month before, perhaps annoyed by Bauman's block passes for teaching, his constant travels throughout State, he'd strip-searched him at A-block's gate as other inmates went filing past. Today, curiosity perhaps having been satisfied, perhaps only wanting to stay out of the wind, Pruhasko remained in his booth, waved Bauman and Cousins through the fence gate into North.

As they turned down North walkway toward the blocks, the wind eased, and seemed to warm. ". . . Lee, the reason I think we need to move fast as we can on this— I'll tell you something. I don't know how many of these little dramas—like the one we just had up in that elevator? I don't know how many of them we're good for. I doubt if we're good for very many. And the longer we go around State sticking our nose into people's business, the more these little incidents are going to multiply. So, let's do our damnedest to get this manhunt over with as fast as possible, in the next few days. All right? Sooner we find the asshole responsible—at least for killing your Mr. Metzler—the sooner we're out from under."

"What about your friend, Spencer?"

"He wasn't a friend, O.K.? He was an acquaintance. A business acquaintance. And since apparently Spencer was killed by the same person or persons who murdered Metzler—and we haven't found any other reason for anyone to want him dead—it seems to me he probably knew something about Metzler's murder, and was killed to silence him."

"Maybe. Maybe that's right. But you know, Charles, we're leanin' pretty hard on maybes."

"I know it. But maybes and money are all we have."

Cousins didn't reply, walked along in silence—recalling, Bauman supposed, Manny Elk Antler's firm grip, his lewd, searching left hand, his right poised with its tiny rectangle of bright steel. Recalling, perhaps, his middle-aged companion in a terrified rage, willing, in order to continue a comforting madness, that Cousins' throat be cut.

"I suppose," Bauman said, "—I suppose Becker will take this as a personal matter."

Cousins stared at him, then started to laugh, laughter pitched higher than his tough tom-boy's speaking voice, so it sounded very much like a girl's, very musical while it lasted.

"Could be he'll take it personal," Cousins said. "—You stickin' a shank up his nose an' cuttin' him, an' right in front of his guys. Could be he's goin' take that personal. We sure ain't goin' be his favorite people."

Bauman—sorry he'd asked, received such sensible and definite confirmation—took several deep breaths as he walked along, and looked about with fresh appreciation at his prison's stretching yards, its girdling wall's grim inherent gray. Not an inconsiderable stage, even for violent nonsense. Perhaps particularly for violent nonsense.

"Course," Cousins said, "him an' his people won't be talkin' about it, neither. One good thing. Population isn' goin' to know about it, if they can help it. Kind of embarrassin'."

Bauman, worried but not displeased, had the notion of naming his knife—as a personality, rather than mascot—retiring, brooding, passive until released by extraordinary circumstance. A soulless instrument, but occasionally lively.

Trajan? Doubtful this would have amused that shy, grudge-holding brigadier, occupied with ambition as with a lovely life-long partner in dancing those years of oblique and artful steps to end at last as emperor, with all dancers bowing but himself.

Some more appropriate name, then. Tigelinus? Horse-dealer, lover, hatchet man. Or, more apropos—Mr. Hyde?

Lunch was bologna, baked beans, two slices of white bread, and pineapple Jell-O. The bologna slices were rimmed with green, but the Jell-O was excellent.

"What the hell you two been doin'?" Scooter, at lunch, chewing the beans. "You look all fucked up."

"Just fooling around," Bauman said.

"Bullshit." Perteet, accepting the gift of Bauman's bologna. "Bullshit. She got smacked, is what happened to her."

"I walked into a door," Cousins said. The area around his right eye was flushed a light rose, had begun to shadow.

"Bullshit," Scooter said. "Pete, you want some beans?"

"No, thanks, man. I don't want any more of them fuckin' beans. They didn' even cook the fuckers."

"So," Scooter to Bauman, "what happened?"

"Scoot, you remember we had an agreement on this? Remember that?"

"Charles, I'm not curious. Hey, it isn' a matter of curiosity. I just wondered you know, what happened, that's all. Stric'ly I was jus' wonderin'."

"Stop wonderin'," Perteet said. "Man wants to tell you, he's goin' to tell you. He don't, he won't."

"Scooter," Cousins said, "—you know that bike you were sayin' I should get? That Ducati?"

"What?" Perteet lifted his great head, swallowed a mouthful of bologna.

"Nothin'," Scooter said. "She's jus' kiddin'." And to Cousins, "—Will you for Chris' sake stop foolin' around about *bikes?* What the hell do you know about 'em? I was talkin' in theory when I mentioned that particular bike. An' that's all. O.K.?"

"What did she mean?" Perteet, starting on his pineapple Jell-O.

"She didn' mean nothin'. She was just kiddin' around."

"I was just kiddin' around," Cousins said.

"You thinkin' about gettin' a bike, you get out?" Perteet said.

"I was thinkin' about it," Cousins said. "Somethin' light, you know. Where you could just go anywhere you want. . . ."

"So what's this Ducati shit?" Perteet said. "Harley makes a nice light bike."

"That's what Scooter told me. He said best to be buyin' American."

"Fuckin' a," Perteet said, finished his Jell-O and looked longingly at Bauman's.

"Forget it," Bauman said. "I'm not giving pineapple away."

Perteet sighed a great gusty sigh, breathing out a composite aroma of White Owl cigar, raisin pruno, stem-and-seed pot, and slightly spoiled bologna. "I'm goin' an' get some Z's." He heaved himself up off his stool, said, "Take it easy," and lumbered away, his massive denimed bottom (grease smeared) looking lonely for a motorcycle's saddle, engine noise, the lightness of velocity. . . .

"I've got to get over to the gym, and I have a visitor coming up this afternoon," Bauman said, he and Cousins climbing the worn stone stairs to B's Ground-tier.

"Right. I remember you told me. Well, I got some stuff to do this afternoon, an' you need to change them pants an' buy a shirt. You shouldn' see a visitor—"

"My wife."

"Well, you shouldn' see her in that shirt, neither."

"Either. And I don't have a clean one left."

"Either," Cousins accepting the correction. "You got the money to buy one?"

"Not just now."

"One of mine wouldn' fit you. Why don't you borrow one off Scooter, an' roll up the sleeves?"

"Probably will."

"You know, fold the sleeves up so it'll look neat."

"Right. Don't worry, I'll change the pants and put on a clean shirt."

On Ground-tier, as they paused to part, Cousins said, "I know what you told me, but I don't like not thankin' you for that over there."

"Forget it. And don't depend on it happening again. I only got away with it because they were surprised; they didn't expect me to be carrying. Next time, they won't be surprised, and I won't be such a hero."

"Well, I'm thankin' you anyway." Cousins apparently annoyed, pale face slightly flushed with anger where Becker's punch hadn't left its darker mark, the bruise serving to emphasize by contrast that facial structure's delicate regularities.

"I have to get to the gym," Bauman said. "—Want to come over? It's all right with Cooper; little man likes you."

"No, I got some stuff to do at the house, an' then I'm suppose' to go to councilin' about attitudes. So I guess I'll see you at dinner."

"After that, we'll go down and try Ramos."

"O.K."

A young con named Chuck Dunfey, a sturdy strutting young hot rock with a shaved scalp and waxed mustache, winked at Cousins as he passed them on his way to the basement stairs, and said, "Hey, Teach, how's it goin'?"

"Fine," Bauman said to him. "Great. . . ."

"Well," Cousins said, "—see you at chow. Hope you have a real good visit."

"See you." Bauman, watching Cousins walk away through the after-lunch crowd, felt ungracious, as if in aborting thanks he'd prevented a celebration—even if of a dubious and temporary triumph. He watched Cousins out of sight, then walked down Ground-tier to the circular stair, and climbed it to Two-tier and home to change his clothes, and for the chore of cleaning his knife's sheath and checking the shank for any blood spot overlooked. Reminded himself, before putting the weapon away, to rub Chapstick along the blade to prevent rust.

Arriving a few minutes after workout had started, Bauman received a terrier's snap from old Cooper for lateness, then found Paco Muñoz on the heavy bag and working hard, sweating even in the gym's barely warmed late autumn air.

Paco, talented fighter, was avoiding the blunder most men made with the heavy bag—to forget that rhythm was the reason for the exercise, even ruling the delivery of such slow weighty blows as this bag invited. The middleweight, crouching, was presenting the big bag first with that thrusting butting forehead brawlers usually employed to position their opponents—and levered from which, like the short battering hooks a bull's horns made, his punches, right and left, came slamming in. Enrique, though not shoved back as Marcantonio could shove him, still was sharply jolted as he held the bag, and Bauman could have seen by only observing him how well Muñoz was doing at this unaccustomed exercise.

While Bauman watched, Paco Muñoz hit the big bag forty-two times—each succeeding blow delivered after a slightly shorter interim than the punch before—so the effect in sound was like the slow, ponderous acceleration of a steam locomotive, its great pistons sliding home in noisy *chuffs* of heated mist, oil, and air in quicker and quicker succession until the noise—storming, continuous—no longer presented intervals.

On the released energy of his last short punch, Muñoz stepped back, straightened up, and hooked high into the bag with his left, came off that with a snapping right, then stepped away entirely, dancing, gloves down, shaking limber muscles out.

"I had a lot of good advice to give you, Paco," Bauman said, "about fighting inside on a man. But watching you work, I think I'll just save my breath."

Muñoz, very pleased at that though he hardly showed it, danced a little more swiftly, tapped his gloves softly together.

"The only thing—and I mean the *only* thing I can think of—is you might need just a little wider stance in case this Dennis Willy is not too dumb to try and sidestep when you come in, to turn you. A slightly wider stance, and you'd move right with him."

"Right," Muñoz said. "Right." His gloves tapped together again. *Tap, tap.*

"You want me," Bauman said, "—I'll be over on the speed bag with Marcantonio."

"Right." *Tap tap tap.*

And, after an hour and a half of the most onerous instruction—example, nagging, example, praise, example, threats and ridicule—Tony Marcantonio was able to keep the speed bag fairly well in play, though complaining constantly and running sweat from the effort involved in accepting and putting to use a sense of rhythm that wasn't in him.

"Pretty good on the meatball," old Cooper said to Bauman, having just refused him permission to shower in the gym for his four o'clock visit. "An' I suppose you think you did great with that spic there, that Muñoz."

"You're goddamned right I did. I did a very good job with him—a better job than you could do. Fact is, Coach, you know a hell of a lot, but what you know about infighting, a bug could shove up his pecker and still piss." This phrase, a favorite of Bauman's old coach at Minnesota, was not strictly accurate, since little Cooper did know at least every dirty trick of infighting—lace-scrubbing, resin-thumbing, butting, and the art of stepping onto an opponent's toe to hold him in place for a punch.

"You're gettin' a real nasty con's mouth on you, Trainer." The bald little man annoyed, red-faced in gray sweatshirt and shorts, his bright lanyarded whistle resting on a pigeon chest.

"Lie down with dogs . . ." Bauman said, and strolled away to the gym's double doors.

Two hacks were working Admin's back entrance. At the top of the steps, a young black man waited with the pass-for-visitors list. A thin white woman named Unger was stationed below. Unger—a useful masturbatory icon for many inmates despite her glasses, her chinlessness, her improbably curly mud-brown hair—was wanding inmates going up for their visits, nudging the portable detector's rod into cons' armpits, then down their chests and bellies to drift very lightly over crotches, more definitely down each leg in turn. The rod then was swept swiftly up over buttocks and back before being withdrawn and poised for the next man, as the line, slow caterpillar, took two steps forward.

The men were showered, clean-shaven (where not bearded, mustached), and wore their best—pressed denims, any street clothes they owned (slacks, jackets, sweaters and windbreakers). Several of them held handmade gifts—simple wooden pull toys made for their children afterhours in the furniture factory, decorated belts and purses for wives and mothers come to visit. A lifer whose name Bauman didn't know, an older man with a cut-throat tattoo—an inked wide-open gash across his throat from ear to ear, from which tattooed blood, bright ruby, spilled down under his shirt collar—carried cradled a lovely schooner made of matchsticks, its set sails (bleached bandannas) bellying in the afternoon's cold breeze as if the boat sailed already, in his arms.

Neither Unger nor the black hack said anything to the inmates while Bauman advanced in line behind a convict named Edwins. Edwins, by repute a dedicated rapist, was holding a small bunch of weather-weary marigolds augmented by carrot greens plucked from one of the mess hall's garbage. Flowers, wreaths, bouquets, were the sideline of a con named Sanchez, gardener to the warden, assistant warden, and senior yard captain, with authentic decorative greens costing extra.

At his turn, Unger probed Bauman's right armpit with her shining wand, poked gently at his chest—allowing the metal to rest there a second or two, as if she were listening to his heart—then stroked it swiftly down his belly, then his right leg.

"Move out," she said, and Bauman went up the steps to have his name checked off the black hack's clipboarded sheet. Passing through a heavy-barred slide gate—another hack perched beside it in an armored booth—Bauman was permitted to climb two flights of stairs, behind Edwins and his small bouquet, to the double doors into Visits.

"Charlie, have you been in a fight?" Susanne—who'd slid through the large room's ructious tides of young women, old women, jittery children and convicts to reach him—stopped just at arm's length, examining his slightly swollen nose, some minor bruising. She'd put her long light-brown hair up into a French knot, showed snowy tender skin just behind her ears where the hair had been lifted away. She wore a heavy-knit white ski sweater, a brown tweed skirt, high brown wool socks and brown loafers. Very coed. He took her into his arms, kissed her lightly. She smelled of autumn and rose verbena. "—Well? Have you? Did you have a fight?"

"No, no fight. I've been very good, sweetheart. Just some sparring with the team." And noticed—had noticed for some time (that phone call from Beth)—how much more smoothly he lied since coming up to State.

" 'Sparring. . . .' Please do me a little favor, Charlie. Don't spar so much, O.K.? It scares me to come up and see you looking so . . . battered. Let these hoodlums beat each other up, O.K.?" She received, for that wifely admonition, an unpleasant look from an older woman, Hispanic, standing just behind her holding a little boy in her arms, apparently waiting for the father's arrival upstairs.

"A little diplomacy is indicated, beautiful," Bauman said, took Susanne by the arm, and steered her back out into the room's center, looking for someplace to sit. " 'Hoodlum' is a no-no. There are some sensitive ladies up here who feel their men have been badly misunderstood, unfairly treated."

"Oh, I'm sorry. . . ." She looked back to find whom she'd offended.

"Never mind. Come on over here." He'd spotted a vacant straight-back chair in a far corner, and towed Susanne that way as quickly as he could without jostling, bumping into anybody.

They edged past two crowded couches, an armchair occupied by one couple, and three straight-back chairs occupied by an Hispanic couple and their two children. The room's furniture was a confusion of worn overstuffed and battered plastic in clashing bright colors—light blue, medium orange, pale pink.

"Are you all right, Charlie? Was that Segregation thing awful? —You know, you don't have to take any crap they want to hand out in here. Bob Christiansen said if there was any harassment, he could try to get you transferred."

"No problem," Bauman said. "—Everything's fine." He led Susanne past a noisy black family ensconced on a battered sofa near the vacant chair—the oldest woman, cheerful, immensely fat, already beginning to produce portions of food from inner pockets of her coat.

Her son, in State's denims, was a lean handsome young man so dark his skin seemed almost midnight blue. His hair had been elaborately corn-rowed, probably by the girls at Sweet Stitches.

"Well, you're very cheerful, Charlie."

"And why the hell not? You're here."

The chair rested unclaimed when they reached it—many inmates and their visitors still greeting in the room's long aisles, hugging, exclaiming, exchanging first long kisses under the eyes of the room's two hacks. One of these, a large ex-farmer named Rossbury, lounged by the visitors' gate, which would be locked at four o'clock, with latecomers out of luck.

Bauman set the chair alongside the wall and facing the back corner, then sat, drew her down onto his lap, and kissed her. Except for the black family across the aisle, whose sofa faced front, he held Susanne in almost privacy.

"Charlie. . . ."

"Is there a problem?"

"No. I just hadn't expected you to be so lively."

"I'm the lively type. How's Braudel?"

"Flourishing, and I think you miss that little monster more than you miss me."

"It's not a question of missing you. It's being only half alive without you."

At which, pleased enough, she relaxed against him. "Well, all right. . . . That ridiculous dog is now on a regular diet of cat food and green beans, any kind of green vegetable. He loves it, gobbles it down and then goes around farting for hours. Really disgusting. And he also comes in the bedroom in the middle of the night."

"Looking for me."

"Don't kid yourself. That's not what that dog is looking for. I woke up Thursday night, night before last, and the little pervert was molesting me. If you ever had a cold nose up your rear end . . ."

"Dare I ask what happened next?"

Susanne punched Bauman sharply on the shoulder. "You creep; you're as bad as he is. Like master, like dog."

"I wouldn't be surprised."

"Anyway, now I wear my pajamas, and I think Braudel is very disappointed. He climbs up on the bed and lies there on his back, farting and whining and carrying on."

"Certainly like master, like dog. And what happened with the amber paper?"

"Well, it seems that Turley couldn't resist the combined bullshit of the Baumans. He said it was O.K. for my thesis."

"A little of my bullshit, a lot of your hard work."

"Oh, listen, I almost got searched!" Susanne enlivened by this near escape, her eyes bright, their green so light, so transparent Bauman had always felt he could see through to the bottom of her, no matter that through that clarity might run fast currents. Beth's brown eyes were one-way eyes, not seen easily into.

"You know that woman guard, the fat one with all the dyed blond hair?"

"Truscott." Bauman amused to find himself annoyed at such careless dismissal of Officer Truscott.

"That's the one. Well, I think she's a little gay. She always looks at me in the strangest way. Well, today she came up and talked to me downstairs—you know, in the dressing room where they're supposed to check people out and search them for drugs and weapons and money and all that good stuff?"

"Right."

"Well, she asked me if I was bringing anything in and so forth, had any drugs or anything, and she made me go through that metal detector thing twice! I thought, Oh-oh, this fat bitch is going to make me take my clothes off. O.K., she didn't do that, but what she did do was search me. And I mean *searched* me. Those fat little hands of hers went all over." Susanne bent closer, murmured in Bauman's ear, "Squeezed my tits. I mean played with them. . . ."

Bauman had the odd notion that fat Truscott—erstwhile stern wrestling opponent and ticketer—had deliberately attended Susanne downstairs. Had admired and fondled her as might in the past an old nursemaid play with a young bride put to bed for her wedding night, or a harem mistress tease and stroke one of her charges to arouse her, warm her for fucking—as if Truscott, fat and aging, and distanced from him by a gulf of authority, might participate in whatever furtive sex they managed here, by proxy.

"I think," Susanne said, "—I think the fat lady is in love." She settled comfortably on Bauman's lap, her slim left arm resting on his shoulders, her buttocks, fairly narrow for a woman, fairly muscular, softened against him, relaxed. Truscott's attentions below, loneliness, three weeks' absence or the visiting room's atmosphere—heated, noisy, vibrant with notions of limited time, of closeness, of sex—had left her restless, anticipatory.

"I brought the money," Susanne said, murmuring the secret into

Bauman's ear. "Thank God that fat lady didn't decide to really get to know me."

"I'm sorry I had to ask you."

"I didn't like it the first time. I suppose I was a real pain about the sacred precincts of my body."

"They are sacred precincts."

"Well, the precincts were holding a hundred and fifty dollars—I brought two extra twenties and a ten—all neatly done up in a little red balloon. And just removed in the ladies' john."

She glanced at the hacks talking in the front of the room, turned on his lap, pretended to adjust her skirt—and from some pocket palmed a little packet and passed it to him.

"—Was that professional, or what?"

"No question it's a developing talent," Bauman said, and slid the thin roll of rubber down under the top of his left sock. "Thank you, sweetheart."

"Least a con's squeeze should do."

Bauman smiled and kissed her, settled her comfortably in his lap, and said, "Give me some other news. How's Pete Quintana doing? Tobey, Chu, the old crowd. They've been very unsatisfactory correspondents."

"Pete asked about you. He wanted to know if it would embarrass you if he came up to visit."

"Asked about me when?"

"At the Youmans'. They had a dinner party, and Pete came over and said, 'I hope Charles is managing to get through this all right.' And I said, 'You bet he is,' and he said, 'Do you think it would embarrass him if I were to go up to visit—if it's all right for just a friend to visit him.' "

"And you said . . ."

"And I said, 'No, it wouldn't embarrass him. What embarrasses him *for* his friends, is that they've proved to be such a bunch of assholes.' "

"Result?"

"A kind of saggy grin, a nerdy little chuckle, 'Heh, heh, heh,' and a really presto departure for the bar."

"Bar? What bar?"

"In their house. Mildred had Donald tending bar in the breakfast nook. Donald's happier with a table between him and the world, anyway, and if the table's got some booze on it, all the better. Oh, and MacClaren's the new dean of humanities."

"No surprise," Bauman said. "—At least he's competent. When did it happen?"

"Conway retired."

"Really retired?"

"That's what everybody says. Ed knows everything that happened, of course, and he said Conway wanted out, and the president said, 'Fine. Goodbye.' "

"It would be nice to have a faculty committee someday that did more than kiss Daley's ass."

"When you get out, Charlie . . ." Susanne bent to kiss him, not as concerned as usual about being observed.

"When I get out, beautiful, it's going to be job-hunt time—and not at Midwest."

"Oh, Charlie, you know I think you're wrong about that. I really think you could get back, if you wanted to. They'd have to give you something."

"No, sweetheart," Bauman said, "—they don't have to give me something, and they won't give me something. For more than a year, Midwest has breathed a sigh of relief to have my nasty little mess over and done with. And believe me, they're not about to have it brought up again."

"Well, I think you're wrong."

"I know you do, and it's wishful thinking. This . . . event has changed my life. Changed our lives. We're not going to be a comfortable faculty couple at a first-class university. Not at Midwest, and not anywhere else really good. —Maybe we'll be something more interesting. Maybe not."

"Charlie, I think they will take you back. I think you underestimate people."

"I think I estimate them quite accurately. And . . . and I'd really rather you didn't go around the campus like mad Carlotta, trying to get Midwest to adopt their troublesome ex-con—because, believe me, they ain't a goin' to do it."

"Well, we'll see."

"To our sorrow. Now, a more immediate subject—your happiness."

"I'm fine."

"Do a little better than that. Just how fine are you?"

"Charlie, I'm getting along all right. I go to classes, and I have my friends, and I work, and I wait for you to get out of here. It just kills me that we're losing this time. That's the only thing that really, really bothers me."

"But otherwise O.K.?"

"Otherwise O.K. But Charlie, what about you? You put on a big act—except when you get jealous and think I'm screwing everybody we ever knew—you put on a big act that this is all just some exotic adventure or something, and you pretend to be so casual, and I know you really don't feel that. Like this afternoon, when I come up here and I know you had a very bad time—and I do know that, because when a place like this punishes somebody, it *punishes* them. And this afternoon you act as if you're doing just great. You act like a kid in summer camp, as if you just won a baseball game or something!—I know you're trying to help me, Charlie, and cheer me up, but I'd really rather you didn't put on this act. Because I know you're not happy, you're not cheerful, it isn't a big adventure. And I want you to stop pretending for me, because I don't believe it, and it makes me imagine this place must be even more horrible than it looks, for you to have to pretend like this."

Bauman, feeling at least cheerful, if not precisely happy—and pleased with what had certainly been an adventure just accomplished—found himself changing his expression to one more mournful, appropriate to his situation.

"I think you're right," he said, "I have been playing it a little too casual."

"A little too casual?"

"All right. I've been terrified every day I've been up here. I'm heartsick at what I've done to both of us. And I'm even beginning to feel sorry for that teenage idiot I ran over."

Susanne sat still in Bauman's lap, leaning close, staring into his eyes as though letters might be forming in their pupils, making words, complete phrases that might be read and understood.

"That isn't exactly what I had in mind."

"Tears?"

"Maybe tears. Tears might help. It just worries me that you're so on guard, Charlie. As if you 're more scared of me than you are of this awful place. As if you 're afraid I'll find out something."

"That's your youth showing, beautiful. All men are afraid women will find out something. And women always do. —As to my apparent contentment, that's probably only pleasure at seeing you. Forgive me a little joy on these occasions."

"My joy too," Susanne said. "My joy." She turned in his lap to hug him, then kissed him, wife to husband, sweetly as if there were no one watching. It still seemed strange to Bauman to think of Susanne as his wife, easier to think of her as Susanne, as herself, as this particular young treasure of delicacy, sweet odor, and limber strength held in his arms. Difficult to think of her as his wife. He supposed, when they let him out of here, he'd have to explain his star of burns to her, be scolded for not having told her of it when it happened. Then, of course, he'd be able to relate the Tale of the Knife, and how he held Becker on its point against the elevator door.

"You son of a bitch! —You white motherfuckah!" So sudden and ferocious a cry that the Baumans and all other visitors and inmates turned to stare at that far side of the room. The two hacks jumped alert, started trotting toward a toppled card table where a huge black man in inmate denims struggled with a small, almost elderly black woman very correctly dressed, as if for rural church, in a tidy dark polka-dotted dress.

Bauman saw it was the heavyweight, Clarence Henry, handling the small woman, restraining her as she lunged and screamed her insult again, staring right across the room. Might have been staring at any of the two dozen men and women near Bauman and Susanne. *"You dirty motherfuckin' white motherfuckah!"*

It was the small woman's last comment. In a concert of masculine action, status as hack or con momentarily irrelevant, Clarence Henry and one of the hacks, murmuring to calm her, half lifted and carried the woman—first still, then struggling, trying to kick, whooping, gathering air for more screaming—to the visiting room's far double doors, and through them and out.

"What . . . what in the *world?*" Susanne's inquiry an unconscious and endearing echo of how many older, decent and proper Indiana ladies—her mother and grandmother certainly. Beth would have said nothing. Would have sat still on his lap, staring after the scene of action with watchful brown eyes, as if *her* mother and grandmother (cautious women of unpredictable men) watched through her, waited to move until certain the trouble was over, trouble having such a predilection for anticlimax.

"Just an entertainment," Bauman said. "—And it's all over."

"God, she was looking right over here!"

"At some ghost or old enemy. Don't worry, sweetheart." Bauman kissed Susanne's ear. "Inmates and their visitors tend to be fairly romantic personalities, not notable for restraint. State's full of marvelous beasts with their fur on inside out."

"Charlie, that's exactly what I mean. You sound as though you're enjoying this—these people."

"I do enjoy them. I like seeing human fundamentals unconcealed. It's very refreshing, after Midwest."

"Refreshing?" Susanne looked startled, stared at Bauman as if he'd just lost a tooth.

"Too bizarre?"

"You bet. Charles, it really is."

Bauman recalled very specifically—in detail including a penetrating odor of ammonia, the sound of a radio jazz program from the jailers' office—recalled his first prison conversation with her, in city jail almost a year and a half before. Susanne, in a visitor's folding metal chair, had watched and listened as Bauman, behind his shield of spit-smeared Plexiglas, talked with her on the telephone. Already, after only hours, the accident—even as accident—had seemed much too complicated to discuss with her, with anyone. Seemed to require half a lifetime of learning to comprehend at all. He was reminded, by that, of the much more than physical barrier unbreachable between them now at State. It seemed to him he swam in an ocean, immense, tumultuous, monstrously inhabited, stormy and becalmed by turns—while Susanne stood distant on the sun-struck beach of a continent of pleasant choices . . . calling to him, then turning her head as she stood barefoot in hot sand, to hear what reply this merman might make shouting from out beyond the breakers, through the surf's roaring separating sound.

Bauman held Susanne as tightly as he could without hurting her, felt the cushioned give of her moderate breasts, felt slender ribs shift slightly under his arms, felt under his hand the neat narrow columns of muscle that in the incurve of her lower back trenched the sides of her spine. He closed his eyes against the room's watery fluorescent light, and concentrated on a kiss that approached Susanne's lips in a measured, unhurried manner, grew reacquainted with her, proceeded very gently along her mouth, rediscovering—felt with the tip of his tongue—the faintest, softest burr of down above her upper lip.

He breathed her odor in as he kissed her, her scent as great a pleasure to him as the touching. There was an odor beneath her milky breath's, beneath the verbena (a toilet water or perfume) at her throat, behind her ears. Beneath these, and warmer, drifted the faint sweet animal odor of her skin.

He felt the fine long muscles of her back move as she shifted position in his lap while he kissed her, touched the right corner of her mouth with his tongue—tickled there until her mouth, slowly come to agreement, grew softer, richer, slacked to allow his tongue to slide into her, slide out. Slide slowly in and out of her again, and then another time, until Susanne pursed her lips to make an echo of her cunt for him, allowed his tongue to force that wide so she had her mouth full, was breathing softly through her nose.

Reaching down with his left hand—his eyes open now, while hers were closed—Bauman lightly lifted the hem of Susanne's skirt, reached above the top of her high wool sock to stroke the faintly rough skin of her left knee. When, after some moments, he felt the muscles of her back relax again, felt her teeth on his tongue, heard her breathing deepen, catch with a little snort of warm air against his cheek, he slowly slid his left hand higher, onto the round smooth-muscled polish of her thigh, and stroked there until she made a sound in her throat, put her hand down on her skirt to find his through it and hold it still.

Bauman took his mouth from Susanne's, let her breathe and rest. His hand held still beneath her skirt by her grip above it, he scratched gently, idly, at the skin of her thigh—so fine in texture it might have been warm glass. Then kissed her again, kissed her as if this were all he intended. All he intended to do.

"Do you love me, Charlie?" This whispered in his ear.

"Every day," Bauman said. "Every night." He kissed her and saw her eyes were still closed, as Cousins' had been when he rested in Manny Elk Antler's arms.

Shifting his position slightly, he slid his right hand down behind her, between her rump and the wall's cool plaster to gather her skirt's material. He worked his fingers, then his hand beneath it, and gripped her right buttock's smooth resilient muscle, slightly slippery under her panties' cotton.

"*Don't.*" Susanne said.

"Shhh. No one can see."

When she stayed sitting slack against him, her lips willing enough to open wide as they kissed again, Bauman lifted his right hand higher beneath her skirt, found the back of her panties' narrow waistband, and with some effort, shifting her slightly on his left knee, holding her up, managed to tug it down, uncovering the cool soft solid rounds of her buttocks.

Susanne murmured something into his mouth—a protest, a request. Bauman bit her lips, licked them, then lifted her a little off his lap and slid his right hand down between her buttocks, rolling her panties farther down, past the smooth closure of her thighs; then he drew his hand back between, turned his palm and fingers up to cup and hold her.

"Don't do that." Having taken her mouth from his to say it, she opened her eyes, sat up in his lap—and looking at the busy bedlam of the room, saw no one interested, none observing.

"No one knows," Bauman said, and held her still, sitting on his still hand.

They sat together, companionable, watching the black family—at an angle a few feet away—happily noisy, jammed together on their weary sofa, enjoying a contraband picnic. Three squirming young children—a girl no more than nine, two small and active boys, much younger—rested uneasily on the grownups' laps.

It was certain that the central figure, a woman massively weighty and black as a Steinway spinet, was the inmate's mother. Certainly she had magisterial authority, was now distributing cold breaded pork chops, large squares of cornbread, and plastic-wrapped wedges of some sort of dark pie, perhaps pecan or sweet-potato. Certainly Southern cooking. It was the first considerable meal Bauman had seen smuggled into Visits, and he assumed that while some of it had been concealed about the lady's person, other portions had been hidden on each child.

"Come on, lean against me," he said to Susanne. "I want you leaning against me."

As if that was what she'd waited to hear, Susanne relaxed against him with a sigh, said, "Don't," again, though he'd done nothing further, and closed her eyes as if the room's heat and clanging radiators, its hubbub, calls, and conversations were making her sleepy.

Bauman sat fairly content under her weight, weight at once light to bear and solid enough to satisfy as to its value. A particular point of value, representing the rest in concentration, lay warm, filling, and furry in his palm—was pressed down into his hand so intimately he could feel, or imagined he felt, a damp kiss at its center.

One of the black family's children—a blue-jeaned little boy of four or five—had climbed down from a lap and now wandered the narrow aisle, a half-eaten pork chop held in his right hand. The child was wearing his winter coat—a hooded article, electric blue with fiercely yellow fleece for lining.

Watching this child, Bauman was suddenly reminded of one of Philly's attempted escapes, prompted one evening by the regulation of bedtime. Four years old, he'd sallied out the back door into the yard to be gone forever—only to stand captive in the back porch's light, fenced firmly in by surrounding dangerous dark, where anything might be. As this child carried food, so Philly had gripped an unpeeled banana, nourishment for the long journey—its direction unknown—all the way to Beth's mother's house.

The small black boy—sensing Bauman's attention, some attendant warmth—trotted over as if he'd been called, and stared up at the two of them.

"Louie," the large woman said, "don't you bother that man."

"That's all right," Bauman said, nodding to the inmate, apparently the child's father. "I've got one of my own." And was worried, once he'd said it, that the black woman might take the subject up and say, "An' your boy don't come see you? His mama don't bring him up?" —while looking with some disapproval at Susanne's lack of escorting children, her youth, her paleness, her probably selfish slimness.

But the large lady said nothing further, merely stared at Bauman as her inmate son did, direct and quickly judging glances that then drifted away, back to their food.

Bauman and the little boy looked at each other, Bauman sensing by a movement of Susanne's head that she was watching the child as well. The boy's coat seemed to Bauman much too warm for him to be wearing indoors, almost a guarantee of a cough or cold. Already the child sported a clear narrow track of snot descending from his right nostril.

"What's your name?" Bauman said. "Louie?"

"My name Mahmoud."

"Didn't I hear that lady call you Louie?"

"Louie my ol' name. My granny call me Louie, but ain' my name."

"O.K. I'll call you Mahmoud. You hot with that coat on, Mahmoud?"

"No."

"He won't be takin' that coat off," the large woman said, her voice a little raised over the room's noise. "Don't waste your time tryin' an' talk sense to that chile. That's his new coat, an' he ain' goin' take it off till he gets tired of it."

"Is that true?" Bauman said to the boy.

"I ain' takin' it off."

"What about when you have a bath? You can't wear your new coat in the bathtub. You'll ruin it."

"Yes, I can."

"No, you won't," the big woman said. "Now come on away from there an' leave that man and that lady alone. They don't want to be wastin' time foolin' aroun' with you."

Mahmoud, not finding enough amusement in Bauman to disobey, turned and walked away, his half-eaten pork chop held firm in a small slightly raised right hand.

Bauman, perhaps by the pleasure of speaking with a child again, was reminded of the elevator's unpleasantness. Easing Susanne in his arms, he looked around the room as he certainly should have looked before, to see if Becker or his men had also come to visit with loved ones. He imagined Becker—tall, tough-looking, his nose swollen, discolored—come into the room to greet a thin, pretty blond girl (wearing glasses, and seeming too gentle, too young for him) bringing their little daughter with her, for Becker to hug and play with. Or Elk Antler come up to greet harder articles, his slight father, a weightier uncle—both very evidently Indian, both at ease in the visitors' room, recalling many visits, recalling being visited themselves.

Bauman looked around carefully, waited for two or three people across the room to stand or sit to clear his line of sight, but saw no Becker, no Indians come up to visit this afternoon. Then, having checked for those enemies, he thought of his others, and looked around the crowded room for Jack Mogle, and for Les Kerwin's distinguished graying hair, the *pro pers'* professional lawyerly air, his sharpened bedspring wire.

Susanne sighed, whispered, "Back-seat lover," into Bauman's ear, and kissed him. "You better unhand me."

He felt her slightly shift position as she sat, and used that change to curl his middle finger beneath her bottom, stroke his fingertip gently back and forth to find through fur a small irregularity that, delicately touched, very slowly opened enough to allow only the tip of a finger.

"Don't, Charlie. Please."

"Shhhh." Bauman kissed her—and tired of waiting, lifted her a little on his lap, used the first and third fingers of the hand beneath her to spread the lips of her cunt slightly apart, gently found the giving place, then slowly thrust his middle finger up into her, into a slippery warm world, and out of this one.

"*Charlie* . . ." She was frowning, her eyes still closed. The finest film of sweat shone on her forehead. "Please, Charlie, I don't want to do this where people can *see*."

Bauman found himself with two Susannes—the one above, sentient, observing, her request resolved out of contradictions—and the Susanne below, mindless, powerful, and direct, a furred mouth (wet and gripping) that cared for nothing but his finger.

"Please don't. . . ."

The voiced Susanne prevailed, and Bauman slowly slid his finger out of her, lifted her to find her panties' waistband and tug them up over her buttocks, then took his hand from beneath her skirt.

She kissed him, murmured in his ear. "Charlie, I want to. I'll go into the bathroom with you. Just not out here."

Bauman sat holding her on his lap, painfully erect beneath her, but not too disappointed. The room seethed around them with a continuous minor uproar of conversation, complaint, and celebration. Children, growing bored, chased and scurried under the pale blue-white of its buzzing fixtures. More than twenty couples sat close in kisses and fondling, or huddled in the back row of chairs. In the front of the room, two long lines had already formed—one for the cons' toilet, the other for the visitors'. The second hack, a young man named Tornquist, was trying to keep track of both lines, trying to prevent husbands, wives, lovers from going into either room together. Tornquist stood in a swirling welter of strained faces and restless bodies, as the two lines, broken here and there by running children, coiled and stretched as if the sexual tension they contained had brought them to life—turned them into immense snakes, each seeking to copulate with its companion.

"Charlie . . . ?"

Bauman looked into Susanne's flushed face, and kissed her, her mouth soft and moist as something to be eaten warm. He smelled the odor of her sex—sharp as fish-glue on his fingers, faintly rank as a vixen fox's, so suited to her face's delicately vulpine cast—and thought it no wonder Braudel had been attracted as if to a goddess bitch. He kissed her again, and considered the effort required to leave the chair and wend through the noisy room, then buck into those toilet lines towing a wife, eager or reluctant, as other men were towing theirs. Then to wait, maneuver, wait once more for the hack's possible distraction, then separate to join again in a toilet, to hope for an empty stall.

"Charlie, I'll go in with you."

"Oh, the hell with it," Bauman said. Then, concerned she might ascribe this reluctance to the fatigue of age, an approaching impotence, said, "You seem a little too special to me this afternoon, to be subjected to that cattle call."

"I don't mind, Charlie. Really I don't."

"But I do mind," Bauman said. "I'll masturbate later, to the memory of you."

Dinner was creamed chicken, white bread, mashed potatoes, and either spinach or some other green—these difficult to differentiate by taste. The mashed potatoes were the dinner's prize, particularly since Gottschalk had made a gravy for them that tasted not bad at all.

The creamed chicken was largely a loss, spoiled for many of the men by the discovery a burglar named Andy Cantrell had made a few weeks previous as part of his portion—a small knot of odorous feathers, an open beak (its tip clipped splintered-short by the farmer when this bird was young), and a single blank blue eye.

Scooter accepted Cousins' portion; Perteet was pleased with Bauman's. Bauman ate his mashed potatoes, the greens, and four slices of bread.

Dinner, otherwise, was not notable. Cousins, right eye now surrounded by bruise purple, asked politely if Bauman had had a good visit—was told he had. And no applause was heard for the elevator incident, for Eddie Becker's injury. That was almost certainly still secret, and if ever known, was likely to be regarded as not the sort of event to be publicly celebrated. Even so, unappreciated, Bauman found himself eating his mashed potatoes and mysterious greens in a sort of rosy anticipation of night and lights-out, in which warmth, relative privacy, relative safety, he might take the day to bed with him as Braudel would a fat bone to cherish and chew on, review and enjoy its riches—Lesnovitch's hideaway (and his exotic maid), the fight with Becker (for it had certainly been a fight), and the curtailed pleasure Susanne had provided (her odor still evident on his unwashed fingers).

A single day's adventures any square john might envy. And the day not over yet.

"Man, you gotta be kiddin'."

"No, we're not kidding, Hector," Bauman said, keeping his voice down. And since the canteen line was already beginning to form behind them, added, "We need to come in there, have a little privacy."

"Fuck you, man. You ain' gettin' in here. Nobody gets in here, man—an' I open up in ten minutes, so you jus' get your ass outta here an' get lost." Hector Ramos stood guard behind his Dutch door, top half swung open, his elbows braced on the lower half-door's serving shelf. He was a tall potbellied man, brown-skinned, brown-eyed, balding—but extremely hairy otherwise, his forearms densely furred, a thick black pelt erupting out of his open shirt collar.

Ramos was manager of the canteen, had held this important position more than three years, an almost unheard-of duration for any inmate, let alone a Latino. This assignment, word was, by courteous agreement among the clubs, a bone to the Zapatistas.

"Hector." Cousins, beside Bauman at the doorway, reached out, put a persuading hand on Ramos' furry forearm. "Vargas says O.K. We just need a few minutes."

"Honey, look—don' bother me, all right? I got ten minutes to open up, an' I don' have time to screw aroun' here."

"No time?" Cousins left his hand where it was. "—Not for a friend?"

"Come on, Lee, give me a break. Ain' nobody gettin' in back here, an' that's that. I let you in, everybody's goin' to wan' in, an' I'm goin' to start losin' stuff."

"Bullshit," Bauman said, wondering if Cousins intended to keep his hand on the man forever. "Why don't you just cut the crap and open the door?"

"Hey, man, who the fuck you think you're talkin' to?"

"Charles," Cousins said, "give us a minute, O.K.?"

"You got it. . . ." Bauman turned away and walked across the basement corridor toward Cernan's phone stand. He supposed he was sulking over Cousins' attempt to persuade. Foolish, since it was the only weapon in the boy's arsenal. The revivifying impact of Gottschalk's mashed potatoes and greens had faded, and Bauman felt a general ache throughout his muscles, if not particularly in his lower back. A little old, apparently, to be playing with knives.—Possibly too old, as well, to play the proper stud with Susanne, for whom effort was still the least consideration in any undertaking.

Cernan was already at his lectern—consulting, as usual, his loose-leaf notebook's tangled schedule of evening long-distance calls incoming, and the very few time-and-phone reservations for outgoing calls, these almost always in reference to some medical emergency outside—a dying mother, wife, child.

"Professor, what can I do for you?" The portly confidence man had a very pleasant and confiding air with everyone, as if he and they had already met earlier in the day, discussed some important and humorous subject, and come to an agreement on it. Bauman, reminded how socially effective Cernan's signals of approval and comradery were, found it difficult to imagine a jury rude enough to have convicted him.

"Phone going to be free in the next half-hour or so?"

"Oh, lord. We are swamped." There was already a short line, callers on all four instruments. "Swamped. But let me see, let me see what I can do for you. . . ." There followed rapid leafings back and forth through his notebook. "Tell you what. I'll tell you what." He stopped at a page, studied with particular care an entry at the bottom. "Shurtliff just got on three. Now, as soon as he's off, Mason is on—and after that I believe we'll have a few minutes if Don Keagan will allow it. Really his time."

"Then if Keagan says all right," Bauman said, "—I'd like to reserve that time. Short call."

"If we can do her, we'll do her," Cernan said, and twinkled at Bauman like a department-store Santa.

"*Charles*." Cousins, across the corridor, beckoned to him, then followed Ramos through the canteen's Dutch door.

Walls of shelves shrank the canteen's interior into a fair-sized closet. Stacks of cigarette cartons tiled thc wall to the left of the door from floor to ceiling. A small cash register and infinite colors of candy bars rested on shelves to the right of the door, and the wall bins above them held stacks of State T-shirts in red, black, and green, along with State baseball caps and racks of bags of corn chips, tortilla chips, pork skins, peanuts, and popcorn. The back wall sported stick sausage, cans of tamales, peaches, Vienna sausages and sardines, and display cases of lighters, pencil flashlights, pens, writing tablets, transistor radios, and watches. Bauman saw two Timex Triathlons—and an empty space beside them where his watch must have rested when Schoonover came to the canteen door seeking a present.

Hector Ramos, discontented, sat on the canteen's freezer chest, a small white metal island filling the center floor space, and containing a great many ice cream sandwiches, Eskimo Pies, and Fruit Pops.

"Now, man, what the fuck do you people wan'? I got to open. . . ." He consulted a steel black-faced pocket watch. "I got to open in eight minutes."

"What we want," Bauman said, "—is to know if someone is buying a lot more down here than they used to. We want to know if someone's suddenly gotten rich."

"None of my business," Ramos said.

"It would be a real big help, Hector," Cousins said.

"None of my business what a dude buys out of here, honey. I don' pay no attention."

"The hell you don't," Bauman said. "You run a store here, and it's none of your business how much a customer buys? Come *on*."

"That's right, man. None of my business. So, if that's what you wan' to come in here for—"

"Hector—"

"No, no." Shaking his head. "Lee, I'm not goin' to start talkin' about my customers in here. Dudes don' wan' no motherfucker—no offense, honey—they don' wan' nobody talkin' about nothin' they do."

"Hector, Vargas O.K.'d this."

"Honey, I don' give a shit what's O.K. Dudes ain' goin' to go after

Vargas. Any dudes get pissed off are goin' to be comin' after *my* ass." He stood up. "So, I don't wan' to say nothin' about buyin' in here." This last directed at Bauman, spoken from Ramos' advantage in height.

"All right," Bauman said. "We've listened to you. Now, you listen to me."

"Charles—"

"Lee, will you please stay out of this for a minute. Let me talk to Mr. Ramos."

"I ain' goin' to listen, man."

"Sure you are." Bauman meant to step over and take Ramos by his shirtfront, perhaps shake him. But as he stepped forward—looking impatient, perhaps angry—Ramos started back, bumped into his freezer, and the edge of its lid catching the back of his knees, sat suddenly down on it again. His large soft brown hands were raised in a sort of warding gesture, though fisted.

"Charles!"

"Relax, I'm not going to do anything."

"*Cabron,*" Ramos said, started to get up, then didn't. He sat rather erect on the freezer, fists held in his lap as if he were saving them for later.

"Have I got your attention?" Bauman said.

Ramos didn't answer; his eyes were blinking a slow metronomic tic.

"If I have your attention, Hector—let me show you this, first. You heard about this . . . ?" Bauman unbuttoned his left shirt cuff, then pushed his left jacket and shirt sleeves up above his forearm. He picked at the adhesive tape for a moment, then pulled the bandage half off. He'd been worried the scramble in the elevator might have done some damage, but not so. The neat pattern of burns was still scabbed and healing.

"See this ridiculous insignia?" Bauman said. "This star? Believe me, I didn't go through this very painful nonsense to fuck around with you." He taped the bandage back on, then tugged his sleeves down and buttoned his shirt cuff. "Now, if you don't give us the information we want, we're going straight to Jaime Vargas, to Ganz, to Perkins—and we'll get word to Nash, too—that you are telling each one of them they can kiss your ass."

"Man—"

"Then, *then,* when Wiltz comes calling on you, or Monte Fitch, or one of Perkins' people. When that old man of Vargas'—the one with the face like a turtle—when those people come to talk to you, believe me you'll wish to Christ you'd talked to us, instead."

"Hector," Cousins said, "—please. Be a smart guy."

"I'm goin' to get in trouble," Ramos said, looking mournful on his freezer lid, his fists resting in his lap.

"Wrong," Bauman said. "You already are in trouble. Question is, are you smart enough to get out?"

"Hector, all we want to know is, did some inmate get real rich all of a sudden, last couple of months, start buyin' a lot of stuff? That's all we want to know."

"Oh, that's all? Jus' wan' me to talk about people's business."

"That's exactly right," Bauman said. "And I advise you to get to it."

"Hector, did a guy get rich out there last couple of months?"

"You got rich," Ramos said, and to Bauman, "She got rich, man, you wan' to know somebody was spendin' money! You know what she did, man? She come here an' put on account two hundred an' fifty bucks scrip for that old man, Billy Burnside, so he can buy any kin' of shit. An' she buys radios and all kin' of shit. An' I know what she's doin'. She's sellin' that shit short to get street money. That's how rich she is, man."

"Lee . . . ?"

"Mr. Metzler left me fifteen hundred dollars."

"So," Bauman said, "Marty Sarasote wasn't quite such a liar, after all."

"I told you I inherited some money."

"You said 'two, three hundred bucks.' You're full of surprises. All right, Hector, never mind about her. Who else?"

"I don' know, man. Maybe that Murray buyin' a lot."

"Murray who?"

"Is that Fitz Murray?" Cousins said.

"Right. He buys a lot of shit."

"Charles, we can forget him. I know Murray. His people send him money. They got some hack bringin' it in."

"All right then, skip Murray. Who else?"

"Casmaier."

"He's a lifer, isn't he?"

"George Casmaier always has a lot of bread, Charles," Cousins said. "—He's a protection guy, an' he deals, too. Kyle Smith works for him."

"So it's nothing new for him to have money?"

"No. George always has lots of bread."

"That's about it," Ramos said. "An' that Armenian."

"Kavafian?"

"Yeah."

"Same thing as with Casmaier," Bauman said. "Kavafian always has money. You're going to have to do a lot better than this, Hector."

"Shit, man, that's all I know. An' Teppman, he's spendin' some."

"I'll bet he is. In the last few weeks?"

"Spendin' a lot, lately."

"Right. No surprise. And who else, Hector?"

"Nobody, man."

"Come on. Who else?"

"Nobody. —That library ding. He paid out for a thirty-buck watch first thing last week."

"Schoonover," Cousins said.

"Forget it." Bauman displayed his watch. "It was a present for me. And he couldn't really afford it."

"Then give us another name, Hector. Please?"

"That's it. I got to open up, man; I got customers out there!"

"One more name," Bauman said.

"That's it. Ain' nobody else come down here spendin' more'n usual, man. Maybe that Ferguson. He's spendin' pretty good. I heard he put in for a new TV, a VCR an' all that shit."

"Ferguson. . . ."

"Sonny Ferguson?" Cousins said.

"No, the other one. An', man, that's a dude didn' have a pot to piss in, man. Big deal for that asshole to come down an' buy a bag of corn chips. Thinks he's funny—always sayin' spic, sayin' greaser."

"You're talking about the fighter? Ferguson, the boxer?"

"That's that asshole. Thinks he's a *muy malo*—"

"I didn't think Ferguson was dealing. I don't think he does anything but jock around."

"He don't have no business I know about," Cousins said.

Someone rapped hard on the closed Dutch door, the sudden sound startling.

"One more name, Hector."

"I don' have no more goddamn names. Ain' nobody else throwin' money aroun'. I tol' you what I could, man, an' only reason is them club guys said O.K. Otherwise, I wouldn' have tol' you shit."

Another sharp knock on the canteen door. A muffled "Open the fuck up!"

Ramos stood up from his freezer lid. His fists had relaxed into hands.

"I know that, Hector, and we appreciate it," Bauman said. "We'll keep this to ourselves."

"You fuckin' better, man. 'Cause I'll tell you, other people can go talk to Jaime Vargas. You know what I'm sayin'? You better keep this shit to yourself." And he went to unbolt his serving door. "Why don' the both of you jus' get the fuck out of here." He glanced at Cousins. "I thought you was a lady, man. But you only a whore."

"It was real important, Hector."

"Jus' get out of here," Ramos said, and swung the top of the Dutch door open. The broad flat face and massive upper torso of an armed robber and cop-killer named Bricknel filled the opening.

"What you doin', Hector? You an' him fuckin' Miss Nancy in there, or what? People out here got some business."

"Jus' a minute." Ramos unbolted the bottom half of the door, gestured Bauman and Cousins through.

"Oooh, I think I'm in love," Bricknel said as Cousins went past him. Several men in line behind him laughed.

"O.K. O.K., Mike, what do you wan'?" Ramos closed and bolted the bottom half of the door.

"Gimme a couple cartons of Camels, an' four Mars bars."

Bauman waited until he and Cousins had walked several yards up the corridor to a shallow alcove just past the phones. "Lee—just one more little surprise, like this lying about what Metzler left you. One more like that, and you're on your own. —This whole bizarre playing-detective bit is dangerous enough without my having to deal with a liar for partner. You understand me? For a lot of inmates in here, fifteen hundred street dollars are a very good reason to kill a man. And don't think it doesn't occur to me you might have had Barney Metzler killed just to get your hands on that inheritance—then started all this who-done-it crap to cover your ass."

"If that's what you think—"

"It's one of the things I think."

"I wasn't goin' to talk to you about my money! Charles, you just don't have no idea the kind of big deal money is in here. You just don't get it. It's more important in here than outside! If you get trouble, then unless you're a real big guy, or real tough, you got to have some bread. If you got it, you can buy protection. —But if you got money an' you don't have protection, then you're goin' to lose the money. A con's got cash an' he can keep it, he can buy anything he wants, exceptin' out. An' some walls, some states, you *can* buy out."

"So? Why lie to me? Why not just tell me it was none of my business? Why that 'two, three hundred bucks' bullshit?"

"I didn' know you at the time. Not enough to tell you about my money. An' not enough to tell you it wasn't none of your business, neither."

"Any more lies?"

"No. Now, I won't lie to you about nothin'."

"Wonderful. . . ."

"Somethin' else botherin' you, right?"

"No."

"Then how come you went to push Ramos around? —Tell you somethin', Charles, you better not try an' do that with Teppman, we see him tomorrow."

"I'm not a fool, Lee. I can tell the difference between Hector Ramos and Bud Teppman. And in case you're wondering, I haven't let that elevator scene go to my head. I know exactly how lucky we were up there."

"I hope you do. An' Charles, while we're talkin' this way, clearin' up the air? You need to realize I got some relationships in here. Long-standin', you know?"

"Like with Ramos."

"That's exactly right. You gotta understan' that, or we can't be goin' around together. —You want to know what was goin' with Hector?"

"Not particularly."

"I think you do, an' I'll tell you. I was chippin' in A-block, an' Ramos was a john for me. You know what that means?"

"Of course I know what it means."

"Well, it shouldn' upset you, 'cause it's all over. He was just a client, you know?"

"I understand. I told you I understood. It's none of my business."

"You wanted to know, so I told you. Hector used to come around with stuff from the canteen, stuff he ripped off, claimed damage an' shit like that? An' I'd blow him, or sometimes he'd fuck me. Cost him two cartons, cost him candy an' some other stuff, dependin' if I was high. Sometimes I'd blow him for ten bucks, scrip. He's a nice guy, an' he never hurt me."

"None of my business."

"But you wanted to know, right?"

"No, I didn't."

"Now you're doin' the lyin'. —You think I don't know what guys want to know about me? I know that real good, Charles."

"Let's drop it. You don't lie to me, and I'll mind my own business."

"I'm not ashamed what I did. You get curious, you ask me. Better do that than tryin' to beat up on guys."

"I think we can drop the subject, can't we? Can't we drop the subject?"

"Sure, we can drop the subject. So, tomorrow we go see Teppman, an' we go over to the infirmary, see Tiger."

"That's right. Any ideas from the canteen?"

Two young cons walked by the alcove, both glancing at Bauman and Cousins as they passed. One called back. " 'At's keepin' the bitch in line, dude!"

It was a moment before Bauman realized the remark referred to Cousins' black eye.

"Assholes."

"Some ladies is real jealous of this eye, Charles," Cousins said, smiling. "Figure you're awesome husban' material."

"Wonderful. I have an ex-wife who'd love to hear that. O.K. Getting back to Ramos' contribution. What about Casmaier?"

"Casmaier an' that Armenian are business guys. Casmaier could be would kill somebody, you know, a contract. But he makes real good money just dealin'."

"And if there is a mysterious hired killer, paid from outside, spending some of his big fee? —Who?"

"It was always just a chance to find the guy."

"Who?"

"O.K. Maybe Schoonover. Maybe Ferguson."

"Schoonover bought this watch for me, sent it over to Seg. He has very little money."

"So he tells you, right? An' you don't call him no liar."

"I've known Schoonover a long time."

"You know him up here a year, an' the guy's a crazy ding. I know he's a buddy. He treated me nice, an' he acts like a decent guy. But you got to remember somethin'; he ain't up here for nothin'."

"Not an innocent man, like Metzler?"

"That's exactly right. Mr. Metzler killed some people in his business. But he didn't do that one they got him for."

"So he told you, and he 'treated you nicely and acted like a decent guy. . . .' "

"Right. O.K., I see the point you're makin', Charles. Except I know people in here different from the way you know 'em. You need to give me some credit for that, 'cause it's a fact."

"Woman's intuition?"

"You tryin' to hurt me, you ain't doin' it. Because that's exactly right."

"Lee, I wasn't trying to hurt you."

"So you say."

"Well, I wasn't. —And if I did, I apologize."

"O.K., all right. So, what about that Ferguson?"

"Do you know him?"

"Charles, I try an' stay away from guys like that."

"Well, he's a wonderful boxer. And I don't doubt he'd kill anybody, if it would entertain him to do it. Seems to me, though, he'd be very hard to deal with. I'd hate to try to hire Ferguson to do anything, let alone kill somebody."

"Somebody gave him bread for doin' somethin'."

"So it seems."

"So, we talk to him?"

"Tomorrow. I can see it'll be an interesting day."

"Charles, today was a interestin' day."

"And worth it to you? Perhaps getting killed over who killed Barney Metzler? No second thoughts?"

"You're damn right. Let me ask you somethin'. —You was in hell, burnin', an' a man came an' gave you a glass of cold water, took care of you so you never got hurt no more. You goin' to forget that man, say, 'Fuck him, I got mine'?"

"I suppose not."

"Damn right, not. Guy killed Mr. Metzler is goin' to be sorry he did it. An' that's that."

"Great. . . . All right. Tomorrow, Teppman first."

"Tomorrow," Cousins said, and walked away toward the corridor gate to A.

Cernan, alert to please, saw Bauman coming back to the phones and waved him cheerfully on. "In a minute, just a minute, Professor. Keagan says O.K., so you'll have your phone."

"I appreciate this very much, Mr. Cernan."

"Tony."

"—Tony."

"My pleasure. Always help if I can."

Bauman, at the third phone, dialed Beth's number, heard the phone ring several times, and had just decided she was out, gone to dinner with someone, when the phone was picked up.

"Hello?"

"Philly? It's Dad." Bauman's heart drumming . . . drumming. "Phil?"

Silence. Silence on the line.

"—It's Dad, Phil. I'm just calling to make sure everything's O.K."

No answer to that. Bauman supposed the boy was about to hang up. "—Is everything all right?"

"I guess so."

"No more trouble with that jerk from up here? You know—"

"I don't think so."

"You don't think so. You've seen him again?"

"I don't know. I saw that dooby Chevy van a couple of times, Friday—you know, driving around the school? But I couldn't tell if it was the weirdo or what."

"Did you tell your mother?" Bauman stepped closer to the wall phone, bent his head so he could rest his forehead on its cool steel, slightly warmer black plastic.

"No."

"Well, he won't bother you. He won't come near you or talk to you or anything. I'm taking care of it."

"Is he a friend of yours?"

"No. He's not a friend."

"Great."

"I'll tell you all about it when I get out of here."

"Sure."

"Are you all right? I can't— I can't tell you, there are no words to tell you, son, how ashamed I am to have acted the way I did. This mess. . . . But most of all leaving your mother, leaving you both. There aren't any words for it, it was so bad, such a crappy thing to do. I'm terribly sorry. I suppose it's no big news adults can be so stupid, much dumber than kids."

"No big news. I have to go."

"Right. O.K. Don't worry about the weirdo, I—"

"I won't tell Mom."

"I mean besides that, don't worry about him."

"I have to go."

"Your mom's out to dinner?"

"I have to go."

"Well, if she's out somewhere—"

"I don't think it's any of your business what Mom does. Why don't you— Why don't you just go fuck yourself." And hung up.

Bauman held the silent receiver to his ear for a few moments, then hung up and walked back past Cernan's lectern. " 'How sharper,' " he said to the confidence man, " '—How sharper than a serpent's tooth . . .' "

Cernan, who frequently saw men come from his phones in tears, shook his head in commiseration. "Sad, but true," he said.

Chapter ELEVEN

Breakfast was powdered eggs, hot chocolate, and toast. The chocolate tasted unpleasant; a sort of gritty sludge ran beneath the surface of the liquid onto the drinker's tongue. Perteet had wanted no seconds of it, a rare refusal.

"Teppman?" Cousins, smelling of some scented soap, stood beside Bauman as they dumped the edible refuse from their trays into the mess-hall's garbage cans.

"Teppman," Bauman said. "—And I'm not looking forward to it."

"Meet you at the kitchen gate, after count," Cousins said. His eye looked very bad this morning; the whole area bruised dark blue. "—An' I'm not lookin' forward to it, neither. . . ."

Three-tier on C-block was vibrating to two clashing morning musics—a twanging country-western, and hard rock so hard, so blasting, it seemed to make the tier's steel hum.

Bud Teppman shared a four-man house with two dealers and an older man, a serial killer named Carl Hurlburt, a celebrity at State for his claimed seventeen victims—though only nine of these had assayed-out, their bones actually uncovered by police. Hurlburt, spare, pale, and graying—an affable man, not at all aggressive—possessed an extensive repertoire of old-fashioned traveling-salesman jokes. Months before, he'd entertained Bauman with these while they waited in line at the infirmary for tetanus-typhoid shots, Bauman assuming he'd done the same for the hitchhikers he'd later murdered.

Hurlburt, this morning, lay stretched on the house's left-side lower bunk, reading *Newsweek*.

Teppman, neat in blue denims and white T-shirt, was sitting at a furniture-factory table smoking a joint and working on a delicately intricate model, ivory-white, of a fairy-tale castle. The bank robber, resembling—with his heavy blond pigtail, the naked Oriental girl tattooed on his left forearm—an early-nineteenth century sailor, was absorbed in his construction. This structure of tiny courts, wards, yards, walls, curtain walls, and donjon keep—all made from toothpicks—was topped with miniature toothpick towers, from which bright minuscule banners flew. The model filled the small table almost edge to edge, and rose over two feet high.

After waiting with Cousins in the house's doorway for some time, Bauman flicked one of the door bars with a fingernail. Teppman and Hurlburt heard that faint sound through C-block's uproar, and looked up.

"What do you want?" Teppman said through elegantly coiling pot smoke, then looked back down at his work. He spent nearly a minute carefully dabbing a toothpick tip into the end of a small tube of glue, then fitting the toothpick to almost complete the grating of the castle's miniature portcullis, this half-raised to permit any Lilliputian horsemen passage.

Teppman finished that, looked up.

"Need to talk with you, if it's O.K.," Bauman said.

"About what?"

"The club people have asked us to get some information."

"Snitch huntin'?"

"That's right."

"You're not sayin' I'm one." A statement, not a question.

"No," Bauman said.

"O.K." Teppman pushed his stool back carefully, so as not to disturb his castle, its fresh-cemented toothpicks. "Come in."

Bauman led Cousins into the house, where they were offered no refreshments, no place to sit.

"You're not sayin' ol' Carl's a snitch, either."

"No."

Hurlburt, in his lower bunk, acknowledged this compliment with a negligent wave of his left hand.

"O.K.," Teppman said. "What do you want from me?"

Cousins said nothing, stood a silent shadow at Bauman's right shoulder.

"Bud—"

"Hey, stop right there. You call me Mr. Teppman or Teppman. My friends call me Bud."

"O.K. Teppman, we've been given a job by the club leaders. And to do it, there're some things we need to know."

Teppman, square-built, stocky (Bauman's height, in fact), sat on his stool relaxed as his blocky musculature allowed, and watched Bauman talk—seemed more interested in watching than listening—his blue eyes clear and steady as if he'd been flash-frozen.

"So," he said, "—let's see what you got."

Disconcerted by this, Bauman supposed Teppman might be asking for a fee for cooperation. Then Cousins said to him softly, "Where they burned you."

"Right," Bauman said. "—Right." And now used to the display, unbuttoned his shirt cuff, pushed his jacket and shirt sleeves up, and tugged off his bandage to show his left forearm's stellar brand.

"Any dude did that to me," Teppman said, "God help him. In fact, God wouldn' be able to help him."

After that, he appeared to have nothing more to say, and sat at ease smoking his pungent pot, inhaling slow, almost endless lungfuls, the joint's narrow tip burning as bright a cherry as the straight cigarettes had, when burning Bauman.

"We have a couple of questions. . . ." Bauman smoothed his bandage on, pulled down his shirt and jacket sleeves, and buttoned his cuff. "First, we'd like to know if it's true you're collecting on bets for the lifers."

"That's right," Teppman said, "—I am. An' that means I collect all official booked bets, period, 'cause lifers is the book in this joint."

"I see."

"You got somethin' else, get to it, 'cause I got work to do," indicating by the barest inclination of his head the model castle, fragile and lovely, stacked on his table like a spun-sugar cake.

"Nice castle," Bauman said. "I saw two just like it along the Rhine."

"This one come out of a book," Teppman said, apparently regarding that as superior provenance. "An' I asked you was there somethin' else you want to know."

"Yes. The collecting job—"

"Position."

"—Position. That was taken over from Becker?"

"That's right."

"Did Becker have a say?"

"He didn' have no say to me," Teppman said. "That breed's out, is all."

"And may I ask who made that decision."

"Sure you may ask. A Lifer Club officer made that decision."

"Metzler?"

"He was dead."

"Dead before the decision?"

"I guess so. —Unless they talked it over with him before he was offed."

"And Shupe told you about this, about Becker being out?"

"I was told, an' it's official, an' what else is none of your business. So anybody got any problem with that, they can just come see me about it and that problem's goin' to get straightened out quick. O.K.? You got any more questions?"

"One. Kenneth Spencer, man was killed over in B. Could that have been a collection matter, if the man was betting?"

"That coon never done business with me, so he sure as shit never crossed me. Could have welshed out on another dude, private bet. Could have snitched him a jacket. I wouldn' know. You got any more questions?"

"No."

"No? Sis, there, got any questions?"

Cousins cleared his throat. "Did you try for that position before Mr. Metzler was killed?"

"Yeah, I asked him last year. He told me to take a hike."

"And you let that go?" Bauman said.

"Hey, that position is a organizational position. An' Metzler was a senior club officer. You understand that? An' what the fuck does that have to do with anybody snitchin' people over?"

"It was just a question," Bauman said, "in case some information started leaking to the corrections people about bets and collecting."

"Shit, those C.O.'s do a lot of bettin' themselves. —You get anybody layin' out some tongue, it'll be those Indian motherfuckers lost their work. Those motherfuckers forget they had this country once, an' they got their asses whipped an' they lost it. This is fuckin' white man's country now, an' they need to remember that, just like some niggers need to learn it."

"Well," Bauman said, noticing how much more difficult it was to gracefully leave where one had been unwelcome. "Well, that's all we had. We'll be going."

"Good," Teppman said, hitched his chair back to his worktable, put his joint roach carefully down at the table's edge, and picked a single toothpick from a small square box of them. Then, concentrating, he leaned over his castle like some outrageous pigtailed ogre—grown huge as in the most fantastic tales—and come to crush the fortress and carry away a perfect fainting infinitesimal princess.

"That could have been worse." Bauman, on reaching C-block's Ground-tier.

"It went all right," Cousins said. "I was scared he'd just say, screw you, an' not tell us nothin'."

"And, of course, he could have been lying."

"He wasn't lyin' about askin' for that job. I know he asked for that job two, three months ago, an' I know Mr. Metzler told him no. I just didn' know he got the job now, after all."

"And he couldn't have gotten it by murdering Metzler?" Bauman said. "Putting pressure on the other lifer officers?"

"No way. Teppman's a real hard rock, but he isn't like, you know, like Wiltz is, or Nash. Them people—"

"They're something else."

"That's right. They're somethin' else."

"And so, where are we?"

"I don't think Teppman killed Mr. Metzler, or your friend Spencer, neither."

"Either."

"—Either."

"And not my friend," Bauman said. "—Just an acquaintance. And you're sure about Teppman?"

"If Bud Teppman had killed my dad, killed that Spencer, it would have made him happy to be talkin' about them bein' killed. If he did it, he would've liked talkin' to us about it. Would have enjoyed it—you know?—and not ever admit he did it."

"But the subject bored him."

"Right," Cousins said. "He didn' care one way or another."

"Hey, Teach . . . !" The call, rather high-pitched, almost a yodel, came echoing down from C-block's Two-tier.

Bauman looked up but saw no one shouting, leaning over the railing. "—I agree," he said. "I don't think Teppman killed either man. He simply wasn't interested."

"*Hey . . . Teach!*" Bauman looked up along Two-tier again and saw

Fatty Fanning, denimed but barefooted, waddling in great haste—his fat roiling about him under a billowing shirt—to the circular staircase and down it, making the steel vibrate and tremble, forcing men on the steps to lean back to the rail as he came thundering past.

"Hey. *Hey!*" he called, apparently to hold Bauman and Cousins where they were until he could reach them.

"Hey. . . ." Fanning surged up to them, and having arrived had to pause, panting, to catch some breath to speak with.

"Take it easy, Matthew. We're not going anywhere."

"We . . . we got a lesson. Hey, where you goin'?"

"I'm sorry, Matt. I should have let you know. I don't have time for our lesson today. There're some things I have to do."

"Hey, c'mon! I got my mirror an' everythin' all set up. I got a whole one page I can write right out like anythin', man. C'mon."

"Can't do it this morning, Matt."

"But we got my lesson *scheduled*."

Bauman, confronted by this immense anxious disappointed baby—fat bare feet spatulate and stubby-toed on Ground-tier's concrete—felt an absurd sense of guilt, as if teaching even such students, and so few, and in such surroundings, were all the more important by virtue of their being such students, and so few, and in such surroundings.

"I can't, Matthew, not this morning. But I'll tell you this, you're the best student I've got. In a few days, I'll expect to see you write out that whole page for me."

"Ah, shit. You know McNeil wants his lesson, too. You got people need their lessons on this block, man. —You can't let this shit slide."

"I know that. You're absolutely right. You just give me the next two, three days, then we'll get right back on it."

"O.K., O.K." The fat man turned slowly away, pouting. "I'm holdin' you to that, now. Three days. . . ."

"Matthew, it's a promise," Bauman said, and watched Fanning lumber away back toward the circular stair.

"Best student you got?"

"Lee, let me tell you something. Any man with a severe learning disability has to work about five times harder, learning to read and write. Fanning has put in his time, and it'll pay off for him."

"But not your best student."

"My best student's Wayman Thompson."

"I know Wayman," Cousins said. . . .

Kyle Smith was on C's courtyard gate with Carson, the hack. Carson—sturdy, middle-aged, pale eyes unpleasant behind rimless glasses—ignored Cousins and said to Bauman, "They still giving you passes to run around these blocks?" Then patted him only carelessly, after all, before motioning them out of C and down the steps into the courtyard.

Bauman noticed that these gate checks and pat-downs were bothering him less than they used to—struck him as casually routine, and didn't frighten him, even carrying the knife. He seemed to pass through the prison with greater ease and comfort now, as if the whole complex of granite buildings and spacious yards was becoming territory familiar, his home.

"Infirmary?" Cousins said, as they walked. The block buildings' courtyard, though walled from the wind, possessed its own sort of chill, its air motionless, scented by stone.

"Why not?" Bauman said. "It seems more than a little strange that Burdon should have checked out right after we talked with him. I'd say it was too much of a coincidence, wouldn't you?"

"Oh, yeah, way too much. Had to be somethin' real bad, though, make that dude waste himself."

"I agree, and no doubt we'd be a lot safer avoiding that 'something real bad.' Unfortunately, it's a little too late, now, for good sense to operate." They went up B-block's kitchen steps, through the back door, and into the odor of lunch in preparation.

"Jesus! What *is* that?" Cousins startled by the smell.

"Fish sticks," Bauman said, as they dodged through kitchen gofers up the aisle of ovens and great cooking kettles.

"Doesn' smell like fish."

"Believe me, it's fish sticks."

"Charles, really, you need to come over an' eat in West. That's what we should have done, is had you come over, eat with me. This Gottschalk dude cannot cook. That's just a fact."

"Shhh."

The chef himself had bustled into view, face red as his tattooed hair from the heat of the ovens. "Hey, how's it goin'?" he said, and was past them.

"What I was about to say," Bauman said, "—was, all right, I'm stuck with this so-called investigation, for various reasons. And you want to know what happened to Mr. Metzler. You have an obligation there; I understand that. . . ." They walked out into the mess hall, saw a trio of bikers—Bump, Winchell, and Fitch—sitting at a table against the wall, having coffee, and walked on through the double doors to the basement steps. "—However, if this manhunt starts getting simply suicidal, we may need to figure out a way to cut our losses, satisfy the club people somehow, and try to get out of it alive."

"Charles, I don't want to die."

"I'm relieved to hear it."

Truscott was the hack on B's side gate, and she patted Cousins fairly thoroughly, her fat strong little hands marching up and down that slender body, but, it seemed to Bauman, less roughly than usual.—And when she turned from Cousins, was quite casual, patting Bauman very lightly.

As this sturdy lady touched him, Bauman imagined her touching Susanne the day before, caressing in the name of duty those long, strong legs, the outline of the girl's thighs beneath her woolen skirt. Then, in the privacy of some alcove below the visiting room, reaching up to trace the outline of Susanne's bra, and more lightly still, trail plump fingers over the girl's sweater, testing the softness of her breast under the sweater's softness . . . to barely touch the nipple, almost hold it for an instant between thumb and forefinger. Then pressed her hand against Susanne's belly, and held it there to feel her breathe.

Bauman grew a slow erection as he walked alongside Cousins across East yard, then down through the yard gate into South toward the infirmary. He concluded he'd been a fool not to have fucked Susanne the day before, while she was warm and willing. While she was present.

The trouble of getting into a toilet together, then finding an empty stall, now seemed no trouble at all. The humiliating wait for only the possibility of hurried privacy now appeared simply a delicious pause before pleasure. He could have had her step out of her skirt, pull the white sweater over her head, unbutton her blouse. Could have had her take off her bra and panties, so she stood naked in front of him wearing only her loafers and high wool socks. He might have had her perform, asked her to sit on the toilet, raise her knees, then slowly spread them wide. Have asked her then to masturbate for him until, after a while and a while longer, her head fell slowly back, her mouth opened at last as she panted in slow time to her fingers' liquid fetches.

This fancy left him troubled, and troubled more by Cousins walking silently beside. Lee had, after all, done everything men wanted. Bauman imagined Cousins glancing down, noticing, moving closer, so their arms brushed every now and then as they walked. Imagined Cousins saying, after they'd walked a little farther, "At the infirmary, you want to ask Tiger if we can go in the back? I could help you, Charles. It's somethin' I want to do. . . ."

"I'll pay Tiger this time," Cousins said, confusing Bauman for a moment. "—He isn' goin' to tell us nothin' without gettin' paid. Dude has the heaviest pruno business goin'; I got no idea what he does with all that bread."

"Maybe," Bauman said, and paused to clear his throat, "maybe he bets."

"Charles, Tiger wouldn' risk a dime."

"Ten bucks, street."

"Oh, come off it," Bauman said. "Ten street dollars to see a damn bathroom?"

"That is my price," Tiger said, with some dignity. "—An' considerin' you two was the last people mess with that man before he went, I think it's a damn good price. You got any idea the bullshit I had to put up with yesterday? State cops up here, the A.W. an' all them assholes messin' up my infirmary? I should be chargin' you twenny!"

"We just talked to him, Tiger," Cousins said.

"That the case, sweet thing, I sure as shit don't want you two talkin' to *me*. Ten bucks, street, an' here an' now. . . ."

The patients' bathroom, just off the chronic ward, was larger than Bauman expected. Three toilets ranked down a narrow white-tiled room across from two showers. Three sinks stood in a row to the left of the door. The room smelled of ammonia, was cleaner than most State toilets.

"You keep a clean bathroom, Tiger."

"Teach, that Irma bitch keeps this bathroom clean. I wouldn' touch the mother. We had AIDS dudes losin' everything in here."

"Bullshit. I saw you with Teddy Rawlins' blood all over you."

"That's different, man. That's carin' for a patient. That's a medical thing; a professional risk."

"He hung himself from one of them showers?" Cousins.

"Hell, no. Look, see that gratin' up over the firs' toilet? Well, that's the sucker right there. That stupid shit strung him some line—twine from the furniture factory? Stood on the toilet, strung him some twine up through that gratin', made a knot, put a loop aroun' his neck—an' went an' jumped off that toilet."

"Seems to me," Bauman said, "—a man could change his mind even after he did that. If he could kick himself around, get his feet back on the toilet so his weight wasn't hanging on that line, then he'd be all right. Get the twine off his neck."

"If he wanted to. . . ." Cousins.

"Shit. You see that mother, you know he can't do that shit. That twine? It was dug into that nigger's neck. Once the fool had tied that end up there? An' jumped off? Shit, that twine was dug in *deep*. You couldn' even see that twine. He ain't never goin' get that off."

Bauman pictured Jomo Burdon—weighty with muscle, skin soot-black against white shorts, white T-shirt—strung up on such a slender cord, exploding, spinning, strangling, trying to grip the thin taut line above his head, kicking a silent Cossack dance, bare feet elegantly arched as he strained for the toilet's cracked porcelain, for a chance to stand, to dig into his throat's flesh for that sunken noose.

"Bad way to go."

"You'd think so, man, you saw him. Dude's eyes was poppin', an' I mean *poppin'*. Ol' Irma, she had about all the shit she can take las' couple weeks. Them ladies don't like seein' that kin' of shit. Firs' Rawlins, an' now this stupid son of a bitch."

"When did he do it?" Cousins said. "How come nobody walked in on him?"

"Middle of the night," Tiger said. "Cargill come in here in the mornin', started yellin'. . . ."

"And there was no indication he was upset, that he was thinking of doing something like this?"

"Hell, no! Teach, did I think a patient was goin' to off himself, I shit sure wouldn' have left the mother on the ward. That mother would have been put in the security room, an' I mean quick. An' I wouldn' be axin' Michaelson or Tracy about it, neither. I don't need some small-town doctor be tellin' me how to run this infirmary."

"I can't think of a reason why Jomo'd do it," Cousins said, looking at the toilet, the air above it, as if Burdon still swung there—face a black balloon, eyes a furious devil's.

"And no one saw him come in here?" Bauman said. "Nobody heard a sound?"

"That's it. You got it."

Bauman walked over to the toilet and stepped up onto the narrow curving porcelain rim, balanced precariously in his running shoes. He reached up, was almost an inch short of being able to touch the heavy steel grillwork, its checkerboard of sizable spaces. "How tall was Burdon?"

" 'Bout five-eleven," Tiger said. "I measured that fool when he come in here. A little bit more'n five-eleven, an' about one ninety-five."

"Well, I guess he could do it."

"Oh, he shit sure done it, man."

"Ghostses?" Cousins said.

"What? Listen, you two can jus' stop tryin' to run a line on me," Tiger said. "You the ones talked to the mother jus' before he did it. Ain' nobody else come see him. —You got somethin' to say, you jus' tell me what the fuck is goin' down aroun' this infirmary!"

"Nothing to do with the infirmary, Tiger," Bauman said, and stepped down from the toilet.

"Well, is it this snitch shit people are talkin' about, or what?"

"You really want to know?" Cousins said.

"You goddamn right I want to know."

"O.K.," Cousins said, "—it'll cost you twenty bucks, street."

Tiger—almost as large as Bauman and Cousins together, and looking larger in his spotless whites—stood astonished at such a charge, at being charged at all. "Twenny *dollars?* You have got to be kiddin', sweet thing. I ain' payin' no twenny dollars for nothin'! An' talkin' 'bout askin' questions, you ain' neither one of you ax me the right question yet."

"And what question is that, Tiger?"

"Cos' you two jus' twenny-five—be clued about that question jive. . . ."

"I ain'," Cousins doing a fair imitation, walking up South yard, "—I ain' payin' no twenny dollars for nothin'!"

"Tiger'd be a cheap date," Bauman said, and was rewarded by Cousins' laugh, that very pleasant springing chortle rising alto to soprano—a laugh to be expected from some girl, husky-voiced, surprised by the punchline of a joke.

"And there's something else, Lee," Bauman said, "—about Tiger. I think he's big enough, strong enough, to have taken Burdon in there—or found him in there—and strangled him, then hanged him."

"Charles," Cousins no longer laughing, "—I sure wish you hadn' thought of that one."

"Something to think about."

"I don't think Tiger'd do that. What would his reason be?"

"Money?"

"Charles, I sure wish you hadn' thought of that one."

"Well, probably nothing to it. Just occurred to me. . . ."

Bauman heard other footsteps on the walk, looked up and saw Tony DiMarco—forger and State's artist in residence—walking toward them with Chris Magliotta.

"Hi," and "How's it goin'?" were exchanged in passing, and the two cons went their way.

"He wanted me to pose for him."

"DiMarco?"

"Right. He wanted me to pose for him naked an' all made up an' everything, for a paintin'."

"And you said?"

"I said no. And he said, 'O.K., how about I take some pictures with the camera? An' I'll pay you.' —You know, he meant with me doin' somethin' with a guy."

"And you said?"

"I told him I wasn' that kind of a girl." A fresh laugh at that, Cousins in a merry mood.

They walked side by side up to C, then to the right along the building's front to the fence gate into East yard. Elroy the farmer sat in the narrow guard box, on outside duty again.

"You're going to get pneumonia sitting yard duty all winter, Elroy," Bauman said to him. "What's the problem? You've only worked inside once in the last three months."

"I know it," Elroy said and came out of his hutch to pat casually at Bauman's arms, his chest. "You talk to Captain Vermillier for me, Professor. That's what you need to do. Some of these people, I jus' don't get along with. Some of these people are not my idea of regular friendly people. I'm used to folks would give you the shirt off their backs, you in need. Ain't true in here."

"State's a harsh environment, Elroy. It's difficult for people to remain pleasant."

Elroy—long farmer's face freshly reddened by the afternoon's chill—sighed in agreement, motioned them through without patting Cousins, then retreated to his booth.

"Charles, you want me to carry that shank?"

Bauman, touched by the offer, was tempted. Cousins, after all, seemed almost never to be thoroughly searched, his androgynous aspect apparently discouraging both male and female hacks, Truscott excepted. Though touched, and welcoming the relaxation of knowing it would be someone else taking the double ticket on discovery, going to Seg for ten and ten, Bauman found himself deciding against it. Perhaps out of concern for Cousins, perhaps only reluctance to be deprived of Mr. Hyde.

"Lee, that's a generous offer. But if I want the knife, then I should take the chance."

"Be smarter for me to be carryin'."

"If we were smart, we wouldn't be here."

"Yeah, but even in here, there's smart guys and there's dumb guys, Charles."

"Really? Show me a smart con. Show me one person in here who's really intelligent in action, as well as bullshit."

"My dad."

"Lee, Mr. Metzler's dead. And probably killed by some moron with a grudge, or a bet he couldn't pay off. That doesn't say much for real smarts."

"I understan' that, and I'm still sayin' my dad was the most intelligent guy they had in here, Charles."

"Well, you knew him, and I didn't."

Bauman heard footsteps, soft, rapid, coming up the walkway behind them. He and Cousins turned together, saw a small black man in a gray sweatsuit jogging up to them. They stepped aside as he ran by, taking nice springy high-stepping paces as he passed.

"A lot of in-shape guys in prison," Bauman said, as he and Cousins walked on.

"All they got to do, Charles, run an' stuff. Work out on weights an' get big."

"If they'd work out with books, they might do themselves some real good."

"An' speakin' of that—gettin' smart—you was sayin' you didn't think my dad was all that bright a guy."

"I didn't say that."

"You ever talked to him, you'd know just how smart a guy he was. He could have talked to you on a strictly even basis, Charles. Professor or not. You an' him could have talked on a strictly even basis."

"That, I don't doubt."

"An' he figured somethin' even you couldn' figure."

"Umm."

"Which is, how to get out of this penitentiary."

"Lee, I've heard a hundred ways to get out of this prison. My favorite one is Scooter's. —Make two hundred pounds of black powder, or have it shipped in as concrete mix. Then make a big rocket out of old gas tanks from the truck shop, by welding two or three tanks into one long tube. Pack the rocket with the gunpowder, and prop the whole thing up against the side of the shop, angled to aim just over the wall. Then sit up in front wearing a motorcycle helmet—there'd be a handle welded there to hang on to—and have a buddy light the other end."

When Cousins laughed, his girlhood was almost convincing.

"—No, I'm serious, Charles."

"So's Scooter."

"The milk truck."

"What about the milk truck?"

"That's *how*. It delivers once a week. They drive in full, an' valve out maybe a hundred gallons into steel barrels—old milk, just for cookin', not drinkin'; drinkin' milk comes in them little cartons. Truck drives in, goes over to the truck shop, valves out that little bit, then drives out again. Takes maybe a half-hour, maybe forty minutes. Then, guys roll those barrels over to West mess."

"And nobody checks the truck?"

"Oh, yeah, Charles, they check the hell out of it. They check it comin' in South gate, an' I mean they check it. They got a . . . like a hand dolly, with mirrors? They look all under it with that. An' a hack goes up to that top hatch on the tank, an' opens it an' looks in there with a flashlight. An' he looks in there at that milk real good."

"All right. —That's in."

"That's in. An', Charles, when the truck goes out, they look it over harder. They really look it over—check under the hood, see some con isn' layin' in there on the engine. An' the hack goes up on top, he looks down there with a flashlight a long time, makin' sure some dude isn' in there under the milk, holdin' his breath."

"Sounds to me as if that would do it."

"Well, it wouldn't do it, way dad had it figured."

"O.K. . . ."

"Dad has— He had a buddy, Bruce Toledano. O.K., Mr. Toledano gets to the dairy middle of the night. Milk truck's parked out there right beside the barn, no hacks, no nothin'. Nobody lookin' out for it. An' Mr. Toledano gets up there an' drops two sets of scuba stuff down in the milk; got more'n four foot deep of milk in there. He drops in two little one-tank sets—weight belt to hold you down, that one little tank, an' a regulator an' mouthpiece."

"Jumping Jesus. . . ."

"So, next day the milk comes in, an' the scuba stuff is down under there. Truck pulls in the shop to valve out that hundred gallons. Lot of guys always workin' in the truck shop, screwin' around. —Now, there's one of two ways it could go. It looks good, just one hack around—an' that's the usual—then a couple of guys could talk him away for a minute. Or, if there is more'n one hack at the shop, then in the middle of they're unloadin', two, three guys get in a hassle—

a serious thing, wrenches an' stuff. A bad fight, an' a guy down an' bleedin' and everybody's yellin'."

"And the hacks are busy."

"More'n busy; they're on their radios yellin' for help. An' right then, two cons get up on that truck, an' they just drop down inside."

"Wade around, find the scuba sets."

"—Wade around, find the stuff, an' take their time puttin' it on. Then they go under the milk. Still got almost four foot of milk in there. Stuff all stirred up an' foamin' 'cause of the valvin' out, so breathin' bubbles won't even show."

"Good God almighty. . . ."

"They're under there, an' they stay under. Hacks at the gate check out the truck real good, take their time, especially if the guys had to start a fight over at the shop, make some trouble. Hacks get nervous all over the joint, that happens. Hack goes up with a flashlight an' looks down in there maybe a minute, maybe more, make *sure* a dude isn' in there holdin' his breath. Then, out the truck goes."

"Out it goes. . . ."

"Truck pulls in the dairy, an' Mr. Metzler's friend—"

"Toledano."

"Mr. Toledano is waitin' parked over in the parkin' lot other side of the milk shed. Driver an' them trusties go inside the buildin' there for lunch, one o'clock on the dot, an' Mr. Toledano comes over a five-foot fence, opens the hatch, an' out comes me an' Mr. Metzler with that scuba stuff, and back over the fence into Mr. Toledano's car. An' gone."

"Gone. . . . But why not wait till dark to get out of the truck? Wouldn't it be safer?"

"Afternoons, they take that truck into Garlin, to the bakery in there? An' they unload some milk, an' then they go back out to the dairy, pump out the rest for the pigs. Then they steam-clean that tank. —So, only time to get out is one o'clock on the dot. An' over the fence an' gone."

"Gone. . . ."

"O.K., Charles. What do you think about that?"

"What do I think? I think Metzler figured a way out of State. I really believe—unless we're missing something—I believe he actually figured a way out of State. Of course there could be a problem there, something that could go wrong. But why the hell didn't he use it? Why the hell didn't he *go?*"

"I told him to, but he wouldn' do it. He just wouldn' do it."

"Why the hell not?"

" 'Cause I got maybe another year, an' then I'm out. I'm short time, like you. You know escape'll cost you five years additional, if they catch you? He said it didn' make no sense at all for me to go."

"And he wouldn't leave without you?"

"He was scared what would happen if he wasn' here."

"Well, Jesus Christ. The man's gone now anyway, and nothing terrible has happened to you."

"I got a year left."

"But the man could have been out, unless there's something he hadn't figured with the truck, something—"

"Mr. Metzler figured everythin'. —An' I told him to go. I told him an' *told* him." Tears in Cousins' voice. "But he jus' said, 'After you, my dear.' Every time I said that, he jus' said, 'After you, my dear. . . .' " Tears in Cousins' eyes, too, when Bauman glanced over as they walked. "He was goin' to wait till I was out straight, an' then come out an' we could go to Indiana. Some little town on a river, where they just got farms an' some stores. Lots of trees, right in the town."

"Indiana. . . ."

"An' I was goin' to be his daughter, an' we'd have this little house under some trees, an' I could maybe be a waitress, or work in a store or somethin', an' he could work in the gas station; he was real good with engines. He was goin' to be Mr. Jepson, an' I was goin' to be Lee Anne Jepson, his kid. Mr. Toledano was goin' to get us Social Securities an' birth certificates an' everythin'." Cousins looked over at Bauman, gray eyes any weeping woman's. "—Sounds real weird, right?"

"It sounds like a pretty good life, to me," Bauman said. "A quiet life."

"An'," Cousins took a sighing breath, "after a while I would go somewhere an' get my operation. Then, when I came back, if there was somebody nice, maybe I'd meet a nice guy in the town, get married. An' nobody would ever know nothin'. I'd just be Lee Anne—except I couldn' have no kids an' we'd have to adopt. An' Mr. Metzler would be a gran'father. An' nobody would ever know."

"It sounds like a very good life. —But you're sure you want that surgery, hormones, all that? You know, Lee, once you're out of here you'll have a choice, more of a choice than State's given you. So you need to be sure you want to be a woman that badly."

"I got to be somethin'." Cousins took a small white handkerchief from his trouser pocket, blew his nose. "—An' I sure as shit don't want to be a man."

To which, Bauman had nothing to say.

When they reached B-block's side gate, Cousins said, "Well, I guess you know stuff now, you didn' know before. Right?"

"Right," Bauman said.

Lunch was fish sticks, peas, white bread. Graham crackers for dessert.

While Bauman was trying to save at least one Graham cracker from Perteet, who was desperate for them—had already begged one each from Cousins and Scooter—Kavafian came over to their table, his albino housemate, silent Carlo, tagging along.

"Hear you had some lady trouble yesterday, Teach, up in visiting."

Bauman, confused, thought Kavafian might be referring to his minor difficulties with Susanne—to get her panties down, deal with her in public—all apparently observed and reported. "Not much," he said.

"From what I hear, if she got to you, you'd have had plenty of trouble with her." Kavafian was smiling.

"Kavvy, what the hell are you talking about?"

"The black lady, I heard she was after your ass up there."

"Black lady?"

"Called you a motherfucker, was goin' after your ass, if Clarence Henry hadn't stopped her." Kavafian seemed to think it was very funny.

"I remember that," Bauman said. "—That didn't have a goddamned thing to do with me." Was chilled by the news, though, as if any threatened assault, however misguided or absurd, might here be transmogrified to deadly. "She wasn't yelling at me."

"Not what I hear," Kavafian said. And grinning—an outsider's noisy complaint only an amusing item—strolled away before Bauman could ask his question.

"Who the hell was she? What's this shit about?"

Since Kavafian and Carlo had moved on, the question was addressed to the table, and Perteet, apparently in the know, answered it through a small beige blizzard of cracker crumbs.

"What I hear, that was only that little nig Spencer's old lady. Figured it was you chopped him 'cause he owed you money, is all." He chewed and swallowed. "Ain't nothin' to that shit."

"Jesus Christ, the man only owed me fifteen dollars!"

"Fifteen, street?" Perteet seemed impressed by the amount. "Any cocksucker owed me fifteen white bucks an' wouldn' pay, I'd damn sure cowboy his ass. You was right to do it. —You goin' to eat that cracker?"

"I didn't do it! —And yes, I'm going to eat my cracker."

"Pete, he didn' do it," Cousins said.

"My roomie's a fuckin' professor, man." Scooter's contribution.

"Poor woman's out of her mind," Bauman said. "And I hadn't even done the work yet. I was just going to write a few letters for that idiot. He didn't even owe the money yet; he was just supposed to get it."

"Well," Perteet said, "dude didn' owe it, that's another matter." The huge man's gaze was locked on Bauman's last Graham cracker, a regard fixed and hopeful as a hungry dog's, some animal powerful enough to tear the possessor's throat out, but reduced by gentleness to begging.

"Oh, take the fucking cracker. . . ."

"It's just a mistake, Charles." This remark by Cousins very poor comfort at State, where mistakes accounted for all and everyone.

"Well, I'm sorry for her, but Jesus, who the hell was she in visiting? Henry was over there. —Don't tell me she's his mother."

"She's his aunt." Scooter.

There was a short silence at the table.

"And how the hell do you know that?" Bauman said, remembering as he said it, Clarence Henry's slow storm-cloud frown as he'd spoken to Bauman in the gym showers: "An' worse'n snitches. Killin' folks. . . ."

"Clarence wouldn' think you'd do something like that," Cousins said. "—Off his uncle." Bauman wished she'd kept her mouth shut, as if even mentioning the possibility might make it so.

"Truth is, it isn't funny. I'm going to have to talk with Clarence Henry."

No one at the table commented on that.

"Christ, I work with the man nearly every afternoon. He could have just come up and talked to me about it." No comments. "And," Bauman said to Scooter, "—how the hell did you know Spencer was Henry's uncle?"

"I jus' knew it. I thought everybody knew that."

"I knew it," Perteet said. "That's how come nobody messed with that nerdy little nigger. Scared of Henry, 'cause them's the niggers raised him."

"Charles, Clarence Henry isn' goin' to think you had anything to do with killin' Spencer."

"Lee, I want you to do me a big favor."

"Shut up about it?"

"That's it, you've got it. Thank you very much."

A quiet table for the last of the lunch.

B-block's Ground-tier was busy as a bus station with after-lunch traffic as Bauman and Cousins walked through it—men holding conversations, calling to each other, starting to move toward the circular stair to get up to their houses for lock-'n'-count.

"The troubling thing about this, besides having Clarence Henry possibly break my back for me, the troubling thing about it—"

"Is the guy killed Spencer wasn' worried about Clarence Henry."

"Lee, let me finish my own sentences, all right?"

"O.K. I'm sorry."

A thief named Urngrauer caught up with them, ostensibly to talk with Bauman, though he kept his eyes on Cousins.

"Say, Teach, I was talkin' to a buddy works in property— Pardon me if I'm interruptin'."

"That's all right. Go ahead." Bauman found it more and more annoying to be the cover for cons' oblique conversations with Cousins.

"He jus' got that big watch of yours in there—Rolex?"

"So?"

"Jus' wanted to let you know the hacks turned it in, an' it's tagged an' in your envelope. So they didn' rip it off." Urngrauer was sweating slightly, standing with them by one of Ground-tier's clanging radiators. He was staring at Cousins, tried a friendly smile.

"Tell your buddy I appreciate the news, Barry. O.K.? I owe him."

"Yeah, I'll let him know." And to Cousins, "How you doin'?"

No reply from Cousins.

"You know, Cousins, case you're interested, my buddy got his hands on some real nice shit in that property room, tags or no tags. Jewelry and everythin'. You name it, he can get it, if you know what I mean. Very, very nice stuff. All I'm sayin', you understand, could be just a gift if you're short. Pay later, whatever. No problem."

"Thanks, Barry," Bauman said. "But we have to be going."

"Oh, yeah. Well, I gotta go, too."

"Take it easy," Bauman said, and Urngrauer, reluctantly, with an awkward half-wave of farewell, turned away into the crowd.

"That dweeb," Cousins said, 'dweeb' apparently an ultimate insult. "That dweeb worked up his nerve maybe all day just to come up like that an' talk. An' you know what he's goin' to do now?"

"No."

"He's goin' up to his house, an' he's goin' to jerk off—in the daytime." A grimace at the notion. "Charles, I'll tell you somethin'. I don't know how women can stand it, guys always tryin' that crap on 'em."

"Well, it's all a little more desperate in here."

"Yeah. —O.K. What were we sayin'?"

"We were saying the killer didn't give a damn about Clarence Henry."

"That's it," Cousins said, and had nothing more to add.

"Of course, it's possible the killer didn't know the two men were related. I didn't know it."

"Possible."

"You don't believe it."

"I said, possible."

"You don't believe it," Bauman said, "and I don't believe it, either. Maybe it was a hack, after all. Somebody who wasn't worried about Henry breaking his back, who wouldn't have to worry so much about that."

"Maybe. Or maybe just a con wasn' scared of Henry. —I got to go for count."

"All right."

"Listen, Charles, Clarence Henry's got nothin' against me. Why don't I go over to the gym, talk to him. I'll set him straight you didn' have nothin' to do with waxin' his uncle."

"Forget that. You can just forget that."

"Hey, wait a minute. This is my business too, Charles. You don't tell me what I can do. It makes sense. Clarence Henry don't have nothin' against me. He isn' goin' to hurt me; an' when I'm over there, I can talk to Ferguson, too, see how come he got so rich all of a sudden."

"No way. I *mean* it, now." Bauman seeing again Ferguson's odd abstracted stare—a welterweight cat with a mouse in view—when Cousins, days before, had walked with Bauman into the gym. "Please leave Ferguson alone. Don't talk to him; don't go near him."

"Ferguson? I know he's bad, but he isn' that bad."

"If you'd heard some of the stories he likes to tell on the team bus, you wouldn't get within a mile of him. Look, do me a personal favor, Lee. All right? I'm asking you to please wait, and go over there with me."

"All right. All right, if it's such a big deal. —I don't like nobody tellin' me what to do, Charles."

"I'm not telling you what to do. I'm asking you."

"All right. So we're goin' over after count?"

"We'll go right over. I'll meet you out on East walkway."

"O.K.," Cousins said, "—but I meant what I told you, Charles." And, annoyed, went on his way, Bauman watching that slight figure wending out of sight to the block gate, watching as if Ferguson or another like him was already come ahunting.

"*Charles.*" Betty Nellis, barefoot in vanilla slacks and denim shirt—dyed aquamarine from blue—waved Bauman over to her house.

"I have to go up for count."

"Jus' a minute, jus' a minute. You an' Lee goin' come to the adoption?" Behind her, as she stood in her doorway, Bauman saw a domestic scene. Young Onofrio, the image of adolescence—rawboned in messy denims, his dark hair falling tangled to his shoulders—sat in the Nellises' rocker, staring up at their TV. Marky Nellis, glasses' lenses glinting in that blue light, lay in the upper bunk, propped on his elbow, reading a magazine.

"You two comin'? Goin' be in nine days, over at the chapel."

"We wouldn't miss it."

"I know," her voice lowered, "—I know I had troubled feelin's. But not no more."

"I'm glad. You'll see, everything's going to work out all right."

"It was makin' me angry, you know? But I figured out where them feelin's was comin' from."

"Well, it'll be a change, but you and Marky can handle it."

"Oh, I know that, Charles. I know that."

"I've got to go."

"I'll tell you somethin', you know. You ain' goin' to like me sayin' it—but I'm a little bit sorry I got you an' that Lee together. Nothin' against her, Charles. She's beautiful, an' that's all right. I jus' hope she's takin' good care of you, you know?"

"Everything's fine."

"That's what you sayin' like a gentleman about her, an' I understan' that, Charles. But I see you got beat up boxin' Paco Muñoz, an' I wouldn' have let you do that in a million years, you an' me had a intimate relationship. You understan'? An' Marky's worried about you. He don' tell me nothin' about no trouble now, 'cause, you know, I guess he don' want to worry the boy. An' the boy's always in here, an' that's one of the problems, Charles, I'll be hones' with you. But I can tell Marky's worried about you, couple times I mention your name."

"What did he say?"

"He don' say nothin'. That's how come I know he's worried about you. So you look out, now. Don' go get beat up no more, fightin' over in that gym—tryin' to show that Lee you a young guy or somethin'. You fine the way you are; she don' like that, fuck her."

"I've got to go."

"Don' be mad. I'm jus' talkin' to you like I was your sister—jus' like that."

"I'm not angry, honey."

"So, how come you don' come see me no more?"

He took her plump left hand, held it in both of his. "I've been busy, but I haven't forgotten my friends. I'll come visit, soon."

"O.K. . . ."

He let go of her hand and left her, climbed the ringing circular stair up to Two-tier, stepped off, and walked into his house.

"Look at this shit," Scooter said, recumbent, commenting on the TV at the foot of his bunk.

Bauman leaned against the upper bunk rail to see the President of the United States, wearing a pilot's helmet, sitting grinning in the cockpit of a fighter-bomber.

The count buzzer sounded through the block; a hack below called, "*Fingerrrs. . . .*"

The afternoon, warmed almost to late summer again by bright sun through still air, had brought the population out to stroll and deal, buy and sell along the walkways, to lean against block-building walls observing more active inmates at play out in the yards. Touch football, baseball, Frisbee.

"That was a real bad lunch." Cousins, thoughtful at Bauman's side, halfway across East field. "Them fish sticks was fierce."

"And West mess food's really better?"

"Hell yes, Charles. Clifford bakes bread over there! It isn' real good, but it's fresh-baked."

"Gottschalk's grilled cheese sandwiches aren't bad."

Cousins gave him the ruined-shirt look. "I ate that lunch with you when we had them sandwiches."

"But Gottschalk has a certain style to him."

"Not in front of no stove, he don't."

Sawyer was the duty hack at the gym doors, a very short man, grizzled-bald and burly, one of the few good-humored veterans.

"What is this? Is this love or what? I heard you two was an item."

"We're not an item, Fred."

"So you say, Teacher, so you say, but what does the lady say?" And he patted Bauman very lightly, paid some attention to his jacket collar.

"We're just friends, Fred," Cousins said. "—How's Emmaline? Is she doin' O.K.?"

Emmaline Sawyer had bone cancer, and had been a long time dying of it. The Sawyers were well liked at State, even by savage men, and Emmaline, a retired waitress, had received several presents from the cons during her illness—silkscreened scarves run off by Giant Jerry in the Lifer Club office; many blossoms and bouquets sent by Sanchez; some needlework by several inmates, with embroidered quotations concerning hope, courage, and comfort; and an orange afghan crocheted by a B.N.A. captain, Ronald Baye.

"Oh, Emma's lots better," Sawyer said. "She sleeps a good deal now, drifts off, you know. Then she comes back to me an' she's her old self. Just like her old self." Finished with the jacket collar, he stooped to check the top of Bauman's right sock.

"Tell her we're all prayin' for her," Cousins said.

"I will, Lee," Sawyer straightened with a soft grunt. "Now you two go on, an' behave yourselves. . . ."

There was no one in the gym except two cons—Admin clerks, playing pickup basketball, the vaulted vacant space echoing each dribble, thunk thunk thunk—and Enrique, mopping down the first ring's canvas with hot soapy water and bleach.

"Where is everybody?"

"Afternoon off. Coach figured they was losin' their edge, give 'em the day. Got six more days to the fight."

"Great."

"Goin' be right back here tomorrow. He ain' givin' 'em no two days off—not for Joliet."

"I don't think we better wait to be talkin' to Henry," Cousins said.

"What you wan' to talk to him for?"

"Never mind, Enrique," Bauman said. "It doesn't look as though you got the other side very well; it's still sweat black over there."

"I'll get it." Enrique steered away behind his mop.

"Charles, don't you think we better be talkin' to Henry before tomorrow?"

"Lee," Bauman keeping his voice low, "—I know we need to talk to him. I suppose we should go on over to D, see if he's home. I have no idea where his house is."

"He used to room with Greg Broughton on Three-tier. I don't know if he still does. But, Charles, I can't be goin' up there to D-block."

"You can't go up there? —Oh, all right. I understand, and no reason you should. I'm up there teaching Wayman all the time. It's no big deal."

"You shouldn' be goin' to see Henry alone, but I just can't go up there. Isn't I'm scared. I got— I got a kind of ex-husban' up there. I'm just not supposed to be goin' up there; that was the agreement."

"I understand. Don't worry about it."

"There're some people up there—"

"I told you, don't worry about it."

"It would just cause real bad trouble. We got this agreement I'd stay off D-block. That was the deal."

"I understand that. All right. But in that case, I would like to know— I'd just like to know how you happened to show up in the kitchen with your buddy Colonel Perkins, and his merry men. You hadn't been up to D-block, then?"

"I got Reggie McCann carry in a message for me," Cousins said, leaned against the side of the ring, and waited for an apology.

"Sorry," Bauman said.

"That's O.K. I know you don't trust me."

"I do. I do trust you." Bauman, making the expected reply, found himself enjoying the exchange, the demanded reassurance so familiar from a thousand dealings with women.

"Sure," Cousins said. "—I don't blame you. You don't know me, an' that's all there is to it."

"I do trust you." Keeping his voice down, though Enrique, across the ring, seemed absorbed in his mopping.

"No."

"I *do*. And I know all I need to know about you, Lee. I trust you, but you need to keep in mind this little investigation we're running here can get the both of us killed, but quick. If I check up—then I check up, and I expect you to do the same. It's not a personal thing. And I do trust you; I trust you more than anybody else in this place." Not really true, Bauman realized as he said it. He trusted Scooter more, and Betty; trusted Schoonover more too, provided metaphysics weren't involved.

"You got people you trust more'n me," Cousins said.

"No, I don't."

"Sure. . . ."

"I trust you, and that's that."

"So, what now?"

"All right, let me go over to D-block and see Clarence Henry. I was in the shower with the man a couple of days ago. If he wanted to put me away, he could have done it then."

"But he talked to his aunt yesterday."

"I know, but I doubt if she drove him into a frenzy. If he starts foaming at the mouth, I'll just get the hell out of there."

"An' while you're doin' that, what am I supposed to do? You don't want me talkin' to Ferguson—"

"Look, the only reason I said that about Ferguson is, if you want to know, he gave you a very bad look the time we came over here."

"You got no idea the looks I get, Charles, a hundred times a day."

"I'm not talking about sex. I'm talking about murder. So please, do me a favor and stay away from Ferguson. He's not just another con. He's a special item."

A sigh from Cousins, a dark look around the almost empty gymnasium, as a girl might gaze discontented, bored by her date, wishing her steady boyfriend (the young lifer with the weightlifter's shoulders?) would suddenly appear, rudely order her into his car, and drive away, leaving this dweeb in the street.

"O.K., Lee? As a favor?"

"All right. You want to do all the work, that's fine with me. I won't talk to nobody."

"Fine. Then tomorrow, we can both come over here and ask Ferguson how come he's suddenly wealthy."

"All right with me. . . ." Sullen. Cousins, it seemed, in addition to the martyrdom of beauty isolate in State, also suffered from its occasional opposite, a surfeit of admiration and spoiling.

"—And I'll let you know at dinner if Clarence Henry has anything constructive to say, if he has any idea at all who did kill his uncle. And for what reason."

"I'm goin' over to the library." A pause, apparently to see if Bauman would take it upon himself to object to this visit with mad Schoonover.

"Fine," Bauman said. Then, though he expected trouble for it, couldn't prevent himself from adding, casually as possible, "If he starts acting odd, just get the hell out." Saying this as much to protect himself from guilt over any mischance, as from concern for Cousins.

"Listen," Cousins said, "don't keep tellin' me how to act with people. I don't like it."

"Right," Bauman said. "Just keep your voice down. Perfect. I give a shit if some maniac strangles you to death. So just fucking *sue* me, all right? We're either going to look out for each other during this absolute bullshit *you* helped get us into, or it's 'Fuck you and tough titty,' whatever happens. You want to operate that way? Fine. Just say so."

The beauty stood glowering, silent—a truce, but no surrender. On the far side of the ring, Enrique lifted his wet mop, slapped it down, and recommenced slow foamy circular scrubbing.

On the long walk over to D-block, Bauman savored the familiar comedy of that exchange with Cousins, so like others with women, and with Philly as well, once he'd entered adolescence. Frictions, as protection rubbed freedom the wrong way. Cousins, as they left the gym, had taken the walk's right fork, headed for North yard and the library, and hadn't answered when Bauman said, "See you at dinner. . . ."

And considering protection, as during this visit to D-block, Bauman wondered if it might be possible to see Colonel Perkins, and request an escort to Clarence Henry's house in case the heavyweight had accepted Bauman's guilt, and decided on execution. An approach to Colonel Perkins, however, with the colonel on his home ground, in his house, in the midst of his army, seemed as frightening as meeting Clarence Henry—a fighter, after all, whom Bauman had often commanded in training.

If not Perkins, then perhaps Wayman—who, as a student, should be visited in any case. Wayman for directions, and possibly an escort. . . .

D-block was quieter than ordinary, the afternoon fine enough for many of the men to have wandered out to the walkways and yards, absent with those few others lucky enough to have work at the license plant or furniture factory.

The block's musics this afternoon were appropriately subdued—easy blues, Alabama guitars, and a lively even-tempered rap echoing down the tiers.

"You still comin' around here, Bauman?" Harrison, the hack at D-block's gate. "Let me see that bullshit pass again." He took the block pass and went into the gate office with it, leaving the other two hacks, a stranger and a C.O. named DuBois—tall, black, uncommunicative—to regard Bauman with no sign of interest.

Standing by the gate, Bauman watched through the guard office's yellow armored glass while Harrison, holding the pass, referring to it, made a call. Spoke, listened. Spoke, listened, then put the phone down, came to the guard-office door, and beckoned Bauman in.

"Wants to talk to you."

The armored space, smaller than it looked from outside, smelled of after-shave and cigarette smoke.

"Bauman?"

"Who is this?"

"Lieutenant Gorney, Bauman. I understand you and that Cousins have been asking around."

"That's right."

"I have some news for you."

Bauman apparently supposed to ask what the news might be.

"Bauman?"

"Yes?"

"News is, you and Gerald Burdon—Jomo Burdon? You were both going to be called before the sitting grand jury in St. John's as material witnesses in Kenneth Spencer's death. Was going to be both of you; now it's just you. That will be submitted in about ten days' time. If I were you, I'd move on this real soon and come up with something, or you're going to be too late. Just a word to the wise."

Bauman hung up.

"Hope the lieutenant gave you the word, jerk," Harrison said, and gestured Bauman out of the guard office ahead of him. At the gate, he handed back the pass. "—Here. An' I don't care what kind of a pass you got, you got no business on this block. You keep in mind I got an eye on you, Mr. Wise-ass."

"Wise-ass?" Bauman said. "—Wise-ass? Officer Harrison, I didn't call you a dickless wonder. I didn't say that as a C.O., you were just a sack of shit. If I'd said anything like that, I could understand your calling me a wise-ass. But since I didn't, I don't think it's fair to accuse me of having an attitude problem."

It took Harrison a moment to digest that; DuBois and the other hack got it sooner.

"You get the fuck away from this gate," Harrison said. "I'm goin' to see you again, another time. I'm goin' to see you again, Bauman. . . ."

On through the high white steel gate, and down Ground-tier toward the circular stair—taking care not to jostle anyone walking by, taking care not to trip over the outstretched legs of the few men staying indoors, sitting with their backs to Ground-tier's side wall. At the circular stair, after a courteous wait for three black cons to precede him, Bauman climbed the steps hoping his student—a neglected student the last two weeks—would be home, wouldn't have gone outdoors to the sunny walkways with his immense roommate Roy, or the other two always-absent anonymous.

Someone on Ground-tier was cooking on an illegal hot plate. Bauman smelled the rich oily odor of frying mess-hall meat drifting up the staircase, meat probably breaded with stale toast crumbs, sizzling, smoking in a few spoonfuls of that reliable contributor to kitchen workers' income—a handful of lard smuggled out in a small plastic bag.

Layered over this odor, from another realm of senses, the rap music thumped and rattled along Two-tier as Bauman climbed up to it, the lyric muttering, commenting in rhyme on "the shame . . . of the name . . . of a loser at the game." Of love, apparently.

As he stepped up behind the conversational trio climbing above him, Bauman, recalling the incident of his last visit—brushing past the black inmate on the stair, the man's shouted threats—now stopped to look behind him, attempting to recall the taller man's face, the con who'd proved to be the shouter, the offended one. It would be comic to have come over on his errand of investigation, dangerous enough, only to be stabbed in the kidneys by a casual stranger who'd been brooding over being accidentally nudged weeks before. Murderous grudges—like their opposites, desperate loves—being the spice of captive lives.

He saw no one behind him on the stairs, noticed no attention from any of the cons lounging along Ground-tier—and turned and climbed again, resenting the Bauman who'd drawn his knife on Becker the day before, and made today's Bauman that much more a coward.

On Three-tier, he avoided the eyes of a black inmate coming toward, then passing him, and walked down to number eleven. There, with great relief, he saw both Wayman and Roy—with another smaller, younger black man, probably one of the two disappearing roommates—comfortably at home, sitting at a crate table playing three-handed cards. A single modest tap on the door bars, and all three men looked up, alert as combat infantrymen.

"Mr. Bauman." Wayman, startled, seemed to fear a forgotten appointment for a lesson, a lesson certainly unprepared for.

"Uh-oh. You in trouble, man." Roy, his almost four hundred pounds resplendent in fancy-beaded denims.

"No lesson, Wayman. I'm sorry I haven't gotten over to work with you. We need to talk."

At which the third man—his skin the polished blue-black Bauman recalled from a few African students at Midwest—laid down his cards, got up, and walked out of the house without a word.

Roy, not so shy, stood up, lumbered to his lower bunk, and sank down upon it with a sigh echoed by the bed's as it took his weight.

There he lay smiling, a mountainous Buddha, observing Bauman with small bright black eyes.

"Come in, come on in, Mr. Bauman," Wayman said, and rose—tall, his skin dark lemon—to indicate one of the fruit-crate chairs. "Sit on down."

"How's it going, Roy?" Bauman said as he sat.

"Goin' all right," Roy said, and as if either the question or his reply had been funny, giggled. "Goin' allll right."

"Glad to hear it," Bauman said.

"What can I do for you, Mr. Bauman?" Wayman said. "We isn' goin' have a lesson, today?"

"Not today, Wayman. What was the last assignment I gave you?"

"Read that story—that High-Low story 'bout that basketball game."

"High-Low?" Roy said from his bunk, and drifted into another giggle.

"This man ain' talkin' to you no more, fool. So why'nt you jus' shut up."

At which rebuke, Roy suddenly wiggled his eyebrows, apparently a customary indication of comic submission, since Wayman smiled one of the few smiles Bauman had seen from him and said, "I mean it, now."

"Have you read the basketball book, Wayman?"

"I did, I did read that book, but now I forgets it."

"Well, don't worry. Learning to read and write is hard work, and if you don't keep on it, it's easy to let some things slip out of your mind. When I have time again—in a few days—we'll make another appointment, and then I'll come over and we'll read the book together."

"Tha's good. That'll be real good." Much relieved at not being subjected to a surprise quiz.

"The reason I came over today, Wayman—you remember when Colonel Perkins came over to B-block?"

Nod.

"Well, this is about that. I need to talk to Clarence Henry, and he wasn't over at the gym, this afternoon. Team's having some time down for the Joliet fight."

Wayman sat alertly watching Bauman across the table, as if certain there'd soon be a point to this, so strict attention needed to be paid.

"And so, I need to know where his house is." Bauman had meant to add, '—And I'd appreciate it if you'd go up there with me.' But he hadn't, and now found it difficult to say.

"He on this tier," Wayman said, "way down at the en'. Secon' house from the en'."

"Good. O.K. . . . Thanks."

"You want me to go down there with you, Mr. Bauman?"

"No, no," Bauman said—and couldn't imagine why he was being so stupid. "No, thanks Wayman. That's not necessary."

Having said that, he found himself reluctant to leave the house for that short journey, and stayed seated on Wayman's uncomfortable crate chair, elbows on Wayman's shabby crate table. "—You don't need to worry about that basketball book. Don't be concerned I'll get on your case about any assignment I give you. Some people you need to keep after, or they won't do their work."

"Tha's true. Plenty dudes like that."

"But it's not true of you. I know you'll do your work; that's why you're learning so fast."

"I'm tryin'."

"I know it. . . ." Looking around, Bauman noticed no change in Wayman's house's decor. The same photographs of black celebrities—athletes, fighters, TV stars, the reverends Martin Luther King and Jesse Jackson, album covers of rap groups. The only white face presented was still the girl's displayed in the act of fellatio in torn triptych photographs on the wall above the opposite lower bunk. Dark hair cut fairly short, gray eyes wide, slim shoulders naked.

Something in Bauman's throat recognized Cousins before he did.

'*. . . Told him I wasn' that kind of a girl.*'

"Wayman, I have to go."

"You want some smoke, Mr. Bauman? I gots to say I did forget a lot about that basketball book. . . ."

"No. No, thank you." Bauman got up. "—I better get going, see Clarence Henry. Tell you what, Wayman, you just look over that book again, and we'll meet next week. What about Wednesday?"

"That be fine."

Bauman went to the door. "O.K., I'll come up Wednesday afternoon." He couldn't help glancing at the photographs once more, then stepped out of the cell and started away down the tier.

'*Told him I wasn' that kind of a girl.*' —But must have been, at least for a while. . . .

Bauman went past two houses before he realized it was the wrong direction and had to turn back, walk past Wayman's house again. He grinned at Wayman and Roy, shook his head at his error, went on by, and walked down nearly to the tier's end, to Clarence Henry's house.

There, at the back of a four-man house Bauman had momentarily thought might be empty, he saw Clarence Henry's great denimed bulk standing dark as fate. Beside him in murmurous conversation was a con Bauman was pleased to recognize—an ex-student and fencing master, the illiterate imam who'd traded for Bauman's lessons with instruction in knife fighting. The priest—a tall muscular brown rope of a man with soft brown eyes and a modest Afro—turned from the heavyweight, and seemed as relieved to see Bauman as Bauman to see him.

Clarence Henry shifted his attention as well, then—as if he'd just mentioned a demon in casual conversation, only to have the thing appear with a faint pop as the air gave way to its awfulness—Henry stood stock still and staring.

"Oooh," he said, voice sounding reedy from its punch-damaged larynx. "*Oooooh*. . . ."

"Now, brother—now, now, my brother," said the priest, plucking at Henry's left shirt sleeve. "The Prophet, may—"

And as Bauman stepped inside the house—and why he'd done that, he was never sure—Clarence Henry came at him so swiftly he blotted out the light like a series of enormous posters of motion and blackness that snapped into place one two three, larger and larger each time, and there he was.

This Benin bronze—mountainous, dark eyes burning bloodshot—loomed over Bauman making slow ponderous gestures, odd as Chinese writing, and said, "Don', oh, don' *make* me be killin' you, Mr. Bauman! Don' you say nothin'. You say somethin', I'm goin' *kill* you, an' I said I never would again. . . ." During this speech, spoken in a high-pitched hoarse voice, Clarence Henry's hands, improbably large to be human, made what Bauman, otherwise paralyzed, saw were the most elaborate gestures of supplication, as if Clarence, transported, were praying in a primitive church.

Bauman, frightened in the most fundamental way—as though this talking cliff with hands, its dark face pouring sweat, might lean that little bit farther over him, then fall—felt with his fear a sudden cool wind of enjoyment. In this chill place, like climbing an overhang pitch, its singing gulf below, he and Clarence Henry stood alone together, almost companions, second by very slow second, the giant's terrified eyes becoming more terrifying as he waited for Bauman to make just the mistake he'd been warned against.

"*Don' don' say nothin'* to *me!*"

Bauman, scalp tingling, mouth caked with sudden dust, was silent, and allowed himself to be guided by what didn't think. He stood staring up at Clarence Henry with no expression whatsoever, then slowly reached down under his trouser waistband, found Mr. Hyde's handle with fingers made of wood, and tugged the knife slowly up and out, displayed it to Clarence Henry—who still chanted, still loomed gesticulating in a storm of sweat—then tossed the blade with a motion easy as gift-giving, over onto the blanket of a lower bunk.

The huge man, only slightly distracted by this, still noticed the knife—watched its course through the air, saw it come to rest—and as if by this small interruption rather than the presented notion of disarmament, began to achieve some control, began to calm, if only a little.

Bauman was certain of this only when he began to distinguish, past Henry's bulk, the Muslim priest still standing at the back of the cell, as if the man had been severely out of focus.

In perhaps half a minute—perhaps much less, all clocks beginning to run faster—the heavyweight was only muttering, his great hands paddling through the air like the paws of a swimming dog, a massive animal, perhaps a Newfoundland, which upon reaching shore might or might not prove safe company.

As Clarence began to quiet—still glaring down at Bauman, frowning meaningfully as if warning of a social solecism—Bauman slowly raised his own hands. He noticed how essential signs, grimaces (or their lack), and gestures had been in this most delicate of encounters, and felt fairly confident as he raised his hands, held them up empty, palms out, and kept them there in a suppliant's posture, until the heavyweight had nothing more to mutter, no gestures of his own to make . . . until at last he stood silent.

"Mommmuh . . . !" The imam, from the cell's depths, produced this apparent comment and period to the drama.

When Bauman felt he could speak, gave himself permission to speak, he found it difficult at first, as if words had been long out of use, were only of marginal value.

"Kenneth Spencer," he said, "—and I, got along fine. I didn't hurt him, and I never would have hurt him. And I didn't help anyone else to hurt him, either."

"Money. . . ." Clarence Henry said.

"I was going to charge your uncle fifteen dollars, street, after I helped him write some letters to people—to some black ministers—to help get him a new trial. He must have told your aunt on the phone he was going to need some money for me. Then he got killed, and she must have thought that was why—"

"That wasn' why," the heavyweight said. "Wasn' that money. —

It's a shitload more money than writin' letters or some shit like that."

Bauman heard this rude reply with great relief at Henry's use of customary language, none of that chanting . . . begging.

"Not more money for me, Clarence," he said. "—Not one damn dime I know about, except that fifteen dollars. I've worked with you for nearly a year, worked my ass off in that gym right with you. Have I ever lied to you about anything? Did I ever lie to you about boxing?"

The heavyweight gave that some thought, then thought of something else, turned to his companion, and said, "You go on, you go on, brother."

The imam seemed happy enough to do it, patted Henry's great shoulder as he passed him, nodded a relieved and complicit nod to Bauman, and left.

"What's that?" Henry said when the man was gone, gone back up the tier, by the soft sounds of news-giving, hushed conversations. The heavyweight's terrible pleas must have reached a fair audience. "What's that . . . ?" Henry said.

At first, Bauman thought he meant those murmurs along the tier, then he saw the big man staring at his knife. Mr. Hyde lay as if asleep, slender and shining, on the bunk's blanket.

"My knife. —Shank," Bauman said.

"You carryin' 'cause of that snitch shit?"

"No. I'm carrying because I'm supposed to be looking for the people who killed your uncle, and killed Barney Metzler, too. The club people—Nash, Perkins, and the rest of them—are making me look for whoever it was." Bauman found some pleasure—as he had in confessing his boyhood cowardice to Muñoz after their two rounds—found some pleasure in revealing this tattered secret to such an overwhelming and reticent monument, as if Clarence Henry, in his size and might, represented some even more prepotent figure, capable of understanding thoroughly, whether or not it cared to judge, or even remember.

"Dude came at my uncle—tol' him to tell me."

"Who? Tell you what?" Bauman—no longer frightened, and apparently quite safe—now suddenly felt a tide of nausea flow up, so severe a sickness that he saw the cell and Clarence Henry begin to slowly revolve, a turning, a revolution that continually commenced but never completed itself. Bauman's hands buzzed, tingled, and he had to swallow and swallow in order not to vomit. "Clarence, I need to sit down. . . ." He stepped to the near bunk without permission, and sat down beside his knife.

"Man, you O.K.? You doin' all right?"

Already, just by sitting with his eyes closed, taking deep slow breaths—already beginning to feel better, feeling the nausea slowly recede, Bauman was touched by this solicitude. He imagined Clarence Henry watching with some concern while an object of his wrath withered away, as if cursed, before him.

"I'm all right," Bauman said. Soon almost was, and opened his eyes to see Henry's face close above him, a looming mahogany moon.

"You O.K.?"

Bauman heard himself sigh as if he were waking. "I'm fine. . . ." He took a deep breath, and after several more deep breaths, felt very well. "—Just seem to be developing a weak stomach." He stood, and found himself steady on his feet. His illness had come and gone, a motion sickness, he supposed, from traveling too swiftly from terror to relief. Bauman picked up his knife, and tucked it carefully under his trouser waistband and down into its sheath. "Who was it went to see your Uncle Spencer, Clarence?"

"He said man tole him 'Don' say.' "

"—And he didn't say?"

"Uncle Kenny was real scared."

"Ghostses?"

"Huh?"

"Nothing. All right, but you said something else."

No response. The heavyweight stood puzzled.

"A minute ago, before I got sick, you said something about a lot of money, 'a shitload of money.' "

Prompted, Clarence Henry said, "Shit lot more'n fifteen dollars."

"That's it. —What money? Was that what the man was talking to Spencer about?"

The boxer went to the opposite bunk and sat down to a clamor of springs. "Tha's right. My auntie figured you was in it, said you mus' be baggin' for that dude fucked up my Uncle Kenny. Dude wanted," he said very softly, "—dude wanted to get me dump my fight."

As slowly as time had passed during Henry's rage, so now it began to gallop in the fine old sportive way it used to when Bauman had some problem of history—sources, interpretation or conclusion—by the throat. He recalled his office, was reminded of the soft light allowed by its single tall window, and felt immediately thereafter a mean scholar's pleasure at Cousins' absence from this discovery. That sullen beauty now to be casually informed of the motive, probably, for both murders. —Money. To be earned by what else, considering location, but a criminal conspiracy?

"I want to be certain I understand this. . . ."

"You ain' goin' tell."

"Not unless you say O.K., Clarence. But let me be sure I've got this straight. A man—con or hack?"

"Wasn' no hack."

"All right. A con went to your uncle and told him to get you to dump this next fight, the big fight with Joliet, with Wajid Coleman?"

"Tha's it. Damn straight. An' I can beat that motherfucker."

Bauman, impressed, his first flush of triumph passed, sat silent opposite Clarence Henry. How much money bet in State, across the state, and in major walls throughout the country on this fight, the last big fight of the season between two unbeaten heavyweights—their two unbeaten teams? Thirty thousand? Fifty thousand street dollars? And the source of Ferguson's sudden wealth, probably some small advance payment for throwing his fight, as the second star in State's boxing firmament.

Bauman wondered if the enterprising fixer, who'd so frightened Kenneth Spencer, had approached any of the other fighters. —Muñoz? It would seem to require a singularly daring and dangerous man to feel free to fix a major fight against the wagers of thousands of murderers, armed robbers, psychopaths, rapists, assaulters of every degree throughout the country, walled into San Quentin, Folsom, Walla Walla, Leavenworth, Cannon City, Atlanta, Attica, Sing Sing—names almost ennobled by the dread they inspired, their medieval and bloody histories.

"Henry, you hear of any other people on the team having this happen?"

"Did, they didn' say nothin' to me—an' I shit sure ain' sayin' nothin' to them. Dudes in here kill any motherfucker they even jus' heard could be dumpin' a fight, take they money."

"What about old Cooper. You didn't tell him?"

"Tell him? Tell *him?* Man, you got to be crazy." The giant's expression one Bauman had never seen on him, an almost comic apprehension. "I ain' tellin' that shit to Coach."

"All right. All right. Henry, why didn't this con come direct to you with this deal?" Stupid question, Bauman instantly recalling Henry in volcanic uproar, pleading, gesticulating, grimacing in his rage beyond rage. "Dumb question. —O.K. So he went to Kenneth Spencer, your uncle, and told him to talk to you?"

"Tha's it. Right."

"But Spencer wouldn't tell you who."

"He scairt. But I tol' him, tell that motherfucker kiss—my—ass!"

"And then that con, and maybe with some buddies, threatened to kill your uncle if you didn't go along."

"Tha's it. You got it. Tha's what that motherfucker tol' my Uncle Kenny. Tol' him he was goin' get waxed, I didn' dump that fight. Shit, I never have dumped no fight in my life! 'I don' *give* a shit, man'; tha's what I tol' him, tol' my Uncle Kenny. I tol' him I ain' never dumped no fight in my life." The principle stated, the heavyweight sat silent.

"Clarence, what was all that about your hand? Your hand being injured?"

"Shit, that was about that shit. I figured dude heard I was hurt, them bets'd be off, you know? But that didn' help nothin'."

"Well, I'm sorry, Clarence. I liked your uncle. Spencer was a very nice man, a gentle man. —But you know, it wasn't your fault. You had no idea the man would actually kill him."

"Fuck I didn'," Henry said, and shook a huge and sorrowful head. "—I jus' didn' give a shit. Didn' give no shit at all, an' my Uncle Kenny raise' me, him an' my auntie. But I never done that, dumped no fight. Tha's the one thing I ain' *never* done."

"So then this con, and possibly with other people, killed him."

"Oh, yeah. Oh, yeah. Kilt my Uncle Kenny like he was a fuckin' bug on the wall, man, an' me not knowin' who the fuck the motherfucker was. I wish I did know. . . ."

"You remember Barney Metzler?"

"That nasty ol' white man? No offense."

"That's the one."

"I didn' know him. Not personal."

"Did you know the same weapon killed your uncle, killed Barney Metzler, too?"

"No shit?"

"That's right. That's a fact."

"Well, I don' know nothin' 'bout that."

"And your uncle didn't tell you anything, not *anything* about the man who threatened him on this? Didn't describe him—black, white, Spanish?"

"He wouldn' a tol' me that dude was green, Mist' Bauman. Didn' say nothin' ceptin' he was a bad man."

"That's not much of a help in here, is it, Clarence?"

"That's the God's truth," said Clarence Henry.

. . .

Which left of the mystery only the question of who. Bauman pondering this as he trotted, triumphant, back down the ringing circular stair, recapitulating in speedy reverse his journey up from odor to music, another rap tape now sending him on his way, muttering about "stayin' cool, and don't be playin' the fool."

Bauman smelled frying meat, reached Ground-tier, and went walking down it imagining the powers of state and State impressed with such results achieved in peril—Gorney's bullying phone call answered so swiftly; the bitch Grace Hilliard (public servant and state's attorney), presented with the motive of this killer of killers, and soon with the creature himself. Nash, in Segregation's stronghold, Shupe, Ganz, Colonel Perkins and Vargas all forced to acknowledge the usefulness of an educated mind—aided, of course, by Cousins' knowledge of State.

He turned down the narrow corridor to D's courtyard entrance, not caring, in this moment of at least partial triumph, to risk Harrison again at the block's main gate, and the possibility of a vengeance strip-search uncovering Mr. Hyde. At the corridor's end, he waited while a group of black cons went out before him, then walked through the courtyard door and was passed at the gate without fuss by a white hack, Haley, and a tall B.N.A. soldier with a shaved scalp.

He went down the steps into a cold late afternoon (its light, silvered glass) and saw Cousins standing to the right, against the building's back wall, waiting for him.

"How come you're over here, Lee? I thought you were going to the library."

"Oh, Schoonover was busy puttin' books away . . . an' I figured we was in this together an' I should stick around."

"Good. Glad you did." And saying so, Bauman recalled the photographs taped to Wayman's wall—unable not to remember the theatrical eye makeup, naked throat, naked shoulders, Cousins' mouth forced wide.

"You O.K.?"

"Fine," Bauman said. "I'm fine, and I have some news."

"All *right* . . . . You didn' have no trouble?" Lively, sulks apparently over, Cousins fell into step beside him as they walked out into the courtyard.

"Not much. Clarence Henry didn't kill me—he just came close. Just scared the living shit out of me, that's all. I would have been delighted to see Becker and his Pawnee friend; I would have run right into their arms. Clarence did think I was involved in killing Spencer."

"Doesn' now?"

"No, not anymore. And," Bauman said, keeping his voice down, "—I have a little sports report."

"Sports?"

"The magic word. According to Clarence Henry, a con approached his uncle, Spencer—and threatened him, to try to get Clarence to go in the tank for the Joliet fight."

"Awe-*some*. . . . Charles, that's real serious stuff."

"Yes, it is. And when Clarence Henry balked, the fixer apparently did just what he'd threatened to do, and killed Spencer."

"Who was it?"

"A mystery con, unfortunately, but definitely a con, not a hack. Spencer was too scared to tell—and, it seems, with good reason."

"*Man*. . . . Charles, you know how much money is involved, they could do somethin' like that?"

"More than enough for murder."

"Damn right, more'n enough. An' Clarence didn't have no idea who it was?"

"No." Bauman, recalling they were crossing lifer territory in mid-courtyard, looked over his shoulder on the odd chance Jack Mogle was walking out to finish their interrupted quarrel. —There was no one behind them.

"—An' could be my dad was offed 'cause he wouldn' go along, wouldn' rip off cons trusted his book."

"I think that's likely. Same killer, and the try at fixing the fight is the only connection Spencer and your Mr. Metzler could have had."

"*Money*," Cousins said. "It was for the bread, all the time. You were right, Charles, an' I was wrong. Wasn' my dad's old partner, or anybody outside. It was in here, an' it was for money."

"Well, I could be wrong, but it all seems to add up. Metzler killed first, because he wouldn't go along, then Kenneth Spencer—poor little man—murdered as a lesson to Clarence Henry. And by the way, we also have Ferguson as a possible fixee."

"That's right, he already got some cash. That's where he got it; he got cash up front!"

"Maybe, and maybe not. We need to be careful not to jump the gun on this. Clarence Henry didn't know of any other boxer being approached, Ferguson or anyone else."

"Where else is that nut-case goin' to get bread, Charles? Who's goin' to give him money? An' whoever, maybe he tried to get some other boxers to dive, too."

"I don't think so. The more men he tried, more chance it would blow up in his face, the word would get out. And he wouldn't need any more. With both Clarence Henry and Ferguson losing, we could never beat Joliet."

"An' what about Jomo Burdon, Charles?"

"Damned if I know—unless our mystery fixer was Tiger. Ghosts wear white. . . ."

"Wow. . . . Heavy shit, Charles."

"Don't I know it. And Burdon might simply have hanged himself in the infirmary—period. I'd like to know if he had a history of mental problems, suicide attempts. Or maybe was having trouble with his family, outside. Wife leaving him, or a child dying."

There was no longer much need to beware Jack Mogle. They'd walked out of lifer territory, crossed a faded painted yellow line to safety in B-block's biker country.

"We could check that, I guess."

"I think we'd better. The club people aren't going to want any loose ends."

"You know," Cousins said, "—it feels real weird to be talkin' like this about my dad. It's like it makes him deader; you know what I mean?"

"I know. But Lee, I'll tell you something, and this happened for me with my mother, who's been gone for years. At first when you talk about them, each time they seem more vanished, deader. Then, as time goes by, in a way they slowly come to life again, just a little. They rejoin you, is what happens. Something of my mother seemed to come to rest in me, if you see what I'm saying."

"I get that. I see that."

"They come back to you in that delicate sort of way, and then they stay with you. Just that much. Not a lot, maybe, but for good. And that'll happen with Mr. Metzler; he'll come back to you, in a way. Then he'll be with you the rest of your life."

"Man, I hope that's what'll happen."

"You'll see."

"An', I also don't feel so bad knowin' he got killed 'cause he wouldn' put it to other cons. 'Cause Charles, fixin' a fight on cons, an' them bettin' what most of 'em can't afford to bet; that really shits."

"I'd say it shits. —And how much would that fix cost losers? What would the total be?"

"Wow . . . somethin' humongous. Forty thousand, I guess. Minimum forty, they lay off the bets real careful. Maybe up to fifty, maybe even sixty thousand if California bets in heavy, an' New York. An' could be that much, too, 'cause rollers got to bet this fight; biggest team fight goin'. Tell you this, Charles—for inside, you're talkin' real major bread. Course, they're goin' to have to spend some of that to collect on the rest."

"But reason enough for a killing. . . ."

"Reason for a bunch of killin's."

They walked up the courtyard steps and into B-block's kitchen, and were struck at once by a powerful odor of turpentine.

"Oh-oh," Bauman said. "Rudy's Mexican Supper."

"Smells like paint or somethin'."

"Lee, that's the sauce."

"Jesus. We got to get over in West mess, Charles. I know you like Rudy an' all, but the guy's poisonin' everybody over here!"

"Not everybody; he doesn't eat his own cooking."

"Are you kiddin' me, or what? —He don't eat what he cooks?"

"Absolutely not. You haven't noticed? He eats out of the canteen. Vienna sausage, crackers, peanuts, ice cream sandwiches. . . ."

"We got to get over to West mess, Charles. Clifford isn't no big genius behind a stove, but he turns out better food than this." The last phrase spoken softly, as Rudy Gottschalk, very busy, stormed past them with a huge rusty can labeled tomato puree cradled in his arms.

"How's it goin'?" he said, and was past and gone.

"Now," Bauman said, leading Cousins through the mess-hall doors, "—let's go down the list. The question being, Who?"

"O.K."

The mess hall, almost emptied by the fine weather outside, contained no hack, and only four bikers at a back table. Gooch and Bad Bob, a big man named Mooney, and Monte Fitch, Ganz's youthful enforcer, handsome despite his dyed orange rooster-comb of hair.

Bad Bob appeared to have gotten hold of some bad dope (or good dope), and was collapsed forward onto their table, speaking to himself very softly. The other three men looked up at Bauman and Cousins, then looked away, continued their conversation.

"Lee, want to try some East-mess pruno?"

"Man . . . Charles, I don' know."

"Come on, how bad can it be?"

"I'm scared to find out."

"You'll love it. Take a table over by the side wall. Not in the back."

"Don't have to tell me that," Cousins said, and walked away.

At the serving counter, Bauman waited until B.B. came by with a gray plastic tub of pots to scrub, called him over and asked for pruno, two cups. And sugar for both; he supposed Cousins liked his drinks sweet.

"I don' know, Teach—all we got is cooked front-kettle shit, got grass in it. It's pretty rough."

"Two cups; we'll take a chance."

B.B., after a short journey behind a row of ovens, came back with a yellow plastic screw-top pitcher. "Ain' suppose' to sell this shit, it didn' age. Charge you a buck, scrip—two cups."

"Deal. Put it on my tab."

"You ain' got a tab, do you?"

"Then it's time I did."

". . . I guess that's O.K." B.B. took the top off the pitcher, carefully poured out two china coffee cups of the stuff, pouring slowly to keep the yeast from coming up. The Styrofoam cups, so useful otherwise, had proven incapable of holding really mature pruno, tending to melt away beneath it.

"Don't use no sugar," Cousins said, when Bauman slid the little paper packet across their table. "An' you shouldn' use none either. Mr. Metzler always said refined sugar was the absolute worst thing you could put in your stomach. He used to say he was fightin' a weight problem all his life, an' the big reason was refined sugar."

"Don't doubt it for a minute," Bauman said, and poured two sugars into his pruno. " 'Live fast, die young, and make a good-looking corpse.' "

"I never heard that one. That's pretty good."

"Supposedly an old Chicago saying."

"That wouldn' be O.K. for me. I don't want no more trouble. I want to live real slow an' quiet. That would make me the most happy, if I could do that." Cousins took a sip of his pruno, looked unpleasantly surprised.

"Bad?"

"Bad don't cover it, Charles."

"Want some coffee, instead?"

"No, no. This is O.K. I had worse than this—I think."

Bauman took a swallow of his drink, found the dark yellow-green liquid to have a disturbing undertaste—spoiled prunes?—spoiled cabbage? "They don't use cabbage making this stuff, do they?"

"Not in West mess."

"Well, this is drinkable."

"Oh, yeah. I'm sure I had worse than this, sometime."

"You were saying, you know, Lee? About a quiet life? Well, there's nothing to prevent you from having just that, once you get the hell out of here."

"But I'm goin' to be out there alone. That's different than havin' somebody with you, somebody to be with."

"Hell, you're very young.—I'll tell you what's going to happen. You'll get out of here pretty soon, finish your parole, and then you'll go to some small quiet town in Indiana. A little farm town with trees, on a river, just the way you and Mr. Metzler had it planned. And you'll go there as a girl or a guy, whichever you decide makes you most comfortable. And you'll get a job, and you'll start to make friends. In a year or a little more, it'll be as if you were never in State at all. This will be only a bad dream, fading away. And when it is a dream, that's when you'll be free to really be yourself, stay in that little town or leave it—and find someone you care about, who cares about you."

Cousins put his coffee cup down. "Charles, you sounded just like my dad. That is just exactly what he would be sayin' to me if he was here right now."

"It's only common sense. Lee, the truth of the matter is you're simply too young to let two or three years, even up here, wreck your life. You let that happen, by self-pity or whatever, and it would be the same as spitting in Mr. Metzler's face."

"I know that. I know it. . . ."

"Doesn't mean it's going to be easy." Bauman, breathing out through his nose as he drank, managed to finish his pruno.

"You got that right."

Bauman found himself wanting to mention Wayman's photographs—a way to take some of their weight from his memory, he supposed. But he couldn't think how to do it, how to bring the subject up so it might be bearable.

"Lee, another drink?"

"No way, Charles."

"I'm going to have celebratory seconds."

At the serving counter, Bauman had to wait for B.B. to return from the back of the kitchen. He received his refill, saw B.B. laboriously print out some sort of letter-and-number code on a greasy sheet of white paper clipboarded beneath the counter.

"Got you down for three drinks—front-kettle stuff."

Back at the table with his cup, Bauman sat and said, "O.K. Let's get to work, go down the list. —I can't believe we're really getting a handle on this. You realize it looks as though we're actually going to solve two murders?"

"If we don't go out like that Chicago dude—young an' nice-lookin'."

"Not possible for me, in any case. O.K. Let's get started on Who. Schoonover. . . ."

"He wouldn' do that. You was right about him, Charles. Not his thing to be doin' that."

"O.K. —Teppman. You're sure not Teppman?"

"No. He wouldn' never think of somethin' that tricky. An' I could tell the way he was talkin' up there he didn' off my dad or your friend, neither."

"Either."

"—Or your friend, either."

"All right. —Tiger? Tiger loves money."

"That's a white guy's game, Charles. Black dude, even Tiger, can't be collectin' on big sports bets in State. Not in this joint. Not yet, anyways."

"All right. What about the bikers? I doubt if Ganz is afraid of anything. And Bump's got the smarts."

"I don' know. . . ."

"They have Pokey Duerstadt playing both sides. And with Nash locked up, this could be their big move against the lifers. —Works either way. Either the fix goes in, in which case the bikers get rich—or, if it's found out, the lifers, who hold the official book, would get the blame. And with the associates of half the incarcerated hoodlums in the country on their tails, that would leave the lifers too busy to fight the bikers for State."

"I don' know."

"What's wrong with it?" Bauman found the pruno tasting better, second time around.

"I'll tell you, I'll tell you what I think's wrong with that, Charles. You got to understand, guys been in the joint awhile get real set, you know? Get, umm . . ."

"Conservative?"

"That's right. They get real conservative. An' I'll tell you, we would have heard about it if the bikers was movin' in on sports bettin' in here. It's not their thing, you know? Dope an' stuff is their thing."

"And there's Teppman, collecting."

"See? No way Bud Teppman's workin' for bikers. He's a Lifer Club guy right down the line."

"So, it's not bikers. Not Ganz."

"That's right. Not them."

"Well, who does that leave?" Bauman heard someone snap his

fingers behind them. He looked over his shoulder and saw Gooch, risen from the back table, strolling toward them, grinning.

The finger snap again. And having this time caught Gooch's attention, Monte Fitch motioned him back to their table, said, "Get back here an' leave 'em alone." While Gooch did as he was told, Fitch sat watching Bauman and Cousins, until Bauman realized Fitch was only watching Cousins, a gaze the more disturbing for its gentleness, its encompassing nature, as if Cousins were a mystery of mysteries. It came to Bauman that Fitch was in love. —And that, of course, the reason for his intervention against Jack Mogle in the courtyard. Not to save Bauman a beating, not to uphold biker territorial rights, but simply because Mogle had offended Lee Cousins, and so offended Fitch.

Understanding this, Bauman saw Cousins had understood it long before, was sitting and looking into his coffee cup as he was being looked at and into by Monte Fitch.

"Lee, want to get out of here?"

"No. It's O.K." Not having to ask Bauman whom he was concerned about. "He isn' goin' to bother us."

From this small encounter—hardly an encounter at all—Bauman saw that Lee Cousins' difficulties would run deep, in State or out of it. Here, the vagaries of love—loves of very desperate sorts, and occasionally sweet—must have complicated his captivity into realities so various, concentrated, and particular, as to be almost unmatchable in freedom.

"All right, Lee, let's go on down the line. —Vargas. Zapatistas?"

"Oh. . . ." Cousins, distracted by having been so powerfully seen, so closely observed and valued, took a moment to think, and put down his coffee cup. "Oh, I'll tell you, Charles. Problem there is, Spanish guys don't have the muscle to be movin' in on that action. I mean they'd like it—but those guys are still beggin' jobs from the other clubs."

"Colonel Perkins?"

"Same thing with the B.N.A. people as Tiger or bikers. No way they could try an' take sports bettin' without this joint goin' up—an' I mean up in smoke. That, that'd be a real move, you know."

"All right, Lee. Then what about a couple of wild cards. How about Sarasote?"

"That creepo's too lazy. He isn' scared of nothin', but he's a ding. An' most important, he's lazy, a rich kid. He don't want to work for nothin'. Con set this up, had to go 'round an' really work at it."

"So, you say not Sarasote?"

"Right. Not him."

"I agree with you. —But you realize if we're guessing wrong, it could very easily get us killed."

"Charles, guessin' right could get us killed, too."

"O.K. Next, Ferguson. He's a lone wolf. He's clever. He's got the guts for it. And he's come into money."

"What do you say?"

". . . I'd say no. Ferguson's a loner. I don't think he's interested in organizing anything, or anybody."

"Right on. You just said it, Charles. Dude's too much of a loner. An' by the way, that's a good reason Schoonover an' Tiger didn't do it, neither—either. I mean I guess they could try an' run somethin' like that all alone, no backin'—"

"But not likely."

"No, not real likely."

"Very well. Now, what do we have? Mr. Metzler, the lifers' bookie, is killed. Metzler's collector is out, and the lifers have a new collector of bets, not the kind of man to object to much. Then Spencer is threatened, and finally murdered to persuade his nephew of the seriousness of the situation, that it might be wise to dump his fight. And another fighter, Ferguson, turns up bonus rich."

"So, Charles, who's the guy gave Teppman his job?"

"Good question, partner—absolutely right. Who gave Bud Teppman his job, after Metzler was so conveniently out of the way? Becker and his Indians out of the way as well."

"Teppman told us a Lifer Club officer."

"And Lee, I believe him."

"An' me too. An' I am sayin' it was that shit, Shupe."

"All by himself?" The pruno did taste better the second time around, but there was a slippery texture to it, as if vegetable oil had been added during the brewing process.

"No way all by himself, Charles."

"Right. No way. So, who else to give Shupe a little extra spine? Someone fierce enough to pressure Clarence Henry, and deal with Ferguson. Someone bad enough to murder a fellow club officer for the chance of making a lot of money on set-up bets."

"Wiltz."

"The very man. —Brian Wiltz, Lifer-Club Vice President, Accounts Receivable."

"Oh, wow. We're gettin' in *real* deep."

"I've been trying to tell you that for some time."

"Wiltz. . . . Brian's one of the worst guys in here."

"Our man'd have to be, wouldn't he?"

"I guess so."

The bikers had left their table, went trooping past—Bad Bob, still half out of it, staggering, leaning on Mooney. Fitch didn't glance at Cousins as he walked by, very light-footed for a young man in boots.

"Now," Bauman said, "here's another question for you. If it was Wiltz—and keep in mind we could be wrong—but if it *was* Wiltz, with Shupe undoubtedly along for the ride, then was this fix being planned just for the money?"

"Just for the money . . . ?"

"Any other reason they might have? Something they'd need the money to do?"

"Oh, man, they could do a lot with that kind of bread. They could hire more muscle, you know, buy a lot of guys."

"And why would they want to do that? Hire the muscle to do—what?"

"Oh, shit, I don' know. Take over the club or somethin'."

"Exactly right! Nash is locked down in Seg, but he's still running the Lifer Club. I got the impression when I was in their office, that Shupe and Wiltz were getting tired of that arrangement."

"Well, there you could be right, Charles. I wouldn' be surprised if you was right. An' that club, man; lifers still just about run this joint."

"Worth one scam—even a very dangerous one—to get the money to buy control of the club?"

"Oh, yeah, in the long run, you bet. An' those guys got nothin' but the long run."

"Well, here we have motive, and a criminal motive, criminal even by prison standards."

"That's right. Rippin' off club brothers, even."

"We have two men in the position to do it, and one of them with the nerve to do it. And did a hack help them?"

"Wouldn' have to."

"No? It seems to me, after all, a hack probably had to help them. I'm thinking of the lights, and how Wiltz was able to get out of his house here in B, middle of the night."

"You want to know how? I been thinkin' about that, an' Charles, you are not the only intelligent person aroun' here. I'm goin' to tell you somethin'—then I'm goin' to ask you somethin'."

"Go ahead."

"I'm goin' give you a hint. A loser, O.K.?"

"All right—that's the hint?"

"That's the hint. Now Charles, all the doors on all the houses in State open an' close an' lock an' unlock on like a kind of lever an' counterweight thing. An' there's a electric motor powers that, head of every tier. Trips 'em all. An' all that machinery is under steel covers—can't get at it without you shut the system down, take it apart a couple of days."

"Right."

"Now, if a hack wants to open just one house, right? He don't want the whole tier openin'."

"Then he uses his key, and hauls the door."

"Right, but he couldn' open all of 'em that way, could he? Case of emergency—a fire or somethin'—an' that circuit could be out. So they got a second system; they got a backup in case of emergency. Same electric motors, but they get tripped on a second circuit, completely separate. An' that circuit board can be set, an' it'll open all them houses—or one. Guy's just got to get in the yard captain's post, A-block gate, bust into the circuit, an' set it. Set it for any house, any time—an' she'll open."

"Just 'get in the yard captain's post'? There're one or two hacks in there day and night. And it's an armored post."

"Right. Right. Them screws are in there, but do they know what the con's doin' when he does it?"

"You mean, what do they know about electrical circuits."

"Right."

"So a man could have gone in on an electrical repair—"

"Now you got it."

"Lesnovitch. The big loser. —That was the way the man paid off!"

"That's what I think. A hack didn' have nothin' to do with it."

"A big loser, and master electrician. Mr. Hunting Prints."

"Right. That's how he paid off them thousands he owed. That's what I think, anyway. Mr. Lesnovitch goes all over this joint, even crippled up."

"That's very good. —Of course, we could be mistaken. We could be wrong about Shupe and Wiltz, too."

"I don't think so, Charles."

"Well, it seems to fit. . . ."

"You like that, with Mr. Lesnovitch?"

"I do. I like that a lot."

"Yeah, but Charles, big question is—what now? We turn Shupe

an' Wiltz over, they're dead. Nash an' them other club leaders, they're goin' to kill those guys. They got to, 'cause their people are goin' to be mighty pissed off. Far as we know, the fix is still in."

"Not with Henry, it isn't."

"Maybe still is with Ferguson, though, an' maybe another guy we don't know about. Could have gone with another guy when Henry said no."

"We'll find out about Ferguson. See him at the gym, tomorrow morning."

"—'Cause if we figured wrong, Charles, this is a real heavy responsibility, here."

"I know, I know. Sure you don't want some more of this juice?"

"No, thanks. I had enough. This stuff's pretty rough, Charles. —An' I think they jus' ground up stems an' seeds an' shit right in it, didn' cook nothin'. You come over to West mess with me sometime, try Clifford's raisin brandy."

"Why not? Wait a minute. . . ." Bauman got up, walked across the mess hall to the serving counter, and saw Rudy Gottschalk bent over, smelling the contents of a steel steam tray.

"How bad is it, Rudy?"

"What are you talkin'?" Gottschalk said. "This stuff is great. Jus' checkin' for seasonin'."

"Wonderful. How about some more of this fabulous brew?"

"You guys, always takin' advantage. Cost you half a buck, scrip. An' you shouldn' even be drinkin' it, 'cause that's not real aged stuff."

"Put it on my tab."

"Teach, since when you got a tab?"

"Since now. B.B. entered it."

"Gimme the cup." Rudy walked back into the kitchen to his supply. "—I want you to tell me," his voice raised, "you taste too much grape jelly in there. An' look out drinkin' that, we don't get a cop comin' in. Vanderlyn is suppose' to be kitchen hack this shift, an' where the fuck is he? Lazy bums. . . ." Returned from behind his ovens, he handed the filled cup over.

"I haven't tasted any grape jelly in there, Rudy. I'd be happy to taste some grape jelly in there." Bauman, feeling a little high, left the serving counter and went back to the table.

"If I can learn to drink this," he said as he sat down, "I can learn anything. . . . All right. Responsibility. It's a nice question, Lee, and you're right; we need to be sure. So first, we'll check with Ferguson over at the gym in the morning. He may be a little easier to deal with in that setting; he's used to doing what I tell him to, over there. And if it turns out he took a first payment on a bribe—and we think he did—then maybe he'll confirm it was Shupe or Wiltz who offered it to him."

"An' if he won't say nothin'?"

"Anything."

"Right, anything."

"If he's got nothing to say, then we go back to Ed Lesnovitch, back to Mr. Hunting Prints, and find out if you were right about his rigging the lights to short out, and setting Wiltz's house door to open."

"Supposin' he says 'Get lost'?"

"Then, Lee, I'll say to him what I said to Ramos down in the canteen. He doesn't want to talk to us? —Fine. Then he can have conversations with the people Nash and Ganz and Perkins and Vargas send to see him. . . . Lesnovitch will talk to us."

"O.K."

"Fair enough?"

"Yeah, that's fair. I— You know, I don't want some guys didn' do nothin', to be gettin' hurt."

"Lee, everyone's done *something*. And in here, usually several somethings. All right, once that's done, once we're absolutely certain, then you should be satisfied as far as Mr. Metzler's death goes—and I will be off the hook. Off two hooks, if I can manage it. And then I intend to fade way, way back into the woodwork, or what passes for woodwork in this joint. I'm going to do what I should have done when I came up here, what I was told to do. I'm going to become a piece of clear glass, and no one's going to be able to see me. Do you know I've managed, in just over a year, to make enough enemies—and the kinds of enemies—to scare the crap out of Wyatt Earp? I do not intend to make any more." The pruno seemed to have gotten more and more oily; there was certainly no taste of grape jelly. It—or the grass in it—was having at least some effect, a light buzz, feeling of well-being.

"Charles, who you considerin' enemies?"

"All right. Les Kerwin, for one."

"Jailhouse lawyer—guy blinded that guy?"

"That's right. Man thinks I owe him money. . . . Then there's Jack Mogle, just because I had to mouth off out there in the courtyard."

"That probably isn' real serious."

"Then Becker and those two Indians."

"O.K. That's serious. That's serious for both of us. That's the worst of 'em, Charles."

"Don't I know it. I've got a sore neck from looking behind me all the time."

"That one, you know, we can't jus' let go. That one, we need to get settled soon as this bettin' thing is cleared up."

"Oh, I agree."

"What we need to do, Charles, we need to go talk to Becker about it. Maybe I should go an' talk to him."

"No."

"Excuse me, I forgot. I'm not allowed to talk to bad guys. —O.K., Charles. Then, when this other thing is settled, we both go talk to him."

"I agree. Maybe we can keep my TV heroics from escalating into killing, which otherwise I'm afraid they might. And once this fix-the-fight thing, and the trouble with Becker, are settled, Charlie Bauman is going to become the little man who isn't there."

"What about your teachin'?"

"I'll work with the people I already have, but I won't take on any more. Then, I'm just going to wait out release. And when I do get out, I intend to leave a good deal of my stupidity behind."

"You aren't stupid. You're as smart as Mr. Metzler."

"If I wasn't stupid, Lee, I wouldn't be here. And I threw other things away, besides my freedom, before I ever came up. One of which, as it happens—and you're the first to hear this little confession, probably prompted by pruno—was the life of the young girl I killed."

"Charles, people know about that up here, think it was jus' bad luck. An accident, is what it was. That wasn' no crime."

"If she'd been your sister, or my daughter, you can be goddamned sure *we'd* call it a crime. Some jerk fresh out of a party with three solid martinis under his belt—and taking no special care, Lee. No special care. . . ."

"Charles—"

"And that's the secret; that's the key phrase. You think I'm O.K. to drive, right now?"

"I would say you're O.K. to drive."

"Not drunk, right?"

"Right. Not drunk."

"Legally maybe, maybe not. But I'd need to take a little extra care, not so?"

"Could be."

"Well, I didn't do it. I drove that fucking Volvo when I shouldn't even have driven it, and I drove as if I hadn't had drink one. Nothing. I didn't take even a little extra care, drive a little slower, more cautiously. And I'm not talking about the law and blood-alcohol levels. I'm talking about responsibility. Which means I belong right where I am. Period." Bauman put his cup of pruno down. The stuff tasted too bad to finish. "—If Karen Silber, if she'd been my daughter, if it had been my boy, Phil, I'd barely be satisfied if the motherfucker who did it was rotting up here for twenty years. And all the more because he ran—*ran*, when he saw her mother coming out to the street. Coming to see what that poor . . . poor woman saw."

Cousins reached out to place his slender right hand over Bauman's left. Cousins' hand was cool, light as a leaf.

"—Lee, the fact of the matter is, you're looking at one of State's strictly-guilty-as-charged."

"I don't like you talkin' yourself down, Charles. You're a major person." Lifted his hand away.

"Wrong. Most of me is good IQ, hard study, enjoyment of teaching, and front. There are dozens of me at every major university at a dime a dozen. Maybe, maybe when I get out of State I'll be worth a little more. A real graduate. . . . Though, of course, there is a mitigating circumstance—some Indian blood, good deal of Indian blood, actually; half Indian . . . difficulty metabolizing alcohol. Odd, it's really amusing when you think about Becker and me wrestling around that elevator—two breeds, when you come right down to it, me half Chippewa, him half whatever."

"Don't. You don't need to be hurtin' yourself, talkin' like that."

"Well . . . I certainly don't need to be talking so much. Enough said. You know, if we actually—and I know it's hard to believe—but if we do actually solve this thing, if we really have it solved, then there won't be any reason to be meeting."

"Yeah, that's right. Except like friends."

"Except like friends."

"Too bad, you know. I don't like you eatin' this lousy food over here. Clifford isn' no restaurant cook, but at least the guy can make pruno."

"Well, Lee, that's not really fair. I was warned this was fresh stuff."

"I don't know, I jus' don't trust a guy got tattooed hair."

"At least he can't shed in the soup."

"Hey, that's right." Cousins put his head back and laughed, revealing a throat smooth and white as Alabama marble, save for the short thread of scab where Manny Elk Antler had slid his razor blade. "—That's pretty good. I never thought of that. That's ol' Rudy's one advantage in cookin'."

Bauman, perhaps because of the smoothness of Cousins' throat, or his laughter—so much more girlish than his talk—or perhaps recalling the photographs on Wayman's wall, grew restless, finished his last swallow of pruno after all, and stood up, empty cup in hand. "O.K. You on for dinner over here, tonight? Or would you rather skip it, meet me in the morning?"

"Oh, what the hell," Cousins said, standing up, "I'll stick with you. I got a good digestion."

"Want to come upstairs until dinner?" Bauman led the way to the serving counter to drop off their cups, then through the mess hall's corridor doors.

"No, I got some stuff to wash out over at the house. I'll see you down here, though, dinnertime."

In the basement corridor, there was a slightly awkward pause between them—usual, Bauman realized, when they parted—and he held out his hand, received Cousins' elegant one.

"Congratulations, Lee; I think maybe we got the job done, and we're still alive."

"So far," Cousins said, and smiled.

Dinner was Rudy's Mexican Supper.

That difficult meal was followed by an easy evening—with Bauman lying in his underwear on his bunk listening to Schubert's Quartet in A minor, and watching Scooter pace up and down the house smoking a half-an'-half (half pot, half Bull Durham), and apparently talking with great animation.

After dinner, after good-nights to Perteet, to Cousins, Scooter had begun a long complaint of some inequality in assignment at the truck shop. He'd been, it seemed, required to bath-clean parts instead of being allowed to re-bore cylinders, a much more responsible position.

This complaint had lasted up the circular stair, on into their house, and continued there—but in dumb-show, once Bauman put his Walkman's earphones on.

Lying through the evening after count, attempting once to set the lap-timer on his Timex, Bauman smoked a couple of Winstons while listening to music. He tried a William Schuman piece (embarrassing, following the Schubert), and was feeling quite at home, relaxed, except he found himself tempted to reveal his triumph of investigation—his and Lee's—if only to Scooter. It would be pleasant to have at least his housemate appreciate what had been done, and under such conditions—surely the first investigation *by* a criminal, of criminal behavior in an environment thoroughly criminal in every sense of the word. Perhaps Vidocq's cases in the slums of nineteenth-century Paris might be compared. . . .

An achievement, and one—if complete, the murderer identified beyond question—that should get him nicely off the state's attorney's hook. And off the clubs' hook as well, Nash certain to be pleased at having a usurping Wiltz destroyed.

An easy evening—Scooter at last at rest above him, watching TV—and ending, when the tier's lights were switched from yellow to dull ruby, with a long, long, swerving descent into sleep.

. . . He dreamed much later, early in the morning, when the steel lattices of State seemed to stretch and creak, resting from their efforts of containment. In these earliest of morning hours, the dream commenced with a scream—raucous, penetrating, with none of the musical effect, the warbling *tessitura* poor Spencer had achieved. This was the shriek of a jungle bird, large, blaze-red and cobalt blue, its bill a heavy hook.

In his dream, Bauman realized this was the predator, not the prey, and that cry the more dreadful for the object's silence, as if its voice had already been torn out, its life to follow.

He dreamed that call was a summons to the infirmary, at Tiger's request. Notwithstanding, Tiger (appearing even larger than life in his medical whites) demanded one hundred dollars, street, to let him in.

Once inside—the dark corridors had no ceilings, were open to the night sky—Tiger assigned Bobby Basket to come and show Bauman the way to the security room. Bobby (a long sausage lump in his gray knit stocking) appeared at once, ghosting down dark infirmary halls a few feet off the floor, supported along his stocking by the safety-pinned strings of seven or eight small gas-filled balloons, whose colors (persimmon, chalk, lime, tan, mauve, spruce and licorice-black) shed their own light as he sailed along.

Bobby paused, suspended, then suddenly bent, doubled, and turned back the way he'd come—gliding away, his balloons softly rubbing and thudding against each other in the wind of his passage.

Bauman hurried to keep up. But, when he reached the door he was looking for, Bobby was gone, perhaps up into the air, where powdered drifts of stars glimmered where the ceilings used to be. The room's door opened its upper half with an inappropriate sound, a soft sliding on steel, and Bauman saw a person he almost recognized. A short, stocky Latino, almost naked, round-faced, stubble-bearded and sweating, stared at Bauman with muddy eyes. The man said something in a Spanish difficult to understand, then, baring teeth yellow as a horse's, made an effort, and spoke in English.

"Oh, Charles. . . . Will you look at what they done to me?" There was lipstick on the lips, a sticky red.

"Betty?" Bauman said. "—Betty?" And saw as he said it, small plump breasts, and a woman's frail white panties stretched around a thick and muscular waist—barely containing heavy buttocks and weighted groin. But beneath were lovely legs, shifting, naked, slim and sleek, the toenails painted to match the lipstick's red.

"Oh, Jesus, Charles, they took my medicine awayyyy," the creature sang. Caught so mournfully mid-change, like a werewolf by an eclipse of the moon, it said, "Charles, am I pretty?" And waited, staring into Bauman's face. Then, despairing of his answer, it turned to wander naked back into the shadows of the room—reaching out as it went, to trail sharp red-painted fingernails scribbling along the padded canvas wall.

Bauman woke with the morning, and remembering his dream, was content to wake even to the clamor of State.

Chapter TWELVE

Bauman stretched and lay relaxed for a few moments, listening to the block's rising racket and reviewing the investigative triumph of the day before. He was distracted by Scooter's gangling leap out of the upper bunk, then threw back his own covers to swing his legs out and sit up. As he did, as if the swirl of sheet and blanket had been an introductory curtain, he saw black printing high on the wall beside his bunk. **BETTER BUTT OUT**

It seemed to have been done in Magic Marker, the letters large, awkwardly made. Shadowed by Scooter's bunk just above, the **BETTER** began on the wall at the other side of the photograph of the blond girl lying, legs spread, on her sunny beach. From there, the phrase sprawled across her picture to end almost above Bauman's pillow.

Staring at these words as if their meaning couldn't be so plain, as if they must hold some secret having nothing to do with him, Bauman hadn't even a second's comfort imagining Scooter might have written them for a joke or sophomoric warning against the publicized snitch hunt. Scooter would never have defaced the photograph.

"Need to be gettin' up, Charles, you want some breakfast."

"Right. . . ." As he stood, Bauman saw that Scooter's tangled sheet and blanket hung low enough to hide the printing fairly well. He was very anxious Scooter not see it, witness it. He didn't want to hear exclamations, discussion, questions—all of which would only increase the words' weight. Above all, he wanted time to think of something else the phrase might mean, than what it seemed to.

He saw—for example, just on first consideration—saw no way the words could have been written except by someone come into the house, leaning over him as he slept. . . .

He delayed finishing dressing long enough for Scooter—calling to him, "Better get movin', roomie!"—to amble on out of the cell to the tier walk and circular stair, crowded with men going down to breakfast.

When the last cons had filed off the tier, Bauman bent over his bunk to examine the words again. BETTER BUTT OUT And printed very crudely, apparently by a man in a hurry, the E's and R particularly badly done. A man in a hurry, and writing, of course, in near darkness. There was no way it could have been accomplished by reaching in through the door bars. The BETTER began almost five feet from them.

"A hand writing on the wall," Bauman said aloud. "—Very biblical." Then was sorry he'd said it. He hurried to the sink, wet Scooter's grimy washcloth, and came back to lean in under the upper bunk and scrub at the writing. "Not indelible," he said as an incantation, and was rewarded when the printing began to fade as the cloth rubbed over it. He tore down the girl's photograph, crumpled it into a ball, and went to stuff it down into their trash box. Then he stopped at the sink to wet the cloth again for more scrubbing, breathless, rushing to get it done as if the words themselves were dark magic, and must be expunged.

When he'd wiped away what he could, only an occasional very faint line or angle could be seen—no phrase, no words at all, nothing for anyone to notice. And, of course, he could tape up one or two new pictures.

It was a relief to have the words gone, a relief to go behind the toilet curtain to lean against the back wall in dim privacy. It was difficult to bear the notion of someone (Wiltz, almost certainly) standing inside their house in rubiate darkness, grinning, listening to Bauman's slow breathing in sleep, and holding his Magic Marker in a hand that would as comfortably have held a knife. It was very difficult to bear the certain knowledge that their prison cell, seeming to offer at least the security of its enclosure, offered no such thing—though, of course, both Metzler and poor Spencer had borne it. But worst, was that an opponent who'd only been imagined, was now real as death.

"Oh, man," Bauman said to himself, and leaned back against the wall as if it were a strong friend. "Oh, man," he said, "I'm so scared," and comforted by hearing this confession, raised his hands to a face contorted as a sorrowful child's, and cried a few painful, relieving tears. "You little motherfucker," he said through damp fingers, realizing, once he'd said it, he meant his son—an ignorant hostage, and ungrateful. . . .

"Charles, you O.K.?" Cousins, come up with Scooter after breakfast as Bauman just finished making his bunk. "—Your back botherin' you?" The skin around Cousins' injured cheek and eye, still slightly swollen, was mottled fading yellow and blue.

"No, back's fine. I just got a slow start, and it didn't seem worthwhile to hurry down for Rudy's breakfast. Now don't tell me it was great; don't tell me I missed a fabulous breakfast."

"You didn' miss no fabulous breakfast," Cousins said.

"Shredded wheat an' bananas," Scooter said. "Hey, man, you made up my bunk!"

"So, you owe me. And I put your washcloth in the laundry bag. That washcloth was starting to crawl around the floor."

"Sure you're O.K., Charles?" Cousins said.

"I'm fine."

"Know who we're gettin'?" Scooter.

"Getting where?"

"Up here, comin' up on the chain, couple days."

"Scoot, I couldn't guess."

"Grant *Briscoe's* comin' up."

"Briscoe? —Oh, Briscoe." Grant Briscoe, a rural bully from upstate, had kicked his way into a family's mobile home, shotgunned them to death, then, curious or famished, had sliced meat from the small of the dead girl's back, fried and eaten it—this nastiness receiving enormous publicity.

"Famous guy," Scooter said.

"Shouldn't mind Rudy's cooking, anyway," Bauman said, and sent Cousins laughing on his way over to A for count.

B's lock-'n'-count lasted longer than usual because of a noisy altercation on Three-tier, where a block sergeant and two other hacks, apparently at the watch commander's orders, were turning a house belonging to four heavy dealers. The noise—of wreckage, protest, threats, and counterthreats—continued well past the usual counting time, until the whole block simmered in dull uproar, cons calling insults to every hack walking by and, in some cases, throwing items that could be spared. Had to be spared, since it was a rule that anything thrown through bars was confiscated and destroyed.

This disturbance, which interested Scooter mightily, continued until half an hour past the usual time for cells-open. It only subsided after the victim dealers (contraband having been discovered) were brought down the circular stair, demanding contact with Inmate Grievance, the A.W., and their *pro pers* counsel.

The block's doors then slid rumbling open, and, the first flood of inmates down the circular stair subsiding, Bauman and Scooter went to Ground-tier and separated, Scooter off to the truck shop. Bauman threaded through inmates to B's side gate, was nodded past by a disinterested hack, Patterson, and trotted down the steps into a shady winter morning, its slow breeze frigid, frost stippling the stretches of the yard.

Cousins, slim arms crossed over his denim jacket's front as if he had breasts to keep from the cold, stood stamping his gray running shoes on the building's walkway, impatient and annoyed.

"Charles, where the hell you been, man? I been out here freezin' for an hour!"

"Sorry. Some dealers got their house turned, and we were all locked down."

"That's some ridiculous block you got yourself on. Isn' nobody botherin' to run it. You got a few lifers, an' independents, an' that bunch of bikers don't do nothin' but deal. They don't give a shit how things are runnin'. Never know what's happenin' on that block; it's real inconvenient. . . ."

"Sorry you had to wait."

"I wouldn' mind, it wasn' so cold out here. Not your fault anyway, Charles."

"Well, I apologize just the same. You know what we need? We need to get prescriptions for leather jackets." Bauman's breath clouded in the cold, reminded him of Colonel Perkins and the meat locker.

"Prescriptions easier to get than payin' for them fancy leather jackets." Cousins falling into step on the East-yard walkway.

"Tell you what, if we can't afford leather, we'll get down jackets. I used to have one. They're light, and they're warm. Don't cost as much. Susanne can shop for us."

"I don't know. . . ."

"We'll call it a Christmas present. They aren't that expensive. I'll spring for the damn things."

"No, no thanks, Charles. It's a real nice thought, an' I appreciate it, but I need to be gettin' out of the habit takin' presents from guys—even friends, you know? I got thc bread for a jacket, an' I need to be spendin' some, instead of just hangin' onto it like it was my big security. Like all I'm ever goin' to have is that money Dad left me."

"All right, Lee; I understand that. I'll find out if we need prescriptions for down jackets. And if we do—which we shouldn't, they're not that big a macho deal—we'll get them. I think I can talk to Michaelson about it; I'll try bronchitis."

"Smarter to go through Tiger, Charles."

"Then we'd have to pay that bloodsucker, too."

"Yeah, but even with that, it's smarter. Doin' that—gettin' guys prescriptions for stuff—that's one of them things Tiger does."

Two Indians were walking toward them, heading for B-block. Bauman reached down into his waistband with his right hand, barely touched the tip of Mr. Hyde's handle, and watched them come. Both big men —not the round-shouldered one, not the Pawnee—but certainly their friends.

"O.K., Lee, we'll see Tiger. Then we'll figure an angle to get you up to visiting—Cooper could send you up there to mop—and you can talk to Susanne about it, tell her what style you'd like. Not that any of them are very stylish—" Bauman stopped talking as the Indians met them. He thought he might be able to yank Cousins out of the way with his left hand, leave his right free for Mr. Hyde.

"I wouldn' want to bother your wife, Charles."

The Indians walked past. Bauman listened to their footsteps fading away.

"You wouldn't be bothering her. Susanne's very nice; you'll like her, and she'll like you."

"I bet she's nice, Charles. An' she's your wife, so I'm goin' to like her. —But she isn' goin' to like me. That's just a fact."

"Oh, bullshit."

"No, there's some things you don't understan', Charles. What ladies like an' all. None of 'em like me in here with their guys; an' that's just a fact. Even if there isn' no sex goin' on or anything. Better believe it; it's just natural, a natural thing. I don't blame 'em."

"I think you underestimate the ladies."

"No, I don't."

"Well, then you tell me what kind of jacket you want, and she'll go shopping for you. If you don't want to meet her, that's O.K. Maybe another time."

"Right. Another time. . . . Charles, I wonder do you mind my askin' you somethin'?—You get bad news from home? Not my business, but I know somethin's botherin' you. I knew it first thing this mornin'."

"All right. I suppose you should know. —Hell, I'm sure you should know. I had a visitor last night who left me, or us, a little message printed across the wall over my bunk. '*Better butt out.*' Short and to the point."

"Who was it?"

"Lee, I was asleep. I don't know, but I assume it was Wiltz."

"Holy *shit*. . . ."

Bauman was interested to see Cousins' bruised and elegant face marked by just the fear he'd felt himself, behind the toilet curtain.

"It looks as though your theory about our killer being able to get in and out of cells, is proved."

"He didn' hurt you?"

"Didn't touch me; didn't wake either of us. And by the way, Scooter doesn't know anything about it. That's what I was doing during breakfast—scrubbing that message off the wall. What does surprise me, was he was able to open the cell door quietly."

"That's nothin'. Unlock it easy, an' slide it open real, real slow. You don't have to make a lot of noise with them doors. —This scare you, Charles, like it scares me?"

"Well, I went behind our toilet curtain and cried. So I think you could say it scared me." Had frightened them, Bauman noticed, into beginning to walk faster, as if already pursued.

"I just didn' figure, you know, about really meetin' up with him. You know?"

"You and me both, kid. But there is one thing, the message that Wiltz left—probably Wiltz, anyway—wasn't that we were good as dead. If he'd wanted that, I'd *be* dead. It was a warning, almost a friendly warning when you think about it."

"I never heard about Wiltz givin' out a warnin'."

"Well, since he was one of the club people who gave us the case to begin with, maybe he feels a warning is fair."

"I never heard about Wiltz bein' fair with anybody, neither."

"Either."

"—Either. Isn' no doubt about it, Charles, we're in real bad trouble."

"Lee, we've been in trouble from the start."

"Sayyyy Teach!" Bauman heard fast footsteps behind them on the walkway, turned and saw mad Hull, stalky in dirty denims, galloping toward them, a frost of breath trailing out behind him like a steam locomotive's smoke.

"Comes one of your dings, Charles."

A few yards from them, Hull shook to a stop and suddenly began to draw great, angled letters in the air, properly reversed for Bauman to read.

I . . . AM . . . HULL.

"Now," Bauman said, "—that is really good. A sentence! Write me some more."

The long right arm, its dirty hand, rose again, slowly described more letters through the air.

MY . . . FRIEND . . . IS . . . WITH . . . ME.

"Wonderful. *Wonderful*, Mr. Hull. I'd say your friend has taught you to read and write."

"Fuckin' a," Hull said. "He's teachin' me better'n you ever could."

"I'm sure that's true. You remember I invited you to come up to my house for a lesson? Two-tier, B-block. Right off the stairs."

"Yeah, yeah, I remember. We both of us remember, but we don't like goin' inside for no reason whatsover."

"Well, I can understand that. But your friend wants to go inside to sleep and get warm, doesn't he? And have something to eat?"

"Oh, yeah, he goes inside for that. Dude's not fuckin' nuts, man."

"I'll bet what your friend is doing, is getting you ready to leave State in a few years, so you'll be O.K. on the outside without him. —You know, so you'll be O.K. on your own."

"Yeah?"

"That's it. Because he's a double-lifer, isn't he? He won't ever be able to leave State."

"No?"

"No. When you leave, your friend is going to have to stay behind. And I think what he's doing, is making sure you're ready to go, making sure you'll do just fine out on the street."

"Jesus, that's scary," Hull said. "I never thought of that, man. I figured, you know, him an' me was a team."

"You are a team—in State. And when you do get out, then you'll know just how good a friend your buddy was. Teaching you things—how to read and write again, and clean yourself up so you look nice. And how to talk to people, how to do steady work and get paid for it. Let me tell you something, Mr. Hull—it takes a very good friend to leave you with gifts like that, when he says goodbye."

"I'll say," Hull said. "You're full of shit, but you got that right.

You better believe I know that's right," and suddenly stamped his heel like a guardsman on parade, performed a neat about-face—in a military mood, today, apparently—and breaking into his head-tossing gallop, flung away down the walk, kicking and high-stepping, making pretty good time as he went.

"You figure that did any good?"

"Lee, I doubt it. But it feels better to play the learning game on their own ground, wherever they choose. At least Hull's friend has his attention."

"Charles, that there's a major geeky ding."

"—But his imaginary friend may be very sensible."

"Charles, tell you what I'm learnin'. I'm learnin' it isn' no use arguin' with you. Dealin' with you, it's got to be 'yes' or 'no' or 'maybe.' Period."

"And when it comes to whether or not we keep on with this little investigation—whether you keep on with it, anyway—is it 'yes', 'no', or 'maybe'?"

"It's 'yes,' Charles. Because only thing really happened is he let us know he knows, an' he wants us to back off, an' he's showin' he can get to us. An' we already knew all that, pretty much. We jus' didn' have it pushed in our faces."

"Think again, Lee. Be really sure you want to stay with this. There are— I have reasons I can't just drop it. But you could, and I think you should."

"An' why should I?"

A con named Toby Collins came down the walk, nodded to Bauman as he passed.

"Because it's goddamned dangerous, and you don't *need* to be doing it."

"All right. You got reasons; I got reasons. I told you my reason; the fuck killed my dad, an' I'm stayin'."

"Lee, I think you're making a mistake, a serious mistake . . . but I'm grateful for the company."

"O.K. We goin' to have to stay awake all night now, Charles?"

"Nice question. . . ."

"What about leanin' some stuff against the inside of our door bars—you know, in between the head of the bunk an' the bars? Lights out, lay a stool down so the legs are jammed in there between the bunk an' the door bars—so one of them legs is pokin' out between the bars just enough they can't move. He sure as shit's goin' to make noise tryin' to get that stool out of there, get that door open."

"Not bad, Lee, that's not bad. Wedge it in there hard after lights out, then in the morning, just pull it free so the door'll open. Not bad. I don't think Scooter'd even notice, if I kept some books on it."

"No use us makin' it easy for the fuck." They started up the gym steps. There was no hack at the doors.

"That'll help for the next night or two," Bauman said, "—though our killer could still come after us in the daytime. For that matter, he might just throw some gas on us through the bars, then toss in a match. . . . Tell you what I think. I think we'd better have our man cold by tomorrow or the day after, and our case proved and passed on to the club leaders. Because what that message really said—"

"Said we're runnin' out of time."

"Lee, do me a favor; please don't finish my sentences for me." And led through the double doors.

The gym was warm, steamy, smelling only nostalgically of sweat this early in the day. November's morning sun was not yet high enough to shine directly in through the building's clerestory windows, so the basketball court, empty as the rising bleachers to each side, was dark as evening. Only the lights beyond the backboard were on, revealing, as in a theater, the boxing team's exercises. Not, Bauman supposed, much different, except for weapons play, from those in a gladiatorial school off the *campus martius* before important games.

"I can't believe it—I can't believe it!" Little Cooper's raucous call. "My assistant ('athithtant') got up this mornin' an' come on over to work!"

"God knows you people need me," Bauman said, as he and Cousins walked from gloom into light. "You have to have somebody out here isn't a danger to society."

Boos at this familiar witticism. —A chorus in which Bauman noticed Clarence Henry joining, as if they'd had no portentous conversation the afternoon before. Relieved of his information, having discussed his uncle's death, Clarence Henry appeared to have set it aside.

Old Cooper came bustling over, bright whistle glittering on his small sweatshirted chest. "Hey, girlie."

"Mr. Cooper."

"Remember now, remember now, no chippin' on my boys."

"No, sir."

"Now, Mr. Trainer, what I want for you to do, is take a good look at that big wop you was braggin' about how he's handlin' the speed bag. You look again, an' then you tell me how great he's comin' along."

"O.K., Coach, I'll check him out. First, I'd like to talk to Ferguson for a minute."

"He's suppose' to spar."

"Just for a minute, away from the other people."

"All right, all right. Make it fast. We don't have no trouble with Ferguson. Guy he's fightin'—Turner—Ferguson could take that yo-yo apart best day he ever saw. Don' know why Burt Cafone even put that boy on; gotta be real weak at welter."

"Just for a minute."

"Well, hurry it up, hurry it up," Cooper said, and trotted away on scarred little legs to instruct the lightweights already boxing, quick as fighting roosters, in ring one.

Bauman walked with Cousins across to the second ring, beside which Ferguson—pale, lean, and limber, beautifully muscled in black shorts, black high-lace boxing shoes—was having his neat fists neatly taped by Enrique.

"Todd. . . ."

Ferguson looked up, then glanced at Cousins. "Teach," he said. "You got some hints for me, how I should kick a little Joliet ass?"

"No," Bauman said, "I don't. Just fight your fight. This man isn't going to give you any trouble."

"Sounds like you wish he would give me some trouble." Smiling.

"I am looking forward to somebody beating the shit out of you, Todd. I think one very good beating is all you need to make a really fine fighter."

"That's pretty funny," Ferguson said. "—That weird coon, Mc-Elvey, used to say the same thing. Before your time."

"I know McElvey, and he was right. You're a fine natural fighter, but you always dog it when you can. I'd love to see you in there someday, with a man you'd have to fight all the way."

"You find him, I'll fight him."

"Deal. And Todd, we'd like to have a private word with you before you start sparring."

"You got it." Ferguson glanced at Cousins again, then intently down at his left fist as Enrique finished taping it. "That's good," he said to Enrique. "—That's good," and raising his taped fists, examined them in that direct, searching, wary way an infantryman checked his weapon, a woman, her decorated face. Satisfied, the welterweight (coordinated as a strolling cat) ambled after Bauman and Cousins to a place just out of the light, under the near end of the bleachers.

"We'd like to ask you a question, Todd."

"Why not? Don't hurt to ask."

"You say you're going to beat this Joliet fighter?"

"Damn straight."

"—Then you're not going to dump the fight?"

"No way." Ferguson's answer immediate, uninflected, untroubled.

"But you did take some money, didn't you? Didn't somebody give you some money, Todd?"

"Bread's bread, Teach. I only got a thousand up front, anyway. Big bread's when I lose."

"But," Cousins said, "—but you're sayin' you won't never get that big money."

"Right. 'Cause I ain't goin' to lose no fight."

"But couldn't you get your throat cut, crossing whoever gave you the thousand?"

"Teach, I don't worry about that shit. Worryin' about shit is a waste of time." Ferguson's eyes, a frosted grey, were direct, candid, untroubled as a child's. They'd likely been so when, downstate, he'd butchered the pregnant woman before her bound husband, silent, stunned, and staring.

"Todd," Bauman said, "would you mind telling us who suggested you dump this fight?"

"Old guy, couple months ago. That Lifer Club dude, Metzler. Old guy got offed? He told me not to spend the thousand right away—but fuck that. I needed a tape deck an' a lot of shit. I don't care for a man tellin' me what to do, in any case."

"*You*," Cousins said, "*you are a dirty fuckin' liar!*" Loud enough for everybody to hear.

"*Lee.*" Bauman put his hand on Cousins' arm—had it briskly knocked away.

"Hey, hey, little honey," Ferguson said. "What's your problem?"

"Lee—"

"And fuck you, big mouth—Mr. Big Brain. An' you're full of shit too!" And on that, Cousins started away.

"Great," Bauman said. "—And where the hell are you going?" Took Cousins by the arm, and held him as he tried to pull away. "You can't run away from it!"

Cousins instantly, spitting like a cat, pivoted around that grip and hit Bauman a cracking forehand slap across the face. Then released, walked away into the dark, footsteps sounding across the basketball court. . . .

Laughter and loud cheers from the team, happy to pause in their work. "*Pussy trouble, pussy trouble. Teach is havin' pussy trouble* . . . !" This chant the source of even more amusement. "Hey, man, you took a cross. How come you didn' block that punch?—how come you didn' slip that punch?" These inquiries punctuated at last by the distant slam of the gym's double doors—then Cooper's immediate shrill whistle.

"You people shut the fuck up an' get back to work!"

"Wow, Teach," Ferguson said, amused. "I didn' mean to get you in trouble there with your squeeze. I mean what the fuck got into her?"

"A personal thing," Bauman said. "Metzler was a friend."

"Oh, yeah. Right. I heard they was an item. But shit, that old dude's dead an' gone."

"You, Ferguson!" Cooper arrived, quivering with rage.

"Yeah?"

" 'Yeah'? You get your dead ass over in that Two-ring an' start sparrin'. We'll see are you good enough to be wastin' time chippin' with some cunt when you suppose' to be trainin' for a fuckin' fight!"

"I wasn'—"

"Shut up an' move."

Ferguson strolled away back to the ring, into a number of catcalls, inquiries as to what had happened to piss that punk chick off—an' how come she hit Teach?

Cooper, a furious little gargoyle, turned to Bauman. "I tol' you an' I *tol'* you—no friggin' chippin' in this gymnasium!"

"She wasn't—Coach, it was another matter."

"We don't have no other matter in this gymnasium! You keep that cunt out of here an' away from my boys. I tol' you an' I *tol'* you. I tol' the both of you. No friggin' . . . whatever. Nothin' in this gymnasium. An' just a few friggin' days before a fight! —You lookin' for trouble? You lookin' for trouble with me?"

"No, sir."

"You better not be. That's all I got to say to you, fish. You better not be."

"I'm not."

"All right. All right. . . ."

"Coach, I think we need to talk."

"I don' need to talk."

"I think we better, somewhere private."

"Private? That's a laugh (but lowered his voice, nonetheless). Private, an' you just messin' with one of my boys, upsettin' him, an' gettin' your face fuckin' slapped. Slapped! Woman never laid a hand on me all my life long since I was ten years old. You can't see a fuckin' slap comin' an' block it, Trainer, you are sad shit for a guy used to box."

"Coach, some people have tried to fix the Joliet fight."

"So? What else is new? Is that what's so fuckin' private?"

" 'What else is *new*'?"

"That's right. Guys have tried an' fix fights in here two, three times, last thirty years. So what? Tried it in nineteen an' sixty-one. Tried it in nineteen an' seventy-three. —Why, you worried about that? That's the big deal you an' that girlie been fartin' aroun' gumshoein'? You think I don't know what's goin' on in this penitentiary?"

"You don't care about it . . . ?"

Cooper, a small vulture, bald and shriveled in gray shorts and sweatshirt, stood staring up at Bauman out of his good eye as if expecting, momentarily, the return of common sense—then being disappointed. "You jus' don't get it, do you, Trainer? Swear to God I don't think you or that girlie, either one of you muffins even *belong* in here. You see, it don't make no difference if guys try an' pay one of my boys to lose a fight. Don't make no difference at all—which you should know, 'cause you boxed a little. Don't make no difference, 'cause I would know it if one of my boys did a dive, an' that asshole wouldn' ever box again at State, an' not in no other walls, neither. You understan' what I'm sayin'? I'm sayin' that boxin' is all my boys got. Only thing they can do. Only thing they're any good for, in here. An' not a man of 'em dumb enough to dump no fight—get 'em kicked off the boxin' team forever. No way. Not for any kind of bread."

The vulture head tilted, looked up in inquiry. "You understan' that, Mr. Assistant?"

"I understand it, Coach."

"Well, I got to tell you it's a relief findin' out you ain't stupid clear through. —Now, here's what I want you should do. You forget whichever asshole is wastin' his time tryin' an' scam my fights nowadays, an' you get your college ass in gear over there on that wop, that Marcantonio, who—so help me God—is missin' hittin' the speed bag, for Christ's sake!"

"O.K."

Cooper started to strut away, halted after three snappy steps to say, "That Ferguson one of the guys worryin' you?"

Bauman said nothing.

Little Cooper grinned, exposing his false teeth. "An' you think Ferguson could go in a ring an' not try an' kill the boy he's fightin'?" He laughed a swift, wheezing laugh. "Mr. Trainer, ain't enough gelt in the world to be buyin' that nut-case to lose no fight." And shaking his head in amusement at such naivete, marched away. . . .

"Tony, listen to me." Bauman's left cheek was still hot from Cousins' slap. "—What the hell are you trying to do to that bag?" And waiting for the sweating cruiser-weight's slow reply, sank as deep as he could into the familiar resilient mattress, cool sheets, and plump pillows of teaching, even this limited instruction.

"I'm hittin' the fuckin' bag!"

"You're missing it, too. Now why is that, Tony?"

"Fuck if I know."

"Well, I know," Bauman said—and reflected that in the Great Investigation he'd apparently known too much, too easily, that wasn't so. Had believed that Shupe and Wiltz were fixing fights . . . had thought that Wiltz had left the message on his wall. "Tony, what you're doing is trying to hit the bag with individual punches. To do that, you need quicker hands than you've got. That's a featherweight's thing, to be choosing shots off a speed bag."

"Well, what do I do? Assholes are laughin' at me over there."

"This time, I'm the one they're laughing at, Tony. Forget them and listen to me, O.K.?—What do we do? We learn the bag. Watch me." Bauman stepped to the bag, put both fists up to nudge it, judge height and distance, then closed his eyes and began a slow regular milling motion against that taut light clapper of leather, feeling, as he boxed the bag, its rapid responses tapping back into his knuckles, tuppa tuppa tuppa, as he struck it.

"See my eyes are closed, Tony?"

"Yeah."

"You don't even have to watch it. It's like jerking off. You look at your dick when you do that?"

"No. I ain't stupid."

"I never thought you were. —Well, you don't have to look at the bag either, though people usually do. You just play with it, get used to the rhythm," demonstrating a fairly accomplished roll, "—just get used to the rhythm it's picking up. Hear that?"

Tuppa tuppa tuppa, tuppa tuppa tuppa.

"Yeah, O.K. I know *you* can do that shit."

"Here, Tony, come up here. Stand . . . stand *up* to the damn thing. It's just a little leather bag; it's no big deal. Now, give me your hands.

. . . All right, close your eyes. Keep them closed, O.K.? I want you to just start tapping the bag, gently, gently, left hand, right hand—keep your eyes closed."

"I am."

"—Left hand, left left left. Right hand, right right right. Good. Now easy, left and right and left and right, and left left left, and right right right, that's it . . . very good. Speed it up and double it up; and it's left left right right, right right left left, and now you're going, now you're going, speed it up and speed it up. Hey—fabulous! You're going and you're going and you're *going*! You know, Tony, could be you'd fight better blind."

"Ha, ha," Marcantonio said, and eyes tight shut, with only an occasional mis-hit, began to bat the little bag into a blur.

Bauman, after almost an hour with the cruiser-weight, spent some time checking on Muñoz' body punching, judging his slightly wider stance, then stood ringside for a while watching Clarence Henry and Bubba Betts spar ponderously, assailing each other with slow thudding punches that made night-skinned meat and muscle shiver.

The morning passed, ended with Bauman helping Enrique to sweep, mop, then load a mound of dirty towels, shorts, socks, T-shirts and jock-straps into the locker room's antique washer. After which, he walked down the gym steps into a bright and frosty noon, satisfied at least with work decently done. Not sufficient, of course, to blunt the embarrassment of having misjudged Mr. Metzler—of taking a daughter's word on the old thug's reformation—and in the process making a public ass of himself, doubly an ass to be smacked across the face by an hysterical girl (or whatever) in front of Cooper and the whole team. That little incident certainly already vined to common knowledge throughout State.

Not the only fool, to be sure, even exempting Cousins on grounds of blind affection. And no question, alas, that Ferguson's casual identification—uncaring, unconcerned—carried complete conviction. Still, Metzler, and whoever had planned the fight-fixing with him, had grievously misjudged and underestimated the importance fighting held for men who could only *be* fighters. —The professorial clown therefore by no means the only booby in the matter. Clowns on both sides of the mystery—and why not? What but garish fantasy, foolishness, childish cruelty, criminal carelessness, headlong blunders and mis-fired plots had packed the tiers and blocks of State? Why assume his fellows, however sinister, had become more competent within their walls?

Comforted not to be the only fool, Bauman went down the long walkway across East yard, managing after all to enjoy the bright noon's silver-plate light against sky blue. Enjoying cold air moving past and around him only as fast as he chose to walk through it, enjoying the barely sufficient warmth of his denim jacket.

As he walked, he looked ahead at the distant figures, still or in motion, of inmates enjoying even this chill air, and supposed that among them might be the man (a mystery once more) who'd come to write the warning on his wall. Bauman then imagined he saw Cousins' slight stature among those loiterers. Cousins, sorry for what he'd done, waiting against B-block's wall for Bauman to walk nearer, when he would come out to greet him and apologize—or simply fall into step, silent, and go in with him to lunch.

Lunch was ham sandwiches, not bad with the slippery spoiling ham removed, handed over to Perteet, and the rest eaten as a mustard, mayonnaise, and lettuce sandwich. Lunch was several of these sandwiches, iced tea (to be served more and more frequently as winter settled in), and cherry Jell-O.

"Where is she?" Perteet, while eating the ham.

"Angry," Bauman said. "—Personal matter."

"Shit, I know that," Perteet said, and certainly did, as did everyone else, since several cons had moaned theatrically when Bauman came into the mess hall, *"Pussy trouble, pussy trouble,"* reminding Bauman forcibly of the chanting half-beasts of Doctor Moreau.

"So, where is she?"

"I think she's at the other mess hall, Pete. Can we drop it?"

"Charles," Scooter contributing, "—guy should know when he's got a good thing goin'. Really, man."

"Scoot, Pete's too big for me. You're not."

"I didn' mean nothin' insultin'. Wow, talk about touchy. . . ."

After lunch, Bauman went up the circular stair early, to have a few moments of privacy before Scooter came in for lock-'n'-count. He put on the Walkman's earphones, slid Stravinsky's *Agon* into the machine to buffer the block's noises, and lay on his bunk. He'd intended to consider the puzzle left by the revelation of Metzler as the fixer—but instead replayed the scene in the gym. Cousins' outburst, his own foolishness in trying to hold Lee still to face what needed to be faced. The slap. Remarkable, really, how consistent Cousins proved. Not a punch—a slap. Bauman suspected that Betty, or any other of State's changelings, would have made that reactive blow a very competent punch indeed.

Cousins, back in West mess enjoying Clifford's superior cooking, possibly had really been angry at Bauman for having been weak, for having gone along, for accepting a daughterly revision of Mr. Metzler's character too easily—allowing the unpleasant truth, when it came, to come as a shock instead of only confirmation.

And would the spoiled beauty have liked it better if Bauman had always argued the old monster a monster, had insisted on keeping him among the likely suspects—and been vindicated by Ferguson, rather than surprised himself? Very doubtful. In either case, Cousins would now be eating in West mess, would be injured, furious, and sullen. It was fatiguing to discover at State—accepted as a most savage and grimly masculine stronghold—precisely the familiar feminine festival of veils, sweet mysteries obscured by quibbles, complaints, outrage and pouting, as if the female principle were a universal constant, bound to appear even in the restricted company of murderous men.

Bauman wondered if he should take a nap, sleep through count, let the rest of this unlucky day go safely by—but that possibility vanished when Scooter appeared, clutching a new motorcycle magazine arrived in B-block's mail. He said something, and Bauman turned his Stravinsky down.

"Letter for you, roomie." Scooter, unfolding his magazine, handed Bauman a short envelope, then climbed up into his bunk. —This an unusual event, since Bauman's friends rarely wrote, and he'd been to considerable pains to keep this particular address from various professional organizations, diverting that stream of letters, bulletins, and papers to Susanne.

He recognized his father's large rounded script in the address.

> Dear son,
>
> Since I haven't heard from you, I guess everything is as O.K. as it can be. If I know you, and you're a chip off the old block, you're probably running that place. And you'll be out of there pretty soon, regardless. If they had put people in jail for having a few drinks and driving in the old days, your dad would have been in for about a century!
>
> It was a good idea to move to St. Cloud, and this little studio apartment thing here is fine. There are a lot of old crocks got it worse than me. I will say this, though, it is a big surprise to wake up and find out you're an old man. Wow, talk about big surprises!
>
> There's an old fart up here in the next unit called Ray Bohannin, got the dirtiest mouth you ever heard, but he's good company and he's always getting us out on these dates to go

shopping with some of the old ladies from their units. And I'll tell you, boy, some of them look pretty good!

But there's not one of them can hold a candle to your mom. We had our good times and our bad times, but she's the gal I dream about, just the same. Once you lose the love of your life, boy, half the love of life goes right out with her, and that's the truth.

Beth calls me once a week, regular as clockwork, and puts that grandson of mine on the phone to tell me what's going on.

I know you're very busy down there, Charlie, so don't worry about writing to me or anything. I know you're thinking about your dad, because he's thinking about you. Tell you something funny before I close. I dreamed I was down there with you in that place, and don't think the Baumans weren't showing those clowns what's what!

Yours,
Dad.

Bauman folded his father's letter, reached back to slide it under his pillow, and lay listening to the Stravinsky—its swift building-blocks unconcerned with any time but time's divisions and the rhythms of dividing. *Ars longa*.

He lifted his earphones a bit, to settle them more comfortably, just in time to hear their house door sound a single click, and released, commence to roll weightily shut as a hack below, a black man by his voice, shouted, "Watch them fingerrrrs. . . !"

Bauman fitted his earphones, and enjoyed a serendipitous conjunction of the steel door's crash closed with a Stravinskyan fanfare. He shook a Winston out of his pack, lit it, and lay imagining he was pretending to sleep, very late at night—lying, eyes almost closed, with Mr. Hyde held in his hand. —Then, having heard the slightest sound in the door lock, the faintest sliding as the steel drew back, suddenly rolling from the covers to be struck in dim red light, hacked at, then thrown sideways into a wall. Slugging, stabbing, wrestling in a brutal fight filling their small house (Scooter, terrified, shouting down from his bunk), Bauman finally managing—cut, but not too badly cut—to twist his right arm free, strike the center of that moving darkness with his knife, and kill the man.

It would serve to teach Cousins a lesson he'd remember once he was out of State, whether he was wearing a skirt or trousers. *'Mr. Big Brain. An' you're full of shit, too. . . .'*

"Not the only one," Bauman said, and because of the Walkman's muffling earphones, apparently said it out loud. Scooter, reading his motorcycle magazine in the bunk above, abruptly changed position and hung his head over the rail.

" 'Not the only one' what?" Asked loud enough to be heard over the Stravinsky.

Bauman tugged the earphones free, turned the tape player off.

"Nothing, Scooter. I was talking to myself."

"Bad habit, dude," Scooter said. "—Bad habit. Start that shit in here, you never stop." He hung upside down, goggling at Bauman a moment more to emphasize the seriousness of that advice, then withdrew back up into his bunk and lay silent, reading about engines, frames, tires, fuel, or techniques of riding—whichever. All to be revealed to Bauman at some early opportunity, and discussed with him at length, as if he must be interested.

The watch sergeant, Hanks, absent the past two weeks or so, probably on leave, was the hack conducting count. Bauman could hear his hoarse voice advancing along Ground-tier below, counting inmates in a loud, slow, carefully articulated series. "Seventy-nine . . . eighty . . . eighty-one . . ."

After Hanks had climbed the circular stair to Two-tier, and stepped to their bars, Bauman was labeled his customary ninety-seven, Scooter his usual ninety-eight.

Hanks paused at their door after ninety-eight. A young black hack Bauman didn't know stood beside him, this a probable fish cop, just up to State.

"An' in here—asshole on the bottom bunk, Bauman, is a cutie, likes to attack corrections officers. Last try got him a little of this," Hanks displaying to the young hack a large mottled fist, "—plus a little time in Seg to cool him off. Would you believe a professor in a college? Believe that? Look at the guy, you want to know why education is in big trouble."

The young black man, very neat in starched new khakis and polished black oxfords, stared through the bars at number ninety-seven. Bauman, propped on his elbow, stared back. "You will find," he said to the young hack, "—that in State there are some inmates who are very decent people, and some C.O.'s who aren't."

"What the fuck you mean by that, Bauman?" Hanks said. "Is that abusive talk or what?"

"It's 'what.' "

Hanks paused, thinking about it. "That's—that's abusive talk. You do any more, an' your college ass is goin' right down to Gorney, an' before that I'm comin' in there an' break your fuckin' jaw!"

Bauman smiled at the young hack. "Welcome to State," he said.

"Oh, hey, Charles!" Betty in her doorway, beckoning him out of the crowd trooping down from the tiers.

"Hi, sweetie."

"Charles, don' be in such a hurry. Come an' talk to me."

"I'm always happy to talk to you."

"Come in, come in. You want coffee?"

"No coffee, but I'm starving. I'm not eating enough of that crap Rudy's serving. Perteet's getting fat, and I'm starving to death."

"Sit down. You sit down. I'm goin' give you cheese san'wiches." And, tomboyish in illicit side-zipper jeans rolled up to her calves, new white court shoes, and a man's dress shirt—dyed plum and worn tails out—she bustled away to her sink, began sorting through a stack of cigar boxes.

"You've had your hair done. . . ." Bauman sat in the house's rocking chair, found he'd missed its easy back and forth. He noticed a movement higher, glanced up and saw in shadow the gleaming rounds of Marky's glasses, the master of the house looking down benignly from his habitual upper bunk.

"I got a haircut. You know that Gloria? Alphonso, was her name. She cut it."

"Looks nice," Bauman said. "Very nice, very uptown. How are things going, Marky?"

"Goin' fine." Nellis' voice soft, uninflected as his manner. "Had some trouble with that ham at lunch?"

"Gottschalk's sliced ham is just too risky."

"Talkin' risky," Nellis said, "—talkin' risky, you want to watch out for that Manny, that Oklahoma guy."

Surprised by this remark, Bauman for an instant couldn't make sense of it, then recalled Manny Elk Antler and the freight elevator.

"Who?" Betty, from the sink. "Who you talkin' about, Marky?"

"Nobody, hon," Nellis said. This useful denial, at Betty's accepting silence, dismissed the subject.

But not for Bauman, who ceased his rocking and sat still, feeling a prickle of gooseflesh down his forearms. He recalled Manny Elk Antler's narrow dark dull eyes, his large high-bridged nose, the protuberant upper lip almost attached to it to present a toucan's profile. He recalled the Pawnee's readiness to cut Cousins' throat.

"Here you go, Charles." Betty, ministering angel, round, brown as a gingerbread girl, came to deposit in Bauman's lap a paper plate on which five Tom's Cheese Sandwich crackers had been arranged around a small red apple, slightly withered.

"This is really nice," Bauman said, and realized after he'd said it, what a habit he'd made of battening on Betty—the careless bachelor feeding with married friends. No question a social debt was owed, and likely one to Kavafian as well, for his poker evenings.

"—Listen, Scooter and I want to give a party. I especially owe you two for your very generous hospitality over many months. I want you to know I appreciate it." Bauman was amused to find himself imagining Cousins as his hostess—smiling, content, all anger and disappointment gone—dressed prettily to welcome their guests.

"Always welcome in here," Marky Nellis said.

"Havin' a party sounds real nice." Betty stood watching him eat his first cheese sandwich cracker. "I don' want to say nothin', but how come that Lee isn' feedin' you up, Charles? You got them passes, you could go to her house."

"We've been busy," Bauman said, and ate another cracker.

"I don' care. I don' want to say nothin' against her—"

"Then don't say nothin' against her." Marky, from his upper bunk. "—Leave the folks alone, work out their own thing."

"I ain' saying nothin' against her."

"Good. Don't say nothin'."

"All I'm—"

"*Hey.*"

"All right, all right. I ain' sayin' nothin'. . . ."

This interchange, so familiarly domestic, brought grimly to Bauman's mind his dream of Betty imprisoned in the infirmary's security room—half changed, a monster trapped between sexes. He'd intended to ask after young Onofrio, the putative adoptee, but decided not to, as if that dark dream and the message on his wall were signs so ominous that his simple inquiry might spark a tragedy. He ate another cracker.

Betty stood for a few moments watching him, then said, "I got somethin' nice for you," hurried back to her sink, searched rapidly through the cigar boxes, then came back with a fresh paper plate. Bending, she presented a Mother Monroe miniature pecan pie, still in its little windowed box. The box had been roughly opened, carelessly reclosed—certainly by one of the mail hacks, to probe the tiny pie for who knew what contraband.

"Too much," Bauman said, and had to swallow a mouthful of cracker. "—I can't take that."

"You can too. Marky's brother sent up a whole package of them pies an' everything."

"Go on, try that pie." Marky, from above. "Them little pies is real good, better'n canteen shit."

"No, no. This is special. Really, I don't need to be eating you two out of house and home. You save these for yourselves."

"We ain' savin' nothin' from frien's," Betty said. "You eat that pie, or I'm goin' get mad at you."

"Eat up, Teach," Marky said. "You see if that ain't better'n canteen shit."

The pecan pie was a three-bite treat, so sweet it made Bauman's throat ache as if he were weeping. "Fabulous," he said when he'd finished it. "That is the best thing I ever put in my mouth."

"You tell that Lee to be feedin' you, Charles."

"Betty—"

"Marky, I ain' sayin' nothin' bad about her. I know she's pretty. . . ."

Walking down through the kitchen to B-block's back gate, Bauman tried to think of when, during his visit, he might have reintroduced the subject of Marky's warning about the Pawnee, and asked Nellis to enlarge on it. It was disturbing that Marky'd mentioned only Manny Elk Antler—not Becker, not the other man. Which could only mean that the Pawnee was regarded by the knowledgeable as more dangerous.

All an insight, Bauman supposed, to the conditions of bronze age and early iron-age tribalism, where any one male, sufficiently formidable, might tilt the balance of battle, and so, of war.

"How'd you like that ham at lunch?" Rudy Gottschalk, sweat stippling his tattooed scalp, beaming, expectant. "That ham was two months old."

"It was something special, Rudy—really special."

"It's slow bakin' does it, man. That ham has got to cook for a full six hours, or it tastes like shit an' don't last."

"I believe that. . . ."

The afternoon, like morning's big brother, confronted Bauman with full winter's white and even light, its freezing air, as he walked down the kitchen steps and out across the courtyard to C-block's back gate, keeping an eye out for Jack Moglc as hc went.

Kyle Smith, become a regular lifer sentinel, stood at C's back gate talking with Carlyle. It was the first time in more than a year at State that Bauman had seen that veteran hack on duty out of doors. Carlyle's khaki uniform coat, three-quarter length, was buttoned up to a plump chin, the afternoon's cold having spanked even more scarlet into the old man's cheeks, the tip of his nose. Carlyle, fat, snowy-haired, rosy, played Santa Claus for the C.O.'s children—and the inmates' children, too, when they came up to visit two days before Christmas.

"Looky who we got here." Smith lean and rakish with his long dark hair, dark mustache. He was wearing a stylish leather jacket, zipped to his throat.

"What are you doing out in the cold, Carlyle?" Bauman said, and stood by the fence gate while Carlyle patted him carelessly with gloved hands.

"I as't for it, any of your business. Got tired of smellin' you people's farts in them blocks."

"What do you want in C, Bauman?" Smith said, as if he had every right to ask.

"I want to talk to your officers," Bauman said.

"Oh, you want to talk to club officers? An' what about?"

"None of your business, Smith," Bauman said. "So stop screwing around."

"Hey, man, you don't talk to fuckin' me like that!"

"I just did," Bauman said, surprised at his confidence Smith would make nothing of it. It seemed he might be learning to judge the men at State.

"Well, fuck you, man."

"Hey, you people take it easy," Carlyle said.

"Kyle, just lead me in."

"You better have fuckin' business in here," Smith said, and turned to lead Bauman up the steps.

There were only a few loungers in the Lifer Club corridor; it was steamy hot, radiators hissing. Smith knocked on the office door, walked in and closed the door behind him. After a moment, he came out into the hall, said, "You better watch your mouth in there, man." Held the office door open for Bauman, then shut it behind him.

The Lifer Club office was almost as it had been, except for the absence of Jerry the Giant, and the different positions occupied by

Shupe and Wiltz. This afternoon, Brian Wiltz was seated behind the desk. Jim Shupe—denims pressed, short russet beard neatly trimmed—was standing by the back wall taking down old posters, charts, and notices, sorting through them, placing rejects in a large brown metal wastebasket.

"Here he is, our very own cop," Wiltz said, smiling, small dark gray eyes sighting past the large adenoidal nose. He was wearing a tan civilian windbreaker with a sweater-knit collar, his long black hair carefully combed straight back.

"Come in an' take a load off, detective. Sit down. What can we do for you?"

"Answer a couple of questions, if you will." Bauman pulled a straight-back chair out a little way from the front of the desk, then sat—but didn't cross his legs, and so slow a reach under his waistband for the knife.

"What do you think, Jimmy?" Wiltz said. "Think we're under arrest?"

"I don't think so," Shupe wadded up a notice of some sort, and threw it in the wastebasket.

Wiltz slid a handsome silver cigarette case out of his left windbreaker pocket, took out a cigarette, put the case away, and lit up with a wooden match from a box of Blue Tips on his desk. He sat smoking, watching Bauman.

"The questions—"

"Don't think they're goin' to be any surprise," Wiltz said. "Do you, Jimmy?"

"No, I don't."

"Jim boy thinks you're real smart, Professor. Guess he don't hold any grudge for almost gettin' his hearin' damaged."

"That's nice," Bauman said.

"Where's your girlfriend?"

"Had something else to do."

"Uh-oh. Not as smart as you thought, Jim boy," Wiltz said. "Lyin' to us already." And to Bauman, "You think we don't know you had a little lovers' quarrel? You lost her, sport; an' that's a sweet piece of ass to lose, as who should know better then us right here in this room. Let me ask you somethin', just satisfy my curiosity as to your relationship. You fucked that sugar, yet?"

"No."

"Told you, Jimmy. Our investigator here hasn't screwed her. Was I right, or what?"

"You were right," Shupe said.

"Right about this, too. She tell you she came up here three, four evenings ago? After chow?"

"No."

"Right again, Brian," Shupe said, folded a small cardboard chart, and slid it down into the wastebasket.

"Well, Professor, she did. Came over here to talk about Billy Burnside; some people been rippin' the old man off for candy."

"Right," Shupe said.

"Unfortunately," Wiltz said, "—my duties of office as a lifer vice president in charge of accounts receivable, require me to act bad as possible, keep my reputation up. An' therefore, I was unable to do a favor without requestin' a favor in return."

"What favor?"

"Hear that, Jimmy? He couldn't help askin' that one."

"Guess not."

Wiltz took a deep drag on his cigarette, swiveled the desk chair slightly to the side, and exhaled the smoke in a long, long breath. "Now," he said, "—subject interests you is history. Interests President Nash, also. But the subject interests me is human nature; you can put a lifetime study into that an' still get surprised. For example, here's this punk comin' over to ask for a favor—and do a favor, if she has to. An' of course she has to, has to put out to help her senile ol' buddy."

"Wiltz," Bauman said, "you are a piece of shit."

"My, my," Shupe said.

"Is our cop, here, brave or what, Jimmy?" Wiltz said. "But I'll tell you somethin' funny, Professor—what I mean by human nature. The dick don't lie. Get my meaning? The dick—don't—lie. An' when a punk is suckin' on somethin', and her pants goes down and there's a hard-on, well, you just have to figure the lady likes it. An' after a little while she steps out of them pants, an' is lyin' on this desk right here," he reached out, tapped the desktop, "—is lyin' across this desk, them pants off, suckin' Jimmy's dick an' stickin' that cute ass in the air, well, my interest in human nature tells me this lady likes what she thinks she shouldn' be likin'. So, she makes excuses with herself, you know, and comes up here just to do an old con a favor. An' if she has to do some stuff—hey, not her fault."

"How's he doing?" Shupe said.

Wiltz laughed. "Come over here. —You should see this face. Professor don't know whether to shit or go blind." He tapped a long ash off his cigarette into the small State souvenir ashtray. "Don't get too distressed now; punk can't help what she can't help. An' if you been too dumb to chip off a piece, well, that's not her fault, is it? You got no business bein' mad at her."

"I'm not."

"He's mad at you, Brian."

"Mad at both of us, Jim boy. I'm goin' to do you a real favor, Professor, 'cause I can see you like the punk—you know, in a spiritual kind of a way. You know why you probably had some trouble with her today? An' I don't mean whatever the argument was about. Know why you had trouble with her? Probably kind of continuous? —It's because she don't know where she's at with you; because what she's got is her face an' her ass. That's it. An' you haven't even tried for some of what she's got, an' you're pissin' her off. Ladies like to be *tried*, Professor."

"Now, let me tell you what I don't like," Bauman said. "—I don't like wasting my time sitting and listening to hoodlums like you pretend they have thought processes. What the hell happened to those good old-fashioned hoods who just grunted, and took what they could get away with?"

"Oh, man, that's rude," Wiltz said. "You must have been a real pain in the ass in a classroom."

"I've listened to you people's horseshit over in Segregation, in houses, in the movies, and in a fucking meat locker—and it's unbelievably boring. As for you, you're lucky you have a talent for breaking people's heads—at least when you come up on them from behind. Give any of the men in here a free choice, and they'd flush you down a toilet."

Wiltz laughed and put his cigarette out in the ashtray. "Any comment on that extreme loss of cool, Jim boy? Think the professor's in love?"

"Sure does care. Maybe he's just in like." Shupe crumpled some paper to throw away. "Hard to say he's wrong on the facts."

Wiltz sighed. "It's a shame for a man to put himself down, but I got to agree. We do have these leadership raps we run. An' I am a naughty guy; it's just somethin' I got to live with. So, change of subject, Professor—those questions you came over here to ask. You really need to ask 'em? Did you finally get it figured ol' Jim an' me didn' wax Barney Metzler, or the little nigger either?"

"So it seems."

"You figure that fight-fixin' shit wasn't us?"

"Oh, I figured that one out. It was Nash, wasn't it? Nash and Metzler decided to give that a try."

"Didn't I tell you?" Shupe said, picked up the full wastebasket and carried it out the office door. Closed the door behind him.

"Well," Wiltz said, "—he did tell me, Professor. He thought you an' the punk'd figure that one out."

"Which leads to my first question, Wiltz. Why?"

"Oh, the bread would have helped him hang on to the club, even from over in Seg. An' also because of the niggers. With our president, it's always the niggers. He figures we build a big enough war chest, we can hold the coons down, no matter they come floodin' into the place."

"But you don't agree?"

"Hell, no. He's givin' 'em too much credit. Listen, Professor, little lesson in human nature. —You know about the numbers? Big city gamblin' on horse-race results, whatever?"

"I know about the numbers."

"Well, there's a very interestin' thing about the numbers. Almost everybody in that is black. Did you know that? Customers, runners, banks, just about everybody's black, an' the locations are right in the middle of black neighborhoods."

"So I understand."

"But, not in one fuckin' city do the blacks run the numbers. Not one. Detroit, Chicago, Philadelphia, New Orleans, New York—you name the city. Wise guys run it; those rednecks down South—Memphis an' Atlanta—they run it; Spanish guys run it in Miami, L.A. Everybody but the blacks."

"And your point. . .?"

"My point, Professor, is they won't be runnin' shit in here, either, no matter how many come in. We don't need a war chest—an' if we do, we'll raise it out of black pockets."

"Then according to you, Nash was way off base—the boxing scam being an example of how far off base—and Metzler equally foolish to try and run it for him."

"Takin' the words out of my mouth."

Shupe walked into the office with the emptied wastebasket, and closed the door behind him.

"Professor's takin' the words right out of our mouths, Jimmy."

"Not surprising."

"Second question," Bauman said. "If Metzler was a problem, going along with Nash on that, obviously paying more attention to Nash than to you two, then why not kill him? After all, Nash is locked down in Segregation and might never be released. With Metzler out of the way, that would be the last of the old guard. You two'd be free to cut up the cake."

"Last of this bullshit." Shupe reached high to tear down a multi-colored chart, crumple it, and stuff it into the wastebasket.

"Well, you know, Professor," Wiltz said, "that wouldn' ever have been necessary."

"No?"

"No. You teach that nutso kid, don't you? Sarasote?"

"Yes."

"Well, one evenin' we was down in the showers, an' that kid came in an' braced Barney about some payout. Now, let me tell you some-thin'. Old days, Barney Metzler would have taken that kid apart right there. Right *there*. —But he didn' do it; didn' do a fuckin' thing. 'Well,' I said to myself, '—we got an old guy here.' Joint politics is a young guy's game, an' Barney was past it. Sad fact."

"Cousins thinks Metzler was changing into a decent man."

"Could be, could be. Amounts to the same thing, right? Effect's the same in here, right? Guy gets old, loses his balls. Same thing if he gets sweet. Man's no fuckin' good to us, either way."

"Not worth killing, is what you're saying."

"You got it. Not worth the trouble. We ever had a hassle with old Barney, we could have just leaned on his punk. Barney would have folded quick, we put Cousins in a cross."

"And Kenneth Spencer?"

"That little nig didn' have a fuckin' thing to do with us."

"But the same weapon killed both of them," Bauman said. "Surprised?"

"Now," Wiltz leaned forward in his swivel chair. "—Now you're tellin' me shit I didn' know. You know what a smart king does?"

"No, I can't say I do know what a smart king does." Struck by the hierarchical and royalist references so common to leadership at State.

"I'll tell you. A smart king gives silver to the dude brings him good news. But dude brings bad news—gets gold."

"Bad news more valuable, of course. Am I going to get some money out of this?"

"That's interesting," Shupe said from the wall. "Definitely same weapon?"

"That's what my expert says."

"Somethin' to think about," Wiltz said. "Isn' it, Jimmy? Maybe this fish is gettin' to be a real cop after all."

"Could be."

"It's the connection puzzles me," Wiltz said. "Barney Metzler, an' a little nothin' nigger. . . ."

"And," Bauman said, "—Metzler's the man who threatened Spencer in the first place."

"Right. Clarence Henry's uncle," Shupe said. "Metzler'd try to get to Henry that way. Makes sense."

"Then, both those men are killed with the same weapon," Bauman said. "And almost certainly by the same man."

"It's interesting." Shupe.

"It's a pain in the ass," said Wiltz.

"What I haven't found—we haven't found—is any trace of a hack being involved."

"Let me tell you somethin', Professor," Wiltz said. "We got one bought hack, an' a couple rented ones. An' they tell us no hack was up for that, no way. —But that still don't explain how some con got out to do that night job on Spencer."

"We think we know how that was done."

"We?" Wiltz said. "Meanin' you an' the punk?"

"And how was it done?" Shupe, tearing the last two notices off the wall.

"It was Cousins' idea," Bauman said. "We think Lesnovitch got into the captain's office and reset the backup system for the cell doors. Set the killer's door to unlock in the middle of the night. And unlocked the victim's, too."

"Oooh, cute," Shupe said. "Cute."

"—If true, Jim boy." Wiltz stubbed his cigarette out in the ashtray. "Not so fuckin' easy, even for the electrician, be screwin' around that office. Those hacks are in there all the time. For me, it's more like a maybe."

"I think more than a maybe," Bauman said, "—since I had a visitor last night who left me a little message across the wall over my bunk. Said, 'Better butt out.' "

"My, my, my." Shupe.

"Sure it wasn't your roomie?" Wiltz said. "That biker kid?"

"It wasn't. So, with the electrician—or some other way—a con's getting out of his house at night, and into other people's. That word needs to get out to the club leaders."

"Lots of bad asses going to be sleeping light tonight," Shupe said, amused.

"—I'll also give Pokey Duerstadt the news. Since he's everybody's official bigmouth, he can have the pleasure of playing switchboard for you club people from here on out."

Wiltz sighed. "That'll be O.K., Professor. —Now, we had our councilin' an' information session here. Time for you to get up an' get out, an' go on lookin' for whoever. Keep in mind Lifer Club did *not* wax Barney Metzler. Which, it's my guess, is what Nash wanted to know from the start—if Jim an' me offed his old buddy, gettin' ready to take over the club."

"Aren't you going to take the club over?"

"Hell, yes. Let me tell you somethin', Mr. College. You think Nash is ever goin' to get out of Seg? No way. Never. Our president always was a little dingy, an' now he's gettin' dingier. Pretty soon he's goin' to be givin' orders—an' nothin' at all is goin' to happen over here. That's just how it goes. It's natural, isn' it?"

"If you can get away with it. I'd say Nash would be dangerous in his grave, let alone over there in Seg."

"Hey, I didn' say we had a risk-free run, here."

"And that's why Teppman's in, collecting—and Becker's out?"

"You got it, Professor. New broom. Becker was the old guys' guy."

"I see. —And what about my son in all this nonsense?"

"Our man's not goin' to bother your kid," Wiltz said. "He likes him. I hear he thinks that's a very good-lookin' boy you got there. Nice kid, an' a good ballplayer. —You just go on detectin', you an' the punk. Find the fuck who offed old Barney, an' we'll call it square."

"Not good enough. Your creep's too close; he's still hanging around my boy's school. I want him called off and far away."

"An' if we decide not to rush doin' that? Keep you on the string?"

"Then we'll all be taking a serious risk. Because if your man loses control of himself and hurts my son—then I will certainly try my very best to get to you two, in here. I'm an intelligent man. I'm sure I'll be able to think of a way to find each of you alone sometime, somewhere in State."

"You buy that, Jimmy?"

"Not for much," Shupe said.

"Jimmy doesn't think you'd do somethin' like that, Professor."

"He's wrong. I'd have no choice."

Wiltz sat relaxed, looking at Bauman with something of the opaque encompassing stare that Nash (soon likely to be the Lear of Segregation) had employed. "O.K. We'll do you the favor. But you stop workin' for us on this, the creep gets called right back—an' not just to hang around."

"Deal," Bauman said, pushed back his chair, and stood up. "I do have one last question."

"Oh, hey, by all means."

"Which one of you is going to run the lifers?"

"Good question. What do you say, Jimmy?"

"Oh, Brian's going to run the club," Shupe said, pinning what looked like a fresh notice to the wall. "No doubt about it. In here, might definitely makes right."

"There you go," Wiltz said. "Great exec. . . ."

"Wiltz," Bauman said, "—you're already in trouble." He walked out of the office and closed the door gently behind him.

Carlyle was still on C-block's courtyard gate. Smith was gone.

"I have a message for Gorney," Bauman said, while Carlyle carelessly stroked down his left arm, then his right.

"That so?"

"Tell him Nash and Metzler tried to fix the Joliet fight, and muffed it. Metzler and Spencer may have been killed in connection with that, though probably not by other lifer officers. In any case, they were killed by the same person or persons, using the same weapon. And whoever the killer is, he may get out of his cell at night by having the backup door circuits reset."

Carlyle now looked almost alert. "No shit?" He felt along Bauman's collar.

"No shit. And you can also tell Gorney that if he or anybody else threatens me with that grand jury just once more, then I'm out of it, and he can take this little murder case and shove it right up his ass."

"He isn' goin' to like that kind of talk, Bauman."

"That's the idea, Carlyle. —Why don't you wake up?"

An inmate named Porter called to Bauman as he came through the kitchen's double doors out into the mess hall, still chill from the courtyard's cold.

"Teach, you got a call-back. Cernan's runner was lookin' for you."

"Thanks, Terry." Bauman went on through the mess hall, then past the basement's stone steps and down the corridor to the phones. There was a long line for the canteen, a shorter line for the phones.

Cernan, standing behind his lectern, saw Bauman coming up alongside the line. "Call come in for you, Professor! Operator fourteen, Fort Wayne. You go on and use number three when Carson's through."

"Thank you, Mr. Cernan."

Once in the phone line, with nothing to do but wait, Bauman found he could no longer avoid picturing Cousins in the Lifer Club office—betrayed by a boy's natural heat into playing the kind of girl he wished not to be. Bauman thought of it, imagined the scene, and was relieved to have no erection.

It took Carson a few seconds more than nine minutes, by Bauman's Timex, to finish his call and leave the phone.

"Hello?"

"Hello."

"Beth? —Beth?"

"Charlie."

"Nothing wrong?"

"No, nothing's wrong. Phil's fine."

"O.K. What is it? Are you all right?"

"Charlie, I'm fine."

"All right."

"Charlie, the reason I'm calling is that Phil and I had a talk. He told me you called—and he told me what happened, what he said to you."

"Oh, hell, that . . . that's nothing. It was my fault. I was out of line; I kept asking about you, and it made him angry. Stupid, and my fault. Neither one of you should worry about that for a minute. Truth is, I have no damn business calling either one of you. I understand that."

"Charlie, that isn't so, and it's not why I'm calling. I had a long talk with Phil about this—at last—and I think, and he agrees, that the situation as it's been going is very unhealthy. Very bad for him, and probably for all of us. Grim as it is up there, and I'm sure it's dreadful, what he's been imagining is probably worse. I think he needs to see his father, even under these circumstances. What do you think?"

"He wants to come up?"

"Let's say he needs to come up—and Charles, believe me I'm grateful that glacier is beginning to melt. I was . . . I've been worried sick about him."

"And you'd come up with him?"

"I called the assistant warden's office—he's that nice man who let me call you before?—and he told me I'd have to come up and go in with Phil, according to regulations."

"Right, that's right. When? When were you thinking?"

"In a couple of weeks? I wouldn't want to interfere with Susanne's going up to see you."

"Don't worry. Don't worry about that. You two plan to come up whenever you want, and I'll take care of it. Don't worry about it."

"All right. I just wanted to ask you, Charlie—I just wanted to ask if I should prepare him for, you know, for how bad it might be?"

"And prepare yourself?"

"Yes. If you could just tell me what it's like. . . ."

"I'll tell you exactly what it's like, and you tell Philly. State's really very interesting, it's such an old-fashioned joint. . . . It's like coming to visit a huge old fortress—a castle—shabby, weary, but still formidable. It's very crowded and very noisy, but in Administration and the visiting room there's nothing to be frightened of, just a lot of families talking, getting together, kids running around. Some couples kissing, making whatever love they can."

"Should I bring something? Some food?"

"No, no, don't bring anything in at all. People do bring food in, but it's against regulations. They'll give you a pamphlet downstairs, and a corrections officer will make a little speech on what's permitted and what's not. They won't let you take your purse in, for example. Tell Philly that a hack—a corrections officer—will probably look you both over, and might pat you down."

"God. Pat me?"

"It'll be a woman, just making sure you're not bringing in a machine gun or a kilo of coke."

"Well, I'm glad you warned me."

"So . . . and you're sure he really wants to come up?"

"It seems like a good idea. Don't you think so?"

"I think it's wonderful. A wonderful idea."

"All right. Well, two weeks?"

"Two weeks. Sunday afternoon visiting."

"Is that the best time?"

"The best time."

"And you're sure it won't inconvenience Susanne?"

"Don't worry about that. It won't inconvenience her."

"Well, all right. We'll see you then."

"See you then."

"Take care."

"You take care," Bauman said, and listened until she hung up. Then he called over to Cernan. "Mr. Cernan! May I make a call?"

"Short call, please, Professor. . . ."

Bauman dialed Norman Silber's office number.

"Silber and Hillman, Locations."

"I have a message for Mr. Silber."

"Who's calling, please?"

"Charles Bauman."

"You— You were told never to call here again."

"This is the last time I'll call, and the message is fairly short. Please write it down. Tell Mr. Silber I had too much to drink to drive safely. Too much to drink. . . . And having done that and driven the car, I'm responsible for his daughter's death. Responsible for her death . . . and for driving away from the scene of that crime. Please tell Mr. Silber I deserve to be where I am . . . and that he won't be hearing from me again. Did you get all that?"

". . . Yes."

"Goodbye." Bauman hung up, waved a thanks to Cernan, and walked across the corridor to the canteen line. He had to wait quite a while, almost half an hour, before he got to Ramos' Dutch serving door.

"What the fuck you wan'?"

"I want three Bit-O'-Honey's, a big almond Hershey, box of Cracker-Jack, and two cans of Vienna sausage—and one of those State baseball caps. It's for a fourteen-year-old. They adjustable?"

"Yeah, medium'll fit a kid."

"All gray?"

"They all gray, man."

"O.K. Give me one with the guard tower and searchlight on it."

Dinner was beef stew, two slices of white bread, peas, and strawberry Jell-O. Cousins didn't come to East mess for the meal.

Scooter gave Perteet his peas, but Bauman, hungry, refused to part with anything. Scooter distracted Perteet from that disappointment by engaging him in an endless and circular discussion of unfair and discriminatory motorcycle-helmet laws—laws enacted by faggots whose own skulls were too soft to survive a finger-flip.

His dinner finished, Bauman went to the end of the serving counter to scrape his tray into the garbage. Scooter and Perteet remained behind in discussion, Perteet arguing that a pair of cow horns screwed to a war-surplus German army helmet made very safe and crash-resistant headgear.

As he handed his tray across the counter to B.B., Bauman heard someone laughing at a table two tables behind him, glanced back, and saw Pokey Duerstadt in merriment with a bearded young biker called Lucky—in for life for invading an elderly couple's motor home in search of cash, tormenting his bound victims with his lighter for an hour or so, then, exasperated, cutting their throats with his Buck knife.

Bauman walked back to that table and sat at the nearest of two empty places.

"Hey, Teach, you want somethin', or what?" Duerstadt—dwarfish, piratical with his red bandanna headband, long oily black hair, the thin gold ring piercing his right cheek—leaned back from his joke-telling still smiling, and seemed as ready to be amused by what Bauman might have to say.

"I want a word with you, Pokey, if you have the time."

"Oh, I got the time."

"Lucky," Bauman said, "—would you excuse us, please? Business." That last word, a talisman in any American situation, levered Lucky up and off his stool.

"I'm takin' off," he said, and to Pokey, "Later, dude." And ambled away.

"What business?"

"Switchboard business, Pokey. I have a report I want you to make for me."

"What are you talkin' about, man?"

"Pokey, I don't know, and I don't give a damn what you tell the lifers about the bikers or vice versa. But since you do obviously talk to the leadership in both clubs, I assume you can arrange to talk to the leadership in the other clubs as well."

"So what?"

"So I want you to forward whatever I tell you, starting tonight—to your own boss, Ganz, and to Colonel Perkins over in D-block, and Vargas in A."

"Me, man? Why the fuck me?"

"Keep your voice down. You, because Shupe named you as my contact for the lifers. And you, because when Bump showed you off in the movies as the bikers' own, you had some fun with me about it. Fine, you've got such a generally accepted mouth—you use it. I'm sick of listening to those club people's crap, so you can spread the word from here on out. I'll tell you—and you'll tell them."

"Fuck that, man. An' fuck you." But kept his voice down.

"Nash and Barney Metzler tried to fix the Joliet fight."

"*Jesus*—" Pokey started to stand up, but Bauman reached across the table, gripped the biker's thick left wrist, and was just able to hold on to it.

"Where you going, Pokey? It's news."

"You better let go."

"Sit down," Bauman said, and took his hand from Duerstadt's wrist.

"You are fuckin' out of your mind, motherfucker," Duerstadt said, and sat.

"I'm just tired of kissing ass in here. I'm tired of talking to these people. Now, listen. Nash and Metzler tried to fix the Joliet fight for a lot of bucks. It didn't work. There is no fix. But in trying it, Metzler threatened Clarence Henry's uncle. Spencer."

"I ain't hearin' none of this."

"Sure you are. For some reason, connected to the fix or not, both Barney Metzler and Spencer were killed by the same weapon, by the same man. And that man has found a way to get out of his house at night, and get into anybody else's—maybe by setting the backup circuits for the cell doors, maybe some other way."

"*Christ*. I ain't listenin'."

"Shhhh. From here on out," Bauman said, and got up from the table, "—any Lifers or B.N.A. or Zapatistas ask me about this little investigation, I'm going to refer them to the Switchboard. You're going to be the dude who knows everything."

"You're lookin' to get hurt real bad, man."

"By you? —Get in line," Bauman said, and walked away to the mess-hall doors and out.

My Dear,

We've always known, I think, our pleasures to be temporary. My year in prison—and the year and more to follow—offer, it seems to me, a natural progression of goodbyes.

These years will also give you time to regain your balance and your youth's proper freedom—so carelessly interfered with—and give me time to achieve what may be more precious, my proper age.

You've allowed me to walk back down the hallway of my life's house to the passions of young manhood. I've lived again in those fresh and sunny rooms beside you, a rare dispensation. But now I believe I hear my family at the door, and hope to walk back up the hall once more to join them. And if not to join them, then wait to be there if they do return.

You've been many things to me, Susanne, as I've been to you. We've been lovers, husband and wife (our least convincing performance), and, at times, father and daughter. I don't regret a moment of it, and neither I hope, do you.

A convict here, womanly in many ways, has lost a man he

loved. I told him the murdered man would return to him as memory, and remain.

So I hope it will be with us. I know I carry, and will always carry something of your summer in me. Perhaps one day, you may find my autumn still with you—if only to recall the colors of the leaves.

It would be best if you didn't answer this, didn't call, didn't write. Go to Bob Christiansen and tell him I've decided to divorce. Have him send the papers to me. I trust your good judgment, as I trust mine, to spare us both the indignity of denying either reason or love.

Goodbye, dear heart.
Charlie

Having finished this letter, Bauman lay rereading it, startled as if it had been written by a stranger. It seemed a mighty risky letter. He felt the greatest relief it hadn't been sent, that it might remain a secret—Susanne never knowing about it. Beth never knowing about it, either.

It appeared there was a Charlie Bauman to guard against, probably the same romantic who'd pulled a knife on Eddie Becker.

Bauman got up, reached under his bunk, and slid the two notebook pages under the front cover of *Numbers and Statistics in the Ancient World* (a remarkably unhelpful volume, since the ancient world had produced practically no reliable numbers or statistics).

"I'm going down to shower, Scoot."

"Shit," Scooter peering past his motorcycle magazine from the upper bunk. "I'm startin' smell like a armpit. I'll go down with you."

"Well, let's get moving. We've got forty minutes to lights."

"I sure hope," Scooter said, clambering down, "—I sure hope that faggot, Peaches, ain't the duty hack. Always lookin' at my dick. . . ."

That night was noisy on B-block, an inmate down Two-tier waking yelling at some dream motherfucker who'd offended or frightened him. And later, a subdued argument—or lovemaking—sounding from the tier above.

Bauman lay listening to these and other noises, restless, turning, trying to sleep, then turning again. Before lights-out, he'd casually set their stool over by the head of his bunk and stacked two books on it—*Dog's-head, Hinge of Empire,* and Garramore's *Pompey's Road*—as if for intended reading. Then, when the lights were off, the night-lights' faint strawberry glowed along the tier, he'd reached over and lifted the books off the stool's seat. Covering any scraping sound with a couple of coughs, he'd turned the stool on its side and wedged it in between the head of the bunk and the door bars, so one of the stool's legs stuck out across the bars' track, to block their movement.

Then, barricaded, feeling fairly secure, he'd tossed his thin pillow to the other end of the bunk, tucked Mr. Hyde (sheathed) beneath it, and turned to lie that way, feet to the door bars, throat out of reach of even the longest arm.

He lay restless for an hour or two, imagining—as he grew sleepy—a long shadow (barely defined, cast along the bars by dim night-lights) that slowly, slowly stretched down the tier as his visitor came calling. He slept lightly, woke once and slept again—until in early morning he fell into a dream, deep, mournful, and richly detailed, in which he visited Schoonover's little bureaucrat of the future, Kwal Katchak, at his home by the sea, on a planet with two dark-orange suns. . . .

Bauman woke to the uproar of State's waking—got up onto his knees and leaned over the other end of the bunk to tug the stool free, and set it upright. Then he lay back down to recall (while he could) Katchak's marvelous home, from his dream of it. The house, sunk in sand to avoid a constant wind, had been set at the crest of a great dune that overlooked a sea gray-green as glacial ice. The house's rooms were a neat, buried maze of stripe-walled smaller and smaller chambers, whose oval windows gave onto a garden. The dining room—also a library—had been oddly shaped with no angles at all, except, in the room's center, a transparent aquarium cube of tiny fish and things like fish—all colorless, pallid as frosted glass, but each with its own motion of swimming, so they gyrated, spun, jiggled, raced and retreated like parts of a jigsaw puzzle seeking sense. . . .

Above, from the upper bunk, Scooter's pale stork's legs were thrust abruptly out, then the boy, in underpants, came flailing down to the cold concrete floor.

Breakfast was cornflakes and canned pitted prunes.

Cousins came in for coffee.

"Hey, welcome stranger!" Scooter, as Cousins sat down holding his Styrofoam cup.

Perteet roused from his prunes. "What's the matter, sweetie, ain't you eatin' no breakfast?"

"No, Pete; you want my breakfast?"

"Shit, yes," Perteet said, and heaved himself up to go claim it at the counter.

"The eye looks better," Bauman said.

"It's fine," Cousins said. "—My trouble is my mouth an' my manners, dealin' with friends. Blamin' other people, when I'm the one screwed up."

"We didn' have no trouble," Scooter said. "You an' me didn' have no fight."

Cousins reached over to pat Scooter's hand. "No, we didn't, Scoot. It was your roomie, here; I was out of line an' smacked him."

"Hit Charles?"

"Scooter," Bauman said, "—it was no big deal. You really don't need to know everything that goes on."

"Oh, hey, say no more. You don't have to say no more. Stuff ain't my business, ain't my business, an' that's just the way I want it, man."

"Good."

Bauman found the rest of breakfast as peaceful as if he and Cousins had resolved their quarrel absolutely, resolved it in those remarks to Scooter without their speaking to each other about it at all.

When they'd finished their coffee, Bauman and Cousins got up together, leaving Scooter and the returned Perteet to divide Cousins' breakfast unevenly—all to Perteet, except for one prune, a little juice.

Bauman paused at the garbage can to scrape his tray. "No visitor last night, Lee?"

"No. An' you?"

"No. He may be waiting a day to see whether we back off or keep asking questions."

"I heard you went over to the lifers yesterday, Charles."

"I got lucky," Bauman said as they went out through the mess-hall's double doors. "I caught Wiltz in a merry mood. He and Shupe claimed, and I believed it, they had nothing to do with the fight-fixing."

"That's right; I know that's right. It was Nash an' Mr. Metzler, after all."

"You know, your dad might not have had a choice. Nash would have threatened you, if Barney hadn't gone along. You think of that?"

"That's nice. It's a nice thing to be sayin', but I don't believe it for a minute."

They started up the worn stone steps to Ground-tier, a distance behind several inmates going up to the block for count.

"Oh, it's very possible," Bauman said, his voice lower, and he turned to look back, make certain there was no one on the stairs behind them. ". . . I would say it's probable. For example, I started on this whole manhunt because the corrections people threatened to keep me in here a few extra years if I didn't snitch to them about those killings. And then, I also agreed to work for Nash, because he had some creep outside to get to my boy if I didn't. —So you can believe me, Lee, when I tell you exactly the same pressure was probably put on your dad, through you."

Cousins had nothing to say to that, climbed silent beside him to the empty landing. Then, as they turned there to climb again, said, "You're a nice man, Charles," and reached out to take Bauman's hand and hold it as they went on up the stairs. Very pleased by this—Cousins' grip relaxed and confident as a child's—Bauman still hoped Lee would let go before they reached Ground-tier's witnesses.

And so Cousins did, slipping his hand away as they reached the top of the stairs. Ground-tier was noisy, the after-breakfast crowd moving toward the circular stair to Two-tier and Three.

"You don't mind associating with a snitch?"

"What I like, Charles, is associatin' with a person trusts me. Now I better be gettin' over to A, for count."

"I'll walk you to the gate."

"I didn' have no business hittin' you, Charles," Cousins said as they threaded their way through the crowd.

"And I had no business trying to hold you anywhere you didn't want to be."

"So," Cousins keeping his voice down, "—So, Wiltz an' Shupe an' them didn' have no hand in it?"

"No. No relish shown."

"What?"

"No pleasure. Wiltz took no pleasure in talking about those killings."

"Right. Guys like that—they do somethin', they want to let you know, some way."

"How's it goin', Teach?" George Esterhaz, erstwhile hijacker of truck cargoes.

"Fine, Big G," Bauman said, noticed Esterhaz' backward glance at Cousins as he walked away.

At B's gate, Cousins stepped a little aside, said softly, "Charles, I know I got you in some major shit, runnin' my mouth about dad—an' some hack offin' him an' so forth."

"You, and my own vanity, my big mouth. —And, let's face it, we're having an adventure here, aren't we? More interesting than playing checkers and watching TV?"

"I guess."

"Lee, it's making the time go by. And we may actually catch a murderer in here who needs catching—if he doesn't get us first."

"That's true. An' Shupe an' them people didn' have nothin' else to say . . . about nothin' else?"

"They had nothing else to say."

"O.K. So, what now, Charles? We don't have much left to be goin' on."

"We still have Lesnovitch, if you were right about an electrician being the man to let our killer out of his house at night. Also, after count I think we should go over to the infirmary and pay Tiger twenty dollars."

"Pay him for what?"

"Pay him for that question he said we should have asked, but didn't."

"Charles, the dude was just foolin' aroun' about that."

"Let's go and find out."

"Cost us twenty."

"Lee, it's going to cost us more than twenty. He'll take twenty to tell us the question—then he'll charge another twenty to answer it."

"Oh, right. That's exactly right, Charles. Goin' to cost us forty bucks—an' for bullshit!"

"I've got it."

"No, no, we'll split it. I'll go twenty."

"O.K."

"I won't be buyin' no down coat this winter, Charles; I'm tellin' you that. We been spendin' money here like it's goin' out of style."

"You'll get that coat; don't worry about it. All right, if you want to meet me in East yard after count, we'll go down there."

Kavafian and Carlo walked by, both nodding pleasantly as they passed. Bauman thought Carlo was smiling, certainly the first smile he'd seen on the albino.

"See that?"

"Yeah," Cousins said. "—Carlo was smilin'."

"O.K. We meet in East yard, go down to the infirmary."

"An' go over to Ed Lesnovitch after that?"

"Makes sense, Lee."

"Don't have much chance gettin' him in the electrician office, this early. He's out workin'."

"Still? When we saw him, the man looked barely able to get off that sofa."

"Charles, he got a stroke, but he can move aroun'. How you think he gets down to that fancy apartment? Guy rooms Ground-tier in A, eats in West—he gets aroun' pretty good."

"Good enough to have done the killings himself? Tiger said it looked as though the murderer had some problem getting the right position on his man."

"No way. He could help out with electrician stuff—but nothin' else."

"And why not?"

"Man's too rich, Charles. Rich people don't do their own killin'. . . ."

East yard was almost deserted—even determined walkway yo-yos discouraged by the morning's cold, its thumping rough wind, which seemed to spring directly off the wall.

"Jesus." Lee walking with his jacket-collar turned up, his hands jammed into his trouser pockets.

It occurred to Bauman that he'd never, in more than a year at State, gone to the wall's base to touch the great blocks of granite that made it up—appeared to make it up. The wall, never having been physically tested by any inmate Bauman knew of, might as well have been only a clever and massive holograph, a Potemkin wall of coherent light, projected from the four towers—which might also not be stone, but only scrawny scaffolds of aluminum, topped with fragile lights for the illusion.

It would explain the winds that seemed to blow from the wall—hot, dry, drifting air in summer . . . then autumn's, cool, wet, gusty. Now, a furious bullying cold—but in a few months, spring's sweetest warming winds, smelling of earth and prairie grasses. Each season introduced by breezes that seeming to blow from the wall by some quirk of aerodynamics, perhaps actually blew through its false substance, betraying a wall that was only a wall's ghost—with nothing to prevent the convicts, after stupid years of belief, from doubting just once, approaching, and walking through only a gauze, a shade, a shadow. Walking through that—and out onto sunny, wide, black-earthed farm fields, tree-bordered, smelling of manure. The fields bordered, as well, by small houses on narrow country roads, from which distant cars and trucks might be seen spinning down the busier highway almost two miles distant.

"Ever touched the wall, Lee?"

"Touched it? No, I never did."

"Ever occur to you it might be just an illusion, like a projected film? That maybe there's nothing to keep us in at all? You make something look that overwhelming, who's going to walk up and try to kick their way through it? A man could spend half a century in here, and never even bother to go up and touch the thing."

"They got a wall-line, Charles. —Dude's liable to get shot just crossin' that line."

"That's what I mean. If the wall was real, why would they need a dead line? But if it isn't—if it just looks like a wall—they'd have to have a line to stop you before you got close enough to find out."

"Man. . . . Charles, you got a out-of-sight imagination. You don't want to be sayin' that stuff in the mess hall. There's a few people would go runnin' right out there, try an' find out if you're right."

"And if they just kept going? Ran right through it?"

"Charles, if that ever happened in here, an' people found out they been put-on that bad? There'd be blood runnin' off them tiers. Cons'd cut the heads right off them hacks. —An' that'd just be the start of it."

"Then I suppose we better keep it to ourselves. We have another option, anyway." Bauman pointed down South yard, where the left side of South's huge gate was already sliding slowly closed behind an entering truck. The dairy's milk truck—its cab painted white, its long milk-tank stainless steel—rolled slowly down the narrow access road toward West yard and the truck shop. A hack was coming in with it, standing on the passenger-side running board.

"That's it," Cousins said. They both stopped walking and watched the big truck on its way, until the bulk of C-block concealed it.

"Nice-looking machine. . . ."

"That's the new truck," Cousins said. "Old one was real beat up; not as big, neither."

"Either."

"—Either."

Wind came buffeting, bounding at them as if the opening and closing of the gate had signalled more icy breezes in.

"Cold."

"*Cold?* Charles, it's freezin' out here."

"All right, let's get warm. —I'll race you over to the deadline. We'll test the wall."

"Are you kiddin'? Over the line?"

"No, not over. Just to it. We can throw a rock or something, see if the wall's real."

"Charles, you are definitely gettin' weird in here."

"Don't I know it. You ready . . . ?"

"We're goin' get in trouble."

"Wouldn't be surprised. What's the matter—you can't beat an old man, running? From the looks of you, you can run like a deer."

"Charles, I can beat you runnin'."

"Prove it. —On three."

"Man, we're goin' to get in trouble. They don't like you even gettin' close to there!"

"And we know why, because the fucking thing is fake! One—Two—"

"Charles. . . ."

"*Three!*" Bauman was already sprinting away as he called out. He thought for a few seconds he was running alone—and wasn't disappointed, was enjoying his furious motion, the frost-stiff grass spanking the soles of his shoes, the cold wind beating at his face. Then, he heard footsteps coming up behind him. Light, light footsteps—a pattering rhythm he recalled from high-school football, when some tailback came racing to interception. These footsteps drumming the turf in the quickest kind of rhythm, almost perfectly even, the beat hardly accented left or right at all, as if a small, beautifully balanced horse was running, no off-kick to its gallop.

Bauman put his head down into the wind and ran harder, forcing the muscles of his legs—so stocky, so sturdy—to hammer into the yard's stiff turf, to drive him, drive him along, arms pumping, leaning forward as he sprinted, running as if his life depended on it. He imagined an animal behind him—a leopard flowing over the ground in chase, bounding along in that lovely swift elastic romping style that had caught so many men and almost-men for eating in the last two million years.

That helped a little. He pounded swiftly along—traveling, it seemed to him, at a fairly clipping rate, if not too efficiently. He was just beginning to worry about his wind when Cousins stepped past him, almost courteously—glanced back with an apologetic smile—then looked ahead, tending to business, and ran away as if Bauman were lugging some ghost convict's cannonball as he labored along.

Cousins ran like a talented woman racer, narrow-hipped, stepping high with each stride, almost bouncing, elbows bent, swinging easily at his sides. Just dancing, dancing along ten yards in front, and pulling away as if Bauman were a permanent fixture.

Cousins crossed the last few hundred feet of South yard—running exactly as fast as he'd run at the start, a perfectly extended sprint—

reached the single painted yellow stripe twenty feet from the wall, and stopped, running casually in place to cool down, waiting for Bauman to catch up.

It took an annoying time for Bauman to do that; it seemed to him he chugged along for half a minute at least, being watched by Cousins, being smiled at, not unpleasantly.

"Lee . . . you are . . . really fast," Bauman, at the yellow line at last, bent over slightly, resting his hands on his thighs while he caught his breath. "You have to have run track."

"I ran in high school, first three years."

"Well, you had a good coach."

"Mr. Howard."

"I don't know much about track, but I'd say Mr. Howard knew his business."

"YOU . . . ! WHAT THE HELL YOU PEOPLE . . . ?"

Bauman looked up, and saw at the top of the wall, outlined against a sky only slightly lighter gray, two hacks staring down at them. One held a bullhorn. The other man, an M-16 rifle.

"—An' with fuckin' telescope sights!" Scooter, describing the wall-guards' armament some months before.

"Wall's got to be real, Charles," Cousins said. "Them hacks is standin' on it."

"WHAT THE HELL YOU PEOPLE THINK YOU'RE DOING? —RUNNING THAT WAY?"

Bauman waved, conciliatory, smiled broadly enough to be seen smiling, then turned and walked with Cousins away from the line, angling toward the infirmary.

"NOT FUNNY . . . ASSHOLE. . . ." Echoed after them.

It struck Bauman that the voice of the God that Moses heard, must have been similar—stentorian, condescending, impatient, and armed.

"Wasn' smart," Cousins said, face flushed to more lively beauty from exercise. "—But it was fun, runnin'."

"Fun for you, humiliation for me. You know, Lee, State might be able to field quite a team in track. Give people who don't enjoy violence something to do. Get them out of those damn blocks."

"Charles, I'll tell you somethin'. You're a lot like Mr. Metzler, one way. You can't leave nothin' alone. Always got to be a better way, somethin' new needs doin'. Let me tell you somethin'—you won't get mad?"

"No."

"Most inmates, most dudes in here, best thing could happen to

’em? What they’d like? What they’d like, day they come up here, is just go to sleep an’ stay asleep, an’ then have some hack wake ’em up, say, ‘—You done your time.’ ”

“ ‘They,’ hell; that’s what I’d like. . . .”

Paul, Irma’s small husband—terrier-quick and courageous, though only a forger—was the white coat in the infirmary’s hall when Bauman and Cousins walked in. He was carrying a double armload of dirty linens.

“How’s it going, Paul?”

“Hey, Teach, Lee. —Teach, you haven’t got no matches on you, I hope.”

“Not this trip. Is Tiger working?”

“He’s upstairs. Michaelson’s puttin’ a cast on that nigger’s arm where the jack slipped. In the truck shop?”

“Never heard about it. —Bad?” Bauman noticing, through the open door of the chronic ward, the TV flickering at the room’s distant end, the small white mound of Bobby Basket in his bed.

“It isn’t shit. A broken arm is all it is.”

“What the hell you people doin’ in my infirmary?” Tiger, coming down the stairs. “—And what the hell you doin’, Paul, standin’ ’roun’ beatin’ your meat when you suppose’ to pick up them linens an’ count ’em for the laundry?”

“Don’t get your ass in an uproar,” Irma’s husband said. “—See you people.” And walked to a room across the hall, went in, and closed the door behind him.

“Wasn’ for Irma, I wouldn’ have that little son-of-a-bitch in this place. Acts like writin’ bounce checks is *real* bad.” Tiger walked up to them, looming in his snowy whites. “An’ what the fuck are you two doin’ here now? I ain’ had nobody else be killin’ himself, an’ that’s jus’ the way I like it.”

“Well, first,” Bauman said, “—we want to check whether we need prescriptions to get down jackets for the winter.”

“Only thing you need prescriptions for, is leather. You can buy any other kin’ of shit you want.”

“All right. Second,” Bauman said, keeping his voice low, “we have some money for you, Tiger.”

“Do tell . . . ?” Tiger also speaking softly, possibly out of respect for the subject.

“Twenty dollars, street,” Cousins said, “—for that question you said we should have asked you before.”

"Ohhhh." Very pleased. "*That* question. That question, we goin' have to go to my treatment room." Tiger turned and lumbered swiftly away down the corridor, Bauman and Cousins following after, each taking almost two steps to Tiger's one.

The treatment room, with its white-painted walls, cabinets, stools and examining table, was bright as Bauman remembered it. —This visit apparently also reminding Tiger of the one previous.

"How them burns?"

"Very good," Bauman said, and shoved a white-painted stool over for Cousins to sit on. "No infection, nothing. You did a good job cleaning them up."

"You was lucky, man. Burns ain't nothin' to be foolin' with."

"Twenty dollars, street," Cousins said.

"Now, honey," Tiger said, "—I know this man didn' give you that black eye."

"No," Cousins said, "he didn'."

"You don't have no trouble seein' out of that eye? You don't have no headaches?"

"No, I don't. Twenty dollars, Tiger, an' that's it."

"All right. All right." Tiger put his hands on the examining table behind him, lifted himself easily to sit on it. "Now the question, question you two should have as't me, is, 'Was they anybody *else* offed jus' like Metzler an' that little Spencer was?' "

"*Damn* it."

"Hey, Teach, don' be mad, now. Can't nobody be thinkin' of everythin'."

"Well," Cousins said, "—was there?"

"Now, sugar, you know that a diff'rent question. I'm goin' have to charge for that one, separate."

"All right," Bauman said. "A second twenty."

"Street."

"Street. Now answer the damn question."

"Well, I can't be sure about much pas' last two, three years, 'cause these records here don't go back no farther. Records do that are over in Admin. —But accordin' to these right here, they was at least two other inmates got it jus' the same way. Dude name of Blake, little wimp burglar, got it in the showers in C."

"I remember that," Cousins said. "That was this year. February."

"March eleven." Tiger, massively black and white, rocked slowly back and forth on his examining table, heavy white-trousered legs swinging. "An' another dude got it three years ago. Dude name' Martin. He got cut up in the supply room over at the license plant."

"Before my time," Cousins said.

"Before my time too, honey," Tiger said. "I been up here three years—but that was a month, two months before I come up."

"And you're certain they were killed exactly the same way?"

"I don't know about 'exactly,' Teach, but they was sure as shit killed similar."

"All right," Bauman said, "let's think about this for a minute. You're saying—and I'd bet it's true—that at least two more cons have gone the way Barney Metzler and Spencer did."

"Same shit, man, cut up like with a razor or somethin', when they was alone. An' had that grease on their han's, too. At least that Blake did. Other report didn' say nothin' about it."

"And not club killings, or the usual kind of thing at all."

"Right. Ain' usual."

"And there's no way to connect Barney Metzler and Spencer and that burglar, Blake—and the other man—to any particular scam or bets?"

"Other man Martin," Tiger said. "An' I never did buy that shit you two was out huntin' no snitch."

"No way to connect them at all," Bauman said. "I doubt if there is a reasonable connection. You know, this is getting more and more interesting. . . ."

"It's a ding." Cousins sat hunched on the stool, face pale beside the fading colors of his bruised right eye.

"And you know, if we could get to those stored records, it's very possible we'd find several more people killed the same way—all just assumed to be club killings or whatever, through the years."

"There's a nut-case in here," Cousins said. "Killin' people. Killed my dad, for one. . . ."

"So it would seem," Bauman said. "But the murdered cons have to have something in common. Even madmen have their reasons."

"An' guess who we heard say just exactly that?" Cousins said. "—Your real good buddy in the library. There's a ding, man."

"I don't believe it."

"You don't want to believe it, Charles, an' I know just how you feel, too. 'Cause I didn' want to believe stuff about Mr. Metzler, neither."

"Now," Tiger said, "—I don't want to hear no more of *this* shit, that's for damn sure, 'cause it ain' no business of mine." He slid down from his examining table. "First thing is, where's my forty dollars?"

"Charles, want to find out if Mr. Lesnovitch is even over there?"

"You have a phone in here, Tiger?"

"There's a phone in here, official use only. An' locked."

"We need to call the electrician's office."

"Where's my forty-*five* dollars?"

"For Christ's sake. . . . All right, forty-five."

Tiger walked over to a small white-painted metal desk, unsnapped a key from the ring at his belt, and unlocked the desk drawer. Then lifted out a battered black phone, found a smaller key on his ring, and removed the receiver's dial lock. "—An' hurry it up," he said. "Electrician is two-seven."

Bauman went to the desk, dialed, and after several rings, heard the phone picked up.

". . . Yeah?"

"This is Charlie Bauman. Is Lesnovitch in the office, or downstairs?"

"No."

"Well, is he going to be in?"

"Could be."

"When?"

"Maybe an hour."

"Well, would you tell him Cousins and I are coming over to see him, and ask him to stay until we get there? O.K.?"

"I'll tell him." Click.

"Who'd you talk to, Charles?"

"I think it was old Waggoner."

"Firs' thing," Tiger locked the phone receiver, put the instrument away, and locked the drawer. "—Where's my forty-five dollars?"

Cousins stood up from his stool. "All right. I need to use your bathroom."

"Never mind, Lee," Bauman said, "I'll use the damn bathroom. You can pay me later."

"—An' secon' thing I got to say is, whoever's offin' folks sure as shit knows you two been lookin'. So you two is already overdue. —An' third an' last thing I got to say is, I want your asses the fuck out of my infirmary, an' I do not want to be seein' you in here for a long, long time. Now, Teach, you go in that toilet down the hall there, an' you get me my money, an' don't you be messin' that toilet up, 'cause *I* clean that motherfucker."

Chapter THIRTEEN

The morning wind that had blown so steadily from the wall when they'd gone to the infirmary, now blew at cross purposes over South yard as they were walking back, gusting one way, then another. The air seemed heavier than summer air, its cold giving it weight.

"You know, Lee, our trouble is time—having time enough to work this damn puzzle out before our killer loses patience with us."

"I know. 'Better butt out.' "

"Advice that's looking more and more attractive, since my first solution to the murders was such a flop."

"Our solution. We both figured it that way, Charles."

"In any case, we now have a situation where the killer knows us, and we don't know him—a very unhealthy state of affairs. So unhealthy, that it seems to me it might be time to cut our losses in here. And since I'm an official snitch—and I've passed on what we do know to Carlyle—maybe the corrections people would do us the favor of getting us the hell out of State to some other walls. That might get me off the hook with the lifers, as well. If I'm transferred out, I'm transferred out; there's nothing I can do about that."

"Charles, we didn' find out nothin' to trade—except some ding is offin' people in here, an' maybe how he's gettin' out of his house to do it. You got a weird idea about Admin, you think they're goin' to be happy you just tell 'em stuff like that, an' that's it. Isn' goin' to make no difference to them club guys neither—either. All they're goin' to say, an' Admin too, is 'Great. Now, go find out who.' None of 'em want to let up no pressure on us. They *want* us in a cross."

"That has the unpleasant ring of reality."

"—An' I'll tell you somethin' else. I know you won't snitch your library buddy over, tell 'em it could be him doin' it."

"Lee, Schoonover is very unlikely to have killed those people. They wouldn't *mean* anything to him, wouldn't do him any good. —They wouldn't be a sacrifice."

"That's what you say. But I'll tell you, Charles, you think you got things all figured out, but you got no way of knowin' what Schoonover or any ding is thinkin'. They got their own way to go. You're a real intelligent man, but nut-cases don't even live in this world."

"And how the hell would Larry Schoonover get out of his cell at night?" Bauman noticed they'd been walking faster and faster, keeping pace with their argument, he supposed.

"Same way we figured anybody could do it, Charles."

"Lesnovitch."

"That's right, electrician. Isn' no other way it could get done."

"And what does Schoonover have to bribe Lesnovitch with? Man has practically no money, has no deals going in here. . . ."

"Maybe he gets library stuff for Lesnovitch. All them real old books in that fancy apartment. That's got to be worth somethin'. Maybe Schoonover got him all them old books."

". . . That's so bizarre, it might be true. I suppose we ought to check on Schoonover. He seems very unlikely to me, precisely because he's known to be disturbed."

" 'Disturbed' don't really say it, Charles. Face it. I know you like him. He's a nice guy, an' he's smart enough so you can have a real conversation with him—which I know damn well you can't have with me, just for an example, since I didn' even finish high school. You can talk to Schoonover, I understan' that—but Charles, it don't mean you know everything the dude's got inside his head."

"All right . . . all right. We'll go over to the library and push Larry a little, see what happens. But before we do that, let's go and have another talk with Mr. Hunting Prints. —And by the way, you can forget that crap about not finishing high school, and we can't have a conversation and so forth. I've known many idiots with graduate degrees, but I've hardly ever heard of a person going through the hell you've gone through, and coming out of it more, rather than less, sensible. You could earn a high school equivalency and go on to college in a year, if you wanted to do it—and I'd help. So spare me any more of that I'm-just-a-dumb-young-con bullshit."

Cousins walked along silent until they reached the shelter of D-block's granite; there the wind eased, breezing lightly. Several leaves—shades of brown and gold, and blown over the wall from some tree outside—rustled past them a few feet off the ground, a weary flock sinking in slow air.

"I never said I was dumb, Charles."

"Well, you're not. And speaking of intelligence, let's try to exercise some. What could your Mr. Metzler have had in common with my Kenneth Spencer—or that burglar, Blake, or Martin?"

"Nothin'. Nothin' in common with Spencer—little black dude, a rapo. Nothin' in common with him, that's for sure. Them others, I wouldn' know about. He never said nothin' about them."

"Then we're missing it. Those men had to have something in common—the motive, the reason why whoever-it-is killed them. And try this out, try adding Jomo Burdon to that list."

"You sayin' he was offed, too?"

"I'm saying I can't imagine that man killing himself, 'ghostses' or no 'ghostses.' "

"Well, I'll tell you, Charles, only way my dad an' that Spencer was alike, was Spencer told you he didn' do that crime—right?"

"Right. Spencer claimed he hadn't raped anybody. Woman lived in the building where he was the super, and she accused him. But Lee, almost every con in State says he didn't do whatever crime.—He didn't do it; it was a bum beef, or he didn't get a straight trial because his lawyer did a deal with the prosecutor and screwed him. If denials, excuses, and complaints were a cause for murder, there wouldn't be anyone left alive in here."

Two young black cons, their hair braided into long dreadlocks, came down the walk, glanced at Bauman and Cousins, and walked on by.

"—I'm not talkin' about that, Charles. I'm not talkin' about bullshit. I'm talkin' about guys really didn' do what they got sent up for."

"All right. All right, let's take that seriously. Your Mr. Metzler stated definitely that despite everything else he'd done—and that was plenty—he hadn't committed the murder he was convicted and sentenced for."

"That's right. That's absolutely right."

"O.K. And Spencer had me convinced he might be innocent. —He really didn't seem the rapist type."

"O.K."

"Then what about the burglar, Blake? What about Martin—whoever he was?"

"Charles, I don't know about them. But I'll tell you, Jomo wasn' sent up here innocent."

"His murder might have been different; he may have seen or heard a little too much of our ghost. But as far as Blake is concerned, I think I do remember Betty Nellis talking about him a few weeks ago. He was killed in the showers."

"That was him. In C."

". . . Then, Lee, I think you may have something. Because I remember Betty mentioning that the man was going around claiming to be innocent."

"An' if that's so?"

"—If that's so, you've been a lot smarter than this professor. We'll check with Betty, but I think I do remember that. . . ."

"It's a connection, isn' it, Charles?"

"It could be. Which, even so, wouldn't answer the question of who killed them, or why."

They turned the southwest corner of D, walked up to West yard's fence gate.

Elroy was the hack on duty.

"Elroy," Bauman said, "are they trying to give you pneumonia or what? Nine times out of ten, your ass is posted out of doors. Maybe you need to see a lawyer."

"I need to see somebody," Elroy said, stepped out of his booth and into the wind to pat Bauman very lightly.

"If we still had a chaplain, you could see him."

"I need to see somebody," Elroy said, long farmer's face flushed with windburn. "I need to see somebody, that's for sure."

"Tell Vermillier we said to assign you indoors for a month."

"That's right," Cousins said. "—You tell him."

"That yard captain don't pay no attention to nothin' I say." Elroy swung the fence gate open for them. "I don't think the man's a Christian, name like that. I know he ain't no Lutheran. . . ."

"We're here to see Lesnovitch."

The elderly electrician, Waggoner, stood silent behind the office's back counter, seemed to be considering whether to acknowledge having spoken to them, acknowledge knowing his chief's name. Bauman noticed again the inflammation where the gold bar of the old man's glasses bit into the bridge of his nose, ancient angry little irritation.

"Mr. Waggoner," Cousins said, "it's pretty important."

Reluctantly, after a last sidelong glance at Bauman, Waggoner walked down the counter, reached under it and picked up a phone. He dialed, said something into the receiver, then listened for a long while.

"I think the old guy forgot meetin' you before, Charles. An' I think he forgot you just called, too."

"I'd say you're right."

"Poor old guys, cons like that. They ought to just let them old people out. No way they're the same guys did what they did before."

"Lee, where would they go? They'd be lost out there."

Cousins, watching Waggoner, looked mournful as a Renaissance angel observing mortality. —This angel freshly fallen, perhaps, its long golden hair burned short and dark by that passage, its robe of light scorched dull to denim.

Waggoner put down the phone, came slowly back up the counter to them, and said, "He isn' answerin'." Having delivered that message, the old man walked away, picked up a typed list—and turning to the section of pegboard behind him, located a series of coils of fine wire, and began to check them off against his sheet, lips moving as he counted.

"Could be Ed's got Marcia down there with him again," Cousins said.

"Let's just wait. We won't have time, anyway, to talk to Schoonover until after lunch. And I'll tell you, I'm not looking forward to that. I'd rather not lose a friend."

"I don't want to be hurtin' Schoonover neither, Charles. But seems to me we got to at least ask him some questions."

"Either. —Oh, we're going to do it. I'll do it. . . ."

After a minute or so, his entries complete, Waggoner walked stiffly back to them.

"I know who you are. You're one of them coaches with the boxers."

"That's right. They call me Teach, Mr. Waggoner."

"I know who you are. Berman, right?"

"Bauman."

"Right. Call you Teach."

"Yes."

"You goin' to let that white boy box next Saturday?"

"Marcantonio?"

"The wop. White boy."

"There're a couple of white boys boxing, Mr. Waggoner."

"Big one. The wop."

"Right. He's going to fight."

"It's a damn shame," the old man said. "White boys set to fightin' niggers, an' them niggers got thick heads so white boys can't hurt 'em."

"That's not true," Bauman said. "You're old enough to know better than that crap about thick skulls. A man can take a punch or he can't—black, yellow, white, or brown."

"Well, maybe."

"No 'well, maybe' about it. Man your age talking nonsense like that. . . ."

Waggoner, challenged in this way, suddenly assumed a sly surrender, ducked his head, seemed to grow slighter, more ancient. "I ain't arguin', chief. You say it—O.K."

Bauman wondered on what occasion, many years before, Waggoner—previously a terror—had, to his own astonishment, suddenly crumpled like damp paper during a no more than ordinarily perilous disagreement. And had instantly been marked a different man, cowardly and old.

"I know some people believe that about blacks, Mr. Waggoner, but it isn't true."

"Then how come most of them boxers is niggers?"

The phone under the counter rang twice.

"Because they're better athletes, not because they have thick skulls."

"Mr. Waggoner," Cousins said, "I think the phone rang."

"Did it ring, sugar, I'd a heard it! Now, Berman, you're a coach, so I ain't goin' to argue with you. I'll jus' say one name—Jack Dempsey."

"What about him?—and by the way, the phone did ring."

"Was there a nigger could beat him?"

"Probably one or two; Dempsey didn't fight them."

"I want— I got to get this straight. You sayin' Jack Dempsey wasn't no great fighter?"

"I think he was a very great fighter—but you know, Dempsey was half black."

Waggoner stood goggling at Bauman, astounded.

"What? What? Jack *Dempsey*?"

"His mother was a black lady named Rhoda Montade."

"Well, there you go," Waggoner said. "See? He had that thick head on him!"

The phone under the counter rang again. One ring, abbreviated.

"Mr. Waggoner," Cousins said, "the phone—"

"I heard it, I heard it! Fuckin' punks is worse'n women. . . ." But when he'd gotten down the counter, picked the receiver up and listened, he said, "There ain't nobody on this phone."

"Mr. Waggoner," Bauman said, "—is it all right if we just go down?"

"Hell, go on down. I don't give a damn what you people do. If that phone had been ringin', I would have heard it. . . ."

"Was that so, about that fighter—what's his name?" Cousins inquiring in the darkness of the staircase down to Lesnovitch's den.

"Dempsey. No."

"Well, Waggoner's real old. . . ."

"Think I should have just let it go, not called him on the 'thick-skulled niggers' bit?"

"No. But you know, you got a quick tongue, Charles. —Watch out, here's the bottom. You got a edge over most people, you know, like a strong guy's got a different kind of a edge."

"And I shouldn't take advantage."

"That's up to you, like with a guy who's real strong, you know?"

"O.K., O.K. I'll apologize to the old fart when we go back up there. Being with you—where the hell's the light down here?—being with you, Lee, presents all the disadvantages of marriage, and few of the benefits."

And was rewarded by pleasant laughter that might, in this darkness, have been a girl's, as if Cousins' feminine portion assumed more strength, more beauty, the less the light.

Lee led, Bauman followed after, as they threaded their way in darkness through the crate-crowded basement. No light lit here, either, to assist them. Only the small red bulb still burned in the furnace room, as they walked down the few steps into it.

Lesnovitch's door was closed. The other door, smaller, white paint peeling, stood half open to darkness across the furnace room.

When Bauman knocked three times—the three spaced impacts traditional, he supposed, at obscure entrances—there was no response from Lesnovitch. After a pause, listening, he knocked again.

Cousins leaned close to the door panels. "*Mr. Lesnovitch* . . ."

Bauman knocked again, harder, listened for a moment, then tried the door.

"It's open."

"Maybe we better wait. He could be in the bathroom or somethin'."

"The hell with it." Bauman pushed the door open and stepped into golden light.

Lesnovitch sat where he'd sat before, haloed by the lambent glow of his floor lamps and table lamps, sat on his small sofa dressed in civilian clothes—loafers, slacks, tweed sports coat, a white dress shirt open at the throat. A sturdy country gentleman, at least a weekend country gentleman, fallen into age.

Fallen farther than that.

The telephone receiver lay in Lesnovitch's lap. His chin glittered with saliva; his head tilted against the sofa's back, jaw gaping. Only his eyes were alive. They swam and rolled and glared in his soft slack face as if they and only they had ever been fully alive in him, and now were trapped in their sockets to rot. Lesnovitch was heaving in slow snoring breaths.

"Jesus Christ."

"What is it?" Cousins said. "What happened?"

"I think he's had another stroke, a very bad one."

Cousins went to kneel by the sofa. "Mr. Lesnovitch, can you hear me talkin' to you?"

No response, except perhaps an attempt by the man's eyes to discover what might be the source of what might be sound. The eyes searched desperately, then seemed to focus just over Cousins' head. The snoring continued, harsh with effort.

"Mr. Lesnovitch!" Cousins picked up the man's dead hands, stroked and patted them. "—Charles, what do we *do?*"

"I can tell you what we won't do; we'll never ask him another question. —We need to call the infirmary, get a hack down here. I think he's dying." He bent to pick up the phone receiver from Lesnovitch's lap, closing his eyes for an instant as he did, to keep from seeing the man's face so close.

"He was callin' upstairs for help is what he was doin'. He was callin' for help. . . ." Cousins still knelt before the sofa, stroking the soft white hands, trying to warm them.

Bauman raised the receiver to call upstairs—and found himself the butt of a primitive practical joke. The phone wire had been cut, snipped cleanly through, so he stood like a fool with the receiver to his ear, its wire dangling.

"Look at this," he said, and as he said it, heard a distant soft metallic crash, a muted cymbal sound through the open door behind him.

Bauman supposed he stared wide-eyed as Cousins was staring at him, in identical startlement.

"*He* did it," Cousins said, and pointed at the cut phone wire as if Bauman hadn't yet noticed it. "—Didn't he do it? So Mr. Lesnovitch couldn' call!"

Bauman started to remark that Lesnovitch couldn't call anybody in any case, when he heard that soft dropped-metal sound again—outside, beyond the furnace room's light.

"That's him!" Cousins said.

"It might be, if Lesnovitch called him, told him we were coming over. Just—just hold on a moment."

"He was here an' that's *him*. That's the motherfucker killed my dad!" Cousins called the last like a trumpet—and was past Bauman and out of the room.

"Wait a minute—*wait* a minute!" Very reluctant to run, shout, do all that on only a possibility, Bauman went at the door to call again, then saw the smaller door beyond the furnace wide open, heard Cousins' rapid footsteps, and was annoyed at such thoughtless dramatics. If the killer had been there, it was certainly better to think a moment before rushing into the dark.

"*Lee!* Wait up, god damn it!" Then had no choice but to follow the sounds of running through that doorway and into a very narrow tunnel crowded with ancient piping on either side, and dark. A chase stupidly premature, accidental—no thinking, no deciding to it at all. And frightening.

The passage smelled of damp rot, with a varying odor of dead rats. There was a little light, either from behind him or somewhere in front, and Bauman ran down the tunnel fast as he could, bent a little to avoid a large ventilator duct hung with clotted dust. He straightened slightly to run faster and hit the duct hard with his head, sounding a sudden tinny thump. He staggered, felt an urge to giggle at the spectacle he was making, then ran on with his forehead hurting, greasy dust in his eyes.

"*Lee!* God damn it, hold the fuck up!" And thought he heard, as the echoes of that died away, Cousins call something back to him. Bauman stumbled to a stop in gritty mud, felt a faint drizzle of condensation from a leak in an old pipe higher up. Holding his breath to still his panting, he heard some distant noise ahead and started to run again, had to run faster and faster to keep on hearing that sound, until the weak light behind him had turned to none. He ran on into darkness, with only a hint of light, its distant possibility, presented where some small work bulb burned far down the passageway.

He was running fast, running stooped over—brushed the side of the tunnel for an instant, bumped into pipes—and correcting, had taken a few more strides when he ran out onto darkness and fell through an open hatchway he saw only as he fell through it, and down onto iron stairs. He hit the descending metal steps with a ringing crash and swift impacts to his knees, forearms, and right side, which felt as if a shelf of iron had struck it.

Bauman lay still, sprawled head down on rust-smelling metal, thinking he'd broken an arm, smashed his knees. He called out, "You stupid little *shit!*" and lay there a few moments longer, reluctant to find out how badly he was hurt. He supposed Cousins had seen well enough to have jumped over the hatchway, even in this darkness. "Little shit . . ." Saying that softly, worried he'd already sounded like a jackass, shouting for Cousins to wait, *wait!* An old, slow jackass, and afraid.

He felt for the iron steps below him to orient himself—then moving carefully, turned half around, got to his feet, and slowly climbed back up to the passageway. His arms seemed all right after all, but his knees were hurting badly, his right side sore as he breathed.

Standing crouched in the tunnel, Bauman bent on aching knees to trace the hatchway's edges, then inched his way past the opening—which he could have jumped across easily if he'd seen it—and started to run again, painfully, keeping his head down and listening through his own footfalls, his own breathing, for some sound ahead. His right knee hurt the most.

The light ahead grew slowly brighter, and he was glad of it. Running underground in the dark seemed more work, sore knees aside, than running in the open air. He entered zones of richer light with great relief, and trotted out at last into an empty space where he could stand erect, the passage ceiling and its great duct now arching four or five feet overhead. This small chamber formed a sort of intersection with another, larger tunnel, cutting across left to right. Everything here was lit dim yellow by a small bulb screwed into conduit in the ceiling. Four large green-painted two-by-four racks held pipe sections stacked along the left-side wall. Several massive steel angle irons leaned against them. Along the right wall, a rank of dusty black pipes ran to the wider passageway, then bent to follow it.

Bauman stood listening, and thought he heard a sound to the right. It was very dark in that larger tunnel, with only a suggestion of light much farther down. He held his breath, and after a moment certainly did hear something. Someone calling? And under that, muffled, the steady thrumming of two of State's ancient exhaust fans, trembling as they labored in some narrow sub-basement.

"Lee?"

A soft metallic clashing sound from the right-hand tunnel.

"*Lee . . . ?*" Bauman took a deep breath and started running down that wider passage, crouching, keeping his head down as the ceiling and ductwork began to lower. He ran as fast as he could, stumbled once, almost fell—then kept running toward that distant spark of light as if he might run past anything bad, run right through trouble.

He heard the fans' deep rich droning, and this time saw a hatchway (wider, longer than the other) and skirted it. Below, the huge machines roared in darkness, one's tuning slightly different from its companion's, so they sang a thundering harmony.

Past the hatchway—this wider tunnel floored with slippery mud—Bauman began to run again as fast as he could, bent, worried about hitting his head on the duct. He'd run a few yards farther, the light no brighter up ahead, when something suddenly appeared, moved at the left side of the tunnel—and he grunted in surprise and ducked away from it, fumbling at his waistband for the knife. Then he saw it was Cousins standing there, leaning against a rack of piping.

"What the *fuck*—what the fuck do you think you're *doing?*"

Cousins, slight, his face a pale oval, stood in deep shadow and seemed to shake his head, had nothing to say. He was holding his left arm at an odd angle, elbow out, hand pressed against his throat.

"Is something wrong? You hurt?"

Nod. Cousins nodded at that.

"All right . . ." Bauman took Cousins gently by his right arm to lead him back down the passage. "—You're lucky you didn't kill yourself, running in here like that! Definitely dumb . . ."

Bauman felt something wet flick his right cheek, and looking closer, saw the front of the boy's jacket soaked black.

"What is it?—What is it?" He put an arm around Cousins' waist, and began to maneuver the boy back along the tunnel, walking fast—then, after a few yards, stepped clumsily with him past the noise and vibration of the fans' hatchway, and into slightly more light. There, Cousins lowered his left arm and hand to show Bauman a neat small black slit at the base of his throat—a wound that pulsed and spat more blood while Bauman stared at it.

"No," Bauman said, as if he'd been asked a question. He pulled the boy stumbling along into the intersection's dull yellow light. Cousins tripped, and would have fallen if Bauman hadn't held him up. "Come on. Come on, now. —What the hell *happened?*"

Cousins put his left hand back to his throat and opened his mouth as if he were going to answer—but only spilled a little blood from a bright red tongue, and took a deep, deep breath that rumbled with liquid. Then he tried to smile, and shrugged in apology.

"Tiger," Bauman said, as if the big man represented all medicine and healing, and might be conjured to them. Then, as Cousins fell against him, got his left arm under the boy's knees, picked him up, and carried him across the chamber and into the narrower tunnel leading back to the furnace room. "*—I'll be back for you, motherfucker!*" This called over his shoulder as if the promise were firm enough to hold captive whoever had cut Cousins' throat, until Bauman returned for him.

Moving almost as fast carrying Cousins as he had before, unburdened, Bauman ran from the intersection and down the passageway, hearing liquid sloshing softly in the boy as he was jolted. All the time he was running—crouching a little, head bent—Bauman reminded himself to be careful of the open hatchway he'd fallen into. He reminded himself of that as he ran—but hadn't reached it, hadn't gotten close when Cousins suddenly writhed and kicked in his arms until Bauman, staggering from side to side against the tunnel's walls, had to stop, let the boy slide down to wet dirt.

"Lee, be still. Will you be *still?*" Bauman bent down to see Cousins' face in near dark. "—Don't do that. Just lie still. Just lie still, and I'll carry you out!"

Cousins' reply was a soft gargling, and a whooping indrawn breath. Then the liquid sound again, louder. The boy's legs pumped, kicking out into the tunnel's mud.

His right knee reluctant to bend, Bauman got his arms under Cousins and picked him up again—had him half up, but Lee was arched so severely back, was thrashing so that he couldn't hold him.

"Please, please, *please* listen to me! You're getting blood in your lungs. Stop trying to breathe! You can live for a long time—minutes, *minutes*, a long time without breathing. Just let me carry you, just let me carry you . . ." And took the boy up in his arms whether he wanted it or not, got him up—Cousins convulsing, struggling, making now a constant gargling sound—and trotted heavily on toward distant light, trying to remember the open hatchway. The boy heaved in Bauman's arms so he tripped and fell against the tunnel's right wall before he recovered and stumbled on, head down to avoid the duct. He saw the open hatchway, slowed, and holding Cousins close, edged past, then began to try to run again.

Bauman went like that some distance, the darkness beginning to fade, the pipes along the sides of the passage now dimly visible. Then Cousins commenced a new motion in his arms—a tremor he felt very clearly, a shuddering steady as an engine's, so fundamental it shook

Bauman too as he carried the boy only a little farther, when that machinery of tremor eased, lessened . . . until only one of Cousins' slender arms, outstretched, shook.

"I told you," Bauman said. "—Didn't I tell you?" and stopped and stood still for a moment, staring at the distant furnace-room light, rose-red—then abruptly sat down in the wet and saw the red point of light as a thousand points that swam and circled in his sight. He sat resting for a moment, with Cousins in his arms, and thought he heard him whispering, saying something. But when Bauman bent to hear, the boy had nothing more to say.

"No, no." Not denying, only attempting to order different events for just the past two or three minutes, Bauman cradled Cousins—lying quite slack now, very easy to handle—and stroked his hair.

He supposed he should have run after Lee at once . . . not hesitated, not have been so surprised and slow, so frightened.

"Happened a little too fast for me," Bauman said, "—and that's the truth. If I were younger, I'd probably have been out that door before you were. . . ." Cousins—so dimly lit, pale and pretty—looking at last like nothing but a girl, seemed to shift as if to be comfortable, and settled into his arms like stone.

Not unhappy to be alone, certainly happier with Lee still and silent, no longer dying, Bauman sat for a while, resting. This peaceful time ended with a rattling noise back up the tunnels. Then a soft, metallic chime.

Bauman was astounded that the man who'd killed Cousins might still be within reach. He'd assumed the killer had ignored his shouted threat, had long ago run deeper into the maze beneath State.

The notion that the man was nearby—perhaps having decided to kill them both—made Bauman very angry. He shoved Cousins roughly off his lap into the dirt, stood up, reached beneath his waistband and drew Mr. Hyde.

He went trotting back up the passage, bent beneath the duct, running from dimness into darkness—jumped across the hatchway—then into dimness again that became the intersection's weary yellow light. And through that chamber down the larger tunnel to the right, and into darkness again—the knife held up as if it were lighting his way, was towing him irresistibly along to stick and slice anything he might encounter, however fast or fierce or sudden, so long as the steel could get into it.

Then, while he trotted through the dark to the deep voices of the fans, something—as if tired of being chased—came hissing and hit him a splitting blow across his face, caught his left cheek and tugged at it, then sliced itself away.

Mr. Hyde instantly yanked Bauman around and back the way he'd come, hauled his arm up into the air so that Bauman flailed the steel left and right, and was hit again by something whirring down out of the dark, that struck his left side and stuck there.

The knife found it, hacked at it, knocked it away; and Bauman, blind in the darkness, turned and caught something greasy, slippery slender with his left hand—something that trembled, then whipped away and cut his hand wide open as it went.

He heard it slide, ring softly on metal, then heard thumping from the tunnel's roof and leaped up at the sound and drove his knife into the air to clang at its first stroke—then smack at its second as the steel struck up through the big duct's soft tin, stuck through it, twisted, and cut its way free, leaving a startled "*Fuck!*" echoing behind.

Bauman fell back with his knife to the muddy floor, and crouched, not breathing, willing his heart to quieter beating. He listened, listened past himself . . . set all his body's minor sounds aside. He listened, and heard metal creaking softly over his head, heard it—and leaped up and struck hard enough so the knife blade was driven up into the tin again, and through it.

Great commotion in the duct—and a murmurous echo down it back toward the passages' intersection, with Bauman trotting along beneath, shaking blood from his left hand. Until, well into that work-lit higher-ceilinged chamber, those sounds of movement stopped, and the duct was hit hard from inside, so it rumbled like theatrical thunder.

Then was struck again from inside, so sharply that a wide grill along the ductwork was sprung, driven half out, groaning. This was hit again, or kicked, and fell away down to the tunnel's mud.

A tentacle—very slender, black, and limber—came whipping out, more than two yards long. It swept the space from side to side, ruffling the air, then stopped, still flexing slightly, and hung still. A small bright hook of blade was fixed to its tip.

Out of the gap where the duct grill had been, a pale large-knuckled hand came holding the thick whipcorded butt of the instrument. Then a short, bare, muscle-knotted arm. A small bald head.

"What a shitty thing to happen," old Cooper said, lisping the "shitty." He hung half out of the big duct's side, blinking down at Bauman as his eyes accustomed themselves to even such dim yellow light.

"What a shitty thing . . ." The wand he held, so long, slim, and supple, bowed slightly as it was swung idly left to right, then right to left. It made a very faint sighing sound.

Bauman judged the little man at least nine feet from the ground at this intersection—difficult to reach. And might, if he chose, scurry further along his duct—might get away.

"That girlie's dead, isn' she?"

"Yes."

"God *dammit*. I was afraid of that, way I caught her." Cooper's other hand came out, wiped his little gargoyle's face, his bald scalp. "Swing jus' caught her wrong—hard workin' through these friggin' duct vents. She hadn' kept after me, comin' so fast, it wouldn' have happened. But I'm real sorry, *real* sorry, Trainer."

"Come down," Bauman said.

"Not while you got that shiv, I'm not comin' down. Not while you're still so fuckin' hot about it."

Bauman tried to drop his knife, but his right hand was cramped closed.

"Poor sweetie," Cooper said. "It was just an accident, an' that's all it was. But it wasn' no accident you stuck that shiv up in the duct. I never had nobody do that—an' I never figured you for carryin', anyway. I didn' hold no stock you stuck that half-breed in the nose. Con believes all the shit gets shoveled at State, he'll believe anything."

"Come down," Bauman said, and tried again to let go of the knife.

But the little man—his T-shirt filthy, his elbows wrapped in fat bandages of cloth—stayed up where he was, a ceiling gnome, and swung his resilient weapon at ease, its slender length coated glistening with grease (too slippery to grip, to hold) and armed at its tip with the bright neat curved blade.

"You kill them all?" Bauman said, and had to clear his throat. His sliced cheek was draining blood into his mouth. "—Killed them with that thing, through the ventilator grills in their houses."

"What's that 'all' shit?" Cooper the coach, irascible at a silly question. "I tol' you the girlie was a mistake, an' I apologized. However, however, when you think about it, she didn' belong here no more, neither." The rod swung left to right again.

"And Lesnovitch? He let you out at night, didn't he, so you could get into one of those ceiling ducts off Three-tier. . . ." Bauman hoped to talk the little man down where he could reach him, imagined himself conversational, persuading a cautious cat down from a tree.

"I didn' do not a damn thing to Ed Lesnovitch. He called me you two was comin' over, an' then when I come over in the ducts an' was talkin' to him, he got sick."

"Just talking to him. . . ."

"That's right, wise-ass."

"You cut the phone cord."

"—So he'd listen! You wouldn' believe how much that guy went downhill, last year or two."

"And Metzler—he didn't belong here, either?"

"That's one hundred percent right. Barney was a real convict, an' I respected the man personally. But he didn' no more belong at State than the fuckin' bishop of Chicago. Barney no more killed that grease-ball than you did. An' I ought to know, 'cause I had that checked out, but good." Having said that, and apparently finding his position cramped, Cooper turned a little in the vent opening, must have straightened his small legs in the duct; it boomed softly.

Bauman again found his mouth filled with blood, bent to spit it out. "—And Spencer the same?"

"You betcha. That sorry coon never rap'd nobody."

"Come down," Bauman said. "You look ridiculous, sitting up there."

"You get rid of that shiv, an' I will come down."

"All right." Bauman tried to open his hand, and found it difficult. He couldn't open his right hand, and he couldn't close his left. He lifted his left hand, and saw by dim lemon light that the palm was cut open—a neat row of small white sections of bone appearing when he shook the blood away, then disappearing beneath a swift film of more. It didn't hurt at all, only felt very odd.

"That hand looks bad," Cooper said from the ceiling.

"It is bad," Bauman said. "I'm not going to be boxing with this for a while."

"Well, no offense, but you wasn' much even with two hands, Trainer. You goin' get rid of that shiv or what? 'Cause I'm not comin' down until you do."

"All right," Bauman said, managed to open his cramped right hand, and tossed the blade glinting away into the dark.

"I never saw such shit in my life." The little man, upset, was lisping badly. "—A fuckin' fish an' a girlie-punk stickin' their noses in what ain't none of their business. An' I wrote you to butt out, too." Cooper wriggled free of his duct, then swung suddenly out and down to hang an improbable moment from one hand—a small, pale, baldheaded ape—then dropped the distance to the dirt. It was a remarkable performance for a man his age, and reminded Bauman what a splendid boxer, what a quick and savage fighter the little man must have been.

Cooper stood relaxed, very small in grease-stained shorts, sweaty T-shirt, and running shoes. Thick pads of cloth had been wrapped around his knees. He still held his slender wand, no doubt fine hand-wrapped fiber-glass—a fly rod, a remnant of his old fishing-pole business—and so supple it bent slightly of its own blade-weighted tip.

"—Taped a marker on the end, to write that note," Cooper said, and shook his instrument slightly, so it nodded.

"And Blake, and a few others through the years. They didn't belong here, either?" Bauman, spitting another mouthful of blood, took a step nearer to Cooper.

"Every single asshole who didn' have no friggin' business whatsoever in here. —An' they wasn' that many. Maybe eleven, twelve guys all together. People I could really check on. I missed a few, I'll tell you that. . . ."

"I see." Bauman thought if he was quick enough, Cooper might be able to hit him only once with that edged hook.

"People said, 'Fine—Cooper, you stay in here rest of your life.' So I say, 'O.K. You got it.' But I figured to choose my own fuckin' company—an' that means no square johns allowed whatsoever, didn' do their crimes. They say guilty can't get outta here—I say not-guilty can't stay in. Sauce for the goose is friggin' sauce for the gander. That make sense to you, Trainer? 'Cause it shit sure makes sense to me."

"It makes sense. You get the idea when they took you out of that furniture crate? Fixed your legs, then sent you back?"

"You never mind when that idea come to me."

Bauman spit out a little blood, took a half-step nearer Cooper as he did. He wasn't sure yet what to do, felt the greatest reluctance to do anything—a yearning to talk with Cooper for a while, then leave the tunnels with him, walk over to the gym. . . .

"And Burdon?"

"That was a entirely different matter. That nigger could have said somethin' to compromise security. —An' if you think it's easy gettin' anythin' done in this joint, then you don't know much. You try an' lie in some two-foot-square ductin' nine fuckin' nights in a row, waitin' for a dumb nigger to come in alone, take a shit on the first pot in line. You think that asshole didn' use every other toilet in that can before I got loop on him? You think that's funny?"

"I know it's funny," Bauman said. "—And by the way, I assume you never doubted I belonged here."

"You assume fuckin' right, Mr. College. You're one of them guys did a yellow-belly crime—no offense. You belong in here, but good."

"Yes, I do," Bauman said, spit a little more blood and took four long steps to get his right hand on the little man. He was cut once across his chest, doing it—ducked the thing when it came whipping back at his face—and caught Cooper after being hit once more, on his raised left arm just below the useless hand. That time, the hooked blade bit in and clicked against the bone.

Reaching with his right hand for a grip, almost bitten by chattering furious false teeth, Bauman caught Cooper by the throat and drove him across the wide tunnel to its other side, into deeper dark, and was kicked several times doing it—hard, swift, swinging kicks at his groin.

Gasping, grunting with effort, Bauman just managed to hold on to the little man, who bucked and twisted, clawed at the gripping hand as if to tear its skin and tendons away. Cooper made odd rasping sounds, his false teeth clicking, snapping once close to Bauman's face as the two of them hit the tunnel's opposite wall, locked together.

Staring down his right arm's length at that small face—convulsed, enraged, much less and more than human—Bauman grew swiftly more frightened than furious, and held harder, gripped, squeezed Cooper's throat out of terror he might get loose.

Squeezing, squeezing, his finger joints aching from effort, Bauman heaved Cooper slightly up off the tunnel floor—and holding him out thrashing at arm's length, kicked at the small body, felt the impacts against his running shoes. Then he heaved him back into the tunnel's wall and kicked at the small scarred legs until at last he had the old man down in shade more peaceful than the wearying light, and was able to concentrate on his grip, his right hand—that old and trusted friend, maker of useful fists, lover in the night, handy holder in rock cracks at considerable heights. Bauman prayed to his hand, prayed first to its subsidiary angels—his right shoulder, his arm, even his weight—as he leaned down and was hit a series of short punches, a boxing lesson in themselves, that cracked and smacked up into his face, into his head when he tried to slip the blows.

Once, wrestling again, the little man managed with a monstrous effort to tug Bauman's hand almost away from his throat, and croaked, "*We . . . got a match . . . comin' up!*" as if tired of rough play.

At last, though, worn out by Bauman's pressing weight, by the strangling grip at his throat—worn out by his age as well as many years of damage from boxing, from so many savage fights—Cooper found breathing impossible. He bucked beneath Bauman as furiously as Cousins had struggled in Bauman's arms, then—a cartilage cracking in his scrawny throat—turned slowly dark as the shadow they were fighting in, stuck out a swollen tongue, and died.

. . . None of that was as difficult as Bauman's work thereafter. He labored one-handed, groaning aloud, his sliced cheek blubbering strands of spit and blood, his left hand, ruined, wrapped in his bloody jacket.

First he picked up Cooper's slender weapon, broke the blade away and threw it into the dark, then slid the limber shaft against a wall to molder. Something was sticking from the pocket of the little man's grimy shorts, and Bauman bent and tugged a tiny flashlight free—Cooper not quite a perfect creature of darkness, after all.

He left the old man lying and went down the narrower tunnel, amazed to have even a slender thread of light to carry with him. Then, the flashlight held in his teeth, he half carried, half dragged Cousins the long, long way back to the intersection and brighter light, where Bauman closed his eyes so as not to see the boy. —Then down the wider passage to the second, larger hatchway, where the great fans roared. Clambering down those steep steel steps, dragging the dead boy after him one-handed, Bauman hauled him deep into the cramped space beneath the second machine. There, it was so perfectly dark that the little flashlight's beam only emphasized the lack of light.

Crawling through a gale of exhaust—State's stale air the fan was sucking forth—crawling through puddles of spill and condensation, Bauman parted curtains of blanketing dust, and tugged and slid Cousins' body down into the fan's long concrete sump of oil and drainage water, two feet deep and dark past any reflection.

After that, though Bauman kept up his groaning, and twice had to lie down in the tunnel's mud to rest, he managed to drag Cooper to the same place. He lifted the drapery of oily dust aside, wriggled under, having the little man along then pushed him down into the sump, deep under the oil and water beside the boy.

Bauman then went back for four of the big steel angle irons stacked at the tunnels' intersection, and hauled these one by one down to the fans' hatchway—first weeping at the effort, then feeling so sick he fainted, or slept, and lay on the hatchway steps for a while. He shoved each of these angle irons under the second fan, sliding them into the oily water to weigh Cousins and his companion down.

It was only after these tasks—a lifetime's work—were done, that Bauman realized he intended a sort of escape for both the dead.

Staggering back down the tunnel, he scraped and scuffed at the floor's mud and dirt to obscure all the blood he could until drip water soaked it away. He did that back to the intersection, scuffed and scraped with even more energy under the work light—which now seemed bright as the sun to him—then tried to do the same retracing the much longer, narrower way back to the furnace room. He remembered to skirt the first hatchway, and tossed the little flashlight clattering down it.

Bauman stepped from the tunnel—emerged, legs trembling—and felt he was wading out into the furnace room's warm red light, a sunset pond that seemed an affirmation of all rich sights. He walked past Lesnovitch's fine furnished room, hugging his jacket-wrapped left hand tight to his chest to keep from spattering. Through the doorway he saw the electrician sitting where he'd been left, sitting on his sofa in the molten glow of his lamps.

There was no hack having coffee or reading a paper in the office and supply room, though Bauman had forgotten there might be as he climbed the stairs—sometimes crouching to help himself with his right hand, so he went on threes. Only old Waggoner, and a young black con Bauman didn't know, were standing behind the long counters.

"Go down to Lesnovitch," Bauman said to them as they stared at him. "Cousins and I were never here. *Nobody* was here. . . ." Then, feeling so sick he couldn't see clearly, was having difficulty walking, he managed to get out of the office and into wonderful daylight—cold, windy, and bright as a mirror through light rain.

He woke in the infirmary's security room, recognized it by the stained brown canvas of its padded walls, by his being there alone.

After a while he recalled waking days before, greeting two hacks with tears of pleasure when they'd discovered him in the evening (absent from two counts) lying in an icy puddle behind discarded plywood sheeting at the back of the truck shop. He'd been delighted to see them, to see any humans alive, walking in open air. He would have been happy to have been their friend for life.

Bauman recalled very clearly being discovered behind the plywood sheeting. But he couldn't remember crawling there, could remember almost nothing of his trip to Garlin, to the local hospital—a trip outside, and mostly forgotten, wasted. He remembered that a young doctor with yellow-tinted glasses had hurt his hand for an hour. For more than an hour.

After recalling that, Bauman slept for a long time, woke again—and found the A.W. and Vermillier were easy to recall, and a police officer, a detective of some sort. Those three had sat in the security room with him for a long time, asking questions, then making threats—useless threats, since Bauman had been so glad to have their company he would have said anything to please them, to make their lives easier and more rewarding. But the only truth they wanted, wasn't his to tell.

Gorney had come in yesterday.

"Everybody's heard the crap you laid on the A.W.," he'd said, sitting by the locked door on a white-painted infirmary chair. "—But I don't believe it, and I don't think any experienced officer in here believes it. I have a special reason to figure you intended to go out with those two, and I'm going to follow up on this real carefully, see if I can't get you at least two years additional, for attempted escape."

"Very thoughtful," Bauman had said.

"That crap about you trying to prevent the boy from going out with Cooper convinces me not one little bit. You got cut all right, but not trying to prevent. You got cut trying to go with them, take Cooper's place or the boy's, and use one of those scuba sets yourself. And I'd say old Cooper stuck you to stop you."

"Could have happened that way," Bauman had said. "But it didn't."

Gorney—very neat, crewcut, his khaki uniform perfectly pressed—had sat silent in his white chair, watching Bauman for some time with eyes the color of tea, as if Bauman were bound to have something more to say.

"If you think," Gorney finally said, "—if you think the administration of this prison isn't going to follow up and investigate and lean on every single person who even could have been involved in the only, the *only* successful run out of this establishment in many years, you got another think coming. —And I'll give you a little sample, just for starters. How would you like it, for example, if the population was to hear that you been snitching hard as you were able. Think they'd like to hear that?"

"I think they'd enjoy hearing that," Bauman said. "Inmates love it when corrections falls on its ass. Let me clue you in, Gorney. I've been snitching to every club in this joint—on exactly the subject I snitched to you. Why do you think I'm still alive?"

Gorney had sat and digested that. "And," he'd said, "that horseshit about the old man doing those killings—which I couldn't believe my ears—and supposedly those inmates didn't belong here, were *innocent*, for Christ's sake? Even Vermillier didn't swallow that one."

"Ask Cooper, when you see him."

"Oh, we'll see him."

"I'll even tell you where to look, at least for Cousins. —If I were you, I'd look for Lee Cousins in Indiana. He'll be in a small town on a river, a small town with lots of trees. And for that matter, Cooper might be there with him."

Gorney had gotten up from his white-painted chair, then, and come to Bauman's cot. He'd looked down almost fondly, as if Bauman were one of those difficulties requiring handling by professionals, one of those difficulties for which professionalism had been developed.

"No inmate I like better," he'd said, "—than a man who thinks he's real smart, thinks he can ride his IQ out of here. Oh, we'll check on that Indiana thing, just in case you're being a little too smart. We'll check on that. And furthermore, as far as I'm concerned, you're still on the hook: You will tell us about the inmate who really killed those people, or you're going to be talking to grand juries up here the next three years."

Bauman had been tired, and his hand was hurting. "Oh, kiss my ass, Gorney," he'd said. "I can do three standing on my head."

This defiance, once Gorney was gone, had dissolved into sniffles, tears on Bauman's pillow. He felt tender as a child, so easily hurt.

There'd been no other visitors in the day or two following, except for Michaelson on his rounds, and Tiger and his aides. Irma, particularly, was agog at the escape, at the notion of one of State's ladies on the loose—proved brave enough, clever enough to have done what many desperate men had failed to do. She confided to Bauman a dream, a vision of Cousins—inspired by the feminine principle—swimming through State's great walls under a magical pool of milk. "A milky-way out," she said, lingering, having delivered Bauman's breakfast—a tray of cold and congealed powdered eggs garnished with what looked like carrot tops, and accompanied by damp toast and a tangerine, its frail segments crowded with seeds. The tangerine, a rare treat, evidence of Rudy Gottschalk's regard.

Reporting general rejoicing by the population at the escape, "—a early Christmas present," Irma also recounted State's triumph over Joliet. This victory only marred by Marcantonio's humiliation at the gloves of a light-heavy named Manuel Farouz, who'd outpointed him astronomically while avoiding that slow and monstrous right hand.

"A hundred dollars," Bauman said, "—a hundred dollars, street, Tony didn't hold the center of that ring."

"I wouldn' know," Irma said. "I didn' watch. There's enough violence in this world without manufacturin' it." And gently touched the tips of the fingers of Bauman's left hand, where they peeped out the end of the palm support and thick bandage.

"Oooh, nice an' warm, Charles. You're circulatin' in that hand like *mad*. That doctor did a wonderful job. Tiger went in with you; you remember that?"

"No."

"Well, he did. Went right in with you—him an' that hack, Sawyer—an' watched the surgery an' everything. He said that young doctor was a ace. I picture him as one of those real cold young gods, you know, that can just drag you right out of death's arms? An' Tiger said that was about right, said he was a very nice-lookin' young man. I just don't understand how those boys can learn so much and be so *young*."

"Want some toast?"

"Charles, you must be jokin'. I eat Clifford's West-mess food, and Clifford's food is the only food I eat."

The conversation was then interrupted by Irma's husband, Paul, the fierce forger accusing her unfairly of flirting, preparatory to a blowjob or its equivalent—something of which she'd apparently been guilty months before—and escorting her out of the room in a storm of angry tears.

The tangerine eaten, Bauman felt almost well except for the mild, steady pain in his left arm and hand. His cheek, stiff with stitches he could feel on its inside with his tongue, was numb, didn't hurt except when he chewed food carelessly.

His chest, his side, both also stitched, didn't hurt at all. "Minor . . . minor," Irma'd said with a gracefully dismissive wave of her hand. And the old bandage had been removed from his left forearm, revealing the pattern of burn scars, round, pink, forming their intended star.

He lay examining the infinite variations of brown in the padded canvas covering his small room's walls. It seemed to him, after a while, that there might not be as great an essential difference between the cardinal colors as between the collective infinite variations of tone within any one of them.

He thought about that for some time—testing his thesis by closing his eyes to imagine blue . . . red, then opening them to look at the range of mottled tans, umbers, coffees, in the room's rich browns. He did this for some time, took a long nap, and then ate lunch—a grilled cheese sandwich (cold, so smelling better than usual), two small sweet pickles, and a half-pint carton of milk. The tray was carried in by a bad-tempered Tiger, tired of strife on his staff.

After lunch, Bauman set himself to considering History's present crisis, one historians only sixty or seventy years before could hardly have imagined. Overwhelming documentation—so plentiful, so exponentially expanding that selection became the crucial part of the process, besides which, interpretation shrank to minor.

He could see History slivering inevitably into small and diverse hunting tracks, down which specialists trailed ever and ever slighter causes of more and more petty effects—leaving the grander formulations to travelers' tales, myths, and dynastic dreams, where, of course, the whole discipline had begun.

These considerations kept Bauman occupied fairly well till dinner, which was broiled liver (bleeding a dark yellow juice), watery cabbage, and really good cherry Jell-O.

After dinner—a silent injured Irma carrying the tray briskly in, as briskly out—Bauman found he was no longer able to avoid thinking of Cousins. He rolled awkwardly onto his right side and wept into his pillow for some time. Then, recovering, he blew his nose on a spare paper napkin, and lay imagining that old Cooper with Cousins, their spoiling bodies lying together—one having been young and beautiful, the other opposite in age and ugliness—that these bodies buried so deep beneath this fortress might, in another fifty, another hundred years, mingle to give magical birth out of oil and dark water to a new and perfect convict, innocent of memory. A man of middle height, middle age, a wonderful runner and savage fighter, in whom kindness, patience, and ferocity were so perfectly blended that corrections—upon his naked appearance, still damp—would recognize in him the convict complete. And, that recognized, would assume their records in error, would enroll him and keep him close as the choicest of their killers to watch over the many, many years, as this gentle and dangerous golem's promise was fulfilled.

Bauman thought of this for a long time, then slept and dreamed of Cousins' Indiana town, saw its small contented river—dark with runoffs of chocolate earth and cattle's rich manure, decorated with young trees swept from fragile banks in storms, and refreshed by streams, creeks, runs, and springs contributing from the hills as it flowed through. Bauman dreamed of Lee Cousins in a light blue summer dress—her dark hair grown longer, brushed almost to slim shoulders—walking, after lunch at the small house she shared with old Cooper, back to work across an elderly iron bridge. A small dark-green car, crossing the bridge from the near side, slowed, and its driver leaned a little out its window to talk, make some joke that left Lee smiling, before it pulled away.

A block or two past the bridge, where Bauman couldn't see—but Cousins would, and would wave to him, walking by—Cooper, tiny, ancient, withered as Tithonus, would be trotting up and down the green border of a football field, augmenting his employment as assistant janitor by assistant-coaching JV high school football. Would also be offering usefully nasty advice to any farm-boy boxers longing for state championships. . . .

Bauman woke deep into the night, tried to recover his dream, but only slept.

The next day was very slowly measured through by a breakfast of icy oatmeal, a morning spent reading a comically inept Western (in which all characters spoke like modern middle-class Californians), a fair lunch of a peanut-butter sandwich, milk, and tapioca pudding, and a long afternoon (broken by one visit from Tiger) in which Bauman lay on his cot enjoying being alone, and trying to digest unfairness—the awkward abruptness of Cousins' death, that canceled all plans for companionship, for down jackets, and marked as well a loss of simple physical beauty, that greatest rarity at State.

Bauman was wondering if the nonsensical notion of a god had been required above all to explain unfairness—so that a monster of contradictions was created to be wondered at, feared, blamed, and forgiven for unfairness—when Billings, the tall young fish hack, came into the security room to see him up and dressed in new-issue denims, then escort him back to B-block in time for dinner.

Tiger was busy preparing slides for Michaelson, so only Paul and Irma stood at the infirmary's second-floor entrance—a couple arm in arm, their quarrel composed—to formalize the discharge and say goodbye. Irma adjusted Bauman's sling and warned against showers, at least for two more days. The stitches due out of the cheek, chest, and side in six days or seven—out of the left arm and hand, later. "An' they're goin' to take you into Garlin for that," she said. "Won't that be nice . . . ?"

"It'll be nice."

South yard at dusk was empty, cold, and still. Frozen grass crunched and collapsed beneath their shoes as Bauman and Billings crossed an angle of lawn to the walkway. Bauman's hand ached slightly at every step.

"Christmas decorations supposed to be goin' up next week," Billings said. He looked away as he spoke, perhaps to avoid viewing Bauman's sewn left cheek.

"You see them last year, Billings?"

"No. Got hired after that."

"Well, they're pretty. They string lights all along the wall, up the towers and so forth. Very festive. . . ." It seemed to Bauman as he walked and talked, that his heart was beating faster, that some transparent obstruction was rising around him that muffled sound and would prevent his touching anything but the grass he walked across. Billings, when he glanced over at him, appeared to be only a two-dimensional figure, which, suddenly turned, might disappear into a tall folded line in the air. Bauman heard his heartbeat echoed through the ground—someone running up behind them, who then ran past, and was Cousins. Lee looked back just once, smiled in apology.

"Are you O.K.?" the fish hack said.

"I'm fine. . . ." Lee ran like a talented woman racer, narrow-hipped, knees high, almost bouncing at each stride. . . .

"Mister Bauman?"

"I'm fine." Frightened, Bauman closed his eyes as he walked, took several deep breaths, and said to himself, "Lee's dead." Then he slowly opened his eyes again, to discover Cousins no longer running in the yard, the air now not quite so substantial, sound reaching him more clearly, and that Billings, striding alongside, seemed solid at least.

"Goin' to be my first Christmas up here, an' goin' to be my last one, too," Billings said.

"Wish I could say the same," Bauman said. "—Not happy in your work?"

"Let me tell you somethin', Mr. Bauman, this is the worst job in the world. Even for good money it's the worst job in the world, an' the money isn' good, neither."

"Either."

"An' the money isn' no good, either."

"People get used to it," Bauman said.

"That's jus' my point. I don't want to get used to it. I don't blame those two people for runnin' out of here."

"And what's your alternative?"

"I can get into a tech school over in Kinross, learn insulation an' air conditionin'."

"Go to it," Bauman said. "This is a dangerous place to stay, if you don't fit in."

"Well, I sure don't fit in," Billings said. "People call me names just like I wasn't a guard. They don't respect me even a little bit."

"If I were you, I'd go for the voc-tech."

"Well, I think I'm goin' to."

"You married?"

"Yes, I am."

"And your wife wants you to go into air conditioning?"

"She sure does."

"Sounds like a smart girl. If I were you, I'd do it."

"Well, I think I'm goin' to," Billings said. "That's what I think I'm goin' to do."

. . .

There was hardly a pause in conversation, barely a momentary silence, when Bauman walked into the mess hall late. Associated with a grand event, an escape—but that association clouded—he was treated with appropriate caution. There were glances, but no comments, no welcome except at his table, when he came to it balancing his tray on his right arm.

"Oh, shit, Charles!" Scooter, awkward, half rose off his stool to take the tray, then hugged Bauman and hurt his slung left arm, its touchy hand. "My roomie is back!"

"Hey, man." Perteet, mouth full of dubious sweet potato, smiled and extended a huge and grimy hand.

"Want my sweet potato, Pete?" Bauman taking great comfort from these two. These friends.

"Yeah. . . . You can spare that, I'll take it."

"Jesus Christ, Charles Bauman!" Scooter, marveling. "I mean it is strictly none of my business, man. But whatever, you know, whatever went down, we are on the fuckin' TV, man. We are on the *tube*. State is fuckin' news, dude!"

"Sorry," Perteet said. "—I mean it's good news an' all, but you lost your squeeze, didn' you?"

"Lost a friend, anyway," Bauman said. With the sweet potato gone, the piece of Swiss steak and portion of green beans didn't look too threatening. Dessert was orange Jell-O.

"—Real pretty, too. Nice havin' a lady at the table. She ain't goin' to be here no more, though." Perteet folded his Swiss steak with his fingers, tucked it all into his mouth, and chewed it, reflecting. "Lady's goin' to be missed. . . ."

Bauman, surprised by sudden tears, cleared his throat and put his hand up to his eyes. "Goddamn fucking headache," he said.

"Charles," Scooter said, "—you want a aspirin? I got two aspirin up in the house."

"No, don't waste them," Bauman said. "The lights are bright in here, that's all. I was in the security room at the infirmary. Dim light." He noticed Scooter looking at the stitched scar on his left cheek.

"Don't know why the fuck they givin' *you* a hard time," Perteet said. "That shit-ass Cooper is the one needs a hard time if they ever catch the little fuck, which I hope they don't—don't catch him, I mean. Little shit didn' need to cut you so bad."

"I agree one hundred percent on that," Bauman said, and tried the green beans.

"Hey, that old guy was a animal," Scooter said. "—Nobody fucked with that old guy. But give the dude credit where credit is due. Man's gone. —*Gone.*"

"In Canada now, I bet," Perteet said, and finished his beans.

"No way." Scooter paused for effect. "What I heard, was New Orleans. Man, you can ship out of there for any-fuckin'-where."

"You got bread, you can ship out," Perteet said, looking at Bauman's Swiss steak.

"Pete, you want some of this Swiss steak?"

"No, man. You need your stren'th, you got cut."

"Sure?"

"You need your stren'th, man. I don't want none of that steak. You eat all that."

"Oh, hey Charles," Scooter hasty to start chewing his own portion of Swiss steak before Perteet transferred his attention to it. "—Cernan sent a dude up a couple days ago, said two different women was callin' in for you, tryin' an' see was you all right."

"Thanks."

"An' you know that hack, Sawyer? Well, he came over yesterday, said to tell you the A.W.'s been talkin' to your wife—your family, whatever—an' told 'em you could be in trouble, but physically you was goin' to be fine."

"O.K."

"Shouldn' be in trouble." Perteet, finishing his bread.

"You kiddin'? Only guys they had run out of here for maybe twenty, thirty years? —An' who they still got in this hole to hand some shit to? My roomie, that's who."

The Swiss steak had tasted better than it looked; Bauman chewed his last bite as long as he could.

"The friggin' milk truck . . ." Perteet said, and shook his great, bearded head. "I seen that truck a lot of times, comin' in an' goin' out, an' I never thought nothin' of it."

"Me too," Scooter said. "An' you tell me why Lee'd want to run when she didn' have no more'n maybe another year? Them fuckers catch her now, it'll be five. Five fuckin' years jus' for fuckin' escape. Why? is what I'm askin'. This ain't no honor farm. We ain't in here on our word of honor, that's for sure."

"A point," Bauman said. "Man's got a point. Any honor we have, we have to earn in here."

"You goin' to eat your bread?" Perteet said.

"I'll have one slice, Pete; second one's yours."

"Reason I ask, bread don't do nothin' to give you blood, you know, from bein' cut. Steak's real good for that. Bread don't do nothin'."

"You enjoy the bread, Pete," Bauman said, finished his slice and stood up, maneuvering to pick up his tray.

"Charles," Scooter said, "—put the friggin' tray down. You jus' leave that tray. I'll take it over for you. You don't have to do nothin'; you jus' go on up to the house an' take it easy."

"Thanks. See you for breakfast, Pete."

"You got it."

Rudy Gottschalk—flushed from cooking, his tattooed hair crimson—was waiting by the mess-hall doors, and beckoned Bauman over, led him around the end of the serving counter and into the kitchen. "You college guys," he said, apparently in a merry mood. "—Talk about blowin' corrections' *mind*. I don't know what other shit went down, man, but I know it was your fuckin' notion to go the fuck swimmin' out of State. A fuckin' classic!"

"Not my idea."

"Oh, sure—the chick's, right? None of my business, none of my business. Just want to congratulate you, man—an' I wasn't surprised that little ding crossed you, shanked you to take the swim. Didn't surprise me at all."

"Shit happens."

"Ain't it the truth? An' now you got no squeeze, an' that was a punk-chick had eyes only for you, man. Don't know how a old guy like you got that lucky." He patted Bauman's back. "That punk's goin' to be waitin' for you outside, man. See you explain *that* to your old lady."

"Be a problem. . . . By the way, Rudy, that Swiss steak wasn't bad."

"You like that Swiss steak?"

"Not bad," Bauman said, and saw a flash of secret pleasure in Gottschalk's eyes. "—Why? What was it?"

"Nothin'," Gottschalk said. "Just good stuff," and started to laugh.

"Rudy, what was in the Swiss steak?"

"Nothin'." Laughter. "Hey, Teach, if you liked it—you liked it!"

"What was it?"

"Why should I break your heart an' tell you. I don't tell nobody what I cook."

"You eat some?"

"You gotta be kiddin'," Gottschalk said, and put a forefinger to his lips. "Reason I got you back here, besides congratulations and all that shit, is you got a friend come over here to see you." He hooked a thumb toward the back of the kitchen. "—An' for Christ's sake get rid of him quick. He don't need to be here on them bikers' shift."

Bauman found Wayman behind the last row of steam kettles—trying, in imperfect light, to read the maintenance tag on a freezer chest.

"Mist' Bauman . . ." Wayman's face and hands almost sulfur yellow under the kitchen's flickering fluorescents.

Shaking the young man's hand—its grip a tool's grip—Bauman felt again the bloom of warmth he'd felt at the dinner table, as if Wayman also were a friend.

"How are things going, Wayman. You ready to talk about that basketball book?"

"I am ready. I read all that book."

"Damn, man. You're not going to leave me anything to teach you!"

Wayman, very pleased at that, shook his head in modesty. "They's plenty shit I don' know yet."

"There's plenty of shit I don't know either, Wayman."

". . . Reason I'm here, is I'm bringin' a message over from the colonel. —Colonel Perkins?"

"I remember him."

"He said an' tell you he's real sorry about the lady. '*Real* sorry,' is what he said. An' he said he 'preciated your solution of the problem, an' he will pass that solution on." Wayman drew a breath and paused to be certain of his recall. " '—Will pass that on, on a stric' need-to-know basis.' " Then sighed the breath out in relief.

Bauman went upstairs comforted by Colonel Perkins' knowledge—probably gained from the young black con who'd been working the electrician's office with Waggoner. Perkins' sharing of the secret so relieving, so much easier than bearing it alone.

Bauman leafed through *Numbers and Statistics in the Ancient World* for his letter to Susanne, then lay on his bunk to read it. He found the block's uproar made concentration difficult, got up to get a pen and his Walkman, adjusted its earphones one-handed, and lay down again to read and listen to Bach's Italian Concerto on harpsichord, its cascading notes lending more weight to the letter than it deserved.

He read it, read it through again, then added a postscript:

> Susanne—Despite the pomposity of the above, it's essentially accurate and should be acted on. Forget the 'no phone call' nonsense. I will have been in touch before you get this, and will remain in touch as long as you care to hear from me.
>
> As you've already heard, I was hurt, but not very seriously.
>
> Yours,
> Charlie

Breakfast was cornflakes, stony raisins, and hot chocolate. Perteet asked for any unwanted raisins around the table, and was disappointed by all—Bauman, Scooter, and a grim young gunman named Richy Ames, who, a few months before, had shot and crippled a police officer in Holmesbridge. This tough fish, still probationary as a Biker Club member, was bound to be accepted, according to Scooter, "—because the dude's too fuckin' mean not to get in."

Ames usually ate with the second shift—had either come down at the wrong time, or been curious about the escape.

"Wouldn' let you run with 'em, huh?" he suddenly said to Bauman through a mouthful of cornflakes, muddy brown eyes seconding the query.

"Damned if I remember," Bauman said. Ames stared at him a moment longer, then bent to his cereal again.

"You ought to know better, motherfucker," Perteet said to Ames. "—You ought to know better'n ask a man a question like that. What the fuck joints you been in, it's all right to ask a man a question like that?"

Ames put his orange plastic spoon down in his cereal bowl, and looked up at Perteet with exactly the calm measuring gaze Bauman had seen on boxers, in the seconds before the first round's bell. It was a professional judgment being made—a very rapid and competent one—in which the factors of Perteet's size, strength, and quickness were being nicely assessed.

Scooter leaned back on his stool, away from the table.

"I didn' mean nothin' by it," Ames said, picked up his spoon, and continued to eat.

After breakfast, Bauman and Scooter climbed the stone steps to Ground-tier, Bauman imagining Cousins would be waiting for him there. He looked for Lee in the morning crowd, to further the fantasy.

Just as they reached the foot of the circular stair, Bauman heard Betty's chirp behind him, gestured Scooter on up, and walked back to the Nellis house.

Betty, barefoot in contraband blue slacks and white blouse, stood in her doorway, beckoned Bauman, then—a first—reached out, drew him to her, and hugged him, hurting his hand. Over her soft shoulder, Bauman saw Nellis lying on his accustomed upper bunk, surveying the embrace with no sign of annoyance, his glasses' lenses reflecting in miniature the morning light rectangled by narrow white bars.

"You come in, Charles," Betty said. "You wan' somethin' to eat?"

"No, thanks. I had a pretty good breakfast."

"Sit down, sit down in that rockin' chair."

Bauman sat, surprised to find his legs grateful for the rest after only climbing some stairs. "I really don't want anything to eat."

"Well, you gettin' somethin', jus' the same," Betty said, went to her sink and began searching, diligent as a squirrel, through her cigar boxes.

"I really don't need anything."

"Well, I need to be givin' you somethin', so you jus' take it," Betty said, and marched down the cell with a small Snickers candy bar in her right hand and a Hostess Twinkie in her left. "Which one you want firs'?"

"Honey, I don't want either one of them."

"You're goin' to have 'em anyway, so which one you want now? You take the other one with you."

"Pick one, Professor," Nellis said from his bunk, "—so we can have some peace in here."

"I'll have the Twinkie."

"O.K." Betty handed the Twinkie over, then bent to slip the Snickers into Bauman's jacket pocket. "You eat that later."

"Thank you," Bauman said. "Where's the boy?"

"Oh, Chris is off with a couple buddies. He's a real nice boy," Betty said. "Me an' Marky is proud he's turnin' out so good. He's always runnin' aroun' doin' somethin', but he checks with Marky all the time, you know, so he don' screw up."

"Glad to hear it."

"How's that hand? Is that hand hurtin' you?"

"Not much."

Betty sat on her lower bunk, reached out to arrange her green bed curtains. "Now, you ain' got no girl no more," she said. "You mind I mention that?"

"No."

"You don' mind?"

"No."

"I tell you, I don' know why that Lee would run. Jus' one more year to go, an' she runs. I'm not sayin' anything against that girl. Lee's pretty, real pretty, but runnin' like that don' show good sense. An' it means she's leavin' you alone. . . ."

"That's life," Bauman said.

"I know you don' want to hear nothin' like this. Too soon after she gone an' all that. But Charles, I blame myself, tyin' you two together—you know?"

"Betty . . ." Nellis said.

"Well, I do. Now I think about it, I jus' don' think she was right for you, Charles. She's real classy, you know, but I don' think she was the right person for you."

"Betty—" Nellis again.

"Well, I *don'*."

Bauman took a bite of the Twinkie.

"Isn' that good?"

"Very good."

"An' they good for you, Charles. Nourishin'."

"Um-hmm."

"Tell you somethin', an' I know it's too soon. —You don' want to hear it, right?"

"Probably not," Bauman said. "I need to be going up for count."

"Well, if you don' want to hear, I won't say nothin'."

"I want to hear," Bauman said, and finished the Twinkie.

"O.K. Otherwise, I wouldn' say nothin'. —That Marcia Simms?"

"Oh, god."

"*Betty*."

"I'm jus' sayin' what she *said*. She said she thought you was a real gentleman."

"Oh, god. . . ."

"I apologize for my wife," Nellis said, from the upper bunk.

"Well, she did say that!"

"Honey," Bauman said, "I really do appreciate it, and Marcia's beautiful. But I think I need some alone time, just for a while."

"Oh, sure, I know that. I wasn' sayin' right away. I know you miss that Lee."

"That's right."

"See, don' you miss her? An' you didn' want nothin' to do with her. But I'm tellin' you, Charles, Marcia is a more steady person. She ain' goin' to be runnin' out of here with no little ding."

"Probably not."

"You goin' to be coachin', now?" Nellis said, by way of rescue.

"Christ—I hope not."

"They don't have nobody else, with the little guy gone. Leaves you, Professor."

"That's a grim thought."

"Who else they got?" Nellis said. "Nobody, that's who."

"I don't know enough boxing, and this hand—"

"Who else they got?" Nellis said. "Face it, you're elected."

"That's goin' be real nice," Betty said. "—You goin' be a coach!"

"You want a Snickers?"

Scooter, watching television in his bunk, held out a hand to receive the candy, then complained about rude inmates who wouldn't let people eat breakfast in peace. "Thought Pete Perteet was goin' to stop that asshole's clock, man. . . ."

Bauman, lying on his bunk—and grateful to be there, his slung arm and hand aching—closed his eyes as if to allow himself relief from events, scenes, grotesqueries too humorous for tragedy. He thought how amused Cousins would have been at Betty's new matchmaking, imagined Lee joking with him about the beautiful Marcia Simms, warning him about Marcia's temper, her known unfortunate habit of biting off noses when distressed by careless treatment, a rude remark, or short payment. Bauman pictured Lee walking with him across South field, stalking along, imitating Marcia's high-fashion Nubian style—and promising him a silver nose if the affair ended badly. . . . Bauman, eyes closed, smiled in his bunk.

After count, he walked Scooter to B's gate, encouraging him to be more firm at the truck shop—firm within reason—about constant assignment to the scrub tub. Then, Scooter sent on his way, Bauman walked back along Ground-tier to the basement steps, and down them to the basement corridor.

He passed the morning mail line—received a few stares from cons curious about his injuries, about the celebrated escape—and paused to slip his letter to Susanne into the slot. Then he stepped into the canteen line behind Kavafian's housemate, Carlo. The albino—serene in his dark glasses—turned to nod, then turned back. It took some time for the line to diminish to Ramos' serving door.

"Two Bit-O'-Honeys, two almond Hersheys," Bauman said.

Ramos took his scrip, made change, then selected the candy and handed it over.

"Keep movin', you," he said. "—I don' got all day."

"Mind your manners, Hector," Bauman said. "I can kick your ass, one-handed." And on that civilized note, some status maintained, he moved on, unwrapped a Bit-O'-Honey, and ate it while waiting for another con to finish talking with Cernan. Then, he asked that major domo for an afternoon phone reservation, long-distance, an out-of-state call to Fort Wayne.

"Oh, certainly, certainly. No problem," Cernan said, smiling, maintaining his warm eye contact, seeming not to notice Bauman's bandages, his sutured cheek. "I'll enter you for three o'clock on the dot. . . ."

Passed for the first time in two weeks through B-block's main gate—free now of Mr. Hyde's telltale iron—Bauman walked down the building steps and out into a morning sunny, windless, and bitter cold. He thought of his knife (tossed aside, its fine steel left to rust away) and considered going back down to get it—in a few days. Then decided not. He was afraid he'd smell a subtler spoilage than dead rats, was afraid the tunnels would never fade if he refreshed his recollection of them . . . was afraid he might find himself dead in red-clotted mud, and now only dreaming of life.

The sunshine had fooled some younger cons into confusing light with warmth. Shivering, their denim jackets and civilian windbreakers buttoned or zipped up, necks wrapped in knit scarves sent from home, they'd formed loose confederacies for touch football. —At a signaled '*hike*' as Bauman walked past, they galloped away over crisp frozen grass, calling to receive the pass.

Bauman supposed a man of honor, of an earlier day, would have had his wife order a warm down jacket, then would have taken that to the dank basement, the tunnels—and deeper, into that chamber where the exhaust fans thundered in dripping condensation. Then would have reached down through oil and water for the boy, lifted him up to gently wrestle the fine jacket onto him to keep him warm, then lowered him back. —Would have left mad Cooper chill.

As he'd done when he first came up to State, Bauman examined the wall while he walked across North yard, and thought about climbing it. A very possible climb, it had seemed to him then—if worked deep into a corner. And seemed so now, if he could have a section to practice on. And, of course, if his left hand was able.

Truscott, on duty at the desk in the library entrance, rose and patted him down carefully—examined the sling, and checked his left hand's splint and bandages for signs of tampering before stooping with a soft grunt to run her fingers around the top of his left sock, then his right.

She stood, said, "You can go on up," and went back to her desk as he climbed the stairs.

Schoonover—alone in the library, as usual—was repairing books at his worktable, and glanced up when Bauman came in. "Charles, you look god-awful."

"I don't doubt it."

"Come and sit down."

"No, rather stand. I've been lying down for days."

"Well, you've had your adventures—which, I suppose, is what you were after all the while." Schoonover pressed a blue book cover between two small sheets of cardboard, holding the cover together while glue set.

"Larry, I don't have the least idea what I was after—something stupid, no doubt." Bauman walked over to watch the work. "Which ones are you trying to mend?"

"Don't you want to sit down? I understand you have a very bad hand, there."

"Tiger tells me I'm supposed to get an eighty-five-percent recovery of motion. If I do the exercises. —Which books are you doing?"

"Current fiction, of course. They read the covers right off the trashier examples. At least I assume they do, since after the weekly orders are filled—by those few courageous enough to dare the library and its 'ding'—I get very little feedback. For all I know, they're smoking them." He set the blue cover aside and picked up a small gray book, sadly worn.

"You might have more luck stocking videos, taking some of that business away from the entrepreneurs. And you could lend music tapes, too."

"I might—if I could persuade some institution or company to donate a few hundred."

"Ask them to include a little Mozart."

"Charles, I'm only—was only—a high school teacher, but even I saw through that eighteenth-century elevator music long ago." Having examined the gray book's covers, finding them unsalvageable, Schoonover tore them off.

"Mozart is not elevator music."

"Oh, some of his things are wonderful; but a great many of them, as far as I'm concerned, are tediously clever variations on hack work."

"Oh, bullshit, Larry."

"—And speaking of which, Charles, did you ever, in the midst of your adventures, remember to write the Midwest library people about some possible deacidification, just as a charity to preserve some trashy reading for trashy readers?"

"I apologize, Larry. I haven't done that, but I will. —I'll write to Ned Abnerson tonight. He's a decent guy; I think he'll be able to do something."

"Well, that would be very much appreciated. And to get back to our discussion of music, I wonder if it's occurred to you that our civilization—American civilization—will most likely be remembered, above all, for its love songs."

"No, Larry, it hadn't occurred to me."

"Well, it should have. We've produced more love songs than the rest of the world together—and wonderful melodies. I used to sing some of them to Edna when we were in bed in the evening, just before we went to sleep. 'Stardust' . . . 'September Song' . . . 'Someone to Watch Over Me.' All too popular for a high academic to appreciate, I suppose."

"I appreciate them, Larry. They're beautiful songs—and you may be right about their being very important, culturally."

". . . I suppose you miss the boy?"

"Yes, I do."

"Such—such foolishness." Schoonover searched his desktop, found pieces of cardboard sized to fit the damaged book. "Why in the world a boy like that—with what? a year? about a year to go? Why in the world would that boy run?"

"Everyone has his reasons."

"Yes, but Cousins out there with that . . . little creature, being hunted. . . ." Schoonover fitted the cardboard to the book, folded it for front and back covers, and carefully tore those pieces free, almost neat as cutting. "I imagine you'll find it lonely here, without him—though I suppose you weren't lovers."

"No, we weren't lovers."

"Then you've lost a friend," Schoonover said, and stirred his small pot of glue. "Which is bad enough."

"Bad enough," Bauman said.

"I'm certain you did the very best you could for him, Charles, whatever the circumstances. —And I'm not fool enough to think I know the circumstances. But a teacher who fails to try to protect a boy like that . . . I'm glad you were hurt, Charles, if you'll forgive me for saying so." Schoonover spread glue neatly down the book's exposed spine, and fitted a strip of backing tape to that.

"You're forgiven."

"The reason being—"

"I know the reason."

"The reason *being*, that I know you tried."

"I knew the reason, Larry. And, as it happens, I tried too late. I was slow—and I was slow because I was frightened. So I let that boy slip through my fingers, fall, and break."

"I see," Schoonover said, and bent to his work, stroked his backing tape firmly down, then tried his cardboard covers for fit.

"—It seems I'm not to be trusted with the young. A subtle irresponsibility—and, after all, the reason I'm here."

"Charles, I'm so sorry. . . ."

"Makes two of us, Larry. —Now, any new histories come in?"

". . . Three books came in last week. Nothing fabulous, a history of flight—"

"Christ."

"—and a grade school history of Alaska, and something more serious about the Hanoverians. It's shelved."

Bauman walked back past five long seven-shelf stacks of fiction, then turned left into the sixth, where history was kept.

Someone had come into the library. Bauman heard soft conversation, Schoonover's voice.

He slid *The House of Hanover*—a big book and a nice piece of work, if dated—from a shelf at eye level, looked through it, then put it back and reached down another book, with a faded yellow cover. *The Sicilian Campaign*, an example of those dubious divisional histories of the Second World War, crowded with slightly inaccurate maps and blurred photographs of Colonel This and General That, usually posed peering through binoculars. One of the innumerable 'histories' of the fighting, in which Allied commanders' miraculous good judgment was presented with no reference to the certain intelligence placed on their desks every few days—sometimes every day—courtesy of British code breakers.

Walled in by books, his oldest friends, Bauman remembered Cousins standing by the fiction shelves leafing through *Beach Red*. The boy had found its atmosphere—fevered, claustrophobic, dangerous—too similar to State's.

"Larry," Bauman said to footsteps coming down the aisle, "you need some decent history." As he started to turn, he was prevented, his right arm gripped hard and held. Then he heard a small sharp cracking noise as his right eye exploded in his head.

"Trying to run?—and fucking still owing *me?!"*

Something stuck into Bauman's left cheek—hardly disturbing him in that instant, his entire attention locked to his right eye's agony, overwhelming as a grand climax of music. But when he flailed into motion, tried to put his tethered left hand up, that thing jerked out of his cheek, flew into his left eye and stung him so he screamed, thrashed, freed his right arm, made a fist and hit something. Someone grunted.

Bauman felt a tugging in his head—a thin pulling of pain too personal to bear—and hit out again, wishing for his left hand.

Then he was let go, swung with his right again and felt a hard whack against his knuckles—someone's head, and jumped after that and punched again, missed and punched again and hit the same man, he was certain, in the back. Then Bauman heard something howling—a deep baying, as if a beast had come into the library. Certainly not his noise. He could feel his mouth tight-closed, teeth clenched together to hold in or out some of the pain that flashed and scintillated through him. Then his eyes seemed to splinter and knock him sideways into what must be shelves of books. He fell—which he had to do to try and leave some agony behind him in the air—hit a table edge, then felt the floor against his chest and belly, smelled dust and floor wax, felt falling books. He heard wood being broken, being smashed. . . .

Truscott came up the steps faster than she'd ever climbed stairs, and ran straight on into sounds that would have made most men pause and be careful. Even so, she came too late to prevent Schoonover, howling, from beating Les Kerwin to death with a library chair, smashing that inmate attorney's skull so severely that his brains—a pale wrinkled puff—showed bloody at the back of his head.

Truscott ran to Schoonover, shoved him back, spoke sharply to him, and took away the last of his chair—a length of splintered yellow oak. Then she watched him turn away, walk slowly across the library to his ladder, and climb it. He settled himself at the top and sat silent and thoughtful, gazing out over fiction.

In library quiet, Truscott (panting softly from exertion, from fear) stared down at dead Kerwin curled on his right side, his handsome graying head, shaped oddly now, stuck in a dark, reflecting puddle. She was startled by slight sounds from the back of the room—and radioing "*Assist officer!*" trotted heavily that way past aisles of shelves.

She found Bauman, face running blood, struggling to rise from fallen books.

"Oh, sweet Jesus." Truscott bent to help him. She went to her knees, then sat awkwardly amid the books with Bauman in her arms, her uniform soon stained with red.

"Beth?" the blind man said.